After descending the steps from the throne platform, Sithel knelt beside the cleric and carefully turned him over. "What did you see?" he asked urgently. "Tell me—I command you!"

Vedvedsica took his hands from his face. His eyebrows were singed, his face blackened. "Five words . . . I saw only five words, Highness," he said falteringly.

"What were they?" Sithel nearly shook the fellow in his haste to know.

"The Tobril said, 'They both shall wear crowns . . .' "

Sithel frowned, his pale, arching brows knotting together. "What does it mean? Two crowns?" he demanded angrily. "How can they both wear crowns?"

"It means what it means, Twice-Blest."

The Speaker of the Stars looked into the brazier, its coals still glowing. A few seconds' glimpse into the great book had nearly cost Vedvedsica his sight. What would the knowledge of Gilean's prophecy cost Sithel himself? What would it cost Silvanesti?

WHEN TRADITIONS ARE BROUGHT INTO QUESTION AND WAR LOOMS, THE SONS OF THE SPEAKER OF THE STARS MUST ACCEPT THE MANTLES OF LEADERSHIP.

OR LOSE ALL THEIR PEOPLE HAVE STRUGGLED FOR.

PAUL B. THOMPSON & TONYA C. COOK

ELVEN EXILES

Sanctuary
Alliance
Destiny

DOUGLAS NILES

DWARF HOME

The Secret of Pax Tharkas
The Heir of Kayolin
The Fate of Thorbardin
(August 2009)

THE ELVEN NATIONS TRILOGY

PAUL B. THOMPSON & TONYA C. COOK
DOUGLAS NILES

FIRSTBORN

THE KINSLAYER WARS

THE QUALINESTI

THE ELVEN NATIONS OMNIBUS

©2009 Wizards of the Coast, Inc.

Cover art by Brom
This Edition First Printing: January 2009

Firstborn originally published February 1991
The Kinslayer Wars originally published August 1991
The Qualinesti originally published November 1991

9 8 7 6 5 4 3 2 1

ISBN: 9780-7869-5187-1
620-25202740-001-EN

U.S., CANADA,
ASIA, PACIFIC, & LATIN AMERICA
Wizards of the Coast, Inc.
P.O. Box 707
Renton, WA 98057-0707
+1-800-324-6496

EUROPEAN HEADQUARTERS
Hasbro UK Ltd
Caswell Way
Newport, Gwent NP9 0YH
GREAT BRITAIN
Save this address for your records.

Visit our web site at www.wizards.com

Introduction to the 2004 edition

It's hard for us to believe, but more than a decade has passed since we wrote the book you're holding. Strange to think how much things have changed for us personally—Paul got married and is a daddy to adorable Sara; after nine years in upstate New York, Tonya returned to her hometown—yet how much they've remained the same professionally. We're still collaborating (and collaborating on Dragonlance, no less); no serious disagreements have marred our teamwork (not to say there haven't been some free and frank exchanges of opinion, but all bloodshed has thus far been confined to our books).

The Elven Nations books marked at least two "firsts" for us: our first foray into a multi-book story and our first attempt to delve into the culture of one of Krynn's nonhuman races. Doug Niles had the formidable task of bringing the Kinslayer Wars to life in book two; we, like Speaker Sithel, were "Twice Blest," having been asked to write the other two books in the trilogy. Facing the challenge of following characters over a long span of time, through more than one book, certainly helped prepare us to write our own first trilogy, The Barbarians, as well as the current one, The Ergoth Empire. And, although our previous books had included nonhuman characters gnomes, dwarves, and the like we had never written an entire book from the perspective of a nonhuman race. It was a fascinating and somewhat daunting experience. On the one hand, we wanted the elves to be, well, *elves.* That is, we wanted them to be their own unique selves, distinct from the other races in the book. Yet, at the same time, we needed to be sure their motivations and emotions would be understandable and more importantly, *believable* to an audience that is, at least as far as we know, totally human.

We hope we succeeded. The very fact that you're holding a new edition of the book tells us we must've gotten something right.

So, if you're returning to Silvanost for another visit, thanks for coming back! And if you're journeying there for the first time, then sit back and allow us to whisk you away to a city of a thousand shining marble towers, where griffons wheel in the sky and an ancient race dwells on the banks of the slow-flowing Thon-Thalas.

Paul B. Thompson
Tonya C. Cook

Prelude

Year of the Dolphin (2308 PC)

The great river Thon-Thalas flowed southward through the forests of Silvanesti. Three-quarters of the way down its length, the broad waterway branched and twin streams flowed around an island called Fallan. On this island was the capital city of the elven nation, Silvanost.

Silvanost was a city of towers. Gleaming white, they soared skyward, some dwarfing even the massive oak trees on the mainland. Unlike the mainland, Fallan Island had few trees. Most had been removed to make way for the city. The island's naturally occurring marble and quartz formations had then been spell-shaped by the Silvanesti, transforming them into houses and towers. Approaching the island from the west on the King's Road, a traveler could see the marble city gleaming with pearly light through the trees. At night, the city absorbed the starlight and moonlight and radiated it softly back to the heavens.

On this particular night, scudding clouds covered the sky and a chill rain fell. A brisk breeze swirled over the island. The streets of Silvanost, however, were full. In spite of the damp cold, every elf in the city stood outside, shouting, clapping, and singing joyfully. Many carried candles, hooded against the rain, and the dancing lights added to the strange yet festive air.

A wonderful thing had happened that evening in the capital. Sithel, Speaker of the Stars, ruler of all Silvanesti, had become a father. Indeed the great fortune of Speaker Sithel was that he had two sons. He was the father of twins, an event rare among

3

elves. The Silvanesti began to call Sithel "Twice Blest." And they celebrated in the cool, damp night.

The Speaker of the Stars was not receiving well-wishers, however. He was not even in the Palace of Quinari, where his wife, Nirakina, still lay in her birthing bed with her new sons. Sithel had left his attendants and walked alone across the plaza between the palace and the Tower of the Stars, the ceremonial seat of the speaker's power. Though common folk were not allowed in the plaza by night, the speaker could hear the echoes of their celebrations. He strode through the dark outlines of the garden surrounding the tower. Wending his way along the paths, he entered the structure through a door reserved for the royal family.

Circling to the front of the great emerald throne, Sithel could see the vast audience hall. It was not completely dark. Six hundred feet above him was a shaft in the roof of the tower, open to the sky. Moonlight, broken by clouds, filtered down the shaft. The walls of the tower were pierced by spiraling rows of window slits and encrusted with precious jewels of every description. These split the moonlight into iridescent beams, and the beams bathed the walls and floor in a thousand myriad colors. Yet Sithel had no mind for this beauty now. Seating himself on the throne he had occupied for two centuries, he rested his hands on the emerald arms, allowing the coolness of the stone to penetrate and soothe his heavy heart.

A figure appeared in the monumental main doorway. "Enter," said the speaker, He hardly spoke above a whisper, but the perfect acoustics of the hall carried the single word clearly to the visitor.

The figure approached. He halted at the bottom of the steps leading up to the throne platform and set a small brazier on the marble floor. Finally the visitor bowed low and said, "You summoned me, great Speaker." His voice was light, with the lilt of the north country in it.

"Vedvedsica, servant of Gilean," Sithel said. "Rise."

Vedvedsica stood. Unlike the clerics, of Silvanost, who wore white robes and a sash in the color of their patron deity, Vedvedsica wore a belted tabard of solid gray. His god had no temple in the city, because the gods of Neutrality were not officially tolerated by the priests who served the gods of Good.

Vedvedsica said, "May I congratulate Your Highness on the birth of his sons?"

Sithel nodded curtly. "It is because of them that I have called you here," he replied. "Does your god allow you to see the future?"

"My master Gilean holds in his hands the *Tobril*, the *Book of Truth*. Sometimes he grants me glimpses of this book." From the priest's expression it appeared this was not a practice he enjoyed.

"I will give you one hundred gold pieces," said the speaker. "Ask your god, and tell me the fate of my sons."

Vedvedsica bowed again. He dipped a hand into the voluminous pockets of his tabard and brought out two dried leaves, still shiny green, but stiff and brittle. Removing the conical cover from the brazier, he exposed hot coals and held the leaves by their stems over the dully-glowing fire.

"Gilean, the Book! Gray Voyager! Sage of Truth, Gate of Souls! By this fire, open my eyes and allow me to read from the book of all-truth!" The cleric's voice was stronger now, resonating through the empty hall. "Open the Tobril! Find for Speaker Sithel the fates of his two sons, born this day!"

Vedvedsica laid the dry leaves on the coals. They caught fire immediately, flames curling around them with a loud crackle. Smoke snaked up from the brazier, thick, gray smoke that condensed as it rose. Sithel gripped the arms of his throne and watched the smoke coil and writhe. Vedvedsica held up his hands as if to embrace it.

Gradually the smoke formed into the wavering shape of an open scroll. The back of the scroll faced Sithel. The front was for Vedvedsica only. The cleric's lips moved as he read from the book that contained all the knowledge of the gods.

In less than half a minute the leaves were totally consumed. The fire flared three feet above the golden brazier, instantly dispelling the smoke. In the flash of flame, the priest cried out in pain and reeled away. Sithel leaped up from his throne as Vedvedsica collapsed in a heap.

After descending the steps from the throne platform, Sithel knelt beside the cleric and carefully turned him over. "What did you see?" he asked urgently. "Tell me—I command you!"

Vedvedsica took his hands from his face. His eyebrows were singed, his face blackened. "Five words . . . I saw only five words, Highness," he said falteringly.

"What were they?" Sithel nearly shook the fellow in his haste to know.

"The Tobril said, 'They both shall wear crowns . . .'"

Sithel frowned, his pale, arching brows knotting together. "What does it mean? Two crowns?" he demanded angrily. "How can they both wear crowns?"

"It means what it means, Twice-Blest."

The Speaker looked at the brazier, its coals still glowing. A few seconds' glimpse into the great book had nearly cost Vedvedsica his sight. What would the knowledge of Gilean's prophecy cost Sithel himself? What would it cost Silvanesti?

5

Spring—Year of the Hawk
(2216 PC)

1

Clouds scattered before the wind, bright white in the brilliant sunshine. In the gaps of blue that showed between the clouds, a dark, winged form darted and wheeled. Far larger than a bird, the creature climbed with powerful strokes of its broad wings. It reached a height above the lowest clouds and hovered there, wings beating fast and hard.

The beast was a griffon, a creature part lion, part eagle. Its magnificent eagle's head and neck gave way to the torso and hind-quarters of a lion. A plumed lion's tail whipped in the wind. Behind the beast's fiercely beaked head and unblinking golden eyes, the leather straps of a halter led back to a saddle, strapped to the griffon's shoulders. In the saddle sat a helmeted figure clad in green and gold armor. An elven face with brown eyes and snow-colored hair peered out from under the bronze helmet.

Spread out below them, elf and griffon, was the whole country of Silvanesti. Where wind had driven the clouds away, the griffon rider could see the green carpet of forests and fields. To his right, the wandering silver ribbon of the Thon-Thalas, the Lord's River, flowed around the verdant Fallan Island. On this island was Silvanost, city of a thousand white towers.

"Are you ready, Arcuballis?" whispered the rider to his mount. He wound the leather reins tightly around his strong, slender hand. "Now!" he cried, drawing the reins sharply down.

The griffon put its head down and folded its wings. Down they plummeted, like a thunderbolt dropped from a clear sky. The

6

young elf bent close to the griffon's neck, burying his fingers in the dense, copper-hued feathers. The massive muscles under his fingers were taut, waiting. Arcuballis was well trained and loyal to its master; it would not open its wings again until told to do so. If its master so desired, the griffon would plunge straight into the fertile soil of Silvanesti.

They were below the clouds, and the land leaped into clear view. The rich green canopy of trees was more obvious now. The griffon rider could see the pines and the mighty oaks reaching up, connecting soil to sky. It was a view of the land few were ever granted.

He had dropped many thousands of feet, and only a few hundred remained. The wind tore at his eyes, bringing tears. He blinked them away. Arcuballis flexed its folded wings nervously, and a low growl sounded in its throat. They were very low. The rider could see individual branches in the trees, see birds fleeing from the griffon's rapidly growing shadow.

"Now!" The rider hauled back sharply on the reins. The broad wings opened slowly. The beast's hindquarters dropped as its head rose. The rider felt himself slide backward, bumping against the rear lip of the tall saddle. The griffon soared up in a high arc, wings flailing. He let the reins out, and the beast leveled off. He whistled a command, and the griffon held its wings out motionless. They started down again in a steep glide. The lower air was rough, full of eddies and currents, and the griffon bobbed and pitched. The rider threw back his head and laughed.

They skimmed over the trees. Abruptly the woods gave way to orderly rows of trees, orchards of cherry, plum, and fima nuts. Elves working in the orchards saw only a large object hurtle over their heads, and they panicked. Many tumbled down ladders, spilling baskets of fruit. The rider put a brass horn to his lips, sounding a shrill note. The griffon added its own eerie call, a deep, trilling growl that was also part lion, part eagle.

The rider urged the beast up. The wings beat lazily, gaining a few dozen feet of height. They banked right, swooping over the slow-flowing waters of the Thon-Thalas. There were many watercraft plying the river—flat log rafts poled by sturdy, sunbrowned elves, piled high with pots and cloth to be traded in the wild south; the slender dugouts of the fishers, the bottoms of which were silvered with the morning's catch. The griffon swept over them in a flurry of wings. The rafters and fishers looked up idly from their work. As travelers up and down the great waterway, they were not easily impressed, not even by the sight of a royal griffon in flight.

On they flew, across the river to Fallan Island. The rider wove his flying steed among the many white towers so skillfully that

7

the griffon never once scraped a wingtip. Their shadow chased them down the streets.

The rider approached the center point of the city, and the center point of every elf's life and loyalty, the Tower of the Stars. At six hundred feet, it was the tallest spire in Silvanost and the seat of power of the Speaker of the Stars.

He steered the griffon in a quick circle around the white marble tower. The horn was at his lips again, and he blew a rude, flat warning. It was a lark, a bit of aerial fun, but halfway around the tower the rider spied a lone figure on the high balcony, looking out over the city. He reined back and sideslipped Arcuballis toward the tower. The white-haired, white-robed figure was no one less than Sithel, Speaker of the Stars.

Startled, the rider clumsily turned the griffon away. His eyes met those of the elven monarch for a moment, then Sithel turned and re-entered the tower. The griffon rider shook his head and made for home. He was in trouble.

North of the tower, across the ornate Gardens of Astarin, stood the Palace of Quinari. Here the descendants of Silvanos, the House Royal, lived. The palace stood clear of the trees and consisted of three, three-story wings radiating from a rose-colored marble tower. The tower soared three hundred feet from base to pinnacle. The three wings of the palace were faced with beautiful colonnades of green-streaked marble. The columns spiraled gracefully upward from their bases, each in imitation of a unicorn's horn.

The rider's heart raced as the palace came into view. He'd been away four days, hunting, flying, and now he had an appointment to keep. He knew there would be trouble with the speaker for his insolent behavior at the Tower of the Stars, but for now thoughts of his upcoming rendezvous made him smile.

He brought the griffon in with firm tugs on the reins. He steered toward the eastern wing of the palace. Lion's claws behind and eagle's talons in front touched down on the cool slate roof. With a tired shudder, Arcuballis drew in its wings.

Servants in sleeveless tunics and short kilts ran out to take the beast's bridle. Another elf set a wooden step ladder against the animal's side. The rider ignored it, threw a leg over the griffon's neck, and nimbly dropped to the rooftop. More servants rushed forward, one with a bowl of clean water, the other with a neatly folded linen towel.

"Highness," said the bowl bearer, "would you care to refresh yourself?"

"A moment." The rider pried off his helmet and shook his sweat-damp hair. "How goes everything here?" he asked, dipping his hands and arms in the clean water, once, twice, three times. The water quickly turned dingy with dirt.

"It goes well, my prince," the bowl bearer replied. He snapped his head at his companion, and the second servant proffered the towel.

"Any word from my brother, Prince Sithas?"

"In fact, yes, Highness. Your brother was recalled yesterday by your father. He returned from the Temple of Matheri this morning."

Puzzlement knit the rider's pale brows. "Recalled? But why?"

"I do not know, my prince. Even now, the speaker is closeted with Prince Sithas in the Tower of the Stars."

The rider tossed the towel back to the servant who'd brought it. "Send word to my mother that I have returned. Tell her I shall see her presently. And should my father and brother return from the tower before sunset, tell them the same."

The servants bowed. "It shall be done, my prince."

The elf prince went briskly to the stair that led from the rooftop into the palace. The servants hastened after him, sloshing dirty water from the bowl as they went.

"Prince Kith-Kanan! Will you not take some food?" called the bowl bearer.

"No. See to it Arcuballis is fed, watered, and brushed down."

"Of course—"

"And stop following me!"

The servants halted as if arrow-shot. Prince Kith-Kanan rattled down the stone steps into the palace. As it was early summer, all the window shutters were open, flooding the interior corridors with light. He strode along, scarcely acknowledging the bows and greetings of the servants and courtiers he met. The length of the shadows on the floor told him he was late. She would be angry, being kept waiting.

Kith-Kanan breezed out the main entrance of the palace. Guards in burnished armor snapped to attention as he passed. His mood lightened with every step he took toward the Gardens of Astarin. So what if his father dressed him down later? It wouldn't be the first time, by any means. Any amount of lecturing was worth his hurried flight home to be on time for his rendezvous with Hermathya.

The gardens bulked around the base of the great tower. Not long after Silvanos, founder of the elven nation, had completed the Tower of the Stars, priests of the god Astarin asked for permission to create a garden around the structure. Silvanos gladly granted their request. The clerics laid out a garden in the plan of a four-pointed star, each point aligned with one of the cardinal directions. They wove spells granted to them by Astarin, the Bard King, spells that formed the trees and flowers in wonderful ways. Thornless red and white roses grew in delicate spirals around the trunks of evergreen oaks. Wisteria dripped purple blossoms into still, clear pools of water. Lilacs and camellias drenched the air with their perfume. Broad leaves of ivy spread over the garden paths, shading them and protecting strollers from all but the harshest rains. And most remarkably, laurels and cedars grew in circular groves, their tops coming together to form perfect shelters, where elves could meditate. Silvanos himself had favored a grove of laurels on the west side of the garden. When the august founder of the elven nation had died, the leaves on the laurels there changed from green to gold, and they remained that way ever after.

Kith-Kanan did not enter the Gardens of Astarin by one of the paths. In his deerskin boots, he crept silently beside the shoulder-high wall of spell-shaped mulberry. He hoisted himself over the wall and dropped down on the other side, still without a sound. Crouching low, he moved toward the grove.

The prince could hear the impatient rustle of footsteps inside the golden grove. In his mind he saw Hermathya pacing to and fro, arms folded, her red-gold hair like a flame in the center of the gilded trees. He slipped around to the entrance to the grove. Hermathya had her back to him, her arms folded tight with vexation. Kith-Kanan called her name.

Hermathya whirled. "Kith! You startled me. Where have you been?"

"Hurrying to you," he replied.

Her angry expression lasted only a moment longer, then she ran to him, her bright blue gown flying. They embraced in the arched entry of Silvanos's retreat. The embrace became a kiss. After a moment, Kith-Kanan drew back a bit and whispered, "We'd best be wary. My father is in the tower. He might see us."

In answer, Hermathya pulled the prince's face down to hers and kissed him again. Finally, she said breathlessly, "Now, let us hide." They entered the shelter of the laurel grove.

Under the elaborate rules of courtly manners, a prince and a well-born elf maiden could not consort freely, as Kith-Kanan and Hermathya had for the past half-year. Escorts had to accompany both of them, if they ever saw each other at all. Protocol demanded that they not be alone together.

"I missed you terribly," Hermathya said, taking Kith-Kanan's hand and leading him to the gray granite bench. "Silvanost is like a tomb when you're not here."

"I'm sorry I was late. Arcuballis had headwinds to fight all the way home." This was not strictly true, but why anger her further?

Actually Kith-Kanan had broken camp late because he had stayed to listen to two Kagonesti elves tell tall tales of adventures in the West, in the land of the humans.

"Next time," Hermathya said, tracing the line of Kith-Kanan's jaw with one slender finger, "take me with you."

"On a hunting trip?"

She nipped at his ear. Her hair smelled of sunshine and spice. "Why not?"

He hugged her close, burying his face in her hair and inhaling deeply. "You could probably handle yourself right enough, but what respectable maiden would travel in the forest with a male not her father, brother, or husband?"

"I don't want to be respectable."

Kith-Kanan studied her face. Hermathya had the dark blue eyes of the Oakleaf Clan and the high cheekbones of her mother's family, the Sunberry Clan. In her slender, beautiful face he saw passion, wit, courage—

"Love," he murmured.

"Yes," Hermathya replied. "I love you too."

The prince looked deep into her eyes and said softly, "Marry me, Hermathya." Her eyes widened, and she pulled away from him, chuckling. "What is funny?" he demanded.

"Why talk of marriage? Giving me a starjewel will not make me love you more. I like things the way they are."

Kith-Kanan waved to the surrounding golden laurels. "You like meeting in secret? Whispering and flinching at every sound, lest we be discovered?"

She leaned close again. "Of course. That makes it all the more stimulating."

He had to admit his life had been anything but boring lately. Kith-Kanan caressed his lover's cheek. Wind stirred through the gilded leaves as they drew closer. She entwined her fingers in his white hair. The prince thought no more of marriage as Hermathya filled his senses.

* * * * *

They parted with smiles and quiet touches on each other's faces. Hermathya disappeared down the garden path with a toss of bronze-red hair and a swish of clinging silk. Kith-Kanan stood in the entrance of the golden grove and watched her until she was lost from sight. Then, with a sigh, he made for the palace.

The sun had set and, as he crossed the plaza, the prince saw that the servants were setting lamps in the windows of the palace. All Silvanost glimmered with light by night, but the Palace of Quinari,

11

with its massive tower and numerous tall windows, was like a constellation in the heavens. Kith-Kanan felt very satisfied as he jauntily ascended the steps by the main doors.

The guards clacked their spears against their shoulder armor. The one on Kith-Kanan's right said, "Highness, the speaker bids you go to the Hall of Balif."

"Well, I'd best not keep the Speaker waiting," he replied. The guards snapped to, and he passed on into the deep, arched opening. Even the prospect of a tongue-lashing by his father did little to lower Kith-Kanan's spirits. He still breathed the clean, spicy scent of Hermathya, and he still gazed into the bottomless blue depths of her eyes.

The Hall of Balif, named for the kender general who had once fought so well on behalf of the great Silvanos, took up an entire floor of the central tower. Kith-Kanan swung up the broad stone stairs, clapping servants on the back and hailing courtiers heartily. Smiles followed in the elf prince's wake.

Oddly, two guards stood outside the high bronze doors of the Hall of Balif. The doors were not usually guarded. As Kith-Kanan approached, one guard rapped on the bronze panel behind him with the butt of his spear. Silently Kith-Kanan stood by as the two soldiers pushed the heavy portals apart for him.

The hall was indifferently lit by a rack of candles on the oval feasting table. The first face Kith-Kanan saw did not belong to his father, Sithel.

"Sithas!"

The tall, white-haired young elf stood up from behind the table. Kith-Kanan circled the table and embraced his twin brother heartily. Though they lived in the same city, they saw each other only at intervals. Sithas spent most of his time in the Temple of Matheri, where the priests had been educating him since he was a child. Kith-Kanan was frequently away, flying, riding, hunting. Ninety years they'd lived, and by the standards of their race they were barely adults. Time and habit had altered the twins, so much so that they were no longer exact copies of each other. Sithas, elder by scant minutes, was slim and pale, the consequence of his scholarly life. His face was lit by large hazel eyes, the eyes of his father and grandfather. On his white robe he wore a narrow red stripe, a tribute to Matheri, whose color it was.

Kith-Kanan, because of his outdoor life, had skin almost as brown as his eyes. The life of a ranger had toughened him, broadened his shoulders and hardened his muscles.

"I'm in trouble," he said ruefully.

"What have you done this time?" Sithas asked, loosening his grip on his twin.

"I was out flying on Arcuballis—"

"Have you been scaring the farmers again?"

"No, it's not that. I was over the city, so I circled the Tower of the Stars—"

"Blowing your horn, no doubt."

Kith-Kanan sighed. "Will you let me finish? I went round the tower, very gently, but who should be there on the high balcony but Father! He saw me and gave me that look."

Sithas folded his arms. "I was there too, inside. He wasn't pleased."

His twin lowered his voice to a conspiratorial whisper, "What's this all about? He didn't call me here to chastise me, did he? You wouldn't be here for that."

"No. Father called me back from the temple before you came home. He's gone upstairs to fetch Mother. He's got something to tell you."

Kith-Kanan relaxed, realizing he wasn't going to get dressed down. "What is it, Sith?"

"I'm getting married," said Sithas.

Kith-Kanan, wide-eyed, leaned back on the table. "By E'li! Is that all you have to say? 'I'm getting married?' "

Sithas shrugged. "What else is there to say? Father decided that it's time, so married I get."

Kith-Kanan grinned. "Has he picked a girl?"

"I think that's why he sent for you and Mother. We'll all find out at the same time."

"You mean, you don't know who it is yet?"

"No. There are fourteen suitable clans within House Cleric, so there are many prospective brides. Father has chosen one based on the dowry offered—and according to which family he wants to link with House Royal."

His brother's eyes danced with merriment. "She will probably be ugly and a shrew, as well."

"That doesn't matter. All that matters is that she be healthy, well-born, and properly worship the gods," Sithas said calmly.

"I don't know. I think wit and beauty ought to count for something," Kith-Kanan replied. "And love. What about love, Sith? How do you feel about marrying a stranger?"

"It is the way things are done."

That was so like him. The quickest way to insure Sithas's cooperation was to invoke tradition. Kith-Kanan clucked his tongue and walked in a slow circle around his motionless twin. His words rang off the polished stone walls. "But is it fair?" he said, mildly mocking. "I mean, any scribe or smith in the city can choose his mate himself, because he loves her and she loves him. The wild

13

elves of the woods, the green sea elves, do they marry for duty, or do they take as mate a loving companion who'll bear them children and be a strength to them in their ancient age?"

"I'm not any smith or scribe, much less a wild elf," Sithas said. He spoke quietly, but his words carried as clearly as Kith-Kanan's loud pronouncements. "I am firstborn to the Speaker of the Stars, and my duty is my duty."

Kith-Kanan stopped circling and slumped against the table. "It's the old story, isn't it? Wise Sithas and rash Kith-Kanan," he said. "Don't pay me any heed, I'm really glad for you. And I'm glad for me, too. At least I can choose my own wife when the time comes."

Sithas smiled. "Do you have someone in mind?"

Why not tell Sithas? he thought. His twin would never give him away.

"Actually," Kith-Kanan began, "there is—"

The rear door of the hall opened, and Sithel entered, with Nirakina at his side.

"Hail, Father," the brothers said in unison.

The speaker waved for his sons to sit. He held a chair out for his wife, then sat himself. The crown of Silvanesti, a circlet of gold and silver stars, weighed heavily on his brow. He had come to the time in his life when age was beginning to show. Sithel's hair had always been white, but now its silky blondness had become brittle and gray. Tiny lines were etched around his eyes and mouth, and his hazel eyes, the sign of the heritage of Silvanos, betrayed the slightest hint of cloudiness. All these were small, outward signs of the great burden of time Sithel carried in his lean, erect body. He was one thousand, five hundred years old.

Though past a thousand herself, Lady Nirakina was still lithe and graceful. She was small by elven standards, almost doll-like. Her hair was honey brown, as were her eyes. These were traits of her family, Clan Silver Moon. A sense of gentleness radiated from her, a gentleness that soothed her often irritable husband. It was said about the palace that Sithas had his father's looks and his mother's temperament. Kith-Kanan had inherited his mother's eyes and his father's energy.

"You look well," Nirakina said to Kith-Kanan. "Was your trip rewarding?"

"Yes, Lady. I do love to fly," he said, after kissing her cheek.

Sithel gave his son a sharp glance. Kith-Kanan cleared his throat and bid his father a polite greeting.

"I'm glad you returned when you did," Sithel said. "Has Sithas told you of his upcoming marriage?" Kith-Kanan admitted he had. "You will have an important part to play as well, Kith. As the brother of the groom, it will be your job to escort the bride to the Tower of the Stars—"

"Yes, I will, but tell us who it is," insisted the impatient prince.

"She is a maiden of exceptional spirit and beauty, I'm told," Sithel said. "Well-educated, well-born—"

"Father!" Kith-Kanan pleaded. Sithas himself sat quietly, hands folded on his lap. Years of training in the Temple of Matheri had given him formidable patience.

"My son," Sithel said to Sithas, "Your wife's name is Hermathya, daughter of Lord Shenbarrus of the Oakleaf Clan."

Sithas raised an eyebrow approvingly. Even he had noticed Hermathya. He said nothing, but nodded his acceptance.

"Are you all right, Kith?" Nirakina asked. "You look quite pale."

To her surprise, Kith-Kanan looked as if his father had struck him across the face. The prince swallowed hard and nodded, unable to speak. Of all the eligible daughters, Hermathya was to marry Sithas. It was incomprehensible. It could not happen!

None of his family knew of his love for her. If they knew, if his father knew, he'd choose someone else.

"Ah," Kith-Kanan managed to say, "who—who else knows of this?"

"Only the bride's family," said Sithel. "I sent Shenbarrus acceptance of the dowry this morning."

A sinking feeling gripped Kith-Kanan. He felt like he was melting into the floor. Hermathya's family already knew. There was no going back now. The speaker had given his word. He could not, in honor, rescind his decision without gravely offending Clan Oakleaf.

His parents and brother began to discuss details of the wedding. A tremor passed through Kith-Kanan. He resolved to stand up and declare his love for Hermathya, declare that she was his and no one else's. Sithas was his brother, his twin, but he didn't know her. He didn't love her. He could find another wife. Kith-Kanan could not find another love.

He rose unsteadily to his feet. "I—" he began. All eyes turned to him.

Think, for once in your life! he admonished himself. What will they say to you?

"What?" said his father. "Are you ill, boy? You don't look well."

"I don't feel too well," Kith-Kanan said hoarsely. He wanted to shout, to run, to smash and break things, but the massive calm of his mother, father, and brother held him down like a thick blanket.

He cleared his throat and added, "I think all that flying has caught up with me."

Nirakina stood and put a hand to his face. "You do feel warm. Perhaps you should rest."

"Yes. Yes," he said. "That's just what I need. Rest." He held the table edge for support.

"I make the formal announcement when the white moon rises tonight. The priests and nobles will gather in the tower," Sithel said. "You must be there, Kith."

"I—I'll be there, Father," Kith-Kanan said. "I just need to rest."

Sithas walked with his brother to the door. Before they went out, Sithel remarked, "Oh, and leave your horn at the palace, Kith. One act of impudence a day is enough." The speaker smiled, and Kith-Kanan managed a weak grin in reply.

"Shall I send a healer to you?" asked Nirakina.

"No. I'll be fine, Mother," Kith-Kanan said.

In the corridor outside, Sithas braced his brother's shoulders and said, "Looks as if I'm to be lucky; both brains and beauty in my wife."

"You are lucky," Kith-Kanan said. Sithas looked at him in concern. Kith-Kanan was moved to say, "Whatever happens, Sith, don't think too badly of me."

Sithas frowned. "What do you mean?"

Kith-Kanan inhaled deeply and turned to climb up the stairs to his room. "Just remember that nothing will ever separate us. We're two halves of the same coin."

"Two branches of the same tree," Sithas said, completing the ritual the twins had invented as children. His concern deepened as he watched Kith-Kanan climb slowly up the stairs.

Kith-Kanan didn't let his brother see his face contort with pain. He had only a scant two hours before Solinari, the white moon, rose above the trees. Whatever he was going to do, he had to think of it before then.

*　*　*　*　*

The great and noble of Silvanesti filed into the open hall of the Tower of the Stars. Rumors flew through the air like sparrows, between courtier and cleric, noble clan father and humble acolyte. Such assemblies in the tower were rare and usually involved a matter of state.

A pair of young heralds, draped in bright green tabards and wearing circlets of oak and laurel, marched into the hall in perfect step. They turned and stood on each side of the great door. Slender trumpets went to their lips, and a stirring fanfare blared forth. When the horns ceased, a third herald entered.

"Free Elves and True! Give heed to His Highness, Sithel, Speaker of the Stars!"

Everyone bowed silently as Sithel appeared and walked to his emerald throne. There was a spontaneous cry of "All hail the speaker!" from the ranks of the nobles; the hall rang with elven voices. The speaker mounted the steps, turned, and faced the assembly. He sat down, and the hails died.

The herald spoke again. "Sithas, son of Sithel, prince heir!"

Sithas passed through the doorway, bowed to his father, and approached the throne. As his son mounted the seven steps to the platform, Sithel held out his hand, indicating his son should stand to the left of the throne. Sithas took his place, facing the audience.

The trumpets blared again. "Lady Nirakina, wife, and Prince Kith-Kanan, son of Sithel!"

Kith-Kanan entered with his mother on his arm. He had changed to his courtly robes of sky-blue linen, clothing he rarely wore. He moved stiffly down the center aisle, his mother's hand resting lightly on his left arm.

"Smile," she whispered.

"I don't know four-fifths of them," Kith-Kanan muttered.

"Smile anyway. They know you."

When he reached the steps, the pommel of Kith-Kanan's sword poked out from under his ceremonial sash. Nirakina glanced down at the weapon, which was largely concealed by the voluminous folds of his robe.

"Why did you bring that?" she whispered.

"It's part of my costume," he replied. "I have a right to wear it."

"Don't be impertinent," his mother said primly. "You know this is a peaceful occasion."

A large wooden chair, cushioned with red velvet, was set in place for the speaker's wife on the left of Prince Sithas. Kith-Kanan, like his twin, was expected to stand in the presence of his father, the monarch.

Once the royal family was in place, the assembled notables lined up to pay their respects to the speaker. The time-honored ritual called for priests first, the clan fathers of House Cleric next, and the masters of the city guilds last. Kith-Kanan, far to the left of Sithel, searched for Hermathya in the press of people. The crowd numbered some three hundred, and though they were quiet, the shuffling of feet and the rustle of silk and linen filled the tower. The heralds advanced to the foot of the speaker's throne and announced each group as they formed up before Sithel.

The priests and priestesses, in their white robes and golden headbands, each wore a sash in the color of their patron deity—silver for E'li, red for Matheri, brown for Kiri Jolith, sky blue for Quenesti Pah, and so on. By ancient law, they went barefoot as well, so they would be closer to the sacred soil of Silvanesti.

The clan fathers shepherded their families past the speaker. Kith-Kanan caught his breath as Lord Shenbarrus of Clan Oakleaf reached the head of the line. He was a widower, so his eldest daughter stood beside him.

Hermathya.

Sithel spoke for the first time since entering the Tower of the Stars. "Lady," he said to Hermathya, "will you remain?"

Hermathya, clad in an embroidered gown the color of summer sunlight, her striking face framed by two maidenly braids—which Kith-Kanan knew she hated—bowed to the speaker and stood aside from her family at the foot of the throne platform. The hiss of three hundred whispering tongues filled the hall.

Sithel stood and offered a hand to Hermathya. She went up the stair without hesitation and stood beside him. Sithel nodded to the heralds. A single note split the air.

"Silence in the hall! His Highness will speak!" cried the herald.

A hush descended. Sithel surveyed the crowd, ending his sweep by looking at his wife and sons. "Holy clerics, elders, subjects, be at ease in your hearts," he said, his rich voice echoing in the vast open tower. "I have called you here to receive joyous news. My son, Sithas, who shall be speaker after me, has reached the age and inclination to take a wife. After due consultation with the gods, and with the chiefs of all the clans of House Cleric, I have found a maiden suitable to be my son's bride."

Kith-Kanan's left hand strayed to his sword hilt. A calm had descended over him. He had thought long and hard about this. He knew what he had to do.

"I have chosen this maiden knowing full well the disappointment that will arise in the other clans," Sithel was saying. "I deeply regret it. If this were a barbarian land, where husbands may have more than one wife, I daresay I could make more of you happy." Polite laughter rippled through the ranks of the nobles. "But the speaker may have only one wife, so one is all I have chosen. It is my great hope that she and my son will be as happy together as I have been with my Nirakina."

He looked at Sithas, who advanced to his father's side. Holding Hermathya's left hand, the speaker reached for Sithas's right. The crowd held its breath, waiting for him to make the official announcement.

18

"Stop!"

The couple's fingers were only a hairsbreadth apart when Kith-Kanan's voice rang out. Sithel turned in surprise to his younger son. Every eye in the hall looked with shock at the prince.

"Hermathya cannot marry Sithas!" Kith-Kanan declared.

"Be silent," Sithel said harshly. "Have you gone mad?"

"No, Father," Kith-Kanan said calmly. "Hermathya loves me."

Sithas withdrew his hand from his father's slack fingers. In his hand he held a starjewel, the traditional betrothal gift among elves. Sithas knew something had been brewing. Kith-Kanan had been too obviously troubled by the announcement of his bride-to-be. But he had not guessed at the reason.

"What does this mean?" demanded Lord Shenbarrus, moving to his daughter's side.

Kith-Kanan advanced to the edge of the raised floor. "Tell him, Hermathya. Tell them all!"

Sithas looked to his father. Sithel's gaze was on Hermathya. Her cheeks were faintly pink, but her expression was calm, her eyes cast down.

When Hermathya said nothing, Sithel commanded, "Speak, girl. Speak the truth."

Hermathya lifted her gaze and looked directly at Sithas. "I want to marry the speaker's heir," she said. Her voice was not loud, but in the tense silence, every sound, every word was like a thunderclap.

"No!" Kith-Kanan exclaimed. What was she saying? "Don't be afraid, Thya. Don't let our fathers sway you. Tell them the truth. Tell them who you love."

Still Hermathya's eyes were on Sithas. "I choose the speaker's heir."

"Thya!" Kith-Kanan would have rushed to her, but Nirakina interposed herself, pleading with her son to be still. He gently but firmly pushed her aside. Only Sithas stood between him and Hermathya now.

"Stand aside, Brother," he said.

"Be silent!" his father roared. "You dishonor us all!"

Kith-Kanan drew his sword. Gasps and shrieks filled the Tower of the Stars. Baring a weapon in the hall was a serious offense, a sacrilegious act. But Kith-Kanan wavered. He looked at the sword in his hand, at his brother's and father's faces, and at the woman he loved. Hermathya stood unmoving, her eyes still fixed on his twin. What hold did they have on her?

Sithas was unarmed. In fact no one in the hall was armed, except for the flimsy ceremonial maces some of the clan fathers carried. No one could stop him if he chose to fight. Kith-Kanan's sword arm trembled.

With a cry of utter anguish, the prince threw the short, slim blade away. It skittered across the polished floor toward the assembled clerics, who moved hastily out of its way. It was ritually unclean for them to touch an edged weapon.

Kith-Kanan ran from the tower, blazing with frustration and anger. The crowd parted for him. Every eye in the hall watched him go.

Sithas descended to the main floor and went to where Kith-Kanan's sword lay. He picked it up. It felt heavy and awkward in his unpracticed hand. He stared at the keen cutting edge, then at the doorway through which Kith-Kanan had departed. His heart bled for his twin. This time Kith had not merely been impudent or impetuous. This time, his deeds were an affront to the throne and to the gods.

Sithas saw only one proper thing to do. He went back to his father and bride-to-be. Laying the naked blade at Sithel's feet, he took Hermathya's hand. It was warm. He could feel her pulse throbbing against his own cool palm. And as Sithas took the blue starjewel from the folds of his robe, it seemed almost alive. It lay in his hand, throwing off scintillas of rainbow light.

"If you will have me, I will have you," he said, holding the jewel out to Hermathya.

"I will," she replied loudly. She took the starjewel and held it to her breast.

The Tower of the Stars shook with the cheers of the assembled elves.

Later That Night

2

Sithel strode with furious energy down the corridors of the Palace of Quinari. Servants and courtiers backed away from him as he went, so fierce was the anger on his face. The assembly had ended on a triumphant note, but the Speaker of the Stars could not forget the outrage his own son had committed.

The corridor ended at the palace's great central tower. Sithel approached the huge bronze doors that closed off the private rooms of his family from the rest of the palace. The doors were eighteen feet high, inlaid with silver runes that kept a protective spell on them. No one not of the blood of Silvanos could open the doors. Sithel hit one door with each palm. The immense portals, delicately balanced, swung inward.

"Where is he? Where is Kith-Kanan?" he demanded, setting his feet wide apart and planting his fists on his hips. "I'll teach that boy to shame us in front of a public assembly!"

Within the chamber, Nirakina sat on a low, gilded couch. Sithas bent over her, proffering a goblet of sweet nectar. The prince straightened when his father entered, but neither he nor his mother spoke.

"Well?" demanded Sithel.

Nirakina looked up from her goblet. Her large amber eyes were full of sadness. "He is not in the palace," she said softly. "The servants looked for him, but they did not find him."

Sithel advanced into the room. His hard footsteps were lost in the deep carpets that covered the center of the floor, and his

21

harsh words were muffled by the rich tapestries covering the cold stone walls.

"Servants, bah, they know nothing. Kith-Kanan has more hiding places than I've had years of life."

"He is gone," Sithas said at last.

"How do you know that?" asked his father, transferring his glare to his eldest son.

"I do not feel his presence within the palace," Sithas said evenly. The twins' parents knew of the close bond that existed between their sons.

Sithel poured a goblet of nectar, using this simple task to give himself time to master his anger. He took a long drink.

"There is something else," Sithas said. His voice was very low. "The griffon, Arcuballis, is missing from the royal stable."

Sithel drained his cup. "So, he's run away, has he? Well, he'll be back. He's a clever boy, Kith is, but he's never been out in the world on his own. He won't last a week without servants, attendants, and guides."

"I'm frightened," said Nirakina. "I've never seen him so upset. Why didn't we know about this girl and Kith?" She took Sithas's hand. "How do we know she will be a good wife for you, after the way she's behaved?"

"Perhaps she is unsuitable," Sithas offered, looking at his father. "If she were, perhaps the marriage could be called off. Then she and Kith-Kanan—"

"I'll not go back on my word to Shenbarrus merely because his daughter is indiscreet," Sithel snapped, interrupting his son's thoughts. "Think of Hermathya, too; shall we blacken her reputation to salve Kith's wounded ego? They'll both forget this nonsense."

Tears ran down Nirakina's cheeks. "Will you forgive him? Will you let him come back?"

"It's outside my hands," Sithel said. His own anger was failing under fatherly concern. "But mark my words, he'll be back." He looked to Sithas for support, but Sithas said nothing. He wasn't as sure of Kith-Kanan's return as his father was.

*　*　*　*　*

The griffon glided in soundlessly, its mismatched feet touching down on the palace roof with only a faint clatter. Kith-Kanan slid off Arcuballis's back. He stroked his mount's neck and whispered encouragement in its ear.

"Be good now. Stay." Obediently the griffon folded its legs and lay down.

Kith-Kanan stole silently along the roof. The vast black shadow of the tower fell over him and buried the stairwell in darkness. In his dark quilted tunic and heavy leggings, the prince was well hidden in the shadows. He avoided the stairs for, even at this late hour, there might be servants stirring about in the lower corridors. He did not want to be seen.

Kith-Kanan flattened himself against the base of the tower. Above his head, narrow windows shone with the soft yellow light of oil lanterns. He uncoiled a thin, silk rope from around his waist. Hanging from his belt was an iron hook. He tied the rope to the eye of the hook, stepped out from the tower wall, and began to whirl the hook in an ever-widening circle. Then, with practiced ease, he let it fly. The hook sailed up to the third level of windows and caught on the jutting stonework beneath them. After giving the rope an experimental tug, Kith-Kanan started climbing up the wall, hand over hand, his feet braced against the thick stone of the tower.

The third level of windows—actually the sixth floor above ground level—was where his private room was located. Once he'd gained the narrow ledge where his hook had wedged, Kith-Kanan stood with his back flat against the wall, pausing to catch his breath. Around him, the city of Silvanost slept. The white temple towers, the palaces of the nobles, the monumental crystal tomb of Silvanos on its hill overlooking the city all stood out in the light of Krynn's two visible moons. The lighted windows were like jewels, yellow topaz and white diamonds.

Kith-Kanan forced the window of his room open with the blade of his dagger. He stepped down from the sill onto his bed. The chill moonlight made his room seem pale and unfamiliar. Like all the rooms on this floor of the tower, Kith-Kanan's was wedge-shaped, like a slice of pie. All the miscellaneous treasures of his boyhood were in this room: hunting trophies, a collection of shiny but worthless stones, scrolls describing the heroic deeds of Silvanos and Balif. All to be left behind, perhaps never to be seen or handled again.

He went first to the oaken wardrobe, standing by an inside wall. From under his breastplate he pulled a limp cloth sack, which he'd just bought from a fisher on the river. It smelled rather strongly of fish, but he had no time to be delicate. From the wardrobe he took only a few things—a padded leather tunic, a pair of heavy horse-riding boots, and his warmest set of leggings. Next he went to the chest at the foot of his bed.

With no concern for neatness, he stuffed spare clothing into the sack. Then, at the bottom of the chest, he found something he hadn't wanted to find. Wrapped in a scrap of linen was the starjewel he'd bought for Hermathya. Once exposed, it glittered in the dim light.

Slowly he picked it up. His first reaction was to grind the delicate gem under his heel, but Kith-Kanan couldn't bring himself to destroy the beautiful scarlet gem. Without knowing exactly why, he slipped it into the fisher's bag.

From the rack by the door he took three items: a short but powerful recurved bow, a full quiver of arrows, and his favorite boar spear. Kith-Kanan's scabbard hung empty at his side. His sword, forged by the priests of Kiri Jolith, he'd left in the Tower of the Stars.

The prince put the arrows and the unstrung bow in the sack and tied it to the boar spear. The whole bundle he slung from his shoulder. Now for the door.

The latch whispered backward in its slot. Kith-Kanan pulled the door open. Directly across from his room was Sithas's sleeping chamber. A strip of light showed under his brother's door. Kith-Kanan lowered his bundle to the floor and reached out for the door handle.

Sithas's door opened silently. Inside, his white-robed twin was kneeling before a small table, on which a single cut rose lay. A candle burned on the fireplace mantle.

Sithas looked up. "Come in, Kith," he said gently, "I was expecting you." He stood, looking hollow-eyed and gaunt in the candlelight. "I felt your presence when you returned. Please, sit down."

"I'm not staying," Kith-Kanan replied bitterly.

"You need not leave, Kith. Beg Father for forgiveness. He will grant it."

Kith-Kanan spread his hands. "I can't, Sith. It wouldn't matter if he did forgive me, I can't stay here any longer."

"Because of Hermathya?" asked Sithas. His twin nodded. "I don't love her, Kith, but she was chosen. I must marry her."

"But what about me? Do you care at all how I feel?"

Sithas's face showed that he did. "But what would you have me do?"

"Tell them you won't have her. Refuse to marry Hermathya."

Sithas sighed. "It would be a grave insult to Clan Oakleaf, to our father, and to Hermathya herself. She was chosen because she will be the best wife for the future speaker."

Kith-Kanan passed a hand over his fevered eyes. "This is like a terrible dream. I can't believe Thya consented to all this."

"Then you can go upstairs and ask her. She is sleeping in the room just above yours," Sithas said evenly. Kith-Kanan turned to go. "Wait," Sithas said. "Where will you go from here?"

"I will go far," Kith-Kanan replied defiantly.

Sithas leaped to his feet. "How far will you get on your own? You are throwing away your heritage, Kith! Throwing it away like a gnawed apple core!"

Kith-Kanan stood still in the open doorway. "I'm doing the only honorable thing I can. Do you think I could continue to live here with you, knowing Hermathya was your wife? Do you think I could stand to see her each day and have to call her 'Sister?' I know I have shamed Father and myself. I can live with shame, but I cannot live in sight of Hermathya and not love her!"

He went out in the hall and stooped to get his bundle. Sithas raised the lid of a plain, dark, oak chest sitting at the foot of his bed.

"Kith, wait." Sithas turned around and held out his brother's sword. "Father was going to have it broken, he was so angry with you, but I persuaded him to let me keep it."

Kith-Kanan took the slim, graceful blade from his brother's hands. It slid home in his scabbard like a hand into a glove. Kith-Kanan instantly felt stronger. He had a part of himself back.

"Thank you, Sith."

On a simultaneous impulse, they came together and clasped their hands on each other's shoulders. "May the gods go with you, Brother," said Sithas warmly.

"They will if you ask them," Kith-Kanan replied wryly. "They listen to you."

He crossed the hall to his old room and prepared to go out the window. Sithas came to his door and said, "Will I ever see you again?"

Kith-Kanan looked out at the two bright moons. "As long as Solinari and Lunitari remain in the same sky, I will—see you again, my brother." Without another word, Kith-Kanan stepped out of the window and was gone. Sithas returned to his sparsely furnished room and shut the door.

As he knelt again at his small shrine to Matheri, he said softly, "Two halves of the same coin; two branches of the same tree." He closed his eyes. "Matheri, keep him safe."

On the ledge, Kith-Kanan gathered up his rope. The room just above his, Sithas had said. Very well then. His first cast fell short, and the hook came scraping down the stone right at his face. Kith-Kanan flinched aside, successfully dodging the hook, but he almost lost his balance on the narrow ledge. The falling hook clattered against the wall below. Kith-Kanan cursed soundlessly and hauled the rope back up.

The Tower of Quinari, like most elven spires, grew steadily narrower as it grew taller. The ledges at each level were thus correspondingly shallower. It took Kith-Kanan four tries to catch his

25

hook on the seventh floor ledge. When he did, he swung out into the cool night air, wobbling under the burden of his sack and spear. Doggedly he climbed. The window of the room above his was dark. He carefully set the bundle against the outside wall and went to work on the window latch with his dagger.

The soft lead of the window frame yielded quickly to his blade. He pushed the crystal panes in.

Already he knew she was in the room. The spicy scent she always wore filled the room with a subtle perfume. He listened and heard short sighs of breathing. Hermathya was asleep.

He went unerringly to her bedside. Kith-Kanan put out a hand and felt the soft fire of her hair. He spoke her name once, quietly. "It is I, my love."

"Kith! Please, don't hurt me!"

He was taken aback. He rose off his knees. "I would never, ever hurt you, Thya."

"But I thought—you were so angry—I thought you came here to kill me!"

"No," he said gently. "I've come to take you with me."

She sat up. Solinari peeked in the window just enough to throw a silver beam on her face and neck. From his place in the shadows, Kith-Kanan felt again the deep wound he'd suffered on her account.

"Go with you?" Hermathya said in genuine confusion. "Go where?"

"Does it matter?"

She pushed her long hair away from her face. "And what of Sithas?"

"He doesn't love you," Kith-Kanan said.

"Nor do I love him, but he is my betrothed now."

Kith-Kanan couldn't believe what he was hearing. "You mean, you *want* to marry him?"

"Yes, I do."

Kith-Kanan blundered backward to the window. He sat down hard on the sill. It seemed as though his legs would not work right. The cool night air washed over him, and he breathed deeply.

"You cannot mean it. What about us? I thought you loved me!"

Hermathya walked into the edge of the shaft of moonlight. "I do, Kith. But the gods have decided that I shall be the wife of the next Speaker of the Stars." A note of pride crept into her voice.

"This is madness!" Kith-Kanan burst out. "It was my father who decided this marriage, not the gods!"

"We are all only instruments of the gods," she said coolly. "I love you, Kith, but the time has come to lay aside pranks and secret garden passions. I have spoken with my father, with your father.

You and I had an exciting time together, we dreamed beautiful dreams. But that's all they were—dreams. It's time to wake up now and think of the future. Of the future of all Silvanesti."

All Kith-Kanan could think of at this moment was his own future. "I can't live without you, Thya," he said weakly.

"Yes, you can. You may not know it yet, but you can." She came toward him, and the moonlight made her nightdress no more than a cobweb. Kith-Kanan squeezed his eyes shut and balled his hands into tight fists.

"Please," Hermathya said. "Accept what will happen. We can still be close." Her warm hand touched his cold, dry cheek.

Kith-Kanan seized her wrist and shoved her away. "I cannot accept it," he said tersely, stepping up on the windowsill. "Farewell, Lady Hermathya. May your life be green and golden."

The irony of his words was not lost on her. 'May your life be green and golden' was what elven commoners said when taking leave of their lords.

Kith-Kanan shouldered his sack and slipped over the stone ledge. Hermathya stood for several seconds, gazing at the empty window. When the tears came she did not fight them.

*   *   *   *   *

Faithful Arcuballis was his only companion now. Kith-Kanan tied the sack to the saddle pillion and stuck the boar spear into the lance cup by his right stirrup. He mounted Arcuballis, strapped himself to the saddle, and turned the beast's head into the wind.

"Fly!" he cried, touching his heels into the griffon's brawny breast. "Fly!"

Arcuballis unfolded its wings and sprang into the air. Kith-Kanan whistled, and the griffon uttered its shrill cry. The least he could do, Kith-Kanan decided, was to let them know he was going. He whistled again and once more the griffon's trilling growl echoed between the white towers.

Kith-Kanan put the waxing red moon on his right hand and flew southwest, across the Thon-Thalas. The royal road stood out misty gray in the night, angling away north from the city and south to the seacoast. Kith-Kanan urged the griffon higher and faster. The road, the river, and the city that had been his home vanished behind them. Ahead lay only darkness and an endless sea of trees, green-black in the depths of night.

The Next Day

3

Kith-Kanan had no plans except to get away from Silvanost. More than anything, he craved solitude right now. He pointed Arcuballis's beak southwest, and gave the griffon its head.

Kith-Kanan dozed in the saddle, slumped forward over the griffon's feathered neck. The loyal beast flew on all night, never straying from the course its master had set. Dawn came, and Kith-Kanan awoke, stiff and groggy. He sat up in the saddle and surveyed the land below. There was nothing but treetops as far as the eye could see. He saw no clearings, streams, or meadows, much less signs of habitation.

How far they had flown during the night Kith-Kanan could not guess. He knew from hunting trips down the Thon-Thalas that south of Silvanost lay the Courrain Ocean, the boundaries of which no elf knew. But he was in the East; the rising sun was almost directly ahead of him. He must be in the great forest that lay between the Thon-Thalas on the east and the plains of Kharolis to the west. He'd never ventured this far before.

Looking at the impenetrable canopy of trees, Kith-Kanan licked his dry lips and said aloud, "Well, boy, if things don't change, we can always walk across the trees."

They flew for hours more, crisscrossing the leafy barrier and finding no openings whatsoever. Poor Arcuballis was laboring, panting in deep, dry grunts. The griffon had been flying all night and half the day. When Kith-Kanan lifted his head to scan the horizon, he spied a thin column of smoke rising from the forest, far off to his left. The prince turned Arcuballis toward the smoke. The gap closed with agonizing slowness.

Finally, he could see that a ragged hole had been torn in the tapestry of the forest. In the center of the hole, the gnarled trunk of a great tree stood, blackened and burning. Lightning had struck it. The burned opening was only ten yards wide, but around the base of the burning tree the ground was clear and level. Arcuballis's feet touched down, its wings trembled, and the beast shuddered. Immediately the exhausted griffon closed its eyes to sleep.

Kith-Kanan untied his sack from the pillion. He crossed the narrow clearing with the sack over one shoulder. Dropping to his feet, he squatted down and started to unpack. The caw of a crow caught his ear. Looking up at the splintered, smoldering trunk of the shattered tree, he spied a single black bird perched on a charred limb. The crow cocked its head and cawed again. Kith-Kanan went back to his unpacking as the crow lifted off the limb, circled the clearing, and flew off.

He took out his bow and quiver, and braced a new bowstring. Though only three feet long when strung, the powerful recursive bow could put an iron-tipped arrow through a thick tree trunk. Kith-Kanan tied the quiver to his belt. Taking the stout boar spear in both hands, he jammed it as high as he could into the burned tree. He stuffed his belongings back in the sack and hung the sack from the spear shaft. That ought to keep his things safe from prowling animals.

Kith-Kanan squinted into the late afternoon sun. Using it as a guide, he decided to strike out to the north a short distance to see if he could flush any game. Arcuballis was safe enough, he figured; few predators would dare tangle with a griffon. He put his back to the shattered tree and dove into the deeply shadowed forest.

Though the elf prince was used to the woods, at least the woods around Silvanost, he found this forest strangely different. The trees were widely spaced, but their thick foliage made it nearly as dim as twilight down below. So dense was the roof of leaves, the forest floor was nearly barren. Some ferns and bracken grew between the great trees, but no heavy undergrowth. The soil was thickly carpeted with dead leaves and velvety moss. And even though the high branches stirred in the wind, it was very still where Kith-Kanan walked. Very still indeed. Rings of red-gilled mushrooms, a favorite food of deer and wild boar, grew undisturbed around the bases of the trees. The silence soon grew oppressive.

Kith-Kanan paused a hundred paces from the clearing and drew his sword. He cut a hunter's sign, a "blaze," into the gray-brown bark of a hundred-foot-high oak tree. Beneath the bark, the white flesh of the tree was hard and tough. The elven blade chipped away

29

at it, and the sound of iron on wood echoed through the forest. His marker made, Kith-Kanan sheathed his sword and continued on, bow in hand.

The forest seemed devoid of animals. Except for the crow he'd seen, no other creature, furred or winged, showed itself. Every thirty yards or so he made another blaze so as not to lose his way, for the darkness was increasing. It was at least four hours until sunset, yet the shadowed recesses of the forest were dimming to twilight. Kith-Kanan mopped the sweat from his brow and knelt in the fallen leaves. He brushed them aside, looking for signs of grazing by deer or wild pigs. The moss was unbroken.

By the time Kith-Kanan had made his tenth blaze, it was dark as night. He leaned against an ash tree and tried to see through the closely growing branches overhead. At this point he'd just as soon have squirrel for dinner as venison. That was growing more likely too.

Tiny points of sunlight filtered through the leaves, dancing as the wind stirred the branches. It was almost like seeing the stars, only these points of light moved. The effect was quite hypnotic, which only made Kith-Kanan more tired than he already was. He'd dozed only fitfully in the saddle and had eaten nearly nothing since the day before. Perhaps he'd stop for a moment. Take a bit of rest. Overhead the points of light danced and swayed.

Kith-Kanan's sword, resting in the crook of his arm, slipped from his grasp and fell to the ground, sticking point first in the soft soil.

Points of light. Dancing. How very tired he was! His knees folded, and he slid slowly down the trunk until he was sitting on his haunches, back against the tree. His gaze remained on the canopy of leaves overhead. What an odd forest this was. Not like home. Not like the woods of Silvanost

As in a dream, the prince saw the airy corridors of the Palace of Quinari. The servants bowed to him, as they always did. He was on his way to a feast in the Hall of Balif. There would be simmered roasts, legs of lamb, fruits dripping with juice, fragrant sauces, and delicious drafts of sweet nectar.

Kith-Kanan came to a door. It was just a door, like any other in the palace. He pushed the door open, and there, in loving embrace, were Sithas and Hermathya. She turned to face him, a smile on her face. A smile for Sithas.

"No!"

He leaped forward, landing on his hands and knees. His legs were completely numb. It was pitch dark around him, and for a few seconds Kith-Kanan didn't know where he was. He breathed deeply. Night must have fallen, he realized. But the dream had seemed so real! The elf's senses told him he'd broken some spell, one that had come over him as he looked at the patterns of light and shadow up in the trees. He must have been dreaming for hours.

After a long minute waiting for the feeling to return to his legs, Kith-Kanan cast about for his sword. He found it sticking in the moss. He freed the weapon and shoved it into its scabbard. A vague sense of urgency turned him back to the blasted clearing. His last blaze was visible in the night, but the second to last was almost gone. New bark was covering the cut he'd made. The next mark was a mere slit, and the one after that he found only because he remembered the oddly forked trunk of the ash tree he'd hacked it into. There were no more to find after that. The cuts had healed.

For a moment the elf prince knew fear. He was lost in the silent forest at night, hungry, thirsty, and alone. Had enough time passed for the cuts to heal naturally, or was the grove enchanted? Even the darkness that surrounded him seemed, well, darker than usual. Not even his elven eyesight could penetrate very far.

Then the training and education of a prince reasserted itself, banishing much of the fear. Kith-Kanan, grandson of the great Silvanos, was not about to be bested on his first night in the wilderness.

He found a dry branch and set about making a torch to light his way back to the clearing. After gathering a pile of dead leaves for tinder, Kith-Kanan pulled out his flint and striker. To his surprise, no sparks flew off the iron bar when he grated the flint against it. He tried and tried, but all the fire seemed to have gone out of the flint.

There was a flutter of black wings overhead. Kith-Kanan leaped to his feet in time to see a flock of crows take up perches on a limb just out of reach. The dozen birds watched him with unnerving intelligence.

"Shoo!" he yelled, flinging a useless branch at them. The crows flapped up and, when the branch had passed, settled again in the same place and posture.

He pocketed his flint and striker. The crows followed his movements with unblinking eyes. Tired and bewildered, he addressed the birds directly. "I don't suppose you can help me find my way back, can you?"

One by one, the birds took wing and disappeared into the night. Kith-Kanan sighed. I must be getting desperate if I'm talking to birds, he concluded. After drawing his sword, he set off again, cutting new blazes as he hunted for the clearing where he had left Arcuballis. That way, at least he could avoid walking in circles.

31

He smote the nearest elm twice, chipping out palm-sized bits of bark. He was about to strike a third time when he noticed the shadow of his sword arm against the gray tree trunk. Shadow? In this well of ink? Kith-Kanan turned quickly, sword ready. Floating six feet off the ground, more than a dozen feet away, was a glowing mass the size of a wine barrel. He watched, half anxious, half curious, as the glowing light came toward him. It halted two feet from his face, and Kith-Kanan could clearly see what it was.

The cool yellow mass of light was a swarm of fireflies. The insects flew in circles around each other, creating a moving lamp for the lost prince. Kith-Kanan stared at them in shock. The glowing mass moved forward a few yards and halted. Kith-Kanan took a step toward them, and they moved on a bit farther.

"Are you leading me back to the clearing?" the prince asked in wonder. In response, the fireflies moved another yard forward. Kith-Kanan followed warily, but grateful for the soft sphere of light the fireflies cast around him.

In minutes, they had led him back to the clearing. The blasted tree was just as he remembered but Arcuballis was gone. Kith-Kanan ran to the spot where the griffon had lain to rest. The leaves and moss still carried the impression of the heavy beast, but that was all. Kith-Kanan was astonished. He couldn't believe Arcuballis had flown off without him. Royal griffons were bonded to their riders, and no more loyal creatures existed on Krynn. There were tales of riders dying, and their griffons following them into death out of sheer grief. Someone or something must have taken Arcuballis. But who? Or what? How could such a powerful creature be subdued without sign of a struggle?

Sick in his heart, Kith-Kanan wandered to the lightning-seared tree. More bad news! His boar spear remained stuck in the trunk, but the sack containing his possessions was gone. Angrily, he reached up and wrenched the spear free. He stood in the clearing, gazing at the dark circle of trees. Now he was truly alone. He and Arcuballis had been companions for many years. More than a means of transport, the griffon was a trusted friend.

He sagged to the ground, feeling utterly wretched. What could he do? He couldn't even find his way around the forest in broad daylight. Kith-Kanan's eyes brimmed, but he steadfastly refused to weep like some abandoned child.

The fireflies remained by his head. They darted forward, then back, as if reminding him they were there.

"Get away!" he snarled as they swooped scant inches from his nose. The swarm instantly dispersed. The fireflies flew off in all directions, their tiny lights flitting here and there, and then were gone.

* * * * *

"Won't you come in? You'll catch a chill."

Sithel drew a woolen mantle up over his shoulders. "I am warmly dressed," he said. His wife pulled a blanket off their bed, wrapped it around her own shoulders, and stepped out on the balcony with him.

Sithel's long white hair lifted off his neck as a chill wind passed over the palace tower. The private rooms of the speaker and his consort took up the penultimate floor of the palace's tower. Only the Tower of the Stars provided a higher vantage point in Silvanost.

"I felt a faint cry not long ago," Sithel said.

"Kith-Kanan?" The speaker nodded. "Do you think he is in danger?" asked Nirakina, drawing her blanket more closely about herself.

"I think he is unhappy. He must be very far away. The feeling was faint."

Nirakina looked up at her husband. "Call him, Sithel. Call him home."

"I will not. He offended me, and he offended the noble assembly. He broke one of our most sacred laws by drawing a weapon inside the Tower of the Stars."

"These things can be forgiven," she said quietly. "What else is it that makes it so hard for you to forgive him?"

Sithel stroked his wife's soft hair. "I might have done what he did, had my father given the woman I loved to another. But I don't approve of his deed, and I will not call him home. If I did, he wouldn't learn the discipline he must have. Let him stay away a while. His life here has been too easy, and the outside world will teach him to be strong and patient."

"I'm afraid for him," Nirakina said. "The world beyond Silvanost is a deadly place."

Sithel raised her chin so their eyes met. "He has the blood of Silvanos in his veins. Kith-Kanan will survive, beloved, survive and prosper." Sithel looked away, out at the dark city. He held out his arm. "Come, let us go in."

They lay down together, as they had for more than a thousand years. But while Nirakina soon fell asleep, Sithel lay awake, worrying.

Three Days Later

4

After three sunrises, Kith-Kanan was in despair. He'd lost his griffon and his spare clothing. When he tried his flint and striker again, he managed to start a small fire. It comforted him somewhat, but he found no food whatsoever to cook. On his third morning in the forest, he ran out of water, too.

There was no point remaining in the clearing, so he shouldered his spear and set out to find food and water. If the maps he remembered were correct, the Kharolis River lay to the west. It might be many miles, but at least it was something to aim for.

The only animals he saw on the way were more crows. The black birds stayed with him, flitting from tree to tree, punctuating their flight with short, sharp caws. The crows were Kith-Kanan's only company, so he started talking to them. It helped keep his spirits up.

"I don't suppose you know where my griffon is?" he asked. Not surprisingly, the birds didn't answer, but continued to fly from tree to tree, keeping up with him.

The day dragged on and grew hotter. Even down in the eternal shade of the deep forest, Kith-Kanan sweltered, because no breeze stirred the air. The lay of the land grew rougher, too, with hills and gullies running north to south along his line of march. This encouraged him at first, because very often springs and brooks could be found at the bottom of ravines. But as he scrambled up one hill and down another, he found only moss and stones and fallen trees.

After skidding down a hillside into the nineteenth gully, Kith-Kanan paused to rest. He sat on a fallen tree, dropping the spear in front of him. He licked his dry lips again and fought down the rising feeling that he had made a grave mistake by running away. How could he have been so foolish to abandon his life of privilege for this? As soon as he asked himself the question the vision of Hermathya marrying his brother rose up in his mind, horribly vivid. Pain and loss welled up inside. To dispel the image, he stood up abruptly and started off again, shouldering his boar spear. He took two steps across the bottom of the ravine, and his feet sank an inch or so into mud, covered by a thin layer of dead leaves.

Where there's mud, there's water, he realized happily. Kith-Kanan went along the ravine to his right, looking for the water that must be there somewhere. He could see the ravine widen up ahead. Perhaps there was a pool, a pool of clear, sweet water. . . .

The ravine converged on several others, making a steepsided bowl in the hills. Kith-Kanan slogged through the increasingly wet mud. He could smell water ahead. Then he could see it a small pool, undisturbed by a ripple. The sight drew him like magic. The mud rose above his knees but he plunged on, right to the center of the pool. Cupping his hands, he filled them with water and raised them to his lips.

Immediately he spit the water out again. It tasted vile, like rotted leaves. Kith-Kanan stared down at his reflection in the water. His face twisted with frustrated rage. It was no use. He would just have to keep going.

His leg wouldn't come up out of the pool. He tried the other. It was also stuck. He strained so hard to pull them up, he nearly lost his balance. Arms flailing, Kith-Kanan twisted his hips from side to side, trying to work himself free. Instead he sank deeper into the mire. He glanced around quickly for a tree branch to grab, or a trailing vine. The nearest trees were ten feet away.

The mud was soon up to his waist. He began to sink even faster. "Help!" he cried desperately. "Is there anyone to hear?"

A flock of crows settled on the hillside facing Kith-Kanan. They watched with unnerving calm as he foundered in the killing mud.

You won't pick my eyes, he vowed silently. When the end comes, I'll duck under the mud before I let you black carrion eaters pick me over.

"They're not really so bad once you get to know them," said a voice. Kith-Kanan jerked as if struck by lightning.

"Who's there?" he shouted, looking around at the still trees. "Help!"

35

"I can help you. I don't know that I will." It was a high, childish voice, full of smugness.

In replying, the speaker had given himself away. Kith-Kanan spotted him, to his left, in a tree. Sitting comfortably on a thick branch, his back propped against the ancient oak trunk, was a slender young person, clad in mottled green-brown tunic and hose. A hood was drawn up over his head. The tan face that showed under the hood was painted with loops and lines, done in bright red and yellow pigment.

"Help me!" Kith-Kanan shouted. "I can reward you handsomely!"

"Really? What with?"

"Gold. Silver. Jewels." Anything, he vowed to himself. Anything in all of Krynn.

"What is gold?"

The mud was halfway up Kith-Kanan's chest. The pressure against his body made it difficult to draw breath. "You're mocking me," he gasped. "Please! I haven't much time!"

"No, you haven't," noted the hooded figure uninterestedly. "What else would you give me if I help you?"

"My bow! Would you like that?"

"I can pick that out of the mire once you're gone."

Blast the fellow! "I haven't anything else!" The cold muck was nearly at his shoulders. "Please, for the gods' sake, help me!"

The hooded figure rolled nimbly forward onto his feet. "I will help you, for the gods' sake. They often do things for me, so it seems only fair I do something for their sake now and again."

The stranger walked heel to toe along the branch until he was almost directly over Kith-Kanan. The prince's shoulders were in the mud, though he held his arms above his head to keep them free until the last possible second. The fellow in the tree unwrapped a belt from his waist. It had circled his slim body several times and, when unwound, was over ten feet long. Lying flat on the branch, he lowered the leather strap to Kith-Kanan. The prince caught it in his left hand.

"What are you waiting for? Pull me out!" Kith-Kanan ordered.

"If you can't pull yourself out, I cannot do it for you," his rescuer remarked. He looped the belt around the tree limb a few times and secured it with a knot. Then he lay on the branch, his head propped on one hand, awaiting the outcome.

Kith-Kanan grimaced and started to haul himself out by the strap. With much gasping and cursing, Kith-Kanan climbed out of the deadly mire and pulled himself up to the tree branch. He threw a leg over the branch and lay panting.

"Thank you," he finally said, a little sarcastically.

The young fellow had moved several feet back toward the oak tree and sat with his knees drawn up. "You're welcome," he replied. Behind the barbarous face paint, his eyes were brilliant green. He pushed back his hood, revealing himself to be a boy with a shock of bone-white hair. His high cheekbones and tapered ears bespoke his heritage. Kith-Kanan sat up slowly, astride the branch.

"You are Silvanesti," he said, startled.

"No, I am Mackeli."

Kith-Kanan shook his head. "You are of the race of the Silvanesti, as am I."

The elf boy stood on the branch. "I don't know what you mean. I am Mackeli."

The branch was too narrow for Kith-Kanan to stand on, so he inched his way forward to the tree trunk. The deadly mud below was hidden once more under its covering of water. He shuddered as he looked down upon it. "You see we are alike, don't you?"

Mackeli, hopping nimbly along the branch, glanced back at Kith-Kanan and said, "No. I don't see that we are alike."

Exasperated and too tired to continue, Kith-Kanan gave up that line of conversation.

They climbed down to solid ground. Kith-Kanan followed the scampering boy slowly. Even so, he lost his grip on the trunk and fell the last few feet. He landed on his rear with a thud and groaned.

"You are clumsy," Mackeli observed.

"And you are rude. Do you know who I am?" the prince said haughtily.

"A clumsy outlander." The elf boy reached around his back and brought back a gourd bottle, laced tightly with deerskin. He poured a trickle of clear water into his open mouth. Kith-Kanan watched intently, his throat moving with imaginary swallows.

"May I may I have some water?" he pleaded.

Mackeli shrugged and handed him the bottle. Kith-Kanan took the gourd in his muddy hands and drank greedily. He drained the bottle in three gulps.

"May the gods bless you," he said, handing the empty container to the boy.

Mackeli upended the bottle, saw that it was indeed completely dry, and gave Kith-Kanan a disgusted look.

"I haven't had any water in two days," Kith-Kanan explained. "Nor have I eaten. Do you have any food?"

"Not with me. There is some at home."

"Would you take me there?"

Mackeli raised his hood again, hiding his startlingly white hair. With it covered, he was superbly camouflaged, blending into the forest. "Won't know if that would be right. Ny might not like it."

"I appeal to you, friend. I am desperate. I have lost my steed and my way, and I cannot seem to find any game in this accursed forest. If you don't help me, I shall starve in this wilderness."

The elf boy laughed, a pleasant sound in the still air. "Yes, I heard there was an outlander blundering about in these parts. The corvae told me about you."

"Corvae?"

Mackeli pointed to the crows, still watching from the nearby hillside. "They know everything that happens in the forest. Sometimes, when something strange occurs, they tell me and Ny about it."

Kith-Kanan remembered the unnerving attention the crows had paid him. "Do you truly speak with birds?"

"Not only birds." Mackeli held up a hand and made a shrill cawing sound. One of the black birds flew over and alighted on his arm, like a falcon returning to its master.

"What do you think?" the boy asked the bird. "Can I trust him?" The crow cocked its head and uttered a single sharp screech. Mackeli frowned. The whorls above his eyes contracted as he knitted his brow together.

"He says you carry an object of power. He says you cut the trees with it."

Kith-Kanan looked down at his mud-caked scabbard. "My sword is not magical," he said. "It's just an ordinary blade. Here, you can hold it." He reversed his grip and held the pommel out to Mackeli. The elf boy reached out tentatively. The crows chorused as if in warning, but Mackeli ignored them. His small hand closed over the diamond-shaped pommel.

"There is power here," he said, snatching his hand back. "It smells like death!"

"Take it in your hands," Kith-Kanan urged. "It won't hurt you."

Mackeli grasped the handle in both hands and lifted it out of the prince's hand. "So heavy! What is it made of?" he grunted.

"Iron and brass." Mackeli's face showed that he did not know iron or brass, gold or silver. "Do you know what metals are, Mackeli?"

"No." He tried to swing Kith-Kanan's sword, but it was too heavy for him to control. The point dropped to the ground.

"I thought as much." Gently the prince took the sword back and slid it into its sheath. "Are you satisfied I'm not dangerous?"

Mackeli sniffed his hands and made a face. "I never said you were dangerous," he said airily. "Except maybe to yourself."

He set off and kept up a brisk pace, slipping in and out of the big trees. Mackeli never walked straight more than a few yards.

He pushed off from the massive trunks, hopped over fallen limbs, and scampered like a squirrel. Kith-Kanan trudged along, weighed down by hunger and several pounds of stinking mud. Several times Mackeli had to double back to find the prince and guide him along. Kith-Kanan watched the boy's progress through the forest and felt like a tired old man. He'd thought he was such a fine ranger. This boy, who could be no more than sixty years old, made the foresters of Silvanost look like blundering drunkards.

The trek lasted hours and followed no discernible path. Kith-Kanan got the strong impression Mackeli didn't want him to know where they were going.

There were elves who dwelt entirely in the wilderness, the Kagonesti. They were given to the practice of painting their skin with strange patterns, as Mackeli did. But they were dark-skinned and dark-haired; this boy's features were pure Silvanesti. Kith-Kanan asked himself why a boy of the pure blood should be out here in the deep forest. Runaway? Member of a lost tribe? He finally imagined a secret forest hideaway, inhabited by outlaws driven from Silvanost by his grandfather Silvanos's wars of unification. Not everyone had followed the great leader to peace and unity.

Suddenly Kith-Kanan realized that he no longer heard Mackeli's light tread in the carpet of fallen leaves. Halting, he looked ahead, then spied the boy a score of yards away, on his right. Mackeli was kneeling, his head bowed low. A hush had fallen over the already quiet forest.

As he observed the boy, wonderingly, a feeling of utter peace flowed over Kith-Kanan, a peace he'd never known before. All the troubles of recent days were washed away. Then Kith-Kanan turned and saw what had brought this tranquility, what had brought Mackeli to his knees.

Framed by ferns and tree trunks wrapped in flowering vines was a magnificent animal with a single white horn spiraling from its head. A unicorn rarest of the rare, more scarce than the gods themselves. The unicorn was snowy white from her small, cloven hooves to the tips of her foaming mane. She radiated a soft light that seemed the essence of peace. Standing on a slight rise of ground, fifteen yards away, her eyes met Kith-Kanan's and touched his soul.

The elf prince sank to his knees. He knew he was being granted a rare privilege, a glimpse of a creature thought by many to be only legend.

"Rise, noble warrior." Kith-Kanan raised his head. "Rise, son of Sithel." The voice was deep and melodic. Mackeli, still bowed, gave no sign that he had heard.

Kith-Kanan stood slowly. "You know me, great one?"

"I heard of your coming." So enticing was the majestic creature, he wanted very badly to approach her, to see her more closely, to touch her. Before he could put the thought into action, she said sharply, "Stand where you are! It is not permitted for you to come too near." Kith-Kanan involuntarily took a step back. "Son of Sithel, you have been chosen for an important task. I brought you and the boy Mackeli together, so he could be your guide in the forest. He is a good boy, much skilled in the ways of beast and bird. He will serve you well!"

"What do you wish me to do?" Kith-Kanan asked with sudden humility.

The unicorn tossed her head, sending pearly waves of mane cascading along her neck. "This deep forest is the oldest in the land. It was here that leaf and limb, animal and bird first lived. The spirits of the land are strong here, but they are vulnerable, too. For five thousand risings of the sun, special ones have lived in the forest, protecting it from despoilers. Now a band of interlopers has come to this land, bringing fire and death with them. The spirits of the old forest cry out for help to me, and I have found you as the answer. You are the fated one, the one who carries iron. You must drive the despoilers out, son of Sithel."

At that moment, Kith-Kanan would have fought armies of dragons had the unicorn but asked. "Where will I find these interlopers?" he said, his hand coming to the pommel of his sword.

The unicorn took a step backward. "There is another, who lives with the boy. Together, you three shall cleanse the forest."

The unicorn took another step backward, and the forest itself seemed to close around her. Her alabaster aura shone briefly, and then she was gone, vanished into the secret depths of the greenwood.

After a few seconds Kith-Kanan recovered himself and ran to Mackeli. When he touched the boy's shoulder, Mackeli shook himself as if coming out of a trance.

"Where is the Forestmaster?" he whispered.

"Gone," said Kith-Kanan regretfully. "She spoke to me!"

A look of awe spread over Mackeli's sharp face. "You are greatly favored, outlander! What did the Forestmaster say?"

"You didn't hear?" Mackeli shook his head. Apparently the unicorn's message was for him alone. He wondered how much to tell the boy and finally decided to keep his own counsel.

"You are to take me to your camp," he said firmly. "I will need to learn everything you know about living in the woods."

"That I will gladly teach you," Mackeli said. He shivered with excitement. "In all my life, I have never seen the Forestmaster!

There were times I sensed her passing, but never have I been so close!" He grasped Kith-Kanan's hand. "Come! Let's hurry. I can't wait to tell Ny about this!"

Kith-Kanan glanced at the spot where the Forestmaster had stood. Flowers had burst up where her hooves had touched the ground. Before he could react, Mackeli had jerked him into motion. At breakneck speed, the sure-footed boy drew Kith-Kanan deeper into the forest. The undergrowth got thicker, the trees larger and closer together, yet Mackeli never faltered. At times he and Kith-Kanan had to wriggle through gaps in the trees so tight and low they had to go on hands and knees.

Just before sunset, when the crickets had begun to sing, Mackeli reached a large clearing and stopped.

"We are home," said the boy.

Kith-Kanan went to the center of the open space, more than forty paces across, and turned a circle on one heel. "What home?" he asked.

Mackeli grinned, the effect weirdly emphasized by the red lines of paint dabbed on his cheeks. Jauntily he walked forward to the base of a truly massive oak. He grasped at a patch of relatively smooth bark and pulled. A door opened in the trunk of the tree, a door made from a curving section of oak bark. Beyond the open door was a dark space. Mackeli waved to Kith-Kanan.

"Come in. This is home," the boy said as he stepped into the hollow tree.

Kith-Kanan had to duck to clear the low opening. It smelled like wood and spice inside, pleasant but strange to his city-bred nose. It was so black he could barely make out the dim curve of the wooden walls. Of Mackeli he could see nothing.

And then the boy's hand touched his, and Kith-Kanan flinched like a frightened child. "Light a candle or a lamp, will you?" he said, embarrassed.

"Do what?"

"Light a never mind. Can you make a fire, Mackeli? I can't see a thing in here."

"Only Ny can make fire."

"Is Ny here?"

"No. Gone hunting, I think."

Kith-Kanan groped his way along the wall. "Where does Ny build his fires?" he asked.

"Here." Mackeli led him to the center of the room. Kith-Kanan's foot bumped a low hearth made of rocks plastered together with mud. He squatted down and felt the ashes. Stone cold. No one had used it in quite a while.

"If you get me some kindling, I'll make a fire," he offered.

"Only Ny can make fire," Mackeli repeated doubtfully.

"Well, I may not be the stealthiest tracker or the best forester, but, by Astarin, I can make fire!"

They went back out and gathered armfuls of windblown twigs and small, dead branches. A weak bit of light cut into the hollow tree through the open door as Kith-Kanan arranged the dry sticks in a cone over a heap of bark and shavings he had whittled off with his dagger. He took out his flint and striker from the pouch at his waist. Leaning on his knees on the stone hearth, he nicked the flint against the roughened iron striker. Sparks fell on the tinder, and he blew gently on them. In a few minutes he had a weak flicker of flame and not long after that, a crackling fire.

"Well, boy, what do you think of that?" the prince asked Mackeli.

Instead of being impressed, Mackeli shook his head. "Ny's not going to like this."

Lightened by the fire, the interior of the hollow tree was finally visible to Kith-Kanan. The room was quite large, five paces wide, and a ladder led up through a hole to the upper branches and the outside of the tree. Smoke from the fire also went out through this hole. The walls were decorated with the skulls of animals rabbit, squirrel, a fierce-looking boar with upthrust tusks, a magnificent eight-point buck, plus a host of bird skulls Kith-Kanan could not identify. Mackeli explained that whenever Ny killed an animal not killed before, the skull was cleaned and mounted on a peg on the wall. That way the spirit of the dead beast was propitiated and the god of the forest, the Blue Phoenix, would grant success to future hunts.

"Which of these did you kill?" Kith-Kanan asked.

"It is not permitted for me to shed the blood of animals. That's Ny's work." The elf boy slipped back his hood. "I talk to the animals and listen to what they say. I do not shed their blood."

Kith-Kanan sat down on a pallet filled with moss. He was weary and dirty and very hungry. Mackeli fidgeted about, giving the prince frequent looks of displeasure. Eventually, Kith-Kanan asked Mackeli what was wrong.

"That's Ny's place. You must not sit there," the boy said irritatedly.

Kith-Kanan heaved himself off. "This Ny has more privileges than the Speaker of the Stars," he said, exasperation clearing his voice. "May I sit here?" He indicated the floor of the hollow tree, which was covered with pine needles. Mackeli nodded.

Soon after that exchange, Kith-Kanan asked for something to eat. The elf boy scampered up the ladder and, leaning out to the center of the hollow space, pushed aside various gourds and skin bags that hung by thongs from the ceiling. He found the one he wanted and brought it down. Sitting cross-legged beside Kith-Kanan, Mackeli bade the prince hold out his hands. He did, and the boy filled them with roasted wild chestnuts, neatly peeled.

"Do you have any meat?" Kith-Kanan asked.

"Only Ny eats meat."

The prince was getting tired of the litany of things only Ny could do. Too tired, in fact, to dispute with the boy, Kith-Kanan ate chestnuts in silence. He was grateful for whatever he could get.

"Do you know," he said at last, "you've never asked me my name?"

Mackeli shrugged. "I didn't think you had one."

"Of course I have a name!" The elf boy rubbed his nose, getting yellow paint on his fingers. "My name is Kith," the prince said, since Mackeli obviously wasn't going to ask.

Mackeli shook more chestnuts into his paint-stained palm. "That's a funny name," he noted and popped a chestnut into his mouth.

Five Weeks Later

5

"Lady Nerakina, wife of the Speaker," annnounced the maidservant. Hermathya looked up from her mirror and nodded. The servant opened the door.

"Time is short, Lady," Nirakina cautioned as she entered.

"I know." Hermathya stood motionless in the center of a maelstrom of activity. Servants, dressmakers, and perfumers dodged and weaved around her, each trying to make final, finishing touches before the wedding ceremony began.

"You look beautiful," Nirakina said, and she was not merely being polite to her daughter-to-be. The finest creators of beauty in Silvanost had labored for weeks to make Hermathya's wedding gown and to compound the special oils and perfumes that would be hers alone.

The gown was in two parts. The first was an overdress in sheerest linen, too light to be worn alone and maintain modesty. Beneath this, Hermathya was wrapped in a single swath of golden cloth, many yards long. Six members of the Seamstress Guild had begun the winding Hermathya wore at her neck. A huge drum of gold was slowly wound around her, closely over her breasts and torso, more loosely over hips and legs. She had been forced to stand with her arms raised for two hours while the elf women worked.

Her feet were covered by sandals made from a single sheet of gold, beaten so thin it felt and flexed like the most supple leather. Golden laces crisscrossed her legs from ankle to knee, securing the sandals.

The elf's hair and face had been worked over, too. Gone were the maidenly braids framing her face. Her coppery hair was waved, then spread around her shoulders. In the elven custom, it was the husband who gave his new wife the first of the clasps with which she would ever after bind her tresses.

The bride's skin was smoothed of every roughness or blemish with aromatic oils and bone-thin soapstone. Her nails were polished and gilded, and her lips were painted golden. As befitted her noble rank and wealthy family, Hermathya wore sixteen bracelets ten on her right arm and six on her left. These were all gifts from her parents, her siblings, and her female friends.

"That's enough," Nirakina said to the agitated servants. "Leave us." With much bowing and flourishing, the mob funneled out the doors of the Hall of Balif. "All of you," said the speaker's wife. The regular palace servants withdrew, closing the doors behind them.

"So much work for such a brief ceremony," Hermathya said. She turned ever so slowly, so as not to disturb her hair or gown. "Is this as great as your wedding, Lady?"

"Greater. Sithel and I were married during the Second Dragon War, when there was no time or gold to spare on fancy things. We didn't know then if we'd be alive in a year, much less know if we'd have an heir to see married."

"I have heard stories of those times. It must have been terrible."

"The times make those who live in them," Nirakina said evenly. Her own dress, as the speaker's wife and mother of the groom, was quite conservative white silk embroidered in silver and gold with the arms of House Royal. But with her honey-brown hair and liquid eyes she had a serene beauty all her own.

There was a loud, very masculine knock at the door. Nirakina said calmly, "Come in."

A splendidly attired warrior entered the hall. His armor was burnished until it was almost painful to look at. Scarlet plumes rose from his helmet. His scabbard was empty the ceremony was one of peace, so no weapons were allowed but his fierce martial splendor was no less imposing.

"My ladies," announced the warrior, "I am Kencathedrus, chosen by Lord Sithas to escort you to the Tower of the Stars."

"I know you, Kencathedrus," replied Nirakina. "You trained Prince Kith-Kanan in the warrior arts, did you not?"

"I did, my lady."

Hermathya was glad she was facing away. Mention of Kith-Kanan brought a rush of color to her powdered face. It wasn't so much that she still loved him, she decided. No, she was over that, if she ever did truly love him. But she knew that Kencathedrus, a mere soldier, was performing the duty Kith-Kanan should be doing. To escort the bride was a duty brother owed to brother.

Hermathya composed herself. This was the moment. She turned. "I am ready."

In the corridor outside the Hall of Balif an honor guard of twenty warriors was drawn up, and farther down the hall twenty young elf girls chosen from the families of the guild masters stood ready to precede the honor guard. And beyond them, filling the other end of the corridor, were twenty elf boys dressed in long, trailing white robes and carrying sistrums. The size of the escort took Hermathya back for a moment. She looked out at the sea of expectant faces. It was rather overwhelming. All these people, and thousands more outside, awaited her. She called upon the core of strength that had carried her through troubles before, put on her most serene expression, and held out her hand. Kencathedrus rested her hand on his armored forearm, and the procession to the Tower of the Stars began.

Nirakina walked three steps behind them, and after her the honor guard fell in with the clank and rattle of armor and metal sandals. The boys led the procession in slow step, banging their sistrums against their hands. To this steady rhythm the elf girls followed, strewing flower petals in the path of the bride.

Outside, the sun was high and bright, and every spire in Silvanost boasted a streaming banner. When Hermathya appeared on the steps of the Palace of Quinari, the assembled crowd let out a shout of greeting.

"What do I do?" Hermathya murmured. "Do I wave?"

"No, that would be vulgar. You must be above it all," said Nirakina softly.

A phalanx of pipers, clad in brilliant green, formed in front of the sistrum-bearing boys and played a bright fanfare. The music settled into a march as the procession wound around the Gardens of Astarin, following the circular road. According to ritual, the bride was first taken to the temple of Quenesti Pah, where she underwent a rite of purification. At the same time, the groom was receiving similar rites in the temple of E'li. Then the two came together before the speaker in the Tower of the Stars, where they exchanged golden rings shaped to resemble twining branches and where their joining was finally accomplished.

The sun shone down from a spring sky unsullied by a single cloud, and the marble buildings glowed in the midst of velvety green foliage. The crowd cheered mightily for the spectacle. Perhaps, Hermathya thought idly, in time they will cheer so for me. . . .

"Careful, Lady," warned Kencathedrus. The flower petals were being trodden to mush, and the road was getting a bit treacherous. Hermathya's golden sandals were stained with the crushed pulp. She lifted the hem of her diaphanous white gown out of the debris.

The squat, conical tower of the Temple of E'li appeared ahead on her right. Hermathya could see Sithas's guard of honor-at least a hundred warriors-drawn up on the. Steps. Just as her own attendants were bedecked in gold and white, so Sithas's attendants wore gold and green. She tried to keep her eyes straight ahead as they passed the temple, but she was drawn irresistibly to look in the open doors. It was dark inside the house of worship, and though she could see torches blazing on the wall, she could see neither Sithas nor anyone else within.

As the bride's entourage rounded the curve, the press of the crowd became greater and the cheering intensified. The shadow cast by the Tower of the Stars fell across the street. It was thought to be good luck to stand in the structure's shadow, so hundreds were crammed into the narrow space.

On a sudden impulse, Hermathya abandoned her distant, serene demeanor and smiled. The cheering increased. She raised her free hand and waved, once to the people of Silvanost. A roar went up such as the 'City had never heard, a roar that excited her.

In the Temple of E'li, Sithas heard the roar. He was kneeling before the high priest, about to be anointed with sacred oils. He raised his head slightly and turned one ear toward the sound. The warrior who knelt behind him whispered, "Shall I see what is the matter, Lord?"

"No" replied Sithas levelly. "I believe the people have just met the bride."

* * * * *

The Temple of Quenesti Pah, goddess of health and fertility, was a light, airy vault with a roof of transparent tortoiseshell. There was no great central tower, as in most of the other temples. Instead, four thin spires rose from the comers of the roof, solid columns of rock that reached skyward. Though not as imposing as the House of E'li, or as somber as the Temple of Matheri, Mermathya thought the Temple of Quenesti Pah the prettiest building in Silvanost.

The pipers, sistrum players, and flower girls all turned aside and flanked the entrance to the temple. The honor guard halted at the foot of the steps.

Nirakina stepped up beside Hermathya. "If you have finished performing for the crowd, we will go in." In her tone could be detected a sharpness, and Hermathya hid a smile. Without reply-ing, Hermathya gave the crowd one last wave before she entered the temple.

Nirakina watched her ascend the steps. She was really trying to get along with the girl, but every passing moment added to her irritation. For Sithas's sake, she wanted the marriage to be a suc-cess, but her overwhelming feeling was that Hermathya was a spoiled child.

Inside, the ritual was brief, consisting of little more than prayers and the washing of Hermathya's hands in scented water. Nirakina hovered over her, her distaste for the younger woman's behavior just barely concealed. But Hermathya had understood Nirakina's annoyance, and she found that she enjoyed it. It added to her sense of excitement.

The ritual done, the bride rose to her feet and thanked Miritelisina, the high priestess. Then, without waiting for Nirakina, she walked swiftly from the temple. The crowd was waiting breathlessly for her reappearance, and Hermathya did not disappoint them. A thunder of approval built from the back of the crowd, where the poorest elves stood. She flashed them a smile, then moved with quick grace down to Kencathedrus. Nirakina hurried after her, looking harassed and undignified.

The procession reformed, and the pipers played "Children of the Stars," the ancient tune that every elf knew from childhood. Even Hermathya was surprised, however, when the people began to sing along with the pipers.

She slowed her pace and gradually stopped. The procession strung out until the pipers in the fore realized that those behind had halted. The music swelled higher and louder until Harmathya felt that she was being lifted by it.

With little prelude, the bride sang. At her side, Kencathedrus looked at her in wonder. He glanced over his armored shoulder to Lady Nirakina, who stood silent and straight, arms held rig-idly at her sides. Her voluminous sleeves covered her tightly clenched fists.

Some in the crowd ceased their own singing that they might hear the bride. But as the last verse of the song began, they all joined in; once more the sound threatened to raise the city from its founda-tions. When the last words of "Children of the Stars" faded in the throats of thousands, silence fell over Silvanost. The silence seemed more intense because of the tumult earlier. Everyone assembled in the street, every elf on rooftops and in tower windows had his or her eyes on Hermathya.

Casually the bride took her hand from Kencathedrus's arm and walked through the procession toward the Tower of the

Stars. The flower girls and sistrum-bearers parted in complete silence. Hermathya walked with calm grace through the ranks of the pipers. They stood aside, their silver flutes stilled. Up the steps of the Tower of the Stars she moved, appearing in the doorway alone.

Sithas stood in the center of the hall, waiting. With much less fanfare, he had come from the Temple of E'li with his retainers. Farther inside, Sithel sat on his throne. The golden mantle that lay on the speaker's shoulders spread out on the floor before him, trailing down the two steps of the dais, across the platform and down the seven steps to where Sithas stood. In front of the throne dais was an ornate and intricately carved golden tray on a silver stand. On the tray rested the golden rings the couple would exchange.

Hermathya came forward. The silence continued as if the entire elven nation was holding its breath. Part of the sensation was awe, and part was amazement. The bride of the speaker's heir had broken several traditions on her way to the tower. The royal family had always maintained an aloofness, an air of unbreachable dignity. Hermathya had flaunted herself before the crowd, yet the people of Silvanost seemed to love her for it.

Sithas wore ceremonial armor over his robe of gold. The skillfully worked breastplate and shoulder pieces were enameled in vibrant green. Though the cuirass bore the arms of Silvanos, Sithas had attached a small red rosebud to his sleeve, a small but potent symbol of his devotion to his patron deity.

When Hermathya drew near, he said teasingly, "Well, my dear, has the celebration ended?"

"No," she said, smiling sweetly. "It has just begun."

Hand in hand, they went before Sithel.

* * * * *

The feasting that began that evening continued for four days. It grew quite wearing on the newlyweds, and after the second day they retired to the fifth floor of the Quinari tower, which had been redecorated as their living quarters. At night, Hermathya and Sithas stood on their balcony overlooking the heart of the city and watched the revelries below.

"Do you suppose anyone remembers what the celebration is for?" asked Hermathya.

"They don't tonight. They will tomorrow," Sithas said forcefully.

Yet he found it difficult being alone with her. She was so much a stranger to him and always, in the back of his mind, he wondered if she compared him to Kith-Kanan. Though they were nearly identical in looks, Sithel's heir knew that he and his brother were worlds apart in temperament. Sithas grasped the balcony rail tightly. For the first time in his life he was at a loss as to what to do or say.

"Are you happy?" Hermathya asked after a long, mutual silence.

"I am content," he said carefully.

"Will you ever be happy?" she asked coyly.

Sithas turned to his wife and said, "I will endeavor to try."

"Do you miss Kith-Kanan?"

The calm golden eyes clouded for a moment. "Yes, I miss him. Do you, Lady?"

Hermathya touched the starjewel she wore pinned to the throat of her gown. Slowly she leaned against the prince and slipped an arm about his waist. "No, I don't miss him," she said a little too strongly.

The Same Day, in the Forest

6

Shorn of his armor and city-made clothes, Kith-Kanan padded through the forest in a close-fitting deerskin tunic and leggings such as Mackeli wore. He was trying to circle Mackeli's house without the boy hearing him.

"You're by the gray elm," Mackeli's voice sang out. And so Kith-Kanan was. Try as he might, he still made too much noise. The boy might keep his eyes closed so he wouldn't see the heat of Kith-Kanan's body, but Mackeli's keen ears were never fooled.

Kith-Kanan doubled back six feet and dropped down on his hands. There was no sound in the woods. Mackeli called, "You can't steal up on anyone by sitting still."

The prince stepped only on the tree roots that humped up above the level of the fallen leaves. In this way he went ten paces without making a sound. Mackeli said nothing, and the prince grinned to himself. The boy couldn't hear him! At last.

He stepped far out from a root to a flat stone. The stone was tall enough to allow him to reach a low limb on a yew tree. As silently as possible, he pulled himself up into the yew tree, hugging the trunk. His green and brown tunic blended well with the lichen-spotted bark. A hood concealed his fair hair. Immobile, he waited. He'd surprise the boy this time!

Any second now, Mackeli would walk by and then he'd spring down on him. But something firm thumped against his hood. Kith-Kanan raised his eyes and saw Mackeli, clinging to the tree just three feet above him. He nearly fell off the branch, so great

51

was his surprise.

"By the Dragonqueen!" he swore. "How did you get up there?"

"I climbed," said Mackeli smugly.

"But how? I never saw "

"Walking on the roots was good, Kith, but you spent so much time watching your feet I was able to slip in front of you."

"But this tree! How did you know which one to climb?"

Mackeli shrugged his narrow shoulders. "I made it easy for you. I pushed the stone out far enough for you to step on and climbed up here to wait. You did the rest."

Kith-Kanan swung down to the ground. "I feel like a fool. Why, your average goblin is probably better in the woods than I am."

Mackeli let go of the tree and fell in a graceful arc. He caught the low branch with his fingertips to slow his descent. Knees bent, he landed beside Kith-Kanan.

"You are pretty clumsy," he said without malice. "But you don't smell as bad as a goblin."

"My thanks." said the prince sourly.

"It's really just a matter of breathing."

"Breathing? How?"

"You breathe like this." Mackeli threw back his shoulders and puffed out his thin chest. He inhaled and exhaled like a blacksmith's bellows. The sight was so absurd, Kith-Kanan had to smile. "Then you walk the way you breathe." The boy stomped about exaggeratedly, lifting his feet high and crashing them into the scattered leaves and twigs.

Kith-Kanan's smile flattened into a frown. "How do you breathe?" he asked.

Mackeli rooted about at the base of the tree until he found a cast-off feather. He lay on his back and placed it on his upper lip. So smoothly did the elf boy draw breath, the feather never wavered.

"Am I going to have to learn how to breathe?" Kith-Kanan demanded.

"It would be a good start," said Mackeli. He hopped to his feet. "We go home now."

Several days passed slowly for Kith-Kanan in the forest. Mackeli was a clever and engaging companion, but his diet of nuts, berries, and water did not agree with the elf prince's tastes. His belly, which was hardly ample to start with, shrank under the simple fare. Kith-Kanan longed for meat and nectar. Only Ny could get meat, the boy insisted. Yet there was no sign of the mysterious "Ny."

There was also no sign of the missing Arcuballis. Though Kith-Kanan prayed that somehow they could be reunited, he knew there was little hope for this. With no idea where the griffon had been taken and no way of finding out, the prince tried to accept that Arcuballis was gone forever. The griffon, a tangible link with his old life, was gone, but Kith-Kanan still had his memories.

These same memories returned to torment the prince in his dreams during those days. He heard once more his father announce Hermathya's betrothal to Sithas. He relived the ordeal in the Tower of the Stars, and, most terrible of all, he listened to Hermathya's calm acceptance of Sithas. Kith-Kanan filled his days talking with and learning from Mackeli, determined to build a new life away from Silvanost. Perhaps that life would be here, he decided, in the peace and solitude of the ancient forest.

One time Kith-Kanan asked Mackeli where he'd been born, where he'd come from.

"I have always been from here," Mackeli replied, waving absently at the trees.

"You were born here?"

"I have always been here," he replied stubbornly.

At that, Kith-Kanan gave up. Questions about the past stymied the boy almost as much as queries about the future. If he stuck to the present and whatever they were doing at the moment he could almost have a conversation with Mackeli.

In return for Mackeli's lessons in stealth and survival, Kith-Kanan regaled his young friend with tales of Silvanost, of the great wars against the dragons, and of the ways of city-bred elves.

Mackeli loved these stories, but more than anything, metal fascinated him. He would sit cross-legged on the ground and hold some object of Kith-Kanan's his helmet, a greave, a piece from his armor and rub his small brown fingers against the cold surface again and again. He could not fathom how such hard material could be shaped so intricately. Kith-Kanan explained what he knew of smithy and foundry work. The idea that metal could be melted and poured absolutely astounded Mackeli.

"You put metal in the fire," he said, "and it doesn't burn? It gets soft and runny, like water?"

"Well, it's thicker than water."

"Then you take away the fire, and the metal gets hard again?" Kith-Kanan nodded. "You made that up!" Mackeli exclaimed. "Things put in the fire get burned."

"I swear by E'li, it is the truth."

Mackeli was too slight to handle the sword, but he was able to draw the bow well enough to shoot. He had an uncanny eye, and Kith-Kanan wished he would use some of that stealth to bring down a deer for dinner. But it was not to be; Mackeli didn't eat meat and he refused to shed blood for Kith-Kanan. Only Ny . . .

On a gray and rainy morning, Mackeli went out to gather nuts and roots. Kith-Kanan remained in the hollow tree, stoking the fire, polishing his sword and dagger. When the rain showed signs of letting up, he left his weapons below and climbed the ladder to the upper part of the oak tree. He stood on a branch thicker around than his waist and surveyed the rain-washed forest. Drops fell from the verdant leaves, and the air had a clean, fertile smell. Deeply the prince inhaled. He had found a small measure of peace here, and the meeting with the Forestmaster had foretold great adventure for his future.

Kith-Kanan went back down and immediately noticed that his sword and dagger were gone. His first thought was that Mackeli had come back and was playing a trick on him, but the prince saw no signs the boy had returned. He turned around and was going back up the tree when something heavy struck him from behind, in the middle of his back.

He crashed against the trunk, spun, and saw nothing. "Mackeli!" he cried, "This isn't funny!" Neither was the blow on the back of his head that followed. A weight bore Kith-Kanan to the ground. He rolled and felt arms and legs around him. Something black and shiny flashed by his nose. He knew the move of a stabbing attack, and he put out both hands to seize the attacker's wrist.

His assailant's face was little more than a whorl of painted lines and a pair of shadowed eyes. The flint knife wavered, and as Kith-Kanan backhanded the knife wielder, the painted face let out a gasp of pain. Kith-Kanan sat up, wrenched the knife out of its owner's grasp, and pinned his attacker to the ground with one knee.

"The kill is yours," said the attacker. His struggles faded, and he lay tense but passive under Kith-Kanan's weight.

Kith-Kanan threw the knife away and stood up. "Who are you?"

"The one who is here. Who are you?" the painted elf said sharply.

"I am Kith, formerly of Silvanost. Why did you attack me?"

"You are in my house."

Understanding quickly dawned. "Are you Ny?"

"The name of my birth was Anaya." There was cool assurance in the voice.

He frowned. "That sounds like a female name."

Anaya got up and kept a discreet distance from Kith-Kanan. He realized she was a female elf of the Kagonesti race. Her black hair was cut close to her head, except in back, where she wore a long braid. Anaya was shorter than Kith-Kanan by a head, and much slimmer. Her green-dyed deerskin tunic ended at her hips, leaving her legs bare. Like her face, her legs were covered with painted lines and decorations.

Her dark, hazel eyes darted left and right. "Where is Mackeli?"

"Out gathering nuts, I think," he said, watching her keenly.

"Why did you come here?"

"The Forestmaster sent me," the prince stated flatly.

In less time than it takes to tell, Anaya bolted from the clearing. She ran to an oak tree and, to Kith-Kanan's astonishment, ran right up the broad trunk. She caught an overhead limb and swung into the midst of the leaves. Gaping, he made a few flatfooted steps forward, but the wild elf was completely lost from view.

"Anaya! Come back! I am a friend! The Forestmaster "

"I will ask the Master if it is so." Her clear, high voice came from somewhere above his line of sight. "If you speak the truth, I will return. If you say the Master's name in vain, I will call down the Black Crawlers on you."

"What?" Kith-Kanan spun around, looking up, trying to locate her. He could see nothing. "Who are the Black Crawlers?" But there was no answer, only the sighing of the wind through the leaves.

* * * * *

Night fell, and neither Mackeli nor Anaya had returned. Kith-Kanan began to fear that something might have happened to the boy. There were interlopers in the forest, the Forestmaster had said. Mackeli was clever, but he was innocent of the ways of ambush and murder. If the boy was in their hands . . . and Anaya. There was a strange creature! If he hadn't actually fought with her, felt the solidity of her flesh, he would have called her a wraith, a forest spirit. But the bruise on his jaw was undeniably real.

Growing tired of the closeness of the hollow tree, the prince cleared a spot in the leaves to build a fire outside. He scraped down to bare soil and laid some stones for a hearth. Soon he had a fine fire blazing. The smoke wafted into the darkness, and sparks floated up, winking off like dying stars.

Though it was summer, Kith-Kanan felt a chill. He held his hands out to the fire, warming them. Crickets whirred in the dark beyond the firelight. Cicadas stirred in the trees, and bats swooped into the clearing to catch them. Suddenly the prince felt as if he was in the center of a seething, crawling pot. His eyes flicked back and forth, following odd rustlings and scrapings in the dry leaves. Things fluttered overhead, slithered behind his back. He grasped the unburned end of a stick of wood and pulled it out of the fire. Dark things seemed to leap back into the shadows when Kith-Kanan brought the burning torch near.

55

He stood with his back to the fire, breathing hard. With the blazing brand before him like a noble blade, the elf kept the darkness at bay. Gradually the incessant activity lessened. By the time Solinari rose above the trees, all was still.

After throwing the stump of the burned limb back on the dying fire, Kith-Kanan sat down again and faced the red coals. Like a thousand lonely travelers before him, the prince whistled a tune to keep the loneliness away. It was a tune from his childhood: "Children of the Stars."

The chorus died when his lips went dry. He saw something that froze him completely. Between the black columns of two tree trunks were a pair of red staring eyes.

He tried to think what it could be. The possibilities were not good: wolf, bear, a tawny panther. The two eyes blinked and disappeared. Kith-Kanan jumped to his feet and snatched up a stone from the outside edge of his campfire. He hurled it at the spot where he'd last seen the eyes. The rock crashed into the underbrush. There was no other sound, Even the crickets had ceased their singing.

Then Kith-Kanan sensed he was being watched and turned to the right. The red eyes were back, creeping forward a foot or so off the ground, right toward him.

Darkness is the enemy, he suddenly realized. *Whatever I can see, I can fight.* Scooping up a double handful of dead leaves, he threw them on the embers of the fire. Flames blazed up. He immediately saw a long, lean body close to the ground. The advance of the red eyes stopped, and suddenly they rose from the ground.

It was Anaya.

"I have spoken with the Forestmaster," she said a little sulkily, her eyes glowing red in the light from the flames. "You said the truth." Anaya walked sideways a few steps, never taking her eyes off Kith-Kanan. Despite this good news, he felt that she was about to spring on him. She dropped down on her haunches and looked into the fire. The leaves were consumed, and their remains sank onto the heap of dully glowing ashes.

"It is wise you laid a fire," she said. "I called the Black Crawlers to watch over you while I spoke with the Forestmaster."

He straightened his shoulders with studied nonchalance. "Who are the Black Crawlers?"

"I will show you." Anaya picked up a dead dry branch and held it to the coals. It smoked heavily for an instant, then burst into flame. She carried the burning branch to the line of trees defining the clearing. Kith-Kanan lost his hard-won composure when Anaya showed him what was waiting beyond the light.

Every tree trunk, every branch, every square inch of ground was covered with black, creeping things. Crickets, millipedes, leaf hoppers, spiders of every sort and size, earwigs, pill bugs, beetles up to the size of his fist, cockroaches, caterpillars, moths, flies of the largest sort, grasshoppers, cicadas with soft, pulpy bodies and gauzy wings . . . stretching as far as he could see, coating every surface. The horde was motionless, waiting.

Anaya returned to the fire. Kith-Kanan was white-faced with revulsion. "What sort of witch are you?" he gasped. "You command all these vermin?"

"I am no witch. This forest is my home, and I guard it closely. The Black Crawlers share the woodland with me. I gave them warning when I left you, and they gathered to keep you under watchful eyes."

"Now that you know who I am, you can send them away," he said.

"They have already departed. Could you not hear them go?" she scoffed.

"No, I couldn't." Kith-Kanan glanced around at the dark forest, blotting sweat from his face with his sleeve. He focussed his attention on the fascinating elf woman and blotted out the memory of the Crawlers. With her painted decorations, grime, and dyed deerskin, Kith-Kanan wasn't sure how old Anaya might be, or even what she really looked like. She perched on her haunches, balancing on her toes. Kith-Kanan fed some twigs to the fire, and the scene slowly lightened.

"The Forestmaster says you are here to drive away the intruders," Anaya said. "I have heard them, smelled them, seen the destruction they have caused. Though I have never doubted the word of the great unicorn, I do not see how you can drive anyone away. You are no ranger; you smell of a place where people are many and trees few."

Kith-Kanan was tired of the Kagonesti's casual rudeness. He excused it in Mackeli, who was only a boy, but it was too much coming from this wild woman.

"I am a prince of House Royal," he said proudly. "I am trained in the arts of the warrior. I don't know who or how many of these intruders there are, but I will do my best to find a way to get rid of them. You need not like me, Anaya, but you had better not insult me too often." He leaned back on his elbows. "After all, who wrestled whom to the ground?"

She poked the dancing bowl of flames. "I let you take my knife away," she said defensively.

Kith-Kanan sat up. "You what?"

"You seemed such a clumsy outlander, I did not think you were dangerous. I let you get the advantage to see what you would do. You could not have cut my throat with that flint blade. It was dull as a cow's tooth."

Despite his annoyance, Kith-Kanan found himself smiling. "You wanted to see if I was merciful, is that it?"

"That was my purpose," she said.

"So I guess I really am a slow, dumb outlander," he said.

"There is power in your limbs," she admitted, "but you fight like a falling stone."

"And I don't breathe properly either." Kith-Kanan was beginning to wonder how he had ever lived to the age of ninety, being so inept.

Mentioning breathing reminded the prince of Mackeli, and he told Anaya the boy still hadn't returned.

"Keli has stayed away longer than this before," she said, waving a hand dismissively.

Though still concerned, Kith-Kanan realized that Anaya knew Mackeli's ways far better than he did. The prince's stomach chose that moment to growl, and he rubbed it, his face coloring with embarrassment.

"You know, I am very hungry," he informed her.

Without a word, Anaya went inside the hollow oak. She returned a moment later with a section of smoked venison ribs wrapped in curled pieces of bark. Kith-Kanan shook his head; he wondered where those had been hiding all these weeks.

Anaya dropped down by the fire, in her characteristic crouch, and slipped a slender flint blade out of her belt pouch. With deft, easy strokes, she cut the ribs apart and began eating.

"May I have some?" the prince inquired desperately. She promptly flung two ribs at him through the fire. Kith-Kanan knew nicety of manner was lost on the Kagonesti, and the sight of the meat made his mouth water. He picked up a rib from his lap and nibbled it. The meat was hard and tangy, but very good. While he nibbled, Anaya gnawed. She cleaned rib bones faster than anyone he'd ever seen.

"Thank you," he said earnestly.

"You should not thank me. Now that you have eaten my meat, it is for you to do as I say," she replied firmly.

"What are you talking about?" he said, frowning. "A prince of the Silvanesti serves no one but the speaker and the gods."

Anaya dropped the clean bones in the fire. "You are not in the Place of Spires any longer. This is the wildwood, and the first law here is, you eat what you take with your own hands. That makes you free. If you eat what others give you, you are not a free person; you are a mewling child who must be fed."

Kith-Kanan got stiffly to his feet. "I have sworn to help the Forestmaster, but by the blood of E'li, I'll not be anyone's servant! Especially not some dirty, painted savage!"

"Being a prince does not matter. The law will be done. Feed yourself, or obey me. Those are your choices," she said flatly.

Anaya walked to the tree. Kith-Kanan grabbed her by the arm and spun her around. "What have you done with my sword and dagger?" he demanded.

"Metal stinks." Anaya jerked her arm free. "It is not permitted for me to touch it. I wrapped a scrap of hide around your metal and carried it from my house. Do not bring it in again."

He opened his mouth to shout at her, to rail against her unjust treatment of him. But before he could, Anaya went inside the tree. Her voice floated out. "I sleep now. Put out the fire."

When the fire was cold and dead, the prince stood in the door of the tree. "Where do I sleep?" he asked sarcastically.

"Where you can fit," was Anaya's laconic reply. She was curled up by the wall, so Kith-Kanan lay down as far from her as he could, yet still be in the warmth of the tree. Thoughts raced through his head. How to find Arcuballis and get out of the forest. How to get away from Anaya. Where Mackeli was. Who the interlopers were.

"Don't think so loud," Anaya said irritatedly. "Go to sleep." With a sigh, Kith-Kanan finally closed his eyes.

High Summer, Year of the Hawk

7

Elves from all corners of Silvanesti had come to Silvanost for Trial Days, that period every year when the Speaker of the Stars sat in judgment of disputes, heard the counsel of his nobles and clerics, and generally tried to resolve whatever problems faced his people.

A platform had been built on the steps of the Temple of E'li. Upon it, Sithel sat on a high, padded throne, under a shimmering white canopy. He could survey the entire square. Sithas stood behind him, watching and listening. Warriors of the royal guard kept the lines orderly as people made their way slowly up the line to their ruler. Trial Days were sometimes amusing, often irritating, and always, always lengthy.

Sithel was hearing a case where two fishers had disputed a large carp, which hit both of their hooks at the same time. Both elves claimed the fish, which had been caught weeks before and allowed to rot while they debated its ownership.

Sithel announced his judgment. "I declare the fish to be worth two silver pieces. As you own it jointly, you will each pay the other one silver piece for permitting it to spoil."

The gaping fishers would have complained but Sithel forestalled them. "It is so ordered. Let it be done!" The trial scribe struck a bell, signaling the end of the case. The fishers bowed and withdrew.

Sithel stood up. The royal guards snapped to attention. "I will take a short rest," he announced. "In my absence, my son, Sithas, will render judgment."

The prince looked to his father in surprise. In a low voice he said, "Are you sure, Father?"

"Wy not? It will give you a taste of the role."

The speaker went to the rear of the platform. He watched Sithas slowly seat himself in the chair of judgment. "Next case," declared his son ringingly.

Sithel ducked through a flap in the cloth wall. There he saw his wife, waiting at a small table laden with food and drink. Snowy white linen walled off this end of the platform on three sides. The rear was open to the temple. The formidable facade loomed over them, fluted columns and walls banded with deep blue, bright rose, and grassy green stone. The heat of midday was upon the city, but a breeze wafted through the canopied enclosure.

Nirakina stood and dismissed a serving boy who had been posted at the table. She poured her husband a tall goblet of nectar. Sithel picked a few grapes from a golden bowl and accepted the goblet.

"How is he doing?" Nirakina asked, gesturing to the front of the platform.

"Well enough. He must get used to rendering decisions." Sithel sipped the amber liquid. "Weren't you and Hermathya attending the debut of Elidan's epic song today?"

"Hermathya pleaded illness and the performance was postponed until tomorrow."

"What's wrong with her?" The speaker settled back in his chair.

Nirakina's face clouded. "She would rather visit the Market than remain in the palace. She is proud and willful, Sithel."

"She knows how to get attention, that's certain," her husband said, chuckling. "I hear the crowds follow her in the streets."

Nirakina nodded. "She throws coins and gems to them just often enough for them to cheer her madly." She leaned forward and put her hand over his where it rested on the goblet. "Sithel, did we make the right choice? So much unhappiness has come about because of this girl. Do you think all will be well?"

Sithel released his grip on the cup and took his wife's hand. "I don't think any harm will come of Hermathya's follies, Kina. She's drunk with acclaim right now, but she will tire of it when she realizes how empty and fleeting the adulation of the mob is. She and Sithas should have children. That would slow her down, give her something else on which to concentrate."

Nirakina tried to smile, though she couldn't help but notice how the speaker had avoided mention of Kith-Kanan at all. Her husband had a strong will. His anger and disappointment were not easily overcome.

The sound of raised voices swelled over the square. Sithel ate a last handful of grapes. "Let's see what disturbs the people," he said.

He stepped around the curtain and walked to the front edge of the platform. The crowd, in its orderly lines, had parted down the center of the square. There, between two lines of soldiers, were twenty to thirty newcomers. They were injured. Some were being carried on litters, others wore blood-stained bandages. The injured elves, male and female, approached the foot of the speaker's platform slowly and painfully. Guards moved forward to keep them away, but Sithel ordered that they be allowed to come.

"Who are you?" he asked.

"Great Speaker," said a tall elf at the head of the group. His face was sun-browned and his body muscled from outdoor work. His corn-colored hair was ragged and sooty, and a dirty bandage covered most of his right arm. "Great Speaker, we are all that is left of the village of Trokali. We have come almost two hundred miles to tell you of our plight."

"What happened?"

"We were a peaceful village, great Speaker. We tended our trees and fields and traded with all who came to the market in the town square. But on the night of the last quarter of Lunitari, a band of brigands appeared in Trokali. They set fire to the houses, broke the limbs off our fruit trees, carried off our women and children " Here the elf's voice broke. He paused a moment to master his emotions, then continued. "We are not fighters, great Speaker, but the fathers and mothers of Trokali tried to defend what was ours. We had sticks and hoes against swords and arrows. These here," he waved a hand in the direction of the battered group behind him, "are all that live out of a village of two hundred."

Sithas left the platform and went down the temple steps until he was on the level with the tall elf from Trokali.

"What is your name?" Sithas demanded.

"Tamanier Ambrodel."

"Who were these brigands, Tamanier?"

The elf shook his head sadly. "I do not know, sire."

"They were humans!" cried an elf woman with a badly burned face. She pushed her way through the crowd. "I saw them!" she hissed. "They were humans. I saw the hair on their faces!"

"They weren't all human," Tamanier said sharply. He raised his wounded arm. "The one who cut me was Kagonesti!"

"Kagonesti and humans in the same band?" Sithas said in consternation. Murmurs surged through the crowd. He turned to look up at his father.

Sithel held up his hands. The scribe had to strike his bell four times before the crowd was quiet. "This matter requires further attention," he proclaimed. "My son will remain here for the trials, while I will conduct the people of Trokali to the Palace of Quinari, where each shall give testimony."

Sithas bowed deeply to his father as an escort of twelve warriors formed in the square to convey the survivors of Trokali to the palace. The lame and sick made it a slow and difficult procession, but Tamanier Ambrodel led his people with great dignity.

Sithel descended the steps of the Temple of E'li, with Nirakina by his side. Courtiers scrambled to keep pace with the speaker's quick stride. The murmuring in the square grew as the people of Trokali trailed after.

Nirakina glanced back over her shoulder at the crowd. "Do you think there will be trouble?" she asked.

"There is already trouble. Now we must see what can be done to remedy it," Sithel answered tersely.

In short order they entered the plaza before the palace. Guards at the doors, responding to the speaker's brief commands, summoned help. Servants flooded out of the palace to aid the injured elves. Nirakina directed them and saw to the distribution of food and water.

Out of deference to Tamanier's weakened condition, Sithel took him no farther than the south portico. He bade Tamanier sit, overlooking the protocol that required commoners to stand in the presence of the speaker. The tall elf eased himself into a finely carved stone chair. He exhaled loudly with relief.

"Tell me about the brigands," Sithel commanded.

"There were thirty or forty of them, Highness," Tamanier said, swallowing hard. "They came on horseback. Hardlooking, they were. The humans wore mail and carried long swords."

"And the Kagonesti?"

"They were poor-looking, ragged and dirty. They carried off our women and children . . . " Tamanier covered his face with his hands.

"I know it is difficult," Sithel said calmly. "But I must know. Go on."

"Yes, Highness." Tamanier dropped his hands, but they shook until he clenched them in his lap. A quaver had crept into his voice. "The humans set fire to the houses and chased off all our livestock. It was also the humans who threw ropes over our trees and tore off their branches. Our orchards are ruined, completely ruined."

"Are you sure about that? The humans despoiled the trees?"

"I am certain, great Speaker."

Sithel walked down the cool, airy portico, hands clasped behind his back. Passing Tamanier, he noticed the thin gold band the elf wore around his neck.

"Is that real gold?" he asked abruptly.

Tamanier fingered the band. "It is, Highness. It was a gift from my wife's family."

"And the brigands didn't take it from you?"

Realization slowly came to Tamanier. "Why, no. They never touched it. Come to think of it, great speaker, no one was robbed. The bandits burned houses and broke down our trees, but they didn't plunder us at all!" He scratched his dirty cheek. "Why would they do that, Highness?"

Sithel tapped two fingers against his chin thoughtfully. "The only thing I can think of is they didn't care about your gold. They were after something more important." Tamanier watched him expectantly, but the speaker didn't elaborate. He rang for a servant. When one appeared he told him to take care of Tamanier. "We will talk again," he assured the tall elf. "In the meantime, do not speak of this with anyone, not even your wife."

Tamanier stood, leaning crookedly, favoring his wounded side. "My wife was killed," he said stiffly.

Sithel watched him go. An honorable fellow, he decided. He would do well to keep an eye on Tamanier Ambrodel. The Speaker of the Stars could always use such an honorable man at court.

He entered the palace through a side door. A steady stream of servants trooped by, carrying buckets and soiled towels. Healers, who were clerics of the goddess Quenesti Pah, had arrived to tend the injured. Sithel looked over the bustle of activity. Trokali was two hundred miles from Silvanost. No human raiders had ever penetrated so far. And in the company of Kagonesti elves . . .

The Speaker of the Stars shook his head worriedly.

* * * * *

After finishing the day's trials, Sithas dismissed the court. Though he had listened to each case fairly, he could not keep his thoughts away from the attack on the village of Trokali. When he returned to his rooms in the palace, everyone, from his mother to the humblest servant, was talking about the raid and its portent.

Hermathya waited for him in their room. No sooner had he entered than she jumped to her feet and exclaimed, "Did you hear about the raid?"

"I did," Sithas said with deliberate nonchalance, shrugging off his dusty outer robe. He poured cool water into a basin and washed his hands and face.

"What's to be done?" she prodded.

"Done? I hardly think that's our concern. The speaker will deal with the problem."

"Why do you not do something yourself?" Hermathya demanded, crossing the room. Her scarlet gown showed off the milky paleness of her skin. Her eyes flashed as she spoke. "The entire nation would unite behind the one who would put down the insolent humans."

"The 'one'? Not the speaker?" asked Sithas blandly.

"The speaker is old," she said, waving a dismissive hand. "Old people are beset with fears."

Dropping the towel he'd used to dry his hands, Sithas caught Hermathya's wrist and pulled her close. Her eyes widened, but she didn't shrink back. Sithas's eyes bored into hers.

"What you say smacks of disloyalty," he rumbled icily.

"You want what is best for the nation, don't you?" she replied, leaning into him. "If these attacks continue, all the settlers to the west will flee back to the city, as did the elves of Trokali. The humans of Ergoth will settle our land with their own people. Is that good for Silvanesti?"

Sithas's face hardened at the thought of humans encroaching on their ancient land. "No," he said firmly.

Hermathya put her free hand on his arm. "How then is it disloyal to want to end these outrages?"

"I am not the Speaker of the Stars!"

Her eyes were the deep blue of the sky at dusk as Hermathya moved to kiss her husband. "Not yet," she whispered, and her breath was sweet and warm on his face. "Not yet."

Late Spring, in the Forest

8

Mackeli had been gone three days when Anaya showed Kith-Kanan where she had secreted his sword and dagger. There could be no question now that something had happened to him and that they had to go to his rescue.

"There is your metal," she said. "Take it up. You may have need of it."

He brushed the dead leaves off the slim, straight blade of his sword and wiped it with an oily cloth. It slid home in its scabbard with only a faint hiss. Anaya kept back when he held the weapons. She regarded the iron blades with loathing, as if they were the stinking carcasses of long dead animals.

"Mackeli's been gone so long, I hope we can pick up his trail," Kith-Kanan said. His eyes searched the huge trees.

"As long as Mackeli lives, I will always be able to find him." declared Anaya. "There is a bond between us. He is my brother."

With this pronouncement she turned and went back to the hollow tree. Kith-Kanan followed her. What did she mean brother? Were the two siblings? He'd wondered at their relationship, but certainly hadn't noticed any family resemblance. Anaya was even less talkative on the subject than Mackeli had been.

He went to the door of the tree and looked in. Squatting before a piece of shiny mica, Anaya was painting her face. She had wiped her cheeks clean relatively clean, anyway with a wad of damp green leaves and now was applying paint made from berries and nut shells. Her brush was a new twig, the end of which she'd chewed to make it soft and pliable. Anaya went from one gourd full of pigment to another, painting zigzag lines on her face in red, brown, and yellow.

"What are you doing? Time is wasting," Kith-Kanan said impatiently.

Anaya drew three converging lines on her chin, like an arrowhead in red. Her dark hazel eyes were hard as she said, "Go outside and wait for me."

Kith-Kanan felt anger rising at her casual tone of command. She ordered him about like a servant, but there was nothing for him to do but stew. When Anaya finally emerged, they plunged into the deep shade of the woods. Kith-Kanan found his anger at her dissolving as he watched her move gracefully through the wood. She never disturbed a leaf or twig, moving, as Mackeli had said, like smoke.

They finally paused to rest, and Kith-Kanan sat on a log to catch his breath. He looked at Anaya as she stood poised, one foot atop the fallen log. She wasn't even breathing heavily. She was a muscular, brown-skinned, painted Kagonesti quite savage by Silvanesti standards but she was also practical and wise in the ways of the forest. Their worlds were so different as to be hostile to each other, but he felt at that moment a sense of security. He was not so alone as he had believed.

"Why do you look at me that way?" Anaya asked, frowning.

"I was just thinking how much better it would be for us to be friends, instead of enemies," said Kith-Kanan sincerely.

It was her turn to give him a strange look. He laughed and asked, "Now why are you looking at me like that?"

"I know the word, but I've never had a friend before," Anaya said.

* * * * *

Kith-Kanan would not have believed it, but the place Anaya led him through was even thicker with trees than any part of the forest he'd seen so far. They were not the giants of the old forest where she lived, but of a size he was more accustomed to seeing. They grew so close together, however, that it soon became impossible for him to walk at all.

Anaya grasped an oak tree trunk with her bare hands and feet and started up it like a squirrel. Kith-Kanan gaped at the ease with which she scaled the tree. The leaves closed around her.

"Are you coming?" she called down,

"I can't climb like that!" he protested.

"Wait then." He saw a flash of her red leg paint as she sprang from an oak branch to a nearby elm. The gap between branches was more than six feet, yet Anaya launched herself without a moment's hesitation. A few seconds later she was back, flitting from tree to tree with the ease of a bird. A twined strand of creeper, as thick as the prince's two thumbs, fell from the oak leaves and landed at his feet. This was more to his liking. Kith-Kanan spat on his palms and hauled himself up, hand over hand. He braced his feet against the tree trunk and soon found himself perched on an oak limb thirty feet from the forest floor.

"Whew!" he said, grinning. "A good climb!" Anaya was patently not impressed. After all, she had made the same climb with no vine at all. Kith-Kanan hauled up the creeper, coiling it carefully around his waist.

"It will be faster to stay in the treetops from now on," Anaya advised.

"How can you tell this is the way Mackeli went?"

She gathered herself to leap. "I smell him. This way."

Anaya sprang across to the elm. Kith-Kanan went more slowly, slipping a good deal on the round surface of the tree limb. Anaya waited for him to catch up, which he did by grasping an overhead branch and swinging over the gap. A dizzy glimpse of the ground flashed beneath his feet, and then Kith-Kanan's leg hooked around the elm. He let go of the oak branch, swung upside-down by one leg, and gradually worked his way onto the elm.

"This is going to take a long time," he admitted, panting for breath.

They continued on high in the treetops for most of the day. Though his hands were by no means soft, accustomed as they were to swordplay and his griffon's reins, Kith-Kanan's palms became scraped and sore from grasping and swinging on the rough-barked branches. His feet slipped so often that he finally removed his thick-strapped sandals and went barefoot like Anaya. His feet were soon as tender as his hands, but he didn't slip again.

Even at the slow pace Kith-Kanan set, they covered many miles on their lofty road. Well past noon, Anaya called for a rest. They wedged themselves high in a carpeen tree. She showed him how to find the elusive fruit of the carpeen, yellow and pearlike, hidden by a tightly growing roll of leaves. The soft white meat of the carpeen not only sated their hunger, it was thirst-quenching, too.

"Do you think Mackeli is all right?" Kith-Kanan asked, the worry clear in his voice.

Anaya finished her fruit and dropped the core to the ground. "He is alive." she stated flatly.

Kith-Kanan dropped his own fruit core and asked, "How can you be certain?"

Shifting around the prince with careless ease, Anaya slid from her perch and came down astride the limb where he sat. She took his scraped hand and held his fingertips to her throat.

"Do you feel the beat of my heart?" she asked him.

"Yes." It was strong and slow.

She pushed his hand away. "And now?"

"Of course not. I'm no longer touching you," he replied.

"Yet you see me and hear me, without touching me."

"That's different."

She raised her eyebrows. "Is it? If I tell you I can feel Mackeli's heart beating from far off, do you believe me?"

"I do," said Kith-Kanan. "I've seen that you have many wonderful talents."

"No!" Anaya swept a hand through the empty air. "I am nothing but what the forest has made me. As I am, so you could be!"

She took his hand again, holding his fingertips against the softly pulsing vein in her neck. Anaya looked directly in his eyes. "Show me the rhythm of my heart," she said.

Kith-Kanan tapped a finger of his other hand against his leg. "Yes," she coaxed. "You have it. Continue."

Her gaze held his. It was true between them he felt a connection. Not a physical bond, like the grasp of a hand, but a more subtle connection like the bond he knew stretched between himself and Sithas. Even when they were not touching and were many miles apart he could sense the life force of Sithas. And now, between Anaya's eyes and his, Kith-Kanan felt the steady surge of her pulse, beating, beating . . .

"Look at your hands," urged Anaya.

His left was still tapping out the rhythm on his leg. His right lay palm up on the tree limb. He wasn't touching her throat any longer.

"Do you still feel the pulse?" she asked.

He nodded. Even as he felt the surging of his own heart, he could feel hers, too. It was slower, steadier. Kith-Kanan looked with shock at his idle hand. "That's impossible!" he exclaimed. No sooner had he said this than the sensation of her heartbeat left his fingertips.

Anaya shook her head. "You don't want to learn," she said in disgust. She stood up and stepped from the carpeen tree to the neighboring oak. "It's time to move on. It will be dark before long, and you aren't skilled enough to treewalk by night."

This was certainly true, so Kith-Kanan did not protest. He watched the wiry Anaya wend her way through the web of branches, but the meaning of her lesson was still sinking in. What did it mean that he had been able to keep Anaya's pulse?

He still felt the pain of his separation from Hermathya, a hard, cold lump in his chest, but when he closed his eyes and thought of Hermathya for a moment a tall, flame-haired elf woman with eyes of deepest blue he only frowned in concentration, for there was nothing, no bond, however slight, that connected him with his lost love. He could not know if she was alive or dead. Sadness touched Kith-Kanan's heart, but there was no time for self-pity now. He opened his eyes and moved quickly to where Anaya had stopped up ahead.

She was staring at a large crow perched on a limb near her head. When the crow spied Kith-Kanan, it abruptly flew away. Anaya's shoulders drooped.

"The corvae have not seen Mackeli since four days past," she explained. "But they have seen something else: humans."

"Humans? In the wildwood?"

Anaya nodded. She lowered herself to a spindly limb and furrowed her brow in thought. "I did not smell them sooner because the metal you carry stinks in my nose too much. The corvae say there's a small band of humans farther to the west. They're cutting down the trees, and they have some sort of flying beast, of a kind the corvae have never seen."

"Arcuballis! That's my griffon! The humans must have captured it," he said. In fact, he couldn't imagine how; as far as he could determine they were miles from the spot where he'd first landed, and it would have been very difficult for strangers, especially humans, to handle the spirited Arcuballis.

"How many humans are there?" Kith-Kanan inquired.

Anaya gave him a disdainful look. "Corvae can't count," she stated contemptuously.

They started off again as twilight was falling. For a brief time it actually brightened in the trees, as the sinking sun lanced in from the side. Anaya found a particularly tall maple and climbed up. The majestic tree rose even above its neighbors, and its thick limbs grew in an easy step pattern around the massive trunk. Kith-Kanan had no trouble keeping up with the Kagonesti in the vertical climb.

At the top of the tree Anaya stopped, one arm hooked around the gnarled peak of the maple. Kith-Kanan worked his way around beside her. The maple's pinnacle swayed under his additional weight, but the view was so breathtaking he didn't mind the motion.

As far as the eye could see, there was nothing but the green tops of trees. The horizon to the west was darkening from pink to flame red. Kith-Kanan was enchanted. Though he had often seen great vistas from the back of Arcuballis, his appreciation for such sights had been increased by the weeks he'd spent in this forest, where a glimpse of sky was a rare treat.

Anaya was not enraptured. She narrowed her sharp eyes and said, "There they are."

"Who?"

"The intruders. Do you not see the smoke?"

Kith-Kanan stared in the direction she pointed. To the north, a faint smudge of gray marred the sky's royal blue. Even as he stared at it, Kith-Kanan wasn't sure the smoke was really there. He blinked several times.

"They are burning the trees," Anaya said grimly. "Savages!"

The prince refrained from saying that to most of the civilized people of Krynn, it was she who was the savage. Instead he asked, "Which way to Mackeli?"

"Toward the smoke," she said. "The humans have taken him after all. I will see them bleed!"

Though Kith-Kanan was surprised at the depth of her feeling, he had no doubt she meant what she said.

They stayed in the treetops until the prince had begun to miss his handholds and then nearly fell forty feet to the ground. It was too dark to continue aloft, so Anaya and Kith-Kanan descended to the forest floor once more. They walked perhaps a mile in silence, Anaya gliding through the black tree trunks like a runaway shadow. Kith-Kanan felt the tension rising. He had never fought humans he'd only met a few of them in Silvanost, and all of them were aristocrats. For that matter, he'd never fought anyone for real, in a fight where death was the likely outcome. He wondered if he could do it, actually thrust his sword through someone's body, or use the edge to cut them. . . . He reminded himself that these humans were holding Mackeli prisoner and probably his royal griffon too.

Anaya froze, silhouetted between two large trees. Her hand was out stiffly behind her, a signal for Kith-Kanan to halt. He did and heard what had stopped her. The tinny sound of a flute drifted through the forest, borne along by the smells of wood smoke and roasting meat.

When he looked toward Anaya she'd vanished. He waited. What was he supposed to do? Kith-Kanan shook himself mentally. You, a prince of House Royal, wanting directions from a Kagonesti savage! You are a warrior do your duty!

He charged through the underbrush. At the first gleam of a campfire, Kith-Kanan drew his sword. Another twenty steps, and he burst into a clearing hewn from the primeval woodland. A large campfire, almost a bonfire, blazed in the center of the clearing. A dozen ruddy faces, thickly fleshed human faces, with their low foreheads, broad cheeks, and wide jaws turned toward the elf prince. Some had hair growing on their faces. All stared at him in utter astonishment.

One of the humans, with pale brown hair on his face, stood up. "Terrible spirit, do not harm us!" he intoned. "Peace be with you!"

Kith-Kanan relaxed. These weren't desperate brigands. They were ordinary men and, by the looks of their equipment, woodcutters. He dropped his sword point and stepped into the firelight.

"It's one of them!" declared another human. "The Elder Folk!"

"Who are you?" demanded Kith-Kanan.

"Essric's company of woodmen. I am Essric," said the brown-haired human.

Kith-Kanan surveyed the clearing. Over thirty large trees had been felled in this one place, and he could see a path had been cut through the forest. The very biggest trees were trimmed of their branches and were being split into halves and quarters with wedges and mallets. Slightly smaller trees were being dragged away. Kith-Kanan saw a rough pen full of broad-backed oxen.

"This is Silvanesti land," he said. "By whose grant do you cut down trees that belong to the Speaker of the Stars?"

Essric looked to his men, who had nothing to tell him. He scratched his brown beard ruefully. "My lord, we were brought hither and landed on the south coast of this country by ships commanded by Lord Ragnarius of Ergoth. It is Lord Ragnarius's pleasure that we fell as many trees as his ships can carry home. We didn't know anyone owned these trees!"

Just then, an eerie howl rippled across the fire-lit clearing. The humans all stood up, reaching for axes and staves. Kith-Kanan smiled to himself. Anaya was putting a scare into the men.

A clean-shaven man to Essric's left, who held a broadaxe in his meaty hands, suddenly let out a cry and staggered backward, almost falling in the fire. Instead, he dropped into the arms of his comrades.

"Forest spirits are attacking!" Kith-Kanan shouted. His declaration was punctuated by a hair-raising screech from the black trees. He had to struggle to keep from laughing as the twelve humans were driven from their fire by a barrage of sooty stones. One connected with the back of one man's head, stretching him out flat. Panic-stricken, the others didn't stop to help him, but fled pell-mell past the ox pen. Without torches to light their way, they stumbled and fell over stumps and broken branches. Within minutes, no one was left in the clearing but Kith-Kanan and the prone woodcutter.

Anaya came striding into the circle of light. Kith-Kanan grinned at her and held up a hand in greeting. She stalked past him to where the human lay. The flint knife was in her hand.

She rolled the unconscious human over. He was fairly young and had a red mustache. A thick gold ring gleamed from one earlobe. That, and the cut of his pants, told Kith-Kanan that the man had been a sailor at one time.

Anaya put a knee on the man's chest. The human opened his eyes and saw a wildly painted creature, serrated flint knife in hand, kneeling on him. The creature's face stared down with a ferocious grimace twisting its painted designs. The man's eyes widened in terror, showing much white. He tried to raise an arm to ward off Anaya, but Kith-Kanan was holding his wrists.

"Shall I cut out your eyes?" Anaya said coldly. "They would make fine decorations for my home."

"No! No! Spare me!" gibbered the man.

"No? Then tell us what we want to know," Kith-Kanan warned. "There was a white-haired elf boy here, yes?"

"Yes, wonderful lord!"

"And a griffon a flying beast with an eagle's forepart and a lion's hindquarters?"

"Yes, yes!"

"What happened to them?"

"They were taken away by Voltorno," the man moaned.

"Who's Voltorno?" asked Kith-Kanan.

"A soldier. A terrible, cruel man. Lord Ragnarius sent him with us."

"Why isn't he here now?" Anaya hissed, pushing the ragged edge of her knife against his throat.

"He-he decided to take the elf boy and the beast back to Lord Ragnarius's ship."

Anaya and Kith-Kanan exchange looks. "How long ago did this Voltorno leave?" persisted Kith-Kanan.

"This morning," the unfortunate sailor gasped.

"And how many are there in his party?"

"Ten. S-six men-at-arms and four archers."

Kith-Kanan stood up, releasing the man's hands. "Let him up."

"No," disagreed Anaya. "He must die."

"That is not the way! If you kill him, how will you be any different from the men who hold Mackeli captive? You cannot be the same as those you fight and have any honor. You must be better."

"Better?" she hissed, looking up at the prince. "Anything is better than tree-killing scum!"

"He is not responsible," Kith-Kanan insisted. "He was ordered."

"Whose hand held the axe?" Anaya interrupted.

Taking advantage of their argument, the sailor shoved Anaya off and scrambled to his feet. He ran after his comrades, bleating for help.

"Now you see? You let him get away," Anaya said. She gathered herself to give chase, but Kith-Kanan told her, "Forget those humans! Mackeli is more important. We'll have to catch up with them before they reach the coast." Anaya sullenly did not reply. "Listen to me! We're going to need all your talents. Call the corvae, the Black Crawlers, everything. Have them find the humans and try to delay them long enough so that we can catch up."

She pushed him aside and stepped away. The big fire was dying, and the hacked out clearing was sinking into darkness. Now and then an ox grunted from the makeshift pen.

Anaya moved to the felled trees. She put a gentle hand on the trunk of one huge oak. "Why do they do it?" she asked mournfully. "Why do they cut down the trees? Can't they hear the fabric of the forest split open each time a tree falls?" Her eyes gleamed with unshed tears. "There are spirits in the wildwood, spirits in the trees. They have murdered them with their metal." Her haunted eyes looked up at the prince.

Kith-Kanan put a hand on her shoulder. "There's much to be done. We must go." Anaya drew a shuddering breath. After giving the tree a last gentle touch, she stooped to gather up her throwing stones.

Late Summer

9

Summer was fading. The harvests were coming in, and the markets of Silvanost were full of the fruits of the soil. Market week always brought a great influx of visitors to the city, not all of them Silvanesti. From the forests to the south and the plains to the west came the swarthy, painted Kagonesti. Up the Thon Thalas came thick-walled boats from the dwarven kingdom, tall-masted, deep-sea vessels from the human realms in the far west. All these ascended the river to Fallan Island where Silvanost lay. It was an exciting time, full of strange sights, sounds, and smells. Exciting, that is, for the travelers. For the Silvanesti, who regarded these races flooding their land with distaste and distrust, it was a trying time.

Sithel sat on his throne in the Tower of the Stars, weary but attentive as clerics and nobles filed up to him to voice their complaints. His duties did not allow him respite from the incessant arguing and pleading.

"Great Sithel, what is to be done?" asked Firincalos, high priest of E'li. "The barbarians come to us daily, asking to worship in our temple. We turn them away and they grow angry, and the next day a new batch of hairy-faced savages appears, asking the same privilege."

"The humans and dwarves are not the worst of it," countered Zertinfinas, of the Temple of Matheri. "The Kagonesti deem themselves our equals and cannot be put off from entering the sacred precincts with filthy hands and feet and noxious sigils painted on

75

their faces. Why, yesterday, some wild elves roughed up my assistant and spilled the sacred rosewater in the outer sanctum."

"What would you have me do?" Sithel asked. "Place soldiers around all the temples? There are not enough royal guardsmen in House Protector to do that not to mention that most of them are sons or grandsons of Kagonesti themselves."

"Perhaps an edict, read in the Market, will convince the outsiders not to attempt to force their way into our holy places," Firincalos noted. A murmur of approval ran through the assembly.

"All very well for you," said Miritelisina, high priestess of Quenesti Pah. "How can we who serve the goddess of healing turn away eager supplicants? It is part of our trust to admit the sick and injured. Can we discriminate between Silvanesti and Kagonesti, human, dwarf, and kender?"

"Yes. You must," declared a voice silent until now.

All heads turned to the speaker's left, where Sithas had been standing. He had been listening to the different factions present their views. A long time he'd been listening, and now he felt he must speak. The prince stepped down to floor level, with the assembled clerics, and faced his father.

"It is vital that the purity of our temples and our city be preserved," he said with fervor. "We, the oldest and wisest race of Krynn, the longest lived, the most blessed, must keep ourselves above the hordes of lesser peoples who flood in, trying to partake of our grace and culture." He lifted his hands. "Where there is not purity, there can be no Silvanost and no Silvanesti."

Some of the clerics, not those of Quenesti Pah, bowed in appreciation of Sithas's declaration. Behind them, however, the guildmasters looked distinctly unhappy. Sithel, looking down on his son, was nodding slowly. He looked over the prince's head at the guildmasters, and bade them come forward.

"Highness," said the master of the Jewelers Guild, "the outsiders bring many things we in Silvanesti do not have. The dwarves trade us the finest metal on Krynn for our foodstuffs and nectars. The humans bring expertly carved wood, the softest of leathers, wine, and oil. Even the kender contribute their share."

"Their share of larceny," muttered one of the clerics. Soft laughter rippled through the tower.

"Enough " Sithel commanded. His gaze rested once more on his son. "How do you propose we keep the foreigners out of our temples without losing their trade, which our nation does need?"

Sithas took a deep breath. "We can build an enclave here on Fallan Island, outside the city, and confine all trading to that point. No outsiders except valid ambassadors from other countries will be admitted within Silvanost's walls. If the humans and others wish to pay homage to the gods, let them put up their own shrines in this new enclave."

Sithel leaned back on his throne and stroked his chin. "An interesting notion. Why should the foreigners agree to it?"

"They do not want to lose the goods they get from us," Sithas reasoned. "If they don't agree, they will be turned away." The clerics looked at him with undisguised admiration.

"A perfect solution!" Zertinfinas exclaimed.

"Proof of the wisdom of the speaker's heir," added Firincalos unctuously.

Sithel looked past them to the guildmasters. "What say you, good sirs? Does this notion of my son's appeal to you?"

It did indeed. If the traders had to land at one specified point on Fallan, then the guilds could more easily impose landing fees on them. The various guildmasters voiced their approval loudly.

"Very well, let the plans be made," Sithel decided. "The forming of the docks and walls I leave to the guild of master builders. Once the plans are chosen, the forming of the stones can begin." As Sithel stood up, everyone bowed. "If that is all, then this audience is at an end." The speaker gave Sithas a thoughtful look, then turned and left the hall by the door behind the throne.

The clerics closed around Sithas, congratulating him. Miritelisina asked him if he had a name in mind for the new trading enclave.

Sithas smiled and shook his head. "I have not considered it in such detail yet."

"It should be named for you," Firincalos said exuberantly. "Perhaps 'Sithanost, the city of Sithas'. "

"No," the prince said firmly. "That is not proper. Let it be something the outsiders will understand. 'Thon-car, village on the Thon,' something simple like that. I do not want it named after me."

After freeing himself from the crowd, Sithas mounted the steps and went out the same door by which his father had left. His sedan chair awaited him outside. He climbed in and ordered, "to Quinari, at once." The slaves hoisted the carrying bars to their broad shoulders and set off at a trot.

Hermathya was waiting for him. The news had moved quickly through the palace, and she was brimming with delight at her husband's triumph.

"You've won them," she crowed, pouring Sithas a cup of cool water. "The clerics look upon you as their champion."

"I said only what I believed," Sithas noted quietly.

"True enough, but they will remember what you did, and they will support you in the future," she insisted.

Sithas dampened his fingers in the last drops of the water and touched his face with his fingertips. "Why should I need their support?"

Hermathya looked surprised. "Haven't you heard? Lady Nirakina has suggested to the Speaker that you be appointed as co-ruler, to share the burden of power with your father."

Sithas was taken aback. "You've been listening from balconies again," he said with displeasure.

"I have only your interests in my heart," she said, a trifle coolly.

There was a long silence between them. Not much affection had grown between the firstborn and his beautiful wife since their marriage, and Sithas was growing more skeptical of her devotion with each passing day. Hermathya's ambition was as obvious as the Tower of the Stars and twice as big.

"I will go and speak with my father," Sithas said at last. Hermathya moved to join him. "Alone, Lady. I go alone."

Hermathya turned away from him, her face blazing crimson.

* * * * *

A servant announced the prince, and Sithel gave permission for him to enter. It was mid-afternoon, and the speaker was immersed in a steaming hot pool, his head resting on a folded towel. His eyes were closed.

"Father?"

Sithel opened one eye. "Get in, why don't you? The water is good and hot."

"No, thank you." Sithas took the direct approach. "Father, what is this I hear about mother wanting you to appoint me co-ruler?"

Sithel raised his head. "You do have your spies, don't you?"

"Only one, and I do not pay her. She works on her own account."

"Hermathya." Sithel smiled when the prince nodded. "She has spirit, that girl. I daresay if it were possible she'd want to be co-ruler, too."

"Yes, and bring the rest of Clan Oakleaf to rule with her. She already replaces palace servers with her own relatives. Soon we won't be able to walk the halls without tripping over some Oakleaf cousin or other," Sithas said.

"This is still House Royal," replied his father confidently.

At that, Sithel sat up, roiling the hot mineral water. He reached for a beaker sitting on the rim of the pool, then shook a handful of brown and white crystals into the water. The steam was immediately scented with a rare, spicy musk. "Do you know why your mother asked me to make you co-ruler?"

"No," Sithas replied.

"It was part of a compromise, actually. She wants me to call Kith-Kanan home "

"Kith!" exclaimed Sithas, interrupting his father. "That is an excellent idea!"

Sithel held up a hand. "It would cause great dissent among the clerics and nobles. Kith-Kanan broke some of our most ardent laws. He threatened the very foundations of the House Royal. My anger with him has faded, and I could bring him home if he would properly apologize. There are many, though, who would oppose my lenience."

"But you are speaker," Sithas argued. "What difference do the grumblings of a few priests make to you?"

Sithel smiled. "I cannot tear apart the nation for love of my son. Your mother said that to assuage the clerics I should name you co-ruler. Then they would be assured Kith-Kanan would have no part of the throne after my death." Sithel gazed long into his eldest son's troubled eyes. "Do you still want me to dismiss Lady Nirakina's suggestion to make you my co-ruler?"

Sithas drew a long breath and let it out slowly. He knew that there was only one path to choose. He turned from the window. "If you seat me beside you on the throne, the people will say there is no Speaker of the Stars in Silvanost," he said quietly.

"Explain that."

"They will say great Sithel is old, not strong enough to rule alone. And they will say Sithas is too young and has not the wisdom to be sole speaker. Two halves do not a speaker make." He looked down at his father's strong face. "You are the Speaker of the Stars. Do not relinquish one drop of your power or, as from a pinhole in a waterskin, it will all leak out and you will have nothing."

"Do you know what this decision means?" Sithel demanded.

The prince made a fist and pressed it against his mouth. There were other words he wanted to say; he wanted to have Kith home and let the consequences be damned. But Sithas knew he must not let these words out. The future of Silvanesti was at stake.

"Then I will be Speaker, and will remain sole Speaker until the day the gods call me to a higher plane," Sithel said after a long silence.

"And . . . Kith-Kanan?"

"I will not call him," Sithel said grimly. "He must return on his own, as a supplicant begging for forgiveness."

"Will mother be angry with you?" Sithas asked softly.

The speaker sighed and scooped steaming water up in his hands, letting it trickle down over his closed eyes. "You know your mother," he said. "She will be hurt for a while, then she will find a cause to which she can devote herself, something to help her forget her pain."

"Hermathya will be angry." Of this, Sithas had no doubt.

"Don't let her bully you," counseled Sithel, wiping his face with his hands.

Sithas flushed. "I am your son. No one bullies me."

"I'm glad to hear it." After a pause, Sithel added, "I've just thought of another reason why you ought not want to be speaker just yet. I'm a husband, father, and monarch. So far, you're only a husband." A wry smile quirked his lips. "Have children. That will bring age and hasten wisdom."

Four Days on the Trail

10

Kith-Kanan and Anaya paused in their pursuit of Voltorno's band. The half-human and his followers were headed almost due south, straight for the seacoast. Kith-Kanan was surprised when Anaya called a temporary halt. He was ready for anything, from a stealthy approach to a headlong, pitched battle. True, his feet ached and his hands were covered with cuts, but the knowledge that this Voltorno held not only Mackeli but his griffon steeled the prince to go on.

When he asked if she'd sensed Mackeli was near, Anaya said, "No. I smell animals nearby. It's time to hunt. You stay here and don't move around. I will return soon."

Kith-Kanan settled down with his back against a tree. In short order, he fell asleep. The next thing he knew, Anaya had tossed a brace of rabbits in his lap.

"You snore," she said irritably. "I could have had us venison, but your roaring chased the deer away. All I could get were these rabbits." She frowned at the scrawny little animals. "These must have been deaf."

Quickly Anaya gutted and skinned the animals, then speared them over a twig fire. Kith-Kanan was impressed; her deftness was amazing. She dressed each rabbit in two strokes and started a fire with one nick of her flint against a blue fieldstone. Kith-Kanan doubted he could strike a spark at all against such a common, frangible rock.

She bent to tend the fire. Kith-Kanan watched her back for a moment, then he put down the rabbit. Quietly he unbuckled his sword belt and let it down soundlessly to the ground. He added his dagger to the pile. Then, using the steps Mackeli had taught him, he crept up behind Anaya.

She straightened, still with her back to him. When he was two feet from her, she whirled, presenting the point of her knife to his face.

"You smell better without the metal, but you still breathe too loud," she said.

He pushed the flint knife aside and finished the step that brought them nose to nose. "Perhaps it's not my breathing you hear, but my heart. I can hear yours, too," he said teasingly.

Her brows knotted. "Liar."

Kith-Kanan put a finger to her cheek and began tapping lightly. "Is that the rhythm?" he said. It was, and the look of consternation on Anaya's face was delightful to him. She pushed him away.

"We've no time for games," she said. "Pick up your metal. We can walk and eat at the same time."

She moved on through the trees. Kith-Kanan watched her curiously as he buckled his swordbelt. Funny-looking Anaya, with painted face and most of her hair cropped shorter than his. He found himself taking pleasure in watching the easy way she wove through her forest home. There was a certain nobility about her.

The corvae circled ceaselessly, bringing Anaya news of the humans. Kith-Kanan and Anaya had followed them hotly all day, while the humans moved in a more leisurely manner. The prince felt ragged with fatigue, but he would not show weakness as long as Anaya remained bright and quick. Trouble was, she didn't show any signs of tiring.

It was well past midday, and for the fourth time she had held up her hand and bid Kith-Kanan be still while she scouted ahead. Sighing, he sat down on a lichen-spotted boulder. Anaya vanished into the pallid green saplings as Kith-Kanan took out his dagger and absently began cleaning his fingernails.

Seconds lengthened into minutes, and the prince began to think Anaya was taking too long. Her reconnaissance forays never took more than a minute or two, sometimes only a few seconds. He slipped his dagger into the top of his leggings and listened hard. Nothing.

A crow alighted at his feet. He stared down at the black bird, which regarded him silently, its beady eyes seeming quite intelligent. Kith-Kanan stood up, and the crow flapped into the air, circled around, and settled on his shoulder. He spared a nervous glance at the bird's sharp, pointed beak so close to his face. "You have something to show me?" he whispered. The crow cocked its head first left, then right. "Anaya? Mackeli?" The crow bobbed its head vigorously.

Kith-Kanan set out along the same path Anaya had gone down just a few minutes earlier. The crow actually directed him with pokes of its sharp beak. One hundred paces from a large boulder, Kith-Kanan heard the clinking of metal on metal. Ten steps more, and the faint whiff of smoke came to his nose. The crow plucked at his ear. Its beak stabbed painfully, and Kith-Kanan resisted the urge to swat the bird away. Then he saw what the crow was warning him about.

Ahead on the ground was a net, spread flat and covered with leaves. He knew the type; he'd often set such traps himself, for wild boar. Kith-Kanan squatted by the edge of the net and looked for trip lines or snare loops. He couldn't see any. Circling to his left, he followed the perimeter of the trap until the ground dropped away into a dry wash ravine. From there the smell of wood smoke was stronger. Kith-Kanan skidded a few feet down the bank and crept along, his head just below the level of the ground. Every now and then he would peek up and see where he was going. The third time he did this, Kith-Kanan got quite a shock. He put his head up and found himself staring into the eyes of a human a dead human, lying on his back with his eyes wide and staring. The human's throat had been cut by a serrated knife.

The man wore rough woolen clothing, the seams of which were white with dried salt. Another sailor. There was a tattoo of a sea-horse on the back of the dead man's hand.

Rough laughter filtered through the trees. As Kith-Kanan climbed out of the ravine and made for the sound, the crow spread its wings and flew away.

More ugly, cruel-sounding laughter. Kith-Kanan moved to his right, keeping a thick-trunked pine tree between him and the source of the sound. He dropped down to the ground and looked around the tree.

He saw six men standing in a glade. A smoky little fire burned on the right. On the left, wrapped in the folds of a heavy rope net, was Anaya. She looked defiant and unharmed.

"Are you sure it's female?" queried one of the men who held a crossbow.

"It 'pears to be. 'Ere, tell us what you are!" said another. He poked at Anaya with the tip of his saber. She shrank from the blade.

"What'll we do with her, Parch?" asked a third human.

"Sell 'er, like the other. She's too ugly to be anything but a slave," noted the crossbowman. The men roared with coarse laughter.

Through the loops in the net, Anaya's eyes shone with hatred. She looked past her tormentors and saw, peeking around a tree, Kith-Kanan. He put a hand to his lips. Quiet, he willed her. Keep quiet.

"Smells a bit, don't she?" sneered the crossbowman called Parch, a lanky fellow with a drooping yellow mustache. He put down his weapon and picked up a heavy wooden bucket full of water. He flung the water on Anaya.

Kith-Kanan thought quickly. The leader, Voltorno, didn't seem to be present; these men acted callous and loud, like many soldiers did when their commander was absent. Retreating a few yards, the prince started around the glade. He hadn't gone more than a half-score steps when his foot snagged a trip line. Kith-Kanan dodged a spike-studded tree limb that was released, but the noise alerted the men. They bared their weapons and started into the woods, leaving one man to guard Anaya.

Standing with his back hard against a sticky pine, Kith-Kanan drew his sword. A human came crunching through the fallen leaves, appallingly noisy. The salty-fishy smell of his sailor's jersey preceded him. Kith-Kanan timed the man's steps and, when he was close, sprang out from behind the tree.

"By the dragon's beard!" exclaimed the man. He held out his saber warily. Without any preliminaries, Kith-Kanan attacked. Their blades clanged together, and the human shouted, "Over here, over here!" Other shouts echoed in the forest. In moments, Kith-Kanan would be hopelessly outnumbered.

The human's saber had little point for thrusting, so the elf prince jabbed his blade straight at the man, who gave ground clumsily. He was a seaman, not a warrior, and when he stumbled over a stone as he was backing away, Kith-Kanan ran him through. This was the first person he'd ever killed, but there was no time for reflection. As quietly as he could the prince ran to the glade. The other men were converging on their dead comrade, so that meant only one man stood between him and Anaya.

He hurtled into the glade, sword upraised. The guard the one called Parch gave a shrill cry of fright and reached for his weapon, a crossbow. Kith-Kanan was on him in a flash. He struck the crossbow from Parch's hands with a single sweep of his sword. The man staggered back, groping for the dagger he wore at his waist. Kith-Kanan advanced on him. Parch drew the dagger. Kith-Kanan easily beat aside the far shorter weapon and left poor Parch bleeding on the ground.

"Are you all right?" he shouted to Anaya as he hacked open the net. It spilled open, and Anaya nimbly leaped out.

"Filthy humans! I want to kill them!" she snarled.

"There's too many. Better to hide for now," Kith-Kanan cried.

She ignored him and went to the fire, where her flint knife lay on the ground. Before Kith-Kanan could protest, she drew the sharp stone across her arm, drawing scarlet blood. "They will die!" she declared. And with that, she dashed into the woods.

"Anaya, wait!" Kith-Kanan frantically followed her.

A hoarse scream sounded from his left. Feet churned through the leaves, running. A human, still holding his saber, ran toward the prince, his bearded face a mask of fear. Kith-Kanan stood in his way. The man traded cuts with him briefly, then threw his sword away and ran for his life. Confused, the Silvanesti trotted in the direction from which the bearded man had come, then stumbled upon the corpse of the man who had poked Anaya with his saber. No wonder the bearded human had been terrified. This other man's throat had been cut from ear to ear. Kith-Kanan clenched his teeth and moved on. He found another human, killed in the same manner.

The woods had fallen quiet, and the elf prince stepped carefully, suspecting an ambush. What he found instead nearly stopped his heart. Anaya had caught a third human and killed him, but not before the man had put a crossbow quarrel into her hip. She had dragged herself a few yards and had come to rest with both arms around an oak sapling.

Before Kith-Kanan knelt by her, he shoved his sword in its scabbard and gently pulled the blood-soaked deerskin away from her wound. The head of the quarrel had missed her hip bone, thank E'li, and was buried in the flesh between her hip and ribs. A nasty wound, but not a fatal one.

"I must take the arrow out," he explained. "But I can't pull it out the way it came in. I'll have to push it through."

"Do what must be done," she gasped her eyelids squeezed shut.

His hands shook. Though he had seen hunters and soldiers injured before, never had Kith-Kanan had to deal with their wounds personally. He tore the leather fletching off the arrow and placed his hands on it. Steeling himself, he pushed on the nock end. Anaya stiffened and sucked air in sharply through her clenched teeth. He pushed until he could feel the iron arrow head in his other hand, beneath her body.

She didn't utter a sound, which made Kith-Kanan marvel at her courage. Once the quarrel was free, he threw it away. Then he unslung his waterskin and gently washed the wound clean. He needed something to bind it with. Under the green leather tunic Mackeli had fashioned for him, he still wore his shirt of linen. At last Kith-Kanan pulled off his tunic and tore the fine Silvanost linen into strips.

He tied the longest strips together to make a bandage, then began to wind it around Anaya's waist. Kith-Kanan split and tied the ends of the bandage, then gently hoisted Anaya in his arms. She was very light, and he carried her easily back to the glade. There he laid her in a patch of soft ferns, then dragged the dead men into the covering of the woods.

Anaya called for water. He put the skin to her lips, and she drank. After a few gulps she said weakly, "I heard them say Mackeli and your flying beast had been taken ahead to the ship. They knew we were following them. Their master, Voltorno, is half-human, and by means of magic he knew we were coming after them."

"Half-human?" Kith-Kanan asked. He had heard whisperings of such crossbreeds, but had never seen one.

"Voltorno had his men stay behind to trap us." Kith-Kanan put the skin to her mouth again. When she had finished, she added, "You must leave me and go after Mackeli."

He knew she was right. "Are you sure you will be all right by yourself?"

"The forest won't hurt me. Only the intruders would do that, and they are ahead of us, carrying Mackeli. You must hurry."

With little delay the elf prince left the Kagonesti the waterskin and laid one of the men's abandoned cloaks over her. "I'll be back soon," he promised. "With Mackeli and Arcuballis."

The sun was sinking fast as Kith-Kanan plunged into the brush. He made great speed and covered a mile or more in minutes. There was a salty smell in the air. The sea was near.

Ahead, moonlight glinted off metal. As he ran, Kith-Kanan spied the backs of two men dragging a smaller person through the brush. Mackeli! He had a halter tied around his neck, and he stumbled along behind his much taller captors. The prince shouldered the crossbow and put a quarrel in the back of the human who was leading Mackeli. The second man saw his partner fall and, without pausing, he grabbed the halter rope and ran, jerking Mackeli forward.

Kith-Kanan followed. He leaped over the man he'd shot and let out the wailing cry elven hunters use when on the chase. The weird cry was too much for the man leading Mackeli. He flung the rope away and ran as hard as he could. Kith-Kanan loosed a quarrel after him, but the human passed between some trees and the shot missed.

He reached Mackeli, pausing long enough to cut the strangling rope from the boy's neck.

"Kith!" he cried. "Is Ny with you?"

"Yes, not far away," Kith-Kanan said. "Where's my griffon?"

"Voltorno has him. He put a spell on your beast to make him obey."

Kith-Kanan gave Mackeli the dagger. "Wait here. I'll come back for you."

"Let me go too! I can help!" the boy said.

"No!" Mackeli looked stubborn, so Kith-Kanan added, "I need you to stay here in case Voltorno gets past me and comes back this way." Mackeli's belligerence vanished, and he nodded. He positioned himself on guard with his dagger as Kith-Kanan ran on.

The boom of the surf rose above the sound of the wind. The forest ended abruptly atop a cliff, and Kith-Kanan had to dig in his heels to avoid plunging over the precipice. The night was bright. Solinari and Lunitari were up; moonlight and starlight silvered the scene below. With his keen vision, Kith-Kanan could see a three-masted ship wallowing in the offshore swells, its sails furled tightly against the yards.

A path led down the cliffside to the beach below. The first thing Kith-Kanan saw was Arcuballis, picking its way along the narrow path. The griffon's glow stood out strongly against the fainter ones of its captors. A red-caped figure presumably the half-human Volterno led the griffon by its bridle. A human trailed restlessly behind the beast. Kith-Kanan stood up against the starry sky and loosed a quarrel at him. The man felt the quarrel pass through the sleeve of his tunic, and he screamed. Right away a swarm of men appeared on the beach. They moved out from the base of the cliff and showered arrows up at Kith-Kanan.

"Halloo," called a voice from below. Kith-Kanan cautiously raised his head. The figure in the red cape moved away from the captive griffon and stood out on the beach in plain sight. "Halloo up there! Can you hear me?"

"I hear you," Kith-Kanan shouted in reply. "Give me back my griffon!"

"I can't give him back. That beast is the only profit I'll realize on this voyage. You've got the boy back, leave the animal and go on your way."

"No! Surrender Arcuballis! I have you in my sight," Kith-Kanan warned.

"No doubt you do, but if you shoot me, my men will kill the griffon. Now, I don't want to die, and I'm certain you don't want a dead griffon either. What would you say to fighting for the beast in an honorable contest with swords?"

"How do I know you won't try some treachery?"

The half-human flung off his cape. "I doubt that will be necessary."

Kith-Kanan didn't trust him, but before the elf could say anything more, the half-human had taken a lantern from one of his men and was striding up the steep path to the top of the cliff, leading the griffon as he came. Arcuballis, usually so spirited, hung its head as it walked. The powerful wings had been pinioned by leather straps, and a muzzle made from chain mail covered the griffon's hooked beak.

"You have bewitched my animal," Kith-Kanan said furiously.

Voltorno tied the bridle to a tree and set the lantern on a waist-high boulder. "It is necessary." As the half-human faced Kith-Kanan, the elf studied him carefully. He was quite tall, and in the lantern's glow his hair was golden. A fine, downy beard covered his cheeks and chin, revealing his human heritage, but Voltorno's ears were slightly pointed, denoting elven blood. His clothes and general bearing were far more refined than any of the humans with him.

"Are you sure you have enough light to see?" Kith-Kanan asked sarcastically, gesturing at the lantern.

Voltorno smiled brilliantly. "Oh, that isn't for me. It's for my men. They would hate to miss the show."

When Kith-Kanan presented his sword, Voltorno complimented him on the weapon. "The pattern is a bit old-fashioned, but very handsome. I shall enjoy using it after you're dead," he smirked.

The sailors lined the beach below to watch the duel. They cheered Voltorno and jeered Kith-Kanan as the two duelists circled each other warily. The half-human's blade flickered in, reaching for Kith-Kanan's heart. The elf parried, rolled the slim Ergothian rapier aside, and lunged with his stouter elven point.

Voltorno laughed and steered Kith-Kanan's thrust into the ground. He tried to stomp on the prince's blade, to snap the stiff iron, but Kith-Kanan drew back, avoiding the seafarer's heavy boots.

"You fight well," Voltorno offered. "Who are you? Despite the rags you wear, you are no wild elf."

"I am Silvanesti. That is all you need to know," Kith-Kanan said tightly.

Voltorno smiled, pleasantly enough. "So much pride. You think I am some renegade."

"It is easy to see which race you have chosen to serve," Kith-Kanan said.

"The humans, for all their crudity, have appreciation for talent. In your nation I would be an outcast, lowest of the low. Among the humans, I am a very useful fellow. I could find a place for you in my company. As I rise, so could you. We would go far, elf."

Voltorno spoke in an increasingly obvious lilt. His words rose and fell in a sort of sing-song intonation that Kith-Kanan found peculiar. The half-human was only a few feet from Kith-Kanan, and the elf prince saw that he was making small, slow gestures with his free hand.

"I owe my allegiance elsewhere," Kith-Kanan stated. His sword felt heavy in his hand.

"Pity." With renewed vigor, Voltorno attacked. Kith-Kanan fought him off clumsily, for the very air was beginning to seem thick, impeding his movements. As their blades tangled, Kith-Kanan lost his plan of defense and Voltorno's steel slipped by his hilt and pierced his upper arm, The half-human stepped back, still smiling like a beneficent cleric.

The weapon fell from Kith-Kanan's numb hand. He stared at it in dawning horror. His fingers had no more feeling than wood or wax. He tried to speak, but his tongue felt thick. A terrifying lethargy gripped him. Though in his mind he was yelling and fighting, his voice and limbs would not obey. Magic . . . it was magic. Voltorno had bewitched Arcuballis, now him.

Voltorno sheathed his own sword and picked up Kith-Kanan's. "How splendidly ironic it will be to kill you with your own sword," he noted. Then he raised the weapon

And it flew from his hand! Voltorno looked down at his chest and the quarrel that had suddenly appeared there. His knees buckled, and he fell.

Mackeli stepped out of the dark ring of trees, a crossbow in his hands. Kith-Kanan staggered back away from the half-human. His strength was returning, in spite of the wound in his arm. Like a river freed from a dam, feeling rushed back into his body. He picked up his sword and heard shouts from the beach. The humans were coming to aid their fallen leader.

"So," said the half-human through bloody lips, "you triumph after all." He grimaced and touched his fingers to the quarrel in his chest. "Go ahead, end it."

Already the humans were running up the steep path toward them. "I've no time to waste on you," spat Kith-Kanan contemptuously. He wanted to sound strong, but his narrow escape had left him shaken.

He took Mackeli by the arm and hurried to Arcuballis. The boy hung back as Kith-Kanan removed the muzzle from the griffon's beak and cut the leather pinions from its wings. The fire was returning to the griffon's eyes. The creature clawed the ground with its talons.

Kith-Kanan touched his forehead to the beast's feathered head and said, "It's good to see you, old fellow." He heard the commotion as the humans came roaring up the cliffside. Mounting the griffon, Kith-Kanan slid forward in the saddle and said, "Climb on, Mackeli." The elf boy looked uncertain. "Hurry, the spell is broken but Voltorno's men are coming!"

After another second's hesitation, Mackeli grasped Kith-Kanan's hand and swung into the saddle behind him. Armed sailors appeared on top of the cliff, and they rushed to Voltorno. Behind them came a tall human with a full, red-brown beard. He pointed to the elves. "Stop them!" he cried in a booming voice.

"Hold on!" shouted Kith-Kanan. He slapped the reins across Arcuballis's neck, and the griffon bounded toward the men. They dropped and scattered like leaves in a whirlwind. Another leap and Arcuballis cleared the edge of the cliff. Mackeli gave a short, sharp cry of fear, but Kith-Kanan yelled with pure joy. Some of the humans got to their feet and loosed arrows at them, but the distance was too great. Kith-Kanan steered Arcuballis out over the foaming surf, turned, and gained height. As they swept past the site of the duel, he saw the red-bearded fellow raise Voltorno to his feet. That one wasn't going to die easily, the prince noted.

"It's good to see you!" Kith-Kanan shouted over his shoulder. "You saved my life, you know." There was no response from Mackeli and Kith-Kanan asked, "Are you well?"

"I was weller on the ground," Mackeli said, his voice high with anxiety. He tightened his fierce grip on Kith-Kanan's waist as he asked, "Where are we going?"

"To fetch Anaya. Hold tight!"

The griffon gave voice to its own triumphant cry. The trilling roar burst over the wildwood, announcing their return to the waiting Anaya.

Early Autumn, Year of the Hawk

11

The traditional way across the river to Silvanost was by ferry. Large, flat-bottomed barges were drawn back and forth across the Thon-Thalas by giant turtles. Some time in the distant past, priests of the Blue Phoenix, god of all animal life, had woven the spells that brought the first giant turtles into being.

They had taken a pair of common river turtles, usually the size of a grown elf's palm, and worked their spells over them until they were as big as houses. Thereafter, the priests bred their own giants, creating quite a sizeable herd. The vast green domes of the turtles' shells had become a common sight as the placid beasts gave faithful service for many centuries.

Lady Nirakina stood on the riverbank, watching a barge of refugees, pulled by just such a turtle, arrive from the west bank. Beside her stood Tamanier Ambrodel, his arm still in a sling. A month had passed since the Trial Days, and during that time more and more settlers from the western plains and forests had retreated to Silvanost for protection.

"How many does that make?" asked Nirakina, shading her eyes to see the crowded barge.

Tamanier checked the tally he was keeping. "Four hundred and nineteen, my lady," he said. "And more coming all the time."

The settlers were mostly from the poorer families of Silvanesti who had gone west to work new land and make new lives for themselves. Though largely unharmed, they were footsore, exhausted, and demoralized. Their stories were all the same: bands of humans and Kagonesti elves had burned down their houses and orchards and ordered them to leave. The Silvanesti, unarmed and unorganized, had little choice but to pack their meager belongings and trek back to Silvanost.

Nirakina had received her husband's blessing to organize relief for the displaced settlers. A field along the southern end of the city was set aside for them, and a shanty town of tents and lean-tos had sprung up in the last few weeks. Nirakina had persuaded many of the city guilds and great temples to contribute food, blankets, and money for the care of the refugees.

Sithel was doing all he could for the refugees, too, but his job was made far more complicated by the demands of the state. The Tower of the Stars was filled daily with petitioners who entreated the speaker to call together the army and clear the plains of the raiders. Sithel quite rightly realized this was not a practical solution. A big, slow-moving army would never catch small, mobile raider bands.

"Our neighbors to the west, Thorbardin and Ergoth, would be very unhappy to see an elven army on their borders," Sithel told his more bellicose nobles. "It would be an invitation to war, and that is an invitation I will not countenance."

So the refugees continued to come, first in a trickle, then in a steady stream. As he was acquainted with them and knew first-hand the problems they faced, Tamanier Ambrodel was chosen by Lady Nirakina to be her chief assistant. He proved a tireless worker, but even with his efforts, the camp along the riverbank became dirty and rowdy as more and more frightened settlers swelled its ranks. A pall of smoke and fear hovered over the refugee camp. It did not take long for the residents of Silvanost to lose their sympathy and regard the refugees with disgust.

This day Nirakina had gone down to the water's edge to speak to the refugees as they came ashore. The weary, grimy travelers were amazed to see the speaker's wife waiting on the muddy bank, her richly made gown trailing in the mud, only Tamanier Ambrodel standing beside her.

"They are so sad, so tired," she murmured to him. He stood by her side making notations on a wax tablet.

"It's a sad thing to lose your home and those you love best, my lady." Tamanier filled a square of twenty and blocked it off. "That makes two hundred and twenty in one barge, including sixty-six humans and half-humans." He eyed her uncertainly. "The Speaker will not be pleased that those not of our blood are entering the city."

"I know the Speaker's heart," Nirakina said a little sharply. Her slight figure bristled with indignation. "It is the others at court who want to cause trouble for these poor folk."

An elf woman struggled ashore from a small boat, carrying a baby in her arms. She slipped and fell to her knees in the muddy water. Other exhausted refugees tramped past her. Nirakina, without hesitation, waded into the press of silent people and helped the elf woman to her feet. Their eyes met, and the raggedly dressed woman said, "Thank you, my lady."

With nothing else to say, she held her child to her shoulder and slogged ashore. Nirakina was standing, openly admiring the woman's dogged courage, when a hand touched her arm.

"You'd best be careful, Lady," Tamanier said.

Unheeding, Nirakina replied, "The priests and nobles will fume about this, about the mixed-blood people especially." Her serene expression darkened. "They should all be made to come here and see the poor innocents they would deny comfort and shelter!"

Tamanier gently tugged Lady Nirakina back to the riverbank.

On the other side of the city, the Tower of the Stars rang with denunciations of the refugees.

"When the gods created the world, they made our race first, to be the guardians of right and truth," declared Firincalos, high priest of E'li. "It is our sacred duty to preserve ourselves as the gods made us, a pure race, always recognizable as Silvanesti."

"Well said! Quite true!" The assembly of nobles and clerics called out in rising voices.

Sithas watched his father. The speaker listened placidly to all this, but he did not look pleased. It was not so much that his father disagreed with the learned Firincalos; Sithas had heard similar sentiments espoused before. But he knew the speaker hated to be lectured to by anyone, for any reason.

Since the Trial Days, Sithas had been at his father's side daily, taking a hand in the day-to-day administration of the country. He'd learned new respect for Sithel when he saw how his father managed to balance the pleas of the priests, the ideas of the nobles, and the needs of the guilds against his own philosophy of what was best for Silvanesti.

Sithas had learned respect but not admiration. He believed his father was too flexible, gave in too often to the wrong people. It surprised him, for he had always thought of Sithel as a strong ruler. Why didn't he simply command obedience instead of constantly compromising?

Sithel waved for the assembled elves to be quiet. Miritelisina, high priestess of Quenesti Pah, was standing, seeking the speaker's grant to comment. The hall quieted, and Sithel bade Miritelisina begin.

"I must ask the pure and righteous Firincalos what he would do with the husbands, wives, and children now languishing in huts along the riverbank, those who are not pure in our blood yet who have the deepest ties to some number of our race?" Her rich voice filled the high tower. In her youth, Miritelisina had been a renowned singer, and she played upon her listeners with all her old skills. "Shall we throw them into the river? Shall we drive them from the island, back onto the swords and torches of the bandits who drove them east?"

A few harsh voices cried "Yes!" to her questions.

Sithas folded his arms and studied Miritelisina. She cut a regal figure in her sapphire headband and white robe with its trailing, sky-blue sash. Her waist-length, flaxen hair rippled down her back as she swept a pointing finger over the mostly male crowd of elves.

"Shame on you all!" she shouted. "Is there no mercy in Silvanost? The humans and half-humans are not here because they want to be! Evil has been done to them, evil that must be laid at someone's door. But to treat them like animals, to deny them simple shelter, is likewise evil. My holy brothers, is this the way of rightness and truth of which the honorable Firincalos speaks? It does not sound that way to me. I would more expect to hear such harsh sentiments from devotees of the Dragonqueen!"

Sithas stiffened. The willful priestess had gone too far! Firincalos and his colleagues thought so, too. They pushed to the front of the crowd, outraged at being compared to the minions of the Queen of Evil. The air thickened with denunciations, but Sithel, sitting back on his throne, did nothing to restrain the angry clerics.

Sithas turned to his father. "May I speak?" he asked calmly.

"I've been waiting for you to take a stand," Sithel said impatiently. "Go ahead. But remember, if you swim with snakes, you may get bitten."

Sithas bowed to his father. "This is a hard time for our people," he began loudly. The wrangling on the floor subsided, and the prince lowered his voice. "It is evident from events in the West that the humans, probably with the support of the emperor of Ergoth, are trying to take over our plains and woodland provinces, not by naked conquest, but by displacing our farmers and traders. Terror is their tool, and so far it is working far better than they could have dreamed. I tell you this first and ask you all to remember who is responsible for the situation in which we now find ourselves."

Sithel nodded with satisfaction. Sithas noted his father's reaction and went on.

"The refugees come to Silvanost seeking our protection, and we cannot fail to give it. It is our duty. We protect those not of our race because they have come on bended knee, as subjects must do before their lords. It is only right and proper that we shield them from harm, not only because the gods teach the virtue of mercy, but also because these are the people who grow our crops, sell our goods, who pay their taxes and their fealty." A murmur passed through the assembly. Sithas's calm, rational tone, so long honed in debates with the priests of Matheri, dampened the anger that had reigned earlier. The clerics relaxed from their previous trembling outrage. Miritelisina smiled faintly.

Sithas dropped his hands to his hips and looked over the gathering with stern resolve. "But make no mistake! The preservation of our race is of the greatest importance. Not merely the purity of our blood, but the purity of our customs, traditions, and laws. For that reason, I ask the speaker to decree a new place of refuge for the settlers, on the western bank of the Thon-Thalas, for the sole purpose of housing all humans and half-humans. Further, I suggest that all non-Silvanesti be sent across to there from the current tent village."

There was a moment of silence as the assembly took in this idea, then the tower erupted with calls of "Well spoken! Well said!"

"What about the husbands and wives who are full-blooded Silvanesti?" demanded Miritelisina.

"They may go with their families, of course," replied Sithas evenly.

"They should be made to go," insisted Damroth, priest of Kiri Jolith. "They are an insult to our heritage."

Sithel rapped the arm of his throne with his massive signet ring. The sound echoed through the Tower of the Stars. Instant silence claimed the hall.

"My son does me honor," the speaker said. "Let all he has said be done." The priestess of Quenesti Pah opened her mouth to protest, but Sithel rapped on his throne again, as a warning. "Those Silvanesti who have taken humans as mates will go with their kin. They have chosen their path, now they must follow it. Let it be done."

He stood, a clear signal that the audience was over. The assembly bowed deeply as one and filed out. In a few minutes, only Sithel and Sithas were left.

"That Miritelisina," said Sithel wryly. "She's a woman of extreme will."

"She's too sentimental," Sithas complained, coming to his father's side. "I didn't notice her offering to take the half-breeds into her temple."

"No, but she's spent a third of the temple treasury on tents and firewood, I hear." The speaker rubbed his brow with one hand and sighed gustily. "Do you think it will come to war? There's no real proof Ergoth is behind these attacks."

Sithas frowned. "These are not ordinary bandits. Ordinary bandits don't scorn gold in favor of wrecking fruit trees. I understand this new emperor, Ullves X, is an ambitious young schemer. Perhaps if we confront him directly, he would restrain the 'bandits' now at liberty in our western lands."

Sithel looked doubtful. "Humans are difficult to deal with. They have more guile than kender, and their rapaciousness can make a goblin pale. And yet, they know honor, loyalty, and courage. It would be easier if they were all cruel or all noble, but as it is, they are mostly . . . difficult." Rising from the throne, the speaker added, "Still, talk is cheaper than war. Prepare a letter to the emperor of Ergoth. Ask him to send an emissary for the purpose of ending the strife on the plains. Oh, you'd better send a similar note to the king of Thorbardin. They have a stake in this, too."

"I will begin at once," Sithas assented, bowing deeply.

* * * * *

Usually, diplomatic notes to foreign rulers would be composed by professional scribes, but Sithas sat down at the onyx table in his private room and began the letter himself. He dipped a fine stylus in a pot of black ink and wrote the salutation. "To His Most Excellent and Highborn Majesty, Ullves X, Emperor, Prince of Daltigoth, Grand Duke of Colem, etc., etc." The prince shook his head. Humans dearly loved titles; how they piled them after their names. "From Sithel, Speaker of the Stars, Son of Silvanos. Greetings, Royal Brother."

Hermathya burst into the room, red-gold hair disheveled, mantle askew. Sithas was so startled he dropped a blot of ink on the page, spoiling the fine vellum.

"Sithas!" she exclaimed breathlessly, rushing toward him. "They are rioting!"

"Who's rioting?" he growled irritably.

"The farmers the settlers lately come from the West. Word got out that the speaker was going to force them to leave Silvanost, and they began to smash and burn things. A band of them attacked the Market! Parts of it are on fire!"

Sithas rushed to the balcony. He threw aside the heavy brocade curtain and stepped out. His rooms faced away from the Market district, but through the muggy autumn air he caught the distant sounds of screaming.

"Has the royal guard been turned out?" he asked, returning inside quickly.

Hermathya inhaled deeply, her pale skin flushed as she tried to get her breathing under control. "I think so. I saw warriors headed that way. My sedan chair was blocked by a column of guards, so I got out and ran to the palace."

"You shouldn't have done that," he said sternly. Sithas imagined Hermathya running down the street like some wild Kagonesti. What would the common folk think, seeing his wife dashing through town like a wild thing?

When she planted her hands on her hips, the prince noticed that Hermathya's mantle had slipped down, leaving one white shoulder bare. Her flame-bright hair had escaped its confining clasp and tendrils streamed around her reddened face. Her blush deepened at Sithas's words.

"I thought it important to bring you the news!"

"The news would have come soon enough," he stated tersely. He pulled a bell cord for a servant. An elf maid appeared with silent efficiency. "A bowl of water and a towel for Lady Hermathya," Sithas commanded. The maid bowed and departed.

Hermathya flung off her dusty mantle. "I don't need water!" she exclaimed angrily. "I want to know what you're going to do about the riot!"

"The warriors will quell it," the prince stated flatly as he returned to the table. When he saw that the parchment was ruined, Sithas frowned at the letter.

"Well, I hope no harm comes to Lady Nirakina!" she added.

Sithas ceased twirling the stylus in his fingers. "What do you mean?" he asked sharply.

"Your mother is out there, in the midst of the fighting!"

He seized Hermathya by the arms. His grip was so tight, a gasp was wrenched from his wife. "Don't lie to me, Hermathya! Why should Mother be in that part of the city?"

"Don't you know? She was at the river with that Ambrodel fellow, helping the poor wretches."

Sithas released her quickly, and she staggered back a step. He thought fast. Then, turning to an elegant wardrobe made of flamewood, he pulled his street cloak off its peg and flipped it around his shoulders. On another peg was a sword belt holding a slender sword, the twin of his brother's. He buckled the belt around his waist. It settled lopsidedly around his narrow hips.

"I'm going to find my mother," he declared.

Hermathya grabbed her mantle. "I'll go with you!"

"You will not," he said firmly. "It isn't seemly for you to roam the streets. You will stay here."

"I will do as I please!"

Hermathya started for the door, but Sithas caught her wrist and pulled her back. Her eyes blazed furiously.

"If it weren't for me, you wouldn't even know about the danger!" she hissed.

Voice tight with control, Sithas replied, "Lady, if you wish to remain in my good graces, you will do as I say."

She stuck out her chin. "Oh? And if I don't, what will you do? Strike me?" Sithas felt impaled by her deep blue eyes and, in spite of his anxiety about his mother, he felt a surge of passion. The starjewel at Hermathya's throat flashed. There was color in her cheeks to match the heat in her eyes. Their life together had been so cold. So little fire, so little emotion. Her arms were smooth and warm in Sithas's hands as he leaned close. But in the instant before their lips met, Hermathya whispered, "I will do as I please!"

The prince pushed his wife back and turned away, breathing deeply to calm himself. She used her beauty like a weapon, not only on the commoners, but even on him. Sithas closed the collar of his cloak with a trembling hand.

"Find my father. Tell the speaker what has happened and what I intend to do."

"Where is the speaker?" she said sulkily.

He snapped, "I don't know. Why don't you look for him?" Without another word, Sithas hurried from the room.

On his way out, the prince passed the servant as she returned with a bowl of tepid water and a soft, white towel. The elf maiden stood aside to let Sithas pass, then presented the bowl to Hermathya. She scowled at the girl, then, with one hand, knocked the basin from the servant's hands. The bronze bowl hit the marble floor with a clang, splashing Hermathya's feet with water.

Idyll at the End of Summer

12

Arcuballis lowered its head to the clear water and drank. Not far from the hollow tree, where Anaya and Mackeli lived, a spring welled up from deep underground, creating a large, still pool. The water spilled over the lip of one side of the pool, cascading down natural steps of granite and bluestone.

It was two days after Kith-Kanan had flown them all safely home. He had come to the pool daily since then to bathe his wounded arm. Though tender, it was a clean wound and showed every sign of healing well.

Despite her own injury, Anaya would not let Kith-Kanan carry her to the pool. Instead, she directed Mackeli to bring her certain roots and leaves, from which she made a poultice. As Kith-Kanan watched her chew the medicinal leaves herself, he listened for the fourth time to Mackeli's tale of capture and captivity.

"And then Voltorno told the woodcutters there were no evil spirits in the forest, and they believed him, until they came running back down the trail, screaming and falling on their hairy faces."

"Do you suppose we could give him back?" Anaya interrupted with a bored expression.

"I think so," offered Kith-Kanan. "The ship may not have sailed yet."

Mackeli looked at the two of them open-mouthed. "Give me back!" he said, horrified. Slowly the boy smiled. "You're teasing me!"

"I'm not," said Anaya, wincing as she applied the chewed leaves and root paste to her wound. Mackeli's face fell until Kith-Kanan winked at him.

"Come with me to the spring," the prince said. It was better to leave Anaya alone. Her wound had made her testy.

Kith-Kanan led Arcuballis through the woods by its reins. Mackeli walked beside him.

"There is one thing I'm not clear about," Kith-Kanan said after a time. "Was it Voltorno who cast the spell on me that first night, the night he stole Arcuballis from me?"

"It must have been," Mackeli guessed. "His men were starved for meat, so Voltorno worked up a spell to enthrall any warm-blooded creatures in the area. The deer, rabbits, boar, and other animals had long since fled, warned of the humans by the corvae. All he got for his trouble was your griffon, which he knew was rare and valuable."

As Arcuballis drank its fill, the elf prince and the Kagonesti boy sat on a bluestone boulder and listened to the water cascading from the pool.

"I'm glad you and Ny are getting along," Mackeli noted. "She is not easy to live with."

"That I know."

The Kagonesti tossed a twig into the water and watched as it was drawn down the miniature falls.

"Mackeli, what do you remember about your parents? Your mother and father what were they like?"

Mackeli's forehead wrinkled with deep thought. "I don't know. I must have been a baby when they left."

"Left? Do you mean died?"

"No. Ny always said our parents left us and meant to come back some day," he said.

She and Mackeli looked so completely different, it was hard for Kith-Kanan to believe they were blood relatives.

"You know, Kith, I watched you fight with Voltorno. It was really something! The way you moved, swish, clang, swish!" Mackeli waved his hand in the air, holding an imaginary sword. "I wish I could fight like that."

"I could teach you," said Kith-Kanan. "If Anaya doesn't mind."

Mackeli wrinkled his nose, as if he smelled something bad. "I know what she'll say: 'Get out of this tree! You stink like metal!' "

"Maybe she wouldn't notice." The boy and the prince looked at each other and then shook their heads in unison. "She'd notice," Kith-Kanan said. "We'll just have to ask her."

They walked back to the clearing. Anaya had limped, no doubt painfully, out of the tree into the one sunny spot in the clearing. An ugly smear of greenish paste covered her wound.

"Ny, uh, Kith has something to ask you," Mackeli said quickly.

She opened her eyes. "What is it?"

Kith-Kanan tied Arcuballis to a tree in the shaded end of the clearing. He came to where Anaya was reclining and squatted down beside her.

"Mackeli wants to learn the use of arms, and I'm willing to teach him. Is that agreeable to you?"

"You wish to take up metal?" she said sharply to the boy. Mackeli nodded as his sister sat up, moving stiffly. "A long time ago, I made a bargain with the spirits of the forest. In return for their allowing me to hear and speak with the animals and trees, I was to be their guardian against outsiders, and those who would despoil the forest are my enemies. And the forest told me that the worst of these intruders carried metal, which is soulless and dead, torn from the deep underground, burned in fire, and used only to kill and destroy. In time the very smell of metal came to offend my nose."

"You find it acceptable for me to carry a sword and dagger," noted Kith-Kanan.

"The Forestmaster chose you for a task, and I cannot fault her judgment. You drove the intruders out, saving my brother and the forest." She looked at Mackeli. "The choice is yours, but if you take up metal, the beasts will no longer speak to you. I may even have to send you away."

Mackeli's face showed shock. "Send me away?" he whispered. He looked around. The hollow oak, the shaded clearing, and Anaya were all he had ever known of home and family. "Is there no other way?"

"No," Anaya said flatly, and tears sprang up in Mackeli's eyes.

Kith-Kanan couldn't understand the elf woman's hardness. "Don't despair, Mackeli," he said consolingly. "I can teach swordsmanship using wooden staves in place of iron blades." He looked at Anaya and added a bit sarcastically, "Is that allowed?"

She waved one hand dismissively.

Kith-Kanan put a hand on Mackeli's shoulder. "What do you say, do you still want to learn?" he asked.

Mackeli blotted his eyes on his sleeve and sniffed, "Yes."

* * * * *

As summer lay down like a tired hound and autumn rose up to take its place, Kith-Kanan and Mackeli sparred with wooden swords in the clearing. It was not harmless fun, and many bruises and black eyes resulted from unguarded blows landed on unprotected flesh. But there was no anger in it, and the boy and the prince developed more than fighting skill on those sunny afternoons. They developed a friendship. Bereft of home and family, with no real plans for the future, Kith-Kanan was glad to have something to fill his days.

Early on, Anaya watched them dance and dodge, shouting and laughing as the wooden "blades" hit home. Her side healed quickly, more quickly than Kith-Kanan thought natural, and before long Anaya retreated to the woods. She came and went according to her own whims, often returning with a dressed out hart or a snare line of rabbits. Kith-Kanan believed she had finally come to accept his presence in her home, but she did not join in the easy camaraderie that grew between him and her brother.

One day, as the first leaves were changing from green to gold, Kith-Kanan went down to the spring. Mackeli was off collecting from a rich harvest of fall nuts, and Anaya had been gone for several days. He patted Arcuballis's flank in passing, then plunged into the cool shade along the path to the pool.

His newly sharpened senses caught the sound of splashing in the water halfway down the path. Curious, he slipped into the underbrush. Kith-Kanan crept along soundlessly for his walking and breathing were much improved, also until he came to the high ground overlooking the pool.

Treading water in the center of the pool was a dark-haired elf woman. Her raven-black tresses floated on the surface around her like a cloud of dense smoke. It took Kith-Kanan a moment to realize he was looking at Anaya. Her hair was free of its long braid, and all her skin paint was washed off; he nearly didn't recognize her clean-scrubbed features. Smiling, he sat down by the trunk of a lichen-encrusted oak to watch her swim.

For all her stealth on land, Anaya was not a graceful swimmer. She paddled back and forth, using a primitive stroke. The fishers of the Thon-Thalas could teach her a thing or two, Kith-Kanan decided.

When she climbed out of the water onto a ledge of granite, Kith-Kanan saw that she was naked. Accustomed though he was to the highly prized pallor of city-dwellers, he found her sun-browned body oddly beautiful. It was lithe and firmly muscled. Her legs were strong, and there was an unconscious, easy grace in her movements. She was like a forest spirit, wild and free. And as Anaya ran her hands through her hair and hummed to herself, Kith-Kanan felt the stirrings of emotions he had thought dead months ago, when he'd fled Silvanost.

Anaya lay down on the rock ledge, pillowing her head with one arm. Eyes closed, she appeared to sleep. Kith-Kanan stood up and meant to slip around the far side of the pool in order to surprise her. But the hill was steep, and the vines were green enough to be slippery when his sandals crushed them. That Kith-Kanan was watching Anaya, not his footing, made the going even more treacherous. He took two steps and fell, sliding feet first down the hill into the pool.

He surfaced, choking and spitting. Anaya hadn't moved, but she said, "You go to a lot of trouble just to see me bathe."

"I—" the prince sneezed violently "—heard someone in the spring and came to investigate. I didn't know it was you." Despite the weight of his clothes and sword, he swam in long strokes to the ledge where she lay. Anaya made no move to cover herself, but merely moved over to give him room to sit on the rock.

"Are you all right?" she asked.

"Only my pride hurts." He stood up, averting his eyes from her. "I'm sorry I intruded, I'll go."

"Go or stay. It doesn't matter to me." When he hesitated, Anaya added, "I am not modest in the fashion of your city females."

"Yet you wear clothes," he felt obliged to say. Uncomfortable as he was with her nudity, he felt strangely unwilling to leave her.

"A deerskin tunic is good protection from thorns." Anaya watched Kith-Kartan with some amusement as his gaze flickered over her and away for a third time. "It bothers you. Give me your tunic." He protested, but she insisted, so he removed his wet tunic.

She pulled it over her head. The tunic covered her to her knees. "Is that better?"

He smiled sheepishly. "I can't get over how different you look," he said. "Without lines painted on your face, I mean." It was true. Her hazel eyes were large and darker than his twin's. She had a small, full-lipped mouth and a high forehead.

As if in response, Anaya stretched lazily, like a big cat. She put more into, and seemed to get more out of, a simple stretch than anyone Kith-Kanan had ever seen. "Don't the women of your race adorn themselves?" she inquired.

"Well, yes, but not to the point of disguising themselves," he said earnestly. "I like your face. Seems a pity to cover it."

Anaya sat up and looked at him curiously. "Why do you say that?"

"Because it's true," he said simply.

She shook herself. "Don't talk nonsense."

"I hope you're not angry with me any more for teaching Mackeli how to fight," he said, hoping to draw the conversation out a little longer. He was enjoying talking with her.

She shrugged. "My injury made me short-tempered. I wasn't angry with you." She gazed out at the clear water. After a moment, she said slowly, "I am glad Mackeli has a friend."

He smiled and reached a hand out to touch her arm. "You have a friend, too, you know."

Quickly Anaya rolled to her feet and pulled his tunic off. Dropping it, she dove into the pool. She stayed under so long that Kith-Kanan began to worry. He was about to dive in after her when Mackeli appeared on the other side of the pool, his bag bursting with chestnuts.

"Hello, Kith! Why are you all wet?"

"Anaya went in the water and hasn't come back up!"

Mackeli heaved the heavy sack to the ground. "Don't worry," he said. "She's gone to her cave." Kith-Kanan looked at him blankly. "There's a tunnel in the pool that connects to a cave. She goes down there when she's upset about something. Did you two have words?"

"Not exactly," Kith-Kanan said, staring at the water's surface. "I just told her I liked her face and that I was her friend."

Mackeli scratched his cheek skeptically. "Well, there's no use waiting there. She may not come up for days!" He hoisted the sack onto his narrow shoulder and added, "The cave is Ny's secret place. We can't get in."

Kith-Kanan picked up his tunic and circled around the pool to where Mackeli stood. They walked up the path to the clearing. Every third step or so, Kith-Kanan looked back at the quiet spring. The forest woman was so difficult to understand. He kept hoping she would reappear, but she didn't.

* * * * *

The sun set, and Mackeli and Kith-Kanan roasted chestnuts in the fire. When they were full, they lay on their backs in the grass and watched a fall of stars in the sky. The stars trailed fiery red tails across the black night, and Kith-Kanan marveled at the beauty of the sight. Living indoors in Silvanost, Kith-Kanan had seen only a few such falls. As the elf prince stared into the sky, a gentle wind tickled the branches of the trees and ruffled his hair.

Kith-Kanan sat up to get another handful of chestnuts. He saw Anaya sitting crosslegged by the fire and almost jumped out of his skin.

"What are you playing at?" he asked, irritated at being so startled.

"I came to share your fire."

Mackeli sat up and poked a few roasted nuts from the ashes with a stick. Though they were hot, Anaya casually picked one up and peeled the red husk from the nut meat.

"Your task is long done, Kith," she said in a low voice. "Why haven't you returned to Silvanost?"

He chewed a chestnut. "I have no life there," he said truthfully.

Anaya's dark eyes looked out from her newly painted face. "Why not? Any disgrace you committed can be forgiven," she said.

"I committed no disgrace!" he said with heat.

"Then go home. You do not belong here." Anaya rose and backed away from the fire. Her eyes glowed in the firelight until she turned away.

Mackeli gaped. "Ny has never acted so strangely. Something is troubling her," he said as he jumped to his feet. "I'll ask "

"No." The single word froze Mackeli in his tracks. "Leave her alone. When she finds the answer, she'll tell us."

Mackeli sat down again. They looked into the red coals in silence for a while, then Mackeli said, "Why do you stay, Kith?"

"Not you too!"

"Your life in the City of Towers was full of wonderful things. Why did you leave? Why do you stay here?"

"There's nowhere else I want to go right now, and I've made friends here, or at least one friend." He smiled at Mackeli. "As for why I left " Kith-Kanan rubbed his hands together as if they were cold. "Once I was in love with a beautiful maiden, in Silvanost. She had wit and spirit, and I believed she loved me. Then it came time for my brother, Sithas, to marry. His wife was chosen for him by our father, the Speaker of the Stars. Of all the suitable maidens in the city, my father chose the one I loved to be my brother's bride." He pulled his dagger and drove it to the hilt in the dirt. "And she married him willingly! She was glad to do it!"

"I don't understand," admitted Mackeli.

"Neither do I. Hermathya—" Kith-Kanan closed his eyes, seeing her in his mind and savoring the feel of her name on his lips "—seemed to love the idea of being the next speaker's wife more than being married to one who loved her. So, I left home. I do not expect to see Silvanost again."

The elf boy looked at Kith-Kanan, whose head hung down. The prince still gripped his dagger hilt tightly. Mackeli cleared his throat and said sincerely, "I hope you stay, Kith. Ny could never have taught me the things you have. She never told me the kind of stories you tell. She's never seen the great cities, or the warriors and nobles and priests."

Kith-Kanan had raised his head. "I try not to think beyond today, Keli. For now, the peace of this place suits me. Strange, after being used to all the comforts and extravagances of royal birth . . ." His voice trailed off.

"Perhaps we can make a new kingdom, here in the wildwood."

Kith-Kanan smiled. "A kingdom?" he asked. "Just us three?"

With complete earnestness, Mackeli said, "Nations must begin somewhere, yes?"

Day of Madness

13

Sithas rode up the Street of Commerce at a canter, past the guild hall towers that filled both sides. He reined in his horse clumsily for he wasn't used to riding when he spied the guild elves standing in the street, watching smoke rise from the Market quarter.

"Has the royal guard come this way?" he called at them.

Wringing his hands, a senior master with the crest of the Gemcutters Guild on his breast replied, "Yes, Highness, some time ago. The chaos grows worse, I fear—"

"Have you seen my mother, Lady Nirakina?"

The master gemcutter picked at his long dark hair with slim fingers and shook his head in silent despair. Sithas snorted with frustration and twisted his horse's head away, toward the rising pillar of smoke. "Go back inside your halls," he called contemptuously. "Bolt your doors and windows."

"Will the half-breeds come here?" asked another guild elf tremulously.

"I don't know, but you'd better be prepared to defend yourselves." Sithas thumped his horse's sides with his heels, then mount and rider clattered down the street.

Beyond the guild halls, in the first crossing street of the commoners' district, he found the way littered with broken barrows, overturned sedan chairs, and abandoned pushcarts. Sithas picked his way through the debris with difficulty, for there were many common folk standing in the street. Most were mute in disbelief, though some wept at the unaccustomed violence so near their homes. They raised a cheer when they saw Sithas. He halted again and asked if anyone had seen Lady Nirakina.

"No one has come through since the warriors passed this way," said a trader. "No one at all."

He thanked them, then ordered them off the street. The elves retreated to their houses. In minutes, the prince was alone.

The poorer people of Silvanost lived in tower houses just as the rich did. However, their homes seldom rose more than four or five stories. Each house had a tiny garden around its base, miniature versions of the great landscape around the Tower of the Stars. Trash and blown rubbish now tainted the lovingly tended gardens. Smoke poisoned the air. Grimly Sithas continued toward the heart of this madness.

Two streets later, the prince saw his first rioters. A human woman and a female Kagonesti were throwing pottery jugs onto the pavement, smashing them. When they ran out of jugs, they went to a derelict potter's cart and replenished their supply.

"Stop that," Sithas commanded. The dark elf woman took one look at the speaker's heir and fled with a shriek. Her human companion, however, hurled a pot at Sithas. It shattered on the street at his horse's feet, spraying the animal with shards. That done, the impudent human woman dusted her hands and simply walked away.

The horse backed and pranced, so Sithas had his hands full calming the mount. When the horse was once more under control, he rode ahead. The lane ended at a sharp turn to the right.

The sounds of fighting grew louder as Sithas rode on, drawing his sword.

The street ahead was full of struggling people Silvanesti, Kagonesti, human, kender, and dwarves. A line of royal guards with pikes held flat in both hands were trying to keep the mass of fear-crazed folk back. Sithas rode up to an officer giving orders to the band of warriors, who numbered no more than twenty.

"Captain! Where is your commander?" shouted Sithas, above the roar of voices.

"Highness!" The warrior, himself of Kagonesti blood, saluted crisply. "Lord Kencathedrus is pursuing some of the criminals in the Market."

Sithas, on horseback, could see far over the seething sea of people. "Are all these rioters?" he asked, incredulous.

"No, sire. Most are merchants and traders, trying to get away from the criminals who set fire to the shops," the captain replied.

"Why are you holding them back?"

"Lord Kencathedrus's orders, sire. He didn't want these foreigners to flood the rest of the city."

When the prince asked the captain if he'd seen his mother, the warrior shook his helmeted head. Sithas then asked if there was another way around, a way to the river.

"Keep them back!" barked the captain to his straining soldiers. "Push them! Use your pike shafts!" He stepped back, closer to Sithas, and said, "Yes, sire, you can circle this street and take White Rose Lane right to the water."

Sithas commended the captain and turned his horse around. A spatter of stones and chunks of pottery rained over them. The captain and his troops had little to fear; they were in armor. Neither Sithas nor his horse were, so they cantered quickly away.

White Rose Lane was narrow and lined on both sides by high stone walls. This was the poorest section of Silvanost, where the house-towers were the lowest. With only two or three floors, they resembled squat stone drums, a far cry from the tall, gleaming spires of the high city.

The lane was empty when Sithas entered it. Astride his horse, his knees nearly scraped the walls on each side. A thin trickle of scummy water ran down the gutter in the center of the lane. At the other end of the alley, small groups of rioters dashed past. These groups of three or four often had royal guards on their heels. Sithas emerged from White Rose Lane in time to confront four desperate-looking elves. They stared at him. Each was armed with a stone or stick.

Sithas pointed with his sword. "Put down those things. Go back to your homes!" he said sternly.

"We are free elves! We won't be ordered about! We've been driven from our homes once, and we'll not let it happen again!" cried one of the elves.

"You are mistaken," Sithas said, turning his horse so none of them could get behind him. "No one is driving you from here. The Speaker of the Stars has plans for a permanent town on the west bank of the Thon-Thalas."

"That's not what the holy lady said," shouted a different elf.

"What holy lady?"

"The priestess of Quenesti Pah. She told us the truth!"

So, the riot could be laid at Miritelisina's door. Sithas burned with anger. He whipped his sword over his head. "Go home!" he shouted. "Go home, lest the warriors strike you down!"

Someone flung a stone at Sithas. He batted it away, the rock clanging off the tempered iron blade. One smoke-stained elf tried to grab the horse's bridle, but the prince hit him on the head with the flat of his blade. The elf collapsed, and the others hastily withdrew to find a more poorly armed target.

Sithas rode on through the mayhem, getting hit more than once by thrown sticks and shards. A bearded fellow he took for human

109

swung a woodcutter's axe at him, so Sithas used the edge, not the flat, of his sword. The axe-wielder fell dead, cleaved from shoulder to heart. Only then did the prince notice the fellow's tapering ears and Silvanesti coloring. A half-human, the first he'd ever seen. Pity mixed with revulsion welled up inside the speaker's heart.

Feeling a bit dazed, Sithas rode to the water's edge. There were dead bodies floating in the normally calm river, a sight that only added to his disorientation. However, his dazed shock vanished instantly when he saw the body of an elf woman clad in a golden gown. His mother had a gown like that.

Sithas half-fell, half-jumped from horseback into the shallow water. He splashed, sword in hand, to the gowned body. It was Nirakina. His mother was dead! Tears spilling down his cheeks, the prince pulled the floating corpse to shallower water. When he turned the body over he saw to his immense relief that it was not his mother. This elf woman was a stranger to Sithas.

He released his hold on the body, and it was nudged gently away by the Thon-Thalas. Sithas stood coughing in the smoke, looking at the nightmare scene around him. Had the gods forsaken the Silvanesti this day?

"Sithas. . . . Sithas. . . ."

The prince whirled as he realized that someone was calling his name. He ran up the riverbank toward the sound. Once ashore, he was engulfed by the row of short towers that lined the river-bank. The tallest of these, a four-story house with conical roof and tall windows, was to his right. A white cloth waved from a top floor window.

"Sithas?" With relief the prince noted that it was his mother's voice.

He mounted the horse and urged it into a gallop. Shouts and a loud crashing sound filled the air. On the other side of a low stone wall, a band of rioters was battering at the door of the four-story tower. Sithas raced the horse straight at the wall, and the animal jumped the barrier. As they landed on the other side, Sithas shouted a challenge and waved his sword in the air. Horse and rider thundered into the rioters' midst. The men dropped the bench they had been using as a battering ram and ran off.

Overhead, a window on the street side opened. Nirakina called down, "Sithas! Praise the gods you came!"

The door of the house, which was almost knocked to pieces, opened inward. A familiar-looking elf emerged warily, the broken end of a table leg clutched in his hand.

"I know you," said Sithas, dismounting quickly.

The elf lowered his weapon. "Tamanier Ambrodel, at your service, Highness," he said quietly. "Lady Nirakina is safe."

Nirakina came down the building's steps, and Sithas rushed to embrace her.

"We were besieged," Nirakina explained. Her honey-brown hair was in complete disarray, and her gentle face was smeared with soot. "Tamanier saved my life. He fought them off and guarded the door."

"I thought you were dead," Sithas said, cupping his mother's face in his scratched, dirty hands. "I found a woman floating in the river. She was wearing your clothes."

Nirakina explained that she had been giving some old clothing to the refugees when the trouble started. In fact she and Tamanier had been at the focus of the riot. One reason they had escaped unharmed was that many of the refugees knew the speaker's wife and protected her.

"How did it start?" demanded Sithas. "I heard something about Miritelisina."

"I'm afraid it was her," Tamanier answered. "I saw her standing in the back of a cart, proclaiming that the speaker and high priests were planning to send all the settlers back across the river. The people grew frightened they thought they were being driven from their last shelter by their own lords, sent to die in the wilderness. So they rose up, with the intention of forestalling a new exile."

Fists clenched, Sithas declared, "This is treason! Miritelisina must be brought to justice!"

"She did not tell them to riot," his mother said gently. "She cares about the poor, and it is they who have suffered most from this."

Sithas was in no mood to debate. Instead, he turned to Tamanier and held out his hand. Eyes wide, the elf grasped his prince's hand. "You shall be rewarded," said Sithas gratefully.

"Thank you, Highness." Tamanier looked up and down the street. "Perhaps we can take Lady Nirakina home now."

It was much quieter. Kencathedrus's warriors had herded the rioters into an ever-tightening circle. When the mob was finally subdued, the fire brigade was able to rush into the Market quarter. That occurred far too late, though; fully half of the marketplace had already been reduced to ruin.

*　*　*　*　*

The justice meted out by Sithel to his rebellious subjects was swift and severe. The rioters were tried as one and condemned.

Those of Silvanesti or Kagonesti blood were made slaves and set to rebuilding what they had destroyed. The humans and other non-elven rioters were driven from the city at pike point and forbidden ever to return, upon pain of death. All merchants who participated in the madness had their goods confiscated. They, too, were banished for life.

Miritelisina was brought before the speaker. Sithas, Nirakina, Tamanier Ambrodel, and all the high clerics of Silvanost were present. She made no speeches, offered no defense. Despite his respect for her, the speaker found the priestess guilty of petty treason. He could have made the charge high treason, for which the penalty was death, but Sithel could not bring himself to be that harsh.

The high priestess of Quenesti Pah was sent to the dungeon cells under the Palace of Quinari. Her cell was large and clean, but dark. Layers of inhibiting spells were placed around it, to prevent her from using her magical knowledge to escape or communicate with the outside world. Though many saw this as just, few found the sentencing a positive thing; not since the terrible, anarchical days of Silvanos and Balif had such a high-ranking person been sent to the dungeon.

"Is it right, do you think, to keep her there?" Nirakina asked her husband and son later, in private.

"You surprise me," said Sithel in a tired voice. "You, of all people, whose life was in the balance, should have no qualm about her sentence."

Nirakina's face was sad. "I am sure she meant no harm. Her only concern was for the welfare of the refugees."

"Perhaps she did not mean to start a riot," Sithas said sympathetically, "but I'm not certain she meant no harm. Miritelisina sought to undermine the decree of the speaker by appealing to the common people. That, in itself, is treason."

"Those poor people," Nirakina murmured.

The speaker's wife retired to her bed. Sithel and his son remained in the sitting room.

"Your mother has a kind heart, Sith. All this suffering has undone her. She needs her rest." Sithas nodded glumly, and the speaker went on. "I am sending a troop of fifty warriors under Captain Coryamis to the west. They are to try to capture some of the brigands who've been terrorizing our settlers and to bring them back alive. Perhaps then we can find out who's truly behind these attacks." Sithel yawned and stretched. "Coryamis leaves tonight. Within a month, we should know something."

Father and son parted. Sithel watched the prince descend the far stairs, not the route to the quarters that he shared with Hermathya. "Where are you going, Sith?" he asked in confusion.

Sithas looked distinctly uncomfortable. "My old rooms, Father. Hermathya and I are we are not sharing a bed these days," he said stiffly. Sithel raised one pale brow in surprise.

"You'll not win her over by sleeping apart," he advised.

"I need time to contemplate," Sithas replied. With a gruff good-night, he went on his way. Sithel waited until his son's footsteps had faded from the stone stairwell, then he sighed. Sithas and Hermathya estranged for some reason that fact bothered him more than having to send Miritelisina to the dungeon. He knew his son, and he knew his daughter-in-law, too. They were both too proud, too unbending. Any rift between them was only likely to widen over time. Not good. The line of Silvanos required stability and offspring to ensure its continuation. He would have to do something.

A prodigious yawn racked the speaker's body. For now, though, there was his own bed, his own wife, and sleep.

*　*　*　*　*

In the weeks following the rioting in the Market, a regular patrol of royal guards walked the streets. A squad of four warriors, moving through the city very late one night, spied a body lying on the steps of the Temple of Quenesti Pah. Two elves ran over and turned the body face-up. To their astonishment, they knew the dead elf well. He was Nortifinthas, and he was of their own company, sent with forty-nine other warriors to the western provinces. No word had been heard from the fifty warriors in over two weeks.

The night watch picked up their fallen comrade and hastened to the Palace of Quinari. Other patrols saw them and joined with them as they went. By the time the group reached the main door of the palace, it was over thirty strong.

Stankathan, the major-domo, arrived at the palace door in response to the vigorous pounding of the guards. He stood in the open doorway, holding aloft a sputtering oil lamp.

"Who goes there?" Stankathan said in a voice husky with sleep. The officer who had found Nortifinthas explained the situation. Stankathan looked at the corpse, borne on the shoulders of his fellow warriors. His face paled.

"I will fetch Prince Sithas," he decided.

Stankathan went to Sithas's bachelor quarters. The door was open, and he saw the prince asleep at a table. The elder elf shook his head. Everyone knew that Prince Sithas and his wife were living apart, but still it saddened the old servant.

"Your Highness?" he said, touching Sithas lightly on the back. "Your Highness, wake up; there's been an . . . event."

Sithas raised his head suddenly. "What? What is it?"

"The night watch has found a dead warrior in the streets.

Apparently he is one of the soldiers the Speaker sent out weeks ago."

Sithas pushed back his chair and stood, disoriented by his sudden awakening. "How can that be?" he asked. He breathed deeply a few times to clear his head. Then, adjusting his sleep-twisted robe, the prince said, "I will see the warriors."

The major-domo led Sithas to the main door. There the prince heard the story of the finding of the body from the night watch officer.

"Show me," ordered Sithas.

The warriors laid the body gently down on the steps. Nortifinthas had numerous knife and club wounds, which had sufficed to drain his life away.

Sithas looked over the array of grim, concerned faces. "Take the body to the cellar and lay it out. Tomorrow perhaps the learned clerics can discover what happened," he said in a subdued voice.

Four guards hoisted Nortifinthas on their shoulders and went up the steps. Stankathan showed them the way to the palace cellar. After a time, when Stankathan returned with the bearers, Sithas dismissed the guards. To the major-domo he said, "When the speaker rises tomorrow, tell him at once what has occurred. And send for me."

"It shall be done, Highness."

* * * * *

The day dawned cool, and gray clouds piled up in the northern sky. Sithas and Sithel stood on opposite sides of the table where the body of Nortifinthas had been laid out. Everyone else had been banished from the cellar.

Sithel bent over and began to examine the dead elf's clothes with minute care. He fingered every seam, looked in every pocket, even felt in the corpse's hair. Finally Sithas could contain himself no longer.

"What are you doing, Father?"

"I know Captain Coryamis would not have sent this warrior back to us without some kind of message."

"How do you know he was sent? He could be a deserter."

Sithel stood up. "Not this fellow. He was a fine warrior. And if he had deserted, he wouldn't come back to Silvanost." Just then, Sithel froze. He reached for the shielded candle that was their only source of light, then held it close to the dead elf's waist.

"There!" The speaker hastily thrust the candle holder into Sithas's hand. Eagerly, Sithel unclasped the sword belt from the corpse. He held it up to Sithas. "Do you see?"

Sithas squinted hard at the inside of the belt. Sure enough, there were letters scratched in the dark leather, but they appeared random and meaningless. "I don't understand," he protested. "I see writing, but it's just gibberish."

Sithel removed the empty scabbard from the belt and gently laid it on the corpse's chest. Then he coiled the belt and tucked it inside his robe. "There are many things you have yet to learn, things that only come from experience. Come with me, and I'll show you how the dead can speak to the living without magic."

They left the cellar. An entire corps of courtiers and servants stood waiting for the two most important people in Silvanost to reappear. Sithel promptly ordered everyone to return to their tasks, and he and his son went alone to the Tower of the Stars.

"This palace is like an anthill," Sithel said, striding briskly across the Processional Road. "How can anything remain secret for very long?"

The prince was puzzled, but he covered his bewilderment with the meditative mask he had learned from the priests of Matheri. It was not until they were alone, locked inside the audience hall of the tower, that his father spoke again.

"Coryamis sent the soldier back as a courier," confided Sithel. "Let us see what he brought us."

The emerald throne of the speaker was not simply made of that stone. The natural faceted gems were interspersed with hand-turned columns of rare and beautiful wood. These were of varying lengths and thicknesses, and some were even inlaid with gold and silver. Sithas looked on in mute wonder as his father detached piece after piece of wood from the ancient, sacred throne. Each time he removed a cylinder of wood, he would wind the dead soldier's belt around it, spiral fashion. The Speaker would then stare at the writing on the belt for a second, remove the belt, and re-fit the wooden piece back into the throne. On the fifth attempt, Sithel gave a cry of triumph. He read up the length of the cylinder, turned it slightly, and read the next row of letters. When he was done, the Speaker of the Stars looked up, ashen faced.

"What is it, Father?" Sithas asked. The Speaker handed him the rod and belt as a reply.

Now the prince understood. The message had been written on the belt while it was wound around a shaft of identical thickness to this one. When the belt was removed, the letters became a meaningless jumble. Now Sithas could read the last message sent by Coryamis.

There were many abbreviations in the writing. Sithas read the message out loud, just to be certain he had it right. " 'Great speaker,' " it said, " 'I write this knowing I may not be alive tomorrow, and this is the only chance I have to tell what has happened. Two days ago we were attacked by a body of humans, elves, and mixed-bloods. The horsemen trapped us between the foothills of the Khalkist Mountains and the falls of the Keraty River. There are only fifteen of us left. I will send this message with my best fighter, Nortifinthas. Great speaker, these men and elves are not bandits, they are formidable cavalry. They also knew where to ambush us and how many we were, so I feel, too, that we were betrayed. There is a traitor in Silvanost. Find him or all shall perish. Long live Silvanesti!' "

Sithas stared at his father in horrified silence for a long moment. Finally, he burst out, "This is monstrous!"

"Treachery in my own city. Who could it be?" Sithel asked.

"I don't know, but we can find out. The greater question is, who pays the traitor? It must be the emperor of Ergoth!" declared his son.

"Yes." Surely there was no one else with the money or reason to wage such an underhanded campaign against the elven nation. Sithel looked at the prince, who suddenly seemed much older than before. "I do not want war, Sithas. I do not want it. We have not yet received a reply from the emperor or from the king of Thorbardin regarding our request for a conference. If both nations agree to come and talk, it will give us a chance for peace."

"It may give the enemy the time they need, too," said Sithas.

The speaker took the belt and wooden cylinder from his son. He restored the cylinder to its place in the side of the throne. The belt he fastened around his own waist. Sithel had regained his calm, and the years fell away once more when resolve filled his face.

"Son, I charge you with the task of finding the traitor. Male or female, young or old, there can be no mercy."

"I shall find the traitor," Sithas vowed.

* * * * *

Dinner each night in the Quinari Palace was held in the Hall of Balif. It was as much a social occasion as a meal, for all the courtiers were required to attend and certain numbers of the priestly and noble classes, too. Speaker Sithel and Lady Nirakina sat in the center of the short locus of the vast oval table. Sithas and Hermathya sat on Nirakina's left, and all the guests sat to the left of them in order of seniority. Thus, the person to Sithel's right was always the most junior member of the court. That seat fell to Tamanier Ambrodel nowadays; for saving Lady Nirakina's life during the riot, he'd been granted a minor title.

The hall was full, though everyone was still standing when Tamanier and Hermathya arrived together. Sithel had not yet come, and no one could sit until the Speaker did so himself. For his part, Sithas stood behind his chair, impassive. Hermathya hoped he might react jealously upon seeing her on the arm of the stalwart Tamanier, but the prince kept his pensive gaze focused on the golden plate set before him.

Sithel entered with his wife. Servants pulled the tall chairs for the speaker and Nirakina, and Sithel took his place. "May the gods grant you all health and long life," he said quietly. The vast hall had been constructed so that conversation at one end could be heard by parties at the other. The traditional greeting before meals carried easily to the entire oval table.

"Long life to you, Speaker of the Stars," the diners responded in unison. Sithel sat. With much shuffling and squeaking of chairs, the guests sat down, too.

A troop of servers appeared, bearing a large pot. The pot swung on a long pole supported on the shoulders of two elves. Behind these servants, two more servers carried a slotted bronze box, from which a dull glow radiated. The box was full of large hearthstones that had been banked against the kitchen fires all day. Two servants set the bronze box on a stone slab, and the pot carriers eased the great cauldron onto the box. Now the soup would stay hot all through dinner which could last several hours.

Young elf maidens clad in shifts of opaque yellow gauze slipped in and out among the seated guests, filling their bowls with steaming turtle soup. For those not inclined to soup, there was fresh fruit, picked that morning in the vast orchards on the eastern shore. Elf boys staggered under the weight of tall amphorae, brimming with purple-red nectar. The goblets of the guests were kept full.

With the first course served, Stankathan signaled to the servants at the doors of the hall. They swung them open, and a trio of musicians entered. The players of flute, lyre, and sistrum, arranged themselves in the far corner of the hall as conversation in the room began in earnest.

"I have heard," opened old Rengaldus, guildmaster of the gemcutters, "that there is to be a conclave with representatives of Ergoth."

"That's old news," said Zertinfinas, the priest. He hacked open a juicy melon and poured the seedy center pulp onto his plate. "The dwarves of Thorbardin are invited, too."

"I have never seen a human close up," remarked Hermathya. "Or talked to one."

"You haven't missed much, Lady," Rengaldus replied. "Their language is uncouth and their bodies thick with hair."

"Quite bestial," agreed Zertinfinas.

"Those are your opinions," Tamanier interjected. Many eyes turned to him. It was unusual for the junior noble to speak at all. "I knew humans out on the plains, and many of them were good people."

"Yes, but aren't they inherently treacherous?" asked the guildmaster of the sandalmakers. "Do humans ever keep their word?"

"Frequently." Tamanier looked to his patron, Sithas, for signs of displeasure. The speaker's son, as usual, ate sparingly, picking grapes one at a time from the cluster on his plate. He did not seem to have heard Tamanier's comments, so the favored young courtier continued. "Humans can be fiercely honorable, perhaps because they know so many of their fellows are not."

"They are unredeemably childish in their tempers," Zertinfinas asserted. "How can they not be? With only seventy or so years of life how can they accumulate any store of wisdom or patience?"

"But they are clever," noted Rengaldus. He slurped a mouthful of nectar and wiped his chin with a satin napkin. "A hundred years ago there wasn't a human alive who could cut a diamond or polish a sapphire. Now craftsmen in Daltigoth have learned to work gems, and they have undercut our market! My factors in Balifor say that human-cut gems are selling well there, mainly because they are far cheaper than ours. The buyers care less about quality than they do about the final price."

"Barbarians," muttered Zertinfinas into his cap.

The second course was brought out: a cold salad of river trout with a sweet herb dressing. Murmurs of approval circled the great table. Loaves of pyramid-shaped bread were also provided, smeared with honey, a confection greatly loved by elves.

"Perhaps one of the learned clerics can tell me," Hermathya said, cutting herself a chunk of warm bread, "why humans have such short lives?" Zertinfinas cleared his throat to speak, but from the opposite side of the table, a new voice answered the lady's question.

"It is generally considered that humans represent a middle race, farther removed from the gods and closer to the realm of the animals. Our own race the first created, longer lived, and possessing a greater affinity for the powers of magic is closest to the gods."

Hermathya tilted her head to get a better look at the softspoken cleric. "I do not know you, holy one. Who are you?"

"Forgive me, Lady, for not introducing myself. I am Kamin Oluvai, second priest of the Blue Phoenix." The young elf stood and bowed to Hermathya. He was a striking-looking fellow, in his brilliant blue robe and golden headband, with its inlay of a blue phoenix. His golden hair was long even by elven standards. Sithas studied him circumspectly. This Kamin Oluvai had not been to many royal dinners.

"What about these humans?" complained Zertinfinas loudly, beginning to feel his nectar. "What is to be done about them?"

"I believe that is a matter best left to the Speaker," Sithas replied. One hundred and fifty pairs of eyes looked to Sithel, who was listening with great care while eating his fish.

"The sovereignty of Silvanesti will be preserved," the Speaker said calmly. "That is why the conclave has been called."

The prince nodded, then asked, "Is it true, Ambrodel, that there are more humans living in our western provinces than Silvanesti and Kagonesti?"

"More than the Silvanesti, Highness. But the true number of the Kagonesti is difficult to state. So many of them live in the remote parts of the forest, mountains, and plains."

"Humans breed at any point past age fifteen," blurted Zertinfinas. "They regularly have five and six children in a family!" Whispers of surprise and concern circled the table. Elven parents seldom had more than two children in their entire, lengthy lifetimes.

"Is that true?" Nirakina queried Tamanier.

"At least in the wild country it is. I cannot say what families are like in the more settled areas of Ergoth. But many of the children do not survive into adulthood. Human knowledge of the healing arts is not nearly so advanced as ours."

The musicians completed their program of light tunes and began to play "The Sea-Elf's Lament." The main course was served.

It came rolling in on a large cart, a huge sculpture of a dragon done in golden-brown pie crust. The "beast" reared up five feet high. His back was scaled with mint leaves, his eyes and talons made red with pomegranates. The head and spiky tail of the dragon were covered with glazed nut meats.

The diners applauded this culinary creation, and Sithel himself smiled. "You see, my friends, how the cook is master of us all," he proclaimed, rising to his feet. "For centuries the dragons preyed upon us, and now we have them to dinner."

Stankathan stood by the pastry dragon, a sword in his hand. He jerked his head, and servants positioned a golden tray under the dragon's chin. With a force that belied his age, the servant lopped off the dragon's head. A flight of live sparrows burst from the open neck of the creation, each bird having silver streamers tied to its legs. The assembly gave a collective gasp of admiration.

"I trust the rest of the insides are more thoroughly cooked," quipped Sithel.

The servants bore the head of the dragon to the speaker. With smaller knives, they carved it to pieces. Under the crusty pastry skin, the head was stuffed with delicate meat paste, whole baked apples, and sweet glazed onions.

Stankathan attacked the rest of the pastry like some culinary thespian portraying the mighty Huma slaying a real dragon. The body of the beast was filled with savory sausages, stuffed peppers, whole capons, and vegetable torts. The room filled with noise as every diner commented on the elegance of this evening's feast.

Zertinfinas, rather loudly, called for more nectar. The serving boy had none left in his amphora, so he ran to the door to fetch more. Sithas called to the servant as he passed, and the elf boy dropped to one knee by the prince's chair.

"Yes, Highness?"

"The holy one has had too much to drink. Have the cellar master cut the nectar with water. Half for half," ordered Sithas in a confidential tone.

"As you command, sire."

"The cook really has outdone himself," Hermathya remarked. "It is a wonderful feast."

"Is it a special occasion?" asked Rengaldus.

"The calendar does not list a holiday," Kamin Oluvai noted. "Unless it is a special day for the speaker."

"It is, holy one. By this feast we do honor to a dead hero," Sithel explained.

Nirakina set down her goblet, puzzled. "What hero, my husband?"

"His name was Nortifinthas."

Head wobbling, Zertinfinas asked, "Was he a companion of Huma Dragonsbane?"

"No," Kamin Oluvai assisted. "He sat in the first great Synthal-Elish, did he not?"

"You are both mistaken," Sithel replied. "Nortifinthas was a simple soldier, a Kagonesti who died nobly in service to this house." Conversation around the table had died just as the flutist trilled the high solo from the lament.

"This morning," the Speaker continued, "this soldier named Nortifinthas returned to the city from the western province. He was the only survivor of the fifty warriors I sent out to find the bandits who have troubled our people lately. All his comrades were slain. Even though he was fearfully wounded, the brave Nortifinthas returned with the last dispatch of his commander." Sithel looked around the table, meeting each guest eye to eye. The prince sat very still, his left hand clenched into a fist in his lap. "One of you here, one of you seated at my table eating my food, is a traitor."

The musicians heard this declaration and ceased playing. The speaker waved a hand to them to continue, and they did so, awkwardly.

"You see, the force that wiped out my fifty warriors was not a band of hit-and-run bandits, but a disciplined troop of cavalry who knew where and when my soldiers would come. It was not a battle. It was a massacre."

"Do you know who the traitor is, Speaker?" Hermathya asked with great earnest.

"Not yet, but the person will be found. I spent most of my day compiling a list of those who could have known the route of my warriors. At this point, I suspect everyone."

The Speaker looked around the large table. The gaiety was gone from the dinner, and the diners looked at the delicacies on their plates without enthusiasm.

Sithel picked up his knife and fork. "Finish your food," he commanded. When no one else emulated him, he held up his hands expressively and said, "Why do you not eat? Do you want this fine meal to go to waste?"

Sithas was the first to take up his fork and resume eating. Hermathya and Nirakina did likewise. Soon, everyone was eating again, but with much less good humor than before.

"I will say this," Sithel added pointedly, cutting the glazed pomegranate eye from the pastry dragon's face. "The traitor's identity is suspected."

By now the elf boy had returned, his amphora full of diluted nectar. Into the absolute silence that followed his own last statement, the Speaker said loudly, "Zertinfinas! Your nectar!"

The cleric, his head snapping up at the sound of his name, had to be pounded on the back several times to save him from choking on a piece of pastry.

Sithas watched his father as he ate. The Speaker's every movement was graceful, his face serene with resolve.

While the Speaker Dined

14

The Wildwood slowly regained its lively character. No longer was there that absence of animal life that Kith-Kanan had found so puzzling when he first arrived. Daily, deer came to graze in the clearing. Rabbits and squirrels cavorted in and around the trees. Birds other than the ubiquitous corvae appeared. Bears, boars, and panthers roared in the night. As Mackeli had said, they'd been warned of the humans. Now that the humans were gone, the animals had returned.

On this particular day, Mackeli wedged his tongue between his teeth and concentrated on lashing an arrowhead to a shaft. Kith-Kanan was teaching him the bow now. It was not something to which the boy took readily. As he tied off the end of the whipcord, the flint arrowhead sagged badly out of line.

"That's not tight enough," Kith-Kanan cautioned. He handed the boy his dagger. "Start again and make it tight."

Neither of them had seen Anaya for over a week. It didn't bother Mackeli a whit, but Kith-Kanan found himself missing the strange forest woman. He wondered if he should go and look for her. Mackeli said, and Kith-Kanan did not doubt, that the prince would never find her unless she wanted to be found.

"What do you do if you need her in a hurry?" Kith-Kanan asked ingeniously. "I mean, suppose you got hurt or something. How would you call her?"

"If I really need Ny, she knows it and comes for me." Mackeli had almost finished his tying of the arrow.

"You mean, you just will her to come, and-she does?"

The boy knotted the tough silk string. "Mostly." With a proud smile, he handed Kith-Kanan the newly lashed arrow. Kith shook it to see if the head would loosen. It didn't.

"Good," he said, handing the arrow back. "You only need twenty more to fill your quiver."

* * * * *

Late the next afternoon the Wildwood rang with laughter and splashing as Kith-Kanan and Mackeli swam in the pool. Mackeli was progressing well under the prince's tutelage, so they had decided to finish their day with a swim in the crystal waters.

Mackeli was treading water and looking around the pool for Kith-Kanan. The boy was a better swimmer than his sister, but not so skilled as the elf prince.

"Where'd you go, Kith?" he said, eyeing the surface of the water uncertairnly. Suddenly a hand closed on his left ankle and Mackeli gave a yelp. He found himself lifted up and launched skyward. Laughing and yelling all the way, he flew several feet and landed back in the pool with a loud splash. He and Kith-Kanan surfaced at the same time.

"It's not fair," Mackeli said, flinging his streaming hair from his eyes. "You're bigger than me!"

Kith-Kanan grinned. "You'll catch up someday, Keli," he said. Twisting gracefully in the water, the prince turned and swam toward the granite ledge on shore.

As Kith-Kanan hoisted himself up on the ledge, Mackeli called to him, "I want to learn to swim like you. You move like a fish!"

"Another result of my misspent youth." Kith-Kanan stretched out full length on the warm ledge and closed his eyes.

Minutes later, something moved to block the sunlight. Without opening his eyes, Kith-Kanan said, "I know you're there, Keli. I heard you walk up. You'd better not—Hey!"

With a cry, the prince sat up. A very sharp spear point had been poked into his bare stomach. Squinting in the bright light, he looked up. Several pairs of moccasin-clad feet were gathered around Kith-Kanan, and their owners four dark figures loomed over him.

"Mackeli, my sword!" he called, leaping to his feet.

The boy, still in the pool, looked at his friend and laughed. "Calm down, Kith! It's only White-Lock."

Kith-Kanan stared. Shading his eyes, he realized that the four dark figures were Kagonesti males. They were brown-skinned, hard-muscled, and wore breechcloths of deerskin. Bows, quivers

123

of arrows, and deerskin bags were slung over their muscled backs. Their exposed skin was covered by red, yellow, and blue loops and whorls of paint.

The tallest of the four he topped Kith-Kanan by several inches had a streak of white in his midnight-black hair. He and his comrades were looking at the Silvanesti nobleman with amused curiosity.

Naked and still damp from his swim, Kith-Kanan drew the tattered shreds of his dignity about himself. He pulled on his clothes as Mackeli came out of the pool and greeted the four strange elves.

"Blessings of Astarin upon you, White-Lock, you and yours," Mackeli said. He placed his hands over his heart and then held them in front of him, palms up.

The Kagonesti called White-Lock repeated the gesture. "And upon you, Mackeli," he said to the boy, in a deep and solemn voice, though he continued to watch Kith-Kanan. "Do you now bring the Settled Ones to the sacred forests?"

Kith-Kanan knew that the term "Settled Ones" was meant as an insult. The Kagonesti were nomadic and never built permanent habitations. Before he could retort, Mackeli said, "Kith is my friend and my guest, White-Lock. Do the People no longer value courtesy to guests?"

A smile quirked White-Lock's lips and he said, "Blessings of Astarin upon you, guest of Mackeli."

"Would you and your hunting party honor me with a visit, White-Lock?" Mackeli asked. He pulled his clothes on.

White-Lock glanced at his companions. Kith-Kanan neither saw nor heard any exchange between them, but the tall Kagonesti said, "My companions and I do not wish to intrude upon the Keeper of the Forest."

"It is no intrusion," Mackeli replied politely.

Kith-Kanan was mildly surprised at the change that seemed to have come over the irrepressible boy. He spoke to the Kagonesti in a very composed and adult manner. They, in turn, treated him with great respect. Mackeli went on. "The keeper is away at present. Were she here, I know she would wish to make you welcome. Come, we can share stories. I have had a great adventure since we last met."

White-Lock looked once more to his three companions. After a moment's hesitation, he nodded and they all set out for the clearing.

As they walked, Kith-Kanan brought up the rear and studied these new acquaintances. In his travels around the western provinces of Silvanesti, he had met several Kagonesti. Those elves, however, had given up their nomadic and isolated ways to trade with the humans and Silvanesti who lived in the West. Many of them no longer painted their bodies, and they wore civilized clothing. These four were obviously not of that ilk.

As they made their way to the clearing, Mackeli introduced Kith-Kanan to the others in the group. There was Sharp-Eye, brown-haired and some inches shorter than White-Lock; Braveheart, who had sandy hair; and Otter. The latter was shorter than the rest, a head shorter than Kith-Kanan, and his pale yellow eyes twinkled with inner mirth. He was the only one who smiled outright at the elf prince. It was a merry smile, and Kith-Kanan returned it.

In the clearing, Mackeli bade them all be seated by the oak. He went inside and returned shortly with nuts, berries, and fruit. White-Lock took only a handful of red berries, though his comrades dug in with gusto.

"So, guest of Mackeli, how do you come to be in the wildwood?" White-Lock asked, staring at the Silvanesti prince.

Kith-Kanan frowned. "I am a traveler, White-Lock. And my name is Kith. You would honor me by using it," he replied testily.

White-Lock nodded and looked pleased. Kith-Kanan remembered then that the more primitive Kagonesti didn't believe it was polite to use a person's name unless they'd been given leave to. He cudgeled his brain, trying to recall what else he knew about their race.

"White-Lock!" called a startled voice behind Kith-Kanan. "What in the name of the forest is this?"

They turned. The one called Otter was standing at the far end of the clearing, staring in awe at Arcuballis. The griffon was lying in the shade of a big tree. The beast opened one golden eye and regarded the amazed Kagonesti.

"That is Arcuballis," Kith-Kanan said proudly. With an inward smile, he uttered a sharp whistle. Arcuballis got quickly to its feet, and Otter nearly fell over backward as he stumbled away from the tall beast. Kith-Kanan gave another whistle, at first high-pitched, then sliding down the scale. The griffon unfolded its wings to their full extent and uttered a trilling call in imitation of Kith-Kanan's whistle. Otter jumped back again. At another whistle from the prince, Arcuballis folded its wings and made its way daintily across the clearing, coming to a stop several feet from the group.

Kith-Kanan was pleased to see that even White-Lock looked impressed. The Kagonesti leader told Otter to rejoin the group. "What is this beast, Kith?" White-Lock asked wonderingly.

"Arcuballis is a griffon. He's my mount and my friend." Kith-Kanan whistled once more and Arcuballis lay down where it was. In seconds, the beast closed its eyes in sleep again.

"He is beautiful, Kith!" Otter said enthusiastically. "He flies?"

"He does indeed."

"I should be honored if you would take me for a ride!"

"Otter," White-Lock said sharply.

Regret replaced the joy on Otter's face, and he subsided. Kith-Kanan smiled kindly at the yellow-eyed elf as the Kagonesti called Sharp-Eye spoke into the silence.

"Mackeli, you said you had a tale to share," he said. "Tell us of your great adventure."

All four Kagonesti settled down to listen. Even Otter tore his gaze from Arcuballis and gave his full attention to Mackeli. The Kagonesti were great ones for storytelling, Kith-Kanan knew. They rarely, if ever, wrote anything down. Their history, their news, all was passed orally from one generation to the next. If they liked Mackeli's story, it would be swapped between tribes until years hence, when it might be heard by every Kagonesti on Krynn.

Mackeli's green eyes widened. He looked at each of them in turn and began his story. "I was kidnapped by an evil wizard named Voltorno," he said softly.

Kith-Kanan shook his head bemusedly. Mackeli finally had a fresh audience for his tale. And the boy didn't let them down. None of the four Kagonesti moved so much as a finger during Mackeli's long recital of his kidnap, the pursuit by Kith-Kanan and Anaya, and the prince's duel with Valtorno. The silence was broken only by Otter's exclamation of triumph when Mackeli told how he and Kith-Kanan had flown away from Voltorno's men on Arcuballis.

When the story was finished, the Kagonesti looked at Kith-Kanan with new respect. The prince preened slightly, sitting up straighter.

"You fought well against the humans, Kith," Sharp-Eye concluded. The other Kagonesti nodded.

"We are sorry to have missed the Keeper of the Forest, Mackeli," White-Lock said. "To see the keeper is a great honor and pleasure. She walks with the gods and speaks with great wisdom."

A snort of laughter was surprised out of Kith-Kanan. "Anaya?" he exclaimed in disbelief. He was immediately sorry. The Kagonesti, including the fun-loving Otter, turned looks of stern reproach upon him.

"You are disrespectful of the keeper, Kith." White-Lock glowered.

"I'm sorry. I meant no disrespect," Kith-Kanan said apologetically. "White-Lock, I'm curious. I've met Kagonesti elves before but they weren't like you. They were more—uh—"

"Where did you meet these others?" White-Lock cut in.

"In the West," replied Kith-Kanan. "The western provinces of Silvanesti."

"Settled Ones," Sharp-Eye said with much disgust. Braveheart rubbed his hands together as if washing them, then flung them away from himself.

"Those you met have taken up the ways of the Settled Ones," said White-Lock, his voice hard. "They have turned their backs on the true ways."

Kith-Kanan was surprised by the loathing they all expressed. Deciding it did not behoove him to anger Mackeli's friends, he changed the subject. "Braveheart, how did you come by your name?"

Braveheart gestured to White-Lock. Kith-Kanan wondered if he'd committed another social breach by inquiring about the Kagonesti's name. White-Lock, though, didn't seem upset. He answered, "Braveheart was born mute, but his skill as a hunter and fighter earned him his adult name." Amusement danced in the hunter's eyes. "Are all your people so curious, Kith?"

Kith-Kanan looked chagrined. "No, White-Lock. My curiosity has gotten me in trouble before."

They all laughed, and the four Kagonesti hunters stood up. White-Lock brought his hands up to cover his heart and then held them out palms-up, first to Mackeli and then to Kith-Kanan. The boy and the prince returned the gesture.

"The blessings of Astarin upon you both," White-Lock said warmly. "Give our respects to the keeper."

"We shall, White-Lock. Blessings upon you all," Mackeli returned.

"Good-bye" Kith-Kanan called after them. With a last wave from Otter, the hunters disappeared into the forest.

Mackeli gathered up the uneaten food and stowed it back in the tree. Kith-Kanan remained standing, looking after the departed Kagonesti.

"They're a strange lot," Kith-Kanan mused aloud. "And they certainly don't care for their more 'settled' brothers. I thought the others I met were a lot less primitive." He chuckled. "And the way they talked about Anaya-as if she were a goddess!"

"They are good elves," Mackeli said when he returned. "They only want to live in peace with the forest, as they have for centuries.

But most humans treat them like savages." The green eyes that looked up at Kith-Kanan were hard. "And from what you've told me about your people, the Silvanesti do no better."

* * * * *

Several more weeks went by. The episode of the Kagonesti stayed with Kith-Kanan, and he continued to think on Mackeli's words. However, he was growing more and more worried about Anaya. He questioned Mackeli, but the boy remained unconcerned. Though Kith-Kanan knew she could take care of herself, he still fretted. At night, he began to dream of her deep in the woods, calling to him, saying his name over and over. He would then follow her voice through the black forest, but just when he thought he'd found her, he would wake up. It was frustrating.

After a time Anaya began to monopolize his waking thoughts as well. The prince had told her he was her friend. Was it more than that? What Kith-Kanan felt for the Kagonesti woman was certainly different from what he felt for Mackeli. Could he be in love with her? They had barely gotten to know each other before she'd disappeared. But still the prince worried about her, and dreamed about her, and missed her.

Kith-Kanan and Mackeli were sleeping outside the tree one pleasant night. The prince slept deeply and, for once, dreamlessly until something unseen tugged at his mind. He opened his eyes and sat bolt-upright, turning his head from side to side. It was as if a sudden clap of thunder had wakened him. Yet Mackeli slept on beside him. Night creatures chirped and whirred softly in the forest, also undisturbed.

Kith-Kanan straightened his tunic for he slept fully clothed and lay back down. He was completely awake when the nameless something called to him once more. Drawn by something he couldn't see, the prince got up and crossed the clearing. The going was not easy, since the silver moon had set and the red moon was almost down. It was an eerie crimson orb just barely visible through the trees.

Kith-Kanan followed the path to the spring. Whatever was pulling him brought him to that place, but when he arrived, there seemed to be no one around. He dipped a hand in the cold water and threw it on his face.

As the Silvanesti prince stared at his reflection in the pool, a second dark image appeared in the water next to it. Kith-Kanan leaped back and turned, his hand on his dagger hilt. It was Anaya, standing a few feet away.

"Anaya!" he uttered with relief. "You're all right. Where have you been?"

"You called me," she said evenly. Her eyes seemed to have a light of their own. "Your call was very strong. I couldn't stay away, no matter how I tried."

Kith-Kanan shook his head. "I don't understand," he said truthfully.

She stepped closer and looked up into his eyes. Her unpainted face was beautiful in the red moonlight. "Your heart spoke to mine, Kith, and I could not refuse to come. We were drawn together."

At that moment, Kith-Kanan thought he did understand. The idea that hearts could speak to each other was something he had heard about. His people were said to be able to perform a mysterious summons known as "the Call." It was said to work over great distances and was reputed to be irresistible. Yet Kith-Kanan had never known anyone who had actually done it.

He stepped closer and put a hand to her cheek. Anaya was trembling.

"Are you afraid?" he asked quietly.

"I have never felt like this before," she whispered.

"How do you feel?"

"I want to run!" she declared loudly. But she didn't move an inch.

"You called to me too, you know. I was asleep in the clearing just now and something woke me, something drew me down here to the spring. I couldn't resist it." Her cheek was warm, despite the coolness of the night. He cupped it in his hand. "Anaya, I have been so worried about you. When you didn't come back, I thought something might have happened to you."

"Something did," she replied softly. "All these weeks, I have been meditating and thinking of you. So many feelings were tumbling inside of me."

"I have been troubled also," the prince confessed. "I've lain awake at night trying to sort out my feelings." He smiled at her. "You've even intruded on my dreams, Anaya"

Her face twisted in pain. "It isn't right."

"Why not? Am I so unappealing?"

"I am born of the forest! For ten times the length of your life I have lived in the Wildwood, on my own and of my own. I did not take Mackeli until a short time ago."

"Take Mackeli? Then, he is not your brother by blood, is he?"

Anaya looked at Kith-Kanan desperately. "No. I took him from a farmer's house. I was lonely. I needed someone to talk to . . ."

The emptiness in her eyes, the pain in her voice, touched Kith-Kanan's heart. He gripped Anaya's shoulders with both hands. In return, she put her arms around his waist and embraced him passionately.

After a moment, Anaya pulled back and said softly, "I want to show you something." She stepped into the pool.

"Where are we going?" he asked as he joined her in the cool spring.

"To my secret place." She took his hand and warned, "Don't let go."

They slid under the water's surface. It was as cold and as black as Takhisis's heart in the pool, but Anaya swam down, kicking with her feet. Something hard brushed Kith-Kanan's shoulder; he put a hand out and felt solid rock. They were in a tunnel. After a moment, Anaya planted her feet on the bottom and thrust upward. Kith-Kanan let himself be pulled along. Suddenly their heads broke the surface.

Treading water, Kith-Kanan looked around in wonder. A soft, white light illuminated a vaulted ceiling that rose some fifteen feet above the pool's surface. The ceiling was smooth and pure white. All around the edge of the vault were painted the most beautiful murals Kith-Kanan had ever seen. They showed a variety of woodland scenes: misty glens, roaring waterfalls, and deep, dark forests.

"Come," Anaya said, drawing him along by the hand. He kicked forward until his toes bumped rock. It was not the sloping bottom of a natural pool. Kith-Kanan felt round-nosed steps cut into the rock as he and Anaya climbed out of the water.

The steps and floor of the cave were made of the same stone as the ceiling, a glassy white rock Kith-Kanan couldn't identify.

The cave itself was divided down the center by a row of graceful columns, deeply fluted and tapering to their tops. They appeared to be joined solidly into the floor and ceiling.

Anaya let go of his hand and let him wander forward on his own. He went to the source of the gentle white light, the third column in from the water's edge. A subtle glow and warmth emanated from the column. Hesitantly Kith-Kanan put out a hand to touch the translucent stone.

He turned to the Kagonesti, smiling. "It feels alive!"

"It is," she beamed,

The walls to the right of the colonnade were decorated with remarkable bas-reliefs, raised carvings that depicted elven women. There were four of them, life-sized, and between each relief was a carving of a different type of tree.

Anaya stood close beside the prince, and he put an arm around her waist. "What do these mean?" he said, gesturing at the reliefs.

"These were the Keepers of the Forest," she said proudly "Those that came before me. They lived as I live now, guarding the Wildwood from harm." Anaya went to the image farthest

130

from the pool. "This was Camirene. She was Keeper of the Forest before me." Anaya moved to the right, to the next figure. "This was Ulyante." She slipped sideways to the third figure. "Here is Delarin. She died driving a dragon from the wildwood." Anaya touched the warm stone relief lightly with her fingertips. Kith-Kanan regarded the carved image with awe.

"And this," Anaya said, facing the figure nearest the pool, "is Ziatia, first guardian of the wildwood." She put her hands together and bowed to the image. Kith-Kanan looked from one relief to the next.

"It is a beautiful place," he said with awe.

"When I am troubled, I come here to rest and think," Anaya said, gesturing around her.

"Is this where you've been these past weeks?" he asked.

"Yes. Here, and in the wildwood. I . . . I watched you sleep many nights." She looked deep into his eyes.

Kith-Kanan could hardly take it all in. This beautiful cave, the many answers it provided and the mysteries it held. It was like the beautiful elf woman before him. She had provided him with answers this night, but in her deep eyes were even more mysteries and questions unanswered. For now, he gave himself up to the joy he felt, the joy at finding someone who cared for him, someone that he cared for. And he did care for her.

"I think I love you, Anaya," Kith-Kanan said tenderly, caressing her cheek.

She laid her head on his chest. "I begged the Forestmaster to send you away, but she would not. 'You must make the decision' she said." She clasped Kith-Kanan with frightening strength.

He tilted her face up to his and bent down to kiss her. Anaya was no soft and timid elf maiden. The hard life of the wildwood had made her tough and strong, but as they kissed, Kith-Kanan could feel the tremors echoing through her body.

She broke the kiss. "I will not be a casual love," she vowed, and her eyes bored into his. "If we are to be together, you must swear to be mine always."

Kith-Kanan remembered how he had searched for her in his dreams, how frightened and alone he'd felt when he couldn't find her. "Yes, Anaya. Always. I wish I still had my starjewel, but Voltorno took it with my other belongings. I wish I could give it to you." She did not understand, and he explained the significance of the starjewel.

She nodded. "We have no jewels to give in the wildwood. We make our most sacred vows in blood." She took his hand and knelt by the pool, drawing him down beside her. Laying her palm against the sharp edge of the rock, she pressed down hard. When she pulled her hand back, it was bleeding. Kith-Kanan hesitated a moment, then he too cut his hand on the hard, glassy rock. They joined hands once more, pressing the wounds together. The blood of the Silvanesti House Royal flowed together with that of the forest-born Kagonesti.

Anaya plunged their joined hands into the water. "By blood and water, by soil and sky, by leaf and limb, I swear to love and keep you, Kith, for as long as I walk, for as long as I breathe."

"By Astarin and E'li, I swear to love and keep you, Anaya, for all my life." Kith-Kanan felt light-headed, as if a great weight had been taken from him. Perhaps it was the weight of his anger, laid across his shoulders when he'd left Silvanost in a rage.

Anaya drew their hands out of the water, and the cuts were healed. While he marveled at this, she said, "Come."

Together they moved to the rear of the cave, away from the pool. There, the glassy stone walls ended. In their place was a solid wall of tree roots, great twining masses of them. A sunken place in the floor, oval-shaped, was lined with soft furs.

Slowly, very slowly, she sank into the furs, looking up at him with eyes full of love. Kith-Kanan felt his heart beat faster as he sat beside his love and took her hands into his. Raising them to his lips, he whispered, "I didn't know."

"What?"

"I didn't know that this is what love truly feels like." He smiled and leaned closer to her. Her breath was warm in his face. "And," he added gently, " didn't know that you were anything but a wild maiden, one who liked to live in the woods."

"That's exactly what I am," said Anaya.

* * * * *

She and Kith-Kanan talked of many things in the night and day they spent in the secret cave. He told her of Hermathya and of Sithas, and he felt his heart lighten as he confessed all. The anger and frustration were gone as if they'd never existed. The youthful passion he'd felt for Hermathya was completely unlike the deep love he now felt for Anaya. He knew there were those in Silvanost who would not understand his love for a Kagonesti. Even his own family would be shocked, he was sure.

But he didn't dwell on that. He filled his mind with only good thoughts, happy thoughts.

One thing Kith-Kanan insisted upon, and to which Anaya eventually agreed, was that she tell Mackeli of his true origins. When they left the cave and returned to the oak tree, they found the boy sitting on a low branch, eating his evening meal.

When he saw the couple, he jumped from the branch and landed lightly in front of them. He took in their happy faces and the fact that they walked hand-in-hand, and demanded, "Are you two finally friends?"

Anaya and Kith-Kanan looked at each other, and a rare thing happened. Anaya smiled. "We are much more than friends," she said sweetly.

The three of them sat down with their backs to the broad oak's trunk. As Anaya told Mackeli the truth about his past, the sun dodged in and out of the clouds and red autumn leaves fell around them.

"I'm not your brother?" Mackeli asked when she had finished.

"You are my brother," Anaya replied firmly, "but we are not of the same blood."

"And if I was taken from my parents," he went on slowly, "who were you taken from, Ny?"

"I don't know, and I never shall. Camirene took me from my mother and father, just as I took you." She looked to the ground, embarrassed. "I needed a girl child to be the next Keeper of the Forest. I moved so hastily, I didn't take time to notice that you were a boy."

Kith-Kanan put an arm on Mackeli's shoulder. "You won't be too angry?"

Mackeli stood up and walked slowly away from them. His ever-present hood slipped down, revealing his white, Silvanesti hair. "It's all so strange," he said, confused. "I've never known any other life than the one I've had in the wildwood." He looked at Anaya. "I guess I'm not angry. I'm . . . stunned. I wonder what I would have been if I if Anaya—"

"A farmer," said Anaya. 'Your parents were farmers. They grew vegetables."

She went on to explain that once she realized she'd taken a boy-child instead of a girl, she tried to return the infant Mackeli to his parents, but their house was abandoned when she went back. So she had raised Mackeli as her brother.

Mackeli still seemed dazed by the tale of his abduction, Finally he asked, rather hesitantly, "Will you have to find a girl to raise to be keeper after you?"

Anaya looked beyond him to Kith-Kanan. "No. This time the Keeper of the Forest will give birth to her successor." Kith-Kanan held out a hand to her. When she took it, Mackeli quietly clasped his small hands around both of theirs.

Three Moons' Day, Year of the Hawk

15

The ambassador from Thorbardin arrived in Silvanost on Three-Moons' Day, midway between the autumnal equinox and the winter solstice. The dwarf's name was Durtbarth, but he was called Ironthumb by most who knew him. In his youth he had been a champion wrestler. Now, in old age, he was esteemed as the most level-headed of all the counselors to the king of Thorbardin.

Dunbarth traveled with a small entourage: his secretary, four scribes, four dispatch riders, a crate of carrier pigeons, and sixteen warrior dwarves as his personal guard. The ambassador rode in a tall, closed coach made entirely of metal. Even though the brass, iron, and bronze panels were hammered quite thin, with all the skill characteristic of the dwarven race, the coach was still enormously heavy. A team of eight horses drew the conveyance, which held not only Dunbarth, but his staff. The warrior escort rode sturdy, short-legged horses, not swift but blessed with phenomenal endurance. The dwarven party was met on the western bank of the Thon-Thalas by Sithas and an honor guard of twelve warriors.

"Good morrow to you, Lord Dunbarth!" Sithas said heartily. The ambassador stood on one of the steps hanging below the coach door. From there he was high enough to clasp arms with Sithas without the embarrassment of making the far taller elf bend over.

"Life and health to you, Speaker's son," Dunbarth rumbled. His leggings and tunic were brown cloth and leather, but he sported a short purple cape and broad-brimmed light brown hat. A short

134

feather plumed out from his hatband and matched in color the wide, bright blue belt at his waist. His attire offered a striking contrast to the elegant simplicity of Sithas's robe and sandals.

The prince smiled. "We have arranged ferries for your company." With a sweep of his hand he indicated the two large barges moored at the river's edge.

"Will you ride with me, son of Sithel?" asked Dunbarth importantly.

"I would be honored."

The dwarf climbed back into his coach, then Sithas grasped the handrail and stepped up into the metal wagon. The top was high enough for him to stand erect in. Nevertheless, Dunbarth ordered his secretary, a swarthy young dwarf, to surrender his seat to Sithas. The elf prince sat. The escort filed in behind the coach, pennants whipping from the tips of their gilded pikes.

"A remarkable thing, this coach," Sithas said politely. "Is it made entirely of metal?"

"Indeed, noble prince. Not one speck of wood or cloth in the whole contraption!"

Sithas felt the silver curtains that hung in front of the side windows. The dwarves had woven them of metal so fine it felt like cloth.

"Why build it so?" he asked. "Wouldn't wood be lighter?"

Dunbarth folded his hands across his broad, round belly. "It would indeed, but this is an official coach for Thorbardin ambassadors traveling abroad, so it was made to show off the skills of my people in metal-working," he replied proudly.

With much shouting and cracking of whips, the ponderous coach rolled onto a barge. The team of horses was cut loose and brought alongside it. Finally, the coach and the warrior escorts were distributed on board.

Dunbarth leaned forward to the coach window. "I would like to see the elves who are going to row this ferry!"

"We have no need for such crude methods," Sithas said smoothly. "But watch, if it pleases your lordship."

Dunbarth leaned his elbow on the window edge and looked out over the starboard side of the barge. The ferry master, an elf long in years with yellow hair and mahogany skin, mounted the wooden bulwark and put a brass trumpet to his lips. A long, single note blurted out, sliding down the scale.

In the center of the river, a round green hump broke the surface for an instant, then disappeared again. Large ripples spread out from that point large enough that when they reached the riverbank they all but swamped a string of canoes tied to the stone pier. The great barge rocked only slightly in the swell.

Again the green hump broke the surface, and this time it rose. The hump became a dome, green and glistening, made up of a hundred angular plates. In front of the dome, the brow of a massive, green head appeared. A large, orange eye with a vertical black pupil the size of a full-grown dwarf appraised the stationary barge. At the tip of the triangular head, two nostrils as big as barrels spewed mist into the air.

"It's a monster!" Dunbarth cried. "By Reorx!" His hand went to his waist, reaching for a sword he'd forgotten he did not wear.

"No, my lord," Sithas said soothingly. "A monster it may be, but a tame one. It is our tow to the far shore."

The dwarven warriors on the barge fingered their heavy axes and muttered to each other. The giant turtle, bred by the elves for just this job, swam to the blunt bow of the ferry and waited patiently as the ferry master and two helpers walked across its huge shell to attach lines to a stout brass chain that encircled the monster's shell. One of the turtle's hind legs bumped the barge, knocking the feet out from under the nervous warrior dwarves. The coach creaked backward an inch or two on its iron axles.

"What a brute!" Dunbarth exclaimed, fascinated. "Do such monsters roam freely in the river, Prince Sithas?"

"No, my lord. At the command of my grandfather, Speaker Silvanos, the priests of the Blue Phoenix used their magic to breed a race of giant turtles to serve as beasts of burden on the river. They are enormously strong, of course, and quite longlived." Sithas sat back imperiously in his springy metal seat.

The ferry master blew his horn again, and the great reptile swung toward the shore of Fallan Island, a mile away. The slack went out of the tow line, and the barge lurched into motion. Sithas heard a loud clatter and knew that the warriors had been thrown off their feet again. He suppressed a smile. "Have you ever been to Silvanost before, Lord Dunbarth?" he asked deferentially.

"No, I've not had the pleasure. My uncle, Dundevin Stonefoot, did come to the city once on behalf of our king."

"I remember," Sithas mused. "I was but a boy." It had been fifty years before.

The ferry pitched up and down as they crossed the midpoint of the river. A freshening wind blew the barge sideways, but the turtle paid no attention, paddling steadily on its familiar course. The barge, loaded with tons of coach, dwarves, Dunbarth, Sithas, and the prince's small honor guard, bobbed on its lines like a cork.

Gray clouds scudded before the scouring wind, hurrying off to the north. Sithas watched them warily, for winter was usually the time of storms in Silvanost. Vast cyclones, often lasting for days, sometimes boiled up out of the Courrain Ocean and lashed across Silvanesti. Wind and rain would drive everyone indoors and the sun would appear only once in two or three weeks. While the countryside suffered during these winter storms, the city was protected by spells woven by the clerics of E'li. Their spells deflected most of the natural fury away to the western mountains, but casting them for each new storm was a severe trial for the priests.

Dunbarth took the bumpy ride in good stride, as befits an ambassador, but his young secretary was not at all happy. He clutched his recording book to his chest and his face went from swarthy to pale to light green as the barge rocked.

"Drollo here hates water," Dunbarth explained with an amused glint in his eye. "He closes his eyes to take a bath!"

"My lord!" protested the secretary.

"Never fear, Master Drollo," Sithas said. "It would take far worse wind than this to upset a craft of this size."

The ferry master tooted another command on his horn, and the turtle swung the barge around. Lord Dunbarth's guard rattled from one bulwark to the other, and the horse team whinnied and shifted nervously as the deck moved beneath them. The mighty turtle butted his shell against the bow of the ferry and pushed it backward toward the dock. Elves on the dock guided the barge in with long poles. With a short, solid bump, the ferry was docked.

A ramp was lowered into the barge, and the dwarven guard mustered together to march ashore. They were much disheveled by the bumpy crossing. Plumes were broken off their helmets, capes were stained from the guards' falls into the scupper, armor was scuffed, but with commendable dignity, the sixteen dwarves shouldered their battle-axes and marched up the ramp to dry land. The horses were re-hitched to the coach and, as whips cracked, they hauled the coach up the ramp.

It began to rain as they rolled through the streets. Dunbarth peered through the curtains at the fabled capital of the elves. White towers gleamed, even under the lowering sky. The peaks of the tallest the Tower of the Stars and the Quinari Palace were clothed in murky clouds. Dunbarth, his face as open with wonder as a child's, admired the intricate spell-formed gardens, the graceful architecture, the almost musical harmony embodied by Silvanost's sights. Finally, he drew the curtains tight to keep out the gusting rain, then turned his attention to Sithas.

"I know you are heir to the Speaker of the Stars, but how is it you have the task of greeting me, noble Sithas?" he asked diplomatically. "Isn't it more usual for the younger son to receive foreign ambassadors?"

"There is no younger son in Silvanost," Sithas replied calmly.

Dunbarth smoothed his iron-gray beard. "Forgive me, Prince, but I was told the speaker had two sons."

Sithas adjusted the folds of his rain-spattered robes. "I have a twin brother, several minutes younger than I. His name is Kith-Kanan." Saying the name aloud was strange for Sithas. Though his twin was seldom far from his thoughts, it had been a very long time since the prince had had reason to speak his name. He said it silently to himself: Kith-Kanan.

"Twins are most uncommon among the elven race," Dunbarth was saying. With effort, Sithas focused on the conversation at hand. "Whereas, among humans, they are not at all uncommon." Dunbarth lowered his gaze. "Where is your brother, Speaker's son?" he asked solemnly.

"He is in disgrace." Dunbarth's face registered only polite attention. Sithas inhaled deeply. "Do you know humans well?" he asked, eager to change the subject.

"I have made a number of journeys as emissary to the court of Ergoth. We've had many disputes with the humans over exchange rates of raw iron, copper, tin . . . but that's ancient history." Dunbarth leaned forward, close to Sithas. "It is a wise person who listens twice to everything a human says," he said softly. "Their duplicity knows no bounds!"

"I shall keep that in mind," Sithas responded.

By the time the coach arrived at the palace, the storm had strengthened. There was no flashing lightning or crashing thunder, but a swirling, howling wind drove buckets of rain through the city. The coach pulled up close to the north portico of the palace, where there was some shelter from the wind and rain. There, an army of servants stood poised in the downpour, ready to assist the ambassador with his luggage. Lord Dunbarth stepped heavily down from his conveyance, his short purple cape lashing in the wind. He doffed his extravagant hat to the assembled servants.

"My lord, I think we should dispense with the amenities for now," Sithas shouted over the wind. "Our rainy season seems to have come early this year."

"As you wish, noble prince," Dunbarth bellowed.

Stankathan waited inside for the dwarven ambassador and Sithas. He bowed low to them and said, "Excellent lord, if you will follow me, I will show you to your quarters."

"Lead on," said Dunbarth grandly. Behind him, the drenched Drollo let out a sneeze.

The ground floor of the north wing housed many of the pieces of art that Lady Nirakina had collected. The delicate and life-like statues of Morvintas, the vividly colored tapestries of the Women of E'li, the spell-molded plants of the priest Jin Fahrus all these lent the north wing an air of otherworldly beauty. As the dwarves passed through, servants discreetly mopped the marble floor behind them, blotting away all the mud and rainwater that had been tracked in.

Dunbarth and his entourage were lodged on the third floor of the north wing. The airy suite, with its curtains of gauze and mosaic tile floor in shades of gold and sea-green, was quite unlike any place in the dwarven realm of Thorbardin. The ambassador stopped to stare at a two-foot-long wooden model of a dove poised over his bed. When Drollo set Dunbarth's bags on the bed, the cloth-covered wings of the dove began to beat slowly, wafting a gentle breeze over the bed.

"By Reorx!" exclaimed the secretary. Dunbarth exploded with laughter.

"A minor spell," Stankathan explained hurriedly. "Activated when anything or anyone rests on the bed. If it bothers your lordship, I shall have it stopped."

"No, no. That's quite all right," Dunbarth said merrily.

"If you require anything, my lord, simply ring the bell," said Stankathan.

The elves withdrew. In the hallway beyond Dunbarth's closed door, Stankathan asked when the human delegation was expected.

"At any time," answered Sithas. "Keep the staff alert."

The major-domo bowed. "As you command, sire."

* * * * *

Lord Dunbarth dined that night with the Speaker of the Stars in a quiet, informal dinner that included only the closest confidantes of both sides. They talked for a long time about nothing of importance, taking the measure of each other. Lady Nirakina, in particular, seemed to find the elderly dwarf engaging.

"Are you married, my lord?" she asked at one point.

"No; Lady, never again!" Dunbarth boomed. He shrugged. "I am a widower."

"I am sorry."

"She was a good wife, my Brenthia, but a real terror at times." He drained a full cup of elven nectar. Smoothly, a servant stepped forward to refill his goblet.

"A terror, my lord?" asked Hermathya, intrigued.

"Quite so, Lady. I remember once she burst into the Council of Thanes and dressed me down for being late for supper five nights in a row. It took years for me to live that down, don't you know. The Daewar faction used to taunt me, when I was speaking in the council, by saying, 'Go home, Ironthumb, go home. Your dinner is ready.' " He laughed loudly, his deep bass voice echoing in the nearly empty Hall of Balif.

"Who are these Daewar?" asked Hermathya. "They sound rude."

"The Daewar are one of the great clans of the dwarven race," Sithel explained smoothly. He prided himself on his knowledge of dwarves and their politics. "You are yourself of the Hylar clan, are you not, Lord Dunbarth?"

The ambassador's blue eyes twinkled with happy cunning. "Your Highness is most knowledgeable. Yes, I am Hylar, and cousin to many kings of Thorbardin." He slapped a blunt hand on the back of his secretary, who was seated on his right. "Now, Drollo here, is half-Theiwar, which accounts for his dark looks and strange temperament." Drollo looked studiously at his plate and said nothing.

"Is it usual for dwarves to marry outside their class?" asked Sithas curiously.

"Not really. Speaking of such things," Dunbarth said languorously, "I hear tales that some elves have married humans."

A sharp silence fell in the hall. Sithel leaned back in his tall chair and put a finger to his lips. "It is unfortunately true," said the Speaker tersely. "In the wilds of our western provinces, some of the Kagonesti have taken humans as mates. No doubt there is a shortage of suitable elven spouses. The practice is pernicious and forbidden by our law."

Dunbarth bowed his head, not in agreement, but in recognition of Sithel's admirable powers of restraint. The mixed-race issue was a very sensitive one, as the dwarf well knew. His own people were race-proud too, and no dwarf had ever been known to intermarry with another race.

"I met many half-humans among the refugees who lately came to our city for shelter from bandits," Lady Nirakina said gently. "They were such sad folk, and many were quite presentable. It seems wrong to me to blame them for the follies of their parents."

"Their existence is not something we can encourage," Sithel countered with noticeable vigor. "As you say, they are known to be melancholy, and that makes them dangerous. They often figure in acts of violence and crime. They hate the Silvanesti because we are pure in blood, while they languish with human clumsiness and frailty. I suppose you in Thorbardin have heard of the riot we had in late summer?"

"There were mutterings of such an event," said Dunbarth casually.

"It was all due to the violent natures of some humans and half-humans we had unwisely allowed on the island. The riot was quelled, and the troublemakers driven away." Nirakina sighed noticeably. Sithel ignored his wife as he continued to make his point. "There can never be peace between Silvanesti and human, unless we keep to our own borders and our own beds."

Dunbarth rubbed his red, bulbous nose. He had a heavy ring on each of his fingers, and they glittered in the candlelight. "Is that what you will tell the emissary from Ergoth?"

"It is," Sithel said vehemently.

"Your wisdom is great, Sithel Twice-Blest. My king has given me almost exactly the same words to speak. If we present a united front to the humans, they will have to accede to our demands."

The dinner ended quickly. Toasts were made to the health of the king of Thorbardin and to the hospitality of the Speaker of the Stars. That done, Lord Dunbarth and Drollo withdrew.

Sithas strode to the door after it closed behind the ambassador. "That old fox! He was trying to make an alliance with you before the humans even arrive! He wants to promote a conspiracy!"

Sithel dipped his hand in a silver bowl of rosewater held by a servant. "My son, Dunbarth is a master of his craft. He was testing our eagerness to compromise. Had he behaved otherwise, I would have thought King Voldrin a fool to have sent him."

"This all seems very confusing to me," complained Lady Nirakina. "Why don't you all speak the truth and work from there!"

Sithel did a rare thing. He burst out laughing. "Diplomats tell the truth! My dear Kina, the stars would fall from heaven and the gods would faint with horror if diplomats started speaking the truth!"

* * * * *

Later that night came a knock on Sithas's door. A storm-drenched warrior strode in, bowed, and said in a ringing voice, "Forgive this intrusion, Highness, but I bring word of the emissary from Ergoth!"

"Yes?" said Sithas tensely. There was so much talk of treachery, he feared foul play had befallen the humans.

"Highness, the ambassador and his party are waiting on the bank of the river. The ambassador demands that he be met by a representative of the royal house."

"Who is this human?" Sithas asked.

"He gave his name as Ulwen, first praetor of the emperor of Ergoth," replied the soldier.

"First praetor, eh? Is the storm worse?" Sithas questioned.

"It is bad, Highness. My boat nearly sank crossing the Thon-Thalas."

"And yet this Ulwen insists on crossing immediately?"

The soldier said yes. "You will pardon me, sire, for saying so, but he is very arrogant, even for a human."

"I shall go," Sithas said simply. "It is my duty. Lord Dunbarth was met by me, and it is only just that I greet Praetor Ulwen likewise."

The prince left with the soldier, but not before sending word to the clerics of E'li, to ask them to begin working their spells to deflect the storm. It was unusual for so strong a storm to come before the winter season. The conference promised to be difficult enough without the added threat of wind and water.

While the Storm Raged

16

How wonderful this time is, Kith-Kanan thought. Not only did he have his growing love for Anaya, which was sweeter than anything he'd ever known, but his friendship with Mackeli, as well. They had become a family Anaya, his wife, and Mackeli, like a son.

It was not an easy life, by any means. There was always work to be done, but there was time to laugh too, to swim in the pool, to take short flying excursions on Arcuballis, to tell stories around the fire at night. Kith-Kanan had began to understand the Silvanesti who had left Silvanost to start new lives in the wilderness. The days ran their own course in the forest. There were no calendars and no clocks. There was no social hierarchy either; there were no rich and no poor. You hunted for yourself, provided for your own needs. And no one stood between an elf and the gods. As he looked over a forest glade, or knelt by a brook, Kith-Kanan felt closer to the gods than he ever had in the cold, marble precincts of Silvanost's temples.

No priests, no taxes, no protocol. For a long time, Kith-Kanan had believed that his life had ended the day he'd left Silvanost. Now he knew it had been a new beginning.

As the weeks went by, hunting grew poorer and poorer. Anaya went out, sometimes for two or three days at a time, and returned only with a brace of rabbits, squirrels, or other small game. At one point she had been reduced to catching pigeons, a poor return for her days in the woods. Nothing like this had ever happened before, according to Mackeli. Usually, Anaya went out and set a snare or trap and a likely prize would practically fall into it. Now, the animals were nowhere to be seen. In hopes of adding to the meager hunting, Kith-Kanan worked harder to develop his woodland skills. He hunted frequently, but had yet to bring anything back.

This day a lone hart moved slowly through the forest, its small hooves sinking deep into drifts of fallen leaves. Its black nose twitched as the wind brought smells from far away.

Kith-Kanan, wedged ten feet off the ground into the fork of a linden tree, was motionless. He willed the deer not to smell him, not to see him. Then, as slowly as possible, the prince drew his bow and swiftly let fly. His aim was true. The hart leaped away, but only for a few yards before it collapsed into the leaves.

Kith-Kanan let out a yell of triumph. Eight months in the wild-wood, and this was his first hunting success. He skittered down the tree and ran to the fallen deer. Yes! The arrow had hit the beast right in the heart.

He dressed the carcass. As he slung it over his shoulder, Kith-Kanan realized that he couldn't stop grinning. Wouldn't Anaya be surprised?

The air was chill, and under his burden Kith-Kanan panted, sending little puffs of vapor from his nostrils and mouth. He walked quickly, making a lot of noise, but it didn't matter now. He had made a kill! He'd been walking for some time when the first flakes of snow began to fall. A sort of steady hiss pervaded the forest as the light flakes filtered down through the bare tree limbs. It wasn't a heavy fall, but as the prince's trek continued, the brown leaves on the forest floor gradually acquired a thin frosting of white.

He climbed the hill to the clearing, meeting Mackeli on the way.

"Look what I have!" Kith-Kanan exclaimed. "Fresh meat!"

"Congratulations, Kith. You've worked hard to get it," the boy said, but a frown creased his forehead.

"What's the matter?"

Mackeli looked at him and blinked. "It's snowing."

Kith-Kanan shifted the weight of the carcass to a more comfortable position. "What's wrong with that? It is winter, after all."

"You don't understand," said the boy. He took Kith-Kanan's quiver and bow, and together they proceeded up the hill. "It never snows in our clearing." They gained the crest of the hill. The clearing was already lightly dusted with snow.

With a stone axe, Kith-Kanan removed the rib section and gave it to Arcuballis. The griffon had been brought to the hollow oak, and a roof of hides had been stretched from the overhead limbs to keep the rain off the mount. The noble eagle head of Arcuballis protruded from the crude shelter. The beast repeatedly ruffled its neck feathers and shook its head, trying to shake off the snowflakes. Kith-Kanan dropped the meat at the griffon's feet.

"This is no weather for you, eh boy?" he said, scratching the animal's neck through its thick feathers. Arcuballis made hoarse grunting sounds and lowered its head to its meal.

Kith-Kanan left his dagger and sword in a covered basket inside Arcuballis's shelter. Brushing the snow off his shoulders, he ducked into the tree. It was snug and warm inside, but very close. A small fire burned on the hearth. As the prince sat crosslegged by the fire and warmed his hands, Mackeli scuttled about in the stores of nuts and dried fruit overhead.

After a short time, the bark-covered door swung open. Anaya stood in the doorway.

"Hello!" Kith-Kanan cried cheerfully. "Come in out of the cold. I had good hunting today!"

Anaya pulled the door closed behind her. When autumn arrived, she had changed from her green-dyed buckskins to natural brown ones. Now, coated with snow, she looked small and cold and unhappy. Kith-Kanan went to her and pushed back the hood from her head. "Are you all right?" he asked quietly, searching for an answer in her eyes.

"It's snowing in my clearing," she said flatly.

"Mackeli said that this is unusual. Still, remember that the weather follows its own laws, Anaya." Kith-Kanan tried to soothe the hopeless look on her face; after all, it was only a little snow. "We'll be fine. Did you see the deer I took?" He'd hung the quarters of meat outside to cool.

"I saw it," she said. Anaya's eyes were dull and lifeless. She pulled free of Kith-Kanan's arms and unlaced her rawhide jacket. Still standing by the door, she looked at him. "You did well. I didn't even see a deer, much less take one. Something is wrong. The animals no longer come as they used to. And now snow in the clearing . . ."

The keeper threw her jacket on the floor and looked up at the chimney hole. Dry, cold flakes fell in, vanishing in the column of rising smoke before they reached the fire. "I must go to the cave and commune with the forest. The Forestmaster may know what has happened," she said, then sighed. "But I am so tired now. Tomorrow. I will go tomorrow."

Kith-Kanan sat by the fire and pulled Anaya gently down beside him. When she put her head in his lap and closed her eyes, the prince leaned back against the side of the tree, intending to keep an eye on the fire. He continued to stroke Anaya's face. In spite of her distress over the snow, Kith-Kanan couldn't believe that anything was really wrong. He had seen snow in the streets of Silvanost after many years of none. As he'd said, the weather followed its own laws. Kith-Kanan's eyes closed, and he dozed. The fire shrank in its circle of stones, and the first flakes of snow reached the floor of the tree, collecting on Anaya's eyelashes.

Kith-Kanan awoke with the slow realization that he was cold. He tried to move and discovered he was buried under two bodies Anaya on his left and Mackeli on his right. Though asleep, the need for warmth had drawn them together. Furs were piled up around them, and as Kith-Kanan opened his eyes, he saw that more than half a foot of snow had collected in the tree. The snowfall had extinguished the coals of the fire and drifted around the sleeping trio.

"Wake up," he said thickly. When neither Anaya nor Mackeli moved, Kith-Kanan patted his wife's cheek. She exhaled sharply and turned over, putting her back to him. He tried to rouse Mackeli, but the boy only started to snore.

"By Astarin," he muttered. The cold had obviously numbed their senses. He must build a fire.

Kith-Kanan heaved himself up, pushing aside the inch of snow that had fallen across his lower legs. His breath made a long stream of fog. There was dry kindling in one of the wattle baskets, against the wall and out of the way of the falling snow. He dug the snow out of the hearth with his bare hands and laid a stand of twigs and bark shavings on the cold stones. With a flint and strike stone, he soon had a smoldering pile of tinder. Kith-Karen fanned it with his breath, and soon a crackling fire was burning.

It had stopped snowing, but the bit of sky he could glimpse through the chimney hole was gray and threatening. Reluctantly the prince eased the door open, even against the resistance from the two feet of snow that had drifted against the tree.

The clearing had been transformed. Where formerly the forest had been wrought in green and brown, now it was gray and white. An unbroken carpet of snow stretched across the clearing. All the imperfections of the ground were lost under the blanket of white.

A snuffling sound caught his ear. Kith-Kanan walked around the broad tree trunk and saw Arcuballis huddled under its flimsy shelter, looking miserable.

"Not like your warm stall in Silvanost, is it, old friend?" Kith-Kanan said. He untied the griffon's halter and led it out a few yards from the tree.

"Fly, boy. Warm yourself and come back." Arcuballis made a few faltering steps forward. "Go on. It's all right."

The griffon spread its wings and took to the air. It circled the clearing three times, then vanished upward into the low gray clouds.

Kith-Kanan examined the venison haunches he'd hung up the day before. They were frozen solid. He untied one and braced it on his shoulder.

Back inside the tree, it was already much warmer, thanks to the fire. Anaya and Mackeli were nestled together like spoons in a drawer. Kith-Kanan smiled at them and knelt to saw two cutlets from the venison haunch. It was hard going, but soon he had whittled the steaks out and had them roasting on a spit over the fire.

"Mmm." Anaya yawned. Eyes still closed, she asked, "Do I smell venison roasting?"

Kith-Kanan smiled again. "You certainly do, wife. I am making our dinner."

She stretched long and hard. "It smells wonderful." She yawned again. "I'm so tired."

"You just lie there and rest," he replied. "I'll provide for us this time." The prince gave his attention to the venison cutlets. He turned them carefully, making sure they were cooked all the way through. When they were done, he took one, still on its stick, and knelt by Anaya. "Dinner is served, my lady," he said and touched her shoulder.

Anaya smiled and her eyelids fluttered open. She raised her head and looked at him.

Kith-Kanan cried out in surprise and dropped the steak onto the wet ground.

Anaya's dark hazel. eyes had changed color. They had become. vividly green, like two shining emeralds.

Quartered with a Gentleman

17

Rain, driven sideways by the wind, tore at the elves who stood on the stone pier at the river's edge. The far bank of the Thon-Thalas could not be seen at all, and the river itself was wild with storm-tossed waves. Through this chaos wallowed the great barge, drawn as before by a giant turtle.

The more Sithas saw of the growing storm, the more he was convinced it was not natural. His suspicion fell upon the waiting humans from Ergoth. Their emperor was known to have a corps of powerful magicians in his service. Was this premature, violent storm the result of some dire human magic?

"Surely, Highness, you should not risk this crossing!" warned the commander of the escort standing with Sithas.

The prince held his sodden cloak closed at his throat. "The ambassador from Ergoth is waiting, Captain," he replied. The turtle turned end-on to the storm waves, which crashed in green torrents over its high-domed shell. "It is important that we show these humans we are masters of our own fate," Sithas continued levelly. "Praetor Ulwen does not expect us to venture out in the storm to meet him. If we don't, when the storm ends he can rail long and loud about the timidity of elves." Sithas blotted water off his face with his wet cloak. "I will not cede that advantage to the humans, Captain."

The dark-haired Kagonesti did not look convinced.

The barge was close now. The thick wooden hull squeezed a swell of water between itself and the shore. This swell, some ten feet high, fell over Sithas and his escort, drenching them further.

The guards cursed and muttered, shuffling about the pier. Sithas stood imperturbable, his pale hair running in rivulets down the back of his emerald cloak.

The ferry master shouted from the deck, "I can't moor in this swell, Highness!"

Sithas looked to the captain. "Follow me," he advised. Turning back the flaps of his cloak, Sithas gathered up the lower edge, so as not to entangle his legs. With a running start, he leaped the gap between the pier end and the heaving barge. The prince hit, rolled, and got to his feet again. The soldiers gaped in amazement.

"Come on! Are you fighters or farmers?" Sithas called.

The captain squared his shoulders. If the heir to the throne was going to kill himself, then he would die too. Once the captain was across, he and Sithas stationed themselves to grab the hurtling warriors as they, too, landed on the barge.

The ferry's deck rose and fell like the chest of a breathing beast. When everyone was safely aboard, the ferry master blew his trumpet. The implacable mammoth turtle paddled away from shore.

Rain swirled and lashed at them. The scuppers ran full, and all sorts of loose debris sloshed back and forth on the ferry's deck. The ferocious pounding near the shore lessened as the raft gained the deeper water in the center of the river. Here the danger was from the churning current, as the wind drove the surface water against the natural flow of the river. The thick chains that secured the barge to the towing turtle snapped hard, first the port, then to starboard. The giant reptile rolled with these blows, which sometimes lifted one of its thick green flippers out of the water. As if resenting this challenge to its strength, the turtle put its head down and pulled even harder for the western bank.

The captain of the escort struggled forward to report to Sithas. "Sire, there's a lot of water coming into the boat. Waves are breaking over the sides." Unperturbed, the prince asked the ferry master what they should do.

"Bail," was all he had to say.

The soldiers got on their knees and scooped water in their helmets. A chain was formed, each elf passing a full helmet to the leeward side and handing an empty helmet back to the first fellow bailing.

"There's the shore!" sang out the ferry master. When Sithas squinted into the rain, he could make out a gray smudge ahead. Slowly the shoreline grew more distinct. On the slight hill overlooking the boat landing stood a large tent. A flag whipped from the center peak of the tent.

Sithas spat rainwater and again clutched his cloak tightly at his throat. In spite of their request to be met and conducted into the city here the humans sat, encamped for the night. Already they were leading the speaker's son around by the nose. Such arrogance made Sithas's blood burn. Still, there was nothing to be gained by storming into the ambassador's tent in a blind rage.

He stared at the swimming turtle and then farther ahead at the gently sloping riverbank. With a firm nod to himself, Sithas teetered across the pitching deck to where the soldiers still knelt, bailing out water with their helmets. He told them to hold fast when the barge reached the shore and to be prepared for a surprise. When Sithas informed the ferry master of his idea, that tired, storm-lashed fellow grinned.

"We'll do it, sire!" he said and put his trumpet to his lips. On his first attempt, instead of a blaring call, water spurted out. Cursing, he rapped the trumpet's bell on the bulwark and tried again. The command note cut through the noise of the storm. The turtle swung right, pulling the barge to one side of the pier ahead. The trumpet sounded again, and the turtle raised its great green head. Its dull orange eyes blinked rapidly, to keep the rain out.

There were a half-dozen caped figures on the dock, waiting. Sithas assumed they were the Ergothian ambassador's unfortunate guards, ordered to wait in the rain should the elves deign to show up. When the barge turned aside, they filed off the dock and tried to get in front of the approaching ferry. The turtle's belly scraped in the mud, and its shell humped out of the water a full twenty feet high. The humans scattered before the awesome onslaught of the turtle. The elf warriors on deck let out a cheer.

The ferry master blew a long rattling passage on his horn, and the turtle dug its massive flippers into the riverside mud. The bank was wide and the angle shallow, so the great beast had no problem heaving itself out of the water. The driving rain rapidly cleansed it of clinging mud, and the turtle crawled up the slope.

The bow of the barge hit bottom, and everyone on board was thrown to the deck. The ferry master bounced to his feet and repeated the surging trumpet signal. All four of the turtle's flippers were out of the water now, and it continued up the hill. As Sithas got to his feet, he resisted an urge to laugh triumphantly. He looked down at the human guards, who were running from the sight of the turtle.

"Stand fast!" he shouted decisively. "I am Prince Sithas of the Silvanesti! I have come to greet your ambassador!" Some of the gray-caped figures halted. Others continued to run. One human, who wore an officer's plume on his tall, conical helmet, tentatively approached the beached barge.

"I am Endrac, commander of the ambassador's escort. The ambassador has retired for the night," he shouted up at Sithas.

"Then go and wake him! The storm may last another day, so this is your master's best chance to reach the city without suffering an avoidable, but major delay."

Endrac threw up his hands and proceeded up the hill. He was not much faster than the turtle, weighed down as he was by armor. The giant turtle ground its way up, inexorable, dragging the barge behind it. The warriors were plainly impressed by the feat, for the barge obviously weighed many tons.

Torches blossomed on the top of the hill, all around the elaborate tent of the Ergothian ambassador. Sithas was gratified to see all the frantic activity. He turned to the ferry master and told him to urge the beast along. The elf put the trumpet to his lips once more and sounded the call.

They were quite a sight, rumbling up the hill. The turtle's flippers, each larger than four elves, dug into the soft ground and threw back gouts of mud against the hull of the barge. The chains that shackled the beast to the boat rattled and clanked rhythmically. The giant grunted deep in its chest as the effort began to tell on it.

The ground flattened out, so the ferry master signaled for the turtle to slow down. The barge tilted forward on its flat bottom, jarring the elven warriors. They laughed and goodnaturedly urged the ferry master to speed up again.

The ambassador's tent was only a few yards away now. A cordon of human soldiers formed around it, capes flapping in the wind. They stood at attention, spears against their shoulders. The turtle loomed over them. Endrac appeared.

"You there, Endrac!" Sithas shouted. "You'd best disperse your fighters. Our turtle hasn't eaten lately, and if you provoke him, he might eat your men."

Endrac complied, and his soldiers moved with grateful speed out of the turtle's way.

"There now, ferry master, you'd better rein him in," cried Sithas. A quick blast on the trumpet, and the turtle grunted to a stop.

A human in civilian dress appeared at the door of the tent. "What is the meaning of this?" he demanded.

"I am Sithas, son of Sithel, Speaker of the Stars. Your ambassador sent word he wished to be met. I have come. It will be a grave insult if the ambassador does not see me."

The human drew his cape around himself in a quick, angry motion. "A thousand pardons, noble prince," he said, vexed. "Wait but a moment. I will speak to the ambassador."

The human went inside the tent.

Sithas put one foot on the port set of chains that ran from the ferry to the halter encircling the turtle's shell. The links were as thick as the prince's wrist. No one but an elf could have walked the fifteen feet along the swaying length of chain in the rain, but Sithas did it easily. Once he reached the turtle's back, he was able to move briskly over the shell to the beast's head. The turtle, placid as all his kind were, paid no mind as the elf prince stepped gingerly on its head.

The human appeared again. This close, Sithas could see he was a mature man; his red-brown hair and full beard were sprinkled with gray. He was richly dressed in the vulgar Ergothian style which meant he was clad in strong, dark colors, wine-red and black, with a golden torc at his throat and a fur-lined cape.

"Well?" Sithas demanded from his lofty perch atop the turtle's head.

"The ambassador asks if you would care to come in out of the rain for a short time, while preparations are made to go," said the human more solicitously.

Using the deep creases in the skin of the creature's neck as hand and footholds, Sithas descended the twelve feet to the ground. Once down, he glanced up at the turtle; a huge eye regarded him benignly.

The bearded human was tall for his race. His gray eyes were hard as he bowed. "I am Ulvissen, seneschal to Ulwen, praetor of the empire," he said with dignity.

With a sweep of his arm, Ulvissen indicated Sithas should precede him. The prince strode into the tent.

It was the size of a largish house. The first room Sithas entered featured the imperial standard of Ergoth, a golden axe crossed with a hammer, on a field of dark crimson. The second room was larger and far mare elaborate. Thick carpets covered the ground. In the center of the room, a fire burned on a portable blackiron hearth. Smoke was carried out through a metal chimney, made of sections of bronze pipe jointed together. Couches and chairs covered with purple velvet were scattered around the room. A lap desk full of rolled maps lay open to Sithas's left, and a table laden with decanters of drink stood on his right. Glass-globed oil lamps lit the room as bright as day. Wind howled outside, and rain drummed on the varnished silk roof.

A flap across the room was pulled back, and four thick-armed servants entered, carrying a chair supported by rods through its armrests. Seated in the chair was an ancient human, far older than Ulvissen. His bald head was hunched deep between his shoulders. His skin was the color of egg yolks, and his rheumy eyes seemed to have no distinct color. Sithas did not need to know much about human health to recognize that this was a sick man.

The prince was about to speak to this venerable man when another person entered, a female. She was altogether different from the frail figure in the chair. Tall, clad in a deep red velvet gown, she had dark brown hair that fell just past her shoulders. More voluptuous than any elven maiden, the human woman appeared less than half the age of the man in the chair.

When she spoke, it was with a velvety voice. "Greetings, Prince Sithas. On behalf of my husband, Praetor Ulwen, I greet you." She rested her hands on the back of the old man's chair. "My name is Teralind denCaer," she added.

Sithas bowed his head slightly. "In the name of my father, Speaker of the Stars, I greet you, Praetor Ulwen, and Lady Teralind," he said respectfully.

She came out from behind the chair and went to the table where the decanters were. Teralind poured a pale white liquid into a tall glass goblet. "We did not expect anyone to meet us. Not until the storm was over," she said, smiling slightly.

"I received the ambassador from Thorbardin this morning," Sithas replied. "It was only proper that I come and greet the emperor's envoy as well."

The old man in the chair still had said nothing, and he remained silent as Teralind drank. Then she passed in front of Sithas, gown rustling as she walked. By lamplight, her eyes were a foreign shade of brown, dark like her hair. Teralind sat and bade Sithas sit down, too.

"Excuse me, Lady, but is the praetor well?" he asked cautiously. The old human's eyes were closed.

"Ulwen is very old," she said with a tinge of sadness. "And it is very late."

"I can't help but wonder why the emperor did not choose a younger man for this task," Sithas ventured softly.

Terafind combed through her thick, wavy hair with the fingers of one hand. "My husband is the senior praetor of the empire. Also he is the only member of the ruling council to have dealt with Silvanesti before."

"Oh? When was that?"

"Forty-six years ago. Before I was born, actually. I believe he worked on what was called the Treaty of Thelgaard," she said distractedly.

Sithas tried to remember the obscure treaty, and could only recall that it had something to do with the cloth trade. "I'm sorry I did not have the pleasure of meeting the praetor then," he said. "I must have been away." Teralind looked at the elf oddly for an instant. Humans never could adjust to elven life spans. "In deference to the age of the ambassador," Sithas added, "I would be willing to stay the night here and escort you all to the city tomorrow."

"That is acceptable. Ulvissen will find you a suitable place to rest," Teralind agreed. She rose suddenly to her feet. "Good night, Your Highness," she said courteously, then snapped her fingers. The servants hoisted Ulwen up, turned ponderously, and carried him out.

* * * * *

Sithas was given a bed in a private corner of the great tent. The bed itself was large enough to sleep four grown elves and far too soft for the prince's taste. It seemed strange to him that humans should prize comfort so excessively.

The rain struck the roof of the tent with a rhythmic beat, but that did not lull Sithas to sleep. Instead, his mind wandered to thoughts of Hermathya. He would have to work harder to reconcile their differences, he decided. But his wife's face did not remain long in Sithas's thoughts. Kith-Kanan soon pushed to the forefront. His twin would probably have enjoyed Sithas's little gesture of bringing turtle and barge to the ambassador's very door.

Kith was a long way off now, Sithas thought. So many miles and so much time lay between them. As the prince closed his eyes, he felt the faint but persistent tie that had always existed between him and Kith-Kanan, but now he concentrated on it. The rain grew louder in his ears. It was like a pulse, the beat of a living heart. Feelings began to come to him the smell of the woodland, the sounds of night animals that no longer lived in the more settled parts of Silvanesti. He opened his mind further, and a flood of sensations came to him.

He saw, as in shadow, a dark elven woman. She was strong and deeply connected to the Power, even as the high clerics and the Speaker of the Stars were said to be. But the dark woman was part of an ancient group, different from the gods, but almost as great. Sithas had an impression of green leaves, of soaring trees, and pools of still, clear water. And there was a battle raging inside this woman. She was trying to leave the Power, and it did not want her to go. The reason she wished to leave was clear, too. She loved Kith, and he loved her. Sithas felt that very strongly.

A word came to him. A name.

"Anaya," he said aloud.

The link was broken when he spoke. Sithas sat up, his head swimming with strange, unexplained impressions. There was a struggle going on, a contest for possession of the dark elf woman. The struggle was between Kith-Kanan and the ancient powers of nature. The storm . . . not the work of human magicians, or any magicians. The storm was a manifestation of the struggle.

As Sithas lay back on the ridiculously large bed, a twinge of sadness entered his heart. The short connection had only emphasized how truly far from home his twin had journeyed.

And Sithas knew he dare tell no one what he'd learned.

In the Forest, Year of the Ram
(2215 PC)

18

The changes in the keeper continued. Anaya's toes and fingers, then the points of her elbows, became light green. She felt no pain and suffered no loss of movement, though it did seem she was becoming less sensitive all the time. Her hearing, formerly so acute, became duller and duller. Her eyesight lost its uncanny focus. Her stealthy tread grew slow and clumsy. At first she was short-tempered with the changes, but her spirits gradually lightened. Things the Forestmaster had told her during her long sojourn away from Kith-Kanan were now making more sense, she said. These changes, Anaya believed, were the price of her life joined to Kith-Kanan's. While she might bemoan the loss of her preternatural agility and hunting skill, her new life did make her very happy.

The winter was long and, as the forest was no longer Anaya's to command, very hard. She and Kith-Kanan hunted almost every day that it wasn't actually snowing. They had some success; there were rabbits and pheasants and the occasional deer to be had. But they more often ate Mackeli's nuts and berries. As their bellies shrank and their belts tightened, conversation diminished, too. When the wind howled outside and the snow drifted so high the door became hard to open, the three sat within the hollow tree, each wrapped in his or her own thoughts. Days went by without any of them speaking a single word.

Mackeli, too, was changing, though his metamorphosis was more easily understood. He had reached the time in a young elf's life when the physical limitations of childhood give way to an adult physique. Compared to the great life span of an elf, these changes take place rather quickly. Even without an abundance of food, he grew taller, stronger, and restless and often rude, as well. The boy's impatience was so high that Kith-Kanan forbade him to accompany them hunting; Mackeli's fidgeting scared off the already scarce game.

While his wife and friend changed in outward, tangible ways, Kith-Kanan grew, too, but inside. His values had changed since coming to the forest, certainly, and now his entire attitude toward life was undergoing fundamental change. All his life he had played at being prince. Since his brother Sithas was the heir, Kith-Kanan had no real responsibilities, no true duties. He took up warrior training and hunting as hobbies. He taught Arcuballis tricks and practiced aerial maneuvers. These activities had filled his days.

But it was different now. He could glide through the forest, silent as a wraith. He didn't have to rely on Mackeli's gathering skills or Anaya's hunting any longer. In fact, more and more, they relied on him. This was a good life, the prince decided, and he could now bless the day his father had taken Hermathya from him. Though he had cared for her, Hermathya was much better suited to his twin both of them so correct, proper, and dutiful. And with his forgiveness of his father came a sense of loss. He found himself missing his family. Still, he knew that his life was in the forest, not the city.

Another, more natural, change had come to Anaya. She was pregnant. She and her husband had been staring dreamily into the fire one night when she had told him. At first Kith-Kanan was stunned. His astonishment gave way to a great, heartfilling joy. He embraced her so hard that she squealed in protest. The thought that a new life, one he had helped create, was growing inside of her made Anaya that much more precious to the prince. It made their life together that much richer. He showered her with kisses and declarations of his love until Mackeli grumbled for them both to shut up, since he was trying to sleep.

The day came, not too long after, when the first icicles began to melt off the oak's bare branches. The sun came out and stayed for a week, and all the ice melted and ran off the tree. The snow retreated to the deep shadows around the rim of the clearing.

They emerged from the tree, blinking at the bright sunshine. It was as if this was the first sunny day they'd ever experienced. Anaya moved stiffly, rubbing her arms and thighs. Her hands and feet were fully colored green by this time.

Kith-Kanan stood in the center of the clearing, eyes shut, face turned to the sky. Mackeli, who was nearly as tall as Kith-Kanan now, bounded around like a deer, though certainly not as gracefully.

"We've never had such a winter," Anaya stated, gazing at the snow still hiding at the base of the trees.

"If the weather holds, the hunting will be good," Kith-Kanan noted confidently. "All the hibernating animals will be coming out."

"Free! Ha, ha, free!" Mackeli rejoiced. He grabbed Anaya's hands and tried to dance her around in a circle. She resisted and pulled her hands away with a grimace.

"Are you all right?" asked Kith-Kanan worriedly.

"I am stiff and sore," she complained. She stopped rubbing her arm and stood up straight. "I'll work the cold out of my bones, don't worry."

The novelty, but not the pleasure, of the first spring day wore off, and the trio returned to the tree to eat. In honor of the fine day, Kith-Kanan cut down their last haunch of venison. Kith-Kanan had been teaching Arcuballis to hunt for game and bring back what it caught. The griffon could cover a much wider range than they, and it grew more adept with each hunt. The last time the creature had brought back the very deer Kith-Kanan was carving.

Now, Kith-Kanan took Arcuballis from its hide tent and, with whistles and encouraging words, sent the beast off on another expedition. When the griffon was lost from sight, the elf prince built a fire outside, not an easy task with all the damp wood. He sliced off a sizeable roast from the hard, smoked haunch. While it cooked, Mackeli came out with his usual fare; arrow root, walnuts, dried blueberries, and wild rice. He looked at the brown assortment in his basket, then at the deer roast, sizzling and dripping fat into the fire. He squatted by Kith-Kanan, who was turning the meat on a rough spit.

"Could I have some?" asked Mackeli tentatively. Kith-Kanan gave him an astonished look. "It smells awfully good. Just a small piece?" the boy pleaded.

Kith-Kanan sliced off a thin strip of cooked meat, speared it with his dagger, and put it in Mackeli's basket. The elf boy eagerly picked it up with his fingers and promptly dropped it again. It was quite hot. Kith-Kanan gave him a sharpened twig, and Mackeli snagged the piece of meat and raised it to his mouth.

A look of utter concentration came over his face as he chewed. Kith-Kanan inquired, "Do you like it?"

"Well, it's different." The slice was gone. "Could I have some more?" The elf prince laughed and cut a larger piece.

Anaya came out of the tree, dragging their furs and bedding into the sun. The red and yellow lines she had painted on her face enhanced the already startling green of her eyes. The elf woman glanced over at the two males, crouched by the fire, and saw Mackeli nibbling a slice of venison. She ran over and slapped the meat from his hand.

"It is forbidden for you to eat meat!" she said heatedly.

"Oh? And who forbids me? You?" demanded Mackeli defiantly.

"Yes!"

Kith-Kanan rose to pull them apart, but as one Mackeli and Anaya shoved him back. He sprawled on the wet turf, astonished.

"You did not kill the animal, Keli, so you have no right to eat it!" Anaya said fiercely.

"You didn't kill it either! Kith did!" he countered.

"That's different. Kith is a hunter, you're only a boy. Stick to your nuts and berries." The "boy" Anaya snarled at was now a head taller than she.

"Are those eyes of yours blind?" Mackeli argued. "Nothing is as it was. The spirits of the forest have turned their backs on you. You've lost your stealth, your keen senses, and your agility. You've turned green! I've gotten bigger and stronger. I can shoot a bow. You—" Mackeli was sputtering in his rage "—you don't belong in the forest any longer!"

Within the sharply painted lines, Anaya's eyes grew large. She made a fist and struck Mackeli smartly on the face. He fell on his back. Kith-Kanan realized things had gone too far.

"Stop it, both of you!" he barked. Anaya had advanced over Mackeli, ready to hit him again, but Kith-Kanan pushed her back. She stiffened, and for a moment he thought she would take a swing at him. After a moment, the anger left her and she stood aside.

The prince helped Mackeli to his feet. A smear, of blood showed under the boy's nose.

"I know we've been cooped up together too long, but there's no reason for fighting," Kith-Kanan said severely. "Mackeli is reaching his adulthood, Ny, you can't hold him back." He turned to the boy, who was dabbing at his bleeding nose with his sleeve. "And you have no right saying things like that to her. Not even the Forestmaster herself has said Anaya doesn't belong in the wood any more. So guard your tongue, Keli. If you wish to be a warrior, you must learn self-control."

Suddenly they heard a pair of hands clapping behind them and a voice exclaiming, "Well said."

Kith-Kanan, Anaya, and Mackeli turned abruptly. A score of men holding swords or crossbows flanked the hollow tree. Standing by the door, dressed in elegant but impractical crimson, was the half-human Voltorno as strong and healthy as ever, from the look of it.

"You!" hissed Anaya.

"Stand very still," cooed Voltorno. "I would hate to perforate you after such a touching performance. It really was worthy of the finest playhouse in Daltigoth." He nodded, and the humans fanned out carefully, surrounding the trio.

"So you survived your wound," Kith-Kanan said tersely. "What a pity."

"Yes," he said with calm assurance. "We had a first-rate healer on the ship. We returned to Ergoth, where I made known your interference in our operation. I was commissioned to return and deal with you."

Voltorno flipped back his hip-length cape, exposing a finely wrought sword hilt. He walked to Anaya, looking her up and down. "Bit of a savage, isn't she?" he said with a sneer to Kith-Kanan and turned to Mackeli. "Could this be our wild boy? Grown a bit, haven't you?" Mackeli kept his hands at his sides, but he was breathing hard. Voltorno shoved him lightly with one gloved hand. "You're the one who shot me," he said, still smiling pleasantly. "I owe you something for that." He pushed Mackeli again. Kith-Kanan gathered himself to spring on Voltorno. As if he were reading the prince's mind, Voltorno said to his men, "If either of them moves, kill them both."

The half-human grasped the gilded hilt of his sword and drew the slim blade from its scabbard. He held it by the blade; the pommel bobbed just inches from Mackelis chest. The boy stared at the sword hilt as he backed away. Mackeli's heels crunched in some of the late snow until his back bumped a tree at the edge of the clearing.

"Where will you go now?" asked Voltorno, his gray eyes gleaming.

Kith-Kanan freed his dagger from his belt when the bowmen turned their attention to the half-human. The elf prince realized that only one of them was behind him, about eight feet away. He nudged Anaya lightly with his elbow. She didn't look at him, but nudged him back.

Kith-Kanan turned and hurled the dagger at the bowman. The good elven iron punched through the man's leather jerkin. Without a word, he fell back, dead. Kith-Kanan broke left, Anaya right. The humans started yelling and opened fire. Those on the left shot at Anaya. Those on the right shot at Kith-Kanan. The only thing they hit was each other.

About half of the group went down, shot by their own comrades. Kith-Kanan dived for the muddy ground and rolled to the man he'd killed with his dagger. The human's crossbow had discharged on impact with the ground. Kith-Kanan pulled a quarrel from the dead man's quiver and struggled to cock the bow.

Anaya also threw herself on the ground, drawing her flint knife as she fell. She was a good ten yards from Mackeli and the archers, who were reloading their weapons. Mackeli reacted to the confusion by trying to snatch Voltorno's sword, but the half-human was too quick for him. In no time Voltorno had reversed his grip and thrust his weapon at Mackeli. The boy ducked, and Voltorno's blade stuck in a tree.

"Get them! Kill them!" Voltorno shouted.

Mackeli ran in and out of the trees along the clearing's edge. Quarrels flicked by him.

Across the clearing, Anaya crawled away in the wet turf, using her toes and elbows. As the archers concentrated their fire on Mackeli, she rose and threw herself at the back of the nearest man. Her moves were not as graceful as they once were, but her flint knife was as deadly as ever. One of the men, wounded by a quarrel, managed to sit up and aim his crossbow at Anaya's back. Luckily, Kith-Kanan picked him off before he could shoot.

Mackeli had plunged into the woods. Several of the surviving humans ran after him, but Voltorno called them back.

Anaya also made it to cover in the woods. She ran only a dozen yards or so before dropping to the ground. In seconds, she was buried in the leaves. Two humans tramped right past her.

Kith-Kanan tried to cock the bow a second time. From a sitting position though, it wasn't easy; the bow was too stiff. Before he could get the string over the lock nut, Voltorno arrived and presented him with thirty inches of Ergothian iron.

"Put it down," Voltorno ordered. When Kith-Kanan hesitated, the half-human raked his sword tip over the prince's jaw. Kith-Kanan felt the blood flow as he dropped the crossbow.

"Your friends have reverted to type," said Voltorno with contempt. "They've run off and left you."

"Good," Kith-Kanan replied. "At least they will be safe."

"Perhaps. You, my friend, are anything but safe."

The eight surviving humans crowded around. Voltorno gave them a nod, and they dragged Kith-Kanan to his feet, punching and kicking him. They brought him to the far side of the clearing where they'd first come in and where they'd dropped their baggage. Voltorno produced a set of arm and leg shackles, then chained Kith-Kanan hand and foot.

*　*　*　*　*

Anaya burrowed away from the clearing, worming through the leaves like a snake. In times past, she could have done so without disturbing a single leaf on the surface. Now, to her ears, she sounded like a herd of humans. Fortunately Voltorno and his men were busy on the other side of the clearing.

When she was quite far away, she parted the leaves with her hands and crawled out. The ground was cold and wet, and Anaya shivered.

She wanted to return at once and free Kith-Kanan, but she knew she'd never trick the humans again. Not alone. She would have to wait until it was dark.

A twig snapped behind her, on her right. She kicked the leaves off her legs and faced the sound. Hugging a tree five yards away was Mackeli.

"You're noisy," she criticized.

"You're deaf. I stepped on four other twigs before that last one," he said coolly.

They met each other halfway. The hostility of the morning was gone, and they embraced.

"I've never seen you run like that," she avowed.

"I surprised myself," admitted Mackeli. "Being more grown up does appear to have advantages." He looked clown at his sister. "I'm sorry for what I said," he added earnestly

"You only said what I've thought a thousand times," she confessed. "Now we have to think of Kith. We can go in after dark and take him."

Mackeli took her by the shoulders and dropped to the ground, pulling her down beside him. "Shh! Not so loud, Ny. We've got to be smart about this. A year ago, we could have crept in and freed Kith, but now we're too slow and loud. We have to think better."

She scowled. "I don't have to think to know that I will kill that Voltorno," she insisted.

"I know, but he's dangerous. He used magic when he fought Kith before, and he's very clever and very cruel."

"All right then, what should we do?"

Mackeli glanced quickly around. "Here's what I think. . . ."

* * * * *

When he'd finished ransacking the tree-home, Voltorno supervised his men in setting up traps around the clearing. Where the footpath had been worn in the grass, they strewed caltrops—small, spiky stars designed to stop charging horses. Against the hide leggings Anaya and Mackeli wore, they would be deadly.

In the grass around the tree, they set saw-toothed, spring-loaded traps, such as humans sometimes used to catch wolves. String triggers were strung, a pull on which would send a crossbow quarrel whizzing. Even by the last of the afternoon light the traps were hard to see. Kith-Kanan shuddered as he watched these diabolical preparations and prayed fervently that Anaya's nose for metal had not deserted her completely.

Night fell, and the cold returned strongly enough to remind the raiders that summer wasn't around the next sunrise. Kith-Kanan shivered in the chill while he watched Voltorno's men wrap themselves in Anaya's warm fur.

Voltorno brought a tin plate of stew and sat on a log in front of the prince. "I was a bit surprised to find you still here," the half-human said. He drank beer from a tin cup. In spite of his thirst, Kith-Kanan's nose wrinkled in disgust; it was a drink no true elf would touch. "When I returned to Daltigoth, I made inquiries about you. A Silvanesti, living in the forest like a painted savage. I heard a very strange tale in the halls of the imperial palace."

"I don't believe it," said Kith-Kanan, staring at the fire built some distance in front of the hollow oak. "I don't believe the humans would allow you into the imperial palace. Even human royalty knows better than to let street garbage into their homes."

His face contorted in anger, Voltorno flipped a spoonful of hot stew into Kith-Kanan's already much-abused face. The elf prince gasped and, despite his bound hands, managed to rub the scalding liquid onto the shoulder of his tunic.

"Don't interrupt," said Voltorno nastily. "As I was saying, I heard a strange tale. It seems that a prince of the Silvanesti, the brother of the current heir to the throne, left the city under a cloud. He bared a weapon in the hallowed Tower of the Stars or some nonsense like that." Voltorno laughed. "It seems the prince's father married the son's sweetheart to his brother," he added.

"Sounds like a very sad story," Kith-Kanan said, betraying as little emotion as he could. His shoulders ached from being forced to sit hunched over. He shifted his feet a bit, making the chains clatter as he did.

"It has the quality of an epic about it," Voltorno agreed, stirring his stew. "And I thought to myself: what a prize that son would make. Imagine the ransom the elf prince's family would pay!"

Kith-Kanan shook his head. "You are gravely mistaken if you think you can pass me off as a prince," he said. "I am Silvanesti, yes; a warrior whose nagging wife drove him into the forest for peace and quiet."

Voltorno laughed heartily. "Oh, yes? It's no use, my royal friend," he said. "I've seen portraits of the royal house of Silvanesti. You are this errant son."

A shrill shriek pierced the night air. The humans reached for their arms, and Voltorno went quickly to steady his men. "Keep your eyes open," he cautioned them, "this could be a trick to divert us."

A flaming brand hurtled through the air, tumbling end over end and trailing sparks and embers. It hit the grass twenty feet from the tree. It tripped a trigger string, and a crossbow fired with a dull thud.

"Aahwoo!" came a wailing cry from the dark trees. The humans began to mutter among themselves.

A second flaming brand flew into the clearing, from the opposite side of the forest. Then a third, some yards from the second. And a fourth, some yards from that.

"They're all around us!" one man cried.

"Quiet!" said Voltorno.

Carefully avoiding the wicked caltrops, he strode out on the central path. The men clustered together near him in a fighting circle facing outward from their campfire. From his staked position, Kith-Kanan smiled grimly.

A figure appeared at the end of the path, carrying a burning branch. Voltorno drew his sword. The figure stopped where the caltrops began, some four yards from the half-human. The torch Voltorno held lit Anaya's face. Her face and hands were painted black. A single red stripe ran vertically from her forehead, along her nose, over her chin, and to the base of her neck.

Voltorno turned to his men. "You see? It's just the girl," he crowed. He faced Anaya. "Where's the boy? Hiding?" he asked with a sneer.

"You have come into the wildwood once too often," Anaya intoned. "None of you will leave it alive."

"Someone shoot her," Voltorno said in a bored tone, but the humans were mesmerized. None of them moved. Taking a slow step toward her, the commander declared, "It's you who will die, girl."

"Then enter the forest and find me," she said. "You have bows and swords and iron blades. All I have is a knife of flint."

"Yes, yes, very boring. You'd like us to flounder around in the woods at night, wouldn't you?" remarked Voltorno, moving another step closer to her.

"It's too late," she warned. "One by one, you shall all die." With that, Anaya slipped away into the night.

"Such melodrama," grumbled the half-human, returning to the fire. "I guess one can't expect more from a pair of savages."

"Why didn't you use your great magic, Voltorno?" Kith-Kanan asked sarcastically.

Quite earnestly, one of the terrified humans began to explain. "Our master must be very close to the one he—" This helpful information was abruptly cut off as Voltorno backhanded the speaker. The human fell back, his face bleeding.

Now Kith-Kanan understood. Voltorno's repertoire of magic was probably quite limited. Perhaps he had only the spell of befuddlement he had used in his duel with Kith-Kanan. And he had to be very close to the one he wished to enchant, which was obviously why he had been sidling closer to Anaya.

The next morning Kith-Kanan awoke stiff and groggy. The chill had penetrated his bones, and his chains didn't allow him to rest comfortably. He was trying to stretch the ache from his legs when a shriek of pure horror rang through the clearing. Kith-Kanan jerked toward the sound.

One of the human guards was staring down at the bedroll of one of his comrades. His face was bone-white and his mouth slack. He would have given vent to another scream, but Voltorno arrived at his side and shoved him away.

Voltorno's face registered shock, too, as he looked down at the bedroll. The human who had screamed now babbled, "Master! They cut Gernian's throat! How?"

The half-human rounded on the frantic raider and commanded him to be silent. All the humans now ringed their dead companion. Each of them asked themselves the same questions: How had Anaya and Mackeli killed the man without being seen by the watch? How had they gotten through the traps? Voltorno was rattled, and the humans were close to panic.

Sithas Returns

19

Morning, and the humans stirred half-heartedly through the ambassador's large tent. Sithas heard them, their voices hoarse from sleep, talking in the cloth-walled corridor outside his room. He rose and shook the wrinkles from his clothes.

Ulvissen greeted the prince as he entered the tent's main salon. The seneschal offered him breakfast, but Sithas took only a single apple from a bowl of fruit and forsook the rest. Humans had the habit of eating abysmally heavy meals, he knew, which probably accounted for their thick physiques.

It had stopped raining during the night, though now the wind blew steadily from the south, tearing the solid ceiling of gray clouds into ragged, fluffy pieces. From their vantage point on the hill overlooking the river, it seemed as if the broken clouds were scudding along at eye level. Flashes of early morning sun illuminated the scene as the clouds passed before it.

"Strange weather," Ulvissen remarked as Sithas looked out over the scene.

"We seldom get snow or ice here, but these storms blow in from the southern ocean many times each winter," explained the Silvanesti prince.

The river was alive with small craft taking advantage of the lull. Ulvissen turned up the flaps of his thick, woolen cape as he asked Sithas if river traffic was usually interrupted for the duration of the storm.

"Oh, no. The fishers and barge runners are accustomed to

bad weather. Only the very worst winds will keep them tied to the dock."

Sithas's escort and the ambassador's guards lined up as Ulwen and Teralind came out. The old ambassador looked even worse by daylight. His skin was sallow, with blue veins boldly visible. He moved so little that Sithas might have taken him for a corpse, were it not that his eyes blinked now and then.

The gang of servants fell to and struck the tent. While the windy air resounded with mallet strikes and the thud of falling canvas, Sithas went to the barge. The giant turtle had drawn in his head and legs during the night, and he was still asleep. Sithas rapped on the hull of the barge.

"Ferry master!" he called. "Are you there?"

The elderly elf's head popped out over the bulwark. "Indeed I am, Highness!" He hopped up on the bulwark with a spryness that belied his advanced age. A long pry bar rested on the boatman's shoulder, and he twirled it slightly as he went to where the chains hooking the turtle to the barge were looped over enormous iron hooks, spiked to the bow of the barge. Positioning the flat end of the pry bar under the chain links, he shouted, "Clear away all!"

The soldiers of both races perked up. Sithas, who was walking back to stand with Ulvissen, halted and spun around. The ferry master leaned on his bar, and the first chain slipped off its hook. He shouted to clear the way again and popped the other chain free. The elf prince saw that the humans were watching with rapt interest. He hoped the ferry master knew what he was doing.

The giant shackles fell against the shell of the turtle. This woke the beast, for the front hinge of its carapace, that part that closed in the giant animal's head, opened. The huge green head slowly emerged.

The ferry master raised his trumpet to his lips and sounded a single note. The turtle's legs came out, and he stood up. The rear of the turtle's shell bumped the barge, and the craft began to move.

"Look sharp!" sang out the ferry master.

With rapidly increasing speed, the fifty-foot barge slid down the muddy hill. It already had a natural groove to follow the one it had made coming up the hill the night before. Churning a wave of mud before it, the barge accelerated down the slope. The ferry master played a cavalry charge on his horn.

"Madness!" exclaimed Teralind. "He'll smash himself to bits."

Sithas glanced over his shoulder and saw that the human woman had come forward, leaving her chair-bound husband with Ulvissen. As politeness dictated, he assuaged her fears as best he could. "It is a common thing. Do not fear, lady, the craft is stoutly built." He prayed to Matheri that this was indeed so.

The flat stern of the barge hit the water, throwing up a tremendous wave. Then the barge slid completely off the bank into the river, leaving a cloud of mud in the water around it.

The turtle swung around ponderously. The humans, who had been dismantling the tent, scattered as the great beast swung toward them. With utmost placidity the giant turned and walked down the hill. The incline and slippery mud bothered him not at all. As the ferry master commanded him with trumpet calls, the turtle slid quietly into the river and allowed the chains to be re-attached to the barge.

In another hour, the ambassador's party was ready to board. By the time they moved down a marble-paved path to the water's edge, the wind had slowed and died out completely.

The captain of the elven soldiers shook his head. "The lull's ending," he noted, resignation coloring his comment.

"More rain?" asked Ulvissen.

"And more wind," replied Sithas.

The ambassador's party made it to the island without incident. Waiting for them were three large sedan chairs and two horse-drawn wagons. Spray broke over the dock, soaking the poor porters who stood by the sedan chairs. With scant attention to protocol, the ambassador was bundled into one chair, Lady Teralind into another, and Sithas into the third. The wagons were for the baggage. Everyone else had to walk.

Sithas was surprised when he entered his private rooms in the palace. The window shutters were drawn against the rain, and waiting for him in the dim, unlit room was Hermathya.

"So you're home," she said with irritation. "Was it worth it?"

Her tone was arch, close to anger. Though he had no reason, Sithas felt his own emotions hardening, a fact that surprised him.

"It had to be done," he said smoothly. "As it is, things turned out rather well. We showed the humans of what stuff elves are made."

She trembled and strode past the prince to the shuttered window. Rain was seeping through the slats, pooling on the cool marble floor.

"And what are you made of?" she demanded, temper flaring.

"What do you mean? What's the matter?"

"You risked your life for etiquette! Did you give any thought to me? What would happen to me if you had been killed?"

Sithas sighed and sat in a chair made of intertwined maple saplings. "Is that what's bothering you? It's unworthy of you, Thya. After all, I was in no real danger."

"Don't be so damned logical! You've no idea what I meant." Hermathya turned to the speaker's heir. Through clenched teeth, she said, "I've passed my first fertile time. It's gone, and we missed it."

Sithas finally understood. Even though an elven couple might live as husband and wife a thousand years, they might only be fertile three or four times in their entire lives. These times were very irregular; even the healing clerics of Quenesti Pah couldn't predict a fertile time more than a day or two in advance.

"Why didn't you tell me sooner?" Sithas asked, his voice softening.

"You weren't here. You were sleeping by yourself."

"Am I so unapproachable?"

She fingered the edge of her embroidered collar "Yes, you are."

"You have no problem getting what you want from others," Sithas went on heedlessly. "You collect gifts and compliments as a child picks flowers in a field. Why can't you speak to me? I am your husband."

"You are the elf I married," she corrected, "not the elf I loved."

Sithas stood quickly. "I've heard enough. In the future you—"

She moved toward him. "Will you listen to me for once? If you insist on risking your life on foolish errands, then you must give me a child. Our marriage can mean something then. An heir needs an heir. You want a son; I need a child."

The prince folded his arms, annoyed at her pleading tone. That emotion confused Sithas somewhat. Why did her pleading irritate him? "Perhaps it is the wisdom of the gods that this happened," he said. "It is not a good time to start a family."

"How can you say that?" she asked.

"It is Matheri's own truth. My life is not my own. I have to live for the nation. With all this trouble in the West, I may even have to take up arm for the speaker's cause."

Hermathya laughed bitterly. "You, a warrior? You have the wrong twin in mind. Kith-Kanan is the warrior. You are a priest."

Coldly, Sithas told her, "Kith-Kanan is not here."

"I wish to Astarin he was! He would not have left me last night!" she said harshly.

"Enough!" Sithas went to the door. With unmatched politeness, he said, "Lady, I am truly sorry to have missed the time, but it is done and no peace will come from dwelling on lost chances." He went out. Behind him, Hermathya dissolved in furious tears.

Sithas descended the steps, his face set hard as granite. Servants and courtiers parted for him as he went. All bowed, as was the custom, but none dared speak. Two fine chairs were set up in the audience hall of the Tower of the Stars. One, short-legged and plush, was for Ehmbarth, ambassador from Thorbardin. The second was a tall piece of furniture, its elegantly wrought curves gilded. Here sat Teralind. Her husband, the titular ambassador, sat in his special chair beside her. Praetor Ulwen did not speak and after a while it was easy to forget he was even present.

Sithel sat on his throne, of course, and Sithas stood by his left hand. The rest of the floor was taken up by courtiers and servants. Ulvissen, never far from Teralind and the ambassador, hovered behind the lady's golden chair, listening much and speaking little.

"The territory in question," Sithel was saying, "is bordered on the south by the bend of the Kharolis River, on the west by the city of Xak Tsaroth, on the east by the Khalkist Mountains, and on the north by the region where the Vingaard River is born on the great plain. In the time of my father, this region was divided into three areas. The northernmost was named Vingaardin, the central was called Kagonesti, and the southernmost was Tsarothelm."

Dunbarth waved a beringed hand. "Your Highness's knowledge of geography is considerable," he noted with exaggerated politeness, "but what is the point in your lecture?"

"As I was about to say, in the time of my father, Silvanos, these three provinces were unclaimed by any of our nations. They were ruled, and ruled poorly, by local lords who extorted taxes from the common folk and who warred constantly with each other."

"Such is not the case today," Teralind interjected.

"There is considerable violence in this area still," Sithel replied, "as evidenced by the massacre of fifty of my guard by a large force of mounted men."

Silence ensued. The elven scribes, who had been taking down every word spoken, held their styluses poised over their pages. Dunbarth looked at Teralind curiously.

"You do not object, lady, to the speaker's description of the marauders as 'men'?" he asked pointedly, leaning forward on one elbow.

She shrugged her green velvet clad shoulders, and Ulvissen sidled closer to the back of her chair. "The emperor does not rule the entire race of men," she allowed. Sithas could almost hear the unspoken *yet* at the end of Teralind's statement. "Any more than the king of Thorbardin rules all dwarves. I don't know who these bandits are, but if they are men, they are not men of Ergoth."

"Certainly not," Sithel continued smoothly. "You will not deny, though, that the emperor has done nothing to discourage the large number of human settlers who cross the plain and descend the rivers by boat and raft. They are displacing both the Kagonesti and those Silvanesti who have moved west to live. It must stop."

"There is not room enough in Ergoth for everyone to live and work, nor is there land enough to grow the food needed to feed them all," countered Teralind. "Why is it strange that human settlers should leave the boundaries of the empire and wander east into the region claimed by the Silvanesti, when that region is so sparsely settled?"

"None have tried to settle in Thorbardin," said Dunbarth unhelpfully.

Prince Sithas gestured to a scribe, who brought him a parchment scroll filled with tiny, precise writing. Two large wax seals were affixed to the bottom of the paper. "This is our copy of the agreement made between Speaker Sithel and Emperor Ackal Ergot, dated nearly three hundred years ago. It specifically forbids Ergoth from colonizing Vingaardin without the approval of the Speaker of the Stars."

"Many of the works done by him late in his life were faulty," Teralind commented tactlessly. Ulvissen, who'd been stroking his auburn beard in thought, leaned down and whispered in her ear. She nodded and continued, "No less than six of Ackal Ergot's treaties have been repudiated over the years since his death. The treaty Prince Sithas holds is therefore of doubtful standing." At her side, the aged praetor stirred vaguely. Teralind paid no attention.

Dunbarth slid forward and dropped out of his chair. He tugged his tunic down smoothly over his barrel chest and said, "As I recall, it was Ackal Ergot's plan to invade and conquer Sancrist, but he feared the elven nation would retaliate against his eastern border. For that reason he struck a deal with Speaker Sithel."

The prince had returned the parchment to the scribe. Curious, he asked, "And why did the invasion of Sancrist not take place?"

Dunbarth laughed merrily. "The Ergothian generals pointed out how difficult it would be to rule an island full of gnomes. The drain on the empire's treasury would have been enormous!" Some scattered laughter drifted through the hall. Sithel rapped on the floor with his five-foot-long regal staff, and the snickering died.

"I believe what you say, Lady Teralind," Sithel noted blandly. "His Majesty Ackal Ergot must have been distracted to imagine he could conquer and rule the gnomes, though he did not really seem so when I met him." Teralind flushed slightly at this reminder of the speaker's great life span. "But that doesn't change the fact that human settlers and human bandits have been taking life and land away from my subjects."

"If I may say something," Dunbarth interrupted, walking around the side of his chair. "Many people come to Thorbardin to buy our metals, and we have heard a great deal about the troubles on the Plain. I think it is unfair to say, Your Highness, that it is simply a matter of humans pushing elves out. I understand that many of the bandits are elves themselves, of the Kagonesti race." He rubbed the broad toe of his left boot against the trousers of his right leg to remove a smudge on the brilliant shine. "And some of the bandits are half-elves."

Although this statement was of no surprise to Sithel or Sithas, it was a revelation that set the crowd of servants and retainers to buzzing. Sithas turned his back on the hall and spoke to his father in guarded tones. "What is the matter with that fellow? He acts as if he were the advocate for Ergoth!" Sithas muttered.

"Don't blame Dunbarth. He knows his country will gain the advantage if we and the humans cannot agree. He's thrown out this rubbish about half-humans to muddy the water. It means nothing," Sithel commented wisely.

The prince stood aside, and his father rapped for silence once more.

"Let us not confuse matters with talk of bandits and half-breeds," Sithel said genially. "There really is only one question who rules these three provinces?"

"Who rules them in fact, or rules them by a signet pressed to a dollop of molten wax?" Teralind said testily.

"We must have law, lady, or we shall be nothing but bandits ourselves," counseled Dunbarth. He smiled behind his curled silver beard. "Well-dressed, rich bandits, but bandits nevertheless." More laughter. This time Sithel let the laughter build, for it diffused the tension in the tower.

"There is no doubt the Speaker of the Stars bears an ancient claim to the land," Dunbarth continued, "or that Ergoth has certain rights where so many of its subjects are concerned."

Sithas lifted his eyebrows at this statement. "Subjects?" he asked quickly. "Are the humans living in the three provinces subjects, therefore, of the emperor of Ergoth?"

"Well, of course," conceded Teralind. Ulvissen leaned forward to speak to her, but she waved him away. The lady looked perplexed as she realized belatedly that she had contradicted her earlier statement that the bandits were not Ergothians. "What I mean to say is—"

Ulvissen tapped urgently on her shoulder. Teralind turned and snapped, "Stand back, sir! Do not interrupt me!" The seneschal instantly retreated a pace and stood rigidly at attention.

Sithas exchanged a glance with his father, and murmurs arose in the hall. Teralind's eyes darted around, for she knew she'd made a dangerous admission. She tried to salvage the situation by saying, "There is not a man, woman, or human child in the whole realm of Ansalon who does not owe allegiance to His Imperial Majesty."

Sithel did not try to speak until the murmuring had subsided. In precise, measured tones, he finally said, "Is it your intention to annex our lands?"

Teralind pushed herself back in her chair and frowned. Beside her, the frail form of Proctor Ulwen moved. He leaned forward slightly and began to shake. Tremors racked his frail body, and Ulvissen moved swiftly to his side. The seneschal snapped his fingers at the human contingent of servants loitering by the grand doors.

"Highness, noble ambassadors, I beg your pardon, but the praetor is seized with an attack," he announced in an anxious voice. "He must withdraw."

Dunbarth spread his hands graciously. Sithel stood. "You have our leave to withdraw," the speaker said. "Shall I send one of our healers to the praetor's rooms?"

Teralind's head lifted regally. "We have a doctor of our own, thank you, noble speaker."

The porters took hold of the rails attached to Ulwen's chair and hoisted him up. The Ergothian delegation filed out behind him. When they were gone, Dunbarth bowed and led his dwarves out. Sithel dismissed his retainers and was finally alone with his son in the tower.

"Diplomacy is so tiring," the speaker said wearily. He stood and laid his silver scepter across the throne. "Give me your arm, Sith. I believe I need to rest for a while."

* * * * *

Tamanier Ambrodel walked beside Lady Nirakina through the palace. They had just come from the guild hall of the stone workers, where Lady Nirakina had viewed the plans for the new Market. It was an orderly, beautifully designed place, but its site and purpose depressed her. "It's simply wrong," she told Tamanier. "We are the firstborn race of the world and favored by the gods. As such, it is only right we share our grace with other people, not look upon them as lesser beings."

Tamanier nodded. "I heartily agree, Lady. When I lived in the wilderness, I saw many kinds of people—Silvanesti, Kagonesti, humans, dwarves, gnomes, kender—and no one lived better than his neighbor for any reason but his own hard work. The land doesn't care if it's plowed by human or elf. The rain falls the same on every farm."

They arrived at the door of Nirakina's private rooms. Before he left, Tamanier informed her, "I went to see Miritelisina, as you requested."

"Is she well?" she asked eagerly. "A priestess of such age and wisdom should not be held in a common dungeon."

"She is well," Tamanier said, "though unrepentant. She still does not admit to her crime."

"I do not believe she committed a crime," Nirakina said with fervor. "Miritelisina was moved by compassion. She only sought to warn the poor refugees of the plan to move them. I'm certain she had no idea they'd riot as they did."

Tamanier bowed. "I bear the holy lady no ill will. I tell you, though, that she will not repent—even to gain her freedom. Miritelisina believes that by remaining in prison, she will inspire others who want to help the refugees."

Nirakina gave the young courtier's arm a squeeze. "And what do you think, Tam? Whose cause do you favor?"

"Do you really have to ask? A short time ago, I was one of the poor wretches—homeless, penniless, despised. They deserve the speaker's protection."

"We'll have to see what we can do to win it," Nirakina replied warmly.

She went into her rooms, and Tamanier walked away, his step light. With the speaker's wife fighting for them, the homeless settlers would soon feel the grace of Sithel's favor. And who knew, perhaps Miritelisina would be freed to resume her good works for the poor.

He left the central tower of the palace and strolled the empty corridor balcony of the east wing.

Suddenly he heard voices. Foreign voices. He'd lived among humans long enough to know their speech.

"—play at this silly game?" complained a woman's voice, tight with emotion.

"As long as necessary. It's the emperor's will," a man's strong voice answered.

"The things I do for my father! I hope he appreciates it!"

"He's paying off your gambling debts, isn't he?" said the man dryly.

Tamanier knew he shouldn't eavesdrop, but he was intrigued. He stood very still. Since the humans were in the corridor below him, their voices carried easily to him up the central atrium.

"I don't trust that Dunbarth," asserted the woman. "He switches sides like a click beetle."

"He has no side but his own. Right now Thorbardin isn't ready for war, so he hopes to play us off against the elves. He's clever, but I see what he's doing."

"He annoys me. So does Prince Sithas. How he stares! They say elves have second sight." The woman's voice rose. "You don't think he's reading my mind, do you?"

"Calm yourself," said the man. "I don't think he can. But if it troubles you, I'll speak to our friend about it."

Footsteps echoed on the balcony across the atrium from where Tamanier stood. He tensed, ready to be discovered. The voices below ceased their furtive talk.

Out of the afternoon shadows on the far side of the balcony Tamanier spied the young priest of the Blue Phoenix, Kamin Oluvai. Tamanier was surprised; why was the priest here? Kamin didn't see him, however, so Tamanier withdrew from the balcony rail. The humans he'd heard were certainly Lady Teralind and Ulvissen, but what did their strange conversation mean?

Court intrigue was foreign to him. Who was Teralind really? What was she concealing? Who was the "friend" Ulvissen referred to? Could it be the traitor of which Speaker Sithel had spoken that night at dinner?

Tamanier hurried away. He had to tell someone, and Sithas's room was nearby. The courtier was already feeling slightly relieved; certainly the prince would know what to do.

Day of Metamorphosis

20

The humans were breaking camp and getting ready to return to their ship. They worked with haste, and it was clear to Kith-Kanan that they wanted nothing more than to be away from such an accursed place. While they worked, Voltorno went to the elf prince. He had his men pry the stake out of the ground, then he grabbed Kith-Kanan's shackles and dragged him to the edge of the clearing.

"You out there! Woman and boy! I have your friend here! If any more of my men are so much as scratched, I'll make your royal friend suffer for it. I'll give him something more than a scar on his cheek. How do you think he'd look without an arm, a hand, or a leg? Do you hear me?"

The only answer was the soft sighing of wind in the still bare branches.

"We're ready to go, master," said one of the humans.

"Then get moving, dolt." Voltorno was losing his air of confidence. Despite his aching limbs and the stinging sword cut on his cheek, Kith-Kanan was pleased. The angrier Voltorno got, the greater advantage Anaya and Mackeli would have.

The raiders marched down the path single file, with Kith-Kanan leading. Voltorno gave the prince over to one of his men and moved out ahead as the band left the path and entered the woods.

They snaked silently through the forest. In spite of their master's assurances, the men adopted a crouching walk, swinging their loaded bows slowly from side to side. Their fear was palpable, like a foul odor.

As they reached the old, deep forest, the trees got larger and farther apart. The raiders moved more quickly, using the trail they'd made on their way to the clearing. Occasionally Voltorno scanned the high tree branches, alert to any ambush from above. This added greatly to the alarm of his men. They started glancing up frequently, stumbling and bumping into each other.

Disgusted, Voltorno turned on them. "You make more noise than a pen of squealing pigs!" he hissed.

"And you don't breathe correctly either," Kith-Kanan put in.

Voltorno gave him a venomous glance and turned to resume the march. Just then, a loud cracking sound filled the air. The men stood, paralyzed, trying to find the source of the noise. A tree branch broke off a nearby oak and dropped to the ground ahead. The men started laughing with relief.

Behind them, a figure popped up out of the leaves and aimed a stolen crossbow at the back of the last man in line. The quarrel loosed, the dark figure slipped silently back into the bed of leaves. The wounded man made a gurgling sound, staggered forward a few steps, and collapsed.

"It's Favius! He's been shot!"

"Mind your front! Look for your target before you shoot!" Voltorno barked. The six men remaining formed a ring with Kith-Kanan in the center. Voltorno walked slowly around the ring, staring hard at the empty woods. There was nothing and no one to be seen.

He halted when he noticed one of his men holding an empty bow. "Meldren," he said glacially, "why is your bow not loaded?"

The man named Meldren looked at his weapon in surprise. "I must have triggered it off," he muttered.

"Yes, into Favius's back!"

"No, master! Favius was behind me!"

"Don't lie to me!" Fiercely Voltorno struck the man with the flat of his sword. Meldren dropped his crossbow and fell to the ground. None of the other men offered to help him or supported his story.

Voltorno picked up the man's crossbow and handed it to another of his company. "Meldren will walk in the rear," he ordered. "With any luck, the witch will kill him next."

The raiders relieved the dead man of his weapons and gear and moved on. The wretched Meldren, with only a short sword for defense, brought up the rear.

The trail they followed led them down a draw, between a pair of giant oaks. Voltorno went down on one knee and held up his hand to halt the group. He studied the ground and then looked ahead.

'This has the look of a trap," he said with a wise air. "We'll not go through the draw. Four of you men go along the right edge. The rest follow me on the left."

The draw was a V-shaped ditch, twenty feet wide and eight feet deep at its lowest point. Four men crept along the right rim of the gully while Voltorno, Kith-Kanan, and two others walked along the left. As the half-human circled around, he clucked his tongue triumphantly.

"See?" he said. Leaning against an oak on the left was a thick log, poised to roll down into the draw if anyone disturbed the web of vines attached to it. This web extended down into the draw and covered the ground there. The men on the right came around their oak. Voltorno waved to them. The lead man waved back—and the ground beneath him gave way.

The "ground" they'd been standing on was nothing but a large log, covered loosely with dirt and leaves. Held in place by slender windfall limbs, the log collapsed under the men's weight. With shouts and cries for help, the four tumbled into the gully.

"No!" Voltorno shouted.

The men received only bruises and cuts from falling the eight feet into the ravine, but they rolled onto the mat of vines that was the trigger for the six-foot-thick log poised on the left bank. The vines snapped taut, the log rolled down, and the men were crushed beneath it. Voltorno, Kith-Kanan, and the remaining two raiders could only stand by and watch as this occurred.

Suddenly there was a whirring sound and a thump. One of the two humans dropped, a crossbow quarrel in his back. The last human gave a shriek. He flung down his weapon and ran off into the woods, screaming without letup. Voltorno shouted for him to come back, but the hysterical raider disappeared into the trees.

"It appears you're on your own, Voltorno," Kith-Kanan said triumphantly.

The half-human seized the prince and held him in front of his body like a shield. "I'll kill him, witch!" he screamed into the trees. He turned from side to side, searching madly for Anaya or Mackeli. "I swear I will kill him!"

"You won't live that long," a voice uttered behind him.

In shock, the half-human whirled. Anaya, still painted sooty black, stood nonchalantly before him, just out of sword's reach. Mackeli was behind her, his bow poised. Taking advantage of his captor's obvious shock at seeing these two foes so close by, Kith-Kanan wrenched himself from Voltorno's grasp and jumped away from him.

"Shoot her!" Voltorno cried dazedly. "Shoot her, men!"

Remembering belatedly that he had no one left to command, the half-human lunged at Anaya. Mackeli started to react, but the keeper shouted, "No, he's mine!"

Despite his wife's shouted claim, Kith-Kanan slogged forward under the burden of his chains. The prince was certain that Anaya didn't have a chance against a fine duelist like Voltorno. Her agility was drastically reduced, and the only weapon she carried was her flint knife.

The half-human thrust at her twice, then a third time. She dodged, adequately but without her old preternatural grace. He cut and slashed the air, and as Anaya scampered aside, the Ergothian blade bit into a tree. She ducked under Voltorno's reach and jabbed at his stomach. The half-human brought the sword's hilt down on her head. With a grunt of pain, Anaya sprawled on her face.

"Shoot!" Kith-Kanan cried. As Mackeli's finger closed on the trigger bar, Anaya rolled away from Voltorno's killing strike and repeated her warning to her friends.

"Only I may shed his blood!" she declared.

Voltorno laughed in response, but it was a laugh shrill with desperation.

Anaya got to her feet clumsily and stumbled in the thick leaves and fallen branches. As best she could, she jerked back, out of the way of Voltorno's sweeping slash, but she could not avoid the straight thrust that followed. Mackeli's green eyes widened in shock and he uttered a strangled cry as the blade pierced Anaya's brown deerskin tunic.

Though he saw what happened, Kith-Kanan was more shocked by what he heard—a roaring In his ears. For a moment, he didn't know what he was hearing. Then he realized that the sound was Anaya's pulse. It hammered at the prince like thunder, and he felt as if he would collapse from the pain of it. Time seemed to slow for Kith-Kanan as he watched Anaya. His beloved's face showed no pain, only an unshakable determination.

Voltorno's lips widened in a smile. Though he would surely die himself, at least he'd killed the witch. That smile froze as Anaya grasped the sword that pierced her stomach and rammed it farther in. His fingers still locked around the handle, the half-human was jerked toward her. His puzzlement turned to horror as Anaya brought up her free hand and drove her flint knife into his heart.

Valtorno collapsed. So tightly did he grip the sword that, when he fell backward, he pulled it from Anaya's body. He was dead before he hit the ground.

Kith-Kanan struggled to Anaya's side and caught her as she

collapsed. "Anaya," the prince said desperately. The front of her tunic was covered in blood. "Anaya, please . . ."

"Take me home," she said and fainted.

Mackeli found the key to Kith-Kanan's shackles in Voltorno's belt pouch. Freed of his bonds, the prince lifted Anaya in his arms. Mackeli offered to help.

"No, I have her," Kith-Kanan said brokenly. "She weighs nothing."

He strode away from the gully, past the places where Voltorno's men had died. Inside, Kith-Kanan concentrated on the sound and sensation of Anaya's heartbeat. It was there. Slow, labored, but it was there. He walked faster. At home there would be medicines. Mackeli knew things. He knew about roots and poultices. At the hollow tree there would be medicines.

"You have to live, " he told Anaya, staring straight ahead. "By Astarin, you have to live! We've not had enough time together!"

The sun flickered through the leafless trees as they hurried toward the clearing. By now Kith-Kanan was almost running. Anaya was strong, he repeated over and over in his mind. Mackeli would be able to save her.

In the clearing, Arcuballis reared up on its hind legs and spread its wings in greeting. The beast had returned from hunting to find everyone gone. Kith-Kanan paid it no heed as he rushed toward Anaya's home—their home.

The prince ran to the hollow tree and laid Anaya on a silver wolf pelt that Mackeli had dragged outside. Her eyes were closed and her skin was ice cold. Kith-Kanan felt for a pulse. There was none.

"Do something!" he screamed at Mackeli. The boy stared at Anaya, his mouth open. Kith-Kanan grabbed the front of his tunic. "Do something, I said!"

"I don't know anything!"

"You know about roots and herbs!" he begged.

"Ny is dead, Kith. I cannot call her back to life. I wish I could, but I can't!"

When the prince saw the tears in Mackeli's eyes, he knew that the boy spoke the truth. Kith-Kanan let go of Mackeli's tunic and rocked back on his heels, staring down at the still form of Anaya. Anaya.

Rage and anguish boiled up inside the prince. His sword lay on the ground by the tree, where Voltorno had found and discarded it. Kith-Kanan picked up the blade and stared at it. The half-human had murdered his wife, and he had done nothing. He'd let Voltorno murder his wife and child-to-be.

Kith-Kanan screamed—a horrible, deep, wrenching cry—then slammed the flat of the blade against the oak tree. The cold iron snapped five inches above the hilt. In anger he threw the sword hilt as far as he could.

*　*　*　*　*

Night. Mackeli and Kith-Kanan sat inside the tree, not moving, not talking. They had covered Anaya with her favorite blanket, one made from the pelts of a dozen rabbits. Now they sat in darkness. The broken blade of his sword lay across Kith-Kanan's lap.

He was cursed. He felt it in his heart. Love always eluded him. First Hermathya had been taken away. So be it. He had found a better life and a better wife than Hermathya would ever have been. His life had just begun again. And now it had ended. Anaya was dead. Their unborn child was dead. He was cursed.

A gust of wind blew in the open door, sweeping leaves and dust in tiny whirlwinds around Mackeli's ankles. He sat with his head on his knees, staring blankly at the floor. The shriveled brown oak leaves were lifted from the ground and spun around. He followed their dancing path toward the doorway, and his eyes widened.

The green glow that filled the open entrance to the hollow tree transfixed Mackeli. It washed his face and silver hair.

"Kith," he murmured. "Look."

"What is it?" the prince asked tiredly. He looked toward the doorway, and a frown creased his forehead. Then, throwing the mantle off his shoulders, he got up. With a hand on the door edge, Kith-Kanan looked outside. The soft mound that was Anaya beneath her blanket was the source of the strange green light. The Silvanesti prince stepped outside. Mackeli followed.

The light was cool as Kith-Kanan knelt by Anaya's body and slowly pulled the rabbit-fur blanket back. It was Anaya herself that was glowing.

Her emerald eyes sprang open.

With a strangled cry, Kith-Kanan fell back. Anaya sat up. The strong light diminished, leaving only a mild verdant aura surrounding the elf woman. She was green from hair to toes.

"Y—You're alive!" he stuttered.

"No," Anaya said sadly. She stood, and he did likewise. "This is part of the change. This was meant to happen. All the animal life has left me, and now, Kith, I am becoming one with the forest."

"I don't understand." To speak with his wife when he'd all but resigned himself to never seeing her again brought Kith-Kanan great joy. But her manner, the tone of her words, frightened him more than her death. He couldn't comprehend what was happening.

181

The green Anaya put a hand to his cheek. It was cool and gentle. She smiled at him, and a lump grew in his throat. "This happened to the other keepers. When their time was done, they became one with the forest, too. I am dead, dear Kith, but I will be here for thousands of years. I am joining the wildwood."

Kith-Kanan took her in his arms. "What about us? Is this what you want?" he asked, and fear made his voice harsh.

"I love you, Kith," Anaya said passionately, "but I am content now. This is my destiny. I am glad I was able to explain it to you." She pulled free of his embrace and walked off a few yards.

"I have always liked this spot in the clearing. It is a good place," she said with satisfaction.

"Good-bye, Ny!" Mackeli called tearfully. "You were a good sister!"

"Good-bye, Keli. Live well."

Kith-Kanan rushed to her. He couldn't accept this. It was all too strange. It was happening too quickly! He tried to take Anaya in his arms once more, but her feet were fixed to the ground.

Her eyes rebuked him gently as she said consolingly, "Don't fight it, Kith." Her voice becoming faint, the keeper added, "It is right."

"What of our child?" he asked desperately.

Anaya placed a hand on her belly. "He is there still. He was not part of the plan. A long, long time from now he will be born . . ." The light slowly dwindled in her eyes. "Farewell, my love."

Kith-Kanan held Anaya's face between his hands and kissed her. For a moment only, her lips had the yielding quality of flesh. Then a firmness crept in. The elf prince pulled back and, even as he touched her face for the last time, Anaya's features slowly vanished. What had been skin roughened into bark. By the time Kith-Kanan spoke her name once more, Anaya had found her destiny. At the clearing's edge, the prince of the Silvanesti was embracing a fine young oak tree.

Silvanost, Year of the Ram

21

For a month the ambassadors met with the Speaker of the Stars, yet nothing was accomplished. Nothing, except that Speaker Sithel fell ill. His health had been deteriorating over the preceding weeks, and the strain of the conference had sapped his strength to the point that by the morning of the twenty-ninth day, he could not even rise from his bed. Sickness was so rare for the speaker that a mild panic gripped the palace. Servants dashed about, conversing in whispers. Nirakina summoned Sithas and Hermathya to the speaker's bedside. So grave was her tone, Sithas half-expected to find his father on the verge of death.

Standing now at the foot of his father's bed, the prince could see that Sithel was wan and dispirited. Nirakina sat beside her ailing husband, holding a damp cloth to his head. Hermathya hovered in the background, obviously uncomfortable in the presence of illness.

"Let me call a healer," Nirakina insisted.

"It's not necessary," Sithel said testily. "I just need some rest."

"You have a fever!"

"I do not! Well, if I do, do you think I want it known that the Speaker of the Stars is so feeble he needs a healer to get well? What sort of message do you suppose that sends to our people? Or to the foreign emissaries?" This short speech left him winded, and he breathed heavily, his face pale against the cream-colored pillows.

"Regarding the ambassadors, what shall I tell them?" Sithas asked. "If you cannot attend the conference today "

"Tell them to soak their heads," Sithel muttered. "That devious dwarf and that contentious human female." His words subsided.

"Now, husband, that's no way to talk," Nirakina said agreeably. "There's no stigma to being ill, you know. You'd get well a lot sooner if a healer treated you."

"I'll heal myself, thank you."

"You may lie here for weeks, fevered, ill-tempered—"

"I am not ill-tempered!" Sithel shouted.

Nirakina rose from the bed purposefully. To Sithas she directed her questions. "Who can we get? Who is the best healer in Silvanost?"

From the far wall, Hermathya uttered one word: "Miritelisina."

"Impossible," the prince said quickly, looking at his wife with reproach. "She is in prison, as you well know, Lady."

"Oh, tosh," responded his mother. "If the speaker wants the best healer, he can order her release." Neither father nor son spoke or showed any sign of heeding Nirakina's counsel. "Miritelisina is high priestess of Quenesti Pah. No one else in Silvanost can come near her expertise in the healing art." She appealed to Sithas. "She's been in prison more than six months. Surely that's punishment enough for a moment's indiscretion?"

Sithel coughed, a loud, racking paroxysm that nearly doubled him over in bed. "It's the old delta fever," he gasped. "It's known to recur."

"Delta fever?" asked Sithas.

"A legacy of misspent youth," the speaker said weakly. When he sat up in bed, Nirakina gave him a cup of cool water to sip. "I used to hunt in the marshes at the mouth of the Thon-Thalas when I was young. I caught delta fever then."

Nirakina looked up at Sithas. "That was more than two hundred years before you were born," she said reassuringly. "He's had other, milder attacks."

"Father, send for the priestess," Sithas decided gravely. The speaker raised his brows questioningly. "The negotiations with the dwarves and humans must go ahead, and only a strong, healthy speaker can see that justice is done."

"Sithas is right," Nirakina agreed. She pressed her small hand to Sithel's burning cheek. "Send for Miritelisina."

The speaker sighed, the dry, rattling sound rising from his fevered throat. "Very well," he said softly. "Let it be done."

*　*　*　*　*

Later that morning came a knock at the door. Nirakina called for the person to enter. Tamanier came in, looking downcast.

"Great speaker, I spoke with Miritelisina," he said abjectly.

"Where is she?" asked Sithas sharply.

"She—she refuses to come, my prince."

"What?" said Sithas.

"What?" echoed Nirakina.

"She will not come to Your Highness, nor will she accept pardon from prison," Tamanier announced, shaking his head.

"Has she gone mad?" demanded Sithas.

"No, sire. Miritelisina believes her suffering in prison will bring the plight of the homeless ones to the attention of all."

In spite of his weakness, the speaker began to laugh softly. "What a character!" he said. The laughter threatened to turn into coughing, so he checked himself.

"It's extortion," Sithas said angrily. "She means to dictate her own terms!"

"Never mind, son. Tamanier, have the door of Miritelisina's cell left open. Tell the warders to bring her neither food nor water. When she gets hungry enough, she'll leave."

"What will you do if she doesn't come?" Nirakina asked, bewildered.

"I shall survive," he replied. "Now, all of you go. I wish to rest."

Tamanier went on his errand. Sithas and Nirakina drifted out, looking back frequently at the speaker. Sithas marveled at how small and weak his father looked in the great bed.

Alone, Sithel sat up slowly. His head pounded, but after a moment it cleared. He put his feet on the floor, and the cool marble soothed him. He stood and moved carefully to a window. The whole of Silvanost spread out below him. How he loved it! Not the city, which was just a collection of buildings, but the people, the daily rhythm of life that made Silvanost a living place.

A rainstorm had ended the day before, leaving the air crystal clean with a bite of cold. High, lacy clouds stretched from the horizon to mid-sky, like delicate fingers reaching up to the abode of the gods.

All of a sudden Sithel gave a shudder. The white clouds and shining towers reeled before him. He clutched the curtains for support, but strength faded from his hands and he lost his grip. Knees buckling, he slid to the floor. No one was around to see him fall. Sithel lay still on the marble floor, warmed by a patch of sunshine.

* * * * *

Sithas walked the palace halls, looking for Hermathya. He saw that she had not stayed with the speaker, so fearful was she of catching his illness. Some sort of intuition drew him up the tower stairs to the floor where his old bachelor room was. To his surprise, the prince found his devotional candle lit and a fresh red rose, sacred to Matheri, lying on the table by his bachelor bed. He had no idea who had left it. Hermathya had no reason to come here.

The sight of the rose and candle soothed his worried mind somewhat. He knelt by the table and began to meditate. At last he prayed to Matheri for his father's recovery and for more understanding in dealing with Hermathya.

Time passed. How much, he didn't know. A tapping sound filled the small chamber. Sithas ignored it. It grew louder. He raised his head and looked around for the source of the intrusive noise. He saw his seldom-worn sword, the twin of Kith-Kanan's weapon, hanging in its scabbard from a peg on the wall. The sword was vibrating inside its brass-bound sheath, causing the tapping noise.

Sithas rose and went to the weapon. He looked on in amazement as the length of iron shook itself like a trembling dog. He put out his hand, grasping the sword's hilt to try and still the vibrations. The shivering climbed Sithas's arm, penetrating his body and sending tingles up his arm. He took the sword hilt in both hands

In a flash the speaker's heir had a sudden, clear impression of his twin brother. Great rage, great anguish, heartache, a mortal blow

A loud crack smote his ears, and the sword ceased vibrating. Slightly dazed, Sithas, drew the blade out. It was broken cleanly, about five inches above the hilt.

Fear seized him. Fear for Kith-Kanan. He had no idea how he knew, but as he held the stump of the sword, Sithas knew without a doubt that Kith was in grave danger, perhaps even near death. He had to tell someone—his father, his mother. Sithas rushed to the dark oaken door of his old room and flung it open. He was startled to find someone standing just outside, shadowed by the massive overhang of the stone arch over the door.

"Who are you?" Sithas demanded, presenting the foreshortened sword. The figure seemed ominous somehow.

"Your sword is broken," said the stranger soothingly. "Be at peace, noble prince. I mean you no harm."

The stranger stepped forward into the pale light emanating from Sithas's candle, still burning on the table. He wore a nondescript gray robe. A hood covered his head. The air around him throbbed with an aura of power. Sithas felt it, like heat on his face from a nearby fire.

"Who are you?" the prince repeated with great deliberation. The oddly menacing figure reached up with slim pink fingers to throw back the hood. Beneath the soft gray material, his face was round and good-natured. He was nearly bald; only a fringe of mouse-brown hair covered the sides of his head. His ears were small and tapered.

"Do I know you?" Sithas asked. He relaxed a bit, for the stranger looked like nothing more than a beggarly cleric.

"At a royal dinner some time ago, you met an elf with long blond hair who introduced himself as Kamin Oluvai, second priest of the Blue Phoenix. That was me." The strange elf seemed pleased with Sithas's evident surprise.

"You're Kamin Oluvai? You look nothing like him," said the puzzled prince.

"A simple disguise." He shrugged. "But in truth, Kamin Oluvai is another of my masks. My real name is Vedvedsica, and I am at Your Highness's service." He bowed low.

It was a northern name, such as Silvanesti used in regions near Istar. Such elves were reputed to be deeply involved in sorcery. Sithas watched Kamin Oluvai or was it Vedvedsica?—warily.

"I'm very busy," the prince said abruptly. "What do you want?"

"I came in answer to a call, great prince. For some years I have been of use to your noble father, helping him in certain discreet matters. The speaker is ill, is he not?"

"A seasonal chill," said Sithas stiffly. "Speak plainly and tell me what you want, or else get out of my way."

"The speaker requires a healer to dispel his delta fever." Sithas could not hide his surprise at the fact that Vedvedsica knew the nature of his father's illness. "I have treated the speaker before, banishing the fever. I can do so again."

"You are not a priest of Quenesti Pah. Who do you serve?"

Vedvedsica smiled and stepped farther into the small room. Sithas automatically backed away, maintaining the distance between them. "Your Highness is an elf of great erudition and education. You know the unfairness of Silvanesti law, which only allows the worship of—"

"Who do you serve?" Sithas repeated sharply.

The gray-robed elf dropped his reticence. "My master is Gilean, the Gray Voyager."

Sithas tossed the broken end of his sword on the table. His concern was eased. Gilean was a god of Neutrality, not Evil. His worship was not officially recognized in Silvanost, but it wasn't actively suppressed either.

"My father has consulted with you?" he asked skeptically.

"Frequently." Vedvedsica's face took on a crafty expression, as if he were privy to things even the speaker's heir did not know.

"If you can cure my father, why did you come to me?" wondered Sithas.

"The speaker is an old, noble prince. Today he is ill. Someday, when he is gone, you will be speaker. I wish to continue my relationship with House Royal," he said, picking his words carefully.

Anger colored Sithas's face. He snatched up the broken sword and held the squared-off edge to the sorcerer's throat. His relationship with House Royal indeed! Vedvedsica held his ground, though he tilted his round head away from the blade.

"You speak treason," Sithas said coldly. "You insult me and my family. I will see you in chains in the lowest reaches of the palace dungeons, gray cleric!"

Vedvedsica's pale gray eyes bored into Sithas's furious face. "You wish to have your twin brother home, do you not?" the cleric asked insinuatingly.

The broken sword remained at Vedvedsica's throat, but Sithas's interest was piqued. He frowned.

The sorcerer sensed his hesitation. "I can find him, great prince," stated Vedvedsica firmly. "I can help you."

Sithas remembered the terrible feelings that had swept over him when he'd first grasped the vibrating sword. So much pain and rage. Wherever Kith was, he was in definite trouble.

"How would you do it?" asked the prince, almost too faintly to be heard.

"A simple act," noted the cleric. His gaze flickered down to the blade.

"I'll not break the law. No invocations to Gilean." Said the prince harshly,

"Of course not, Highness. You yourself will do all that needs to be done."

Sithas bade him explain, but Vedvedsica's eyes traveled once more to the blade at his throat. "If you please, Highness—?" Sithas swung the weapon away. The sorcerer swallowed audibly, then continued. "There is in all of us who share the blood of Astarin the ability to reach out to the ones we love, across great distances, and summon them to us."

"I know of what you speak," said Sithas. "But the Call has been forbidden to Kith-Kanan. I cannot break the speaker's edict."

"Ah," said the sorcerer with a wry smile. "But the speaker has need of my services to heal his fever. Perhaps I can strike a bargain!"

Sithas was growing weary of this fellow's impudence. Striking bargains with the speaker indeed! But if there was the slightest hope of getting Kith back—and healing his father—

Vedvedsica remained silent, sensing his best hope lay in letting Sithas come to a decision of his own accord.

"What must I do to call Kith-Kanan home?" Sithas asked finally.

"If you have some object that is strongly identified with your brother, that will help your concentration. It can be a focus for your thoughts."

After a long, tense silence, Sithas spoke. "I will take you to my father," he said. He brought the broken sword up once more to the cleric's throat. "But if anything you have told me is false, I shall turn you over to the Clerical Court Council for trial as a charlatan. You know what they do to illicit sorcerers?" Vedvedsica waved a hand casually. "Very well. Come!"

As Sithas opened the door, Vedvedsica caught his arm. The prince stared furiously at the cleric's hand until Vedvedsica deigned to remove it. "I cannot walk the halls of the palace in plain sight, great prince," the cleric said mysteriously. "Discretion is necessary for someone like myself." He took a small bottle from his sash and pulled the cork. An acrid smell flooded the small room. "If you will allow me to use this unguent. When warmed by the skin, it creates a fog of uncertainty around those who wear it. No one we pass will be certain they see or hear us."

Sithas felt he had no choice. Vedvedsica applied the reddish oil to his fingers and traced a magic sigil on Sithas's forehead. He did the same to himself. The unguent left a burning sensation on Sithas's skin. He had an intense desire to wipe the poisonous-smelling stuff off, but as the gray-clad cleric displayed no discomfort, the prince mastered the impulse.

"Follow me," advised Vedvedsica. At least that's what Sithas thought he said. The words came to his ear distantly, waveringly, as if the cleric spoke from the bottom of a well.

They ascended the steps, passing a trio of handmaids on the way. The elf girls' forms were indistinct to Sithas, though the background of stair and wall was solid and clear. The maids' eyes flickered over the prince and his companion, but no recognition showed on their faces. They continued on down the stair. The "fog of uncertainty" was working just as the cleric had claimed.

On the penultimate floor of the tower, they paused before the doors to the speaker's private rooms. Servants stood outside, idle. They paid no heed to the prince or the cleric.

"Strange," mused Sithas, words falling from his lips like drops of cold water. His own voice sounded muffled. "Why are they not inside with the speaker?"

He opened the door and hurried in. "Father?" he called. Sithas passed through the antechamber, with Vedvedsica close behind. After a glance around the room, he saw his father's crumpled form lying on the stone floor by the window. He shouted for assistance.

"They cannot hear you." Vedvedsica said, wafting into Sithas's line of sight. Desperately the prince knelt and lifted his father.

How light he felt, the great elf who ruled the elven nation! As Sithas placed his father on the bed, Sithel's eyes fluttered open. His face was dazed.

"Kith? Is that you?" he asked in a strange, faraway voice.

"No, Father, it's Sithas," said the elf prince, stricken with anguish.

"You're a good boy, Kith . . . but a willful fool. Why did you bare a weapon in the tower? You know it's a sacred place."

Sithas turned to the waiting Vedvedsica. "Take the spell off us!" he demanded fiercely. The cleric bowed and dampened a cloth at a wash basin, then wiped the prince's forehead clean. Immediately, it seemed, the fog vanished from his senses. Just seconds later the cleric materialized, seemingly out of nowhere.

Swiftly Vedvedsica took some dried herbs from his shoulder pouch and crushed them into a pewter goblet that stood on a table near the speaker's bed. Concerned, Sithas watched him work. The cleric next soaked the crushed dry leaves in crimson nectar, swirled the goblet to mix the ingredients, and held out the goblet to the prince.

"Let him drink this," he said with confidence. "It will clear his head."

Sithas held the goblet to his father's lips. No sooner had the first red drops passed Sithel's mouth, than his eyes lost their rheumy haze. Tightly he gripped Sithas's wrist.

"Son, what is this?" He looked beyond Sithas and espied the sorcerer. Sharply he said, "Why are you here? I did not send for you!"

"But you did, great speaker." Vedvedsica bowed deeply from the waist. "Your fevered mind called to me for help some hours ago. I came."

"Do you know him, Father?" Sithas asked.

"All too well." Sithel sank back on his pillows, so the prince set the goblet aside. "I'm sorry you had to meet him under such circumstances, son. I might have warned you."

Sithas looked at Vedvedsica, his face mixed with gratitude and distrust. "Is he cured?"

"Not yet, my prince. There are other potions I must prepare. They will cure the speaker."

"Get on with it, then," Sithas commanded.

Vedvedsica flinched. "There is the matter of our bargain."

Sithel coughed. "What bargain have you made with this old spider?" the speaker demanded.

"He will cure your fever if you allow me to call Kith-Kanan home," Sithas said honestly. Sithel arched his white brows in surprise, and the prince averted his eyes from his father's intense gaze.

190

"Call Kith?" he asked skeptically. "Vedvedsica, you're no altruist. What do you want for yourself out of this?"

The cleric bowed again. "I ask only that the speaker's heir pay me such an amount as he thinks appropriate."

Sithel shook his head. "I don't see why Kith-Kanan should interest you, but I don't object," he said with a heavy sigh, then turned to his heir. "What will you pay him, Sithas?"

The prince thought once more of the broken sword and the terrible feeling of suffering he'd felt from his twin. "Fifty gold pieces," he said decisively.

Vedvedsica's eyes widened. "A most handsome amount, great prince."

Father and son watched in silence as the cleric compounded his healing potion. When at last it was done, he filled a tall silver beaker with the muddy green fluid. To Sithas's surprise, Vedvedsica took a healthy swig of the mixture himself first and seemed satisfied. Then he held it out to the prostrate speaker.

"You must drink it all," he insisted. Sithas handed the beaker to his father. Sithel raised himself on his elbows and downed the brew in three swallows. He looked expectantly at his son. In turn, Sithas turned to Vedvedsica.

"Well?"

"The effect is a subtle one, great prince, but rest assured, the speaker will shortly be cured of his fever."

Indeed, Sithel's forehead had become cooler to the touch. The speaker exhaled gustily, and sat up straighter. A tinge of color was returning to his pale cheeks. Vedvedsica nodded grandly.

"Leave us, sorcerer," Sithel said tersely. "You may collect your payment later."

Another deep bow. "As the speaker commands." Vedvedsica produced the small bottle of unguent and began to apply it as before.

Holding up a hand, the prince said acidly, "Out the door first, cleric."

Vedvedsica's smile was wide as he departed.

* * * * *

Sithas left his father looking more fit than he had in a month, then proceded to make his way through the palace to spread word of his recovery. Vedvedsica wasn't mentioned. The speaker's recovery was reported as natural, a sign of the gods' favor.

Finally, Sithas went down the tower steps to Kith-Kanan's old room. No one was around. Dust lay thickly over everything for nothing had disturbed it since his brother had left in disgrace. How long ago had it been? Two years?

The room held all sorts of Kith's personal items. His silver comb. His second favorite bow, now warped and cracked from the room's dry air. All his courtly clothes hung in the wardrobe. Sithas touched each item of clothing, trying to concentrate his thoughts on his lost brother. All he felt were old memories. Some pleasant, many sad.

A strange sensation came over the prince. He felt as if he were moving up and away, though his body hadn't stirred an inch. Smoke from a campfire teased his nose. The sound of wind in a forest filled his ears. Sithas looked down at his hands. They were browned by the sun and hardened by work and combat. These were not his hands; they were Kith-Kanan's. The prince knew then that he must try to communicate with his twin, but when he opened his mouth to speak, his throat was tight. It was hard to form words. He concentrated instead on forming them in his mind.

Come home, he willed. *Come home, Kith. Come home.*

Sithas forced his lips to work. "Kith!" he cried.

Speaking his twin's name ended the experience abruptly. Sithas staggered backward, disoriented, and sat down on his twin's old bed. Dust rose around him. Streaks of sunlight, which had reached across the room when he came in, now had retreated to just under the window sill. Several hours had passed.

Sithas shook the queer disorientation out of his head and went to the door. He had definitely made contact with Kith, but whether he had made the fabled Call, he didn't know. It was late now, and he needed to see how his father was doing.

Sithas left the room so hastily he didn't pull the door completely closed behind him. And as he mounted the steps to the upper floor of the palace tower, the prince didn't notice the door to Kith-Kanan's room slowly swing open and remain that way.

Spring, Year of the Ram

22

The days seemed empty. Each morning Kith-Kanan went to sit by the young oak. It was slender and tall, its twining branches reaching heavenward. Leaf buds appeared on it, as they did on all the trees in the forest. But these buds seemed a symbol, a notice that the wildwood was once again furiously and joyously alive. Even the clearing erupted in wildflowers and vibrant green growth. The path to the pool covered over in a day with new grass and nodding thistles.

"There's never been a spring like this." Mackeli exclaimed. "Things are growing while you watch!" His spirits had recovered more quickly than Kith-Kanan's. Mackeli easily accepted that Anaya's change had been fated to happen, and he'd been trying to draw his friend out of his misery.

This beautiful day he and Kith-Kanan sat on a lower limb of the oak tree. Mackeli's gangling legs swung back and forth as he chewed a sweet grass stem and looked over the clearing, "It's like we're besieged," he added. Grass had grown to waist height in little more than a week. The bare ground around the tree, scuffed down to dirt by their daily walking on it, was gradually shrinking as the plants in the clearing grew.

"The hunting ought to be good," Mackeli enthused. His new-found appetite for meat was enormous. He ate twice as much as Kith-Kanan and grew stronger all the time. And since the griffon had grown more skilled in bringing back game for them, they were well fed.

With the explosion of flowering trees and plants had come the onslaught of the insects. Not the Black Crawlers of Anaya's acquaintance, but bees and flies and butterflies. The air was always thick with them now. Kith-Kanan and Mackeli had to keep a fire burning in the hearth at all times to discourage the bees from building a hive in the tree with them.

With Arcuballis bringing in a whole boar or deer once a day, there was little for the two elves to do. Still hoping to divert Kith-Kanan from his grief, Mackeli once more began to ask questions of Silvanost. They talked about the people, their clothing, eating habits, work routines, and more. Slowly, Kith-Kanan was persuaded to share his memories. To his surprise, he found himself feeling homesick.

"And what about—" Mackeli chewed his lower lip. "What about girls?"

Kith-Kanan smiled slightly. "Yes, there are girls."

"What are they like?"

"The maids of Silvanost are well known for their grace and beauty," he said, without much exaggeration. "Most of them are kindly and gentle and very intelligent, and a few have been known to take up horse and sword. Those are rare, though. They are red-haired, blond, sandy-haired, and I've seen some with hair as black as the nighttime sky."

Mackeli drew in his legs, crouching on the balls of his feet. "I would like to meet them! All of them!"

"No doubt you would, Keli," Kith-Kanan said solemnly. "But I cannot take you there."

Mackeli knew the story of Kith-Kanan's flight from Silvanost. "Whenever Ny would get mad at me, I would wait a few days, then go and say I was sorry," he suggested. "Can't you tell your father you're sorry?"

"It's not that easy," Kith-Kanan replied defensively.

"Why?"

The prince opened his mouth to reply, but no words came out. Why, indeed? Surely in the time that had gone by his father's anger would have cooled. The gods knew his own anger at losing Hermathya had withered and died as if it had never been. Even now, as he spoke her name in his mind, no remembered passion stirred inside him. His heart would always belong to Anaya. Now that she was gone, why should he not return home?

In the end, though, Kith-Kanan always decided that he could not. "My father is Speaker of the Stars. He is bound by traditions he cannot flout. If he were only my father and angry with me, perhaps I could return and beg his forgiveness. But there are many others around him who wouldn't want me back."

Mackeli nodded knowingly. "Enemies."

"Not personal enemies, just those priests and guild masters who have a vested interest in keeping things as they've always been. My father needs their support, which is why he married Hermathya to Sithas in the first place. I'm sure my return would cause much unrest in the city."

Mackeli dropped out of his crouch. He swung his legs back and forth in the air. "Seems complicated," he said. "I think the forest is better."

Even with the ache of Anaya's loss in his heart, Kith-Kanan had to agree as he looked over the sunny clearing carpeted with flowers.

*　*　*　*　*

The Call struck him like a blow.

It was evening, four days after the prince's discussion of Silvanost with Mackeli, and they were skinning a mountain elk. Neither Kith-Kanan nor the boy could explain why the griffon had flown two hundred miles to the Khalkist Mountains to catch the elk, but that was the nearest source of such animals. They were nearly finished with the skinning when the Call came.

Kith-Kanan dropped his flint skinning knife in the dirt. He jumped to his feet, hands outstretched as if he'd been stricken blind.

"Kith! Kith, what's wrong?" Mackeli cried.

Kith-Kanan could no longer see the forest. Instead, he saw vague impressions of walls, floor, and ceiling made of white marble. It was as if he'd been lifted up out of his body and set down in Silvanost. He held a hand to his face and in place of his leather tunic and callused palm, he saw a smooth hand and a white silk robe. The ring on his finger he recognized as belonging to Sithas.

A jumble of sensations assaulted his mind: worry, sadness, loneliness. Sithas was calling his name. There was trouble in the city. Arguments and fighting. Humans at court. Kith-Kanan reeled as it came at him in a rush.

"Sithas!" he cried. When he spoke, the Call ended abruptly.

Mackeli was shaking him by his tunic. Kith-Kanan broke the boy's grip and shoved him back.

"What is it?" Mackeli asked, frightened.

"My brother. It was my brother, back in Silvanost . . ."

"You saw him? Did he speak?"

"Not in words. The nation is in peril—" Kith-Kanan pressed his hands to his face. His heart was pounding. "I must go back. I must go to Silvanost." He turned and walked into the hollow tree.

"Wait! Do you have to go now?"

"I have to go. I have to leave now," Kith-Kanan insisted tensely.

"Then take me with you!"

Kith-Kanan appeared in the doorway. "What did you say?"

"Take me with you," Mackeli repeated in a hopeful tone. "I'll be your servant. I'll do anything. Clean your boots, cook your food—anything. I don't want to stay here alone, Kith. I want to see the city of my people!"

Kith-Kanan went to where Mackeli stood, still holding his skinning knife. With the muddle of feelings clearing from his brain, he realized he was glad Mackeli wanted to go with him. He felt closer to him than he had to anyone except Anaya—and Sithas. If he was going back to face who knows what in Silvanost, he didn't want to lose that friendship and support now.

Clapping a hand to the boy's shoulder, Kith-Kanan declared, "You shall go with me, but never as my servant. You can be my squire and train to be a warrior. How does that sound?"

Mackeli was too overcome to speak. He threw his arms around Kith-Kanan and hugged him fiercely.

"When shall we leave?" the boy asked.

Kith-Kanan felt the powerful tug of the Call. *Now, now, now.* It coursed through his body like a second heartbeat. He steeled himself against the insatiable pull. It was late and there were preparations which must be made before they departed. "Tomorrow morning," he decided.

* * * * *

Day came like the cracking of an egg. First all was smooth, unbroken night, then just a chip of sunlight showed to the east. It was enough to rouse the eager Mackeli, who splashed water on his face and announced himself ready to go.

"Is there nothing you want to take with you?" Kith-Kanan wondered.

Mackeli surveyed the inside of the tree. The flint tools, gourd bottles, clay-daubed baskets, none of them were worth taking, he said. Still, they needed food and water, so they loaded a pair of wicker baskets with meat, nuts, berries, and water, balancing the weight so Arcuballis could carry it all. Alone of the three of them, the griffon was still heavily asleep. When Kith-Kanan whistled through his teeth, Arcuballis raised its aquiline head out from under one wing and stood on its mismatched feet. Kith-Kanan gave the beast some water while Mackeli tied the food baskets to the back of the saddle.

A sense of urgency spurred them on. Mackeli chattered incessantly about the things he wanted to do and see. He scrubbed the residue of paint from his face, announcing that he didn't want the city-dwellers to think he was a savage. Kith-Kanan tested the harness fittings under the griffon's neck and chest, and Mackeli climbed onto the pillion. At last, though, Kith-Kanan hesitated.

"What is it?" the boy asked.

"There is one thing I must do!" He cut across the flower-choked clearing to the slender oak that had been Anaya. He stopped two yards away and looked up at the limbs reaching toward the sky. He still found it hard to accept that the woman he loved was here now, in any form. "Part of my heart stays with you here, my love. I have to go back now; I hope you understand." Tears welled in his eyes as he took out his dagger. "Forgive me," he whispered, then reached up and quickly sliced off a four-inch green shoot, well laden with bright green buds. Kith-Kanan cut a small slit in the tough deerhide of his tunic, directly over his heart, and put the shoot there.

The elf prince gazed up at the young tree, then looked around at the clearing where they had been so happy. "I love you, Anaya," he said. "Farewell." Turning, he walked quickly back to the griffon.

Kith-Kanan swung onto Arcuballis's back and settled himself into the saddle. He whistled and touched the griffon with his heels, signaling the creature to be off. As the griffon bounded across the clearing, its strong legs tearing through the new growth, great torrents of petals and pollen flew into the air. At last the mount opened its wings and, in a stupendous bound, leaped into the air. Mackeli yelped with delight.

They circled the clearing, gaining height with each circuit. Kith-Kanan looked down for a few seconds, then he lifted his face and studied the clouds. He turned Arcuballis's head northeast. They leveled out at a thousand feet. The air was warm, and a steady wind buoyed Arcuballis, enabling him to glide for long stretches with hardly a wingbeat.

Mackeli leaned forward and shouted in Kith-Kanan's ear, "How long will it take us to get there?"

"One day, perhaps two."

They passed over a world rapidly greening. Life seemed to be bursting from the ground even as they flew by. The lower air was full of birds, from tiny swallows to large flocks of wild geese. Farther below, the forest thinned, then gave way to plain. As the sun reached its zenith, Kith-Kanan and Mackeli saw the first signs of civilization since leaving the wildwood. There was a village below, laid out in a circle, with a sod wall surrounding it for protection. A pall of smoke hung over the village.

"Is that a city?" asked Mackeli excitedly.

"No, that's barely a village. It looks like they've been attacked." Worry and the edge of fear set Kith-Kanan's heart to pounding as he hauled back on the reins. Arcuballis tipped over in a shallow dive. They flew through the smoke. Coughing, the elf prince steered the griffon in a slow circle around the despoiled village. Nothing moved. He could see the bodies of the fallen lying atop the wall and in between the huts.

"It's terrible," Kith-Kanan said grimly. "I'm going to land and take a look. Be on guard, Keli."

Arcuballis touched down lightly outside the wall, near one of the rents that had been torn in it. Kith-Kanan and Mackeli dismounted. Mackeli had a crossbow, salvaged from Voltorno's band, and Kith-Kanan had his compound bow. His scabbard hung empty by his side.

"You see what they did?" Kith-Kanan said, pointing to the gap in the sod wall. "The attackers used grappling hooks to pull down the wall."

They stepped over the rubble of dried sod and entered the village. It was eerily quiet. Smoke eddied and swirled in the shifting wind. Where once people had talked and argued and laughed, there was now nothing but empty streets. Broken crockery and torn clothing were strewn here and there. Kith-Kanan turned over the first body he came to—a Kagonesti male, slain by sword. He could tell the elf had died not very long before, a day or two at most. Turning the fellow facedown once more, Kith-Kanan paused and shook his head. Horrible. During the Call he had sensed from Sithas that there was trouble in the land, but this? This was murder and raping.

As they continued through the silent village, all the other dead they found were Kagonesti or Silvanesti males. No females, no children. All the farm animals were gone, as was practically everything else of value.

"Who could have done this?" Mackeli asked solemnly.

"I don't know. Whoever it was, they didn't want their identity known. Do you notice, they took their own dead with them?"

"How can you tell?"

Kith-Kanan pointed at the scattering of dead villagers. "These fellows didn't just lay down and die. They died fighting, which means they must've taken a few of their enemies with them."

On the west side of the village, they found a mass of footprints—horses, cattle, and people. The raiders had taken their elven and animal captives and driven them out onto the great plain. Mackeli asked what lay in that direction.

"The city of Xak Tsaroth. No doubt the raiders will try to sell their prizes in the markets there," said Kith-Kanan grimly. He gazed at the flat horizon as if he might catch a glimpse of the bandits who had committed this outrage. "Beyond Xak Tsaroth is the homeland of the Kagonesti. It's forest, much like the wildwood we just left."

"Does your father rule all this land?" Mackeli said curiously.

"He rules it by law, but out here the real ruler is the hand that wields the sword." Kith-Kanan kicked the dry plains soil, sending up a gout of dust. "Come, Keli. Let's go."

They trudged back to the griffon, following the outside curve of the village wall. Mackeli dragged his feet and hung his head. Kith-Kanan asked what was troubling him.

"This world beyond the forest is a dark place," he said. "These folk died because someone wanted to rob them."

"I never said the outside world was all marble cities and pretty girls," Kith-Kanan replied, draping an arm across the boy's shoulders. "Don't be too discouraged, though. This sort of thing doesn't happen every day. Once I tell my father about it, he will put an end to this brigandage."

"What can he do? He lives in a far away city."

"Don't underestimate the power of the Speaker of the Stars."

* * * * *

It was twilight of the second day when the white tops of the city towers first appeared. Arcuballis sensed the end of their journey was near; without Kith-Kanan's urging, the beast quickened its wingbeat. The land raced by. The broad Thon-Thalas, mirroring the deep aquamarine of the evening sky, appeared, approached, and then flashed beneath the griffon's tucked-in feet.

"Hello! Hello down there!" Mackeli called to the boaters and fishers on the river. Kith-Kanan shushed him.

"I may not be coming back to the warmest of welcomes," he cautioned. "There's no need to announce our return, all right?" The boy reluctantly fell silent.

Kith-Kanan found himself experiencing great doubt and no small amount of trepidation. How would he be received? Could his father forgive his outrage? One thing he knew, he was certainly not the same elf he had been when he left here. So much had happened to him, and he found himself looking forward to the time when he could share it with his twin.

Kith-Kanan had noticed the beginning of a settlement on the western bank of the river. From the grid layout, it looked like a town was being built on the river, opposite the piers and docks of Silvanost. Then, as they approached the city from the south, he saw that a large section of the Market was a blackened ruin. This alarmed him, for if the city had been attacked it might not be his father and twin who would be waiting for him when he landed. The prince was only a little relieved when he saw that the rest of the city appeared normal.

For his part, Mackeli leaned far to the side, staring with unabashed amazement at the wonders below. The city glittered in the sunlight. Marble buildings, green gardens, and sparkling pools filled his eyes. A thousand towers, each a marvel to the forest-raised boy, jutted above the artfully manicured treetops. Rising higher than all the rest was the Tower of the Stars. Kith-Kanan circled the great pinnacle and recalled with a pang the day he'd done it last. The number of days was small compared to an elf's entire life, but the gulf it represented seemed as great as one thousand years.

Arcuballis was ready for home. The beast banked away from the tower with only a minimum of direction from Kith-Kanan and headed for the rooftop of the Quinari Palace. A line of torches burned along the flat roof, the flames whipped by a steady wind. The rosy palace tower was tinted a much deeper shade of red by the last rays of the setting sun.

Mackeli held tightly to Kith-Kanan's waist as the angle of descent steepened. A single white-robed figure stood beside the line of torches. The griffon raised its head and wafted its wings rapidly. The mount's forward speed diminished, and its clawed forelegs touched down on the roof. When its hind legs found purchase, Arcuballis folded its wings.

The figure in white, a dozen yards away, lifted a torch from its holder and walked toward the grounded griffon. Mackeli held his breath.

"Brother," Kith-Kanan said simply as he dismounted.

Sithas held up the torch. "I knew you would come back. I've waited here every night since I called you," said his twin warmly.

"I am glad to see you!" The brothers embraced. Seeing this, Mackeli threw a leg over and slid down the griffon's rump to the roof. Sithas and Kith-Kanan drew apart and clapped each other on the shoulders.

"You look like a ragged bandit," Sithas exclaimed. "Where did you get those clothes?"

"It's a very long story," Kith-Kanan replied. He was grinning so widely his face ached; Sithas's expression mirrored his. "And you, when did you stop being a priest and become a prince?" he exclaimed, thumping Sithas's back.

Sithas kept smiling. "Well, a lot's happened since you left. I—" He stopped, seeing Mackeli come up behind Kith-Kanan.

"This is my good friend and companion Mackeli," Kith-Kanan explained. "Keli, this is my brother, Sithas."

"Hello," said Mackeli casually.

"No," Kith-Kanan chided. "Bow, like I told you."

Mackeli bent awkwardly at the waist, bending nearly double. "Sorry, Kith! I meant, hello, Prince Sithas," he said ingenuously.

Sithas smiled at the boy. "You've plenty of time to learn court manners," he said. "Right now, I'll wager you'd both like a hot bath and some dinner."

"Ah! With that, I could die happy," Kith-Kanan said, placing a hand over his heart. Laughing, he and Sithas started toward the stairwell, with Mackeli following a pace behind. Kith-Kanan suddenly halted.

"What about father?" he asked apprehensively. "Does he know you called me?"

"Yes," said Sithas. "He was ill for a few days, and I asked him for permission to use the Call. He consented. A healer brought him through, and he's well now. We've been dealing with ambassadors from Ergoth and Thorbardin, too, so things have been quite busy. We'll go to him and mother as soon as you're presentable."

"Ambassadors? Why are they here?" Kith-Kanan asked. "And, Sith, what happened to the Market? It looks as though it was sacked!"

"I'll tell you all about it."

As the twins reached the steps, Kith-Kanan looked back. Stars were coming out in the darkening sky. The weary Arcuballis had dropped into a sleeping crouch. Kith-Kanan looked from the star-salted sky to the nearby bulk of the Tower of the Stars. Without really thinking about it, his hand went to the sprig of oak he'd snipped from Anaya's tree and drew it out. It had changed. Where there had been tight buds, now the shoot was furnished with perfect green leaves. Even though it had been cut from the tree two days past, the sprig was green and growing.

"What is that?" asked Sithas curiously.

Kith-Kanan drew a deep breath and shared a knowing glance with Mackeli. "This is the best part of my story, Brother." Tenderly he returned the oak shoot to its place over his heart.

Night of Reunion

23

Freshly bathed, clothed, and fed, Kith-Kanan and Mackeli followed Sithas to the Hall of Balif. There the speaker, Lady Nirakina, and Lady Hermathya were having a late, private dinner.

"Wait here," Sithas said, stopping his twin and Mackeli just outside the hall door. "Let me prepare them."

Most of Mackeli's attention was focused on his surroundings. Since entering the palace, he'd touched the stone walls and floor, felt bronze and iron fittings, and goggled at the courtiers and servants that passed by. He was dressed in one of Kith-Kanan's old outfits. The sleeves were too short for him, and even though his ragged hair was combed as neatly as possible, he still looked like a well-costumed scarecrow.

Servants who recognized Kith-Kanan gaped in astonishment. He smiled at the elves, but admonished them in a low voice to go about their business as he stepped close to the hall door and listened. Hearing his father's voice, even so indistinctly, brought a lump to his throat. Kith-Kanan peered around the door, but Sithas held a hand out to him. Straight as an arrow, he walked proudly into the now-silent hall. Then there was a gasp, and a silver spoon rang on the marble floor. Hermathya bent to retrieve the lost utensil.

Sithas stopped Mackeli so that Kith-Kanan could approach the table alone. The wayward prince of the Silvanesti stood across the oval table from his parents and former lover.

Nirakina rose halfway to her feet, but Sithel commanded her

tersely to sit back down. The lady sank back into her chair, tears glistening on her cheeks. Kith-Kanan bowed deeply.

"Great speaker," he began. Then: "Father. Thank you for letting Sithas call me home." Both elf women snapped around to stare at Sithel, for they had not known of the speaker's leniency.

"I have been angry with you a long time," Sithel replied sternly. "No one in House Royal ever shamed us as you did. What have you to say?"

Kith-Kanan dropped to one knee. "I am the greatest fool who ever lived," he said, looking down at the floor. "I know I shamed you and myself. I have made peace with myself and the gods, and now I want to make peace with my family."

Sithel pushed back his chair and stood. His white hair seemed golden in the candlelight. He'd regained some of the weight he'd lost while ill, and the old fire in his eyes was renewed. He strode with firm, even steps around the table to where his younger son knelt.

"Stand up," he said, still in his commanding speaker's voice.

As Kith-Kanan got up, Sithel's stern countenance softened. "Son," he said when they were face to face.

They clasped hands about each other's forearms in soldierly fashion. But it wasn't enough for Kith-Kanan. He embraced his father with fervor, a fervor returned by Sithel. Over the speaker's shoulder, Kith-Kanan saw his mother, still weeping, but now the tears tracked down on each side of a radiant smile.

Hermathya tried to maintain her aloofness, but her pale face and trembling fingers betrayed her. She dropped her hands to her lap and looked away, at the wall, at the ceiling, at anything but Kith-Kanan.

Sithel held the prince at arm's length and studied his sunbrowned features. "I cannot deny you," he said, his voice breaking with emotion. "You are my son, and I am glad to have you back!"

Nirakina came and kissed him. Kith-Kanan brushed away her tears and let her walk him back around the table to where their places were set. They came to Hermathya, still seated.

"You are looking well, lady," Kith-Kanan said awkwardly.

She looked up at him, blinking rapidly. "I am well," she replied uncertainly. "Thank you for noticing." Seeing Kith-Kanan at a loss for words, Sithas moved to intervene. He ushered Mackeli forward and introduced him. Sithel and Nirakina found the boy's rustic manners both charming and amusing.

Now that the news was out, servants were roused from their work, even from bed, and whole troops of them filed into the hall to pay their respects to the returned prince. Kith-Kanan had always been popular with the members of House Servitor for his lively manner and kind heart.

"Quiet, all of you! Quiet!" Sithel shouted, and the throng became still. The speaker called for amphorae of fine nectar, and there was a pause as cups of the sweet beverage were passed through the crowd. When everyone had a share, the speaker raised his goblet and saluted his newly restored son.

"To Prince Kith-Kanan," he exclaimed. "Home at last!"

"Kith-Kanan!" answered the great assembly. They all drank.

All but one. Hermathya held her cup tightly until her knuckles were as white as her face.

*   *   *   *   *

The servants finally dispersed, but the family remained. They surrounded Kith-Kanan and talked for hours, telling him what had happened during his absence. He, in turn, regaled them with his adventures in the wildwood.

"You see me now, a widower," Kith-Kanan said sorrowfully, gazing at the dregs of nectar in his cup. "Anaya was claimed by the forest she had served so long."

"Was this Anaya nobly born?" Nirakina delicately asked.

"Her birth was a mystery, even to her. I suspect she was stolen from her family by the guardian before her, just as she took Mackeli from his parents."

"I'm not sorry she did so," Mackeli said staunchly. "Anaya was good to me."

Kith-Kanan allowed his family to assume Anaya was Silvanesti, like Mackeli. He also kept from them the news of his unborn child. The loss was too recent, and he wanted to keep some memories for himself.

Sithas broke the quiet interlude by commenting on the half-human Voltorno. "It fits with what we already suspect," he ventured. "The emperor of Ergoth is behind the terror in our western provinces. He not only wants our land, but our timber, too." Everyone knew that Ergoth had a sizable navy and needed wood for ships. Their own land was relatively poor in trees. Also, unlike elves, humans tended to build houses out of wood.

"At any rate," the speaker noted, "the emissaries have been here nearly five weeks and nothing's been accomplished. I was ill for a few days, but since my recovery we've made no progress at all."

"I'd be glad to speak to the ambassadors of the things I saw and heard in the forest," Kith-Kanan offered. "Men from Ergoth have been landing on our southern coast to plunder the forest. They would have taken Mackeli to Daltigoth as a slave. That's a fact."

"That's probably what the raiders have done with the other captives," Sithas said darkly. "The wives and children of the Silvanesti settlers."

Kith-Kanan told of the sacked village he and Mackeli had seen on their way home. Sithel was disturbed to hear that a settlement so close to the capital had been attacked.

"You will come to the tower tomorrow," the speaker declared. "I want the Ergothians to hear what you have seen!"

Sithel rose. "It is very late," he said. "The session begins early, so we'd all better take our rest." Mackeli was already snoring. Hermathya, likewise, was dozing where she sat, curled up in her chair.

Kith-Kanan roused Mackeli with a shake, and the boy sat up.

"Funny dream, Kith. I went to a great city, and people lived inside stone mountains."

"Not so funny," Kith-Kanan said, smiling. "Come on, Keli, I can put you in Sithas's old room. Is that well with you, Brother?" Sithas waved his agreement.

Kith-Kanan kissed his mother's cheek and said good night. Her face shone with contentment, which made her look decades younger.

"Good night, son," she said devotedly.

A servant with a candelabrum arrived to conduct Mackeli to his bed. Sithel and Nirakina went out. At last, the brothers stood by the door.

"I'll leave you to your wife," Kith-Kanan said, nodding toward the sleeping Hermathya. Rather awkwardly, he added, "I'm sorry I missed the wedding, Sith. I hope you two are happy."

Sithas stared at his wife's sleeping form for a few seconds, then said, "It has been no bargain being married to her, Kith." Kith-Kanan could not conceal his surprise. He asked in a whisper what was wrong.

"Well, you know how willful she is. She takes every opportunity to make herself known to the people. She throws trinkets from the windows of her sedan chair when she goes out. People follow after her, calling her name." Sithas's mouth hardened to a thin line. "Do you know what the city wits call us? The Shadow and the Flower! I don't suppose I need to explain who is who, do I?"

Kith-Kanan suppressed a wry smile. "Thya always was chaos in motion."

"There's more to it than that. I think—" Sithas cut himself off as a servant came down the corridor toward the open door. The yellow glow of his candles flowed ahead of him like a stolen sunrise.

"Good night, Kith," Sithas said suddenly. He summoned the servant and told him to guide the prince up the dark stairs to his room. Kith-Kanan regarded his twin curiously.

"I shall see you in the morning," he said. Sithas nodded and held the hall door. As soon as Kith-Kanan went out, Sithas shut the door firmly.

Inside the hall, Sithas spoke sharply to Hermathya. "It's very childish, this pretense of sleep."

She sat up and yawned. "Quite a compliment from the master of pretense."

"Lady, have you no respect for us or our position?"

Hermathya pushed her heavy chair away from the table. "Respect is all I do have," she replied calmly. "Heavy, thick, rigid respect."

* * * * *

The Palace of Quinari was sleeping, nearly everyone within it walls exhausted by the homecoming of Kith-Kanan. But in the gallery leading away from the central tower, two figures met in the dark and broke the silence with their whispers.

"He's come back," said the female voice.

"So I have heard," answered the male. "It's not a problem."

"But Prince Kith-Kanan is a factor we hadn't considered." In her distress the female spoke louder than was necessary—or prudent.

"*I* considered him," said the male voice calmly. "If anything, his return will be to our advantage."

"How?"

"Kith-Kanan enjoys a certain popularity with all those who find his brother cold and uninspiring—elves such as the royal guard, for example. Moreover, my evaluation of the errant prince tells me he is more open and trusting than either his father or brother. And a trusting person is always more useful than a doubter."

"You are clever. My father chose well when he picked you." The female voice was once more calm and soft. There was the sound of heavy cloth being crushed and a kiss. "I wish we didn't have to meet in shadows like this."

"Don't you think it's romantic?" murmured the male voice.

"Yes . . . but it annoys me that so many think you are harmless."

"My best weapon. Would you take it away from me?"

"Oh, never . . ."

There was silence for a while, then the female voice said, "How long till sun-up?"

"An hour or so."

"I'm worried."

"What about?" he asked.

"The whole affair is getting too complicated. Sometimes when I'm sitting in the audience hall I want to scream, the tension is so great."

"I know," the male voice said soothingly, "but our task is quite simple. We have only to delay and dissemble and keep the elves talking. Daily, our numbers swell. Time is our ally, my darling. Given enough time, the mighty elven nation will fall!"

Their slippered feet made only the slightest whisper on the cool marble floor as the conspirators stole down the gallery to the steps. They had to get back to their rooms before the palace stirred. No one must see them together, not even the members of their own delegation.

The Day Following

24

The entrance of Kith-Kanan into the Tower of the Stars the next day created a stir. Gone were Kith-Kanan's tattered green buckskins. Now he wore smooth white robes and a silver circlet on his head. With great ceremony he was introduced to Lord Dunbarth. The dwarf doffed his floppy hat and said, "It is a great honor to meet you, Prince. I've heard much about you."

"Perhaps we shall be friends anyway," was the wry reply.

Meeting the human delegation was more forced. Praetor Ulwen sat in his portable chair like a wax image. Only the slight rise and fall of the blanket over his chest testified he was alive. Lady Teralind accepted Kith-Kanan's hand, holding it for a long minute as she assessed this newest addition to the conference. He noted the dark circles under her eyes. The lady hadn't slept very well the night before.

Ulvissen saluted, human fashion. Kith-Kanan imitated his gesture.

"Have we met before?" the elf prince asked, looking carefully at the bearded human.

"I don't think so, noble prince," Ulvissen replied coolly. "I served most of my military career on ships. Perhaps Your Highness met another human who looked like me. I understand it is hard for elves to distinguish one bearded man from another."

"There is much in what you say." Kith-Kanan walked away, but the idea that he'd seen Ulvissen before troubled him still. He paused before his father, bowed, and took his old seat on the speaker's right. A human with a full, red-brown beard—where had he seen him?

"The fifteenth session of the Conference of Three Nations will now begin," said Sithas, acting as his father's herald. "Seated for Silvanesti is Prince Kith-Kanan." The scribes at their tables wrote busily.

Dunbarth stood up—which had the effect of making him shorter, as his chair's legs were longer than his own. "Great speaker, noble princes, Lord Praetor, Lady Teralind," he began. "We have been here many days, and the principal obstacle in the way of peace is this question: Who rules the western plains and the forest? The noble speaker and his heir present as proof of their claim ancient treaties and documents. Lady Teralind, on behalf of the emperor of Ergoth, makes her claim from the point of view of the majority, claiming that most of the people who live in the disputed territory are Ergothians." Dunbarth took a deep breath. "I summarize these positions as I have presented them to my king. I have this day received his reply."

Murmurs of interest rose. Dunbarth unfolded a heavy piece of parchment. The golden wax seal of the king of Thorbardin was visible.

"Ahem," said the dwarf. The muttering subsided. "To my right trusty and well-loved cousin, Dunbarth of Dunbarth, greetings: I hope the elves are feeding you well, cousin; you know how meager their eating habits are . . ." The emissary peered over the parchment at the speaker and winked. Kith-Kanan covered his mouth with one hand to hide his smile.

Dunbarth continued: "I charge you, Dunbarth of Dunbarth, to deliver to the Speaker of the Stars and the praetor of Ergoth this proposal—that the territory lying on each side of the Kharolis Mountains, seventy-five miles east and west, be entrusted to the Kingdom of Thorbardin, to be governed and administered by us as a buffer zone between the empires of Ergoth and Silvanesti."

There was a moment of crystalline silence as everyone in the tower took in the message.

"Absolutely preposterous!" Teralind exploded.

"Not an acceptable proposal," said Sithas, albeit more calmly.

"It's only a preliminary idea," Dunbarth protested. "His Majesty offers concessions, here—"

"Totally unacceptable!" Teralind was on her feet. "I ask the speaker, what do you think of this outlandish notion?"

All eyes turned to Sithel. He leaned back against his throne, his mask of composed command perfect. "The idea has some merit," he said slowly. "Let us discuss it." Dunbarth beamed. Teralind's face got very white, and Ulvissen was suddenly at her elbow, warning her to stay calm.

At that moment Kith-Kanan felt a flash of recognition; he remembered where he'd seen Ulvissen before. It had been the day he'd rescued Mackeli from Voltorno. When the half-human had fallen after their duel, a crowd of humans from his ship had raced up the hillside. The tallest human there had had a full, red-brown beard like Ulvissen's. And since the human had already admitted that he'd spent most of his career aboard ships. . . . The prince started as his twin's voice interrupted his thoughts.

Sithas was asking the speaker what merit he had found in the dwarves' suggestion.

Sithel paused a moment before replying, considering his words carefully. "It is not King Voldrin's offer to rule the troublesome region that I favor," he said. "It is the idea of a buffer zone, independent of not just our rule and the emperor's, but of Thorbardin's as well."

"Are you proposing we create a new country?" Teralind said curiously.

"Not a sovereign state, a buffer state," replied the speaker.

Ulvissen tugged on his mistress's sleeve urgently. Feeling harassed, Teralind turned her back to Sithel for a moment to speak with the seneschal. She then asked the company for a brief adjournment. Dunbarth sat down, carefully tucking the crinkly parchment letter from his king into his brocade vest. Despite the opposition to his king's proposal, he was quite pleased with himself.

Kith-Kanan watched all this with barely contained agitation. He could hardly denounce Ulvissen during a diplomatic meeting—not when such an accusation would violate the law of good behavior in the Tower of the Stars on his first day back in Silvanost! Moreover, could he be certain Ulvissen was the man he'd seen with Voltorno? Bearded humans did tend to look alike. In any event, the elaborate manners and elliptical conversations of the ambassadors struck him as silly and wasteful of time.

"My king suggests a division of rights among the three nations," Dunbarth resumed when Teralind signaled herself ready. "Ergoth to have grazing rights, Silvanesti to have growing rights, and Thorbardin to have the mineral rights."

"Any proposal that puts the territory under any one nation's control is unacceptable," Teralind said shrilly. A strand of dark brown hair had come loose from its confining clasp. She absently looped it behind one ear. "Unless Ergothian rights are guaranteed," she added curtly.

The delegations, mingled as they were behind the chairs of their respective leaders, began to debate among themselves the merits of a joint administration of the disputed land. Their voices got louder and louder. After a moment, Kith-Kanan couldn't stand it any longer. He jumped to his feet.

Sithel raised a hand for quiet. "My son Kith-Kanan would speak," he said. The faintest trace of a smile crossed his lips.

"As you know, I have only just returned to Silvanost," the prince said, speaking quickly and nervously. "For some time I have been living in the wildwood, far to the south, where I came to know all sorts of people. Some, like my friend Mackeli, called the forest home. Others saw it as a place to be plundered. Ships from Ergoth have been lying off the coast while their crews steal inland to cut timber."

"This is outrageous!" Teralind exploded. "What has this to do with the current question? Worse, these charges have no proof behind them!"

For once Sithel cast aside his assumed air of impartiality. "What my son tells you is true," he said icily. "Believe it." The force in his words stifled Teralind's reply, and the speaker bade Kith-Kanan continue.

"The heart of the matter is that while kings and emperors wrestle over problems off national pride and prestige, people— innocent elves and humans—are dying. The gods alone know where the true blame lies, but now we have a chance to put an end to the suffering."

"Tell us how!" said Teralind sarcastically.

"First, by admitting that peace is what we all want. I don't have to be a soothsayer to know there are many in Daltigoth and Silvanost who think war is inevitable. So I ask you, is war the answer?" He turned to Lord Dunbarth. "You, my, lord. Is war the answer?"

"That's not a proper diplomatic question," countered the dwarf uncomfortably.

Kith-Kanan would not be put off. "Yes or no?" he insisted.

The entire company was looking at Dunbarth. He shifted in his chair. "War is never the answer, where people of good will—"

"Just answer the question!" snapped Teralind. Dunbarth arched one bushy eyebrow.

"No," he said firmly. "War is not the answer."

Kith-Kanan turned to the silent, crippled praetor and his wife. "Does Ergoth think war is the answer?"

The praetor's head jerked slightly. As usual, his wife answered for him. "No," Teralind replied. "Not when peace is cheaper."

He turned at last to his father. "What do you say, great speaker?"

"You're being impudent," Sithas warned.

"No," his father said simply, "it's only right he ask us all. I don't want war. I never have."

Kith-Kanan nodded and looked around at the entire group.

"Then, can't some way be found to rule the land jointly, elves, humans, and dwarves?"

"I don't see what the dwarves have to do with this," said Teralind sulkily. "Hardly any of them live in the disputed land."

"Yes, but we're speaking of our entire land border," Dunbarth reminded her. "Naturally, we are concerned with who is on the other side of it."

Sunlight filtered into the hall through the hundreds of window slits up the walls of the tower; a mild breeze flowed in through the doorway. The day beckoned them out of the stuffy debate. Sithel rubbed his hands together and announced, "This is a good time to pause, not only for reflection on the question of peace, but also to take bread and meat, and stroll in the sunshine."

"As ever, Your Highness is the wisest of us all," said Dunbarth with a tired smile.

Teralind started to object, but the speaker declared the meeting adjourned for lunch. The hall rapidly emptied, leaving Teralind, Praetor Ulwen, and Ulvissen by themselves. Wordlessly, Ulvissen gathered the frail praetor in his strong arms and carried him out. Teralind worked to master her anger, tearing one of her lace handkerchiefs to bits.

* * * * *

It was a fine day, and the delegations spilled out the huge front doors into the garden that surrounded the mighty tower. Servants from the palace arrived bearing tables on their shoulders. In short order the processional walkway at the tower's main entrance was filled with tables. Snow-white linen was spread on the tables, and a pleasant array of fruit and meats was set out for the speaker's guests. A cask of blush nectar was rolled to the site, its staves making booming noises like summer thunder as the barrel rolled.

The ambassadors and their delegations crowded around the tables. Dunbarth took a brimming cup of nectar. He tasted the vintage, found it good, and wandered over to inspect the food. From there he spied Kith-Kanan standing at the edge of the garden by himself. Food in hand, the dwarf strolled over to him.

"May I join you, noble prince?" he asked.

"As a guest you may stand where you want," Kith-Kanan replied genially.

"An interesting session this morning, don't you think?" Dunbarth pulled apart a capon and gnawed at a leg. "This is the most progress we've made since we first convened."

Kith-Kanan took a large bite from an apple and regarded the

dwarf with some surprise. "Progress? All I heard was a lot of contentious talk."

The dwarf flipped up the brim of his hat in order to hoist his golden goblet high. He drained the nectar and wiped the sticky liquid from his mustache. "Reorx bless me, Highness! Diplomacy is not like a hunt. We don't track down our quarry, pot him, and cart him home to be eaten. No, noble prince, diplomacy is like an old dwarf combing his hair—every hair that comes out in his comb is a defeat, and every one that stays in his head is a victory!"

Kith-Kanan chuckled and looked around the garden. He missed the weight of a sword at his hip. And even more, he missed the sights and smells of the forest. The city seemed too bright, the air tinged with too much smoke. Odd, he'd never noticed those things before.

"What are you thinking, Highness?" asked Dunbarth.

What was he thinking? He returned his gaze to the dwarf. "The praetor's wife is rather short-tempered, and the praetor himself never speaks. You'd think the emperor would have more able representatives," Kith-Kanan commented. "I don't think Lady Teralind does their cause much good."

Dunbarth looked for a place to throw the capon leg bone, now that he had cleaned it of meat. A servant appeared as if summoned and collected the refuse. "Yes, well, smooth and subtle she's not, but a lot can be accomplished by sheer stubbornness too. Prince Sithas—" Dunbarth quickly recalled to whom he spoke and thought the better of what he had been about to say.

"Yes?" Kith-Kanan prompted him.

"It's nothing, Highness."

"Speak, my lord. Truth is not to be feared."

"I wish I had Your Highness's optimism!" A passing servitor refilled Dunbarth's cup. "I was going to say that Prince Sithas, your noble brother, is a match for Lady Teralind in stubbornness."

Kith-Kanan nodded. "It is only too true. They are much alike. Both believe they have right always on their side."

He and Dunbarth exchanged some further pleasantries, then the dwarf said an abrupt good-bye. He wanted to mingle with the others a bit, he said, and wandered off aimlessly. But Kith-Kanan could read the purpose in his stride. He shook his head. Dwarves were supposedly bluff and hearty, but Dunbarth was more subtle than a Balifor merchant.

The prince strolled off on his own, among the head-high hedges of flowering vines and the artfully molded sculptures of boxwood and cedar. The vigorous spring seemed to have followed him from the wildwood to Silvanost. The garden was a riot of bloom.

He thought of the clearing where he and his little family had lived. Had the bees built their hives in the hollow oak yet? Were the flowering trees dropping their blossoms into the pool that was the entrance to Anaya's secret cave? In the midst of all the splendor and majesty that was Silvanost, Kith-Kanan remembered wistfully the simple life he had shared with Anaya.

His reverie was broken when he rounded a corner in the hedges and found Hermathya seated alone on a stone bench.

Kith-Kanan briefly considered turning and avoiding his former lover, but he decided that he couldn't hide from her forever. Instead of leaving, he went up to her and said hello.

Hermathya did not look up at him, but gazed off into the blossoms and greenery. "I woke up this morning thinking I had dreamed you returned. Then I asked my maidservant, and she said it was true." Her voice was low, controlled, and her hair shone in the sunlight. She wore it pulled back in a jeweled clasp, as befitted a high-born, married elf woman. Her pale arms were bare, her skin smooth and unblemished. He thought she was even more beautiful than when he'd left Silvanost.

She asked him to sit. He declined.

"Are you afraid to sit next to me?" she said, meeting his eyes for the first time. "It was once your favorite place to be."

"Let's not bring up the past," Kith-Kanan said, keeping his distance. "That's over and done with."

"Is it?" Her eyes, as always, caught and held him.

He was intensely aware of her, as near as he was, and she stirred him. What elf could be so close to her flame-bright loveliness and not be moved? However, Kith-Kanan no longer loved Hermathya; he was certain of that.

"I've been married," he said pointedly.

"Yes, I heard that last night. Your wife is dead, isn't she?"

No, only changed, he thought. But he replied, "Yes, she is."

"I thought about you a great deal, Kith." Hermathya said softly. "The longer you were away, the more I missed you."

"You forget, Thya, I asked you to flee with me—and you refused."

She seized his hand. "I was a fool! I don't love Sithas. You must know that," she exclaimed.

Hermathya's hand was smooth and warm, but Kith-Kanan still pulled his hand free of hers. "He is your husband and my brother," he said.

She didn't hear the warning in his statement. She leaned her head against him. "He's a pale shadow of you, as a prince . . . and a lover," she said bitterly.

Kith-Kanan moved away from the bench. "I have no intention

of betraying him, Thya. And you must accept the fact that I do not love you."

"But I love you!" A tear trickled down her cheek.

"If that's true, then I pity you. I have passed into another life since we loved each other, years ago. I'm not the headstrong young fool I once was."

"Don't you care for me at all?" she asked, her face anguished.

"No." he said truthfully, "I don't care for you at all."

One of Dunbarth's dwarven servants came running through the maze of hedges. "Great prince!" he said breathlessly. "The speaker is recalling the assembly."

Kith-Kanan walked away and did not look back at Hermathya, though he could hear her crying until he reached the entrance to the Tower of the Stars.

When he was out of earshot, Hermathya clenched her eyes shut, squeezing the tears from them. "So be it," she hissed to herself. "So be it." She picked up the golden goblet Kith-Kanan had left nearby and bashed the soft metal against the marble bench. The goblet was soon a twisted, misshapen lump.

* * * * *

The afternoon session dragged on as the three sides tried to decide who would govern the proposed buffer state. It was a tricky question, and every suggestion that came up was debated and discounted. Clerics and guildmasters from the city grew tired of the endless discussion and drifted away, thinning the crowd in the audience hall. After a time, Praetor Ulwen's head nodded forward. His wife looked like she wanted a long nap herself.

"I can't agree to give away mineral rights or crop-growing rights," Teralind said testily, for the third time. "How do you expect our people to live? They can't all herd cattle."

"Well, your idea to have enclaves belonging to different nations is no solution," Sithas said, tapping the arm of his chair to emphasize each word. "Instead of one large disputed territory, we'll have scores of tiny ones!"

"Separate communities might be the answer," mused Dunbarth, "if they are able to trade with each other."

"They would fight over the choicest land," the speaker said. He rubbed a hand against his left temple. "This is getting nowhere. Surely one of us can come up with a fair and adequate solution."

No one said anything. Kith-Kanan shifted nervously in his seat. He had said virtually nothing during this session. Something Anaya had mentioned to him once was nagging at him. "I don't meddle with the forest. I just protect it." Perhaps that was the answer.

The prince stood quickly. The sudden movement startled everyone; they'd practically forgotten he was there. Sithel looked at his son questioningly, and Kith-Kanan self-consciously straightened the folds of his white robe.

"It seems to me," he said with dignity, "that the entire problem with the western provinces comes from the fact that new settlers are pushing the old ones out. No one here, I think, would defend such activity." Sithas and Dunbarth glanced at Teralind. She put her nose in the air and shrugged.

Kith-Kanan moved to the center of the floor. Sithas shifted restlessly as all eyes fixed on his brother. "If everyone is agreed upon the principle that all persons, regardless of race, have a right to settle on empty land, then the problem becomes a simple one—how to protect the legitimate settlers from those who seek to drive them off their land."

"I sent soldiers once," said the speaker flatly. "They were betrayed and slaughtered."

"Forgive me, Father," Kith-Kanan said, "but from what I have heard of the incident, they were too few and not the right kind of soldiers. If we are going to share the bounty of these lands, then the burden of protecting them must be shared. Soldiers from the city have no stake in the area; they simply obey the orders of the speaker." The prince looked around at the company. "Do you not see? What's needed is a local force, a militia, in which the farmer has his own shield and spear with which to protect his land and that of his neighbor."

"Militia?" said Teralind with interest. Ulvissen was suddenly at her elbow trying to tell her something.

"Arm the farmers?" asked Dunbarth. The brim of his hat had lost its snap and drooped down over his eyes. He brushed it back.

"Peasants with spears would never stand up to mounted bandits," asserted Sithas.

"They would if they were trained and led by experienced soldiers," Kith-Kanan countered. He was thinking on his feet now. "One sergeant for each company of twenty; one captain for each band of two hundred."

"Are you speaking of all settlers in the disputed lands being armed?" asked Dunbarth. "Even those not of elven blood?"

"Definitely. If we arm one group and not another, it's just an invitation for war. A mixed militia will bind the people together, serving shoulder to shoulder with men of other races."

"I still say farmers and cow herders will never catch a fast-moving party of raiders," Sithas said stiffly.

Kith-Kanan's enthusiasm brought him right up to his brother's chair. "Don't you see, Sith? They don't have to catch the bandits. They only have to be able to fend them off. Why, the ruined village Mackeli and I saw had a sod wall eight feet high all around it. If the villagers had had a few spears and had known how to fight, they all might have been saved."

"I think it is an excellent idea," Sithel remarked.

"I like it, too."

Kith-Kanan swiveled around to see if what he'd just heard was true. Teralind was sitting proudly, hands folded on the lap of her burgundy gown. "I like it," she repeated firmly. "It puts the responsibility on the people living there." Behind her Ulvissen was livid with ill-suppressed anger. "No army need be sent in, yours or ours. The emperor will save much money."

"I have some doubts about the efficacy of such a militia," Dunbarth put in, "but never let it be said that Dunbarth of Dunbarth wasn't willing to give it a try!" The dwarf whipped off his bothersome hat. "I smell peace!" he declared, throwing the hat to the shiny marble floor.

"Don't be hasty," Sithas warned. His cool voice dampened the growing elation in the hall. "My brother's plan has its merits, but it doesn't address the problem of sovereignty. I say, let there be a militia, but only elves may bear arms in it."

Kith-Kanan looked stricken, and Teralind rapidly lost her serene expression. She said, "No! That's impossible. Ergoth will not allow humans to live as hostages among an army of elves!"

"Quite right," said Dunbarth, picking up his hat and dusting it off against his leg.

"We cannot abandon our ancestral right to this land!" Sithas insisted.

"Be still," the speaker said, frowning. Now it was Sithas's turn to look aggrieved. "This is a practical business we're in. If Ergoth and Thorbardin like Kith-Kanan's proposal, I cannot in good conscience throw away the best chance we have for peace."

Sithas opened his mouth to speak, but Sithel stifled him with a glance. The prince turned away, his lips pressed together in a thin line.

After a short while, when more specific details were worked out, a basic agreement was reached. Each of the three nations was to provide a corps of experienced warriors to serve as organizers of the new militia. Armories would be set up, where the warrior officers would reside. And in times of trouble all able bodied settlers within twenty miles would present themselves at the armory to receive weapons and leadership. No single nation would command the militia.

"You expect professional warriors to live in the wilderness, shepherding a motley rabble of farmers?" Sithas asked with ill-concealed irritation. "What will keep them in their place?"

Kith-Kanan folded his arms. "Land," he declared. "Give them a stake in the peace of the country."

"Give them enough to be worth working," said Dunbarth, catching the gist of Kith-Kanan's idea.

"Exactly! Five acres for every sergeant, twenty acres for every captain. A whole new class of gentry will arise, loyal to the land and to their neighbors," Kith-Kanan predicted.

The speaker ordered the scribes to prepare a draft of the decree. Then, as it was nearly dusk, he adjourned the session. Everyone stood while Sithel went out, looking tired but very pleased. Teralind's shoulders sagged, and she was supported on the arm of Ulvissen, who did not look at all happy with events. Neither did Sithas as he left. Kith-Kanan was about to start after him when Dunbarth called to him.

"My prince," he enthused, "Congratulations on your masterful stroke!"

Kith-Kanan watched his twin disappear out the private exit to the palace. "Yes, thank you," he said distantly.

"I praise the gods for bringing you back," continued the dwarf, folding his hands across his round belly. "That's what this problem needed, a fresh perspective." Dunbarth cleared his throat.

"Oh, your pardon, my lord. I'm being rude," said Kith-Kanan, turning his attention to the ambassador from Thorbardin.

"Do not trouble about it." Dunbarth glanced at the rear exit and commented. "Your brother is proud, and he hasn't yet learned the benefit of flexibility. Your father is wise. He understands."

The elf prince's brow furrowed with thought. "I suppose," he replied uncertainly.

Guards opened the vast double doors of the tower. Beyond the entryway, the red rays of the setting sun painted the world scarlet. Only Dunbarth's small retinue, two scribes and his secretary, Drollo, remained, waiting patiently for their master.

Dunbarth's eyes shone as he plopped his hat on his head. "Noble prince, would you dine with me? I have an urge to try some inn in your city tonight—not that the dining is poor in the palace. Far from it! It's just that I crave some hearty, simple fare."

Kith-Kanan smiled. "I know a place, right on the river. Fried catfish, cabbage rolls, a suet pudding . . ."

"Beer?" said the dwarf hopefully. Elves don't drink beer, so the ambassador hadn't had any since coming to Silvanost.

"I think the innkeeper ought to be able to scratch some up," Kith-Kanan assured him.

The elf prince and the dwarven ambassador walked out the high doors and into the crimson evening.

* * * * *

After leaving the Tower of the Stars, Sithas walked through the starlit streets. He wanted to be alone, to think. Anger propelled his steps, and habit steered him to the Temple of Matheri, where so much of his early life had been spent. The crystal dome of the sanctum of the god rose above the sculpted trees like a rising moon, lit a golden yellow from within. Sithas took the steps two at a time. At the door, he dipped his hands in the bowl of rose petals set on a tripod and scattered them on the paving before him.

In quick, barely audible tones, he said, "Wise Matheri, grant me entrance that I may commune with you." The buffed wooden doors parted silently, with no hand to stir them. Sithas went inside.

In the center of the floor, directly under the great dome, the ever-burning lamp of Matheri stood. The silent, smokeless flame cast harsh shadows around the circular room. Along the outer edge of the temple were the meditation chambers of the monks. Sithas knew them well. This was where he had lived for thirty years of his life.

He went to his old cubicle. It was empty, so he entered. Sitting on the hard floor, he crossed his legs. The prince tried to meditate, to find the reason for his resentment of Kith-Kanan's success. As the priests had taught him, he imagined a dialogue with himself.

"You are angry, why?" he asked aloud.

In his mind, he formed a reply. Kith's suggestion is dangerous to the nation.

"Is it? Why?"

It allows the humans to remain on land that rightfully belongs to us.

"They have been there for years. Is their presence intrinsically bad?"

The land belongs to the elven nation. No one else.

"An inflexible attitude. Is this the reason you're angry?"

Sithas paused and considered. He closed his eyes and examined closely the feelings that crowded inside his heart.

No. I've been working at father's side for weeks, discussing, planning, thinking, and re-thinking, yet nothing was accomplished. I should have thought of the militia plan. I have failed.

"You are jealous of Kith-Kanan."

I have no reason to be jealous. I am the speaker's heir. Yet a short time ago I found myself wishing I hadn't called him back.

"Why did you?"

He's my brother. I missed him. I thought father might die—

Before he could ponder his feelings further, the carved rosewood door of the cell swung open. Sithas looked up, ready to lash out at whomever would intrude. It was Hermathya.

"What are you doing here?" he demanded harshly.

She stepped into the little room. Covered from head to toe in a midnight-black cape, she dropped the hood from her head. Diamonds gleamed faintly from her earlobes.

"I knew you would be here," she said in a low voice. "You always come here when you're upset."

Sithas felt an icy mask of resolve fall into place, covering his painful emotions. "I am not upset," he said coldly.

"Tosh, I heard you raving to yourself as soon as I came in."

He stood and brushed the dust from his knees. "What is it you want?" he demanded again.

"I heard what happened at the tower today. It doesn't look good for you, does it? All these days of negotiating for nothing, then Kith solves everything in one day."

She was only reinforcing what his bitter heart had been saying. Sithas moved until he was only inches from her. He could smell the rosewater she'd bathed in. "Are you trying to provoke me?" he asked, staring into her eyes.

"Yes." He felt her breath on his face when she said it. "I'm trying to provoke you into being a prince and not some sort of high-born monk!"

He drew away. "You are as tactful as ever, lady. Leave me to recover my temper. Your advice is not needed or welcome."

Hermathya made no move to go. "You need me," she insisted. "You've always needed me, but you're too stubborn to know it."

Sithas swept a hand over the single candle that lit the cubicle. Darkness, save for a stray shaft of light that slipped in around the closed door, claimed the room. He could see the heat outline of Hermathya, her back to the door, and she could hear his quick breathing.

"When I was a child, I was sent to this temple to learn patience and wisdom. The first three days I was here, I wept all my waking hours because I'd been separated from Kith. I could live without my mother and father, but cut off from Kith . . . I felt like I'd been cut open and part of me had been torn out."

Hermathya said nothing. The diamonds in her ears sparkled like stars in the scant light.

"Later, when we were older, I was allowed to go home to the palace and visit a few days each month. Kith was always doing something interesting—learning to ride, fence, shoot a bow. He

220

was always better than me," Sithas said. Resignation was creeping into his voice.

"There is one thing you have that he hasn't," Hermathya said soothingly, reaching out in the dark for Sithas's hand.

"What's that?"

"Me."

Sithas uttered a short, sardonic laugh. "I daresay he could have you if he wanted you!"

She snatched her hand from his and slapped Sithas hard across the cheek. Her blow stung his face. Forgetting his training, the prince seized his wife roughly and brought their faces together until they were only a finger's width apart. Even in the dim cubicle, he could see her pale features clearly, and she his.

She said desperately, "I am your wife!"

"Do you still love Kith-Kanan?" Despite the coldness of their marriage, Sithas braced himself for her answer.

"No," she whispered fiercely. "I hate him. Anything that angers you, I hate."

"Your concern for me is touching. And quite new," he said skeptically.

"I admit that I thought I might still love him," she whispered, "but since seeing him, I know it's not true." Tremors shivered through her. "You are my husband," Hermathya declared passionately. "I wish Kith-Kanan were gone again, so he couldn't ever make you feel small!"

"He's never tried to make me feel small," Sithas retorted.

"And what if he wins your father's favor completely?" she parried. "The speaker could declare Kith-Kanan his heir if he felt he would do a better job of ruling than you."

"Father would never do that!"

Her lips were by his ear. She pressed her cheek against his and felt his tight grip relax. Quickly she said, "The militia must have an overall commander. Who better than Kith-Kanan? He has the skills and experience for it. With all those square miles to patrol, he could be gone for decades."

Sithas turned his head away, and she knew he was thinking about it. A small, triumphant smile played about her lips. "By then," she murmured, "we will have a son of our own, and Kith could never come between you and the throne."

The prince said nothing, but Hermathya was patient. Instead of prompting him further, she laid her head on his chest. His heartbeat was strong in her ear. After a time, Sithas slowly brought his hand up and stroked her copper-gold hair.

By Next Dawn

25

When it came to the spread of important news, the great city of Silvanost was just like a tiny village.

By the next morning, word of the tentative agreement between the speaker and the representatives of Ergoth and Thorbardin had penetrated every corner of the capital. The city, and the elven nation itself, seemed to let out a long-held breath. Fear of war had been uppermost in the minds of all the people, followed closely by fear that large numbers of refugees would once more be driven back into the city by the bandit raids.

When the new day dawned, rimmed by low clouds and chilly with the threat of rain, the people of Silvanost behaved as if it was a bright, sun-filled day. The nobility, priests, and guildmasters heard cheering as their sedan chairs were carried through the streets.

Kith-Kanan went into the city that morning on horseback with Lord Dunbarth. It was the prince's first chance to see Silvanost since his return. His appetite had been whetted when he and the dwarf had dined at the Inn of the Golden Acorn. There, with good food and drink, stirred by the strains of a bardic lyre, Kith-Kanan had rediscovered his love for the city, dormant for all his months in the wildwood.

He and Dunbarth rode through the crowded streets of the family quarter, where most of Silvanost's population lived. Here the houses were less grand than the guildmasters' halls or the priestly enclaves, but they mimicked the styles of the great homes. Beautifully sculpted towers rose, but only for three or four stories.

Tiny green plots of land in front of each home were molded by elven magic to support dazzling gardens of red, yellow, and violet flowers; shrubs formed into wave patterns like the river; and trees that bowed and twined together like the braids in an elf maiden's hair. Nearly every house, no matter how small, was built in imitation of the homes of the great, around a central atrium that held the family's private garden.

"I didn't realize how much I missed it," Kith-Kanan said, steering his horse around a pushcart full of spring melons.

"Miss what, noble prince?" asked Dunbarth.

"The city. Though the forest became my home, a part of me still lives here. It's like I'm seeing Silvanost for the first time!"

Both elf and dwarf were dressed plainly, without the fine embroidery, golden jewelry, or other outward signs of rank. Even their horses were trapped in the simplest possible style. Kith-Kanan wore a wide-brimmed hat, like a fisher, so that his royal features would be less obvious. They wanted to see the city, not be surrounded by crowds.

Together the duo turned off Phoenix Street and rode down a narrow alley. Kith-Kanan could smell the river even more strongly here. When he emerged in the old Market quarter, ruined by the great riot and now under repair, Kith-Kanan reined up and surveyed the scene. The entire marketplace, from where his horse stood down to the banks of the Thon-Thalas, had been razed. Gangs of Kagonesti elves swarmed around the site, sawing lumber, hauling stones, mixing mortar. Here and there a robed priest of E'li stood, directing the work.

For a large project, like a high tower, magic would be used to shape and raise the stones of the walls and meld the blocks together without need for mortar. In the mundane buildings of the marketplace, more ordinary techniques would be used.

"Where do all the workers come from?" Kith-Kanan wondered aloud.

"As I understand it, they're slaves from estates to the north and west, owned by the priests of E'li," said Dunbarth without inflection.

"Slaves? But the speaker put severe limits on the number of slaves anyone could own."

Dunbarth stroked his curly beard. "I know it may shock Your Highness, but outside of Silvanost the speaker's laws aren't always followed. They are bent to suit the needs of the rich and powerful."

"I'm certain my father doesn't know about this," Kith-Kanan said firmly.

"Forgive me, Highness, but I believe he does," Dunbarth remarked confidentially. "Your mother, the Lady Nirakina, has many times pleaded with the speaker to free the slaves of Silvanesti, to no avail."

"How do you know these things? Aren't they private matters of the palace?"

The dwarf smiled benignly. "It is a diplomat's purpose to listen as well as talk. Five weeks in the Quinari Palace exposes one to all sorts of gossip and idle talk. I know the love lives of your servants and who among the nobility drinks too much—not to mention the sad plight of slaves in your own capital city." With that, Dunbarth's smile vanished.

"It's intolerable!" Kith-Kanan's horse sensed his rider's agitation and pranced around in a half-circle. "I'll put a stop to this right now!"

He tightened the reins and turned his mount's head. Before he could ride over to confront the supervising priests, Danbarth caught his reins and held him back.

"Don't be hasty, my prince. The priesthoods are very powerful. They have friends at court who will speak against you."

Kith-Kanan was indignant. "Who do you mean?"

Dunbarth's gaze was level. "I mean your brother, the noble Sithas."

Kith-Kanan squinted from under the brim of his hat. "My twin is not a slave driver. Why do you say this to me, my lord?"

"I only say what is true, Highness. You know the court; you know how alliances are made. Prince Sithas has become the defender of the temples. In turn, the priests support him."

"Against whom?"

"Anyone who opposes him. The priestess Miritelisina, of the Temple of Quenesti Pah, for one. She tried to defend those who fled from the slaughter on the plains. You know of the riot?" Kith-Kanan knew Sithas's version of the story. He indicated Dunbarth should continue.

"The riot began because Prince Sithas and the priests, along with the guildmasters, wanted to expel the poor farmers from the city. Miritelisina warned them. They misunderstood her and, believing they were to be sent back to the plains, rioted. For that the priestess was put in prison. The speaker has let her go free, but she continues her work for the poor and homeless."

Kith-Kanan said nothing, but watched as three Kagonesti passed by with a ten-inch-thick log braced on their shoulders.

In each one he saw Anaya—the same dark eyes and hair, the same passion for freedom.

"I must speak out against this," he said at last. "It is wrong for one of the firstborn race to own another."

"They will not hear you, Highness," Dunbarth said sadly.

Kith-Kanan put his horse's head toward the palace. "They will hear me. If they don't listen, I'll shout at them till they do."

They rode back at a brisk canter, avoiding the clogged streets in the center of the city and keeping to the riverside roads. By the time they reached the plaza in front of the palace, a light rain had started to fall. Mackeli was standing in the courtyard in his new squire's livery, a studded leather jerkin and helmet. When Kith-Kanan rode up, Mackeli hurried over and held the prince's horse while he dismounted.

"You look splendid," Kith-Kanan said, sizing up Mackeli's new outfit.

"Are you sure this is what squires wear?" asked the boy. He hooked a finger in the tight collar and tugged at the stiff leather. "I feel like I've been swallowed by a steer."

Kith-Kanan laughed and clapped him on the shoulder. "Wait until you put on your first real armor," he said exuberantly. "Then you'll feel like one of our giant turtles has swallowed you!"

The three left the horses for the servants to stable and entered the palace. Maids appeared with dry towels. Kith-Kanan and Dunbarth made perfunctory swipes at their faces, then handed the cloths back. Mackeli dried himself carefully, all the while eyeing the handmaids with frank interest. The girls, both of whom were about the boy's age, blushed under his studied gaze,

"Come along," Kith-Kanan scolded, dragging at Mackeli's sleeve. Dunbarth plucked the towel from his hand and returned it to the servants.

"I wasn't finished," Mackeli protested.

"If you'd dried yourself any longer, you'd have taken hide and hair off, too," observed the dwarf.

"I was looking at the girls," Mackeli said bluntly.

"Yes, like a wolf looks at his dinner," noted Kith-Kanan. "If you want to impress the fair sex, you'd best learn to be a little more discreet."

"What do you mean?"

"He means, don't stare," advised Dunbarth. "Smile at them and say something pleasant."

Mackeli was puzzled. "What should I say?"

Kith-Kanan put a hand to his chin and considered. "Pay them a compliment. Say, 'what pretty eyes you have!' or ask them their name and say, 'what a pretty name!' "

"Can I touch them?" asked Mackeli innocently.

"No!" exclaimed the two in unison.

They spotted Ulvissen in the corridor, accompanied by one of the human soldiers. The Ergothian seneschal was handing the soldier a large brass tube, which the man furtively tucked into a leather bag hung from his shoulder. Ulvissen stood up straight when he saw Kith-Kanan. The soldier with the tube saluted and went on his way.

"How goes it, Master Ulvissen?" the prince asked blandly.

"Very well, Your Highness. I have dispatched a copy of the preliminary agreement we've made to His Imperial Majesty."

"Just now?"

Ulvissen nodded. Behind his beard and graying hair, he looked haggard. Kith-Kanan guessed Lady Teralind had kept him up very late, preparing the dispatch.

"Would you know where my father and Prince Sithas might be?"

"I last saw them in the reception hall, where seals were being put to the copies of the agreement," said Ulvissen courteously. He bowed.

"Thank you." Kith-Kanan and Dunbarth walked on. Mackeli, too, drifted past the tall, elder human, looking at him with curiosity.

"How old are you?" asked Mackeli impetuously.

Ulvissen was surprised. "Forty and nine years," he replied.

"I am sixty-one," said the boy. "Why is it you look so much older than I?"

Kith-Kanan swung around and took Mackeli by the elbows. "Forgive him, Excellency," said the prince. "The boy has lived all his life in the forest and knows little about manners."

"It is nothing," said Ulvissen. Yet he continued to watch with an intense expression as the prince and the dwarf ambassador hustled Mackeli away.

*　*　*　*　*

The reception hall of the palace was on the ground floor of the central tower, one floor below the Hall of Balif. Dunbarth took his leave of Kith-Kanan in the corridor outside. "My old bones need a nap," he apologized.

Mackeli started to follow the prince, who told him to remain behind. The boy objected, but Kith-Kanan said sharply, "Find some other way to be useful. I'll be back soon."

When Kith-Kanan entered, the vast, round room was full of tables and stools, at which scribes were furiously writing. The entire transcript of the conference was being written out in full and copied as quickly as the master scribe could finish a page.

Sithel and Sithas stood in the center of this organized chaos, approving sheets of parchment covered with spidery handwriting. Boys darted among the tables, filling inkpots, sharpening styluses, and piling up fresh stacks of unmarked vellum. When Sithel espied him, he shoved the parchment aside and gestured for the assistant to leave.

"Father, I need to speak with you. And you, Brother," Kith-Kanan said, gesturing to a quieter side of the hall. When they had moved, the prince asked bluntly, "Do you know that gangs of slaves are working in the city, working to rebuild the Market?"

"That's common knowledge," said Sithas quickly. He was especially elegant today, having forsworn his usual robe in favor of a divided kilt and a thigh-length tunic of quilted cloth of gold. His headband, too, was golden.

"What about the law?" asked Kith-Kanan, his voice rising. "No household is supposed to have more than two slaves at a time, yet I saw two hundred or more working away, watched over by clerics from the Temple of E'li."

"The law only applies to those who live in Silvanost," Sithas said, preempting his father again. Sithel kept quiet and let his sons argue. He was curious to see which would prevail. "The slaves you saw come from temple estates on the Em-Bali River, north of the city," added the speaker's firstborn.

"That's an evasion," Kith-Kanan said heatedly. "I never heard of a law that applied only in Silvanost and not to the entire nation!"

"Why all this concern about slaves?" Sithas demanded.

"It isn't right." Kith-Kanan clenched his hands into fists. "They are elves, the same as us. It is not right that elves should own one another."

"They are not like us," Sithas snapped. "They are Kagonesti."

"Does that automatically condemn them?"

Sithel decided it was time to intervene. "The workers you saw were sold into slavery because they were convicted of crimes against the Silvanesti people," he said gently. "That they are Kagonesti is of no significance. Your concern for them is misplaced, Kith."

"I don't think so, Father," his son argued earnestly. "We're all proud of our Silvanesti blood, and that's good. But pride should not lead us to exploit our subjects."

"You have been in the woods too long," said Sithas coolly. "You have forgotten how the world works."

"Hold your tongue," Sithel intervened sharply. "And you too, Kith." The Speaker of the Stars looked rueful. "I am glad to know both my sons feel so passionately about right and wrong. The blood of Silvanos has not run thin, I can see. But this debate serves no purpose. If the slaves in the Market are well treated and do their allotted work, I see no reason to tamper with the situation."

"But, Father—"

"Listen to me, Kith. You've only been back four days. I know you grew used to much freedom in the forest, but a city and a nation cannot operate like a camp in the wildwood. Someone must command, and others must obey. That's how a speaker can protect the weak and rule with justice."

"Yes, Father." When Sithel explained it like that, it almost made sense. Still, Kith-Kanan knew that no amount of logic and lawful argument would ever convince him that slavery was anything but wrong.

Sithas listened to Sithel's words with his arms folded in satisfaction. Kith was not as infallible as he seemed, thought the firstborn. Facing down Kith's sentimental ramblings made him feel every inch the next Speaker of the Stars.

"Now I have a command for you, son," Sithel said to Kith-Kanan. "I want you to lead the new militia."

Utter silence. Kith-Kanan tried to digest this. He was just back home, and now he was being sent away. He looked at Sithas—who glanced away—then back at the speaker. "Me, Father?" he asked, dazed.

"With your experience as a warrior and ranger, who better? I have already spoken with Lady Teralind and Lord Dunbarth, and they agree. A speaker's son, ranger, and a friend of the Kagonesti, you are the best choice."

Kith-Kanan looked to Sithas. "This was your idea, Sith?"

His brother shrugged. "Clear reasoning pointed to you and no one else."

Kith-Kanan ran a hand through his tousled hair. The crafty old Dunbarth knew all through their ride this morning and hadn't said a word. In fact, had he led the way to the Market to show Kith-Kanan the slaves at work there? To prepare him for this?

"You can refuse," noted the speaker, "if you wish." He plainly expected no such reaction from his stalwart son.

A rush of images and thoughts flooded Kith-Kanan's mind. In quick succession he saw the ruined village he and Mackeli had found; Voltorno, roving and plundering at will through Silvanesti; Anaya, mortally stricken, fighting bows and swords with a flint knife; Kagonesti slaves, stripped of their lives.

The prince also heard his own words: "If the people had possessed a few spears, and had known how to fight, they might all have been saved."

Kith-Kanan's gaze remained on his twin for a long moment, then he looked at the speaker.

"I accept," he said quietly.

* * * * *

With Mackeli at his side, Kith-Kanan spent the next few days interviewing members of the royal guard who had volunteered for the militia. As he had predicted, the lure of free land was a powerful inducement to soldiers who seldom owned anything more than the clothes on their backs. Kith-Kanan could select the very best of them as his sergeants.

A great public celebration had been declared, both to honor the new agreement with Ergoth and Thorbardin and to honor Kith-Kanan's ascent to command of the new militia of House Protector. The force was already being called the Wildrunners, after the old name given to the armed bands of Kagonesti who had fought for Silvanos during the wars of elven unification.

*　*　*　*　*

"I still don't understand why we don't just fly out there," Mackeli said, struggling under the weight of real armor and a pot-shaped iron helmet.

"Griffons are reserved as mounts of House Royal," Kith-Kanan said. "Besides, there aren't enough of them for this whole company." He cinched a rope tight around the last bundle of his personal gear. His chestnut charger, Kijo, bore the weight of bedroll and armor well. Kith-Kanan had been pleased to discover that his old mount was still as spirited as ever.

Mackeli regarded the horses skeptically. "Are you sure these beasts are tame?"

Kith-Kanan smiled. "You rode Arcuballis one thousand feet up in the air, and now you're worried about riding on horseback?"

"I know Arcuballis," the boy said apprehensively. "I don't know these animals."

"It will be all right." Kith-Kanan went down the line of horses and warriors. The last knots were made, and the good-byes were being said.

The Processional Road was full of elves and horses. Two hundred and fifty warriors and an equal number of mounts milled about. Unlike Sithel's earlier, ill-fated expedition, Kith-Kanan's band was to be entirely mounted and self-sufficient. This was the largest force to leave Silvanost since the days of the founding wars.

It was a splendid spectacle, and the sides of the street were lined with townsfolk. The warriors had discarded their fancy parade armor in favor of more practical equipment. Each elf wore a hammered iron breastplate and a simple, open-faced helmet. Bronze shields, shaped like hourglasses, hung from each saddlehorn. Every warrior carried a bow, twenty arrows, a sword, a knife, and a heavy javelin that could be used for thrusting or throwing. The horses wore only minimal trapping, as mobility was more important than protection.

Kith-Kanan tucked his gauntlets under his arm as he mounted the steps to the processional entrance of the Tower of the Stars. There stood his father and mother, Sithas and Hermathya, Lady Teralind, Praetor Ulwen in his chair, and Ulvissen. Lord Dunbarth had begged off attending the departure ceremony. He was afflicted with a colic, according to his faithful secretary, Drollo. Kith-Kanan knew that the old rascal had been living it up in the inns and taverns along the riverfront since the treaty had been approved by the emperor of Ergoth and the king of Thorbardin.

The prince ascended the steps in measured tread, keeping his eyes fixed on his father. Sithel was wearing the formal Crown of Stars, a magnificent golden circlet that featured as its central stone the famed Eye of Astarin, the largest emerald in all of Krynn. The gem caught the rays of the midmorning sun and sent flashes of verdant light across the street and gardens.

Beside Sithel stood Lady Nirakina. She was dressed in a gown of palest blue and wore a filigree silver torc around her throat. Her honey-colored hair was held in a silver cloth scarf. There was something sad and remote about her expression—no doubt it was the realization that she was losing her younger son again, after he'd been home less than a month.

Kith-Kanan reached the step just below the landing where the royal family was gathered. He removed his helmet and bowed to his father.

"Noble father, gracious mother," he said with dignity.

"Stand with me," said Sithel warmly. Kith-Kanan made the final step and stood beside his father.

"Your mother and I have something to give you," the speaker said in a private tone. "Open it when you are alone." Nirakina handed her husband a red silk kerchief, the corners of which were tied together. Sithel pressed this into Kith-Kanan's hand.

"Now for the public words," the speaker said with the faintest trace of a smile. Sithel looked out over the crowd. He raised his hand and declaimed, "People of Silvanost! I present you my son, Kith-Kanan, in whose trust I place the peace and safety of the realm." To Kith-Kanan he asked loudly, "Will you faithfully and honorably discharge the duties of lord constable in all parts of our realm and any other provinces you may enter?"

Loudly and clearly Kith-Kanan replied, "By E'li, I swear I will." The crowd roared in approval.

Standing apart on the speaker's left were Sithas and Hermathya. The lady, who was radiantly beautiful in cream white and gold, had a serene expression on her fine-boned face. But Kith-Kanan's twin smiled on him as he approached for a blessing.

"Good hunting, Kith," said Sithas warmly. "Show the humans what elven mettle is like!"

"That I'll do, Sith." Without warning, Kith-Kanan embraced his brother. Sithas returned Kith-Kanan's embrace with fervor.

"Keep yourself safe, Brother," Sithas said softly, then broke away.

Kith-Kanan turned to Hermathya. "Farewell, lady."

"Good-bye," she replied coldly.

Kith-Kanan descended the steps. Mackeli was holding Kijo's reins. "What did the lady say?" he asked, gazing up at Hermathya with rapt admiration.

"You noticed her, did you?"

"Well, yes! She's like a sunflower in a hedge of thistles—"

Kith-Kanan swung into the saddle. "By Astarin! You're starting to sound like a bard! It's a good thing we're getting you out of the city. Anaya wouldn't know you, talking like that!"

The warriors followed Kith-Kanan and Mackeli in ranks of five, wheeling with precision as the prince led them down the curving Processional Road. The assembled Silvanesti let out a roar of approbation, which quickly turned into a steady chant:

"Kith-Ka-nan, Kith-Ka-nan, Kith-Ka-nan . . ."

The chanting continued as the slow procession wound its way to the riverside. Two ferry barges were waiting for the warriors. Kith-Kanan and the Wildrunners boarded the ferries, and the huge turtles towed them away. The people of Silvanost lined the shore and called out Kith-Kanan's name until long after the barges were lost against the dark strip of the western riverbank.

Early Summer, Year of the Ram

26

Lord Dunbarth's party loaded all their possessions onto wagons and formed up to depart. Sithas and his honor guard were there to see the dwarven ambassador off.

"Much better weather than when I arrived," Dunbarth remarked. He was sweating under his woolen coat and vest. Summer was upon Silvanost, and a warm, humid wind blew in from the river.

"It is indeed," Sithas said pleasantly. In spite of Dunbarth's professional caginess, Sithas liked the old dwarf. There was a basic goodness about him.

"You'll find a case of amber nectar in your carriage," said the prince. "With the compliments of Lady Nirakina and myself."

"Ah!" The dwarf looked genuinely touched. "Many thanks, noble prince. I shall be sure to share it with my king. He esteems elven nectar almost as much as Thorbardin ale."

The ambassador's escort, augmented by an honor guard of twenty elven warriors, paraded past the wagon. Dunbarth and his secretary, Drollo, climbed into their closed metal coach. As the ambassador pushed back the fine mesh curtains, he extended a ring-heavy hand to Sithas.

"In Thorbardin we wish friends a long life when parting, but I know you'll outlive me by centuries," Dunbarth said, a twinkle in his eye. "What do elves say when they part?"

"We say, 'Blessings of Astarin' and "May your way be green and golden'," Sithas replied. He clasped the ambassador's thick, wrinkled hand.

"May your way be green and golden, then, Prince Sithas. Oh, and some news for you, too. Our Lady Teralind is not what she pretends to be."

Sithas raised a brow. "Oh?"

"She is the emperor's eldest daughter."

Sithas feigned mild interest. "Really? That's interesting. Why do you tell me this now, my lord?"

Dunbarth tried to hide his smile. "The dealing is done, so there's no advantage to my keeping her identity secret. I've seen her before, you see. In Daltigoth. Hmm, I thought your noble father might like to know so that he could—um—ah, give her a royal send-off."

"My lord, you are wise for one so young," Sithas said, grinning.

"Would that I *were* young! Farewell, Prince!" Dunbarth rapped on the side of the coach. "Drive on!"

* * * * *

When he returned to the palace, Sithas was summoned to the Ergothians' quarters. There he was awaited by his father, his mother, and her courtier, Tamanier Ambrodel. The prince quickly informed them of the dwarven lord's revelation.

At one end of the room, Teralind was giving final orders to her servants in a cross, high-pitched voice. Dresses of heavy velvet and delicate lace were being squeezed into crates, which were then nailed shut. Toiletries rattled into rattan hampers.

The strongbox containing Teralind's jewelry was locked with a stout padlock and given to a soldier to guard personally.

Sithel approached this hectic scene. He halted in the center of the room and clasped his hands behind his back. Lady Teralind had no choice but to leave off her packing and attend the speaker. She combed a strand of hair back from her face and curtsied to Sithel.

"To what do I owe this honor?" she asked in a hurried tone that made it plain she regarded it as no honor at all.

"It's just come to my attention that I have been remiss in my duty," Sithel noted with heavy irony. "I greeted you and your husband as befitted an ambassador, when I should have done you more honor. It is not often I have an imperial princess under my roof."

A twitch passed over Teralind's face. "What?" she murmured.

"Surely you don't deny your father? He is the emperor, after all."

The tension left the woman's shoulders. Her back straightened slightly, and she immediately took on a more relaxed and regal attitude. "It doesn't matter now. You are quite right, Highness. I am Xanille Teralind, first daughter of His Majesty, Ullves X." She looped the stray strand of hair back again. "How did you find out?"

"Lord Dunbarth recognized you. But why did you hide your identity?" asked Sithel curiously.

"To protect myself," she averred. "My husband is a helpless invalid. We traveled a long way from Daltigoth, through regions where my father is not loved. Can you imagine the danger we would have faced if every bandit chief and warlord knew I was an imperial princess? We should have needed a hundred times the escort we came with. And how would Your Highness have felt if we had shown up before Silvanost at the head of a thousand warriors?"

"You are right. I would have thought you were trying to intimidate me," Sithel said genially. He glanced at Tamanier Ambrodel. At the signal, the courtier handed the speaker a small rolled slip of vellum. Although Sithel made a fist around the scroll, he didn't yet open it.

The prince studied his father, mother, and Tamanier. What were they up to? No one had told him what was going to happen— and yet, something was about to happen, that was plain.

"Where, my lady, is your seneschal?" Sithel asked nonchalantly.

"Ulvissen? Seeing to the loading of my baggage. Why?" The question seemed to put Teralind on the defensive.

"Would you summon him? I wish to speak with the man."

In short order Ulvissen himself entered from the courtyard where the Ergothians' wagons were being loaded. He was sweating heavily in his thick wool and leather outfit. In turn he bowed grandly to Teralind and Sithel.

"You wished to speak to me, Highness?" he asked the speaker awkwardly.

"Yes. Since this is a day of revelations, I see no reason why you shouldn't be part of them." Sithel opened his hand, displaying the slip of vellum. "I have here a report prepared by Prince Kith-Kanan before his departure to the West. In it, he describes a half-human bandit he met in the wilderness, Voltorno by name. Many months ago, he encountered this Voltorno in the company of a band of humans. He states that you were one of these men."

Ulvissen looked from the small scroll to the speaker's face, but betrayed no guilt. "No offense intended, great speaker, but your son is mistaken. I have never been to Silvanesti prior to coming as my lady's seneschal," he said evenly.

"Mistakes are possible, even by Kith-Kanan," Sithel said, closing his fingers around the parchment again. "Which is why I had my scribes search the archives of the Temple of Kiri-Jolith. There are kept accounts of all wars and battles fought since the dawn of time. And whose name should be found as high admiral of the Ergothian fleet, but one Guldur Ul Vissen? A name strangely similar to your own, wouldn't you agree? Since your princess saw fit to come here in disguise, it does not tax belief to think you may have also." The speaker clasped his hands behind his back. "What have you to say, Master Ulvissen?"

Ulvissen regarded the Speaker of the Stars with utter coolness. "Your Highness is mistaken," he said firmly. "A similarity of names proves nothing. Vissen is a common name in Ergoth."

"Do you agree, Lady?"

Teralind flinched. "Yes. What is the point? I've told you why I pretended to be someone else. But my seneschal is who he claims to be."

Sithel tucked the parchment into his sash. "As an imperial princess, please go with my best wishes and every hope of safety, but do not bring your 'seneschal' to Silvanost again. Do you understand?" The harsh tone was unusual for the speaker. "Those who despoil my country and kill my subjects are not welcome in my city or my house. Please let this be known when you arrive in Daltigoth, Lady."

With that, the speaker turned on his heel and walked away. Nirakina. Followed. Tamanier bowed and did likewise. Sithas, wide-eyed, went last.

In the rotunda outside the humans' quarters, Sithel turned to his wife with a broad smile on his face. He shook a fist at the ceiling.

"At last!" he said fiercely. "I've given that contentious woman her own back!" He turned to Tamanier. "You have been of great service to me. You shall be rewarded."

Tamanier blinked and bowed. "I seek only to serve Your Highness and Lady Nirakina," he said.

"So you shall." Sithel pondered for a moment, stroking his pointed chin. "I wish to appoint you chamberlain of the court. The management of daily court life shall fall to you. You will be known as Lord Ambrodel, and your clan shall have the right to inherit the title." The speaker folded his arms and asked, "What say you to that, Lord Ambrodel?"

Tamanier gaped like a startled child. At last he collected himself and dropped to one knee. "I thank you, Highness," he said humbly. "I will serve you to the end of my days!"

"I think my days will end before yours," Sithel said wryly. "But you can serve my son after."

Laughing, the royal family and their new chamberlain left the rotunda. Sithas put a hand on Tamanier Ambrodel's arm.

"A word, my new lord," Sithas said in a confidential whisper, pulling him aside.

"Yes?" said Tamanier discreetly.

"Let us go to a more private location."

They left the palace. Outside, the air was sweet with flowers and the marble walks were covered with blossoms fallen from the trees. Sithas said nothing until they were some distance from any observers.

"You know someone in the palace has been giving information to the Ergothians," Sithas said conspiratorially, looking eastward to the fine houses of the nobility. "I would appreciate it if you would help me find out who the traitor is."

"I'll do what I can, noble prince," said Tamanier earnestly.

"Good. As chamberlain, you'll have access to every part of the palace. I want you to use your authority to root out the spy and reveal him to me." Sithas paused and looked straight at Tamanier. "But be wise. I don't want the wrong person accused. And I don't want the culprit alerted."

"Do you have any suspects?" asked Tamanier.

"Officially, no. Personally, yes," Sithas said grimly. "I suspect my own wife, Lady Hermathya."

"Your wife!" Tamanier was so shocked he could hardly believe what he had heard.

"Surely, noble prince, your wife loves you. She would not betray you to the humans!"

Sithas rubbed his hands slowly together. "I only have suspicions. All I can say about Hermathya's motives is that she so loves attention and the cheers of the people, that she spends huge amounts of money to keep their favor. I do not give her coins to scatter in the streets, yet she never seems to lack for money."

Shocked, yet pitying the prince at the same time, Tamanier asked, "Do you suspect anyone else?"

"Yes, and perhaps he is the stronger candidate. His name is Vedvedsica. He is a sorcerer and a priest, he claims, of Gilean the Gray Voyager. My father sometimes uses his clairvoyant skills, but Vedvedsica is a greedy conniver who would do anything for gold or power."

"The emperor of Ergoth has plenty of gold," Tamanier said sagely.

They talked for several minutes more. Tamanier vowed to detect the traitor, and Sithas listened approvingly, nodded, then walked away. The newly created chamberlain was left in the east garden, surrounded by fallen petals and singing birds.

* * * * *

The farmers were apprehensive when they first saw the column of armed warriors ride by, but when they realized who the Wildrunners were, they came to greet these newcomers. Along the way, Kith-Kanan sent troopers to help one farmer to fell a tree, another to free an ox from a boggy ditch, and a third to mend a fence. Word of these kindnesses spread ahead of the Wildrunners' march and increased the number of enthusiastic elves—Silvanesti and Kagonesti—who came out to greet Kith-Kanan and his troops.

For the next few days, the way of the march was lined with grateful farmers and their families, bearing gifts of new nectar, smoked meat, and fruit. Wreaths of flowers were hung around the Wildrunners' necks. Kith-Kanan's mount Kijo was draped with a garland of white roses. At one point, the prince ordered his pipers to play a lively tune, and the Wildrunners passed through the countryside in a swirl of music, flowers, and smiling settlers. It was more like a festival than a military expedition. Some of the more veteran warriors were astonished.

Now, ten days from Silvanost, sitting around the blazing campfire, warriors asked Kith-Kanan why he was making such a show of helping the farmers and herders they met.

"Well," he explained, stirring his soup with a wooden spoon, "if this militia idea is to succeed, the people must see us as their friends and not just their protectors. You see, our ranks will be filled by the same farmers, woodcutters, and herders we help along the way. They will be the troops, and all of you will be their leaders."

"Is it true we're to take in humans and dwarves in the ranks?" asked a captain with some distaste.

"It is," said Kith-Kanan.

"Can we rely on such fighters? I mean, we all know humans can fight, and the dwarves are stout fellows, but will they obey orders to attack and slay fellow humans or dwarves if those orders come from an elf?" asked one of the older sergeants.

"They will, or they'll be expelled from the militia and lose its protection," Kith-Kanan responded. "You ask if humans will serve us by fighting humans. Some will, some won't. We'll be fighting elves, too, I expect. I've heard tales of robber bands made up of humans, Kagonesti, and even mixed-bloods. If they rob, if they kill, then we will bring them to justice. We make no distinctions out here."

Sleep followed dinner, and guards were posted. The horses were corralled in the center of the camp, and one by one the lamps went out in the Wildrunners' tents.

Mackeli usually slept at Kith-Kanan's side, and that night was no exception. Though the boy often slept soundly, the months he'd spent out of the old forest hadn't completely dulled his senses; he was the first one to sense something amiss. He sat up in the dark tent and rubbed his eyes, unsure of what had roused him. He heard nothing, but he saw something very odd.

Pink shadows wavered inside the tent. Mackeli saw his own hand, washed pink by an unknown light. He slowly raised his head and saw that a red circle of light showed through the tent's canvas roof. A glare of heat on his face, Mackeli had no idea what the red glow portended, but he was sure it wasn't friendly. He shook Kith-Kanan awake.

"Wha—What is it?" mumbled the prince.

"Look!" hissed Mackeli.

Kith-Kanan blinked at the red glow. He brushed the long hair from his eyes and threw back his blanket. In lieu of the sword he'd broken in the wildwood, he'd brought along a fine new weapon. Mackeli drew his own sword from its scabbard as, warily, Kith-Kanan lifted the flap on the tent with the tip of his blade.

Hovering over the camp, about twenty feet in the air, was a ball of red fire the size of a cart wheel. The crackling red light covered the camp. Kith-Kanan immediately felt a prickling sensation on his skin when the red glow touched him.

"What is it?" asked Mackeli wonderingly.

"I don't know. . . ."

The elf prince looked across the camp. The sentries were frozen, one foot raised in midstep, mouths open in the act of giving the alarm. Their eyes stared ahead, unblinking. Even the horses were rooted in place, some with hooves raised and necks arched in odd angles.

"They're all paralyzed somehow," Kith-Kanan said in awe. "This is evil magic!"

"Why aren't we paralyzed?" Mackeli asked, but Kith-Kanan had no answer to that.

Through the line of tents shadowy figures moved. Bloodcolored light sparkled on naked sword blades. Kith-Kanan and Mackeli ducked down behind a tent. The shadow figures came on. There were five of them. By their clothing, features, and coloring, Kith-Kanan saw they were raffish Kagonesti. He held a finger to his lips, warning Mackeli to remain silent.

The Kagonesti approached the tent Kith-Kanan and Mackeli had been sleeping in minutes before. "Is this the tent?" hissed one of them.

"Yeah," replied the leading elf. His face was heavily scarred, and instead of a left hand, he had a cruel-looking metal hook.

"Let's be done with it an' get outta here," said a third Kagonesti. Hook-Hand made a snarling sound in his throat.

"Don't be so hasty," he advised. "There's plenty of time for the kill and to fill our pockets besides."

With sign language, Kith-Kanan indicated to Mackeli that he should circle around behind the band of magic-wielding killers. The boy vanished like a ghost, barefoot and wearing only his trousers. Kith-Kanan rose to his feet.

Hook-Hand had just ordered his men to surround the prince's tent. The killers slashed the ropes holding the tent up. As the canvas cone collapsed, the five killers waded in, hacking and stabbing through the tent cloth.

Suddenly, with a shout, Mackeli burst from concealment and bravely attacked the gang. He ran the first one through, even as that elf was turning to face him. Kith-Kanan gritted his teeth. Mackeli had attacked too rashly, so the prince had to rush his own attack. With a shout, Kith-Kanan entered the fray; he felled a mace-wielding killer with his first stroke. Hook-Hand kicked through the slashed canvas of the fallen tent to get clear. "That's him, boys!" he shouted as he retreated. "Finish 'em!"

From five, the villains were now down to three. Two of the Kagonesti went for Mackeli, leaving Hook-Hand and Kith-Kanan to duel. The scar-faced elf cut and thrust with deadly efficiency. Snatching up a cut length of rope with his hook, he lashed at Kith-Kanan. The knotted end stung hard against the prince's cheek.

Mackeli was not doing well against the other two. Already they had cut him on his left knee and right arm. Sweat sheened his body in the weird crimson glow. When the killer on his left thrust straight at him, Mackeli beat his blade and counter-thrust into his opponent's chest. This moment of triumph was shortlived. The other attacker stabbed Mackeli before the boy could free his blade. Cold iron touched his heart, and he fell to the ground.

"I got 'im!" shouted the victorious killer.

"Ya fool, that ain't the prince—this is! Help me get 'im!" Hook-Hand shouted back, out of breath.

But Mackeli managed to heave himself up with great effort and stab his foe in the leg. With a scream, the Kagonesti went down. He fell against Hook-Hand's back, throwing his chief off balance. That was all Kith-Kanan needed. Ignoring the flailing rope, he closed in and rammed his blade through the assassin. Hook-Hand let out a slow, rattling gasp and died as he fell.

Mackeli lay face-down in the dirt. His right arm was outstretched, still clutching his sword. Kith-Kanan threw himself down by the boy. He gently turned him over and then felt his own heart constrict. Mackeli's bare chest was covered with blood.

"Say something, Keli!" he begged. "Don't die!"

Mackeli's eyes were open. He looked at Kith-Kanan, and a frown tugged one corner of his mouth.

"This time . . . I can't obey, Kith," he said weakly. The life left his body with a shuddering sigh. Sightlessly his green eyes continued to gaze up at his friend.

An anguished sob wracked Kith-Kanan. He clutched Mackeli to him and wept. What curse was he under? How had he offended the gods? Now all of his family from the wildwood was gone. All gone. His tears mingled with Mackeli's blood.

A sound penetrated Kith-Kanan's grief; the brute that Mackeli had stabbed in the leg groaned. Kith-Kanan lowered the boy's body to the ground and gently closed his eyes. Then, with a growl, he grabbed the wounded mercenary by the tunic and dragged him to his feet.

"Who sent you?" he snarled. "Who sent you to kill me?"

"I don't know," gasped the elf. He trembled on his injured leg. "Mercy, great lord! I'm just a hireling!"

Kith-Kanan shook him by the shirt front, his face twisted into a hideous mask of rage. "You want mercy? Here's mercy: tell me who hired you, and I'll cut your throat. Don't tell me, and it will take far longer for you to die!"

"I'll tell, I'll tell!" babbled the terrified elf. Kith-Kanan threw him to the ground. The light from the fireball suddenly grew more intense. The elf let out a scream and threw an arm over his face. Kith-Kanan turned in time to see the fiery globe come hurtling at them. As he leaped aside, the fireball hit the wounded elf. There was a thunderclap, and the globe exploded.

Slowly, sight and hearing returned to Kith-Kanan, and darkness reclaimed the camp. The prince raised his head and found that his right arm and leg were scorched from the fireball's impact. The wounded elf was gone, vaporized.

* * * * *

Mackeli was buried in a simple grave on the banks of the Khalkist River. The Wildrunners laid his sword across his chest, as was the custom with elven warriors. At the head of his grave, in lieu of a marker, Kith-Kanan planted the sprig of oak he'd snipped from Anaya's tree. All this time it had remained green. The prince was certain the sprig would grow into a fine tree, and that Mackeli and Anaya would be united somehow in renewed life once more.

As the camp was breaking up, Kith-Kanan fingered the small ring he now wore on his left little finger. This was the ring Silvanos had given to his great general Balif during the Dragon War. Sithel had passed the ring on to his son as a parting gift; it had been wrapped in the red silk handkerchief the speaker had passed to his son. Kith-Kanan had donned the ring with pride, but now he wondered if it was an unintentional portent of tragedy. After all, Balif had been murdered by his rivals, certain high-ranking elves who resented the kender's influence with Silvanos. Now similar treachery had struck at Kith-Kanan and had taken his young friend.

With somber diligence the Wildrunners struck their tents. When they were done, the senior captain, a Kagonesti named Piradon, came to Kith-Kanan.

"Highness, all is ready," he announced.

Kith-Kanan studied the captain's face. Like all the Kagonesti who served in the royal guard, Piradon did not wear skin paint. It made his face seem naked.

"Very well," he said flatly. "The usual columns of four, and I want outriders ahead, behind, and on both flanks. No one's going to surprise us again."

Kith-Kanan put a foot in his stirrup and swung a leg over his horse. He slapped the reins against his horse's rump and cantered down to the road. The golden ring of Balif felt tight on his finger, making his pulse throb in his fingertip. The prince decided then that the feeling would stand as a constant reminder of Mackeli's death and of his own vulnerability.

High Summer, Year of the Ram

27

Deprived of Anaya and bereft of Mackeli, Kith-Kanan threw himself into his duty with a will that would have astonished those who had known him as a callow, self-centered youth. He drove his warriors as hard as he drove himself, and in weeks molded them into a quick-thinking, quick-acting force.

Two months passed. High summer came to the plain, and the days grew very hot. Daily thunderstorms soaked the steaming plains and green forest, quenching the thirsty land so bursting with life. Grass grew on the plain as tall as a grown elf's shoulder; so tall, in fact, that the herders had to cut swaths through it with scythes twice weekly. Vines and bracken choked the paths in the forest, making travel difficult, but the Wildrunners were too busy to complain. Tall mountains of clouds, like castles of white smoke, passed serenely overhead as the Wildrunners set up camp in order to construct a new armory; one Kith-Kanan had already dubbed Sithelbec.

Militia outposts like the one under construction had been established all across the plain in the past eight weeks, and settlers of every race flocked to their standards. Humans, elves, kender, dwarves—they were all tired of being victims, subject to the whims of the roving robbers. The captains and sergeants of the Wildrunners drilled them with pikes and shields, and showed them how to stand up to the mounted brigands. Everywhere Kith-Kanan's force stopped, an armory was founded. Stout stone houses were built by the Wildrunners, and there all the militia's weapons were stored. At the sounding of a gong, all able-bodied people in the locale would rush to the arsenal and arm themselves. In an attack, the Wildrunner officers stationed close at hand would lead them out to repel the raiders.

By a few weeks before midsummer, the south and central plains had been pacified. In most cases, the brigands hadn't even stayed around to fight the new militia. They'd simply vanished. Parnigar, eldest of the sergeants, had pronounced himself dissatisfied with the results of the campaign, however.

"What fault can you find?" Kith-Kanan had asked his trusted aide, the closest person to him since Mackeli's death. "I'd say we were succeeding far better than we could have hoped."

"Aye, that's the problem, sir. The brigands have given up too easily. They've scarcely tried to test us," Parnigar countered.

"Just shows that thieves have no stomach for honest combat." The old soldier nodded politely, but it was plain he had not been convinced.

The construction of Sithelbec began with a stockade of logs around the inner blockhouse of stone. Here, at the edge of the western forest, Kith-Kanan planned to extend law and order.

Inside the forest, however, was a different proposition. There were many elves of the Kagonesti race living in the woods, but they were hardy and independent and did not take kindly to armed soldiers on their land. These woods elves got along much better with their human neighbors than they did with the Kagonesti under Kith-Kanan's command. Worse, the western woods elves scorned the prince's offers of protection.

"Who do we need protection from?" they had asked scornfully when confronted. "The only invaders we see are you."

The woods elves spat on Kith-Kanan's representatives or threw stones at them, then melted into the trees.

The Wildrunners were all for going into the forest and converting the stubborn woods elves at the point of a sword, but Kith-Kanan would not allow it. Their success was built upon the trust the common people had in them; if they turned tyrannical, everything they'd accomplished would be for naught. It would take time, but the prince believed that he could even win over the wild Kagonesti.

As work on Sithelbec continued, Kith-Kanan received a dispatch from his father. The Speaker of the Stars had accepted the prince's invitation to the outpost. Sithel was coming, accompanied by Sithas and a caravan of guards and courtiers.

Kith-Kanan studied the dispatch, penned by his twin. The speaker's retinue was large and slow-moving; it would be at least two weeks before they reached Sithelbec. Even with that grace period, the fortress would not be finished in time. Kith-Kanan exhorted his warriors to do their best, but to save their strength for fighting—even though bandits were becoming as rare as cool breezes in the hot and steamy summer nights.

The work was still unfinished when the banner of the speaker's party appeared on the horizon. Kith-Kanan called in all his patrols and formed his warriors before the gates of Sithelbec.

The Wildrunners looked on in awe as the speaker's party came into view. First came forty guards on horseback, armed with long lances. Pennants fluttered from their lance tips. Behind them came an honor guard of nobles, sixty-two of them, bearing the banners of Silvanos's clan, the city of Silvanost, the great temples, the major guilds, and the lesser towns of Silvanesti. The nobles formed a square behind the line of lancers. Next came Sithas and his entourage, all clad in scarlet and white. Finally, the Speaker of the Stars rode up, flanked by one hundred courtiers wearing the speaker's colors. The tail of the procession consisted of the rest of the guards and all the baggage wagons.

"By Astarin," muttered Kith-Kanan. "Is there anyone left in Silvanost?"

The nobles parted ranks, the lancers moved to one side, and Sithas rode forward. "Greetings, Brother. Is everything in order?" asked the heir to the throne.

Kith-Kanan grinned. "Not everything," he said, looking up at Sithas. "But we're doing well enough."

The leader of the Wildrunners strode through the blocks of mounted elves toward his father. Soldiers, nobles, and courtiers parted for him with mechanical precision. There was Sithel, astride a splendid white charger, his golden mantle draped across the animal's rump. The crown of Silvanos sparkled on his brow.

Kith-Kanan bowed from the waist. "Hail, great speaker!"

"Hail to you, my son." Sithel waved the emerald and ivory scepter of Silvanos, and Kith-Kanan straightened, "How have you been?"

"Mostly well, Father. The militia has been a great success. Incidents of marauding have ceased and, until recently, everyone we met was with us."

Sithel laid the scepter in the crook of his arm. "Until recently?" he asked with a frown.

"Yes. The inhabitants of the woods are not eager for our help. I believe we can eventually win them to our side, though."

The speaker's charger shook its head and did a slow half-circle. A groom ran forward to hold the animal's bridle as Sithel patted his horse's snowy neck.

"I would hear more about this," he said solemnly. Kith-Kanan took the bridle from the groom and led his father's mount toward the unfinished fortress.

* * * * *

The vast formation of soldiers and courtiers dispersed, and a regular tent city grew up on the plain in and around the stockade of Sithelbec. The speaker moved into the incomplete keep, as did Sithas. There, on a rough table of green oak planks, Kith-Kanan served them dinner and told them about the problems they'd been having winning the confidence of the woods elves.

"The impudence of it," Sithas complained vehemently. "I think you should go in and drag the wretches out."

Kith-Kanan couldn't believe his ears. "And make them blood enemies forever, Sith? I know the Kagonesti. They prize freedom above all things and won't submit even with a sword at their throat. Unless we're willing to burn down the whole forest, we'll never flush them out. It's their element; they know every inch of it. Most of all, it's their home."

There was a moment of silence, then Sithel broke it.

"How is the hunting?" he asked pleasantly.

"Outstanding," Kith-Kanan said, glad of the change in subject. "The woods are fairly bursting with game, Father."

They gossiped a bit about life back in the city. Lady Nirakina and Tamanier Ambrodel were continuing their efforts on behalf of the homeless. The new Market was almost finished. Given the huge abundance of the coming harvest, even the new, expanded Market would be taxed to handle the volume.

"How is Hermathya?" Kith-Kanan asked politely.

Sithas shrugged, "As well as always. She spends too much and still craves the adoration of the common folk."

They made plans for a boar hunt that would take place on the morrow. Only a small party would go—the speaker, Sithas, Kith-Kanan, Kencathedrus, another royal guard, Parnigar, and half a dozen favored courtiers. They would assemble at dawn and ride into the forest armed with lances. No beaters or hounds would be used. The speaker viewed such measures as unsporting.

* * * * *

Though the sun had not yet shown itself, there was an early heat in the air, a promise of the stifling day to come. Kith-Kanan stood by a small campfire with Parnigar, eating some bread and porridge. Sithas and Sithel emerged from the half-built keep, dressed in drab brown hunting clothes.

"Good morning," Kith-Kanan said energetically.

"Going to be hot, I think," appraised Sithel. A servant appeared silently at his elbow with a cup of cool apple cider. A second servant offered Sithas similar refreshment.

The courtiers appeared, looking ill at ease in their borrowed hunting clothes. Kencathedrus and Parnigar were more lethal looking. The commander leaned on his lance with an easy grace, seeming fully awake, the benefit of many years rising before the sun. The hunting party ate in relative silence, chewing bread and cheese, spooning porridge quickly, and washing everything down with cider.

Sithel finished first. He thrust his empty cup and plate at a servant and took a lance from the pyramid of weapons stacked outside the keep.

"To horse," he announced. "The prey awaits!"

The speaker mounted with ease and swung the long ash lance in a broad circle around his head. Kith-Kanan couldn't help but smile at his father who, despite his age and dignity, was more expert with horse and lance than any of them, except perhaps Kencathedrus and Parnigar.

Sithas was a fair horseman, but fumbled with the long lance and reins. The courtiers, more used to loose robes and tight protocol, wobbled aboard their animals. The nervous animals were made more so by the lances bobbing and dancing just behind their heads.

Forming a triangle with Sithel in the lead, the party rode toward the forest, half a mile away. Dew was thick on the tall grass, and crickets sang until the horses drew near. The silver rim of Solinari could been seen on the western horizon.

Sithas rode on the speaker's left. Kith-Kanan rode on his father's right, resting the butt of his lance in his stirrup cup. They rode at an easy pace, not wanting to tire the horses too early. If they flushed a boar, they'd need all the speed they could muster from their chargers.

"I haven't been hunting in sixty years," Sithel said, breathing deeply of the morning air. "When I was your age, all the young bucks had to have a boar's head on their clan hall wall to show everyone how virile they were." Sithel smiled. "I still remember how I got my first boar. Shenbarrus, Hermathya's father, and I used to go to the marshes at the mouth of the Thon-Thalas. Marsh boar were reputed to be the fiercest of the fierce, and we thought we'd be the most famous hunters in Silvanost if we came back with a trophy. Shenbarrus was a lot thinner and more active in those days. He and I went down river by boat. We landed on Fairgo Island and immediately started tracking a large beast."

"You were on foot?" asked Kith-Kanan, incredulous.

"Couldn't get a horse on the island, son. It was too marshy. So Shenbarrus and I went in the spikerod thickets, armed with spears and brass bucklers. We got separated and the next thing I knew, I was alone in the marsh, with ominous rustlings in the bushes around me. I called out: 'Shenbarrus! Is that you?' There was no answer. I called again; still no answer. By then I was certain the noise I'd heard was a boar. I raised my spear high and thrust it through the thick brush. There was a scream such as mortal elf never heard, and Shenbarrus came pounding through the spikerod into the open. I'd jabbed him in, hmm, the seat of his robe."

Kith-Kanan laughed. Sithas laughed and asked, "So you never got your marsh boar?"

"Oh, I did!" Sithel said. "Shenbarrus's yells flushed a monster of a pig out of the brush. He ran right at us. Despite his painful wound Shenbarrus stabbed first. The pig thrashed and tore up the clearing. I got my spear back and finished the beast off."

"Who got the head?" asked Sithas.

"Shenbarrus. He drew first blood, so it was only right," said his father warmly.

Kith-Kanan had been in Hermathya's father's house many times and had seen the fierce boar's head in the dining hall over the fireplace. He thought of old Shenbarrus getting poked in the "seat of his robe" and he burst out laughing all over again.

The sky had lightened to pink by the time they reached the dark wall of trees. The party spread out, far enough apart for easy movement, but near enough to stay in sight of one another. All idle talk ceased.

The sun rose behind them, throwing long shadows through the trees. Kith-Kanan sweated in his cotton tunic and mopped his face with his sleeve. His father was ahead to his left, Parnigar slightly behind to his right.

Being in the forest again brought Anaya irresistibly to mind. Kith-Kanan saw her again, lithe and lively, flitting through the trees as silent as a ghost. He remembered her brusque manners, her gentle repose, and the way she felt in his arms. That he remembered best of all.

The heavy rains of summer had washed the sandy soil of the forest away, leaving chuckholes and protruding roots. Kith-Kanan let his horse pick its way along, but the animal misjudged its footing and hit a hole. The horse stumbled and recovered, but Kith-Kanan lost his seat and tumbled to the ground. The stump of a broken sapling gouged him in the back, and he lay there for a moment, stunned.

His vision cleared and he saw Parnigar leaning over him. "Are you all right, sir?" the old sergeant asked concernedly.

"Yes, just dazed. How's my horse?"

The animal stood a few yards away, cropping moss. His right foreleg was held painfully off the ground.

Parnigar helped Kith-Kanan stand as the last of the hunting party passed by. Kencathedrus, in the rear, asked if they needed any help.

"No," Kith-Kanan said quickly. "Go on. I'll see to my horse."

The horse's lower leg was bruised but, with care, it wouldn't be a crippling injury. Parnigar offered Kith-Kanan his horse, so he could catch up to the rest.

"No, thank you, Sergeant. They're too far ahead. If I go galloping after them, I'll scare off any game in the area." He put a hand to his aching back.

Parnigar asked, "Shall I stay with you, sir?"

"I think you'd better. I may have to walk back to Sithelbec from here." His back stabbed at him again, and he winced.

The news that Kith-Kanan had dropped out was passed ahead. The speaker expressed regret that his son would miss the hunt. But this was a rare day, and the expedition should continue. Sithel's course through the trees meandered here and there, taking the path best suited to his horse. At more than one place he paused to examine tracks in the moss or mud. Wild pig, definitely.

It was hot, but the elves welcomed such heat—for it was a good change from the ever-present coolness of the Quinari Palace and the Tower of the Stars. While Silvanost was constantly bathed in fresh breezes, the heat of the plains made the speaker's limbs feel looser and more supple, his head clearer. He reveled in the sense of freedom he felt out here and urged his horse on.

In the far distance, Sithel heard the call of a hunting horn. Such horns meant humans, and that meant dogs. Sure enough, the sound of barking came very faintly to his ears. Elves never used dogs, but humans rarely went into the woods without them. Human eyesight and hearing being so poor, Sithel reckoned they needed the animals to find any game at all.

The horns and dogs would likely frighten off any boar in the area. In fact, the dogs would flush everything—boar, deer, rabbits, foxes—out of hiding. Sithel shifted his lance back to his stirrup cup and sniffed. Humans were so unsporting.

There was a noise in the sumac behind and to his right. Sithel turned his horse around, lowered the tip of his lance, and poked through the bushes. A wild pheasant erupted from the green leaves, bleating shrilly. Laughing, the speaker calmed his prancing horse.

Sithas and a courtier named Timonas were close enough to see each other when the hunting horn sounded. The prince also realized that it meant humans in the woods. The idea filled him with alarm. He tightened his reins and spurred his horse in a tight circle, looking for other members of the party. The only one he could spot was Timonas.

"Can you see anyone?" Sithas called. The courtier shouted back that he could not.

Sithas's alarm increased. It was inexplicable, but he felt a dangerous presentiment. In the heat of the summer morning, the prince shivered.

"Father!" he called. "Speaker, where are you?"

Ahead, the speaker had decided to turn back. Any boar worth bagging had long since left these woods, driven off by the humans. He retraced his path and heard Sithas's call from not too far away.

"Oh, don't shout," he muttered irritably. "I'm coming."

Catching up to him, Sithas pushed through a tangle of vines and elm saplings. As the prince spurred his mount toward the speaker, the feeling of danger was still with him. Out of the corner of his eye, he saw the glint of metal in a stand of cedar.

Then he saw the arrow in flight.

Before Sithas could utter the cry that rose to his lips, the arrow had struck Sithel in the left side, below his ribs. The Speaker of the Stars dropped his lance and pitched forward, but he did not fall from the saddle. A scarlet stain spread out from the arrow, running down the leg of Sithel's trousers.

Timonas rode up on Sithas's left. "See to the speaker!" Sithas cried. He slapped his horse's flank with the reins and bore down on the cedar trees. Lance lowered, he burst through the dark green curtain. A quick glimpse of a white face, and he brought the handguard of his lance down on the archer's head. The archer pitched forward on his face.

The royal guardsman accompanying the party appeared. "Come here! Watch this fellow!" Sithas shouted at him and then rode hard to where Timonas supported Sithel on his horse.

"Father," Sithas said breathlessly. "Father . . ."

The speaker stared in wordless shock. He could say nothing as he reached a bloody hand to his son.

Gently Sithas and Timonas lowered the speaker to the ground. The rest of the hunting party quickly collected around them. The courtiers argued whether to remove the arrow, but Sithas silenced them all as Kencathedrus studied the wound. The look he gave the prince was telling. Sithas understood.

"Father," Sithas said desperately, "can you speak?"

Sithel's lips parted, but no sound came. His hazel eyes seemed full of puzzlement. At last, his hand touched his son's face, and he breathed his last. The hand fell to the ground.

The elves stood around their fallen monarch in abject disbelief. The one who had ruled them for three hundred and twenty-three years lay dead at their feet.

Kencathedrus had retrieved the fallen archer from the guardsman who watched him. The commander dragged the unconscious fellow by the back of his collar to where Sithel lay. "Sire, look at this," he said. He rolled the inert figure over.

The archer was human. His carrot-colored hair was short and spiky, leaving his queerly rounded ears plainly visible. There was a stubble of orange beard on his chin.

"Murder," muttered one of the courtiers. "The humans have killed our speaker!"

"Be silent!" Sithas said angrily. "Show some respect for the dead." To Kencathedrus he declared, "When he wakes we will find out who he is and why he did this."

"Perhaps it was an accident," cautioned Kencathedrus, inspecting the man. "His bow is a hunting weapon, not a war bow."

"He took aim! I saw him," Sithas said hotly. "My father was mounted on a white horse! Who could mistake him?"

The human groaned. Courtiers surrounded him and dragged him to his feet. They were not very gentle about it. By the time they finished shaking and pummeling him, it was a wonder he opened his eyes at all.

"You have killed the Speaker of the Stars!" Sithas demanded furiously, "Why?"

"No—" gasped the man.

He was forced to his knees. "I saw you!" Sithas insisted. "How can you deny it? Why did you do it?"

"I swear, Lord—"

Sithas could barely think or feel. His senses reeled with the fact that his beloved father was dead.

"Get him ready to travel," the prince ordered numbly. "We will take him back to the fortress and question him properly there."

"Yes, Speaker," said Timonas.

Sithas froze. It was true. Even as his father's blood ran into the ground, he was the rightful speaker. He could feel the burden of rulership settle about him like a length of chain laid across his shoulders. He had to be strong now, strong and wise, like his father.

"What about your father?" Kencathedrus asked gently.

"I will carry him." Sithas put his arms under his father's lifeless body and picked it up.

They walked out of the grove, the human with his arms wrenched behind him, the courtiers leading their horses, and Sithas carrying his dead father. As they came, the sound of hunting horns grew louder and the barking of dogs sounded behind them. Before the party had gone another quarter-mile, a band of mounted humans, armed with bows, appeared. There were at least thirty of them, and as they spread out around the party of elves, the Silvanesti slowed and stopped.

One human picked his way to Sithas. He wore a visored helmet, no doubt to protect his face from intruding branches. The man flipped the visor up, and Sithas started in surprise. He knew that face. It was Ulvissen, the human who had acted as seneschal to Princess Teralind.

"What has happened here?" Ulvissen asked grimly, taking in the scene.

"The Speaker of the Stars has been murdered," Sithas replied archly. "By that man."

Ulvissen looked beyond Sithas and saw the archer with his arms pinioned. "You must be mistaken. That man is my forester, Dremic," he said firmly. "He is no murderer. This was obviously an accident."

"Accident? That's not an acceptable answer. I am speaker now, and I say that this assassin will face Silvanesti justice."

Ulvissen leaned forward in his saddle. "I do not think so, Highness. Dremic is my man. If he is to be punished, I will see to it," he said strongly.

"No," disagreed Sithas.

The elves drew together. Some still carried their lances, others had courtly short swords at their waists. Kencathedrus held his sword to the neck of the human archer, Dremic. The standoff was tense.

Before anyone could act, though, a shrill two-tone whistle cut the air. Sithas felt relief well up inside him. Sure enough, through the trees came Kith-Kanan at the head of a company of the militia's pikemen. The prince rode forward to where Sithas stood, holding their father in his arms.

Kith-Kanan's face twisted. "I—I am too late!" he cried in anguish.

"Too late for one tragedy, but not too late to prevent another," Sithas said. Quickly he told his twin what had happened and what was about to happen.

"I heard the hunting horns at Sithelbec," Kith-Kanan said. "I thought there might be a clash, so I mustered the First Company. But this—if only I had stayed, kept up with Father—"

"We must have our man back, Highness," Ulvissen insisted. His hunting party nocked arrows.

Sithas shook his head. Before he'd even finished the gesture, some of the humans loosed arrows. Kith-Kanan shouted an order, and his pikemen charged. The humans, with no time to reload, bolted. In seconds, not one human could be seen, though the sound of their horses galloping away could be heard clearly.

Kith-Kanan halted the militia and called the Wildrunners back to order. Kencathedrus had been hit in the thigh. The unfortunate Dremic had been shot by his own people and now lay dead on the grass.

"We must get back to Silvanost, quickly," Sithas advised, "Not only to bury our father but to tell the people of war!"

Before the confused Kith-Kanan could question or protest, he was shocked to hear his own Wildrunners cheer Sithas's inflammatory words. The humans' cowardly flight had aroused their blood. Some were even ready to hunt down the humans in the forest, but Kith-Kanan reminded them that their duty was to their dead speaker and their comrades back at the fort.

They marched out of the woods, a solemn parade, bearing the bodies of the fallen on their horses. The dead human, Dremic, was left where he lay. A shocked and silent garrison greeted them at Sithelbec. Sithel was dead. Sithas was Speaker. Everyone wondered if the cause of peace had died with the great and ancient leader.

Kith-Kanan readied his warriors in defensive positions in case of attack. Watch was kept throughout the night, but it proved to be a peaceful one. After midnight, when he'd finished his work for the day, Kith-Kanan went to the shell of the unfinished keep, where Sithas knelt by the body of their slain father.

"The Wildrunners are prepared should an attack come," he said softly.

Sithas did not raise his head. "Thank you."

Kith-Kanan looked down at his father's still face. "Did he suffer?"

"No."

"Did he say anything?"

"He could not speak."

Hands clenched into fists, Kith-Kanan wept. "This is my fault! His safety was my duty! I urged him to come here. I encouraged him to go hunting."

"And you weren't present when he was ambushed." said Sithas calmly.

Kith-Kanan reacted blindly. He seized his twin by the back of his robe and hauled him to his feet. Spinning him around, he snarled, "You were there, and what good did it do him?"

Sithas gripped Kith-Kanan's fists and pulled them loose from his shirt. With angry precision, he said, "I am speaker. I am. I am the leader of the elven nation, so you serve me now, Brother. You can no longer fly off to the forest. And do not trouble me about the rights of Kagonesti or half-human trash."

Kith-Kanan let out a breath, long and slow. The twin he loved was swamped by hatred and grief, he told himself as he looked into Sithas's stormy eyes. With equal precision he answered, "You are my Speaker. You are my liege lord, and I shall obey you even unto death." It was the ancient oath of fealty. Word for word, the twins had said it to their father when they'd reached maturity. Now Kith-Kanan said it to his twin, his elder by just three minutes.

Burdened by Command

28

Sithel's body was borne back to his capital with haste. Sithas felt dignity was less important than speed; he wanted to present the nation with the terrible news as quickly as possible. The Ergothians might move at any time, and the elven nation was not ready to meet them.

The dire news flashed ahead of the caravan. By the time Sithel's body was ferried across the Thon-Thalas, the city was already in mourning. The river was so thick with boats, it could be walked across. From the humblest fisher to the mightiest priest, all elves turned out to view the speaker for the last time. By the thousands they lined the street to the Tower of the Stars, bare-headed out of respect. Waiting for the cortege at the tower was Lady Nirakina. She was so stricken that she had to be carried in a sedan chair from the palace to the tower.

There were no hails or cheers as Speaker Sithas walked through the streets, leading the funeral cortege. His father lay in state in the Temple of E'li as thousands of his subjects came to pay him a last farewell. Then, with a minimum of ceremony, Sithel was put to rest beside his own father in the magnificent mausoleum known as the Crystal Tomb.

The very next day, Sithas composed an ultimatum to the emperor of Ergoth. "We consider the death of our father Sithel to be nothing less than deliberate murder," Sithas wrote. "The Elven Nation demands retribution for its speaker's death. If Your Imperial Highness wishes to avoid war, we will accept an indemnity of one million gold pieces, the expulsion of all Ergothian subjects from our western territories, and the surrender of all the men present at the murder of our father, including Ulvissen."

Kith-Kanan had had to delay his departure from Sithelbec. He arrived in Silvanost two days after his father's funeral, incensed that Sithas had acted so precipitously with the last rites and his ultimatum to the emperor of Ergoth.

"Why did you not wait?" he complained to his twin in the Tower of the Stars. "I should have been here to see father's last rites!" Kith-Kanan had just come from a long visit with his mother; her grief and his own weighed heavily upon him.

"There is no time for empty ceremony," Sithas said. "War may be near, and we must act. I have ordered prayers and offerings to our father be made in every temple every night for thirty days, but for now I must rally the people."

"Will the humans attack?" asked Hermathya anxiously from her place at Sithas's side.

"I don't know," the speaker replied grimly. "They outnumber us ten to one."

Kith-Kanan looked at the two of them. It was so unnatural to see them where Sithel and Nirakina had been so often seated. Hermathya looked beautiful, perfectly groomed and dressed in a gown of gold, silver, and white. Yet she was cold. Whereas Nirakina could inspire respect and love with a smile and a nod, all Hermathya seemed capable of doing was looking statuesque. Of course she did not meet Kith-Kanan's eyes.

On the emerald throne, Sithas looked strained and tired. He was trying to make fast and hard decisions, as he felt befitted a monarch in time of trouble. The burden showed on his face and in his posture. He looked far older than his twin at this moment.

The tower was empty except for the three of them. All morning Sithas had been meeting with priests, nobles, and masters of the guilds, telling them what he expected from them in case of war. There had been some patriotic words, mostly from the priests, but in all the tone of the audience had been very subdued. Now only Kith-Kanan remained. Sithas had special orders for him.

"I want you to form the Wildrunners into a single army," he commanded.

"With what purpose?" his twin asked.

"Resist the Ergothian army, should it cross the border into the forest."

Kith-Kanan rubbed his forehead. "You know, Sith, that the whole militia numbers only twenty thousand, most of whom are farmers armed with pikes."

"I know, but there's nothing else to stop the humans between their border and the banks of the Thon-Thalas. We need time, Kith, time for Kencathedrus to raise an army with which to defend Silvanost."

"Then why in Astarin's name are you so eager to start a war with Ergoth? They have two hundred thousand men under arms! You said it yourself!"

Sithas's hands clenched the arms of his throne, and he leaned forward. "What else can I do? Forgive the humans for murdering our father? You know it was murder. They laid a trap for him and killed him! Is it such a coincidence that Ulvissen was in the area and that one of his supposed foresters perpetrated the crime?"

"It is suspicious," Kith-Kanan conceded, with less heat than before. He pulled his helmet on, threading the chin strap into its buckle. "I will do what I can, Sith," he said finally, "but there may be those who aren't as willing to fight and die for Silvanesti."

"Anyone who refuses the speaker's call is a traitor," Hermathya interjected.

"It is easy to make such distinctions here in the city, but on the plains and in the woods, neighbors mean more than far-off monarchs," Kith-Kanan said pointedly.

"Are you saying the Kagonesti will not fight for us?" asked Sithas angrily.

"Some will. Some may not."

Sithas leaned back and sighed deeply. "I see. Do what you can, Kith. Go back to Sithelbec as quickly as you can." He hesitated. "I know you will do your best."

A brief glance passed between the twins. "I'll take Arcuballis," said Kith-Kanan and went quickly.

When the prince had departed, Hermathya fumed. "Why do you allow him to be so familiar? You're the speaker. He should bow and call you Highness."

Sithas turned to his wife. His face was impassive. "I have no doubts about Kith's loyalty," he said heavily. "Unlike yours, lady, in spite of your correct language and empty flattery."

"What do you mean?" she said stiffly.

"I know you hired Kagonesti thugs to murder Kith-Kanan because he would not dishonor me by becoming your lover. I know all, lady."

Hermathya's normally pale face grew waxen. "It's not true," she said, her voice wavering. "It's a foul lie—Kith-Kanan told you, didn't he?"

"No, lady. Kith doesn't know you hired the elves who murdered his friend. When you employed a certain gray-robed sorcerer to contact a band of killers, you didn't know that the same sorcerer also works for me. For gold, he will do anything—including tell me everything about your treachery."

Hermathya's entire body shivered violently. She rose unsteadily from her throne and backed across the platform, away from Sithas. The silver and gold hem of her heavy robe dragged across the marble floor.

"What will you do?" she gasped.

He stared at her for a long minute. "To you? Nothing. This is hardly the time for the speaker to put his wife in prison. Your plot failed, fortunately for your life, so I will let you keep your freedom for now. But I tell you this, Hermathya—" he rose and stood tall and straight before her "—if you so much as frown at my brother, or if you ever have contact with Vedvedsica again, I will shut you away someplace where you'll never see the sun again."

Sithas turned and strode with resolve from the tower. Hermathya remained standing for a moment, swaying to and fro. Finally, her legs gave way. She collapsed in the center of the platform and wept. The rich silver and gold of her robes gleamed in the light from the window slits.

* * * * *

The griffon's wings beat in quick rhythm as Kith-Kanan and Arcuballis flew to the west. An array of armor and arms weighed Arcuballis down, but the powerful beast never faltered in flight. As they passed over the vast southern forest, Kith-Kanan couldn't help but look down at the green canopy and wonder. If Anaya hadn't changed, would he still be down there somewhere, living the free life of a wild elf? Would Mackeli still be alive? These thoughts gnawed at him. His happiest days had been the time spent with Anaya and Mackeli, roaming the wildwood, doing whatever the moment called for. No duty. No onerous protocol. Life had been an eternal, joyous spring.

And just as quickly, Kith-Kanan found himself dismissing these thoughts from his mind. It can't always be spring, and one can't always be young and carefree. He wasn't an ordinary elf after all, but a prince of the blood. His life had held many pleasures and very little had ever been asked of him. Now it was time for him to earn what he had enjoyed. Kith-Kanan fixed his gaze on the distant blue horizon and steeled himself for war.

Introduction

The great mosaic of Krynn's history is populated by many epic components: heroes and villains, great conflicts, simple discoveries, and dramatic acts of immortal retribution. The most significant of these details are events that are based on the decisions of important characters acting out their lives upon the stage that is this world.

It was truly an honor to have the opportunity to write this part of that vast tapestry of stories. The Kinslayer Wars are keystones in the tale of the magnificent fantasy setting that is the Dragonlance world, for these conflicts formed the core histories of two of Krynn's most influential nations. It is a tale based in the world's early history, yet it has ramifications extending even into the Age of Mortals and beyond.

The continuing sagas of Krynn and her most important characters are tied to the fundamental and conflicted relationship, both a bond and a division, between the twin elven realms of Qualinesti and Silvanesti. This is the tale of how the ancient homeland of that oldest of races was sundered, and of how those two lands came into existence. It is also the tale of two brothers, the twins Sithas and Kith-Kanan, and how their bond of brotherhood was strengthened by courage and danger, and eventually fractured by forces that neither of them could control.

Like all good stories, and following in the models established by the first Dragonlance authors, Tracy Hickman and Margaret Weis, this is a tale that embodies a powerful theme. And like all good themes, it has a moral that resonates in the world we all inhabit.

That theme focuses on the powerfully destructive effects of racism. The concept is central to many fantasy realms, of course. In some ways, the racial tensions that are commonly portrayed between elves and dwarves and humans are symbolic of the divisions we feel in our own societies. The differences between fantasy races are perhaps more profound, and more apparent, than those existing in the real world, but they serve as graphic illustrations, and cautionary models, of the destructive power inherent in any kind of xenophobia.

In the Kinslayer Wars, this racial hatred explodes with a force that divides not just entire nations, but individual families, communities, tribes. It kills and it wounds, and where it wounds it leaves scars that will not heal. In this tragic impact it is not terribly different from the racial hatreds that affect our world every day.

But even against the backdrop of tragedy and division, I hope that the reader does not lose sight of the fact that this is also a tale of progress, and of promise. . . that even in the midst of war there can be moments of true goodness . . . that courage is a concept transcending connections of kinship, tradition, and prejudice. . . .

And that even in the depths of darkness, it is possible to love.

Douglas Niles

Prologue

Winter, Year Of the Ram, 2215 (PC)

"The emperor arrives—he enters the fortress at the South Gate!"

The cry rang from the walls of Caergoth, blared by a thousand trumpets and heard by a million ears. Excitement spread through the massive tent city around the great castle, while the towering fortress itself fairly tingled with anticipation.

The carriage of Emperor Quivalin Soth V, sometimes called Ullves, rumbled through the huge gates, pulled by a team of twelve white horses, trailed by an escort of five thousand men. From every parapet, every castellated tower top and high rampart in sprawling Caergoth, silk-gowned ladies, proud noblemen, and courtiers waved and cheered.

Sheer, gray-fronted walls of granite towered over the procession, dominating the surrounding farmlands as a mountain looms over a plain. Four massive gates, each formed from planks of vallenwood eighty feet long, barred the sides of the great structure against any conceivable foe—indeed, they proudly bore the scars of dragonbreath, inflicted during the Second Dragon War more than four centuries earlier.

The interior of Caergoth consisted of winding avenues, tall and narrow gates, stone buildings crowded together, and always the high walls. They curved about and climbed in terrace after terrace toward the heart of the massive castle, forming a granite maze for all who entered.

The carriage trundled through the outer gatehouse with imperial dignity and rolled along the streets, through open gates, and down the widest avenue toward the center of the fortress. Banners, in black and deep red and dark blue, hung from the ramparts. Everywhere the cheering of the crowds thundered around the emperor's coach.

Outside the walls, a vast sea of tents covered the fields around the fortress, and from these poured the men-at-arms of the emperor's—army some two hundred thousand in all. Though they did not mingle with the nobles and captains of the fortress, their joy was no less boisterous. They surged toward the castle in the wake of the emperor's procession, their shouts and hurrahs penetrating the heavy stone walls.

Finally the procession entered a broad plaza, cool and misty from the spray of a hundred fountains. Beyond, soaring to the very clouds themselves, arose the true wonder of Caergoth: the palace of the king. Tall towers jutted up from high walls, and lofty, peaked roofs seemed distant and unreachable. Crystal windows reflected sunlight in dazzling rainbows, filtering and flashing their colors through the shimmering haze of the fountains.

The coach rumbled down the wide, paved roadway to the gates of the palace. These portals, solid silver shined to mirrorlike brilliance, stood open wide. In their place stood the royal personage himself, King Trangath II, Lord of Caergoth and most loyal servant to the Emperor of Ergoth.

Here the royal coach halted. A dozen men-at-arms snapped their halberds to their chests as the king's own daughter opened the door of the gleaming steel carriage. The crowd surged across the plaza, even through the pools of the fountains, in an effort to see the great person who rode within. Around the plaza, from the surrounding walls and towers, teeming thousands shouted their adulation.

The emperor's green eyes flashed as he stepped from the high vehicle with a grace that belied his fifty years. His beard and hair now showed streaks of gray, but his iron will had hardened over his decades of rule until he was known, truthfully, as a ruthless and determined leader who had led his people into a prosperity they had never before known.

Now this regal leader, his robe of crimson fur flowing over a black silk tunic trimmed in platinum, ignored the King of Caergoth, stepping quickly to the three men who stood silently behind that suddenly embarassed monarch. Each of these was bearded and wore a cap and breastplate of gleaming steel plate. Tall boots rose above their knees, and each held a pair of gauntlets under his arm as he waited to greet the most powerful man in all of Ansalon.

The shrieks of the crowd reached a crescendo as the emperor seized each of these men, one after the other, in an embrace of deepest affection. He turned once more and waved to the masses.

Then Quivalin V led the three men toward the crystal doors of the king's palace. The portals parted smoothly, and when they closed, the hysteria beyond fell to a muted rumble.

"Find us a place where we can speak privately," the emperor commanded, without turning to look at King Trangath.

Immediately that royal personage scuttled ahead, bowing obsequiously and beckoning the emperor's party through a towering door of dark mahogany.

"I hope fervently that my humble library will suit my most esteemed lord's needs," the old king huffed, bowing so deeply he tottered for a moment, almost losing his balance.

Emperor Quivalin said nothing until he and the three men had entered the library and the doors had soundlessly closed behind them. A deep black marble floor stretched into the far comers of the huge room. Above them, the ceiling lofted into the distance, a dark surface of rich, brown wood. The only light came from high, narrow windows of crystal; it fell around them as beams of heat and warmth before its reflections vanished in the light-absorbent darkness of the floor.

Though several soft chairs stood along the walls, none of the men moved to sit. Instead, the emperor fixed each of the others with a stare of piercing strength and impelling command.

"You three men are my greatest generals," Quivalin V said, his voice surprisingly soft beneath the intensity of his gaze. "And now you are the hope and the future of all humankind!"

The three stood a little taller at his words, their shoulders growing a trifle more broad. The emperor continued. "We have borne the elven savagery long enough. Their stubborn refusal to allow humans their rightful place in the plains has become too much to bear. The racial arrogance of their Speaker has turned diplomacy into insults. Our reasonable demands are mocked. Silvanesti intransigence must be wiped out!"

Abruptly Quivalin's gaze flashed to one of the trio—the oldest, if his white beard and long hair of the same color were any indication. Lines of strain and character marked the man's face, and his short stature nevertheless bespoke a quiet, contained power.

"Now, High General Barnet, tell me your plans."

The older warrior cleared his throat. A veteran of four decades of service to this emperor—and to Quivalin IV before him—Barnet nevertheless couldn't entirely calm himself in the face of that august presence.

"Excellency, we will advance into the plains in three great wings—a powerful thrust from the center, and two great hooks to the north and south. I myself will command the central wing—a thousand heavy lancers and fifty thousand sturdy footmen with metal armor, shields, and pikes. Sailors and woodsmen from Daltigoth and the south, mainly, including ten thousand with crossbow.

"We shall drive directly toward Sithelbec, which we know is the heart of the elven defense—a place the elven general must defend. Our aim is to force the enemy into combat before us, while the northern and southern wings complete the encirclement. They will serve as the mobile hammers, gathering the enemy against the anvil of my own solid force."

High General Barnett looked to one of his co-commanders. "General Xalthan commands the southern wing."

Xalthan, a red-bearded warrior with bristling eyebrows and missing front teeth, seemed to glower at the emperor with a savage aspect, but this was simply an effect of his warlike appearance. His voice, as he spoke, was deferential. "I have three brigades of heavy lancers, Excellency, and as many footmen as Barnett—armored in leather, to move more quickly."

Xalthan seemed to hesitate a moment, as if embarrassed, then he plunged boldly ahead. "The gnomish artillery, I must admit, has not lived up to expectations. But their engineers are busy even as we speak. I feel certain that the lava cannons will be activated early in the campaign."

The emperor's eyes narrowed slightly at the news. No one saw the facial gesture except for Xalthan, but the other two noticed that veteran commander's ruddy complexion grow visibly pale.

"And you, Giarna?" asked the emperor, turning to the third man. "How goes the grandest campaign of the Boy General?"

Giarna, whose youthfulness was apparent in his smooth skin and soft, curling beard, didn't react to his nickname. Instead, he stood easily, with a casualness that might have been interpreted as insolence, except there was crisp respect reflected in his expression as he pondered his answer. Even so, his eyes unsettled the watchers, even the emperor. They were dark and full of a deep and abiding menace that made him seem older than his years.

The other two generals scowled privately at the young man. After all, it was common knowledge that Giarna's favored status with the emperor was due more to the Duchess Suzine des Quivalin—niece of the emperor, and reputed mistress to the general himself—than to any inherent military skill.

Still, Giarna's battle prowess, demonstrated against rebellious keeps across the Vingaard Plains, was grudgingly admitted even by his critics. It was his mastery of strategy, not his individual courage or his grasp of tactics, that had yet to be proven.

Under ordinary circumstances, General Giarna's army command skills would not have been tested on the battlefield for some years yet—until he was older and more seasoned. However, a recent rash of tragic accidents—a panicked horse bucking, a jealous husband returning home, and a misunderstood command to retreat—had cost the lives of the three generals who had stood in line for this post. Thus Giarna, youthful though he was, had been given his opportunity.

Now he stood proudly before his emperor and replied.

"My force is the smallest, Excellency, but also the fastest. I have twenty thousand riders—horse archers and lancers; and also ten thousand footmen each of sword and longbowmen. It is my intention to march swiftly and come between the Wildrunners and their base in Sithelbec. Then I will wait for Kith-Kanan to come to me, and I will shred his army with my arrows and my horsemen."

Giarna made his report coolly, without so much as a nod to his peers, as if the other two commanders were excessive baggage on this, the Boy General's first great expedition. The older generals fumed; the implication was not lost on them.

Nor on the emperor. Quivalin V smiled at the plans of his generals. Beyond the walls of the cavernous library; within the vast palace, the roar of the admiring crowd could still be heard.

Abruptly the emperor clapped his hands, the sound echoing sharply through the large chamber. A side door to the room opened, and a woman advanced across the gleaming marble. Even the two older generals, both of whom distrusted and resented her, would have admitted that her beauty was stunning.

Her hair, of coppery red, spiraled around a diamond-encrusted tiara of rich platinum. A gown of green silk conformed to the full outline of her breasts and hips, accented by a belt of rubies and emeralds that enclosed her narrow waist. But it was her face that was most striking, with her high cheekbones and proud, narrow chin and, most significant, her eyes. They glowed with the same vibrance as the emeralds on her belt, the almost unnatural green of the Quivalin line.

Suzine Des Quivalin curtsied deeply to her uncle, the emperor. Her eyes remained downcast as she awaited his questions.

"What can you tell us about the state of the enemy's forces?" asked the ruler. "Has your mirror been of use in this regard?"

"Indeed, Excellency," she replied. "Though the range to the elven army is great, conditions have been good. I have been able to see much.

"The elven general, Kith-Kanan, has deployed his forces in thin screens throughout the plain, well forward of the fortress of Sithelbec. He has few horsemen—perhaps five hundred, certainly less than a thousand. Any one of your army's wings will outnumber his entire force, perhaps by a factor of two or three."

"Splendid," noted Quivalin. Again he clapped, this time twice.

The figure that emerged from a different door was perhaps as opposite from the woman as was conceivable. Suzine turned to leave as this stocky individual clumped into the room. She paused only long enough to meet Giarna's gaze, as if she was searching for something in his eyes. Whatever it was, she didn't find it. She saw nothing but the dark insatiable hunger for war. In another moment, she disappeared through the same door she had entered.

In the meantime, the other figure advanced toward the four men. The newcomer was stooped, almost apelike in posture, and barely four feet tall. His face was grotesque, an effect accentuated by his leering grin. And where Suzine's eyes crowned her beauty with pride and dignity, the mad, staring eyes of the dwarf showed white all around the tiny pupils and seemed to dart frantically from person to person.

If he felt any repugnance at the dwarf's appearance, the emperor didn't show it. Instead, he simply asked a question.

"What is the status of Thorbardin's involvement?"

"Most Exalted One, my own dwarves of the Theiwar Clan offer you their unequivocal support. We share your hatred of the arrogant elves and wish nothing more than their defeat and destruction!"

"Nothing more, unless it be a sum of profit in the bargain," remarked the emperor, his voice neutral.

The dwarf bowed again, too thick-skinned to be offended. "Your Eminence may take reassurance from the fact that loyalty purchased is always owed to the wealthiest patron—and here you have no competition in all of Krynn!"

"Indeed," Quivalin added dryly. "But what of the other dwarves—the Hylar, the Daergar?"

"Alas," sighed the Theiwar dwarf. "They have not been so open-minded as my own clan. The Hylar, in particular, seem bound by ancient treaties and affections. Our influence is great, but thus far insufficient to break these ties."

The dwarf lowered his voice conspiratorially. "However, your lordliness, we have an agent in place—a Theiwar—and should be able to ensure that little excess of comfort is delivered to your enemies."

"Splendid," agreed the emperor. If he was curious as to the precise identity of the Theiwar agent, he gave no sign. "A vigorous season of warfare should bring them to heel. I hope to drive them from the plains before winter. The elven cowards will be ready to sign a treaty by spring!"

The emperor's eyes suddenly glowed with dull fire, the calculated sense of power and brutality that had allowed him to send thousands of men to their deaths in a dozen of his empire's wars. They flamed brighter at the thought of the arrogance of the long-lived elves and their accursed stubbornness. His voice became a growl.

"But if they continue to resist, we will not be content to wage war on the plains. Then you will march on the elven capital itself. If it is necessary to prove our might, we will reduce Silvanost itself to ashes!"

The generals bowed to their ruler, determined to do his bidding. Two of them felt fear—fear of his power and his whim. Beads of sweat collected upon their foreheads, dripping unnoticed down cheeks and beards.

General Giarna's brow, however, remained quite dry.

PART I

A Taste of Killing

Late Winter, Year of the Raven

2214 (PC)

1

The forest vanished into the distance on all sides, comfortingly huge, eternal, and unchanging. That expanse was the true heart, the most enduring symbol, of the elven nation of Silvanesti. The towering pines, with lush green needles so dark they were almost black, dominated, but glades of oak and maple, aspen, and birch flourished in many isolated pockets, giving the forest a diverse and ever-changing character.

Only from a truly exalted vantage—such as from the Tower of the Stars, the central feature of Silvanost—could the view be fully appreciated. This was where Sithas, Speaker of the Stars and ruler of Silvanesti, came to meditate and contemplate.

The sky loomed vast and distant overhead, a dome of black filled with glittering pinpoints of light. Krynn's moons had not yet risen, and this made the pristine beauty of the stars more brilliant, more commanding.

For a long time, Sithas stood at the lip of the tower's parapet. He found comfort in the stars, and in the deep and eternal woods beyond this island, beyond this city. Sithas sensed that the forest was the true symbol of his people's supremacy. Like the great trunks of forest giants, the ancient, centuries-living elves stood above the scurrying, scampering lesser creatures of the world.

Finally the Speaker of the Stars lowered his eyes to look upon that city, and immediately the sense of peace and splendor he had known dissipated. Instead, his mind focused on Silvanost, the ancient elven capital, the city that held his palace and his throne.

Faint traces of a drunken chant rose through the night air to disturb his ears. The song thrummed in the guttural basso of dwarves, as if to mock his concern and consternation.

Dwarves! They are everywhere in Silvanost! Everywhere, in the city of elves, he thought grimly.

Yet the dwarves were a necessary evil, Sithas admitted with a sigh. The war with the humans called for extremely careful negotiations with powerful Thorbardin, the dwarven stronghold south of the disputed lands. The power of that vast and warlike nation, thrown behind either human Ergoth or elven Silvanesti, could well prove decisive.

Once, a year earlier, the Speaker of the Stars had assumed the dwarves were firmly in the elven camp. His negotiations with the esteemed Hylar dwarf Dunbarth Ironthumb had presented a unified front against human encroachment. Sithas had assumed that dwarven troops would soon stand beside the elves in the disputed plainslands.

Yet, to date, King Hal-Waith of Thorbardin had not yet sent a single regiment of dwarven fighters, nor had he released to Kith-Kanan's growing army any of the great stocks of dwarven weapons. The patient dwarves were not about to be hurried into any rash wars.

So a dwarven diplomatic mission was a necessity in Silvanost. And now that war had begun, such missions required sizable escorts—in the case of the recently arrived dwarven general Than-Kar, some one thousand loyal axemen.

Surprising himself, Sithas thought with fondness of the previous dwarven ambassador. Dunbarth Ironthumb had fully possessed all the usual uncouthness of a dwarf, but he also had a sense of humor and was self-effacing, traits that had relaxed and amused Sithas.

Than-Kar had none of these traits. A swarthy-complected Theiwar, the general was rude to the point of belligerence. Impatient and uncooperative, the ambassador actually seemed to act as an impediment to communication.

Take, for example, the messenger who had arrived from Thorbardin more than a week ago. This dwarf, after his months-long march, must certainly have brought important news from the dwarven king. Yet Than-Kar had said nothing, had not even requested an audience with the Speaker of the Stars. This was the reason for the conference Sithas had scheduled for the morrow, peremptorily summoning Than-Kar to the meeting in order to find out what the Theiwar knew.

His mood as thick as the night, Sithas let his gaze follow the dark outlines of the river Thon-Thalas, the wide waterway surrounding Silvanost and its island. The water was smooth, and he could see starlight reflected in its crystal surface. Then the breeze rose again, clouding the surface with ripples and washing the chant of the dwarven axemen away.

Seeing the river, the Speaker's mind filled with a new and most unwelcome memory, a scene as clear in its every detail as it was painful in its recollection. Two weeks ago or more it was now, yet it might as well have been that very morning. That was when the newly recruited regiments had departed westward, to join Kith-Kanan's forces.

The long columns of warriors had lined the riverbank, waiting their turns to board the ferry and cross. From the far bank of the Thon-Thalas, they were about to begin their long march to the disputed lands, five hundred miles to the west. Their five thousand spears, swords, and longbows would prove an important addition to the Wildrunners.

Yet, for the first time in the history of Silvanesti, the elves had needed to be bribed into taking up arms for their Speaker, their nation. A hundred steel bounty, paid upon recruitment, had been offered as incentive. Even this had not brought volunteers flocking to the colors, though after several weeks of recruitment regiments of sufficient size had finally been raised.

And then there had been the scene at the riverbank.

The cleric Miritelisina had just recently emerged from the cell where Sithas's father, Sithel, had thrown her for treason a year earlier. The matriarch of the faith of Quenesti Pah, benign goddess of healing and health, Miritelisina had voiced loud objections to the war with the humans. She had had the audacity to lead a group of elven females in a shrill, hysterical protest against the conflict with Ergoth. It had been a sickening display, worthy more of humans than of elves. Yet the cleric had enjoyed a surprisingly large amount of support from the onlooking citizens of Silvanesti.

Sithas had promptly ordered Miritelisina back to prison, and his guard had disrupted the gathering with crisp efficiency. Several females had been wounded, one fatally. At the same time, one of the heavily laden river craft had overturned, drowning several newly recruited elves. All in all, these were bad omens.

At least, the Speaker realized, the outbreak of war had driven the last humans from the city. The pathetic refugees of the troubles on the plains—many with elven spouses—had marched back to their homelands. Those who could fight had joined the Wildrunners, the army of Silvanost, centered around the members of the House Protectorate. The others had taken shelter in the great fortress of Sithelbec. Ironic, thought Sithas, that humans married to elves

274

should be sheltered in an elven fortress, safe against the onslaught of human armies!

Still, in every other way, the city that Sithas loved seemed to be slipping further and further from his control.

His gaze lingered to the west, rising to the horizon, and he wished he could see beyond. Kith-Kanan was there somewhere under this same star-studded sky. His twin brother might even be looking eastward at this moment; at least, Sithas wanted to believe that he felt some contact.

For a moment, Sithas found himself wishing that his father still lived. How he missed Sithel's wisdom, his steady counsel and firm guidance! Had his father ever known these doubts, these insecurities? The idea seemed impossible to the son. Sithel had been a pillar of strength and conviction. He would not have wavered in his pursuit of this war, in the protection of the elven nation against outside corruption!

The purity of the elven race was a gift of the gods, with its longevity and its serene majesty. Now that purity was threatened—by human blood, to be sure, but also by ideas of intermingling, trade, artisanship, and social tolerance.

The nation faced a very crucial time indeed. In the west, he knew, elves and humans had begun to intermarry with disturbing frequency, giving birth to a whole bastard race of half-elves.

By all the gods, it was an abomination, an affront to the heavens themselves! Sithas felt his face flush, and his hands clenched. If he had worn a sword, he would have seized it then, so powerfully did the urge to fight come over him. The elves *must* prevail—they *would* prevail!

Again he felt his distance from the conflict, and it loomed as a yawning chasm of frustration before him. As yet they had received no word of battle, although he knew that nearly a month earlier, the great invasion had begun. His brother had reported three great human columns, all moving purposefully into the plainslands. Sithas wanted to go and fight himself, to lend his strength to winning the war, and it was all he could do to hold himself back. Inevitably his sense of reason prevailed.

At times, the war seemed so far away, so unreachable. Yet, other times, he found it beside him, here in Silvanost, in his palace, in his thoughts . . . in his very bedroom.

In his bedroom Sithas gave a rueful smile and shook his head in wonder. He thought of Hermathya, how months earlier his feelings for her had approached loathing.

Yet with the coming of war, a change had come over his wife as well. Now she supported him as never before, standing beside him

275

every day against the complaints and pettiness of his people . . . and lying beside him every night as well.

He heard, or perhaps he felt, the soft rustle of silk, and then she was beside him. He breathed a deep sigh—a sound of contentment and satisfaction. The two of them stood alone, six hundred feet above the city, atop the Tower of the Stars, beneath the brilliant light shower of its namesake.

Her mouth, with its round lips so unusually full for an elf, was creased by the trace of a smile—a sly, secret smile that he found strangely beguiling. She stood beside him, touching a hand to his chest and leaning her head on his shoulder.

He smelled her hair, rich with the scent of lilacs, yet in color as bright as copper. Her smooth skin glowed with a milky luminescence, and he felt her warm lips upon his neck. A warm rush of desire swept through him, fading only slightly as she relaxed and stood beside him in silence.

Sithas thought of his volatile wife—how pleasant it was to have her come to him thus, and how rare such instances had been in the past. Hermathya was a proud and beautiful elfwoman, used to getting her own way. Sometimes he wondered if she regretted their marriage, arranged by their parents. Once, he knew, she had been the lover of his brother—indeed, Kith-Kanan had rebelled against his father's authority and fled Silvanost when her engagement to Sithas had been announced. Did she ever regret her choice? How well had she calculated her future as wife of the Speaker of the Stars? He did not know—perhaps, in fact, he was afraid to ask her.

"Have you seen my cousin yet?" she asked after a few minutes.

"Lord Quimant? Yes, he came to the Hall of Balif earlier today. I must say, he seems to have an excellent grip on the problems of weapon production. He knows mining, smelting, and smithing. His aid is much needed . . . and would be much appreciated. We are not a nation of weaponsmiths like the dwarves."

"Clan Oakleaf has long made the finest of elven blades," Hermathya replied proudly. "'That is known throughout Silvanesti!"

"It is not the quality that worries me, my dear. It is in the quantity of weapons that we lag sadly behind the humans, and the dwarves. We cleaned out the royal armories in order to outfit the last regiments we sent to the west."

"Quimant will solve your problems, I'm certain. Will he be coming to Silvanost?"

The estate of Clan Oakleaf lay to the north of the elven capital, near the mines where they excavated the iron for their small foundries. The clan, the central power behind House Metalline, was the primary producer of weapons-quality steel in the kingdom of Silvanesti. Lately its influence had grown, due to the necessity of increased weapons production brought on by the war. The mines were worked by slaves, mostly human and Kagonesti elves, but this was a fact Sithas had to accept because of his nation's emergency. Lord Quimant, the son of Hermathya's eldest uncle, was being groomed as the spokesman and leader of Clan Oakleaf, and his services for the estate were important.

"I believe he will. I've offered him chambers in the palace, as well as incentives for the Oakleaf clan—mineral rights, steady supplies of coal . . . and labor."

"It would be wonderful to have some of my family around again!" Hermathya's voice rose, joyful as a young girl's. "This can be such a *lonely* place, with all of your attention directed to the war."

He lowered his hand, sliding it along the smooth silk of her gown, down her back, his strong fingers caressing her. She sighed and held him tighter. "Well, maybe not *all* of your attention," she added, with a soft laugh.

Sithas wanted to tell her what a comfort she had been to him, how much she had eased the burdens of his role as leader of the elven nation. He wondered at the change that had come over her, but he said nothing. That was his nature, and perhaps his weakness.

It was Hermathya who next spoke.

"There is another thing I must tell you. . . ."

"Good news or bad?" he asked, idly curious.

"You will need to judge that for yourself, though I suspect you will be pleased."

He turned to look at her, holding both of his hands on her shoulders. That secret smile still played about her lips.

"Well?" he demanded, feigning impatience. "Don't tease me all night! Tell me!"

"You and I, great Speaker of the Stars, are going to have a baby. An heir."

Sithas gaped at her, unaware that his jaw had dropped in a most unelven lack of dignity. His mind reeled, and a profound explosion of joy rose within his heart. He wanted to shout his delight from the tower top, to let the word ring through the city like a prideful cry.

For a moment, he truly forgot about everything—the war, the dwarves, the logistics and weapons that had occupied him. He pulled his wife to him and kissed her. He held her for a long time under the starlight, above the city that had so troubled him earlier.

But for now, all was right with the world.

* * * * *

The next day Than-Kar came to see Sithas, though the Theiwar dwarf arrived, nearly fifteen minutes after the time indicated in the Speaker's summons.

Sithas awaited him, impatiently seated upon the great emerald throne of his ancestors, located in the center of the great Hall of Audience. This vast chamber occupied the base of the Tower of the Stars, with its sheer walls soaring upward into the dizzying heights. Above, six hundred feet over their heads, the top of the tower stood open to the sky.

Than-Kar clumped into the hall at the head of a column of twelve bodyguards, almost as if he expected ambush. Twoscore elves of the House Protectorate—the royal guard of Silvanesti— snapped to attention around the periphery of the hall.

The Theiwar sniffed his nose loudly, the rude gesture echoing through the hall, as he approached the Speaker. Sithas studied the dwarf, carefully masking his distaste.

Like all Theiwar dwarves, Than-Kar's eyes seemed to stare wildly, with the whites showing all around the pinpoint pupils. His lips curled in a perpetual sneer, and despite his ambassadorial station, his beard and hair remained unkempt, his leather clothes filthy. How unlike Dunbarth Ironthumb!

The Theiwar bowed perfunctorily and then looked up at Sithas, his beady eyes glittering with antagonism.

"We'll make this brief," said the elf coldly. "I desire to know what word has come from your king. He has had time to reply, and the questions we have sent have not been formally answered."

"As a matter of fact, I was preparing my written reply when your courier interrupted me with this summons yesterday. I had to delay my progress in order to hasten to this meeting."

Yes, Than-Kar must have made haste, for he obviously hadn't taken time to run a comb through his hair or change his grease-spattered tunic, thought Sithas. The Speaker held his tongue, albeit with difficulty.

"However, insofar as I am here and taking up the speaker's valuable time, I can summarize the message that I have received from Thorbardin."

"Please, do," Sithas requested dryly.

"The Royal Council of Thorbardin finds that, to date, there is insufficient cause to support elven warmaking in the plains," announced the dwarf bluntly.

"What?" Sithas stiffened, no longer able to retain his impassive demeanor. 'That is a contradiction of everything our meetings with Dunbarth established! Surely you—your people—recognize that the human threat extends beyond mere grazing rights on the plains!"

"There is no evidence of a threat to our interests."

"No threat?" The elf cut him off rudely. "You *know* humans. They will stretch and grab whatever they can. They will seize our plains, *your* mountains, the forest—*everything!*"

Than-Kar regarded him coolly, those wide, staring eyes seeming to gleam with delight. Abruptly Sithas realized that he was wasting his time with this arrogant Theiwar. Angrily he stood, half fearing that he would strike out at the dwarf and very much desiring to do just that. Still, enough of his dignity and self-control remained to stay his hand. After all, a war with the dwarves was the last thing they needed right now.

"This conference is concluded," he said stiffly.

Than-Kar nodded—smugly, Sithas thought—and turned to lead his escort from the hall.

Sithas stared after the dwarven ambassador, his anger still seething. He would not—he *could* not—allow this to be the final impasse!

But what else could he do? No ideas arrived to lighten the oppressive burden of his mood.

Spring
2214 (PC)

2

The horse pranced nervously along the ridgetop, staying within the protective foliage of the tree line. Thick, blue-green pines enclosed the mount and its elven rider on three sides. Finally the great stallion Kijo stood still, allowing Kith-Kanan to peer through the moist, aromatic branches to the vast expanse of open country beyond.

Nearby, two of the Wildrunners—Kith's personal bodyguards—sat alertly in their saddles, swords drawn and eyes alert. Those elves, too, were nervous at the sight of their leader possibly exposing himself to the threat in the valley below.

And what a threat it was! The long column of the human army snaked into the distance as far as the keen-eyed elves could see from their vantage on the ridgetop. The vanguard of the army, a company of heavily armored lancers riding huge, lumbering war-horses, had already passed them by.

Now ranks of spearmen, thousands upon thousands, marched past, perhaps a mile away down the gradually sloping ridge. This was the central wing of the massive Army of Ergoth, which followed the most direct route toward Sithelbec and presented the most immediate threat to the Wildrunners. Kith-Kanan turned with a grim smile, and Kijo pranced into the deeper shelter of the forest.

The commander of the Wildrunners knew his force was ready for this, the opening battle of his nation's first war in over four centuries. Not since the Second Dragon War had the elves of the

House Protectorate taken to the field to defend their nation against an external threat,

The ring on his finger—the Ring of Balifor—had been given to his father as a reminder of the alliance between kender and elves during the Second Dragon War. Now he wore it and prepared to do battle in a new cause. For a moment, he wondered what this war would be named when Astinus took up his pen to scribe the tale in his great annals.

Though Kith-Kanan was young for an elf—he had been born a mere ninety-three years ago—he felt the weight of long tradition riding in the saddle with him. He knew no compelling hatred toward these humans, yet he recognized the threat they presented. If they weren't stopped here, half of Silvanesti would be gobbled up by the rapacious human settlers and the elves would be driven into a small corner of their once vast holdings.

The humans had to be defeated. It was Kith-Kanan's job, as commander of the Wildrunners, to see that the elven nation was victorious.

Another figure moved through the trees, bringing the bodyguards' swords swooshing forth, until they recognized the rider.

"Sergeant-Major Parnigar." Kith-Kanan nodded to the veteran Wildrunner, his chief aide and most reliable scout. The sergeant was dressed in leather armor of green and brown, and he rode a stocky, nimble pony.

"The companies are in place, sir—the riders behind the ridge, with a thousand elves of Silvanost bearing pike behind them." Parnigar, a veteran warrior who had fought in the Second Dragon War, had helped recruit the first wild elves into Kith-Kanan's force. Now he reported on their readiness to die for that cause. "The Kagonesti archers are well hidden and well supplied. We can only hope the humans react as we desire."

Parnigar looked skeptical as he spoke, but Kith suspected this was just the elf's cautious nature. The sergeant's face was as gray and leathery as an old map. His strapping arms rested on the pommel of his saddle with deceptive ease. His green eyes missed nothing. Even as he talked to his general, the sergeant-major was scanning the horizon.

Parnigar slouched casually in his saddle, his posture more like a human's than an elf's. Indeed, the veteran had taken a human wife some years before, and in many ways he seemed to enjoy the company of the short-lived race. He spoke quickly and moved with a certain restless agitation—both characteristics that tended to mark humans far more typically than elves.

Yet Parnigar knew his roots. He was an heir of the House Protectorate and had served in the Wildrunners since he had first learned to handle a sword. He was the most capable warrior that Kith-Kanan knew, and the elven general was glad to have him at his side.

"The human scouts have been slain by ambush," Kith-Kanan told him. "Their army has lost its eyes. It is almost time. Come, ride with me!"

The commander of the Wildrunners nudged Kijo's flanks with his knees, and the stallion exploded into a dash through the forest. So nimble was the horse's step that he dashed around tree trunks with Kith-Kanan virtually a blur. Parnigar raced behind, with the two hapless guards spurring their steeds in a losing struggle to keep pace.

For several minutes, the pair dashed through the forest, the riders' faces lashed by pine needles, but the horses' hooves landing true. Abruptly the trees stopped, exposing the wide, gently rolling ridgetop. Below, to the right, marched the endless army of humankind.

Kith-Kanan nudged Kijo again, and the stallion burst into view of the humans below. The elven general's blond hair trailed in the sun behind him, for his helmet remained lashed to the back of his saddle. As he rode, he raised a steel-mailed fist.

He made a grand figure, racing along the crest of the hill above the teeming mass of his enemy. Like his twin brother Sithas, his face was handsome and proud, with prominent cheekbones and a sharp, strong chin. Though he was slender—like every one of his race—his tall physique lifted him above the deep pommels of the saddle.

Instantly the trumpeters of Silvanost sprang to their feet. They had lain in the grass along this portion of the crest. Raising their golden horns in unison, they brayed a challenge across the rolling prairie below. Behind the trumpeters, concealed from the humans by the crest of the ridge, the elven riders mounted their horses while the bowmen knelt in the tall grass, waiting for the command to action.

The great column of humans staggered like a confused centipede. Men turned to gape at the spectacle, observing pennants and banners that burst from the woods in a riotous display of color. All order vanished from the march as each soldier instinctively yielded to astonishment and the beginnings of fear.

Then the human army gasped, for the elven riders abruptly swarmed over the ridgetop in a long, precise line. Horses pranced, raising their forefeet in a high trot, while banners unfurled overhead and steel lance tips gleamed before them. They numbered but five hundred, yet every human who saw them swore later that they were attacked by thousands of elven riders.

Onward the elven horsemen came, their line remaining parade-ground sharp. On the valley floor, some of the humans broke and ran, while others raised spears or swords, ready and even eager for battle.

From the front of the vast human column, the huge brigade of heavy lancers turned its mighty war-horses toward the flank. Yet they were two miles away, and their companies quickly lost coherence as they struggled around other regiments—the footmen—that were caught behind them.

The elven riders raced closer to the center of the column, the thunder of their hooves crashing and shaking the earth. Then, two hundred feet from their target, they stopped. Each of the five hundred horses pivoted, and from the dust of the sudden maneuver, five hundred arrows arced forth, over the great blocks of humans and then down, like deadly hawks seeking out their terrified victims.

Another volley ripped into the human ranks, and suddenly the elven riders retreated, dashing across the same ridge they had charged down mere moments before.

In that same instant, the humans realized they were going to be robbed of the satisfaction of fighting, and a roar of outrage erupted from ten thousand throats. Swords raised, shields brandished, men broke from the column without command of their captains, chasing and cursing the elven riders. The enraged mob swept up the slope in chaotic disarray, united only in its fury.

Abruptly a trumpet cry rang from the low summit, and ranks of green-clad elves appeared in the grass before the charging humans, as if they had suddenly sprouted from the ground.

In the next instant, the sky darkened beneath a shower of keen elven arrows, their steel tips gleaming in the sunlight as they arced high above the humans, then tipped in their inevitable descent. Even before the first volley fell, another rippled outward, as steady and irresistible as hail.

The arrows tore into the human ranks with no regard for armor, rank, or quickness. Instead, the deadly rain showered the mob with complete randomness, puncturing steel helmets and breastplates and slicing through leather shoulder pads. Shrieks and cries from the wounded rose in hysterical chorus, while other humans fell silently, writhing in mute agony or lying still upon the now-reddening grass.

Again and again the arrows soared outward, and the mob wavered in its onrush. Bodies littered the field. Some of these crawled or squirmed pathetically toward safety, ignored by the mindless rush of the others.

As more of them died, fear rose like a palpable cloud over the heads of the humans. Then, by twos and fives and tens, they turned and raced back toward the rest of the column. Finally they retreated in hundreds, harried back down the newly mud-covered slope by pursuing missile fire. As they vanished, so did the elven archers, withdrawing at a trot over the crest of the ridge.

At last the human heavy lancers approached, and a cheer rose from the rest of the great army. A thousand bold knights, clad in armor from head to toe, urged their massive horses onward. The great beasts lumbered like monsters, buried beneath clanking plates of barding. A cloud of bright pennants fluttered over the thundering mass.

Kith-Kanan, still mounted upon his proud stallion, studied these new warriors from the ridgetop. Caution, not fear, tempered his hopes as the great weight of horses, men, and metal churned closer. The heavy knights, he knew, were the army's most lethal attack force.

He had planned for this, but only the reality of things would show whether the Wildrunners stood equal to the task. For a moment, Kith-Kanan's courage wavered, and he considered ordering a fast retreat from the field a disastrous idea, he quickly told himself, for his hope now lay in steadfast courage, not flight. The knights drew nearer, and Kith-Kanan wheeled and galloped after the archers.

The great steeds rumbled inexorably up the slope, toward the gentle crest where the elven riders and archers had disappeared. They couldn't see the foe, but they hoped that the elves would be found just beyond the ridgetop. The knights kicked their mounts and shouted their challenges as they crested the rise, springing with renewed speed toward the enemy. In their haste, they broke their tight ranks, eager to crush the deadly archers and light elven lancers.

Instead, they met a phalanx of elven pikemen, the gleaming steel tips of the Wildrunners' weapons arrayed as a bristling wall of death. The elves stood shoulder to shoulder in great blocks, facing outward from all sides. The riders and archers had taken shelter in the middle of these blocks, while three ranks of pikemen one kneeling, one crouching, and one standing kept their weapons fixed, promising certain death to any horse reckless enough to close.

The great war-horses, sensing the danger, turned, bucked, and spun, desperate to avoid the rows of pikes. Unfortunately for the riders, each horse, as it turned, met another performing a similar contortion. Many of the beasts crashed to the ground, and still more riders were thrown by their panicked steeds. They lay in their heavy armor, too weighted down even to climb to their feet.

Arrows whistled outward from the Wildrunners. Though

the shortbows of the elven riders were ineffective against the armored knights, the longbows of the foot archers drove their barbed missiles through the heaviest plate at this close range. Howls of pain and dismay now drowned out the battle cries among the knights, and in moments the cavalry, in mass, turned and lumbered back across the ridgetop, leaving several dozen of their number moaning on the ground almost at the feet of the elven pikemen.

"Run, you bastards!" Parnigar's shout was a gleeful bark beside Kith-Kanan.

The general, too, felt his lieutenant's elation. They had held the knights! They had broken the charge!

Kith-Kanan and Parnigar watched the retreat of the knights from the center of the largest contingent. The sergeant-major looked at his commander, gesturing to the fallen knights. Some of these unfortunate men lay still, knocked unconscious by the fall from horseback, while others struggled to their knees or twitched in obvious pain. More humans lay at the top of the slope, their bodies punctured by elven arrows.

"Shall I give the order to finish them?" Parnigar asked, ready to send a rank of swordsmen forward. The grim warrior's eyes flashed.

"No," Kith-Kanan said. He looked grimly at his sergeant's raised eyebrows. "This is the first skirmish of a great war. Let it not be said we began it with butchery."

"But-but they're knights! These are the most powerful humans in that entire army! What if they are healed and restored to arms? Surely you don't want them to ride against us again?" Parnigar kept his voice low but made his arguments precisely.

"You're right the power of the heavy knights is lethal. If we hadn't been fully prepared for their assault, I'm not certain we could have held them. Still . . ."

Kith-Kanan's mind balked at the situation before him, until a solution suddenly brightened his expression, "Send the swordsmen forward but not to kill. Have them take the weapons of the fallen knights and any banners, pennants, and the like that they can find. Return with these, but let the humans live."

Parnigar nodded, satisfied with his general's decision. He raised a hand and the line of pikemen parted, allowing the sergeant-major's charger to trot forward. Selecting a hundred veterans, he started the task of stripping the humans of their badges and pennants.

Kith turned, sensing movement behind him. He saw the pikemen parting there, too, this time to admit someone a grimy elven rider straddling a foaming, dust-covered horse. Through the dust, Kith recognized a shock of hair the color of snow.

"White-lock! It's good to see you." Kith swung easily from his saddle as the Kagonesti elf did the same. The general clasped the rider's hand warmly, searching the wild elf's eyes for a hint of his news.

White-lock rubbed a hand across his dust-covered face, revealing the black and white stripes painted across his forehead. Typical of the wild elves, he was fully painted for war and covered by the grit of his long ride. A scout and courier for the Wildrunners, he had ridden hundreds of miles to report on the movements of the human army.

Now White-lock nodded, deferentially but coolly, toward Kith-Kanan. "The humans fare poorly in the south," he began. "They have not yet crossed the border into elven lands, so slowly do they march."

White-lock's tone dripped with scorn a scom equal to that Kith had heard him use when describing the "civilized" elves of crystalline Silvanost. Indeed, the wild elves of Kagonesti in many cases bore little love for their cousins in the cities antipathy, to be sure, that mirrored the hatred and prejudice held by the Silvanesti elves for any race other than their own.

"Any word out of Thorbardin?"

"Nothing reliable." The Kagonesti continued his report, his tone revealing that dwarves ranked near the bottom on his list of worthwhile peoples. "They promise to assist us when the humans have committed sufficient provocation, but I won't believe them till I see them stand and fight."

"Why does the southern wing of the Ergothian army march so slowly?" Kith-Kanan, through his Wildrunner scouts, had been tracking the three great wings of the vast Caergoth army, each of which was far greater in size than his entire force of Wildrunners.

"They have difficulties with the gnomes," White-lock continued. "They drag some kind of monstrous machine with them, pulled by a hundred oxen, and it steams and belches smoke. A whole train of coal wagons follows, carrying fuel for this machine."

"It must surely be some type of weapon but what? Do you know?"

White-lock shook his head. "It is now mired in the bottomlands a few miles from the border. Perhaps they will leave it behind. If not . . ." The Kagonesti elf shrugged. It was simply another idiocy of the enemy that he could not predict or fathom.

"You bring good news," Kith noted with satisfaction. He planted his hands on his hips and looked at the ridgeline above, where Parnigar and his footmen were returning. Many waved captured human banners or held aloft helmets with long, trailing plumes. Every so often he saw a dejected and disarmed human scuttling upward and disappearing over the ridge as if he still feared for his life.

Today Kith and the Wildrunners had directed a sharp blow against the central wing of the human army. He hoped the confusion and frustration of the elven attack would delay their march for several days. The news from the south was encouraging. It would take months for a threat to develop there. But what of the north?

His worries lingered as the Wildrunners quickly reformed from battle into march formation. They would pass through partially forested terrain, so the elven army moved in five broad, irregular columns. They followed parallel routes, with about a quarter of a mile between columns. If necessary, they could easily outdistance any human army, whether mounted or on foot.

Kith-Kanan, with Parnigar and a company of riders, remained behind until sunset. He was pleased to see the human army encamp at the scene of the attack. In the morning, he suspected, they would send forth huge and cumbersome reconnaissances, none of which would find any trace of the elves.

Finally the last of the Wildrunners, with Kith in the lead, turned their stocky, fast horses to the west. They would leave the field in possession of the foe, but a foe a little more bewildered, a little more frightened, than the day before.

The elven riders passed easily along forest trails at a fast walk, and at a canter through moonlit meadows. It was as they crossed one of these that movement in the fringe of the treeline pulled Kijo up sharply. A trio of riders approached. Kith recognized the first two as members of his guard.

"A messenger, sir from the north!" The guards puffed aside as Kith stared in shock at the third rider.

The elf slumped in his saddle like a corpse that had been placed astride a horse. As he looked toward Kith-Kanan, his eyes flickered with a momentary hope.

"We tried to hold them back, sir to harass them, as you commanded!" the elf reported in a rush. "The human wing to the north moved onto the plain, and we struck them!"

The scout's voice belied his looks. It was taut and firm, the voice of a man who spoke the truth and who desperately wanted to be believed. Now he shook his head. "But no matter how quickly we moved, they moved more quickly. They struck at us, sir! They wiped out a hundred elves in one camp and routed the Kagonesti back to the woods! They move with unbelievable stealth and speed!"

"They advance southward, then?" Kith-Kanan asked, instinctively knowing the answer, for he immediately understood that the human commander of the northern wing must be an unusually keen and agressive foe.

"Yes

"Yes! Faster than I would have believed, had I not seen it myself! They ride like the wind, these humans. They have surrounded most of the northern pickets. I alone escaped."

The messenger's eyes met Kith's, and the elf spoke with all the intensity of his soul. "But that is not the worst of it, my general! Now they sweep to the east of my own path. Already you may be cut off from Sithelbec!"

"Impossible!" Kith barked the denial. The fortress, or city, of Sithelbec was his headquarters and his base of operations. It was far to the rear of the battle zone. "There can't be any humans within a hundred miles of there!"

But again he looked into the eyes of the messenger, and he had to believe the terrible news. "All right," he said grimly. "They've stolen a march on us. It's time for the Wildrunners to seize it back."

That Night in the Army of Ergoth

3

The sprawling tent stood in the center of the vast encampment. Three peaks stood high, marking the poles that divided the shelter into a trio of chambers. Though the stains of the season's campaign marked its sides, and seams showed where the top had been mended, the colorless canvas structure had a certain air about it, as if it was a little more important, a little more proud than the tents flowing to the horizon around it.

The huge camp was not a permanent gathering, and so the rows of straight-backed tents ran haphazardly, wherever the rolling ground, crisscrossed by numerous ravines, allowed. Green pastures, feeding grounds for twenty thousand horses, marked the hinges of the encampment. As dusk settled, the army's shelters lined up in gray anonymity, except for this high, three-peaked tent.

The inside of that structure, as well, would never be mistaken for the abode of some soldier. Here cascades of silken draperies—deep browns, rich golds, and the iridescent black that was so popular among Ergothian nobles—covered the sides, blocking any view of the harsh realities beyond the canvas walls.

Suzine des Quivalin sat in the tent, studying a crystal glass before her. Her coppery hair no longer coiled about the tiara of diamond-studded platinum. Instead, it gathered in a bun at the back of her head, though its length still cascaded more than a foot down her back. She wore a practical leather skirt, but her blouse was of fine silk. Her skin was clean, making her unique among all these thousands of humans.

Indeed, captains and sergeants and troopers alike grumbled about the favors shown to the general's woman—hot water for bathing! A luxurious tent—ten valuable horses were required just to haul her baggage.

Still, though grumbling occurred, none of it happened within earshot of the commander. General Giarna led his force with skill and determination, but he was a terrifying man who would brook no argument, whether it was about his tactics or his woman's comforts. Thus the men kept the remarks very quiet and very private.

Now Suzine sat upon a large chair, cushioned with silk-covered pillows of down, but she didn't take advantage of that softness. Instead, she sat at the edge of the seat, tension visible in her posture and in the rapt concentration of her face as she studied the crystal surface before her.

The glass looked like a normal mirror, but it didn't show a reflection of the lady's very lovely face. Instead, as she studied the image, she saw a long line of foot soldiers. They were clean-shaven, blond of hair, and carried long pikes or thin, silver swords.

She watched the army of Kith-Kanan.

For a time, she touched the mirror, and her vision ran back and forth along the winding column. Her lips moved silently as she counted longbows and pikes and horses. She watched the elves form and march. She noted the precision with which the long, fluid columns moved across the plains, retaining their precise intervals as they did so.

But then her perusal reached the head of the column, and here she lingered. She studied the one who rode at the head of that force, the one she knew was Kith-Kanan, twin brother to the elven ruler.

She admired his tall stance in the saddle, the easy, graceful way that he raised his hand, gesturing to his outriders or summoning a messenger. Narrow wings rose to a pair of peaks atop his dark helmet. His dark plate mail looked worn, and a heavy layer of dust covered it, yet she could discern its quality and the easy way he wore it, as comfortably as many a human would wear his soft cotton tunic.

Her lips parted slightly, and she didn't sense the pace of her breathing slowly increase. The lady did not hear the tent flap move behind her, so engrossed was she in her study of the handsome elven warrior.

Then a shadow fell across her, and she looked up with a sharp cry. The mirror faded until it showed only the lady, her face twisted in an expression of guilt mixed with indignation.

"You could announce your presence!" she snapped, standing to face the tall man who had entered.

"I am commander of the camp. General Giarna of Ergoth need announce his presence to no one, save the emperor himself," the armor-plated figure said quietly. His black eyes fixed upon the woman's, then shifted to the mirror. These eyes of the Boy General frightened her—they were hardly boyish, and not entirely human, either. Dark and brooding, they sometimes blazed with an internal fire that was fueled, she sensed, by something that was beyond her understanding. At other times, however, they gaped black and empty. She found this dispassionate void even more frightening than his rage.

Suddenly he snarled, and Suzine gasped in fright. She would have backed away, save for the fact that her dressing table blocked any retreat. For a moment, she felt certain he would strike her. It would not be the first time. But then she looked into his eyes and knew that, for the moment, anyway, she was safe.

Instead of violent rage, she saw there a hunger that, while frightening, did not presage a blow. Instead, it signaled a desperate yearning for a need that could never be satisfied. It was one of the things that had first drawn her to him, this strange hunger. Once she had felt certain that she could slake it.

Now she knew better. The attraction that had once drawn her to Giarna had waned, replaced for the most part by fear, and now when she saw that look in his eyes, she mostly pitied him.

The general grunted, shaking his head wearily. His short black hair lay sweaty and tousled on his head. She knew he would have had his helmet on until he entered the tent, and then taken it off in deference to her.

"Lady Suzine, I seek information and have been worried by your long silence. Tell me, what have you seen in your magic mirror?"

"I'm sorry, my lord," replied Suzine. Her eyes fell, and she hoped that the flush across her cheeks couldn't be noticed. She took a deep breath, regaining her composure.

"The elven army countermarches quickly—faster than you expected," she explained, her voice crisp and efficient. "They will confront you before you can march to Sithelbec."

General Giarna's eyes narrowed, but his face showed no other emotion. "This captain . . . what's his name?"

"Kith-Kanan," Suzine supplied.

"Yes. He seems alert—more so than any human commander I've faced. I would have wagered a year's pay that he couldn't have moved so fast."

"They march with urgency. They make good time, even through the woods"

"They'll have to stick to the forests," growled the general, "because as soon as I meet them, I shall rule the plains."

Abruptly General Giarna looked at Suzine inquiringly. "What is the word on the other two wings?"

"Xalthan is still paralyzed. The lava cannon is mired in the lowlands, and he seems unwilling to advance until the gnomes free it."

The general snorted in amused derision. "Just what I expected from that fool. And Barnet?"

'The central wing has gone into a defensive formation, as if they expect attack. They haven't moved since yesterday afternoon."

"Excellent. The enemy comes to me, and my erstwhile allies twiddle their thumbs!" General Giarna's black beard split apart as he grinned. "When I win this battle, the emperor cannot help but realize who his greatest warrior is!"

He turned and paced, speaking more to himself than to her. "We will drive against him, break him before Sithelbec! We have assurances that the dwarves will stay out of the war, and the elves alone cannot hope to match our numbers. The victory will be *mine!*"

He turned back to her, those dark eyes flaming again, and Suzine felt another kind of fear—the fear of the doe as it trembles before the slavering jaws of the wolf. Again the general whirled in agitation, pounding his fist into the palm of his other hand.

Suzine cast a sidelong glance at the mirror, as if she feared someone might be listening. The surface was natural, reflecting only the pair in the tent. In the mirror, she saw General Giarna step toward her. She turned to face him as he placed his hands on her shoulders.

She knew what he wanted, what she would—she *must*—give him. Their contact was brief and violent. Giarna's passion contorted him, as if she was the vent for all of his anxieties. The experience bruised her, gave her a sense of uncleanliness that nearly brought her to despair. Afterward, she wanted to reach out and cover the mirror, to smash it or at least turn it away.

Instead, she hid her feelings, as she had learned to do so well, and then lay quietly as Giarna rose and dressed, saying nothing. Once he looked at her, and she thought he was going to speak.

Suzine's heart pounded. Did he know what she was thinking? She thought of the face in the mirror again—that *elven* face. But General Giarna only scowled as he stood before her. After several moments, he spun on his heel and stalked from the tent. She heard the pacing of his charger without, and then the clatter of hooves as the general galloped away.

Hesitantly, inevitably, she turned back to the mirror.

In Pitched Battle

4

The two armies wheeled and skirmished across the flatlands, using the forests for cover and obstruction, making sharp cavalry sweeps and sudden ambushes. Lives expired, men and elves suffered agony and maiming and yet the great bodies of the two armies did not contact each other.

General Giarna's human force drove toward Sithelbec, while Kith-Kanan's Wildrunners countermarched to interpose themselves between the Ergothian army and its destination. The humans moved quickly, and it was only the effort of an all-night forced march that finally brought the exhausted elves into position.

Twenty thousand Silvanesti and Kagonesti warriors finally gathered into, a single mass and prepared a defense, tensely awaiting the steadily advancing human horde. The elven warriors averaged three to four hundred years of age, and many of their captains had seen six or more centuries. If they survived the battle and the war, they could look forward to more centuries, five or six hundred years, perhaps, of peaceful aging.

The Silvanesti bore steel weapons of fine craftsmanship, arrowheads that could punch through plate mail and swords that would not shatter under the most crushing of blows. Many of the elves had some limited proficiency in magic, and these were grouped in small platoons attached to each company. Though these elves, too, would rely upon sword and shield to survive the battle, their spells could provide a timely and demoralizing counterpunch.

The Wildrunners also had some five hundred exceptionally fleet horses, and upon these were mounted the elite—lancers and archers who would harass and confuse the enemy. They wore the grandest armor, shined to perfection, and each bore his personal emblem embroidered in silk upon his breast.

This force stood against a human army of more than fifty thousand men. The humans averaged about twenty-five years of age, the oldest veterans having seen a mere four or five decades of life. Their weapons were crudely crafted by elven standards, yet they possessed a deep strength. The blade might grow dull, but only rarely would it break.

The human elite included riders, numbering twenty thousand. They bore no insignia, nor did they wear armor of metal. Instead, they were a ragged, evil-looking lot, with many a missing tooth, eye, or ear. Unlike their elven counterparts, almost all were bearded, primarily because of a disdain of shaving, or indeed grooming of any kind.

But they carried within them an inner thirst for a thing uniquely human in character. Whether it was called glory or excitement or Adventure, or simply cruelty or savagery, it was a quality that made the short-lived humans feared and distrusted by all the longer-lived races of Krynn.

Now this burning ambition, propelled by the steel-bladed drive of General Giarna, pushed the humans toward Sithelbec. For two days, the elven army appeared to stand before them, only to melt away at the first sign of attack. By the third day, however, they stood within march of that city itself.

Kith-Kanan had reached the edge of the tree cover. Beyond lay nothing but open field to the gates of Sithelbec, some ten miles away. Here the Wildrunners would have to stand.

The reason for falling back this far became obvious to elf and human alike as the Wildrunners reached their final position. Silver trumpets blared to the eastward, and a column of marchers hove into view.

"Hail the elves of Silvanost!"

Cries of delight and welcome erupted from the elven army as, with propitious timing, the five thousand recruits sent by Sithas two months earlier marched into the Wildrunners' camp. At their head rode Kencathedrus, the stalwart veteran who had given Kith-Kanan his earliest weapons training.

"Hah! I see that my former student still plays his war games!" The old veteran, his narrow face showing the strain of the long march, greeted Kith before the commander's tent. Wearily Kencathedrus lifted a leg over his saddle. Kith helped him to stand on the ground.

"I'm glad you made it," Kith-Kanan greeted his old teacher, clasping his arms warmly. "It's a long march from the city."

Kencathedrus nodded curtly. Kith-Kanan would have thought the gesture rude, except that he knew the old warrior and his mannerisms. Kencathedrus represented the purest tradition of the House Royal—the descendents, like Kith-Kanan and Sithas, of Silvanos himself. Indeed, they were distant cousins in some obscure way Kith had never understood.

But more than blood relative, Kencathedrus was in many ways the mentor of Kith-Kanan the warrior. Strict to the point of obsession, the teacher had drilled the pupil in the instinctive use of the longsword and in the swift and repetitive shooting of the bow until such tasks had become second nature.

Now Kencathedrus looked Kith-Kanan up and down. The general was clad in unadorned plate mail, with a simple steel helmet, unmarked by any sign of rank.

"What about your crest?" he asked. "Don't you fight in the name of Silvanos, of the House Royal?"

Kith nodded. "As always. However, my guards have persuaded me that there's no sense in making myself a target. I dress like a simple cavalryman now." He took Kencathedrus's arm, noting that the old elf moved with considerable stiffness.

"My back isn't what it used to be," admitted the venerable captain, stretching.

"It's likely to get some more exercise soon," Kith warned him. "Thank the gods you arrived when you did!"

"The human army?" Kencathedrus looked past the elves, lined up for battle. Kith told the captain what he knew.

"A mile away, no more. We have to face them here. The alternative is to fall back into the fortress, and I'm not ready to concede the plains!"

"You've chosen a good field, it seems." Kencathedrus nodded at the stands of trees around them. The area consisted of many of these thick groves, separated by wide, grassy fields. "How many stand against us?"

"Just a third of the entire Ergoth army—that's the good news. The other two wings have bogged down—more than a hundred miles away right now. But this one is the most dangerous. The commander is bold and adventurous. I had to march all night to get in front of him, and now my troops are exhausted as he prepares his attack!"

"You forget," Kencathedrus chided Kith, almost harshly. "You stand with elves against a force of mere humans."

Kith-Kanan looked at the old warrior fondly, but he shook his head at the same time. "These 'mere' humans wiped out a hundred of my Wildrunners in one ambush. They've covered four hundred miles in three weeks." Now the leader's voice took on a tone of authority. "Do not underestimate them."

Kencathedrus studied Kith-Kanan before nodding his agreement. "Why don't you show me the lines," he suggested. "I presume you want us ready at first light."

As it happened, General Giarna gave Kith's force one more day to rest and prepare. The human army shifted and marched and expanded, all behind the screen of several groves of trees. Kith sent a dozen Kagonesti Wildrunners to spy, counting on the natural vegetation that they used so well to cover them.

Only one returned, and he to report that the human sentries were too thick for even the skilled elves to pass without detection.

The elven force took advantage of the extra day, however. They constructed trenches along much of their front, and in other places, they laid long, sharp stakes in the earth to form a wall thrusting outward. These stakes would protect much of the front from the enemy horsemen Kith knew to number in the thousands.

Parnigar supervised the excavation, racing from site to site, shouting and cursing. He insulted the depth of one trench, the width of another. He cast aspersions on the lineage of the elves who had done the work. The Wildrunners leaped to obey out of respect, not fear. All along the line they dug in, proving that they used the pick and the spade as well as the longsword and pike.

Midafternoon slowly crept toward dusk. Kith restlessly worked his way back and forth along the line. Eventually he came to the reserve, where the men of Silvanost recovered from their long march under the shrewd tutelage of Kencathedrus. That captain stepped up to Kith-Kanan as the general dismounted from Kijo.

"Odd how they work for him," noted the older elf, indicating Parnigar. "My elves wouldn't even look at an officer who talked to them like that!"

Kith-Kanan looked at him curiously, realizing that he spoke the truth. "The Wildrunners here on the plains are a different kind of force than you know from the city," he pointed out.

He looked at the reserve force, consisting of the five thousand elves who had marched with Kencathedrus. Even at ease, they lounged in the sun in neat ranks across the grassy meadows. A formation of Wildrunners, Kith reflected, would have collected in the areas of shade.

The teacher nodded, still skeptical. He looked across the front, toward the trees that screened the enemy army. "Do you know their deployments?" asked Kencathedrus.

"No," Kith admitted. "We've been shut off all day. I'd fall back if I could. They've had too much time to prepare an attack, and I'd love to set those preparations to waste. Your old lesson comes to mind: 'Don't let the enemy have the luxury of following his plan!' "

Kencathedrus nodded, and Kith nearly growled in frustration as he continued. "But I *can't* move back. These trees are the last cover between here and Sithelbec. There's not so much as a ditch to hide behind if I abandon this position!"

All he could do was to deploy a company of skirmishers well to each flank of his position and hope they could provide him with warning of any sudden flanking thrust.

It was a night of restlessness throughout the camp, despite the exhaustion of the weary troops. Few of them slept for more than a few hours, and many campfires remained lit well past midnight as elves gathered around them and talked of past centuries, of their families—of anything but the terrible destiny that seemed to await them on the morrow.

Dew crept across the land in the darkest hours of night, becoming a heavy mist that flowed thickly through the meadows and twisted around the trunks in the groves. With it came a chill that woke every elf, and thus they spent the last hours of darkness.

They heard the drums before dawn, a far-off rattle that began with shocking precision from a thousand places at once. Darkness shrouded the woods, and the mists of the humid night drifted like spirits among the nervous elves, further obscuring visibility.

Gradually the dark mist turned to pale blue. As the sky lightened overhead, the cadence of a great army's advance swelled around the elves. The Wildrunners held to their pikes, or steadied their prancing horses. They checked their bowstrings and their quivers, and made certain that the bucklings on their armor held secure. Inevitably the blue light gave way to a dawn of vague, indistinct shapes, still clouded by the haze of fog.

The beat of the drums grew louder. The mist drifted across the fields, leaving even nearby clumps of trees nothing more than gray shadows. Louder still grew the precise tapping, yet nothing could be seen of the approaching force.

"There—coming through the pines!"

"I see them—over that way!"

"Here they come—from the ravine!"

Elves shouted, pointing to spots all along their front where shapes began to take form in the mist. Now they could see great, rippling lines of movement, as if waves rolled through the earth itself. The large, prancing figures of horsemen became apparent, several waves of them flexing among the ranks of infantry.

Abruptly, as suddenly as it had started, the drumming ceased. The formations of the human army appeared as darker shapes against the yellow grass and the gray sky. For a moment, time on the field, and perhaps across all the plains, across all of Ansalon, stood still. The warriors of the two armies regarded each other across a quarter-mile of ground. Even the wind died, and the mist settled low to the earth.

Then a shout arose from one of the humans and was echoed by fifty thousand voices. Swords bashed against shields, while trumpets blared and horses whinnied in excitement and terror.

In the next instant, the human wave surged forward, the roaring sound wave of the attack preceding it with terrifying force.

Now brassy notes rang from elven trumpets. Pikes rattled as their wielders set their weapons. The five hundred horses of the Wildrunner cavalry nickered and kicked nervously.

Kith-Kanan steadied Kijo. From his position in the center of the line, he had a good view of the advancing human tide. His bodyguards, increased to twelve riders today, stood in a semicircle behind him. He had insisted that they not obstruct his view of the field.

For a moment, he had a terrifying vision of the elven line's collapse, the human horde sweeping across the plains and forests beyond like a swarm of insects. He shuddered in the grip of the fear, but then the swirl of events grabbed and held his attention.

The first shock of the charge came in the form of two thousand swordsmen, brandishing shields and howling madly. Dressed in thick leather jerkins, they raced ahead of their metal-armored comrades, toward the block of elven pikes standing firm in the center of Kith's line.

The clash of swordsmen with the tips of those pikes was a horrible scene. The steel-edged blades of the pikes pierced the leather with ease as scores of humans impaled themselves from the force of the charge. A cheer went up from the Wildrunners as the surviving swordsmen turned to flee, leaving perhaps a quarter of their number writhing and groaning on the ground, at the very feet of the elves who had wounded them.

Now the focus shifted to the left, where human longbowmen advanced against an exposed portion of the Wildrunner line. Kith's own archers fired back, sending a deadly shower against the press of men. But the human arrows, too, found marks among the tightly packed ranks, and elven blood soon flowed thick in the trampled grass.

Kith nudged Kijo toward the archers, watching volleys of arrows arc and cross through the air. The humans rushed forward and the elves stood firm. The elven commander urged his steed faster, sensing the imminent clash.

Then the human advance wavered and slowed. Kith saw Parnigar, standing beside the archers.

"Now!" cried the sergeant-major, gesturing toward a platoon of elves standing beside him. A few dozen in number, these elves wore swords at their sides but had no weapons in their hands. It was their bare hands that they raised, fingers extended toward the rushing humans.

A bright flash of light made Kith blink. Magic missiles, crackling blasts of sorcerous power, exploded from Parnigar's platoon. A whole line of men dropped, slain so suddenly that members of the rear ranks tripped and tumbled over the bodies. Again the light flashed, and another volley of magic ripped into the humans.

Some of those struck screamed aloud, crying for their gods or for their mothers. Others stumbled back, panicked by the sorcerous attack. A whole company, following the decimated formation, stopped in its tracks and then turned to flee. In another moment, the mass of human bowmen streamed away, pursued by another volley of the keen elven arrows.

Yet even as this attack failed, Kith sensed a crisis on his left. A line of human cavalry, three thousand snorting horses bearing armored lancers, thundered through the rapidly thinning mist, The charge swept forward with a momentum that made the previous attacks look like parade-ground drills.

Before the horsemen waited a line of elves with swords and shields, soft prey for the thundering riders. To the right and left of them, the sharp stakes jutted forward, proof against the cavalry attack. But the gaps in the line had to be held by troops, and now these elves faced approaching doom.

"Archers give cover!" Kith shouted as Kijo raced across the lines. Companies of elven longbow wheeled and released their missiles, scoring hits among the horsemen. But still the charge pounded forward.

"Fall back! Take cover in the trees!" he shouted to the captains of the longsword companies, for there was no other choice.

Kith cursed himself in frustration, realizing that the human commander had forced him to commit his pikes against the initial charge. Now came the horses, and his companies of pikes, the only true defense against a wave of cavalry, were terribly out of position.

Then he stared in astonishment. As more arrows fell among the riders, suddenly the horsemen wheeled about, racing away from the elven position before the defenders could follow Kith's orders to withdraw. The astonished elven swordsmen watched the horses and the riders flee, pursued by a desultory shower of arrows. The elven defenders could only wonder at the fortuitous turn of events.

In the back of Kith's mind, something whispered a warning. This had to be a trick, he told himself. Certainly the arrows hadn't been thick and deadly enough to halt that awe-inspiring charge. Less than fifty riders, and no more than two dozen horses, lay in the field before them. His scouts had given him a good count of the human cavalry. Though he had not been able to study these, he suspected he had seen only about half the force.

* * * * *

"Our men fall back as you ordered," reported Suzine, her eyes locked upon the violent images in her mirror. The glass rested on a table, and she sat before it—table, woman, and mirror, all encased in a narrow shroud of canvas, to keep the daylight from the crucial seeing device. She never lost view of the elven commander who sat straight and proud in his saddle, every inch the warrior of House Royal.

Behind her, pacing in taut excitement, General Giarna looked over her shoulder.

"Excellent! And the elves—what do you see of them?"

"They stand firm, my lord."

"What?" General Giarna's voice barked violently against her, filling the small canvas shelter where they observed the battle. "You're *wrong!* They must *attack!*"

Suzine flinched. The image in the mirror—a picture of long ranks of elven warriors, holding their positions, failing to pursue the bait of the human retreat—wavered slightly.

She felt the general's rage explode, and then the image faded. Suzine saw only her own reflection and the hideous face of the man behind her.

* * * * *

"My lord! Let us hit them now, while they fall back in confusion!" Kith turned to see Kencathedrus beside him. His old teacher rode a prancing mare, and the weariness of the march from Silvanost was totally gone from his face. Instead, the warrior's eyes burned, and his gauntleted fist clung tightly to the hilt of his sword.

"It has to be a trick," Kith countered. "We didn't drive them away that easily!"

"For the gods' sakes, Kith-Kanan—these are *humans!* The cowardly scum will run from a loud noise! Let's follow up and destroy them"

"No!" Kith's voice was harsh, full of command, and Kencathedrus's face whitened with frustration.

"We do not face an ordinary general," Kith-Kanan continued, feeling that he owed further explanation to the one who had girded his first sword upon him. "He hasn't failed to surprise me yet, and I know *we* have seen but a fraction of his force."

"But if they fly they will escape! We *must* pursue!" Kencathedrus couldn't help himself.

"The answer is no. If they are escaping, so be it. If they attempt to pull us out of our position to trap us, they shall not."

Another roar thundered across the fields before them, and more humans came into view, running toward the elves with all manner of weaponry. Great companies of longbowmen readied their missiles, while bearded axemen raised their heavy blades over their heads. Spearmen charged with gleaming points extended toward the enemy, while swordsmen banged their swords against their shields, advancing at a steady march.

Kencathedrus, shocked by the fresh display of human might and visor, looked at the general with respect. "You *knew?*" he said wonderingly,

Kith-Kanan shrugged and shook his head. "No—I simply suspected. Perhaps because I had a good teacher."

The older elf growled, appreciating the remark but annoyed with himself. Indeed, they both realized that had the elves advanced when Kencathedrus had desired, they would have been swiftly overrun, vulnerable in the open field.

Kencathedrus rejoined his reserve company, and Kith-Kanan immersed himself in the fight. Thousands of humans and elves clashed along the line, and hundreds died. Weapons shattered against shields, and bones shattered beneath blades. The long morning gave way to afternoon, but the passing of time meant nothing to the desperate combatants, for whom each moment could be their last.

The tide of battle surged back and forth. Companies of humans turned and fled, many of them before their charging ranks even reached the determined elves. Others hacked and slew their way into the defenders, and—occasionally—a company of elves gave way. Then the humans poured through the gap like the surging surf, but always Kith-Kanan was there, slashing with his bloody sword, urging his elven lancers into the breach.

Wave after wave of humans surged madly across the trampled field, hurling themselves into the elves as if to shatter them with the sheer momentum of their charges. As soon as one company broke, one regiment fell back depleted and demoralized, another block of steel-tipped humanity lunged forward to take its place.

The Wildrunners fought until total exhaustion gripped each and every warrior, and then they fought some more. Their small, mobile companies banded together to form solid lines, shifted to deflect each new charge, and flowed sideways to fill gaps caused by their fallen or routed comrades. Always those plunging horses backed them up, and each time, as the line faltered, the elven cavalry thundered against the breakthrough, driving it back in disorder.

Those five hundred riders managed to seal every breach. By the time the afternoon shadows began to lengthen, Kith noticed a slackening in the human attacks. One company of swordsmen stumbled away, and for once there was no fresh formation to take their place in the attack. The din of combat seemed to fade somewhat, and then he saw another formation a group of axemen turn and lumber away from the fight. More and more of the humans broke off their attacks, and soon the great regiments of Ergoth streamed across the field, back toward their own lines.

Kith slumped wearily in his saddle, staring in suspicion at the fleeing backs of the soldiers. Could it be over? Had the Wildrunners won? He looked at the sun—about four good hours of daylight remained. The humans wouldn't risk an encounter at night, he knew. Elven nightvision was one of the great proofs of the elder race's superiority over its shorter-lived counterparts. Yet certainly the hour was not the reason for the humans' retreat, not when they had been pressing so forcefully all along the line.

A weary Parnigar approached on foot. Kith had seen the scout's horse cut down beneath him during the height of the battle. The general recognized his captain's lanky walk, though Parnigar's face and clothes were caked in mud and the blood of his slain enemies.

"We've held them, sir," he reported, his face creasing into a disbelieving smile. Immediately, however, he frowned and shook his head. "Some three or four hundred dead, though. The day was not without its cost."

Kith looked at the exhausted yet steady ranks of his Wildrunners. The pikemen held their weapons high, the archers carried bows at the ready, while those with swords honed their blades in the moments of silence and respite. The formations still arrayed in full ranks, as if fresh and unblooded, but their ranks were shorter now. Organized in neat rows behind each company, covered with blankets, lay a quiet grouping of motionless forms.

At least the dead can rest, he thought, feeling his own weariness. He looked again to the humans, seeing that they still fled in disorder. Many of them had reached the tree line and were disappearing into the sheltering forest.

"My lord! My lord! Now is the time. You *must* see that!"

Kith turned to see Kencathedrus galloping up to him. The elven veteran reined in beside the general and gestured at the fleeing humans.

"You may be right," Kith-Kanan had to agree. He saw the five thousand elves of Silvanost gathered in trim ranks, ready to advance the moment he gave the word. This was the chance to deliver a coup *de grace* that could send the enemy reeling all the way back to Caergoth.

"Quickly, my lord—they're getting away!" Impatiently, his gray brows bristling, Kencathedrus indicated the ragged humans running in small dumps, like sheep, toward the sheltering woods in the distance.

"Very well—advance and pursue! But have a care for your flanks!"

* * * * *

"They *must* come after us now!" General Giarna's horse twisted and pitched among the ranks of retreating humans, many of whom were bleeding or limping, supported by the shoulders of their sturdier comrades. Indeed, the Army of Ergoth had paid a hideous price for the daylong attacks, all of which were mere preliminaries to his real plan of battle.

The general paid no attention to the human suffering around him. Instead, his dark eyes fixed with a malevolent stare on the elven positions across the mud-spattered landscape. No movement yet—but they must advance. He felt this with a certainty that filled his dark heart with a bloodthirsty anticipation.

For a moment, he cast a sharp glance to the rear, toward the tiny tent that sheltered Suzine and her mirror. The gods should damn that bitch! How, in the heat of the fight, could her powers fail her? Why *now*—today?

His brow narrowed in suspicion, but he had no time now to wonder about the unreliability of his mistress. She had been a valuable tool, and it would be regrettable if that tool were no longer at his disposal.

Perhaps, as she had claimed, the tension of the great conflict had proven too distracting, too overpowering for her to concentrate. Or maybe the general's looming presence had frightened her. In fact, General Giarna *wanted* to frighten her, just as he wanted to frighten everyone under his command. However, if that fear was enough to disrupt her powers of concentration, than Suzine's usefulness might be seriously limited.

No matter—at least for now. The battle could still be won by force of arms. The key was to make the elves believe that the humans were beaten.

General Giarna's pulse quickened then as he saw a line of movement across the field.

* * * * *

"Elves of Silvanost, advance!" The captain had already turned away from his commander. The reserve companies started forward at a brisk march, through the gaps in the spiked fence of the elven line. The companies of the Wildrunners, battered and weary, cleared the way for the attackers, whose gleaming spearpoints and shining armor stood out in stark contrast to the muddy, bloody mess around them. Nevertheless, the Wildrunners raised a hearty cheer as Kencathedrus led his troops into the attack.

"On the double—charge!" His horse prancing eagerly beneath him, Kencathedrus brandished his sword and urged his complement forward. The troops needed no prodding. All day they had seen their fellow countrymen die at the hands of these rapacious savages, and now they had the chance to take vengeance.

The panicked humans cast down weapons, shields, helmets—anything loose and cumbersome—in their desperate flight. They scattered away from the charging elves, racing for the shelter of any clump of trees or thick brush they could find.

The warriors of Silvanost, disciplined even at their steady advance, remained in close-meshed lines. They parted at the obstacles, while several who were armed with shortswords pressed into the grove, quickly dispatching the hapless humans who sought refuge there.

But even so, it was clear that the great bulk of the routed troops would escape, so rapid was their flight. The close ranks of the elves could not keep pace. Finally Kencathedrus slowed his company to a brisk walk, allowing the elves to catch their breath as they approached the first large expanse of forest.

"Archers, stand forward to the flanks!" Kith-Kanan didn't know why he gave the order, but suddenly he saw how vulnerable were the five thousand elves in the event that he *had* been tricked. Kencathedrus and his regiment had already advanced nearly half a mile ahead of the main army, while the fleeing humans seemed to melt away before them.

Two blocks of elves—his keenest longbows, some thousand strong each—trotted ahead.

"Pikes—in the middle, quickly!" One more unit Kith-Kanan sent forward, this one consisting of his fiercest veterans, armed with their deadly, fifteen-foot weapons with razor-sharp steel tips. They advanced at a trot, filling some of the gap between the two blocks of longbows.

"Horsemen! To me!" A third command brought the proud elven cavalry thundering to their commander. It seemed to Kith-Kanan that Kencathedrus and his company were now in terrible danger. He had to catch up and give them support.

Flanked by his mounted bodyguards, the commander led his horsemen through the lines, in a wide sweep toward the right of Kencathedrus's company. The elven archers carried their weapons ready. Pikes rattled behind them. Had he done everything that he could to protect the advance?

Kith sensed something in the air as the late afternoon seemed to grow sinister around him. He listened carefully; his eyes studied the opposite tree line, scanned to the right and left to the limits of his vision.

Nothing.

Yet now some of his elves sensed the same thing, the indefinable inkling of something terrible and awesome and mighty. Warriors nervously fingered their weapons. The Wildrunners' horses moved restlessly, shaking off the weariness of many hours' battle.

Then a rumble of deep thunder permeated the air. It began as a faint drumming, but in Kith-Kanan's mind, it grew to a deafening explosion within a few seconds.

"Sound the withdrawal!" He shouted at the trumpeters as he looked left, then right—*where*, by all the gods?

He saw them appear, like a wave of brown grass on the horizon, to *both* sides—countless thousands of humans mounted on thundering horses, sweeping around the patches of woods, across the open prairie, pounding closer, with all the speed of the wind.

The horns blared, and Kith saw that Kencathedrus had already sensed the trap. Now the elves of Silvanost retired toward the Wildrunners' lines at a quick pace. But all who looked on could see that they would be too late.

The archers and pikemen advanced, desperate to aid their countrymen. They showered the human cavalry with arrows, while the long pikes bristled before the archers, protecting them from the charge.

But the elves of Silvanost had no such protection. The human cavalry slammed into them, and rank after rank of the elven infantry fell beneath the cruel hooves and keen, unfeeling steel.

The pikemen and archers fell back slowly, carefully, still shredding the cavalry with deadly arrows, felling the horsemen by the hundred with each volley. Yet thousands upon thousands of the humans trampled across the plain, slaughtering the stranded regiment.

Kith-Kanan led his riders into the flank of the human charge, caring little that there were ten or twenty humans for every one of his elves. With his own sword, he cut a leering, bearded human from the saddle. Horses screamed and bucked around them, and in moments, the two companies of cavalry mingled, each man or elf fighting the foe he found close at hand.

More blood flowed into the already soaked ground. Kith saw a human lancer drive a bloodstained lance toward his heart. One of his loyal bodyguards flung himself from his saddle and took the weapon through his own throat, deflecting the blow that would have surely been fatal. With a surge of hatred, Kith spurred Kijo forward, chopping savagely through the neck and striking the lancer's head from his shoulders. Spouting blood like an obscene geyser, the corpse toppled from the saddle, lost in the chaos of the melee before it struck the ground.

Kith saw another of his faithful guards fall, this time to a human swordsman whose horse skipped nimbly away. The fight swirled madly, flashing images of blood, screaming horses, dying men and elves. If he had paused to think, he would have regretted the charge that brought his riders out here to aid Kencathedrus. Now, it seemed, *both* units faced annihilation.

Desperately Kith-Kanan looked for a sign of the elves of Silvanost. He saw them through the melee. Led by a grim-faced Kencathedrus, the elven reserve force struggled to break free of the deadly trap. Finally they tore from their neat ranks in a headlong dash through the sea of human horsemen toward the safety of the Wildrunner lines.

Miraculously, many of them made it. They scrambled between the thick wall of stakes, into the welcoming arms of their comrades, while the stampeding cavalry surged and bucked just beyond. By the dozens and scores and hundreds, they limped and dodged and tumbled to safety, until more than two thousand of them, including Kencathedrus, had emerged. The captain tried to turn and lunge back into the fray in a foredoomed effort to bring forth more of his men, but he was restrained in the grasp of two sergeants-major.

The archers, too, fell back, and then it was only the riders caught on the field. Isolated pockets of elven cavalry twisted away from the sea of human horsemen, breaking for the shelter of their lines. Kith-Kanan himself, however, after having led the charge, was now caught in the middle of the enemy forces.

His arm grew leaden with fatigue. Blood from a cut on his forehead streamed into his eyes. His helmet was gone, knocked from his head by a human's bashing shield. His loyal guards—the few who still lived—fought around him, but now the outlook was grim.

The humans fell back, just far enough to avoid the slashing elven blades. Kith-Kanan and a group of perhaps two dozen elven riders gasped for breath, surrounded by a ring of death—more than a thousand human lancers, swordsmen, and archers.

With a groan of despair, he cast his sword to the ground. The rest of the survivors immediately followed his example.

* * * * *

As darkness finally closed about them, the humans turned back from the elven line. Kencathedrus and Parnigar knew that it was only nightfall that had prevented the complete collapse of their position. They knew, too, that the exhausted army would have to retreat—now, even before the darkness was complete.

They would have to take shelter in Sithelbec early the following day, before the deadly human cavalry could catch them in the open. The entire force of the Wildrunners could suffer the fate of the unblooded elves of Silvanost.

It seemed to the elven leaders that the day couldn't have been any more disastrous. Despair settled around them like a bleak cloud as they considered the worst news of all: Kith-Kanan, their commander and the driving force behind the Wildrunners, was lost—possibly captured, but more likely killed.

The army marched, heads down and shambling, toward the security—and the confinement—of Sithelbec.

Sometime after midnight, it started to rain, and it continued to pour throughout the night and even past the gray, featureless dawn. The miserable army finally reached Sithelbec, closing the gates behind the last of the Wildrunners, sometime around noon of the following gray, drizzling day.

After the Battle

5

Suzine awakened to a summons from the general, delivered by a bronze-helmed lieutenant of crossbows. The woman felt vague relief that General Giarna hadn't come to her in person. Indeed, she hadn't seen him since before the battle's climax, when his trap had snared so much of the elven army.

Her relief had grown from the previous night, when she had feared that he would desire her. General Giarna frightened her often, but there was something deeper and more abiding about the terror he inspired after he had led his troops in battle.

The darkness that seemed always to linger in his eyes became, in those moments, like a bottomless well of despair and hopelessness, as if his hunger for killing could never be sated. The more the blood flowed around him, the greater his appetite became.

He would take her then, using her like he was some kind of parasite, unaware and uncaring of her feelings. He would hurt her and, when he was finished, cast her roughly aside, his own fundamental needs still raging.

But after this battle, his greatest victory to date, he had stayed away from her. She had retired early the night before, dying to look into her mirror, to ascertain Kith-Kanan's whereabouts. She felt a terrible fear for his safety, but she hadn't dared to use her glass for fear of the general. He mustn't suspect her growing fascination with Kith-Kanan.

Now she dressed quickly and fetched her mirror, safe in a felt-lined wooden case, and then allowed the officer to lead her along the column of tents to General Giarna's shelter of black silk. The lieutenant held the door while she entered, blinking for a moment as she adjusted to the dim light.

And then it seemed that her world exploded.

The file of muddy elven prisoners, many of them bruised, stood at resentful attention. There were perhaps a score of them, each with a watchful swordsman right behind him, but Suzine's eyes flashed immediately to *him*.

She recognized Kith-Kanan in the instant that she saw him, and she had to forcibly resist an urge to run to him. She wanted to look at him, to touch him in all the ways she could not through her mirror. She fought an urge to knock the sword-wielding guard aside.

Then she remembered General Giarna. Her face flushed, she felt perspiration gather on her brow. He was watching her closely. Forcing an expression of cool detachment, she turned to him.

"You summoned me, General?"

The commander seemed to look through her, with a gaze that threatened to wither her soul. His eyes yawned before her like black chasms, menacing pits that made her want to hurriedly step back from the edge.

"The interrogation continues. I want you to witness their testimony and gauge the truth of their replies." His voice was like a cold gust of air.

For the first time, Suzine noticed an additional elven form. This one stretched facedown on the carpeted floor of the tent, a tiny hole at the base of his neck showing where he had been stabbed.

Numbly she looked back. Kith-Kanan stood second from the end of the line, near where the killing had occurred. He paid no attention to her. The elf between him and the dead one looked in grimly concealed fear at the human general.

"Your strength!" demanded General Giarna. "How many troops garrison your fortress? Catapults? Ballistae? You will tell us about them all."

The final sentence was a demand, not a question.

"The fortress is garrisoned by twenty thousand warriors, with more on the way!" blurted the prisoner beside the corpse. "Wizards and clerics, too—"

Suzine didn't need the mirror to see that he lied; neither, apparently, did General Giarna. He chopped his hand once, and the swordsman behind the terrified speaker stabbed at the doomed elf. His blade severed the elf's spinal cord and then plunged through his neck, emerging under the unfortunate warrior's chin in a gurgling fountain of blood.

The next swordsman—the one behind Kith-Kanan—prodded his charge in the back, forcing him to stand a little straighter, as the general's eyes came to rest upon him. But only for, a moment, for the human leader allowed his scornful gaze to roam across the entire row of his captives.

"Which of you holds rank over the others?" inquired the general, casting his eyes along the line of remaining elves.

For the first time, Suzine realized that Kith-Kanan wore none of the trappings of his station. He was an anonymous rider among the elven warriors. Giarna didn't recognize him! That revelation encouraged her to take a risk.

"My general," she said quickly, hearing her voice as if another person was speaking, "could I have a word with you—away from the ears of the prisoners?"

He looked at her, his dark eyes boring into her. Was that annoyance she saw, or something darker?

"Very well," he replied curtly. He took her arm in his hand and led her from the tent.

She felt the mirror's case in her hand, seeking words as she spoke. "They are obviously willing to die for their cause. But perhaps, with a little patience, I can make them useful to us . . . alive."

"You can tell me whether they speak the truth—or not—but what good is that when they are willing to die with lies in their mouths?"

"But there is more to the glass," she said insistently. "Given a quiet place and some time—and some close personal attention to one of these subjects—I can probe deeper than mere questions and answers. I can see into their minds, to the secret truths they would never admit to such as you."

General Giarna's black brows came together in a scowl. "Very well. I will allow you to try." He led her back into the tent. "Which one will you start with?"

Trying to still the trembling in her heart, Suzine raised an imperious hand and indicated Kith-Kanan. She spoke to the guard behind him. "Bring this one to my tent," she said matter-of-factly.

She avoided looking at the general, afraid those black eyes would paralyze her with suspicion or accusation. But he said nothing. He merely nodded to the guard behind Kith and the swordsman beside him, the one who had just slain the fallen elf. The pair of guards prodded Kith-Kanan forward, and Suzine preceded him through the silken flap of General Giarna's tent.

They passed between two tents, the high canvas shapes screening them from the rest of the camp. She could feel his eyes on her back as she walked, and finally she could no longer resist the urge to turn and look at him.

"What do you want with me?" he asked, his voice surprising her with its total lack of fear.

"I won't hurt you," she replied, suddenly angry when the elf smiled slightly in response.

"Move, you!" grunted one of the guards, stepping in front of his companion and waving his blade past Kith-Kanan's face.

Kith-Kanan reached forward with the speed of a striking snake, seizing the guard's wrist as the blade veered away from his face. Holding the man's hand, the elf kicked him sharply in the groin. The swordsman gasped and collapsed.

His companion, the warrior who had slain the elf in the tent, gaped in momentary shock—a moment that proved to be his last. Kith pulled the blade from the fallen guard's hand and, in the same motion, drove the point into the swordsman's throat. He died, his jaw soundlessly working in an effort to articulate his shock.

The dead guard's helmet toppled off as he fell, allowing his long blond hair to spill free when he collapsed, facefirst, on the ground.

Kith lowered the blade, ready to thrust it through the neck of the groaning man he had kicked. Then something stayed his hand, and he merely admonished the guard to be silent with a persuasive press of the blade against the man's throat.

Turning to the one he had slain, Kith looked at the body curiously. Suzine hadn't moved. She watched him in fascination, scarcely daring to breath, as he brushed the blond hair aside with the toe of his boot.

The ear that was revealed was long and pointed.

"Do you have many elves in your army?" he asked.

"No—not many," Suzine said quickly. "They are mostly from the ranks of traders and farmers who have lived in Ergoth and desire a homeland on the plains."

Kith looked sharply at Suzine. There was something about this human woman. . . .

She stood still, paralyzed not so much by fear for herself as by dismay. He was about to escape, to leave her!

"I thank you for inadvertently saving my life," he said before darting toward the corner of a nearby tent.

"I—I know who you are!" she said, her voice a bare whisper.

He stopped again, torn between the need to escape and increasing curiosity about this woman and her knowledge.

"Thank you, too, then, for keeping the secret," he said, with a short bow. "Why did you . . . ?"

She wanted to tell him that she had watched him for a long time, had all but lain beside him, through the use of her mirror.

Suzine looked at him now, and he was more glorious, prouder, and taller than she had ever imagined. She wanted to ask him to take her away with him—right now—but, instead, her mouth froze, her mind locked by terror.

In another moment, he had disappeared. It was several moments longer before she finally found the voice to scream.

* * * * *

The elation Kith-Kanan felt at his escape dissipated as quickly as the gates of Sithelbec shut behind him and enclosed him within the sturdy walls of the fortress. His stolen horse, staggering from exhaustion, stumbled to a halt, and the elf swung to the ground.

He wondered, through his weariness, about the human woman who had given him his chance to flee. The picture of her face, crowned by that glory of red hair, remained indelibly burned into his mind. He wondered if he would ever see her again.

Around him loomed the high walls, with the pointed logs arrayed along the top. Below these, he saw the faces of his warriors. Several raised a halfhearted cheer at his return, but the shock of defeat hung over the Wildrunners like a heavy pall.

Sithelbec had grown rapidly in the last year, sprawling across the surrounding plain until it covered a circle more than a mile in diameter. The central keep of the fortress was a stone structure of high towers, soaring to needlelike spires in the elven fashion. Around this keep clustered a crowded nest of houses, shops, barracks, inns, and other buildings, all within other networks of walls, blockhouses, and battle platforms.

Expanding outward through a series of concentric palisades, mostly of wood, the fortress protected a series of wells within its walls, ensuring a steady supply of water. Food—mostly grain—had been stockpiled in huge barns and silos. Supplies of arrows and flammable oil, stored in great vats, had been collected along the walls' tops. The greater part of Kith-Kanan's army, through the alert withdrawal under Parnigar, had reached the shelter of those ramparts.

Yet as the Army of Ergoth moved in to encircle the fortress, the Wildrunners could only wait.

Now Kith-Kanan walked among them, making his way to the small office and quarters he maintained in the gate-house of the central keep. He felt the tension, the fear that approached despair, as he looked at the wide, staring eyes of his warriors.

And even more than the warriors, there were the women and children. Many of the women were human, their children half-elves, wives and offspring of the western elves who made up the Wildrunners. Kith shared their sorrow as deeply as he felt that of the elven females who were here in ever greater numbers.

They would all be eating short rations, he knew. The siege would inevitably last into the autumn, and he had little doubt the humans could sustain the pressure through the winter and beyond.

As he looked at the young ones, Kith felt a stab of pain. He wondered how many of them would see spring.

Autumn, Year of the Raven

6

Lord Quimant came to Sithas in the Hall of Audience. His wife's cousin brought another elf—a stalwart-looking fellow, with lines of soot set firmly in his face, and the strapping, sinewy arms of a powerful wrestler—to see the Speaker of the Stars.

Sithas sat upon his emerald throne and watched the approaching pair. The Speaker's green robe flowed around him, collecting the light of the throne and diffusing it into a soft glow that seemed to surround him. He reclined casually in the throne, but he remained fully alert.

Alert, in that his mind was working quickly. Yet his thoughts were many hundreds of miles and years away.

Weeks earlier, he had received a letter from Kencathedrus describing Kith-Kanan's capture and presumed loss. That had been followed, barely two days later, by a missive from his brother himself, describing a harrowing escape: the battle with guards, the theft of a fleet horse, a mad dash from the encampment, and finally a chase that ended only after Kith-Kanan had led his pursuers to within arrow range of the great fortress of Sithelbec.

Sithelbec—named for his father, the former Speaker of the Stars. Many times Sithas had reflected on the irony, for his father had been slain on a hunting trip, practically within sight of the fortress's walls. As far as Sithas knew, it had been his father's first and only expedition to the western plains. Yet Sithel had been willing to go to war over those plains, to put the nation's future at stake because of them. And now Sithas, his firstborn, had inherited that struggle. Would he live up to his father's expectations?

Reluctantly Sithas forced his mind back to the present, to his current location. He cast his eyes around his surroundings to force the transition in his thoughts.

A dozen elven guards, in silver breastplates and tall, plumed helmets, snapped their halberds to attention around the periphery of the hall. They stood impassive and silent as the noble lord marched toward the throne. Otherwise the great hall, with its gleaming marble floor and the ceiling towering six hundred feet overhead, was empty.

Sithas looked at Quimant. The elven noble wore a long cloak of black over a silk tunic of light green. Tights of red, and soft, black boots, completed his ensemble.

Lord Quimant of Oakleaf was a very handsome elf indeed. But he was also intelligent, quick-witted, and alert to many threats and opportunities that might otherwise have missed Sithas's notice.

"This is my nephew," the lord explained. "Gamock Ethu, master smith. I recommend him, my Speaker, for the position of palace smith. He is shrewd, quick to learn, and a very hard worker."

"But Herrlock Redmoon has always handled the royal smithy," Sithas protested. Then he remembered: Herrlock had been blinded the week before in a tragic accident, when he had touched spark to his forge. Somehow the kindled coal had exploded violently, destroying his eyes beyond the abilities of Silvanost's clerics to repair. After seeing that the loyal smith was well cared for and as comfortable as possible, Sithas had promised to select a replacement.

He looked at the young elf before him. Ganrock's face showed lines of maturity, and the thick muscle of his upper torso showed proof of long years of work.

"Very well," Sithas agreed. "Show him the royal smithy and find out what he needs to get started." He called to one of his guards and told the elf to accompany Ganrock Ethu to the forge area, which lay in the rear of the Palace of Quinari.

"Thank you, Your Eminence," said the smith, with a sudden bow. "I shall endeavor to do fine work for you."

"Very good," replied the Speaker. Quimant lingered as the smith left the hall.

Lord Quimant's narrow face tightened in determination as he turned back to Sithas.

"What is it, my lord? You look distressed."

Sithas raised a hand and bade Qiumant stand beside him.

"The Smelters Guild, Your Highness," replied the noble elf. "They refuse—they simply *refuse*—to work their foundries during the hours of darkness. Without the additional steel, our weapon production is hamstrung, barely adequate for even peacetime needs."

Sithas cursed quietly. Nevertheless, he was thankful that Quimant had informed him. The proud heir of Clan Oakleaf had greatly improved the efficiency of Silvanost's war preparations by spotting details—such as this one—that would have escaped Sithas's notice.

"I shall speak to the smelter Kerilar," Sithas vowed. "He is a stubborn old elf, but he knows the importance of the sword. I will *make* him understand, if I have to."

"Very good, Excellency," said Lord Quimant, with a bow. He straightened again. "Is there news of the war?"

"Not since the last letter, a week ago. The Wildrunners remain besieged in Sithelbec, while the humans roam the disputed lands at will. Kith has no chance to break out. He's now surrounded by a hundred thousand men."

The lord shook his head grimly before fixing Sithas with a hard gaze. "He must be reinforced—there's no other way. You know this, don't you?"

Sithas met Quimant's gaze with equal steadiness. "Yes—I do. But the only way I can recruit more troops is to conscript them from the city and the surrounding clan estates. You know what kind of dispute that will provoke!"

"How long can your brother hold his fort?"

"He has rations enough for the winter. The casualties of the battle were terrible, of course, but the remainder of his force is well disciplined, and the fortress is strong."

The news of the battlefield debacle had hit the elven capital hard. As the knowledge spread that two thousand of the city's young elves—two out of every five who had marched so proudly to the west!—had perished in the fight, Silvanost had been shrouded in grief for a week.

Sithas learned of the battle at the same time as he heard that his brother had fallen and was most likely lost. For two days, his world had been a grim shroud of despair. Knowing that Kith had reached safety lightened the burden to some extent, but their prospects for victory still seemed nonexistent. How long would it be, he had agonized, before the rest of the Wildrunners fell to the overwhelming tide around them?

Then gradually his despair had turned to anger—anger at the shortsightedness of his own people. Elves had crowded the Hall of Audience on the Trial Days, disrupting the proceedings. The emotions of the city's elves had been inflamed by the knowledge that the rest of the Wildrunners had suffered nowhere near the size of losses inflicted upon the elves of Silvanost. It was not uncommon now to hear voices raised in the complaint that the western lands should be turned over to the humans and the Wildrunner elves, to let them battle each other to extinction.

"Very well—so he can hold out." Quimant's voice was strong yet deferential. "But he *cannot* escape! We *must* send a fresh army, a large one, to give him the sinew he needs!"

"There are the dwarves. We have yet to hear from them!" Sithas pointed out.

"Pah! If they do anything, it will be too late! It seems that Than-Kar sympathizes with the humans as much as with us. The dwarves will never do anything so long as he remains their voice and their ears!"

Ah—but he is not their voice and ears. Sithas had that thought with some small satisfaction, but he said nothing to Quimant as the lord continued, though his thoughts considered the potential of hope. Tamanier Ambrodel, I am depending upon you!

"Still, we must tolerate him, I suppose. He is our best chance of an alliance."

"As always, good cousin, your words are the mirror of my thoughts." Sithas straightened in his throne, a signal that the interview drew to a close. "But my decision is still to wait. Kith-Kanan is secure for now, and we may learn more as time goes on."

He hoped he was right. The fortress *was* strong, and the humans would undoubtedly require months to prepare a coordinated assault. But what then?

"Very well." Quimant cleared his throat awkwardly, then added, "What is the word of my cousin? I have not seen her for some weeks now."

"Her time is near," Sithas offered. "Her sisters have come from the estates to stay with her, and she has been confined to bed by the clerics of Quenesti Pah."

Quimant nodded. "Please give her my wishes when next you see her. May she give birth speedily, to a healthy child."

"Indeed."

Sithas watched the elegant noble walk from the hall. He was impressed by Quimant's bearing. The lord knew his worth to the throne, proven in the half-year since he had come to Silvanost. He showed sensitivity to the desires of the Speaker and seemed to work well toward those ends.

He heard one of the side doors open and looked across the great hall as a silk-gowned female elf entered. Her eyes fell softly on the figure seated upon the brilliant throne with its multitude of green, gleaming facets.

"Mother," said Sithas with delight. He didn't see much of Nirakina around the palace during these difficult days, and this visit was a pleasant surprise. He was struck, as she approached him, by how much older she looked.

"I see you do not have attendants now," she said quietly to Sithas, who rose and approached her. "So often you are busy with the affairs of state . . . and war."

He sighed. "War has become the way of my life—the way all Silvanost lives now." He felt a twinge of sadness for his mother. So often Sithas looked upon the death of his father as an event that had placed the burden of rule on his own shoulders. He tended to forget that it had, at the same time, made his mother a widow.

"Take a moment to walk with me, won't you?" asked Nirakina, taking her son by the arm.

He nodded, and they walked in silence across the great hall of the tower to the crystal doors reserved for the royal family alone. These opened soundlessly, and then they were in the Gardens of Astarin. To their right were the dark wooden buildings of the royal stables, while before them beckoned the wondrous beauty of the royal gardens. Immediately Sithas felt a sense of lightness and ease.

"You need to do this more often," said his mother, gently chiding. "You grow old before your time." She held his arm loosely, letting him select the path they followed.

The gardens loomed around them—great hedges and thick bushes heavy with dewy blossoms; ponds and pools and fountains; small clumps of aspen and oak and fir. It was a world of nature, shaped and formed by elven clerics—devotees of the Bard King, Astarin—into a transcendent work of art.

"I thank you for bringing me through those doors," Sithas said with a chuckle. "Sometimes I need to be reminded."

"Your father, too, needed a subtle reminder now and then. I tried to give him that when it became necessary."

For a moment, Sithas felt a wave of melancholy. "I miss him now more than ever. I feel so . . . unready to sit on his throne."

"You are ready," said Nirakina firmly. "Your wisdom is seeing us through the most difficult time since the Dragon Wars. But since you are about to become a father, you must realize that your life cannot be totally given over to your nation. You have a family to think about, as well."

Sithas smiled. "The clerics of Quenesti Pah are with Hermathya at all times. They say it will be any day now."

"The clerics, and her sisters," Nirakina murmured.

"Yes," Sithas agreed. Hermathya's sisters, Gelynna and Lyath, had moved into the palace as soon as his wife's pregnancy had become known. They were pleasant enough, but Sithas had come to feel that his apartments were somehow less than his own now. It was a feeling he didn't like but that he had tried to overlook for Hermathya's sake.

"She has changed, Mother, that much you must see. Hermathya had become a new woman even before she knew about the child. She has been a support and a comfort to me, as if for the first time."

"It is the war," said Nirakina. "I have noticed this change you speak of, and it began with the war. She, her clan of Oakleaf, they all thrive upon this intensity and activity." The elven woman paused, then added, "I noticed Lord Quimant leaving before I entered. You speak with him often. Is he proving himself useful?"

"Indeed, very. Does this cause you concern?"

Nirakina sighed, then shook her head. "I—no—no, it doesn't. You are doing the right thing for Silvanesti, and if he can aid you, that is a good thing."

Sithas stopped at a stone bench. His mother sat while he paced idly below overhanging branches of silvery quaking aspen that shimmered in the light breeze.

"Have you had word from Tamanier Ambrodel?" Nirakina asked.

Sithas smiled confidentially. "He has arrived at Thorbardin safely and hopes to get in touch with the Hylar. With any luck, he will see the king himself. Then we shall find out if this Than-Kar is doing us true justice as ambassador."

"And you have told no one of Lord Ambrodel's mission?" his mother inquired carefully.

"No," Sithas informed her. "Indeed, Quimant and I discussed the dwarves today, but I said nothing even to him about our quiet diplomat. Still, I wish you would tell me why we must maintain such secrecy."

"Please, not yet," Nirakina demurred.

A thin haze had gradually spread across the sky, and now the wind carried a bit of early winter in its caress. Sithas saw his mother shiver in her light silken garment.

"Come, well return to the hall," he said, offering his arm as she rose.

"And your brother?" Nirakina asked tentatively as they turned back toward the crystal doors. "Can you send him more troops?"

"I don't know yet," Sithas replied, the agony of the decision audible in his voice. "Can I risk arousing the city?"

"Perhaps you need more information."

"Who could inform me of that which I don't already know?" Sithas asked skeptically.

"Kith-Kanan himself." His mother stopped to face him as the doors opened and the warmth of the tower beckoned. "Bring him home, Sithas," she said urgently, taking both of his arms in her hands. "Bring him home and talk to him!"

Sithas was surprised at his own instinctive reaction. The suggestion made surprisingly good sense. It offered him hope—and an idea for action that would unite, not divide, his people. Yet how could he call his brother home now, out of the midst of a monstrous encircling army?

* * * * *

The next day Quimant again was Sithas's first and primary visitor.

"My lord," began the adviser, "have you made a decision about conscription of additional forces? I am reluctant to remind you, but time may be running short."

Sithas frowned. Unbidden, his mind recalled the scene at the riverbank when the first column departed for war. Now more than half those elves were dead. What would be the city's reaction should another, larger force march west?

"Not yet. I wish to wait until . . . " His voice trailed off. He had been about to mention Ambrodel's mission. "I will not make that decision yet," he concluded.

He was spared the necessity of further discussion when Stankathan, his palace majordomo, entered the great hall. That dignified elf, clad in a black waistcoat of wool, preceded a travel-stained messenger who wore the leather jerkin of a Wildrunner scout. The latter bore a scroll of parchment sealed with a familiar stamp of red wax.

"A message from my brother?" Sithas rose to his feet, recognizing the form of the sheet.

"By courier, who came from across the river just this morning," replied Stankathan. "I brought him over to the tower directly."

Sithas felt a surge of delight, as he did every fortnight or so when a courier arrived with the latest reports from Kith-Kanan. Yet that delight had lately been tempered by the grim news from his brother and the besieged garrison.

He looked at the courier as the elf approached and bowed deeply. Besides the dirt and mud of the trail, Sithas saw that the fellow had a sling supporting his right arm and a dark-stained bandage around the leggings of his left knee.

"My gratitude for your efforts," said Sithas, appraising the rider. The elf stood taller after his words, as if the praise of the speaker was a balm to his wounds. "What was the nature of your obstacles?"

"The usual rings of guards, Your Highness," replied the elf. "But the humans lack sorcerers and so cannot screen the paths with magic. The first day of my journey I was concealed by invisibility, a spell that camouflaged myself and my horse. Afterward, the fleetness of my steed carried me, and I encountered only one minor fray."

The Speaker of the Stars took the scroll and broke the wax seal. Carefully he unrolled the sheet, ignoring Quimant for the time being. The lord stood quietly; if he was annoyed, he made no visible sign of the fact.

Sithas read the missive solemnly.

I look out, my brother, upon an endless sea of humanity. Indeed, they surround us like the ocean surrounds an island, completely blocking our passage. It is only with great risk that my couriers can penetrate the lines—that, and the aid of spells cast by my enchanters, which allow them some brief time to escape the notice of the foe.

What is to be the fate now of our cause? Will the army of Ergoth attack and carry the fort? Their horses sweep in great circles about us, but the steeds cannot reach us here. The other two wings have joined General Giarna before Sithelbec, and their numbers truly stun the mind.

General Giarna, I have learned, is the name of the foe we faced in the spring, the one who drove us from the field. We have taken prisoners from his force, and to a man they speak of their devotion to him and their confidence that he will one day destroy us! I met him in the brief hours I was prisoner, and he is a terrifying man. There is something deep and cruel about him that transcended any foe I have ever encountered.

Will the dwarves of Thorbardin march from their stronghold and break the siege from the south? That, my brother, would be a truly magnificent feat of diplomacy on your part. Should you bring such an alliance into being, I could scarce convey my gratitude across the miles!

Or will the hosts of Silvanost march forth, the elves united in their campaign against the threat to our race? That, I am afraid, is the least likely of my musings—at least, from the words you give me as to our peoples' apathy and lack of concern. How fares the diplomatic battle, Brother?

I hope to amuse you with one tale, an experience that gave us all many moments of distraction, not to mention fear. I have written to you of the gnomish lava cannon, the mountain vehicle pulled by a hundred oxen, its stony maw pointed skyward as it belches smoke and fire. Finally, shortly after my last letter, this device was hauled into place before Sithelbec. It stood some three miles away but loomed so high and spurned so furiously that we were indeed distraught!

For three days, the monstrous structure became the center of a whirlwind of gnomish activity. They scaled its sides, fed coal into its bowels, poured great quantities of muck and dust and streams of a red powder into its maw. All this time, the thing puffed and chugged, and by the third day, the entire plain lay shrouded beneath a cloud from its wheezing exhalations.

Finally the gnomes clambered up the sides and stood atop the device, as if they had scaled a small mountain. We watched, admittedly with great trepidation, as one of the little creatures mixed a cauldron at the very lip of the cannon's interior. Eventually he cast the contents of the vessel into the weapon itself. All of the gnomes fled, and for the first time, we noticed that the humans had pulled back from the cannon, giving it a good half-mile berth to either side.

For a full day, the army of Ergoth huddled in fright, staring at their monstrous weapon, Finally it appeared that it had failed to discharge, but it was not until the following day that we watched the gnomes creep forward to investigate.

Suddenly the thing began to chug and wheeze and belch. The gnomes scurried for cover, and for another full day, we all watched and waited. But it was not until the morning of the third day that we saw the weapon in action.

It exploded shortly after dawn and cast its formidable ordnance for many miles. Fortunately we, as the targets of the attack, were safe. It was the gathered human army that suffered the brunt of flaming rock and devastating force that ripped across the plains.

We saw thousands of the humans' horses (unfortunately a small fraction of their total number) stampede in panic across the plain. Whole regiments vanished beneath the deluge of death as a sludgelike wave spread through the army.

For a brief moment, I saw the opportunity to make a sharp attack, further disrupting the encircling host. Even as I ordered the attack, however, the ranks of General Giarna's wing shouldered aside the other humans. His deadly riders ensured that our trap remained effectively closed.

Nevertheless, the accident wreaked havoc among the Army of Ergoth. We gave thanks to the gods that the device misfired; had its attack struck Sithelbec, you would have already received your last missive from me. The cannon has been reduced to a heap of rubble, and we pray daily that it cannot be rebuilt.

My best wishes and hopes for my new niece or nephew. Which is it to be? Perhaps you will have the answer by the time you read this. I can only hope that somehow I will know. I hope Hermathya is comfortable and well.

I miss your counsel and presence as always, Brother. I treat myself to the thought that, could we but bring our minds together, we could *work a way to break out of this stalemate. But, alas, the jaws of the trap close about me, and I know that you, in the capital, are ensnared in every bit as tight a position as I.*

Until then, have a prayer for us! Give my love to Mother!

Kith

Sithas paused, realizing that the guards and Quimant had been studying him intently as he read. A full range of emotions had played across his face, he knew, and suddenly the knowledge made him feel exceedingly vulnerable.

"Leave me, all of you!" Sithas barked the command, more harshly perhaps than he intended, but he was nevertheless gratified to see them all quickly depart from the hall.

He paced back and forth before the emerald throne. His brother's letter had agitated him more than usual, for he knew that he had to do something. No longer could he force the standoff at Sithlebec into the back of his mind. His mother and his brother were right. He needed to *see* Kith-Kanan, to *talk* with him. They would be able to work out a plan—a plan with some hope of success!

Remembering his walk with Nirakina, he turned toward the royal doors of crystal. The gardens—and the stables—lay beyond.

Resolutely Sithas stalked to those doors, which opened silently before him. He emerged from the tower into the cool sunlight of the garden but took no note of his surroundings. Instead, he crossed directly to the royal stable.

The stable was in fact a sprawling collection of buildings and corrals. These included barns for the horses and small houses for the grooms and trainers, as well as stocks of feed. Behind the main structure, a field of short grass stretched away from the Tower of the Stars, covering the palace grounds to the edges of the guild-houses that bordered them.

Here were kept the several dozen horses of the royal family, as well as several coaches and carriages. But it was to none of these that the speaker now made his way.

Instead, he crossed through the main barn, nodding with easy familiarity to the grooms who brushed the sleek stallions. He passed through the far door and crossed a small corral, approaching a sturdy building that stood by itself, unattached to any other. The door was divided into top and bottom halves; the top half stood open.

A form moved within the structure, and then a great head emerged from the door. Bright golden eyes regarded Sithas with distrust and suspicion.

The front of that head was a long, wickedly hawklike beak. The beak opened slightly. Sithas saw the great wings flex within the confining stable and knew that Arcuballis longed to fly.

"You must go to Kith-Kanan," Sithas told the powerful steed. "Bring him out of his fort and back to me. Do this, Arcuballis, when I let you fly!"

The griffon's large eyes glittered as the creature studied the Speaker of the Stars. Arcuballis had been Kith-Kanan's lifelong mount until the duties of generalship had forced his brother to take a more conventional steed. Sithas knew that the griffon would go and bring his brother back.

Slowly Sithas reached forward and unlatched the bottom half of the door, allowing the portal to swing freely open. Arcuballis hesitantly stepped forward over the half-eaten carcass of a deer that lay just inside the stable.

With a spreading of his great wings, Arcuballis gave a mighty spring. He bounded across the corral, and by his third leap, the griffon was airborne. His powerful wings drove downward and the creature gained height, soaring over the roof of the stable, then veering to pass near the Tower of the Stars.

"Go!" cried Sithas. "Go to Kith-Kanan!"

As if he heard, the griffon swept through a turn. Powerful wings still driving him upward, Arcuballis swerved toward the west.

It seemed to Sithas as if a heavy burden had flown away from him, borne upon the wings of the griffon. His brother would understand, he knew. When Arcuballis arrived at Sithelbec, as Sithas felt certain he would, Kith-Kanan would waste no time in mounting his faithful steed and hastening back to Silvanost. Between them, he knew, they would find a way to advance the elven cause.

"Excellency?"

Sithas whirled, startled from his reverie by a voice from behind him. He saw Stankathan, the majordomo, looking out of place among the mud and dung of the corral. The elf's face, however, was knit by a deeper concern.

"What is it?" Sithas inquired quickly.

"It's your wife, the Lady Hermathya," replied Stankathan. "She cries with pain now. The clerics tell me it is time for your child to be born."

Three Days Later

7

The old lamp sputtered in the center of the wooden table. The flame was set low to conserve precious fuel for the long, dark months of winter that lay ahead. Kith-Kanan thought the shadowy darkness appropriate for this bleak meeting.

With him at the table sat Kencathedrus and Parnigar. Both of them—as well as Kith, himself—showed the gauntness of six months at half rations. Their eyes carried the dull awareness that many more months of the same lay before them.

Every night during that time, Kith had met with these two officers, both of them trusted friends and seasoned veterans. They gathered in this small room, with its plain table and chairs. Sometimes they shared a bottle of wine, but that commodity, too, had to be rationed carefully.

"We have a report from the Wildrunners," Parnigar began. "White-lock managed to slip through the lines. He told me that the small companies we have roaming the woods can hit hard and often. But they have to keep moving, and they don't dare venture onto the plains."

"Of course not!" Kencathedrus snapped.

The two officers argued, as they did so often, from their different tactical perspectives. "We'll never make any progress if we keep dispersing our forces through the woods. We have to gather them together! We must mass our strength!"

Kith sighed and held up his hands. "We all know that our 'mass of strength' would be little more than a nuisance to the human army—at least right now. The fortress is the only thing keeping the Wildrunners from annihilation, and the hit-and-run tactics are all we *can* do until . . . until something happens."

He trailed off weakly, knowing he had touched upon the heart of their despair. True, for the time being they were safe enough in Sithelbec from direct attack. And they had food that could be stretched, with the help of their clerics, to last for a year, perhaps a little longer.

In sudden anger, Kencathedrus smashed his fist on the table. "They hold us here like caged beasts!" he growled. "What kind of fate do we consign ourselves to?"

"Calm yourself, my friend." Kith touched his old teacher on the shoulder, seeing the tears in the elven warrior's eyes. His eyes were framed by sunken skin, dark brown in color, which accentuated further the hollowness of the elf's cheeks. By the gods, do we all look like that? Kith had to wonder.

The captain of Silvanost pushed himself to his feet and turned away from them. Parnigar cleared his throat awkwardly. "There is nothing we can accomplish by morning," he said. Quietly he got to his feet.

Parnigar, alone of the three of them, had a wife here. He worried more about her health than his own. She was human, one of several hundred in the fort, but this was a fact that they carefully avoided in conversation. Though Kith-Kanan knew and liked the woman, Kencathedrus still found the interracial marriage deeply disturbing.

"May you rest well tonight, noble elves," Parnigar offered before stepping through the door into the dark night beyond.

"I know your need to avenge the battle on the plains," Kith-Kanan said to Kencathedrus as the latter turned and gathered his cloak. "I believe this, my friend—your chance will come!"

The elven captain looked at the general, so much younger than himself, and Kith could see that Kencathedrus wanted to believe him. His eyes were dry again, and finally the captain nodded gruffly. "I'll see you in the morning," he promised before following Parnigar into the night.

Kith sat for a while, staring at the dying flame of the lantern, reluctant to extinguish the light even though he knew precious fuel burned away with each second. Not enough fuel . . . not enough food . . . insufficient troops. What did he have *enough* of, besides problems?

He tried not to think about the extent of his frustration—how much he hated being trapped inside the fortress, cooped up with his entire army, at the mercy of the enemy beyond the walls. How he longed for the freedom of the forests, where he had lived so happily during his years away from Silvanost.

Yet with these thoughts, he couldn't help thinking of Anaya— beautiful, lost Anaya. Perhaps his true entrapment had begun with her death, before the war started, before he had been made general of his father's—and then his brother's—army.

Finally he sighed, knowing that his thoughts could bring him no comfort. Reluctantly he doused the lantern's flame. His own bunk occupied the room adjacent to this office, and soon he lay there.

But sleep would not come. That night they had had no wine to share, and now the tension of his mood kept Kith-Kanan awake for seeming hours after his two officers left.

Eventually, with the entire fortress silent and still around him, his eyes fell shut—but not to the darkness of restful sleep. Instead, it was as though he fell directly from wakefulness into a very vivid dream.

He dreamed that he soared through the clouds, not upon the back of Arcuballis as he had flown so many times before, but supported by the strength of his own arms, his own feet. He swooped and dove like an eagle, master of the sky.

Abruptly the clouds parted before him, and he saw three conical mountain peaks jutting upward from the haze of earth so far below. These monstrous peaks belched smoke, and streaks of fire splashed and flowed down their sides. The valleys extending from their feet were hellish wastelands of crimson lava and brown sludge.

Away from the peaks he soared, and now below him were lifeless valleys of a different sort. Surrounded by craggy ridges and needlelike peaks, these mountain retreats lay beneath great sheets of snow and ice. All around him stretched a pristine brilliance. Gray and black shapes, the forms of towering summits, rose from the vast glaciers of pure white. In places, streaks of blue showed through the snow, and here Kith-Kanan saw ice as clean, as clear as any on Krynn.

Movement suddenly caught his eye in one of these valleys. He saw a great mountain looming, higher than all the others around. Upon its face, dripping ice formed the crude outlines of a face like that of an old, white-bearded dwarf.

Kith continued his flight and saw movement again. At first Kith thought that he was witnessing a great flock of eagles—savage, prideful birds that crowded the sky. Then he wondered, Could they be some kind of mountain horses or unusual, tawny-colored goats?

In another moment, he knew, as the memory of Arcuballis came flooding back. These were griffons, a whole flock of them!

Hundreds of the savage half-eagle, half-lion creatures were surging through the air toward Kith-Kanan.

He felt no fear. Instead, he turned away from the dwarf-beard mountain and flew southward. The griffons followed, and slowly the heights of the range fell behind him. He saw lakes of blue water below him and fields of brush and mossy rock. Then came the first trees, and he dove to follow a mountain rivulet toward the green flatlands that now opened up before him.

And then he saw her in the forest—Anaya! She was painted like a wild savage, her naked body flashing among the trees as she ran from him. By the gods, she was fast! She outdistanced him even as he flew, and soon the only trace of her passage was the wild laughter that lingered on the breeze before him.

Then he found her, but already she had changed. She was old, and rooted in the ground. Before his eyes, she had become a tree, growing toward the heavens and losing all of the form and the senses of the elfin woman he had grown to love.

His tears flowed, unnoticed, down his face. They soaked the ground and nourished the tree, causing it to shoot farther into the sky. Sadly the elf left her, and he and his griffons flew on farther to the south.

Another face wafted before him. He recognized with shock the human woman who had given him his escape from the enemy camp. Why, now, did she enter his dream?

The rivulet below him became a stream, and then more streams joined it, and the stream became a river, flowing into the forested realm of his homeland.

Ahead he finally saw a ring of water where the River Thon-Thalas parted around the island of Silvanost. Behind, him, five hundred griffons followed him homeward. A radiant glow reached out to welcome him.

He saw another elf woman in the garden. She looked upward, her arms spread, welcoming him to his home, to her. At first, from a distance, he wondered if this was his mother, but then as he dove closer, he recognized his brother's wife, Hermathya.

Sunlight streamed into his window. He awoke suddenly, refreshed and revitalized. The memory of his dream shone in his mind like a beacon, and he sprang from his bed. The fortress still slumbered around him. His window, on the east wall of a tower, was the first place in Sithelbec to receive the morning sun. Throwing a cloak over his tunic and sticking his feet into soft, high leather boots, he laced the latter around his knees while he hobbled toward the door.

A cry of alarm suddenly sounded from the courtyard. In the next moment, a horn blared, followed by a chorus of trumpets blasting a warning. Kith dashed from his room, down the hall of the captain's quarters and to the outside. The sun was barely cresting the fortress wall, and yet he saw a shadow pass across that small area of brightness.

He noted several archers on the wall, turning and aiming their weapons skyward.

"Don't shoot!" he cried as the shadow swooped closer and he recognized it. "Arcuballis!"

He waved his hand and ran into the courtyard as the proud griffon circled him once, then came to rest before him. The lion's hindquarter's squatted while the creature raised one foreclaw—the massive, taloned limb of an eagle. The keen yellow eyes blinked, and Kith-Kanan felt a surge of affection for his faithful steed.

In the next moment, he wondered about Arcuballis's presence here. He had left him in charge of his brother back in Silvanost. Of course! Sithas had sent the creature here to Kith to bring him home! The prospect elated him like nothing else had in years.

* * * * *

It took Kith-Kanan less than an hour to leave orders with his two subordinates. Parnigar he placed in overall command, while Kencathedrus was to drill and train a small, mobile sortie force of cavalry, pikes, and archers. They would be called the Flying Brigade, but they were not to be employed until Kith-Kanan's return. He cautioned both officers on the need to remain alert to any human strategem. Sithelbec was the keystone to any defense on the plains, and it must remain impregnable, inviolate.

"I'm sure my brother has plans. We'll meet and work out a way to break this stalemate!" The autumn wind swirled through the compound, bringing the first bite of winter.

He climbed onto the back of his steed, settling into the new saddle that one of the Wildrunner horsemen had cobbled for him.

"Good luck, and may the gods watch over your flight," Kencathedrus said, clasping Kith's gloved hand in both of his own.

"And bring a speedy return," added Parnigar.

Arcuballis thrust powerful wings, muscular and stout enough to break a man's neck, toward the ground. At the same time, the leonine hindquarters thrust the body into the air.

Several strokes of his wings carried Arcuballis to the top of a building, still inside the fortress wall. He grasped the peaked roof with his eagle foreclaws, then used his feline rear legs to spring himself still higher into the air. With a squawk that rang like a challenge across the plain, he soared over the wall, climbing steadily.

Kith-Kanan was momentarily awestruck at the spectacle of the enemy arrayed below him. His tower, the highest vantage point in Sithelbec, didn't convey the immense sprawl of the Army of Ergoth—not in the way that Arcuballis's ascending flight did. Below, ranks of human archers took up their weapons, but the griffon already soared far out of range.

They flew onward, passing above a great herd of horses in a pasture. The shadow of the griffon passed along the ground, and several of the steeds snorted and reared in sudden panic. These bolted immediately, and in seconds, the herd had erupted into a stampede. The elf watched in wry amusement as the human herdsmen raced out of the path of the beasts. It would be hours, he suspected, before order was restored to the camp.

Kith looked down at the smoldering remains of the lava cannon, now a black, misshapen thing, like a burned and gnarled tree trunk leaning at a steep angle over the ground. He saw seemingly endless rows of tents, some of them grand but most simple shelters of oilskin or wool. Everywhere the flat ground had been churned to mud.

Finally he left the circular fortress and the larger circle of the human army behind. Forests of lush green opened before him, dotted by ponds and lakes, streaked by rivers and long meandering meadows. As the wild land surrounded him, he felt the agony of the war fall away.

* * * * *

Suzine des Quivalen studied the image in the mirror until it faded into the distance, beyond the reach of her arcane crystal. Yet even after it vanished, the memory of those powerful wings carrying Kith-Kanan away—away from *her*—lingered in her mind.

She saw his blond hair, flying from beneath his helmet. She recalled her gasp of terror when the archers had fired, and her slow relaxation as he gained height and safety. Yet a part of her had cursed and railed at him for leaving, and that part had wanted to see a human arrow bring him down. She didn't want him dead, of course, but the idea of this handsome elf as a prisoner in her camp was strangely appealing.

For a moment, she paused, wondering at the fascination she found for this elven commander, mortal enemy of her people and chief opponent of the man who was her . . . lover.

Once General Giarna had been that and more. Smooth, dashing, and handsome, he had swept her off her feet in the early days of their relationship. With the aid of her powers with the mirror, she had given him information sufficient to discredit several of the emperor's highest generals. The grateful ruler had rewarded the Boy General with an ever-increasing array of field commands.

But something had changed since those times. The man who she thought had loved her now treated her with cruelty and arrogance, inspiring in her fears that she could not overcome. Those fears were great enough to hold her at his side, for she had come to believe that flight from General Giarna would mean her sentence of death.

Here on the plains, in command of many thousands of men, Giarna had little time for her, which was a relief. But when she saw him, he seemed so coldly controlled, so monstrously purposeful, that she feared him all the more.

With an angry shake of her head, she turned from the mirror, which slowly faded into a reflection of the Lady Suzine and the interior of her tent. She rose in a swirl of silk and stalked across the rich carpets that blanketed the ground. Her red hair swirled in a long coil around her scalp, rising higher than her head and peaking in a glittering tiara of diamonds, emeralds, and rubies.

Her gown, of blood-red silk, clung to the full curves of her body as she stalked toward the tent flap that served as her door. She stopped long enough to throw a woolen shawl over her bare shoulders, remembering the chill that had settled over the plains in the last few days.

As soon as she emerged, the six men-at-arms standing at her door snapped to attention, bringing their halberds straight before their faces. She paid no attention as they fell in behind her, marching with crisp precision as she headed toward another elegant tent some distance away. The black stallion of General Giarna stood restlessly outside, so she knew that the man she sought was within.

The Army of Ergoth spread to the horizons around her. The massive encampment encircled the fortress of Sithelbec in a great ring. Here, at the eastern arc of that ring, the headquarters of the three generals and their retinues had collected. Amid the mud and smoke of the army camp, the gilded coaches of the noble lancers and the tall, silken folds of the high officers' tents, stood out in contrast.

Before Suzine arose the tallest tent of all, that of General Barnet, the overall general of the army.

The two guards before that tent stepped quickly out of the way to let her pass, one of them pulling aside the tent flap to give her entrance. She passed into the semidarkness of the tent and her eyes quickly adjusted to the dim light. She saw General Giarna lounging easily at a table loaded with food and drink. Before him, sitting stiffly, was General Barnet. Suzine couldn't help but notice the fear and anger in the older general's eyes as he looked at her.

Beyond the two seated men stood a third, General Xalthan. That veteran's face was deathly, shockingly pale. He surprised Suzine by looking at her with an expression of pleading, as if he hoped that she could offer him succor for some terrible predicament.

"Come in, my dear," said Giarna, his voice smooth, his manner light. "We are having a farewell toast to our friend, General Xalthan."

"Farewell?" she asked, having heard nothing of that worthy soldier's departure.

"By word of the emperor—by special courier, with an escort. Quite an honor, really," added Giarna, his tone mocking and cruel.

Instantly Suzine understood. The disaster with the lava cannon had been the last straw, as far as the emperor was concerned, for General Xalthan. He had been recalled to Daltigoth under guard.

To his credit, the wing commander nodded stiffly, retaining his composure even in the face of Giarna's taunts. General Barnet remained immobile, but the hatred in his eyes now flashed toward Giarna. Suzine, too, felt an unexpected sense of loathing toward the Boy General.

"I'm sorry," she said to the doomed wing commander quietly. "I really am." Indeed, the depths of her sorrow surprised her. She had never thought very much about Xalthan, except sometimes to feel uncomfortable when his eyes ran over the outlines of her body if she wore a clinging gown.

But the old man was guilty of no failing, she suspected, except an inability to move as quickly as the Boy General. Xalthan stood in the path of Giarna's desire to command the entire army. General Giarna's reports to the emperor, she felt certain, had been full of the information she had provided him—news of Xalthan's sluggish advance, the ineptness of the gnomish artillerymen, all details that could make a vengeful and impatient ruler lose his patience.

And cause an old warrior who deserved only a peaceful retirement face instead a prospect of torture, disgrace, and execution.

The knowledge made Suzine feel somehow dirty.

Xalthan looked at her with that puppylike sense of hope, a hope she could do nothing to gratify. His fate was laid in stone before them: There would be a long ride to Daltigoth, perhaps with the formerly esteemed officer bound in chains. Once there, the emperor's inquisitors would begin, often with Quivalen himself in attendance.

It was rumored that the emperor received great pleasure from watching the torture of those he felt had failed him. No tool was too devious, no tactic too inhumane, for these monstrous sculptors of pain. Fire and steel, venoms and acids, all were the instruments of their ungodly work. Finally, after days or weeks of indescribable agony, the inquisitors would be finished, and Xalthan would be healed—just enough to allow him to be alert for the occasion of his public execution.

The fact that her cousin was the one who would do this to the man didn't enter into her considerations. She accepted, fatalistically, that this was the way things would happen. Her role in the court family was to be one who remained docile and sensitive to her duties, useful with her skills as seer. She had to play that role and leave the rest to fate.

Just for a moment, a nearly overwhelming urge possessed her, a desire to flee this army camp, to flee the gracious life of the capital, to fly from all the darkness that seemed to surround her empire's endeavors. She wanted to go to a place where troubles such as this one remained concealed from delicate eyes.

It was only when she remembered the blond-haired elf who so fascinated her that she paused. Even though he had gone, flown from Sithelbec on the back of his winged steed, she felt certain he would return. She didn't know why, but she wanted to be here when he did.

"Farewell, General," she said quietly, crossing to embrace the once-proud warrior. Without another glance at Giarna, she turned and left the tent.

Suzine retreated to her own shelter, anger rising within her. She stalked back and forth within the silken walls, resisting the urge to throw things, to rant loudly at the air. For all her efforts at self-control, her vaunted discipline seemed to have deserted her. She could not calm herself.

Suddenly she gasped as the tent flap flew open and her general's huge form blocked out the light. Instinctively she backed away as he marched into her shelter, allowing the flap to fall closed behind him.

'That was quite a display," he growled, his voice like a blast of winter's wind. His dark eyes glowered, showing none of the amusement they had displayed at Xalthan's predicament.

"What—what do you mean?" she stammered, still backing away. She held her hand to her mouth and stared at him, her green eyes wide. A trace of her red hair spilled across her brow, and she angrily pushed it away from her face.

Giarna crossed to her in three quick strides, taking her wrists in both his hands. He pulled her arms to her sides and stared into her face, his mouth twisted into a menacing sneer.

"Stop—you're hurting me!" she objected, twisting powerlessly in his grip.

"Hear me well, wench," he growled, his voice barely audible. "Do not attempt to mock me again—ever! If you do, that shall be the end your power . . . the end of *everything!*"

She gasped, frightened beyond words.

"I have chosen you for my woman. That fact pleased you once; perhaps it may please you again. Whether it does or not is irrelevant to me. Your skills, however, are of use to me. The others wonder at the great intelligence I gain concerning the elven army, and so you will continue to serve me thus.

"But you will *not* affront me again!" General Giarna paused, and his dark eyes seemed to mock Suzine's terrified stare.

"Do I make myself perfectly clear?" Giarna demanded, and she nodded quickly, helplessly. She feared his power and his strength, and she could only tremble in the grip of his powerful hands.

"Remember well," added the general. He fixed her with a penetrating gaze, and she felt the blood drain from her face. Without another word, he spun on his heel and stalked imperiously from the tent.

*　*　*　*　*

The flight to Silvanost took four days, for Kith allowed Arcuballis to hunt in the forest, while he himself took the time to rest at night on a lush bed of pine boughs amid the noisy, friendly chatter of the woods.

On the second day of his flight, Kith-Kanan stopped early, for he had reached a place that he intended to visit. Arcuballis dove to earth in the center of a blossom-bright clearing, and Kith dismounted. He walked over to a tree that grew strong and proud, shading a wide area, far wider than when he had last been here a year before.

"Anaya, I miss you," he said quietly.

He rested at the foot of the tree and spent several hours in bittersweet reflection of the elfwoman he'd loved and lost. But he didn't find total despair in the memory, for this was indeed Anaya beside him now. She grew tall and flourished, a part of the woods she had always loved.

She had been a creature of the woods, and together with her "brother" Mackeli, the forest's guardian as well. For a moment, the pain threatened to block out the happier memories. Why did they die? For what purpose? Anaya killed by marauders. Mackeli slain by assassins—sent, Kith suspected, by someone in Silvanost itself.

Anaya hadn't really died, he reminded himself. Instead, she had undergone a bizarre transformation and become a tree, rooted firmly in the forest soil she loved and had strived to protect.

Then a disturbing vision intruded itself into Kith's reminiscences, and the picture of Anaya, laughing and bright before him, changed slightly. A beautiful elven woman still teased him, but now the face was different, no longer Anaya's.

Hermathya! The image of his first love, now his brother's wife, struck him like a physical blow. Angrily he shook his head, trying to dispel her features, to call back those of Anaya. Yet Hermathya remained before him, her eyes bold and challenging, her smile alluring.

Kith-Kanan exhaled sharply, surprised by the attraction he still felt for the Silvanesti woman. He had thought that impulse long dead, an immature passion that had run its course and been banished to the past. Now he imagined her supple body, her clinging, low-cut gown tailored to show enough to excite while concealing enough to mystify. He found himself vaguely ashamed to realize that he still desired her.

As he shook his head in an effort to banish the disturbing emotion, a picture of still a third woman insinuated itself. He recalled again the red-haired human woman who had given him his chance to escape from the enemy camp. There had been something vibrant and compelling about her, and this wasn't the first time he had remembered her face.

The conflicting memories warred within him as he built a small fire and ate a simple meal. He camped in the clearing, as usual making himself a soft bed. The night passed in peace.

He took to the air at first light, feeling as if he had somehow sullied Anaya's memory, but soon the clean air swept through his hair, and his mind focused on the day's journey. Arcuballis carried him swiftly and uneventfully eastward. After his third night of sleeping in the woods, he felt as if his strength had been doubled, his wit and alertness greatly enhanced.

His spirits soared as high as the Tower of the Stars, which now appeared on the distant horizon. Arcuballis carried him steadily, but so far was the tower that more than an hour passed before they reached the Thon-Thalas River, border to the island of Silvanost.

His arrival was anticipated; boatmen on the river waved and cheered as he flew overhead, while a crowd of elves hurried toward the Palace of Quinari. The doors at the foot of the tower burst open, and Kith saw a blond-haired elf, clad in the silk robe of the Speaker of the Stars, emerge. Sithas hurried across the garden, but the griffon met him halfway.

Grinning foolishly, Kith leapt from the back of his steed to embrace his brother. It felt very good to be home.

PÁRT II

Scions of Silvanos

Midautumn

2214 (PC)

8

"By Quenesti Pah, he's beautiful!" Kith-Kanan cautiously took the infant in his arms. Proudly Sithas stood beside them. Kith had been on the ground for all of five minutes before the Speaker of the Stars had hurried him to the nursery to see the newest heir to the throne of Silvanesti.

"It takes a while before you feel certain that you won't break him," he told his brother, based on his own extensive paternal experience, a good two months' worth now.

"Vanesti—it's a good name. Proud, full of our heritage," Kith said. "A name worthy of the heir of the House of Silvanos."

Sithas looked at his brother and his son, and he felt better than he had in months. Indeed, he knew a gladness that hadn't been his since the start of the war.

The door to the nursery opened and Hermathya entered. She approached Kith-Kanan nervously, her eyes upon her child. At first, the elven general thought that his sister-in-law's tension resulted from the memory of them together. Kith and Hermathya's affair, before her engagement to Sithas, had been brief but passionate.

But then he realized that her anxiety came from a simpler, more direct source. She was concerned that someone other than herself held her child.

"Here," said Kith, offering the silk-swathed infant to Hermathya. "You have a very handsome son."

'Thank you." She took the child then smiled hesitantly. Kith tried to see her in a different light than he did in his memories.

He told himself that she looked nothing like the woman he had known, had thought he loved, those few years earlier.

Then the memories came back in a physical rush that almost brought him to his knees. Hermathya smiled again, and Kith-Kanan ached with desire. He lowered his eyes, certain that his bold feelings showed plainly on his face. By the gods, she was his brother's wife! What kind of distorted loyalty tortured him that he could think these thoughts, feel these needs.

He cast a quick, apprehensive glance at Sithas and saw that his brother looked only at the baby. Hermathya, however, caught his eye, her own gaze sparking like fire. What was happening? Suddenly Kith-Kanan felt very frightened and very lonely.

"You should both be very happy," he said awkwardly.

They said nothing, but each looked at Vanesti in a way that communicated their love and pride.

"Now let's take care of business," said Sithas to his brother. "The war."

Kith sighed. "I knew we'd have to get around to the war sooner or later, but can we make it a little bit later? I'd like to see Mother first."

"Of course. How stupid of me," Sithas agreed. If he had noticed any of the feelings that Kith had thought showed so plainly on his face, the Speaker gave no sign. His voice dropped slightly. "She's in her quarters. She'll be delighted to see you. I think it's just what she needs."

Kith-Kanan looked at his brother curiously, but Sithas did not elaborate. Instead, the Speaker continued in a different vein.

"I've had some Thalian blond wine chilled in my apartment. I want to hear everything that's happened since the start of the war. Come and find me after you've spoken to Nirakina."

"I will. I've got a lot to tell, but I want to know how things have fared in the city as well." Kith-Kanan followed Sithas from the nursery, quietly closing the door. Before it shut, he looked back and saw Hermathya cuddling the baby to her breast. The elf-woman's eyes looked up suddenly and locked upon Kith's, making an electric connection that he had to force himself to break.

The two elves, leaders of the nation, walked in silence through the long halls of the Palace of Quinari. They reached the apartments of their mother, and Kith stopped as Sithas walked silently on.

"Enter," came her familiar voice in response to his soft knock.

He pushed open the door and saw Nirakina seated in a chair by the open window. She rose and swept him into her arms, hugging him as if she would never let him go.

He was shocked by the aging apparent in his mother's face, an aging that was all the more distressing because of the long elven

340

life span. By rights, she was just reaching middle age and could look forward to several productive centuries before she approached old age.

Yet her face, drawn by cares, and the gray streaks that had begun to silver her hair reminded Kith of his grandmother, in the years shortly before her death. It was a revelation that disturbed him deeply.

"Sit down, Mother," Kith said quietly, leading her back to her chair. "Are you all right?"

Nirakina looked at him, and the son had trouble facing his mother's eyes. So much despair!

"Seeing you does much to bring my strength back," she replied, offering a wan smile. "It seems I'm surrounded by strangers so much now."

"Surely Sithas is here with you."

"Oh, when he can be, but there is much to occupy him. The affairs of war, and now his child. Vanesti is a beautiful baby, don't you agree?"

Kith nodded, wondering why he didn't hear more pleasure in his mother's voice. This was her first grandchild.

"But Hermathya thinks that I get in the way, and her sisters are here to help. I have seen too little of Vanesti." Nirakina's eyes drifted to the window. "I miss your father. I miss him so much sometimes that I can hardly stand it."

Kith struggled for words. Failing, he took his mother's hands in his own.

"The palace, the city—it's all changing," she continued. "It's the war. In your absence, Lord Quimant advises your brother. It seems the palace is becoming home to all of Clan Oakleaf."

Kith had heard of Quimant in Sithas's letters and knew his brother considered him to be a great assistance in affairs of state.

"What of Tamanier Ambrodel?" The loyal elf had been his mother's able aide and had saved her life during the riots that had rocked the city before the outbreak of war. Sithel had promoted him to lord chamberlain to reward his loyalty. His mother and Tamanier had been good friends for many years.

"He's gone. Sithas tells me not to worry, and I know he has embarked upon a mission in the service of the throne. But he has been absent a long time, and I cannot help but miss him."

She looked at him, and he saw tears in her eyes. "Sometimes I feel like so much excess baggage, locked away in my room here, waiting for my life to pass!"

Kith sat back, shocked and dismayed by his mother's despair. This was so unlike the Nirakina he had always known, an elf-woman full of vigor, serene and patient against the background of his father's rigid ideas. He tried to bide his churning emotions beneath a lighthearted tone.

"Tomorrow we'll go riding," he said, realizing that sunset approached quickly. "I have to meet Sithas tonight to make my reports. But meet me for breakfast in the dining hall, won't you?"

Nirakina smiled, for the first time with her eyes as well as her lips. "I'd like that," she said. But the memory of her lined, unhappy face stuck with him as he left her chambers and made his way to his brother's library.

"Come in," announced Sithas, as two liveried halberdiers of the House Protectorate snapped to attention before the silver-plated doors to the royal apartment. One of them pulled the door open, and the general entered.

"We wish to be alone," announced the Speaker of the Stars, and the guards nodded silently.

The pair settled into comfortable chairs, near the balcony that gave them an excellent view of the Tower of the Stars, which rose into the night sky across the gardens. The red moon, Lunitari, and the pale orb of Solinari illuminated the vista, casting shadows through the winding passages of the garden paths.

Sithas filled two mugs and placed the bottle of fine wine back into its bucket of melting ice. Handing one mug to his brother, he raised his own and met Kith's with a slight clink.

"To victory," he offered.

"Victory!" Kith-Kanan repeated.

They sat and, sensing that his brother wanted to speak first, the army commander waited expectantly. His intuition was correct.

"By all the gods, I wish I could be there with you!" Sithas began, his tone full of conviction.

Kith didn't doubt him. "War's not what I thought it would be," he admitted. "Mostly it's waiting, discomfort, and tedium. We are always hungry and cold, but mostly bored. It seems that days and weeks go by when nothing happens of consequence."

He sighed and paused for a moment to take a deep draft of his wine. The sweet liquid soothed his throat and loosened his tongue. "Then, when things do start to happen, you're more frightened than you ever thought was possible. You fight for your life; you run when you have to. You try to stay in touch with what's going on, but it's impossible. Just as quickly, the fight's over and you go back to being bored. Except now you have the grief, too, knowing that brave companions have died this day, some of them because you made the wrong decision. Even the right decision sometimes sends too many good elves to their deaths."

Sithas shook his head sadly. "At least you have some control over events. I sit here, hundreds of miles away. I send those good elves to live or die without the slightest knowledge of what will befall them."

"That knowledge is slim comfort," replied his brother.

Kith-Kanan told his brother, in elaborate detail, about the battles in which the Wildrunners had fought the Army of Ergoth. He talked of their initial small victories, of the plodding advance of the central and southern wings. He described the fast-moving horsemen of the north wing and their keen and brutal commander, General Giarna. His voice broke as he related the tale of the trap that had ensnared Kencathedrus and his proud regiment, and for a moment, he lapsed into a miserable silence.

Sithas reached out and touched his brother on the shoulder. The gesture seemed to renew Kith-Kanan's strength, and after drawing a deep breath, he began to speak again.

He told of their forced retreat into the fortress, of the numberless horde of humans surrounding them, barring the Wildrunners against any real penetration, The wine bottle emptied—it may as well have been by evaporation, for all the notice the brothers took—and the moons crept toward the western horizon. Sithas rang for another bottle of Thalian blond as Kith described the state of supplies and morale within Sithelbec and talked about their prospects for the future.

"We can hold out through the winter, perhaps well into next year. But we cannot shake the grip around us, not unless something happens to break this stalemate!"

"Something such as what? More reinforcements—another five thousand elves from Silvanost?" Sithas leaned close to his brother, disturbed by the account of the war. The setbacks suffered by the Wildrunners were temporary—this the speaker truly believed—and together they had to figure out some way to turn the tide.

Kith shook his head. "That would help—*any* reinforcements you can send would help—but even twice that many elves would not turn the tide. Perhaps the Army of Thorbardin, if the dwarves can be coaxed from their mountain retreat . . ." His voice showed that he placed little hope in this possibility.

"It might happen," Sithas replied. "You didn't get to know Lord Dunbarth as did I, when he spent a year among us in the city. He is a trustworthy fellow, and he bears no love for the humans. I think he realizes that his own kingdom will be next in line for conquest unless he can do something now."

Sithas described the present ambassador, the intransigent Than-Kar, in considerably less glowing terms. "He's a major stumbling block to any firm agreement, but there still might be some way around him!"

343

"I'd like to talk to him myself," Kith said. "Can we bring him to the palace?"

"I can try," Sithas agreed, realizing how weak the phrase sounded. Father would have ordered it! he reminded himself. For a moment, he felt terribly ineffective, wishing he had Sithel's steady nerves. Angrily he pushed the sensation of doubt *away* and listened to his brother speak.

"I'll believe in dwarven help when I see their banners on the field and their weapons pointed *away* from us!"

"But what else?" pressed Sithas. "What other tactics do we have?"

"I wish I knew," his brother replied. "I hoped that you might have some suggestions."

"Weapons?" Sithas explained the key role Lord Quimant was playing to increase the munitions production at the Oakleak Clan's forges. "We'll get you the best blades that elven craftsmen can make."

"That's something—but still, we need more. We need something that cannot just stand against the human cavalry but break it. Drive it away!"

The second bottle of wine began to vanish as the elven lords wrestled with their problem. The first traces of dawn colored the sky, a thin line of pale blue on the horizon, but no ready solution came to mind.

"You know, I wasn't certain that Arcuballis could find you," Sithas said after a pause of several minutes. The frustration of their search for a solution weighed upon them, and Kith welcomed the change of conversation.

"He never looked so good to me," Kith-Kanan replied, "as when he came soaring into the fortress compound. I didn't realize how much I missed this place—how much I missed you and mother—until I saw him."

"He's been there in the stable since you left," Sithas said, shaking his head with a wry grin, "I don't know why I didn't think of sending him to you shortly after you were first besieged."

"I had a curious dream about him—about an entire of griffons, actually—on the very night before he arrived. It was most uncanny." Kith described his strange dream, and the two brothers pondered its meaning.

"A flock of griffons?" Sithas asked intently.

"Well, yes. Do you think it significant?"

"If we had a flock of griffons . . . if they all carried riders into combat . . . could that be the hammer needed to crack the shell around Sithelbec?" Sithas spoke with growing enthusiasm.

"Wait a minute," said Kith, holding up his hand. "I suppose

you're right, in a hypothetical sense. In fact, the horses of the humans were spooked as I flew over, even though I was high, out of bowshot range. But who ever heard of an army of griffons?"

Sithas settled back, suddenly realizing the futility of his idea. For a moment, neither of them said anything—which was how they heard the soft rustling in the room behind them.

Kith-Kanan sprang to his feet, instinctively reaching for a sword at his hip, forgetting that his weapon hung back on the wall of his own apartment. Sithas whirled in his seat, staring in astonishment, and then he rose to his feet.

"You!" the Speaker barked, his voice taut with rage. "What are you doing here?"

Kith-Kanan crouched, preparing to spring at the intruder. He saw the figure, a mature elf cloaked in a silky gray robe, move forward from the shadows.

"Wait," said Sithas, much to his brother's surprise. The speaker held up his hand, and Kith straightened, still tense and suspicious.

"One day your impudence will cost you," Sithas said levelly as the elf approached them. "You are not to enter my chambers unannounced again. Is that clear?"

"Pardon my intrusion. As you know, my presence must remain discreet."

"Who is this?" Kith-Kanan demanded.

"Forgive me," said the gray-cloaked elf before Sithas cut him off.

"This is Vedvedsica," said Sithas. Kith-Kanan noted that his brother's tone had become carefully guarded. "He has . . . been helpful to the House of Silvanos in the past."

"The pleasure is mine, and it is indeed great, honored prince," offered Vedvedsica, with a deep bow to Kith-Kanan.

"Who are you? Why do you come here?" Kith demanded.

"In good time, lord—in good time. As to who I am, I am a cleric, a devoted follower of Gilean."

Kith-Kanan wasn't surprised. The god was the most purely neutral in the elven pantheon, most often used to justify self-aggrandizement and profit. Something about Vedvedsica struck him as very self-serving indeed.

"More to the point, I know of your dream."

The last was directed to Kith-Kanan and struck him like a lightning bolt between the eyes. For a moment, he hesitated, fighting an almost undeniable urge to hurl himself at the insolent cleric and kill him with his bare hands. Never before had he felt so violated.

"Explain yourself!"

"I have knowledge that the two of you may desire—knowledge of griffons, hundreds of them. And even more important, I may have knowledge as to how they can be found and tamed."

For the moment, the elven lords remained silent, listening suspiciously as Vedvedsica moved forward. "May I?" inquired the cleric, gesturing to a seat beside their own.

Sithas nodded silently, and all three sat.

"The griffons dwell in the Khalkist Mountains, south of the Lords of Doom." The brothers knew of these peaks—three violent volcanoes in the heart of the forbidding range, high among vast glaciers and sheer summits. It was a region beyond the ken of elven explorers.

"How do you know this?" asked Sithas.

"Did your father ever tell you how he came to possess Arcuballis?" Again the cleric fixed Kith-Kanan with his gaze, then continued as if he already knew the answer. "He got him from me!"

Kith nodded, reluctant to believe the cleric but finding himself unable to doubt the veracity of his words.

"I purchased him from a Kagonesti, a wild elf who told me of the whereabouts of the pack. He encountered them, together with a dozen companions. He alone escaped the wrath of the griffons, with one young cub—the one given by me to Sithel as a gift, and the one that he passed along to his son. To you, Kith-Kanan."

"But how could the flock be tamed? From what you say, a dozen elves perished to bring one tiny cub away!" Kith-Kanan challenged Vedvedsica. Despite his suspicions, he felt his own excitement begin to build.

"*I* tamed him, with the aid and protection of Gilean. I developed the spell that broke him to halter. It's a simple enchantment, really. Any elf with a working knowledge of the Old Script could have cast it. But only I could bring it into being!"

"Continue," said Sithas urgently.

"I believe that spell can be enhanced, developed so that many more of the creatures could be brought to heel. I can inscribe it onto a scroll. Then one of you can take it in search of the griffons."

"Are you certain that it will work?" demanded Sithas.

"No," replied the cleric frankly. "It will need to be presented under precise circumstances and with a great force of command. That is why the person who casts the spell must be a leader among elves—one of you two. No others of our race would have the necessary traits."

"How long would it take to prepare such a scroll?" pressed Kith. A cavalry company mounted on griffons, flying over the battlefield! The thought made his heart pound with excitement. They would be unstoppable!

Vedvedsica shrugged. "A week, perhaps two. It will be an arduous process."

"I'll go," Kith volunteered.

"Wait!" said Sithas sharply. "*I* should go! And I will!"

Kith-Kanan looked at the Speaker in astonishment. "That's crazy!" he argued. "You're the Speaker of the Stars. You have a wife, a child! More to the point, you're the leader of all Silvanesti! And you haven't ever lived in the wilderness before like I have! I can't allow you to take the risk."

For a moment, the twins stared at each other, equally stubborn. The cleric was forgotten for the moment, and he melted into the shadows, discreet in his withdrawal.

It was Sithas who spoke.

"Do *you* read the Old Script?" he asked his brother bluntly. "Well enough to be certain of your words, when you know that the whole future of the realm could depend upon what you say?"

The younger twin sighed. "No. My studies always emphasized the outdoor skills. I'm afraid the ancient writing wouldn't make much sense to me."

Sithas smiled wryly. "I used to resent that. You were always out riding horses or hunting or learning swordsmanship, while I studied the musty tomes and forgotten histories. Well, now I'm going to put that learning to use.

"We'll both go," Sithas concluded.

Kith-Kanan stared at him, realizing the outcry such a plan would raise. Perhaps, he had to admit, this was the reason the scheme appealed to him. Slowly Kith relaxed, settling back into his chair.

"The trip won't be easy," Kith warned sternly. "We're going to have to explore the largest mountain range on Ansalon, and winter isn't far away. In those heights, you can be sure there's already plenty of snow."

"You can't scare me off," answered Sithas purposefully. "I know that Arcuballis can carry the two of us, and I don't care if it takes all winter. We'll *find* them, Kith. I know we will."

"You know," Kith-Kanan said ironically. "I must still be dreaming. In any event, you're right. The sons of Sithel ought to make this quest together."

With a final mug of wine, as the sky grew pale above them, they began to make their plans.

Next Morning

9

Kith-Kanan and his mother rode through the tree-lined streets of Silvanost for several hours, talking only of fond memories and pleasant topics from many years before. They stopped to enjoy the fountains, to watch the hawks dive for fish in the river, and to listen to the songbirds that clustered in the many flowered bushes of the city's lush gardens.

During the ride, it seemed to the elven warrior that his mother slowly came to life again, even to the point of laughing as they watched the pompous dance of a brilliant cardinal trying to impress his mate.

In the back of Kith's mind lurked the realization that his mother would soon learn of her sons' plans to embark on a dangerous expedition into the Khalkist Mountains. That news could wait, he decided.

"Are you going to join your brother at court?" asked Nirakina as the sun slid past the midafternoon point,

Kith sighed. "There'll be enough time for that tomorrow," he decided.

"Good." His mother looked at him, and he was delighted to see that the familiar sparkle had returned to her eyes. She spurred her horse with a sharp kick, and the mare raced ahead, leaving Kith with the challenge of her laugh as he tried to urge his older gelding into catching up.

They cantered beneath the shade of towering elms and dashed among the crystal columns of the elven homes in a friendly race toward the Gardens of Astarin and the royal stables. Nirakina was a good rider, with the faster horse; though Kith tried to spur the last energy from his own steed, his mother beat him through the palace gates by a good three lengths.

Laughing, they pulled up before the stables and dismounted. Nirakina turned toward him, impulsively pulling him into a hug, "Thank you," she whispered. "Thank you for coming home!"

Kith held her in silence for some moments, relieved that he hadn't discussed the twins' plans with her.

Leaving his mother at her chambers, he made his way to his own apartments, intending to bathe and dress for the banquet his brother had scheduled for that evening. Before he reached his door, however, a figure moved out of a nearby alcove.

Reflexively the elven warrior reached for a sword, a weapon that he did not usually carry in the secure confines of the palace. At the same time, he relaxed, recognizing the figure and realizing that there was no threat—at least, no threat of harm.

"Hermathya," he said, his voice oddly husky.

"Your nerves are stretched tight," she observed, with an awkward little laugh. She wore a turquoise gown cut low over her breasts. Her hair cascaded over her shoulders, and as she looked up at him, Kith-Kanan thought that she seemed as young and vulnerable as ever.

He forced himself to shake his head, remembering that she was neither young nor vulnerable. Still, the spell of her innocent allure held him, and he wanted to reach out and sweep her into his arms.

With difficulty, he held his hands at his tides, waiting for Hermathya to speak again. His stillness seemed to unsettle her, as if she had expected him to make the next move.

The look in her eyes left him little doubt as to what response she was hoping for. He didn't open the door, he didn't move toward his room. He remained all too conscious of the private chambers and the large bed nearby. The aching in his body surprised him, and he realized with a great deal of dismay that he wanted her. He wanted her very badly indeed.

"I–I wanted to talk to you," she said. He understood implicitly that she was lying.

Her words seemed to break the spell, and he reached past her to push open his door. "Come in," he said as flatly as possible.

He walked to the tall crystal doors, pulling the draperies aside to reveal the lush brilliance of the Gardens of Astarin. Keeping his back to her, he waited for her to speak.

"I've been worried about you," she began. "They told me you had been captured, and I feared I would go out of my mind! Were they cruel to you? Did they hurt you?"

349

Not half so cruel as you were once, he thought silently. Half of him wanted to shout at her, to remind her that he had once begged her to run away with him, to choose him over his brother. The other half wanted to sweep her into his arms, into his bed, into his life. Yet he dared not look at her, for he feared the latter emotion and knew it was the worst treachery.

"I was only held prisoner for a day," he said, his voice hardening, "They butchered the other elves that they held, but I was fortunate enough to escape."

He thought of the human woman who had—unwittingly, so far as he knew—aided his flight. She had been very beautiful, for a human. Her body possessed a fullness that was voluptuous, that he had to admit he found strangely attractive. Yet she was nothing to him. He didn't even know her name. She was far away from him, probably forever. While Hermathya . . .

Kith-Kanan sensed her moving closer. Her hand touched his shoulder and he stood very still.

"You'd better go. I've got to get ready for the banquet." Still he did not look at her.

For a second, she was silent, and he felt very conscious of her delicate touch. Then her hand fell away. "I . . ." She didn't complete the thought.

As he heard her move toward the door, he turned from the windows to watch her. She smiled awkwardly before she left, pulling the door closed behind her.

For a long time afterward, he remained motionless. The image of her body remained burning in his mind. It frightened him terribly that he found himself wishing she had chosen to remain.

* * * * *

Kith-Kanan's reentry into the royal court of Silvanost felt to him like a sudden immersion into icy water. Nothing in his recent experience bore any resemblance to the gleaming marble-floored hall, and the elegant nobles and ladies dressed in their silken robes, which were trimmed in fur and silver thread and embellished with diamonds, emeralds, and rubies.

The discussions with his family, even the banquet of the previous night, had not prepared him for the full formality of the Hall of Audience. Now he found himself speaking to a faceless congregation of stiff coats and noble gowns, describing the course of the war to date. Finally his report was done, and the elves dissolved smoothly into private discussions.

"Who's that?" Kith-Kanan asked Sithas, indicating a tall elf who had just arrived and now made his way to the throne.

"I'll introduce you." Sithas rose and gestured the elf forward. "This is Lord Quimant of Oakleaf, of whom I have spoken. This is my brother, Kith-Kanan, general of the elven army."

"I am indeed honored, my lord," said Quimant, with a deep bow.

"Thank you," Kith replied, studying his face. "My brother tells me that your aid has been invaluable in supporting the war effort."

"The Speaker is generous," the lord said to Kith-Kanan modestly. "My contribution pales in comparison to the sacrifices made by you and all of your warriors. If we can but provide you with reliable blades, that is my only wish."

For a moment, Kith was struck by the jarring impression that Lord Quimant, in fact, wished for a great deal more out of the war. That moment passed, and Kith noticed that his brother seemed to place tremendous confidence and warmth in Hermathya's cousin.

"What word from our esteemed ambassador?" asked Sithas.

"Than-Kar will attend our court, but not until after the noon hour," reported the lord. "He seems to feel that he has no pressing business here."

"That's the problem!" snapped the Speaker harshly.

Quimant changed the topic. To Sithas and Kith-Kanan, he described some additional expansions of the Clan Oakleaf mines, though the general paid little attention. Restlessly his eyes roamed the crowd, seeking Hermathya. He felt a vague relief that she was not present. He had felt likewise when she didn't attend the previous night's banquet, pleading a mild illness.

The evening passed with excruciating slowness. Kith-Kanan stood tersely as he was plied with invitations to banquets and hunting trips. Some of the ladies gave him other types of invitations, judging from the suggestive tilts of their smiles or the coy lowerings of demure eyelashes. He felt like a prize stag whose antlers were coveted for everybody's mantel.

Kith found himself, much to his astonishment, actually looking back with fondness on the grim, battle-weary conversations he had most nights with his fellow warriors. They might have squatted around a smoky fire for illumination, caked with mud and smelling of weeks of accumulated grime, yet somehow that all seemed so much more real than did this pompous display!

Finally the fanfare of trumpets announced the arrival of the dwarven ambassador and his retinue. Kith-Kanan stared in surprise as Than-Kar led a column of more than thirty armed and armored dwarves into the hall. They marched in a muddy file toward the throne, finally halting to allow their leader to swagger forward on his own.

The Theiwar dwarf bore little resemblance to the jovial Dunbarth Ironthumb, of the Hylar Clan, whom Kith-Kanan had met years before. He found Than-Kar's wide eyes, with their surrounding whites and tiny, beadlike pupils, disturbing—like the eyes of a madman, he thought. The dwarf was filthy and unkempt, with a soiled tunic and muddy boots, almost as if he had made a point of his messy appearance for the benefit of the elven general.

"The Speaker has demanded my presence, and I have come," announced the dwarf in a tone ripe with insolence.

Kith-Kanan felt an urge to leap from the Speaker's platform and throttle the obscene creature. With an effort, he held his temper in check.

"My brother has returned from the front," began Sithas, dispensing with the formality of an introduction. "I desire for you to report to him on the status of your nation's involvement."

Than-Kar's weird eyes appraised Kith-Kanan, while a smirk played on the dwarf's lips. "No change," he said bluntly. "My king needs to see some concrete evidence of elven trustworthiness before he will commit dwarven lives to this . . . cause."

Kith felt his face flush, and he took a step forward. "Surely you understand that all the elder races are threatened by this human aggression?" he demanded.

The Theiwar shrugged. "The humans would say that *they* are threatened by elven aggression."

"*They* are the ones who have marched into elven lands! Lands, I might add, that border firmly against the northern flank of your own kingdom!"

"I don't see it that way," snorted the dwarf. "And besides, you have humans among your own ranks! It almost seems to me that it is a family feud. If they see fit to join, why should dwarves get involved?"

Sithas turned in astonishment to Kith-Kanan, though the speaker remained outwardly composed.

"We have no humans fighting on the side of our forces. There are some—women and children, mostly—who have taken shelter in the fortress for the siege. They are merely innocent victims of the war. They do not change its character!"

"More to the point, then," spoke the ambassador, his voice an accusing hiss, "explain the presence of elves in the Army of Ergoth!"

"Lies!" shouted Sithas, forgetting himself and springing to his feet. The hall erupted in shouts of anger and denial from courtiers and nobles pressing forward. Than-Kar's bodyguards bristled and raised their weapons.

"Entire ranks of elves," continued the dwarf as the crowd murmured. "They resist your imperial hegemony—"

"They are traitors to the homeland!" snapped Sithas.

"A question of semantics," argued Than-Kar. "I merely mean to illustrate that the confused state of the conflict makes a dwarven intervention seem rash to the point of foolishness."

Kith-Kanan could hold himself in check no longer. He stepped down from the platform and stared at the dwarf, who was a foot or more shorter than himself. "You distort the truth in a way that can only discredit your nation!"

He continued, his voice a growl. "Any elves among the ranks of Ergoth are lone rogues, lured by human coin or promises of power. Even the likes of you cannot blur the clear lines of this conflict. You spout your lies and your distortions from the safety of this far city; hiding like a coward behind the robes of diplomacy. You make me sick!"

Than-Kar appeared unruffled as he stepped aside to address Sithas. "This example of your general's impetuous behavior will be duly reported to my king. It cannot further your cause."

"You set a new standard for diplomatic excess, and you try my patience to its limits. Leave, *now*!" Sithas hissed the words with thick anger, and the hall fell deathly silent.

If the dwarf was affected by the speaker's rage, however, he concealed his emotions well. With calculated insolence, he marched his column about and then led them from the Hall of Audience.

"Throw open the windows!" barked the Speaker of the Stars. "Clear the stench from the air!"

Kith-Kanan slumped to sit on the steps of the royal dais, ignoring the surprised looks from some of the stiff-backed elven nobles. "I could have strangled him with pleasure," he snarled as his brother came to sit beside him.

"The audience is over," Sithas announced to the rest of the elves, and Kith-Kanan sighed with concern as the last of the anonymous nobles left. The only ones remaining in the great hall were Quimant, the twins, and Nirakina.

"I know I shouldn't have let him get under my skin like that. I'm sorry," the general said to the Speaker.

"Nonsense. You said things I've wanted to voice for months. It's better to have a warrior say them than a head of state." Sithas paused awkwardly. "What he *did* say—how much truth was there to it?"

"Very little," sighed Kith-Kanan. "We are sheltering humans in the fortress, most of them the wives and families of Wildrunners. They would be slain on sight if they fell into the hands of the enemy."

"And are elves fighting for *Ergoth?*" Sithas couldn't keep the dismay from his voice.

"A few rogues, as I said," Kith admitted. "At least, we've had reports of them. I saw one myself in the human camp. But these turncoats are not numerous enough that we have taken notice of them on the field."

He groaned and leaned backward, remembering the offensive and arrogant Theiwar dwarf. "That *lout!* I suppose it's a good thing I didn't have my sword at my side."

"You're tired," said Sithas. "Why don't you relax for a while. This round of banquets and courts and all-night meetings, I'm sure, takes an adjustment. We can talk tomorrow."

"Your brother is right. You *do* need rest," Nirakina added in a maternal tone. "I'll have dinner sent to your apartments!"

* * * * *

The dinner arrived, as Nirakina had promised. Kith-Kanan guessed that his mother had sent orders to the kitchen, and someone in the kitchen had communicated the situation to another interested party. For it was Hermathya who knocked on his door and entered.

"Hello, Hermathya," he said, sitting up in the bed. He wasn't particularly surprised to see her, and if he was honest with himself, neither was he very much dismayed.

"I took this from the serving girl," she said, bringing forward a large silver tray with domed, steaming dishes and crystal platters. Once again he was struck by her air of youth and innocence.

Memories of the two of them together . . . Kith-Kanan felt a sudden resurgence of desire, a feeling that he thought had been gone for years. He wanted to take her in his arms. Looking into her eyes, he knew that she desired the same thing.

"I'll get up. We can dine near the windows." He didn't want to suggest they go to the balcony. He felt there was something furtive and private about her visit.

"Just stay there," she said softly. "I'll serve you in bed."

He wondered what she meant, at first. Soon he learned, as the dinner grew cold upon a nearby table.

The Morning After

10

Hermathya slipped away sometime during the middle of the night, and Kith-Kanan felt profoundly grateful in the morning that she was gone. Now, in the cold light of day, the passion that had seized them seemed like nothing so much as a malicious and hurtful interlude. The flame that had once drawn them together ought not to be rekindled.

Kith-Kanan spent most of the day with his brother, touring the stables and farriers of the city. He forced himself to maintain focus on the task at hand: gathering additional horses to mount his cavalry forces for the time when the Wildrunnners took to the offensive. They both knew that they would, they *must,* eventually attack the human army. They couldn't simply wait out the siege.

During these hours together, Kith found that he couldn't meet his brother's eyes. Sithas remained cheerful and enthusiastic, friendly in a way that twisted Kith-Kanan's gut. By midafternoon, he made an excuse to leave his twin's company, pleading the need to give Arcuballis some exercise. In reality, he needed an escape, a chance to suffer his guilt in solitude.

The following days in Silvanost passed slowly, making even the bleak confinement in beseiged Sithelbec seem eventful by comparison. He avoided Hermathya, and he found to his relief that she seemed to be avoiding him as well. The few times, he saw her she was with Sithas, playing the doting wife holding tightly to her husband's arm and hanging upon his every word.

In truth, the time dragged for Sithas as well. He knew that Vedvedsica was laboring to create a spell that might allow them to magically ensnare the griffons, but he was impatient to begin the quest. He ascribed Kith-Kanan's unease to similar impatience. When they were together, they spoke only of the war and waited for a message from the mysterious cleric.

That word did not come for eight days, and then, oddly, it arrived in the middle of the night. The twins were wide awake, engaged in deep discussion in Sithas's chambers, when they heard a rustling on the balcony beyond the open window. Sithas drew the draperies aside, and the sorcerous cleric stepped into the room.

Kith-Kanan's eyes immediately fell upon Vedvedsica's hand, for he carried a long ivory tube, the ends capped by cork. Several arcane sigils, in black, marked its alabaster surface.

The cleric raised the object, and the twins instinctively understood, even before Vedvedsica uncorked the end and withdrew a rolled sheet of oiled vellum. Unrolling the scroll, he showed them a series of symbols scribed in the Old Script.

"The spell of command," the priest explained softly. "With this magic, I believe the griffons can be tamed."

* * * * *

The twins planned to depart after one more day of final preparations. With the scroll at last a reality, a new urgency marked their activity. They met with Nirakina and Lord Quimant shortly after breakfast, a few hours after Vedvedsica had departed.

The four of them gathered in the royal library, where a fire crackled in the hearth to disperse the autumnal chill. Sithas brought the scroll, though he placed his cloak over it as he set it on the floor. They all sat in the great leather-backed chairs that faced the fire.

"We have word of a discovery that may change the course of the war—for the better," announced Kith.

"Splendid!" Quimant was enthusiastic. Nirakina merely looked at her sons, her concern showing in the furrowing of her brow.

"You know of Arcuballis, of course," continued the warrior. "He was given to Siithel—to father—by a 'merchant' from the north." According to the strategy he and Sithas had developed, they would say nothing about the involvement of the gray cleric. "We have since learned that the Khalkist Mountains are home to a great herd of the creatures—hundreds of them, at least."

"Do you have proof of this, or is it merely rumor?" asked Nirakina. Her face had grown pale.

"They have been seen," explained Kith-Kanan, glossing over the question. He told Quimant and Nirakina of his dream on the night before he departed Sithelbec. "Right down to the three volcanoes, it bears out everything we've been able to learn."

"Think of the potential!" Sithas added. "A whole wing of flying cavalry! Why, the passage of Arcuballis alone sent hundreds of horses into a stampede. A sky full of griffons could very well rout the whole Army of Ergoth!"

"It seems a great leap," Nirakina said slowly and quietly, "from the knowledge of griffons in a remote mountain range to a trained legion of flyers, obeying the commands of their riders." She was still pale, but her voice was strong and steady.

"We believe we can find them," Sithas replied levelly. "We leave at tomorrow's sunrise to embark upon this quest."

"How many warriors will you take?" asked Nirakina, knowing as they all did the legends of the distant Khalkists. Tales of ogres, dark and evil dwarves, even tribes of brutish hill giants—these comprised the folklore whispered by the average elf regarding the mountain range that was the central feature of the continent of Ansalon.

"Only the two of us will go." Sithas faced his mother, who appeared terribly frail in her overly large chair.

"We'll ride Arcuballis," Kith-Kanan explained quickly. "And he'll cover the distance in a fraction of the time it would take an army—even if we *had* one to send!"

Nirakina looked at Kith-Kanan, her eyes pleading. Her warrior son understood the appeal. She wanted him to volunteer to go alone, leaving the Speaker of the Stars behind. Yet even as this thought flashed in her eyes, she lowered her head.

When she looked up, her voice was firm again. "How will you capture these creatures, assuming that you find them?"

Sithas removed his cloak and picked up the tube from the floor beside his chair. "We have acquired a spell of command from a friend of the House of Silvanos. If we can find the griffons, the spell will bind them to our will."

"It is a more powerful version of the same enchantment that was used to domesticate Arcuballis," added Kith. "It is written in the Old Script. That is one reason why Sithas must go with me—to help me cast the spell by reading the Old Script."

His mother looked at him, nodding calmly, more out of shock than from any true sense of understanding.

Nirakina had stood beside her husband through three centuries of rule. She had borne these two proud sons. She had suffered the news of her husband's murder at the hands of a human and lived through the resulting war that now engulfed her nation, her family, and her people. Now she faced the prospect of her two sons embarking on what seemed to her a mad quest, in search of a miracle, with little more than a prayer of success.

Yet, above all, she was the matriarch of the House of Silver Moon. She, too, was a leader of the Silvanesti, and she understood some things about strength, about ruling, and about risk-taking. She had made known her objections, and she realized that the minds of her sons were set. Now she would give no further vent to her personal feelings.

She rose from her chair and nodded stiffly at each of her sons. Kith-Kanan went to her side, while Sithas remained in his chair, moved by her loyalty. The warrior escorted her to the door. Quimant looked at Sithas then turned to Kith-Kanan as he returned to his chair. "May your quest be speedy and successful. I only wish I could accompany you."

Sithas spoke. "I shall entrust you to act as regent in my absence. You know the details of the nation's daily affairs. I shall also need you to begin the conscription of new troops. By the end of winter, we will have to raise and train a new force to send to the plains."

"I will do everything in my power," pledged Quimant.

"Another thing," added Sithas casually. "If Tamanier Ambrodel returns to the city, he is to be given quarters in the palace. I will need to see him immediately upon my return."

Quimant nodded, rose, and bowed to the twins. "May the gods watch over you," he said then left.

* * * * *

"I have to go. Don't you understand that?" Sithas challenged Hermathya. She stomped about their royal bedchambers before whirling upon him.

"You can't! I forbid it!" Hermathya's voice rose, becoming shrill. Her face, moments before blank with astonishment, now contorted in fury.

"Damn it! *Listen* to me!" Sithas scowled, his own anger rising. Stubborn and untractable, they stared into each other's eyes for a moment.

"I've told you about the spell of bonding. It's in the Old Script. Kith doesn't have the knowledge to use it, even if he found the griffons. *I'm* the only one who can read it properly." He held her shoulders and continued to meet her eyes.

"I have to do this, not just for the good it will do our nation, but for *me! That's* what you have to understand!"

"I *don't* have to, and I won't!" she cried, whirling away from him.

"Kith-Kanan has always been the one to face the dangers and the challenges of the unknown. Now there's something that I must do. I, too, must put my life at risk. For once, I'm not just sending my brother into danger. I'm going myself!"

"But you don't *have* to!"

Hermathya almost spat her anger, but Sithas wouldn't budge. If she could see any sense in his desire to test himself, she wouldn't admit it. Finally, in exhaustion and frustration, the Speaker of the Stars stormed out of the chambers.

* * * * *

He found Kith-Kanan in the stables, instructing the saddle-maker on modifications to Arcuballis's harness. The griffon would be able to carry the two of them, but his flight would be slowed, and they would be able to take precious little in the way of provisions and equipment.

"Dried meat—enough for only a few weeks," recited Kith-Kanan, examining the bulging saddlebags. "A pair of waterskins, several extra cloaks. Tinder and flint, a couple of daggers. Extra bowstrings. We'll carry our bows where we can get at them in a hurry, of course. And two-score arrows. Do you have a practical sword?"

For a moment, Sithas flushed. He knew that the ceremonial blade he had carried for years would be inadequate for the task at hand. Cast in a soft silver alloy, its shining blade was, inscribed with all manner of symbols in the Old Script, reciting the glorious history of the House of Silvanos. It was beautiful and valuable, but impractical in a fight. Still, it rankled him to hear his brother speak ill of it. "Lord Quimant has procured a splendid longsword for me," he said stiffly. "It will do quite nicely."

"Good." Kith took no notice of his brother's annoyance. "We'll have to leave our metal armor behind. With this load, Arcuballis can't handle the extra weight. Have you a good set of leathers?"

Again Sithas replied in the affirmative.

"Well, we'll be ready to go at first light, then. Ah . . ." Kith hesistated, then asked, "How did Hermathya react?" Kith knew that Sithas had put off telling Hermathya that he would be gone for weeks on this journey.

"Poorly," Sithar, said, with a grimace. He offered no elaboration, and Kith-Kanan did not probe further.

They attended a small banquet that night, joined by Quimant and Nirakina. and several other nobles. Hermathya was conspicuously absent, a fact for which Kith was profoundly grateful, and the mood was subdued.

He had found himself anxious throughout these last days that Hermathya would tell her husband about her dalliance with his brother. Kith-Kanan had tried to put aside the memory of that night, treating the incident as some sort of waking dream. This made his guilt somewhat easier to bear.

After dinner, Nirakina handed Sithas a small vial. The stoneware jar was tightly plugged by a cork.

"It is a salve, made by the clerics of Quenesti Pah," she explained. "Miritelisina gave it to me. If you are injured, spread a small amount around the area of the wound. It will help the healing."

"I hope we won't need it, but thank you," said Sithas. For a moment, he wondered if his mother was about to cry, but again her proud heritage sustained her. She embraced each of her sons warmly, kissed them, and wished them the luck of the gods. Then she retired to her chambers.

Both of the twins spent much of the night awake, taut with the prospect of the upcoming adventure. Sithas tried to see his wife in the evening and again before sunrise, but she wouldn't open her door even to speak to him. He settled for a few moments with Vanesti, holding his son in his arms and rocking him gently while night gave way to early dawn.

Day of Departure, Autumn

11

They met at the stables before dawn. As they had requested, no one came to see them off. Kith threw the heavy saddle over the restless griffon's back, making sure that the straps that passed around Arcuballis's wings were taut. Sithas stood by, watching as his brother hoisted the heavy saddlebags over the creature's loins. The elf took several minutes to make sure that everything was secure.

They mounted the powerful beast, with Kith-Kanan in the fore, and settled into the specially modified saddle. Arcuballis trotted from the stable doors into the wide corral. Here he sprang upward, the thick muscles of his legs propelling them from the ground. His powerful wings beat the still air and thrust downward. In a single fluid motion, he leaped again and they were airborne.

The griffon labored over the garden and then along the city's main avenue, slowly gaining altitude. The twins saw the towers of the city pats alongside then slowly fall behind. Rosy hues of dawn quickly brightened to pink, then pale blue, as the sun seemed to explode over the eastern horizon into a crisp and cloudless day.

"By the gods, this is fantastic!" cried Sithas, overcome with the beauty of their flight, with the sight of Silvanost, and perhaps with the exhilaration of at last escaping the confining rituals of his daily life.

Kith-Kanan smiled to himself, pleased with his brother's enthusiasm. They flew above the Thon-Thalas River, following the silvery ribbon of its path. Though autumn had come to the elven lands, the day was brilliant with sunshine, the air was clear, and a brilliant collage of colors spread across the forested lands below.

The steady pulse of the griffon's wings carried them for many hours. The city quickly fell away; though the Tower of the Stars remained visible for some time. By midmorning, however, they soared over pristine forestland. No building broke the leafy canopy to indicate that anyone—elf, human, or whatever—lived here.

"Are these lands truly uninhabited?" inquired Sithas, studying the verdant terrain.

"The Kagonesti dwell throughout these forests," explained Kith. The wild elves, considered uncouth and barbaric by the civilized Silvanesti, did not build structures to dominate the land or monuments to their own greatness. Instead, they took the land as they found it and left it that way when they passed on.

Arcuballis swept northward, as if the great griffon felt the same joy at leaving civilization behind. Despite the heavy packs and his extra passenger, he showed no signs of tiring during a flight that lasted nearly twelve hours and carried them several hundred miles. When they ultimately landed to make camp, they touched earth beside a clear pool in a sheltered forest grotto. The two elves and their mighty beast spent a peaceful night, sleeping almost from the moment of sunset straight through until dawn.

Their flight took them six days. After the first day, they took a two-hour interval at midday so that Arcuballis could rest. They passed beyond the forests on the third day, then into the barren plains of Northern Silvanesti, a virtual desert, uninhabited and undesired by the elves.

Finally they flew beside the jagged teeth of the Khalkist Range, the mountainous backbone of Ansalon. For two full days, these craggy peaks rose to their left, but Kith-Kanan kept them over the dry plains, explaining that the winds here were more easily negotiable than they would be among the jutting summmits.

Eventually they reached the point where they had to turn toward the high valleys and snow-filled swales if they expected to find any trace of their quarry. Arcuballis strained to gain altitude, carrying them safely over the sheer crests of the foothills and flying above the floor of a deep valley, following the contours of its winding course as steep ridgelines rose to the right and left, high above them.

They camped that night, the seventh night of their journey, near a partially frozen lake in the base of a steep-sided, circular valley. Three waterfalls, now frozen into massive icicles, plunged toward them from the surrounding heights. They chose the spot for its small grove of hardy cedars, reasoning correctly that firewood would be a useful, and rare, commodity among these lofty realms.

Sithas helped his brother build the fire. He discovered that he relished the feel of the small axe blade cutting the wood into kindling. The campfire soon crackled merrily, and the warmth on his hands was especially gratifying because his work had provided the welcome heat.

Thus far, their journey seemed to the Speaker of the Stars to be the grandest adventure he had ever embarked upon.

"Where do you think the Lords of Doom lie from here?" he asked his brother as they settled back to gnaw on some dried venison. The three volcanoes were rumored to lie at the heart of the range.

"I don't know exactly," Kith admitted. "Somewhere to the north and west of here, I should say. The city of Sanction lies on the far side of the range, and if we reach it, we'll know we've gone too far."

"I never knew that the mountains could be so beautiful, so majestic," Sithas added, gazing at the awesome heights around them. The sun had long since left their deep valley, yet its fading rays still illuminated some of the highest summits in brilliant reflections of white snow and blue ice.

"Forbidding, too."

They looked toward Arcuballis as the griffon curled up near the fire. His massive bulk loomed like a wall.

"Now we'll have to start searching," Kith commented. "And that might take us a long time!"

"How big can this range be?" asked Sithas skeptically. "After all, we can fly."

* * * * *

Fly they did, for day after grueling, bone-chilling day. The pleasant autumn of the lowlands swiftly became brutal winter in these heights. They pressed to the highest elevations, and Sithas felt a fierce exultation as they passed among the lofty ridges, a sense of accomplishment that dwarfed anything he had done in the city. When the snow blew into their faces, he relished the heavy cloak pulled tight against his face; when they spent a night in the barren heights, he enjoyed the search for a good campsite.

Kith-Kanan remained quiet, almost brooding, for hours during their aerial search. The guilt of his night with Hermathya gnawed at him, and he cursed his foolish weakness. He longed to confess to Sithas, to ask for his forgiveness, but in his heart, he sensed that this would be a mistake—that his brother would never forgive him. Instead, he bore his pain privately.

Some days the sun shone brightly, and then the white bowls of the valleys became great reflectors. They both learned, the first such day, to leave no skin exposed under these conditions. Their cheeks and foreheads were brutally seared, yet ironically the cold air prevented them from feeling the sunburn until it had reached a painful state.

On other days, gray clouds pressed like a leaden blanket overhead, cloaking the highest summits and casting the vistas in a bleak and forbidding light. Then the snow would fly, and Arcuballis had to seek firm ground until the storm passed. A driving blizzard could toss the griffon about like a leaf in the wind.

Always they pushed through the highest summits of the range, searching each valley for sign of the winged creatures. They swung southward until they reached the borders of the ogrelands of Blöten. The valleys were lower here, but they saw signs of the brutish inhabitants everywhere—forestlands blackened by swath burning, great piles of tailings. Knowing that the griffons would seek a more remote habitat, they turned back to the north, following a snakelike glacier higher and higher into the heart of the range.

Here the weather hit them with the hardest blow yet. A mass of dark clouds appeared with explosive suddenness to the west. The expanse covered the sky and swiftly spread toward them. Arcuballis dove, but the snow swirled so thickly they couldn't see the valley floor.

'There—a ledge!" shouted Sithas, pointing over his brother's shoulder.

I see it." Kith-Kanan directed Arcuballis onto a narrow shelf of rock protected by a blunt overhang. Sheer cliffs dropped away below them and climbed over their heads. Winds buffeted them even as the griffon landed, and further flight seemed suicidal. A narrow trail seemed to lead along the cliff face, winding gradually downward from their perch, but they elected to wait out the storm.

"Look—it's flat and wide here," announced Sithas, clearing away some loose rubble. "Plenty of space to rest, even for Arcuballis."

Kith nodded.

They unsaddled the creature and settled in to wait as the winds rose to a howling crescendo and the snow flew past them.

"How long will this last?" asked Sithas.

Kith-Kanan shrugged, and Sithas suddenly felt foolish for the question. They unpacked their bedrolls and huddled together beside the warm flank of the griffon and the cold protection of the cliff wall. Their bows, arrows, and swords they placed within easy reach. Just beyond their feet, the slope of the mountainside plummeted away, a sheer precipice vanishing into the snow-swept distance.

They coped, on their remote ledge, for two solid days as the blizzard raged around them and the temperature dropped. They had no fuel for a fire, so they could only huddle together, taking turns sleeping so that they didn't both drift into eternal rest, blanketed by a deep winter cold.

Sithas was awake at the end of the second day, shaking his head and pinching himself to try to remain alert. His hands and feet felt like blocks of ice, and he alternated his position frequently, trying to warm some part of his body against the bulk of Arcuballis.

He noticed the pace of the griffon's breathing change slightly. Suddenly the creature raised his head, and Sithas stared with him into the snow-obscured murk.

Was there something there, down the path that they had seen when they landed, the one that seemed to lead away from this ledge? Sithas blinked, certain his eyes deceived him, but it *had* seemed as if something moved!

In the next instant, he gaped in shock as a huge shape lunged out of the blowing snow. It towered twice as high as an elf, though its shape was vaguely human. It had arms and hands—indeed, one of those clutched a club the size of a small tree trunk. This weapon loomed high above Sithas as the creature charged forward.

"Kith! A giant!" He shouted, kicking his brother to awaken him. At the same time, purely by instinct, he picked up the sword he had laid by his side.

Arcuballis reacted faster than the elf, springing toward the giant with a powerful shriek. Sithas watched in horror as the monster's club crashed into the griffon's skull. Soundlessly Arcuballis went limp, disappearing over the side of the ledge like so much discarded garbage.

"No!" Kith-Kanan was awake now and saw the fate of his beloved steed. At the same time, the twins saw additional shapes, two or three more, materializing from the blizzard behind the first giant. Snarling with hatred, the elven warrior grabbed his blade.

The monster's face, this close, was more grotesque than Sithas had first thought. Its eyes were small, bloodshot, and very close-set while its nose bulged like an outcrop of rock. Its mouth was garishly wide. The giant's maw gaped open as the beast fought, revealing blood-red gums and stubs of ivory that looked more like tusks than teeth.

A deep and pervasive terror seized Sithas, freezing him in place. He could only stare in horror at the approaching menace. Some distant part of his mind told him that he should react, should fight, but his muscles refused to budge. His fear paralyzed him.

Kith-Kanan rose into a fighting crouch, menacing the giant with his sword. Tears streaked Kith's face, but grief only heightened his rage and his deadly competence. His hand remained steady. Seeing him, Sithas shook his head, finally freeing himself from his immobility.

Sithas leaped to his feet and lunged at the monster, but his foot slipped on the icy rocks, and he fell to the rocks at the very lip of the precipice, slamming the wind from his lungs. The giant loomed over him.

But then he saw his brother, darting forward with incredible agility, raising his blade and thrusting at the giant's belly. The keen steel struck home, and the creature howled, lurching backward. One of its huge boots slipped from the ice-encrusted ledge, and with a scream, the monster vanished into the gray storm below.

Now they saw that the three other giants approached them, one at a time along the narrow ledge. Each of the massive creatures carried a huge club. The first of these lumbered forward, and Kith-Kanan darted at him. Sithas, recovering his breath, climbed to his feet.

The giant stepped back, then swung a heavy blow at the dodging, weaving elf. Kith danced away, and then struck so quickly that Sithas didn't see the movement. The tip of the sword cut a shallow opening in the giant's knee before the elf skipped backward.

But that cut was telling. Sithas watched in astonishment as the giant's leg collapsed beneath it. Thrashing in futility with its hamlike hands, the giant slid slowly over the edge, vanishing with a shriek that was quickly lost in the howling of the storm.

While the other two giants gaped in astonishment, Kith-Kanan remained a dervish of motion. He charged the massive creatures, sending them slipping and sliding backward along the ledge to avoid his keen blade, a blade that now glistened with blood.

"Kith, watch out!" Sithas found his voice and urged his brother on. Kith-Kanan appeared to stumble, and one the giants crashed his heavy club downward. But again the elf moved too quickly, and the club splintered against bare stone. Kith rolled toward this one, rising into a crouch between its stumplike legs. He stabbed upward with all the strength in his powerful arms and shoulders, and then dove out of the way as the mortally wounded giant bellowed its pain.

Sithas raced toward his brother, recognizing Kith's danger. He saw his twin slip as he tried to hug the cliff wall between the dying giant and its sole remaining comrade.

The latter swung his club with strength born of desperate terror. The loglike beam, nearly a foot thick at its head, crashed into Kith-Kanan's chest and crushed his body against the rough stone wall behind him. Sithas saw his brother's head snap back and blood explode from his skull. Slowly the elf sank to the ledge.

The wounded giant collapsed, and Sithas sent it toppling from the brink. The last of the brutes looked at the charging elf, the twin of the warrior he had just felled, and turned away. He bounded along the narrow ledge, descending across the face of the mountain, away from the niche that had sheltered the twins. In seconds, he disappeared into the distance.

Sithas paid no further attention to the monster. He knelt at Kith's side, appalled at the blood that gushed from his brother's mouth and nose, staining and matting his long blond hair.

"Kith, don't die! Please!" He didn't realize that he was sobbing.

Gingerly he lifted his brother, surprised at Kith's frailty—or perhaps at his own desperate strength. He carried him to their niche. Every cloak, every blanket and tunic that they carried, he used to cushion and wrap Kith-Kanan. His brother's eyes were closed. A very faint motion, a rising and falling of his chest, gave the only sign that Kith lived.

Now night fell with abruptness, and the wind seemed to pick up. The snow stung Sithas's face as sharply as did his own tears. He took Kith's cold hand in his and sat beside his brother, not expecting either of them to be alive to greet the dawn.

Dawn

12

Somehow Sithas must have dozed off, for he suddenly noticed that the wind, the snow—indeed, the entire storm—had vanished. The air, now still, had become icy cold, with an absolute clarity that only comes in the highest mountains during the deepest winter frosts.

The sun hadn't risen yet, but the Speaker could see that all around him towered summits of unimaginable heights, plumed with great collars of snow. Gray and impassive, like stone-face giants with thick beards of frost, they regarded him from their aloof vantages.

The brothers' ledge perched along one of the two steep sides of the valley. To the south, on Sithas's left as he looked outward, the valley stretched and twisted toward the low, forested country from which they had come. To the right, it appeared to end in a cirque of steep-walled peaks. At one place, he saw a saddle that, while still high above him, seemed to offer a lone, treacherous path into the next section of the mountain range.

Kith-Kanan lay motionless beside him. His skin had the paleness of death, and Sithas had to struggle against a resurgence of despair. He couldn't allow himself to abandon hope; he was their only chance for survival. The quest for the griffons, the excitement and adventure of the journey he had known before, were all forgotten now, overwhelmed by the simple and basic wish to continue living.

The valley below him, he saw, was not as deep as they had guessed when the storm struck. Their shelf was a bare hundred feet above level ground. He leaned out to look over the edge, but all he saw was a vast drift of snow piled against the cliff. If the bodies of the giants or of gallant, fallen Arcuballis remained down there somewhere, he had no way to know it. No trees grew in this high valley, nor did he see any signs of animal life. In fact, the only objects that met his eyes, in any direction, were the bedrock of the mountain range and the snowy blanket that covered it.

With a groan, he slumped back against the cliff. They were doomed! He could see no possibility of any fate other than death in this remote valley. His throat ached, and tears welled in his eyes. What good was his court training in a situation like this?

"Kith!" he moaned. "Wake up! *Please!*"

When his brother made no response, Sithas collapsed facedown on his cloak. A part of him wished that he was as unconscious of their fate as Kith-Kanan.

For the whole long day, he lay as if in a trance. He pulled their cloaks about them as night fell, certain that they would freeze to death. Kith-Kanan hadn't moved—indeed, he barely breathed. Broken by his own anguish, the Speaker finally tumbled into restless sleep.

It was not until the next morning that he regained some sense of purpose. What did they need? Warmth, but there was no firewood in sight. Water, but their skins of the liquid had frozen solid, and without fire, they couldn't melt snow. Food, of which they had several strips of dried venison and some bread. But how could he feed Kith-Kanan while his brother remained unconscious?

Again the feeling of hopelessness seized him. If only Arcuballis were here! If only Kith could walk! If only the giants . . . He snarled at himself in anger, realizing the idiocy of his ramblings.

Instead, he pushed himself to his feet, suddenly aware of a terrible stiffness in his own body. He studied the route along the narrow ledge that twisted its way from their niche to the valley floor. It looked negotiable—barely. But what could he do if he was lucky enough to reach the ground?

He noted, for the first time, a dark patch on the snow at the edge of the flat expanse. The sun had crested the eastern peaks by now, and Sithas squinted into the brightness.

What caused the change of coloration in the otherwise immaculate surface of snow? Then it dawned on him—water! Somewhere beneath that snow, water still flowed! It soaked into the powder above, turning it to slush and causing it to settle.

With a clear goal now, Sithas began to act. He took his own nearly empty water skin, since Kith's contained a block of ice that would be impossible to remove. As he turned away from the sun, however, he had another idea. He set Kith's water skin in the sunlight, on a flat stone. He found several other dark boulders and placed them beside the skin, taking care that they didn't block the sunlight.

Then he started down the treacherous ledge. In many places, the narrow path was piled with snow, and he used his sword to sweep these drifts away, carefully probing so that he did not step off the cliff.

Finally he reached a spot where he was able to drop into the soft snow below. He pushed his way through the deep fluff, leaving a trench behind him as he worked his way toward the dark patch of slush. The going was difficult, and he had to rest many times, but finally he reached his goal.

Pausing again, he heard a faint trill of sound from beneath the snow, the gurgling of water as it babbled along a buried stream. He poked and pressed with his sword, and the surface of snow dropped away, revealing a flowage about six inches deep.

But that was enough. Sithas suspended his skin from the tip of his sword and let it soak in the stream. Though it only filled halfway, it was more water than they had tasted in two days, and he greedily drained the waterskin. Then he refilled it, as much as possible with his awkward rig, and turned back to the cliff. It took him more than an hour to carry it back up to Kith-Kanan, but the hour of toil seemed to warm and vitalize him.

His brother showed no change. Sithas dribbled some water into Kith's mouth, just enough to wet his tongue and throat. He also washed away the blood that had caked on the elf's frostbitten face. There was even some water left over, since Kith's frozen waterskin had begun to melt from the heat of the sun.

"What now, Kith?" Sithas asked softly.

He heard a sound from somewhere and looked anxiously around. Again came the noise, which sounded like rocks falling down a rough slope.

Then he saw a distinct movement across the valley. White shapes leaped and sprang along the sheer face, and for a moment, he thought they flew, so effectively did they defy gravity. More rocks broke free, crashing and sliding downward. He saw that these nimble creatures moved upon hooves.

He had heard about the great mountain sheep that dwelled in the high places, but never had he observed them before. One, obviously the ram, paused and looked around, raising his proud head high. Sithas glimpsed his immense horns, swirling from the creature's forehead.

For a moment, he wondered at the presence of these great beasts as he watched them press downward. They reached the foot of the cliff, and then the ram bounded through the powder, plowing a trail for the others.

"The water!" Sithas spoke aloud to himself. The sheep needed the water, too!

Indeed, the ram was nearing the shallow stream. Alert, he looked carefully around the valley, and Sithas, though he was out of sight, remained very still. Finally the proud creature lowered his head to drink. He stopped frequently to look around, but he drank for a long time before he finally stepped away from the small hole in the snow.

Then, one by one, the females came to the water. The ram stood protectively beside them, his proud head and keen eyes shifting back and forth.

The group of mountain sheep spent perhaps an hour beside the water hole, each of the creatures slaking its thirst. Finally, with the ram still in the lead, they turned back along the tracks and reclimbed the mountain wall.

Sithas watched them until they disappeared from view. The magnificent creatures moved with grace and skill up the steep face of rock. They looked right at home here—so very different from himself!

A soft groan beside him pulled his attention instantly back to Kith-Kanan.

"Kith! Say something!" He leaned over his twin's face, rejoicing to see a flicker of vitality. Kith-Kanan's eyes remained shut, but his mouth twisted into a grimace and he was gasping for breath.

"Here, take a drink. Don't try to move."

He poured a few drops of water onto Kith's lips, and the wounded elf licked them away. Slowly, with obvious pain, Kith-Kanan opened his eyes, squinting at the bright daylight before him.

"What . . . happened?" he asked weakly. Abruptly his eyes widened and his body tensed. "The giants! Where . . . ?"

"It's all right," Sithas told him, giving him more water. "They're dead—or gone, I'm not sure which."

"Arcuballis?" Kith's eyes widened and he struggled to sit up, before collapsing with a dull groan.

"He's . . . gone, Kith. He attacked the first giant, got clubbed over the head, and fell."

"He must be down below!"

Sithas shook his head. "I looked. There's no sign of his body—or of any of the giants, either."

Kith moaned, a sound of deep despair. Sithas had no words of comfort.

"The giants . . . what kind of beasts do you think they were?" asked Sithas.

"Hill giants, I'm sure," Kith-Kanan said after a moment's pause.

"Relatives of ogres, I guess, but bigger. I wouldn't have expected to see them this far south."

"Gods! If only I'd been faster!" Sithas said, ashamed.

"Don't!" snapped the injured elf. "You warned me—gave me time to get my sword out, to get into the fight." Kith-Kanan thought for a moment. "When—how long ago was it, anyway? How much time has passed since—"

"We've been up here for two nights," said Sithas quietly. "The sun has nearly set for the third time." He hestitated, then blurted his question. "How badly are you hurt?"

"Bad enough," Kith said bluntly. "My skull feels like it's been crushed, and my right leg seems as if it is on fire. "

"Your leg?" Sithas had been so worried about the blow to his brother's head that he had paid little attention to the rest of his body.

"It's broken, I think," the elf grunted, gritting his teeth against the pain.

Sithas's mind went blank. A broken leg! It might as well be a sentence of death! How would they ever get out of here with his twin thus crippled? And winter had only begun! If they didn't get out of the mountains quickly, they could be trapped here for months. Another snowfall would make travel by foot all but impossible.

"You'll have to do something about it," Kith said, though it took several moments before the remark registered in Sithas's mind,

"About what?"

"My leg!" The injured elf looked at his twin sharply then toughened his voice. Almost without thinking, he used the tones of command he had become accustomed to when he led the Wildrunners.

"Tell me if the skin is broken, if there's any discoloration—any infection."

"Where? Which leg?" Sithas struggled to focus his thoughts. He had never been so disoriented before in his life.

"The right one, below the knee."

Gingerly, almost trembling, Sithas pulled the blankets and cloaks away from his brother's feet and legs. What he saw was terrifying.

The ugly red swelling had almost doubled the size of the limb from the knee to the ankle, and Kith's leg was bent outward at an awkward angle. For a moment, he cursed himself, as if the injury was his own fault. Why hadn't he thought to examine his brother two days earlier, when Kith had first been injured? Had he twisted the wound more when he moved the fallen elf into the shelter of the rocky niche?

"The—the skin isn't broken," he explained, trying to keep his voice calm. "But it's red. By the gods, Kith, it's blood-red!"

Kith-Kanan grimaced at the news, "You'll have to straighten it. If you don't, I'll be crippled for life!"

The Speaker of the Stars looked at his twin brother, the sense of helplessness growing inside him. But he saw the pain in Kith-Kanan's eyes, and he knew he had no choice but to try.

"It's going to hurt," he warned, and Kith nodded silently, gritting his teeth.

Cautiously he touched the swollen limb, and then instantly recoiled at Kith's sharp gasp of pain. "Don't stop," hissed the wounded elf. "Do it—now!"

Gritting his teeth, Sithas grasped the swollen flesh. His fingers probed the wound, and he felt the break in the bone. Kith-Kanan cried aloud, gasping and choking in his pain as Sithas pulled on the limb.

Kith shrieked again and then, mercifully, collapsed into unconsciousness. Desperately Sithas tugged, forcing his hands and arms to do these things that he knew must be causing Kith-Kanan unspeakable pain.

Finally he felt the bones slip into place.

"By Quenesti Pah, I'm sorry, Kith," Sithas whispered, looking at his brother's terribly pale face.

Quenesti Pah . . . goddess of healing! The invocation of that benign goddess brought his mind around to the small vial his mother had given them before they departed. From Miritelesina, she had said, high priestess of Quenesti Pah. Frantically Sithas dug through the saddlebag, finally discovering the little ceramic jar, plugged with a stout cork.

He popped the cork from the bottle's mouth and immediately recoiled at the pungent scent. Smearing some of the salve on his fingers, he drew off the cloak and spread the stuff on Kith's leg, above and below the wound. That done, he covered his brother with the blankets and leaned back against the stone wall to wait.

Kith-Kanan remained unconscious throughout the impossibly long afternoon as the sun sank through the pale blue sky and finally disappeared behind the western ridge. Still, no sign of movement came from the wounded elf. If anything, he seemed even weaker.

Gently Sithas fed his brother drops of water. He wrapped him in all of their blankets and lay down beside him.

He fell asleep that way, and though he awoke many times throughout the brutally cold night, he stayed at Kith-Kanan's side until dawn began to brighten their valley.

Kith-Kanan showed no sign of reviving consciousness. Sithas looked at his brother's leg and was appalled to see a streak of red running upward, past his knee and into his thigh. What should he do? He had never seen an injury like this before. Unlike Kith-Kanan, he hadn't been confronted by the horrors of battle or by the necessity of self-sufficiency in the wilds.

Quickly the elf took the rest of the cleric's salve and smeared it onto the wound. He knew enough about blood poisoning to realize that if the venomous infection could not be arrested, his brother was doomed. With no way left to treat Kith-Kanan, however, all Sithas could do was pray.

Once again the water in their skins was frozen, and so he made the arduous trek down the narrow pathway from the ledge to the valley floor. The trough in the snow made by his passage on the previous day remained, for the wind had remained blessedly light. Thus he made his way to his snow-rimmed water hole with less difficulty than the day before.

But here he encountered a challenge: the bitter cold of the night had frozen even the rapidly flowing water beneath the snow. He chopped and chipped with his sword, finally exposing a small trickle, less than two inches deep. Only by stretching himself full-length in the snow, and immersing his hand into the frigid waters could he collect enough to carry back to their high campsite.

As he rose from the water hole, he saw the trail of the sheep across from him and remembered the magnificent creatures. Suddenly he was seized by an inspiration, He thought of his bow and arrows, still up on the ledge with Kith-Kanan. How could he conceal himself in order to get close enough to shoot? Unlike Kith-Kanan, he was not an expert archer. A close target would be essential.

He gave up his ponderings in the effort of making his way back to the ledge. Here he found no change in Kith-Kanan, and all he could do was force his brother once again to take a few drops of water between his lips.

Afterward, he strung his bow, checking the smooth surface of the weapon for flaws, the string for knots or frays. As he did so, he heard a clattering of hooves even as he stewed in his frustration. Once again led by the proud ram, the mountain sheep descended from their slope across the valley and made their way to the faint trickle of water. They took turns drinking and watching, with the ram remaining alert.

Once, when the creature's eyes passed across the cliff where Sithas and Kith lay motionless, the animal stiffened. Sithas wondered if he had been discovered and wrestled with a compulsion to quickly nock an arrow and let it fly in the desperate hope of hitting something.

But he forced himself to remain still, and finally the ram relaxed its guard. Sithas sighed and clenched his teeth in frustration as he watched the creatures turn and plow through the snow back toward their mountain fastness. The powdery drifts came to the shoulders of the large ram, and the sheep floundered and struggled until they reached the secure footing of the rocky slope.

The rest of the day passed in frigid monotony. That night was the coldest yet, and Sithas's own shivering kept him awake. He would have been grateful for even such an uncomfortable sign of life from his brother, but Kith-Kanan remained still and lifeless.

The fourth morning on the ridge, Sithas could barely bring himself to emerge from beneath the cloaks and blankets. The sun rose over the eastern ridge, and still he lay motionless.

Then urgency returned, and he sat up in panic. He sensed instinctively that today was his last chance. If he could not feed himself and his brother, they would not experience another dawn.

He grabbed his bow and arrows, strapped his sword to his back, and allowed himself the luxury of one woolen cloak from the pile that sheltered Kith-Kanan. He made his way down the cliff with almost reckless haste. Only after he nearly slipped fifty feet above the valley floor did he calm himself, forcing his feet to move with more precision.

He pushed toward the water hole, feeling sensation return to his limbs and anticipation and tension fill his heart. Finally he reached the place opposite where the sheep came to drink. He didn't allow himself to ponder a distinct possibility: What if the sheep didn't return here today? If they didn't, he and his brother would die. It was a simple as that.

Urgently he swept a shallow excavation in the snow, fearful that the sheep might already be on their way. He swung his eyes to the southern ridge, to the slope the sheep had descended on each of the two previous days, but he saw no sign of movement.

In minutes, Sithas cleared the space he desired. A quick check showed no sign of the sheep. Trembling with tension, he freed his bow and arrows and laid them before him in the snow. Next he knelt, forcing his feet into the powdery fluff behind him. He took the cloak he had brought and laid it before him, before stretching, belly down, on top.

The last thing was the hardest to do. He pulled snow from each side into the excavation, burying his thighs, buttocks, and torso. Only his shoulders, arms, and head remained exposed,

Feeling the chill settle into his bones as he pressed deeper into the snowy cushion, he twisted to the side and pulled still more of the winter powder onto him. His bow, with several arrows ready, he covered with a faint dusting of snow directly in front of him.

Finally he buried his head, leaving an opening no more than two inches in diameter before his face. From this tiny slot, he could see the water hole and he could get enough air to breathe. At last his trap was ready. Now he had only to wait.

And wait. And wait some more. The sun passed the zenith, the hour when the sheep had come to water on each of the previous days, with no sign of the creatures. Cold numbness crept into Sithas's bones. His fingers and toes burned from frostbite, which was bad enough, but gradually he became aware that he was losing feeling in them altogether. Frantically he wiggled and stretched as much as he could within the limitations of his confinement.

Where were the accursed sheep?

An hour of the afternoon passed, and another began. He could no longer keep any sensation in his fingers, Another few hours, he knew, and he would freeze to death.

But then he became aware of strange sensations deep within his snowy cocoon. Slowly, inexplicably, he began to grow warm. The burning returned to his fingertips. The snow around his body formed a cavity, slightly larger than Sithas himself, and he noticed that this snow was wet. It packed tightly, giving him room to move. He noticed wetness in his hair, on his back.

He was actually warm! The cavity had trapped his body heat, melting the snow and warming him with the trapped energy. The narrow slot had solidified before him, and it was with a sense of exhilaration that he realized he could wait here safely for some time.

But the arrival of twilight confirmed his worse fears—the sheep had not come to drink that day. Bitter with the sense of his failure, he tried to ignore the gnawing in his belly as he gathered more water and made the return to the ledge, arriving just as full darkness settled around them.

Had the sheep seen his trap? Had the flock moved on to some distant valley, following the course of some winter migration? He could not know. All he could was try the same plan tomorrow and hope he lived long enough for the effort.

Sithas had to lean close to Kith-Kanan just to hear his brother's breathing. "Please, Kith, don't die!" he whispered. Those words were the only ones he spoke before he fell asleep.

His hunger was painful when he awoke. Once again the day was clear and still, but how long could this last? Grimly he repeated his process of the previous day, making his way to the streambank, settling himself in with his bow and arrows, and trying to conceal any sign of his presence. If the sheep didn't come today, he knew that he would be too weak to try on the morrow.

Exhausted, despairing, and starving, he passed from consciousness into an exhausted sleep.

Perhaps the snow insulated him from sound, or maybe his sleep was deeper than he thought. In any event, he heard nothing as his quarry approached. It wasn't until the sheep had reached the water hole that he woke suddenly. They had come! They weren't twenty feet away!

Not daring to breathe, Sithas studied the ram. The creature was even more magnificent up close. The swirled horns were more than a foot in diameter. The ram's eyes swept around them, but Sithas realized with relief that the animal did not notice his enemy up close.

The ram, as usual, drank his fill and then stepped aside. One by one the ewes approached the small water hole, dipping their muzzles to slurp up the icy liquid. Sithas waited until most of the sheep had drunk. As he had observed earlier, the smallest were the last to drink, and it was one of these that would prove his target.

Finally a plump ewe moved tentatively among her larger sisters. Sithas tensed himself, keeping his hands under the snow as he slowly reached forward for his bow.

Suddenly the ewe raised her head, staring straight at him. Others of the flock skittered to the sides. The elf felt two dozen eyes fixed upon his hiding place. Another second, he suspected, and the sheep would turn in flight. He couldn't give them that opportunity.

With all of the speed, all of the agility at his command, he grasped his bow and arrows and lurched forward from his hiding place, his eyes fixed on the terrified ewe. Vaguely he sensed the sheep spinning, leaping, turning to flee. They struggled through the deep snow, away from this maniacal apparition who rose apparently from the very earth itself.

He saw the ram plunge forward, nudging the ewe that stood stock-still beside the water hole. With a panicked squeal, she turned and tried to spring away.

As she turned, for one split second, she presented her soft flank to the elven archer. Even as he struggled to his feet, Sithas had nocked his arrow. He pulled back the string as his target became a blur before him. Reflexively he let the missile fly. He prayed to all the gods, desperate for a hit,

But the gods were not impressed.

The arrow darted past the ewe's rump, barely grazing her skin, just enough to spur the frightened creature into a maddened flight that took her bounding out of range even as Sithas fumbled with another arrow. He raised the weapon in time to see the ram kick his heels as that great beast, too, sprinted away.

The herd of mountain sheep bounded through the deep snow, springing and leaping in many different directions. Sithas launched another arrow and almost sobbed aloud in frustration as the missile flew over the head of a ewe. Mechanically he nocked another arrow, but even as he did so, he knew that the sheep had escaped.

For a moment, a sensation of catastrophe swept over him. He staggered, weak on his feet, and would have slumped to the ground if something hadn't caught his attention.

A small sheep, a yearling, struggled to break free from a huge drift. The animal was scarcely thirty feet away, bleating pathetically. He knew then he had one more chance—perhaps the *last* chance—for survival. He held his aim steady, sighting down the arrow at the sheep's heaving flank. The animal gasped for breath, and Sithas released the missile.

The steel-tipped shaft shot true, its barbed head striking the sheep behind its foreleg, driving through the heart and lungs in a powerful, fatal strike.

Bleating one final time, a hopeless call to the disappearing herd, the young sheep collapsed. Pink blood spurted from its mouth and nostrils, foaming into the snow. Sithas reached the animal's side. Some instinct caused him to draw his sword, and he slashed the razor-sharp edge across the sheep's throat. With a gurgle of air, the animal perished.

For a moment, Sithas raised his eyes to the ledge across the valley. The ewes scampered upward, while the ram lingered behind, staring back at the elf who had claimed one of his flock. Sithas felt a momentary sense of gratitude to the creature. His heart filled with admiration as he saw it bound higher and higher up the sheer slope.

Finally he reached down and gutted the carcass of his kill. The climb back to Kith-Kanan would be a tough one, he knew, but suddenly his body thrummed with excitement and energy.

Behind him, atop the ridge, the ram cast one last glance downward and then disappeared.

Fresh Blood

13

Sithas cut a slice of meat from his kill on the valley floor, tearing bites from the raw meat, uncaring of the blood that dribbled across his chin. Smacking greedily, he wolfed down the morsel before he carried the rest of the carcass up the steep trail to their ledge. He found Kith-Kanan as still as when he had left him, but now, at least, they had food—they had hope!

The lack of fire created a drawback, but it didn't prevent Sithas from devouring a large chunk of meat as soon as he got it back to the ledge. The blood, while it was still warm, he dribbled into his unconscious brother's mouth, hoping that the warmth and nourishment might have a beneficial effect, however minimal.

Finally sated, Sithas settled back to rest. For the first time in days, he felt something other than bleak despair. He had stalked his game and slain it—something he had never done before, not without beaters and weapon-bearers and guides. Only his brother's condition cast a pall over the situation.

For two more days, Kith's condition showed no signs of change. Gray clouds rolled in, and a dusting of snow fell around them. Sithas trickled more of the ewe's blood into Kith's mouth, hiked down for water several times a day, and offered prayers to Quenesti Pah.

Then, toward sunset of their seventh day on the ledge, Kith groaned and moved. His eyes fluttered open and he looked around in confusion.

"Kith! Wake up!" Sithas leaned over his twin, and slowly

Kith-Kanan's eyes met his own. At first they looked dull and life-less, but even as Sithas watched they grew brighter, more alert.

"What—how did you . . . ?"

Sithas felt weak with relief and helped his brother to sit up. "It's okay, Kith. You'll be all right!" He forced more confidence into his tone than he actually felt.

Kith's eyes fell upon the carcass, which Sithas had perched near the precipice. "What's that?"

"Mountain sheep!" Sithas grinned proudly. "I killed it a few days ago. Here, have some!"

"Raw?" Kith-Kanan raised his eyebrows but quickly saw that there was no alternative. He took a tender loin portion and tore off a piece of meat. It was no delicacy, but it was sustenance. As he chewed, he saw Sithas watching him like a master chef savoring the reaction to a new recipe.

"It's good," Kith-Kanan said, swallowing and tearing off another mouthful.

Excitedly Sithas told him of stalking his prey—about his two wasted arrows and the lucky break that helped him make his kill.

Kith chuckled with a heartiness that belied his wounds and their predicament.

"Your leg," Sithas said concernedly. "How does it feel today?"

Kith groaned and shook his head. "Need a cleric to work on it. I doubt it'll heal enough to carry me."

Sithas sat back, suddenly too tired to go on. Alone, he *might* be able to walk out of these mountains, but he didn't see any way that Kith-Kanan could even get down from this exposed, perilous ledge.

For a while, the brothers sat in silence, watching the sun set. The sky domed over them, pale blue to the east and overhead but fading to a rose hue that blended into a rich lavender along the western ridge. One by one stars winked into sight. Finally darkness crept across the sky, expanding from the east to overhead, then pursuing the last lingering strips of brightness into the west.

"Any sign of Arcuballis?" asked Kith hopefully. His brother shook his head sadly.

"What do we do now?" Sithas asked.

To his dismay, his brother shook his head in puzzlement. "I don't know. I don't think I can get down from here, and we can't finish our quest on this ledge."

"Quest?" Sithas had almost forgotten about the mission that had brought them to these mountains. "You're not suggesting we still seek out the griffons, are you?"

Kith smiled, albeit wanly. "No, I don't think *we* can do much searching. *You,* however, might have a chance."

Now Sithas gaped at his twin. "And leave you here alone? Don't even think about it!"

The wounded elf gestured to stem Sithas's outburst. "We *have* to think about it."

"You won't have a chance up here! I won't abandon you!"

Kith-Kanan sighed. "Our chances aren't that great any way you look at it. Getting out of these mountains on foot is out of the question until spring. And the months of deep winter are still before us. We can't just sit here, waiting for my leg to heal."

"But what kind of progress can I make on foot?" Sithas gestured to the valley walls surrounding them.

Kith-Kanan pointed to the northwest, toward the pass that had been their goal before the storm had driven them to this ledge. The gap between the two towering summits was protected by a steep slope, strewn with large boulders and patches of scree. Strangely, snow had not collected there.

"You could investigate the next valley," the elf suggested. "Remember, we've explored much of the range already."

"That's precious little comfort," Sithas replied. "We flew over the mountains before. I'm not even sure I could climb that pass, let alone explore beyond it."

Kith-Kanan studied the steep slope with a practiced eye. "Sure you could. Go up on the big rocks off to the side there. Stay away from those smooth patches. They look like easy going, but it's sure to be loose scree. You'd probably slip back farther than you climbed with each step. But if you stay on the good footing, you could make it."

The wounded elf turned his eyes upon his skeptical brother and continued. "Even if you don't find the griffons, perhaps you'll locate a cave, or better yet some herdsman's hut. Whatever lies over that ridge, it can't be any more barren than this place."

The Speaker of the Stars squatted back on his haunches, shaking his head in frustration. He had looked at the pass himself over the last few days and privately had decided that he would probably be able to climb it. But he had never considered the prospect of going without his brother.

Finally he made a decision. "I'll go—but just to have a look. If I don't see anything, I'm coming straight back here."

"Agreed." Kith-Kanan nodded. "Now maybe you can hand me another strip of lamb—only this time, I'd like it cooked a little more on the rare side. That last piece was too well done for my taste."

Laughing, Sithas used his dagger to carve another strip of raw mutton. He had found that by slicing it very thin he could make the meat more palatable—at least; more easily chewed. And though it was still cold, it tasted very, very good.

* * * * *

Kith-Kanan sat up, leaning against the back wall of the ledge, and watched Sithas gather his equipment. It was nearly dawn.

"Take some of my arrows," he offered, but Sithas shook his head.

"I'll leave them with you, just in case. . . ."

"In case of what? In case that ram comes looking for revenge?"

Suddenly uncomfortable, Sithas looked away, They both knew that if the hill giants returned, Kith-Kanan would be helpless to do more than shoot a few arrows before he was overcome.

"Kith . . ." He wanted to tell his brother that he wouldn't leave him, that he would stay at his side until his wounds had healed.

"No!" The injured elf raised a hand, anticipating his brother's objections. "We both understand—we *know*—that this is the only thing to do!

"I–I suppose you're right."

"You *know* I'm right!" Kith's voice was almost harsh.

"I'll be back as soon as I can."

"Sithas—be careful."

The Speaker of the Stars nodded dumbly. It made him feel like a traitor to leave his brother like this.

"Good luck, Brother." Kith's voice came to Sithas softly, and he turned back.

They clasped hands, and then Sithas leaned forward to embrace his brother. "Don't run off on me," he told Kith, with a wry smile.

An hour later, he was past the water hole, where he had stopped to refill his skin. Now the pass loomed before him like an icy palisade—the castle wall of some unimaginably monstrous giant. Carefully, still some distance away from the ascent, he selected a route up the slope. He stopped to rest several times before reaching the base, but before noon, he began the rugged climb.

All the time he remained conscious of Kith-Kanan's eyes on his back. He looked behind him occasionally, until his brother became a faint speck on the dark mountain wall. Before he started up the pass, he waved and saw a tiny flicker of motion from the ledge as Kith waved back.

The pass, up close, soared upward and away from him like a steep castle wall, steeper than it had looked from the safe distance of their campsite. The base was a massive, sloping pile of talus— great boulders that, over many centuries, had been pried loose by frost or water to tumble and crash down the mountainside. Now they teetered precariously on top of each other, and powdery snow filled the gaps between them.

Sithas strung his bow across his back, next to his sword. His cloak he removed and tied around his waist, hoping to maintain full freedom of movement.

He picked his way up the talus slope, stepping from rock to rock only after testing each foothold for security. Once several rocks tumbled away beneath him, and he sprang aside just in time. Always he gained altitude, pulling himself up the sheer face with his leather-gloved hands. Sweat dripped into his eyes, and for a moment, he wondered how, in the midst of this snow-swept landscape, could he get so Abyss-cursed hot? Then a swirl of icy wind struck him, penetrating his damp tunic and leggings and bringing an instant shiver to his bones.

Soon he reached the top. Here he encountered long stretches of loose scree, small stones that seemed to slip and slide beneath each footfall, carrying him backward four feet for every five of progress.

Kith-Kanan, of course, had been right. He was always right! His brother knew his way around in country like this, knew how to survive and even how to move and explore, to hunt and find shelter.

Why couldn't it have been Sithas to suffer the crippling injury? A healthy Kith-Kanan would have been able to care for both of them, Sithas knew. Meanwhile, he wrestled with overwhelming despair and hopelessness, and he was not yet out of sight of their base camp!

Shaking off his self-pity, Sithas worked his way sideways, toward steeper, but more solid, shoulders of bedrock. Once his feet slipped away, and he tumbled twenty or thirty feet down the slope, only stopping himself by digging his hands and feet into the loose surface. Cursing, he checked his weapons, relieved to find them intact. Finally he reached a solid rock, with a small shelf shaped much like a chair, where he collapsed in exhaustion.

A quick look upward showed that he had made it perhaps a quarter of the way up the slope. At this rate, he would be stranded here at nightfall, a prospect that terrified him more than he wanted to contemplate.

Resolutely he started upward again, this time climbing along rough outcrops of rock, After only a few moments, he realized that this was by far the easiest climbing yet, and his spirits rose rapidly.

Stepping upward in long strides, he relished a new sense of accomplishment. The valley floor fell away below him; the heavens—and more mountains—beckoned from above. He no longer felt the need for rest. Instead, the climb seemed to energize him.

By midafternoon, he had neared the top of the pass, and here the route narrowed challengingly. Two huge boulders teetered on the slope, with but a narrow crack of daylight between them. One, or both, could very easily roll free, carrying him back down the mountainside if they didn't crush him between them first.

No other route presented itself. To either side of the massive rocks, sheer cliffs soared upward to the pinnacles of the two mountains. The only way through the pass lay between those two precarious boulders.

He didn't hesistate. He approached the rocks and saw that the gap was wide enough to allow him to pass—just barely. He entered the aperture, climbing upward across loose rock.

Suddenly the ground beneath his feet slipped away, and his heart lurched. He felt one of the huge boulders shift with a menacing rumble. The rock walls to either side of him pressed closer, narrowing by an inch or so. Then the rock seemed to settle into place, and he felt no more movement.

With a quick burst of speed, he darted upward, scrambling out of the narrow passage before the rocks could budge again. His momentum carried him farther up the last hundred yards of so of the ascent until finally he stood upon the summit of the pass,

Trees! He saw patches of green among the snowfields, far, far below. Trees, which meant wood, which meant fire! The slope before him, while steep and long, was nowhere near as grueling as the one he had just climbed. He glanced over his left shoulder at the sun, estimating two remaining hours of daylight.

It would have to be enough. He would have a fire tonight, he vowed to himself.

He plunged recklessly downward, sometimes riding a small, tumbling pillow of snow, at other times leaping through great drifts to soft landings ten or fifteen feet below. Exhausted, sweat-soaked, and bone-weary, he finally reached a clump of gnarled cedars far down in the basin. Now, at last, his spirits soared. He used the last illumination of daylight to gather all of the dead limbs he could find. He piled the firewood before an unusually thick trio of evergreens, where he had decided to make his camp.

A mere touch of his steel dagger to the flint he carried in his belt-pouch brought a satisfactory spark. The dry wood kindled instantly, and within minutes, he relished the comfort of a crackling blaze.

* * * * *

Was this the curse of the gods, thought Kith-Kanan, the punishment for his betrayal of his brother's marriage? He leaned against the cliff wall and shut his eyes, wincing not in pain but in guilt.

Why couldn't he have simply died? That would have made things so much easier. Sithas would have been free to perform the quest instead of worrying about him like a nervous nursemaid worries about a feverish babe.

In truth, Kith-Kanan felt more helpless than a crawling infant, for he didn't have even that much mobility.

He had watched Sithas make his way up the slope until his twin had disappeared from sight. His brother had moved with grace and power, surprising Kith with the speed of his ascent.

But as long as Kith-Kanan lay here upon this ledge, he knew Sithas would be tied to this location by their bond of brotherhood. He would explore their immediate surroundings, perhaps, but would never bring himself to travel far beyond.

All because I'm so damned *stupid!* Kith railed at himself. They had made inadequate preparations for attack! They had both dozed off. Only the sacrifice of brave Arcuballis had given the first warning of the hill giants.

Now his griffon was gone, no doubt dead, and he himself was impossibly crippled. Sithas searched alone and on foot. It seemed inevitable to Kith-Kanan that their quest would be a failure.

* * * * *

Sithas dried his clothes and boots, every stitch of which had been soaked by sweat or melting snow, by the crackling fire. It brightened his night, driving back the high mountain darkness that had previously stretched to infinity on all sides, and it warmed his spirits in a way that he wouldn't have thought possible a few hours earlier.

The fire spoke to him with a soothing voice, and it danced for him in sultry allure. It was like a companion, one who could listen to his thoughts and give him pleasure. And finally the fire allowed him to cook a strip of his frozen meat.

That morsel, seared for a few minutes on a forked stick that Sithas plunged into the flames, emerged from the fire covered with ash, blackened and charred on the outside and virtually raw in the center. It was unseasoned, tough, imperfectly preserved . . . and it was unquestionably the most splendid meal that the elf had ever eaten in his life.

The three pines served as a backdrop to his campsite. Sithas scraped away the small amount of snow here and cleared for himself a soft bed of pine needles. He stoked the fire until he had to back away from the blazing heat.

That night he slept for a few hours, and then awoke to fuel his fire. A mountainous pile of coals radiated heat, and the ground provided a soft and comfortable cushion until the coming of dawn,

Sithas arose slowly, reluctant to break the reverie of warmth and comfort. He cooked another piece of meat, more patiently this time, for breakfast. By the time he finished, sunlight was bathing the bowl-shaped depression around him in its brilliant light. He had made a decision.

He would bring Kith-Kanan to this valley. He didn't know how yet, but he was convinced that this was the best way to insure his brother's recovery.

His course plotted, he gathered up his few possessions and lashed them to his body. Next he took several minutes to gather a stack of firewood—light, sun-dried logs that would burn steadily. He trimmed the twigs off of these so that he could bundle them tightly together. This bundle he then lashed to his back.

Finally he turned his face toward the pass. The slope before him still lay in shadow, as it would for most of the day. Retracing his tracks of the previous afternoon, he forced his way through the deep snow, back toward the summit of the pass.

It took him all morning, but finally he reached the summit. He paused to rest—the climb had been extremely wearying—and sought out the speck of color that he knew would mark Kith-Kanan's presence on the ledge in the distance. He had to squint, for the sunlight reflecting from the snow-filled bowl brutally assaulted his eyes.

He couldn't see the ledge, though he recognized the water hole where he had collected their drinking water. What was that? He saw movement near the stream, and for a moment, he wondered if the sheep had returned, His eyes adjusted to the brightness, and he understood that these could not be sheep. Large humanoid shapes lumbered through the snow. Shaggy fur seemed to cover them in patches, but the "fur" proved to be cloaks cast over broad shoulders.

They moved in single file, some ten or twelve of them, as they crossed the valley floor, taking no notice of the depth of the snow.

With a sickening realization, Sithas understood what was happening: the hill giants had returned, and they were making their way toward Kith-Kanan.

Immediately Following

14

Sithas studied the hill giant that led the column of the brutes, perhaps two miles away and a thousand feet below him. The monster gestured to its fellows, pointing upward. Not toward Sithas, the elf realized, but toward . . . the ledge! His brother's camp! The dozen giants trudged through the snow of the valley floor, making their way in that direction.

Sithas tried to spot his twin, but the distance was too great. Wait . . . there! Kith-Kanan, he realized, must also have seen the giants, for the wounded elf had pulled a dark cloak over himself and was now pressed against the far wall of the ledge, His camouflage seemed effective and would make him virtually invisible from below as the giants headed toward the cliff.

The column of giants waded the stream. The one in the lead gestured again, this time indicating the path in the snow that Sithas had made in his travels back and forth for water. Another giant indicated a different track, the one made by Sithas on the previous day.

That slight gesture gave him a desperate idea. He acted quickly, casting around until his eyes fell upon a medium-sized boulder resting in the summit of the pass and cracked loose from the bedrock below. Seizing it in both of his hands, grunting from the exertion, he lifted the stone over his head. The last of the giants had crossed the stream, and now the file of huge, grotesque creatures was nearing the cliff wall.

Sithas pitched the boulder as hard and as far as he could. The rock plummeted down the steep, rock-strewn pass. Then it hit, crashing into another boulder with a sharp report before bouncing and smashing again and again down the mountain pass, Breathlessly Sithas watched the giants. They *had* to hear the commotion!

Indeed they did. Suddenly the twelve monsters whirled around in surprise. Sithas kicked another rock, and that one too clattered down the pass, rolling between the two huge boulders that he had slipped between on the previous day's climb.

Now the beasts halted, staring upward. Breathlessly Sithas waited.

It worked! He saw the first giant gesturing wildly, pointing toward the summit of the pass, toward Sithas! Kith-Kanan was left behind as the entire band of the great brutes turned and broke into a lumbering trot, pursuing the elf they probably thought they had "discovered" trying to sneak through the pass.

Sithas watched them advance toward him. They plunged through the deep snow in giant strides, each stride taking them farther from Kith-Kanan. Sithas wondered if his brother was watching, if he had seen the clever diversion created by his twin. He lay still, peering around a boulder as the monsters approached the bottom of the pass.

Now what could he do? The giants had almost reached the base of the pass. He looked behind him. Everywhere the valley was blanketed by deep snow. Wherever he went, he would leave a trail so obvious that even the thick-witted hill giants would have no difficulty in following him.

His attention returned to the immediate problem. He saw, with sharp panic, that the giants had disappeared from view. Moments later he understood. They were so close to the pass now that the steepness of the slope blocked his vision.

His head seemed fogged by fear, his body tensed with the anticipation of combat. The thought almost brought a smile to his lips. The prospect of facing a dozen giants with his puny sword struck him as ludicrous indeed! Yet by the same token, that prospect seemed inevitable, so that his amusement quickly gave way to stark terror.

Carefully he crept forward and looked down the pass. All he saw were the two monstrous boulders that had bracketed his ascent of the pass on the day before. As yet there was no sign of the giants.

Should he confront them at those rocks? No more than one at a time could pass through the narrow aperture. Still, with a brutally honest assessment of his own fighting prowess, he knew that one of them was all it would take to squash his skull like an eggshell. Also, he remembered the precarious balance of those boulders.

Indeed, one of them had shifted several inches merely from the weight of his touch.

That recollection gave him an idea. The elf checked his longsword, which was lashed securely to his back. Quickly he unlashed the bundle of firewood and dropped the sticks unceremoniously to the ground. He hefted the longest one, which was about as long as his leg but no thicker than his arm. Still, it would have to do.

Without pausing to consider, Sithas, in a running crouch, crossed through the saddle and started down the slope toward the two rocks. He could see several of the giants through the crack now, and realized with alarm that they were nearly halfway up the steep-sided pass.

In a slide of tumbling scree, Sithas crashed into one of the boulders and felt it lurch beneath his weight. But then it settled back into its place, and he couldn't force it to move farther. Turning to the second rock, he pushed and heaved at it and was rewarded by a fractional shifting of its massive bulk. However, it, too, seemed to be nestled in a comfortable spot and would not move any farther.

Desperately Sithas slid downward through the crack between the boulders. The elf reached beneath the base of the one he judged to be the loosest and began to dig and chop with his piece of firewood.

He pried a large stone loose, and it skittered down the slope. Immediately he began prying at a different rock. A bellow of surprise reached him from below, and he knew that he didn't have much time. He didn't look behind him. Instead, he scrambled back upward between the rocks. He pitched his body against the rock he had worked so hard to loosen and was rewarded by a slight teetering. Then a shower of gravel sprayed from beneath it to tumble into the faces of the approaching giants.

The leader of the monsters bellowed again. The creature was a bare fifty yards below Sithas now and bounding upward with astonishing speed.

After one last, futile push at the rock, Sithas knew that he would have to abandon that plan. His time had run out. Drawing his sword, he dropped through the narrow crack again, prepared to meet the first giant at the mouth of the opening. Grimly he resolved to draw as much blood as possible before he perished.

The beast came toward him, its face split by a garish caricature of a grin. Sithas saw the tiny bloodshot eyes and the stubs of teeth jutting like tusks from its gums. Its huge lips flapped with excitement as the brute prepared to squash the life from this impudent elf.

The thing held one of those monstrous clubs such as the giants had employed in their earlier attack. Now that weapon lashed outward, but Sithas ducked back into the niche, feeling the rock tremble next to him from the force of the blow. He darted outward and stabbed quickly with his steel blade. A sense of cruel delight flared within him as the weapon scored a bloody gash on the giant's forehead.

With a cry of animal rage, the giant lunged upward, dropping its club and reaching with massive paws toward Sithas's legs. The elf skipped backward, scrambling up and away. As he did, he stabbed downward, driving his blade clear through the monster's hand.

Howling in pain, the giant twisted away, shrinking back down the slope to clutch its bleeding extremity. Sithas had no time to reconnoiter, however. The next monster had already caught up. This one had apparently learned from his comrade's errors, for it thrust its heavy club into the crack and stayed out of reach.

Sithas twisted away with a curse as the crude weapon nearly crushed his left wrist. The giant reached in, and Sithas scrambled upward. But then a loose patch of scree caused him to lose his footing, and he slipped downward toward that leering, hate-filled face.

He saw the monstrous lips spread in a leering grin, darkened stubs of ivory teeth ready to tear at his flesh. Sithas kicked out, and his boot cracked into the beast's huge, wart-covered nose.

Desperately Sithas kicked again, pushing himself upward and catching one boot on an outcrop of the rock wall beside him. The giant reached up to catch him, but the elf remained just out of his reach, barely a foot or so above him.

With determination, the broad-shouldered brute pressed into the narrow crack between the boulders. The force of his body pushed the stones outward slightly.

Yet that seemed to be enough. The monster's hand clutched Sithas's foot. Even as the elf kicked and flailed frantically, one of the rocks teetered precariously on the brink of a fall.

The Speaker of the Stars braced his back against one of the rocks and pressed both of his boots against the other. Calling for the blessings of every god he could think of, he pushed outward, straining and gasping to move the monstrous weight.

Slowly, almost gradually, the huge boulder toppled forward. The giant stared upward, his beady eyes nearly bulging out of his skull as the huge load slid forward, then began to roll downward. Tons of rock crushed the life from the brute as the boulder broke free.

His foothold suddenly gone, Sithas slid downward in the wake of the crashing stone. He felt a sickening crunch in the earth and looked up to see the other rock also break free to crash toward the valley floor a thousand feet below. Desperately the elf sprang to one side, feeling the ground shake as the huge stone tumbled past him.

The sounds of the rockslide grew and echoed, seeming to shake the bedrock of the world. Sithas pressed his face into the ground, trying to cling with his hands as the entire wall of the pass fell away. The thunderous volume overwhelmed him, and he expected to be swept away at any second.

But now the gods looked kindly on the Speaker of the Stars, and though the cliff wall a scant twelve inches from his hand plunged below, the rock to which Sithas clung remained fixed, miraculously, to the ridge.

The world crashed and surged around Sithas for what seemed like hours, though in reality it was no more than a few minutes. When he finally opened his eyes, blinking away the dust and grime, he looked down at a scene of complete devastation.

A dust cloud had settled across the formerly pristine snowfields, casting the entire valley in a dirty gray hue. The surface of the cliff gaped like a fresh scar where scree and talus, even great chunks of bedrock, had torn away. He could see none of the twelve giants, but it seemed inconceiveable that any of them could have lived through that massive, crushing avalanche.

The pass was now even steeper than it had been when he climbed it, but the entire surface was clear of snow, and the rock that remained was solid mountain. Thus he had little difficulty in picking his way painstakingly down the thousand feet of descent to the valley floor.

Near the bottom, he came upon the body of one of the giants. The creature was half-buried in rubble and covered with dust.

Sithas stepped carefully along the slope, using handholds to maintain his balance, until he reached the motionless body of the giant. The creature hung over a sharp outcrop of rock, looking like a rag doll that someone had casually cast aside. When the elf reached the monster, he examined it more closely.

He saw that it wore boots of heavy fur and a tunic of bearskin. The creature's beard was long but sparsely grown, adding to the straggled and unkempt appearance of its face. The great mouth hung slackly open, and its long, floppy tongue protruded. Several broken teeth studded its gums alongside a single well-formed tusk of ivory in front. Sithas found himself feeling a spontaneous reaction of compassion as he looked at the pathetic visage.

His reaction changed instantly to alarm when the giant moved, reaching out with one trunklike arm toward him. The elf stepped nervously backward, his longsword in his hand.

Then the giant groaned, smacking his lips and snorting in discomfort before finally forcing open the lid of one blank, bloodshot eye. The eye stared straight at the elf.

Sithas froze. His instincts, as soon as the beast had moved, had urged him to drive his keen steel blade into the creature's throat or its heart.

However, some inner emotion, surprising the elf with its strong compulsion, had held his hand. The blade remained poised before the giant's face, a foot from the end of its blunt and swollen nose, but Sithas didn't drive it home.

Instead, he studied the creature as it opened its other eye. The two orbs crossed ludicrously as it appeared to study the keen steel so close to its face. Slowly the bloodshot orbs came into focus. Sithas sensed the giant tensing, and he knew that he should slay it, if it wasn't already too late! Misgivings assailed him.

Still he held firm. The giant scowled, still trying to understand what had happened, what was going on. Finally the realization came, with a reaction that took Sithas completely by surprise. The monster yelped—a high-pitched gasp of fright—and tried to squirm backward, away from the elf and the weapon.

A large boulder blocked its retreat, and the beast cowered against the rock, raising its massive fists as if to ward away a blow. Sithas took a step forward, and when the beast cried out again, he lowered his blade, bemused by the strange behavior.

Sithas made a casual gesture with his sword. The giant raised its hands to protect its face and grunted something in a crude tongue. Again Sithas was struck by the one perfect tooth bobbing up and down amongst the otherwise ragged gums.

The problem remained of what to do with it. Letting the brute just wander away seemed like an unacceptable risk. Yet Sithas couldn't kill it out of hand, now that it cowered and gibbered at him. It didn't seem like much of a threat anymore, despite its huge size.

"Hey, One-Tooth. Stand up!" The elf gestured with his blade, and after several moments, the giant climbed hesitantly to its feet.

The creature loomed ten feet or more tall, with a barrel-sized chest and stout, sinew-lined limbs. One-Tooth gaped pathetically at Sithas as the elf nodded, pleased. He gestured again with his sword, this time down the pass, toward the valley.

"Come on, you lead the way," he instructed the giant. They started down the mountain, with Sithas keeping his sword ready.

But One-Tooth seemed perfectly content to shuffle along ahead of the elf. On the ground, Sithas found it a great boon to follow in the footsteps of the giant, rather than break his own trail through the snow. Following an elaborate pantomime, he showed

One-Tooth how to drag his feet when he walked, thus making a deeper and smoother path for the elf.

He directed the giant toward the ledge where Kith-Kanan lay helpless. At the bottom, before they picked their way up the steep, treacherous trail, Sithas turned back to the giant.

"I want *you* to carry him," he explained. He cradled his arms as if he was carrying an infant and pointed to the ledge above them. "Do you understand?"

The giant squinted at the elf, his eyes shrinking to tiny dots of bloodshot concentration. He looked upward.

Then his eyes widened, as if someone had just opened the shutters to a dark, little-used room. His mouth gaped happily, and the tooth bobbed up and down in enthusiastic comprehension.

"I hope so," Sithas muttered, not entirely confident about what he was doing.

Now the elf led the way, working his way up the narrow trail until he reached the ledge that had sequestered his brother.

"Well done, Brother!" Kith-Kanan was sitting upright, his back against the cliff wall and his face creased by a grin of amazed delight. "I saw them coming, and I figured that was the end!"

"That thought crossed my mind as well," admitted Sithas.

Kith looked at him with an admiring expression Sithas had never seen in his brother's eyes before. "You could have been killed, you know!"

Sithas laughed self-consciously, feeling a warm sense of pride. "I can't let you have all the fun."

Kith smiled, his eyes shining. "Thanks, Brother!" Clearing his throat, he nodded at One-Tooth. "But what is this—a prisoner or friend? And what idea do you have now?"

"We're going to the next valley," Sithas replied. "I couldn't find a horse, so you'll have to ride a giant!"

Winter, in the Army of Ergoth

15

The rains beat across a sea of canvas, a drumming, monotonous cadence that marked time during winter on the plains. Gray skies stretched over the brown land, encloaked by air that changed from fog to downpour to icy mist.

If only it would freeze! This was the wish of every soldier in the army who had to stand guard, conduct drills, or make the arduous treks to distant woods for firewood or lumber. A hard frost would soldify the viscous earth that now churned underfoot, miring wagon wheels and making the simple act of walking an exhaustive struggle.

Sentries stood shivering on guard duty around the ring of the great human encampment. The great bulk of Sithelbec was practically invisible in the gray anonymity of the twilit gloom. The fortress walls loomed strong; they had been tested at the cost of more than a thousand men during recent months.

Darkness came like a lowering curtain, and the camp became still and silent, broken only by the fires that dotted the darkness. Even these blazes were few, for all sources of firewood within ten miles of the camp had already been picked clean.

Amid this darkness, an even darker figure moved. General Giarna stalked toward the command tent of High General Barnet. Trailing him, trying to control her terror, followed Suzine.

She didn't want to be here. Never before had she seen General Giarna as menacing as he seemed tonight. He had summoned her without explanation, his eyes distant . . . and hungry. It was as if he barely knew that she was present, so intent were his thoughts on something else.

Now she understood that his victim was to be Barnet.

General Giarna reached the high general's tent and flung aside the canvas flap, boldly entering. Suzine, more cautiously, came behind him.

Barnet had been expecting company, for he stood facing the door, his hand on the hilt of his sheathed sword, The three of them were alone in the dim enclosure. One lamp sputtered on a battered wooden table, and rain seeped through the waterlogged roof and sides of the tent.

"The usurper dares to challenge his master?" sneered the white-haired Barnet, but his voice was not as forceful as his words.

"Master?" The black-armored general's voice was heavy with scorn. His eyes remained vacant, and focused on something very far away. "You are a failure—and your time is up, old man!"

"Bastard!" Barnet reacted with surprising quickness, given his age. In one smooth movement, his blade hissed from its scabbard and lashed toward the younger man's face.

General Giarna was quicker. He raised one hand, encased, in its black steel gauntlet. The blade met the gauntlet at the wrist, a powerful blow that ought to have chopped through the armor and sliced off the general's hand.

Instead, the sword shattered into a shower of silver splinters. Barnet, still holding the useless hilt, gaped at the taller Giarna and stepped involuntarily backward.

Suzine groaned in terror. Some unbelievably horrible power pulsed in the room, a thing that she sensed on a deeper level than sight or smell or touch. Her knees grew weak beneath her, but somehow she forced herself to stand.

She knew that Giarna *wanted* her to watch, for this was to be a lesson for her as much as a punishment for Barnet.

The old man squealed—a pathetic, whimpering sound—as he stared at something in the dark eyes of his nemesis. Giarna's hands, cloaked in the shiny black steel, grasped Barnet around the neck, and the high general's sounds faded into strangled gasps and coughs.

Barnet's face expanded to a circle of horror. His tongue protruded, and his jaw flexed soundlessly. His skin grew red—bright red, like a crimson rose, thought Suzine. Then the man's face darkened to a bluish, then ashen, gray.

Finally, as if his corpse was being seared by a hot fire, Barnet turned black. His face ceased to bulge, slowly shrinking until the skin pressed tight around the clear outlines of his skull. His lips stretched backward, and then split and dried into mummified husks.

His hands, Suzine saw, had become veritable claws, each an outline of white bone, with bare shreds of skin and fingernails clinging to the ghastly skeleton.

Giarna cast the corpse aside, and it settled slowly to the floor, like an empty gunnysack that catches the undercurrents of air as it floats downward.

When the general finally turned back to Suzine, she gasped in mindless dread. He stood taller now. His skin was bright, flushed.

But his eyes were his most frightening aspect, for now they fixed upon her with a clear and deadly glow.

*　*　*　*　*

Later, Suzine stared into her mirror, despairing. Though it might show ten thousand signs, to her it was still devoid of that which meant all to her. She no longer knew if Kith-Kanan was even alive, so far distant had he flown.

In the ten days since General Giarna had slain Barnet, the army camp had been driven into furious activity. An array of great stone-casting catapults took shape along the lines. Building the huge wooden machines was slow work, but by the end of winter, two-score of the war machines would be ready to rain their destruction upon Sithelbec.

A hard ground freeze had occurred during the days immediately following the brutal murder, and this had eliminated the mud that had impeded all activity. Now great parties of human riders scoured the surrounding plains, and the few bands of Wildrunners outside Sithelbec's walls had been eliminated or driven to the shelter of the deepest forests.

Wearily Suzine turned her thoughts to her uncle, Emperor Quivalin Soth V. The mirror combed the expanse of the frozen plain to the west, and soon she found what Giarna had directed her to seek: the emperor's great carriage, escorted by four thousand of his most loyal knights, was trundling closer to the camp.

She went to seek her commander and found him belaboring the unfortunate captains of a team sent to bring lumber from a patch of forest some dozen miles away.

"Double the size of your force if you need to!" snarled General Giarna, while six battle-scarred officers trembled before him. "But bring me the wood by tomorrow! Work on the catapults must cease until we get those timbers!"

"Sir," ventured the boldest, "it's the horses! We drive them until near collapse. Then they must rest! It takes two days to make the trip!"

"Drive them until they collapse, then—or perhaps you consider horseflesh to be more valuable than your own?"

"No, General!" Badly shaken, the captains left to organize another, larger, lumbering expedition.

"What have you learned?" General Giarna whirled upon Suzine, fixing her with his penetrating stare.

For a moment, Suzine looked at him, trying to banish her trembling. The Boy General reminded her, for the first time in a long time, of the vibrant and energetic officer she had first met, for whom she had once developed an infatuation. What did the death of Barnet have to do with this? In some vile way, it seemed to Suzine that the man had *consumed* the life force of the other, devoured his rival, and found the deed somehow invigorating.

"The emperor will arrive tomorrow," she reported. "He makes good time, now that the ground is frozen."

"Splendid." The general's mind, she could see, was already preoccupied with something else, for he turned that sharp stare toward the bastion of Sithelbec.

* * * * *

If Emperor Quivalin noticed any dark change in General Giarna, he didn't say anything to Suzine. His carriage had rolled into the camp to the cheers of more than a hundred thousand of his soldiers. The great procession rumbled around the full circumference of the circular deployments before arriving at the tent where the Boy General kept his headquarters.

The two men conferred within the tent for several hours before the ruler and the commander emerged, side by side, to address the troops.

"I have appointed General Giarna as High General of the Army," announced Quivalin, to the cheers of his men, "following the unfortunate demise of former High General Barnet.

"He has my full confidence, as do you all!" More cheers. "I feel certain that, with the coming of spring, your force will carry the walls of the elven fortress and reduce their defenses to ashes! For the glory of Ergoth, you will prevail!"

Adulation rose from the troops, who surged forward to get a close look at the mighty ruler. A sweeping stare from their general, however, held them in their tracks. A slow, reluctant silence fell over the mass of warriors.

"The collapse of my predecessor, due to exhaustion, was symptomatic of the sluggishness that previously pervaded this entire army—a laxness that allowed our enemy to reach its fortress months ago," said General Giarna. His voice was level and low, yet it seemed to carry more ominous power than the emperor's loud exhortations.

Murmurs of discontent rose in many thousands of throats. Barnet had been a popular leader, and his death hadn't been satisfactorily explained to the men. Yet the stark fear they felt for the Boy General prevented anyone from audibly muttering open displeasure.

"Our emperor informs me that additional troops will be joining us, a contingent of dwarves from the Theiwar Clan of Thorbardin. They are skilled miners and will be put to work digging excavations beneath the walls of the enemy defenses. "Those of you who are not engaged in preparations for the attack will begin tomorrow a vigorous program of training. When the time comes to attack, you will be ready! And for the glory of our emperor, you will succeed!"

Two Weeks Later, Early Winter

16

The firelight reflected from the walls of the cave like dancing sprites, weaving patterns of warmth and comfort. A haunch of venison sizzled on a spit over the coals, while Sithas's cloak and leggings dried on a makeshift rack.

"No tenderloin of steer ever tasted so sweet or lay so sumptuously on the palate," announced Kith-Kanan, with an approving smack of his lips. He reached forward and sliced another hot strip from the meat that slow-roasted above the coals.

Sithas looked at his brother, his eyes shining with pride. Unlike the sheep, which he admitted had been slain by dumb luck as much as anything, he had stalked this deer through the woods, lying in wait for long, chilly hours, until the timid creature had worked its way into bow range. He had aimed carefully and brought the animal down with one shot to the neck.

"I have to agree," Sithas allowed as he finished his own piece. He, too, carved another strip for eating. Then he cut several other juicy morsels, piling them on a flat stone that served as a platter, before lifting the spit from the fire.

He turned to the mouth of the shallow cave, where winter's darkness closed in. "Hey, One-Tooth," he called. "Dinner time!"

The giant's round face, split by his characteristic massive grin, appeared. One-Tooth squinted before reaching his massive paw into the cave. His eyes lit up expectantly as Sithas handed him the spit.

"Careful—it's hot. Eat hearty, my friend." Sithas watched in amusement as the giant, who had learned several words of the common tongue—'hot' being high on the list—picked tentatively at the dripping meat.

"Amazing how friendly he got, once we started feeding him," remarked Kith-Kanan.

Indeed, once the hill giant had satisfied himself that the elf wasn't going to slay him, One-Tooth had become an enthusiastic helper. He had carried Kith down the narrow trail from the ledge with all the care that a mother shows to her firstborn babe. The weight of the injured elf hadn't seemed to slow the hill giant at all as Sithas led him back over the steep pass and into this valley.

The trip had been hard on Kith-Kanan, with each step jarring his injured leg, but he had borne the punishment in silence. Indeed, he had been amazed and delighted at the degree of control with which Sithas had seized the reins of their expedition.

It had taken another day of searching, but finally the Speaker of the Stars had discovered this shallow cave, its entrance partially screened by boulders and brush. Lying in the overhang of a rock-walled riverbank, the cave itself was dry and spacious, albeit not so spacious that the giant didn't have to remain outside, A small stream flowed within a dozen feet of its mouth, assuring a plentiful supply of water.

Now that they had reached this forested valley, Sithas had been able to rig a splint for Kith-Kanan's wound.

Nevertheless, it galled the leader of the Wildrunners, who had always handled his own problems, to sit here in forced immobility while his brother, the Speaker of the Stars, did the hunting, wood-gathering, and exploration, as well as the simpler jobs like fire-tending and cooking.

"This is truly amazing, Sithas," Kith said, indicating their rude shelter. "All the comforts of home."

The cave was shallow, perhaps twenty feet deep, with a ceiling that rose almost five feet. Several dense clumps of pines and cedars grew within easy walking distance.

"Comforts," Sithas agreed. "And even a palace guard!"

One-Tooth looked attentive, sensing that they were talking about him. He grinned again, though the juice dribbling from his huge lips made the effect rather grotesque.

"I have to admit, when you first told me that I was going to ride a giant, I thought the cold had penetrated a little too far between your ears. But it worked!"

They had set up a permanent camp here, agreeing tacitly between them that without Arcuballis they were stuck in these mountains at least for the duration of the winter.

Of course, they were haunted by awareness of the distant war. They had discussed the nature of Sithelbec's defenses and concluded that the humans probably wouldn't be able to launch an effective assault before summer. The stout walls ought to stand against a long barrage of catapult attacks, and the hard earth would make tunneling operations difficult and time-consuming. All they could do now was wait and hope.

Sithas had gathered huge piles of pine boughs, which made fairly comfortable beds. A fire built at the mouth of the cave sent its smoke billowing outward, but radiated its impressive heat throughout their shelter. It made the cave into a very pleasant shelter, and—with the presence of One-Tooth—Sithas no longer feared for his brother's safety if he had to be left alone. They both knew that soon enough, Sithas would have to set out on foot to seek the griffons.

Now they sat in silence, sharing a sense of well-being that was quite extraordinary, given the circumstances. They had shelter and warmth, and now they even had extra food! Lazily Sithas rose and checked his boots, careful not to singe their fur-covered surface. He turned them slightly to warm a different part of their soggy surface. Immediately steam began to arise from the soaked leather. He returned to his spot and flopped down on his own cloak. He looked at his brother, and Kith-Kanan sensed that he wanted to say something.

"I think you've got enough food here to last you for a while," Sithas began. "I'm going to search for the griffons."

Kith nodded. "Despite my frustration with this"— he indicated his leg—"I think that's the only thing to do."

"We're near the heart of the range," Sithas continued, with a nod. "I figure that I can head out in one direction, make a thorough search, and get back here within a week or ten days. Even with the deep snow, I'll be able to make some progress. I'll stop back and check on you and let you know what I've found. If it's nothing, I'll head out in a different direction after that."

"Sounds like a reasonable plan," Kith-Kanan agreed. "You'll take the scroll from Vedvedsica, of course."

Sithas had planned on this. "Yes. If I find the griffons, I'll try to get close enough to use the spell!"

His brother looked at him steadily. Kith-Kanan's face showed an expression Sithas was not accustomed to. The injured elf spoke. "Let me do something before you go. It might help on your journey."

"What?"

Kith wouldn't explain, instead requesting that his brother bring him numerous supple pine branches—still green, unlike the dried sticks they used for firewood. "The best ones will be about as big around as your thumb and as long as possible."

"Why? What do you want them for?"

His brother acted mysterious, but Sithas willingly gathered the wood as soon as daylight illuminated the valley, He spent the rest of the day gathering provisions for the first leg of his trek, checking his own equipment, and stealing sidelong glances at his brother. Kith-Kanan pretended to ignore him, instead whittling away at the pine branches, weaving them into a tight pattern, even pulling threads from his woolen cloak to lash the sticks together firmly.

Toward sunset, he finally held the finished creations up for Sithas's inspection. He had made two flat objects, oval in shape and nearly three feet long by a foot wide, The sticks had been woven back and forth into a grid pattern.

"Wonderful, Kith—simply amazing. I've never seen anything like them! But . . . what are they?"

Kith-Kanan smiled smugly. "I learned about them during that winter I spent in the wildwood." For a moment, his smile tightened. He couldn't remember that time without thinking of Anaya, of the bliss they had shared, and of the strange fate that had claimed her. He blinked and went on. "They're called 'snowshoes.' "

Instantly Sithas saw the application. "I lash these to my boots, right?" he guessed. "And then walk around, leaving footprints in the snow like a giant?"

"You'll be surprised, I promise. They'll let you walk on top of the snow, even deep powder."

Indeed, Sithas wasted no time pulling on his boots and affixing the snowshoes to them with several straps Kith had created by tearing a strip from one of their cloaks. He tripped and sprawled headlong as he left the cave but quickly dusted himself off and started into the woods on a test walk.

Though the snowshoes felt somewhat awkward on his feet and forced him to walk with an unusually wide-spread gait, he trotted and marched and plodded through the woods for nearly an hour before returning to the cave.

"Big feet!" One-Tooth greeted him outside, where he had left the giant.

"Good feet!" Sithas replied, reaching up to give the giant a friendly clap on the arm.

Kith awaited him expectantly.

"They're fantastic! I can't believe the difference they make!"

Kith was forced to admit, as he looked at his exhilarated brother, that Sithas no longer seemed to need the assistance of anyone to cope with the rigors of the high mountain winter.

Determined to begin his quest well rested, Sithas tried to force himself to sleep. But though he closed his eyes, his mind remained alert. It leaped from fear to hope to anticipation in a chaotic whirling dance that kept him wide awake as the hours drifted past. He heard One-Tooth snoring at the cave mouth and saw Kith slumbering peacefully on the other side of the fire,

Finally, past midnight, Sithas slept. And when he did, his dreams were rich and bright, full of blue skies swarming with griffons.

* * * * *

Yellow eyes gleamed in the woods, staring at the fading fire in the mouth of the cave. The dire wolf crept closer, suppressing the urge to growl.

The creature saw and smelled the hill giant slumbering at the mouth of the cave. Though the savage canine was huge—the size of a pony, weighing more than three hundred pounds—it feared to attack the larger hill giant.

Too, the fire gave it pause. It had been burned once before, and remembered well the terrifying touch of flame.

Silently the wolf slinked back into the woods. When it was safely out of hearing of the cave, it broke into a patient lope, easily moving atop the snow.

But there was food in the cave. During the lean winter months, fresh meat was a rare prize in this mountain fastness. The wolf would remember, and as it roamed the valleys, it would meet others of its kind. Finally, when the pack had gathered, they would return.

* * * * *

Sithas's first expedition, to the west, lasted nearly four weeks. He pressed along snow-swept ridges and through barren, rock-boundaried vales. He saw no life, save for the occasional spoor of the hardy mountain sheep or the flying speck of an eagle soaring in the distance.

He traveled alone, having persuaded One-Tooth—only after a most intricate series of contortions, pantomimes, threats, and pleas—to remain behind and guard Kith-Kanan. Each day his solitude seemed to weigh heavier on him and become an oppressive, gnawing despair.

Winds tore at him every day, and as often as not, his world vanished behind a shroud of blowing snow. The days of clear weather that had followed Kith's injury, he now realized, had been a fortunate aberration in the typical weather patterns of the high mountains. Winter closed in with a fury, shrouding him in snow and hail and ice.

He pressed westward until at last he stood upon a high ridge and saw ground falling to foothills and plains beyond. He would find no mountainous refuge of griffons in this direction. The route he followed back to Kith-Kanan and One-Tooth diverged somewhat from the trail he had taken westward, but this, too, proved fruitless.

He found his brother and the hill giant in good spirits, with a plentiful supply of meat. Though Kith could not yet bear his weight on his leg, the limb seemed to be healing well. Given time, it would regain most of its prior strength.

After a night of warmth and freshly cooked meat, Sithas began his search to the north. This time his quest took even longer, for the Khalkist Range extended far along this axis. After twenty-five days of exploring, however, he saw that he had left the highest summits of the range behind. Though the trail northward was mountainous and the land uninhabited, he could see from his lofty vantage that it lacked the towering, craggy summits that had been so vividly described in Kith-Kanan's dream. It seemed safe to conclude that the valley of the griffons did not lie farther north.

His return to camp took another ten days and carried him through more lofty, but equally barren, country. The only significant finds he made were several herds of deer. He had stumbled across the creatures by accident and watched them race away, plunging through the deep snow. It was with a sensation approaching abject hopelessness that he plodded over the last ridge and found the camp nestled in its cave and remaining very much as he had left it.

One-Tooth was eager to greet him, and Kith-Kanan looked stronger and healthier, though his leg was still awkwardly splinted. His brother was working on an intricately carved crutch, but as yet he hadn't tried walking with it.

By now the food supply had begun to run short, so Sithas remained for several days, long enough to stalk and slay a plump doe. The deer's carcass yielded more meat than either of his previous kills, and when he returned to camp with the doe, he was surprised to find Kith waiting at the cave mouth *standing* and waiting.

"Kith! Your leg!" he asked, dropping the deer and stepping quickly to his brother's side.

"Hurts like all the fires of the Abyss," Kith grunted, but his teeth, though clenched, forced his mouth into a tight smile. "Still, it can hold me up, with the help of my crutch."

"Call you Three-Legs now," observed One-Tooth dryly.

"Fair enough!" Kith agreed, still gritting his teeth.

"I think this calls for a celebration. How about some melted snow and venison?" proposed Sithas.

"Perfect," Kith-Kanan agreed.

One-Tooth drooled happily, sharing the brothers' elation, The trio enjoyed an evening of feasting. The giant was the first to tire, and soon he was snoring noisily in his accustomed position outside the mouth of the cave.

"Are you going back out?" Kith asked quietly after long moments of contented silence.

"I have to," Sithas replied. They both knew that there was no other alternative.

"This is the last chance," Kith-Kanan observed. "We've come up from the south, and now you've looked to the north and the west. If the valley doesn't lie somewhere to the east, we'll have to face the fact that this whole adventure might have been a costly pipe dream."

"I'm not prepared to give up yet!" Sithas said, more sharply than he intended. Truthfully, the same suspicions had lurked in his own subconscious for many days, What if he found no sign of the griffons? What if they had to march back to Silvanost on foot, a journey that would take months and couldn't begin until snowmelt in late spring? And what if they returned, after all this time, empty-handed?

So it was that Sithas began his eastward search with a taut determination. He pushed himself harder than ever before, going to reckless lengths to scale sheer passes and traverse lofty, precipitous ridges. The mountains here were the most rugged of any in the range, and any number of times they came very close to claiming the life of the intrepid elf.

Every day Sithas witnessed thundering avalanches. He learned to recognize the overhanging crests, the steep and snow-blanketed heights that gave birth to these crushing snowslides. He identified places where water flowed beneath the snow, gaining drinking water when he needed it but avoiding a potential plunge through the ice that, by soaking him in these woodless heights, would amount to a sentence of death by freezing.

He slept on high ridges, with rocks for his pillow and bed. He excavated snow caves when he could and found that the warmth of these greatly improved his chances of surviving the long, dark nights. But once again he found nothing that would indicate the presence of griffons—indeed, of *any* living creatures—among these towering crags.

He pressed for two full weeks through the barren vales, climbing rock-studded slopes, dodging avalanches, and searching the skies and the ridges for some sign of his quarry. He pressed forward each day before dawn and searched throughout the hours of daylight until darkness all but blinded him to any spoor that wasn't directly in front of his nose. Then he slept fitfully, anxious for the coming of daylight so that he could resume his search.

However, he was finally forced to admit defeat and turned back toward the brothers' camp. A bleak feeling of despair came over him as he made camp on a high ridge. It was as he rearranged some rocks to form his sleeping place that Sithas saw the tracks: like a cat's, only far bigger, larger than his own hand with the fingers fully outstretched. The rear, feline feet he identified with certainty, and now the nature of the padded forefeet became clear, too. They might have been made by an incredibly huge eagle, but Sithas knew this was not the case. The prints had been made by the great taloned griffon.

* * * * *

Kith-Kanan squirmed restlessly on his pine-branch bed. The once-soft branches had been matted into a hard and lumpy mat by more than two months of steady use, and no longer did they provide a pleasant cushion for his body. As he had often done before—indeed, as he did a hundred or a thousand times each day—he cursed the injury that kept him hobbled to this shelter like an invalid.

He noticed another sound that disturbed his slumber—a rumble like a leaky bellows in a steel-smelting plant. The noise reverberated throughout the cave.

"Hey, One-Tooth!" Kith snapped. "Wake up!"

Abruptly the sound ceased with a snuffling gurgle, and the giant peered sleepily into the cave.

"Huh?" demanded the monstrous humanoid. "What Three-Legs want now?"

"Stop snoring! I can't sleep with all the racket!"

"Huh?" One-Tooth squinted at him. "Not snoring!"

"Never mind. Sorry I woke you." Smiling to himself, the wounded elf shifted his position on the rude mattress and slowly boosted himself to his feet.

"Nice fire" The giant moved closer to the pile of coals. "Better than village firehole."

"Where is your village?" asked Kith curiously. The giant had mentioned his small community before.

"In mountains, close to tree lands."

This didn't tell Kith much, except that it was at a lower altitude than the valley they now inhabited, a fact that was just as well, considering his brother's ongoing exploration of the highlands.

"Sleep some more," grunted the giant, stretching and yawning.

His mouth gaped, and the solitary tusk protruded until One-Tooth smacked his lips and closed his eyes.

The giant had made remarkable progress in learning the elven tongue. He was no scintillating conversationalist, of course, but he could communicate with Kith-Kanan on a remarkable number of day-to-day topics.

"Sleep well, friend," remarked Kith softly. He looked at the slumbering giant with genuine affection, grateful that the fellow had been here during these months of solitude.

Looking outward, he noticed the pale blue of the dawn sky looming behind One-Tooth's recumbent form.

Damn this leg! Why did he have to suffer an injury now, just when his skills were most needed, when the entire future of the war and of his nation were at stake?

He had regained some limited mobility. He could totter, albeit painfully, around the mouth of the cave, getting water for himself and exercising his limbs. Today, he resolved, he would press far enough to get a few more pine branches for his crude and increasingly uncomfortable bed.

But that was nothing compared to the epic quest undertaken by his brother! Even as Kith thought about making the cave a little more cozy, his brother was negotiating high mountain ridges and steep, snow-filled valleys, making his camp wherever the sunset found him, pressing forward each day to new vistas.

More than once, Kith had brooded on the fact that Sithas faced great danger in these mountains. Indeed, he could be killed by a fall, or an avalanche, or a band of wolves or giants—by any of countless threats—and Kith-Kanan wouldn't even know about it until much time had passed and he failed to return.

Growling to himself, Kith limped to the cave mouth and looked over the serene valley. Instead of inspiring mountain scenery, however, all he saw were steep, gray prison walls, walls that seemed likely to hold him here forever.

What was his brother doing now? How fared the search for the griffons?

He limped out into the clear, still air. The sun touched the tips of the peaks around him, yet it would be hours before it reached the camp on the valley floor.

Grimacing with pain, Kith pressed forward, One-Tooth's forays for wood and water had packed down the snow for a large area around their cave, and the elf crossed the smooth surface with little difficulty.

He reached the edge of the packed snow, stepping into the spring mush and sinking to his knee. He took another step, and another, wincing at the effort it took to move his leg.

Then he froze, motionless, his eyes riveted to the snow before him. His hand reached for a sword that he was not wearing.

The tracks were clear in the soft snow. They must have been made the night before. A pack of huge wolves, perhaps a dozen or more, had run past the cave in the darkness. Luckily he could see no sign of them now as he carefully backed toward the cave.

He remembered the fire they had built the night before and imagined the wolves sidling past, fearful of the flames. Yet he knew, as he studied the silent woods, that sooner or later they would return.

The Next Day

17

Sithas reached upward, pulling himself another eight inches closer to his goal. Sweat beaded upon his forehead, fatigue numbed his arms and legs, and a dizzying expanse of space yawned below him. All of these factors he ignored in his grim determination to reach the crest of the ridge.

The rocky barrier before him loomed high, with sheer sides studded with cracked and jagged outcrops of granite. A month ago, he reflected as he paused to gasp for breath, he would have called the climb impossible. Now it represented merely another obstacle, one that he would treat with respect yet was confident that he would successfully overcome.

High hopes surged in his heart, convincing him to keep on climbing. This *had* to be the place! The night before, those tracks on the ledge had seemed so clear, such irrefutable proof that the griffons lived somewhere nearby. Now doubts assailed him. Perhaps his mind played tricks on him, and this torturous climb was simply another exercise in futility.

Beyond this steep-walled ridge, he knew, lay a stretch of the Khalkist Mountains that he had not yet explored. The region sprawled, a chaos of ridges, glaciers and valleys. Finally he pulled himself up over the rocky summit of the divide. He looked into the deep valley beyond, squinting against the bright sunlight. He no longer wore his scarf protectively across his face. Four months of exposure to wind, snow, and sun had given his skin the consistency and toughness of leather.

No movement greeted his eyes, no sign of life in the wide and deep vale. Yet before him—and far, far below—he saw a wide expanse of dark green forest. Amidst these trees, he glimpsed a sparkling reflection that he knew must be a pond or small lake, and unlike any other body of water he had seen for the last two months, this one was *unfrozen!*

He scrambled over the top of the ridge, only to be confronted by a precipitous descent beyond. Undismayed, he followed the knifelike crest, until at last he found a narrow ravine that led downward at an angle. Quickly, almost recklessly, Sithas slid down the narrow chute. Always he kept his eyes on the heavens, searching for any sign of the magnificent half-lion, half-eagle beasts that he sought.

Would he be able to tame them? He thought of the scroll he had carried during these weeks of searching. When he paused to rest, he removed it and examined its ivory tube. Uncorking the top, he checked to see that the parchment was still curled, well protected, within. From somewhere, a nagging doubt troubled him, and for the first time, he wondered if the enchantment would work. How could mere words, read from such a scroll, have an effect on creatures as proud and free as the griffons? He could only hope that Vedvedsica had spoken the truth,

The ravine provided him good cover and a relatively easy descent that carried him steadily downward for thousands of feet. He moved carefully, taking precautions that his footsteps didn't trigger any slide of loose rock. And though he saw no sign of his quarry, he wanted to make every effort to ensure that it was *he* who discovered *them,* rather than the other way around.

It took Sithas several hours to make the long, tedious descent. Steep walls climbed to his right and left, sometimes so close together that he could reach out his hands and touch each side of the ravine simultaneously. Once he came to a sharp drop-off, some twelve feet straight down. Turning to face the mountain, he lowered himself over the precipice, groping with his feet until he found a secure hold. Very carefully, he braced himself and sought lower grips for his hands. In this painstaking fashion, he negotiated the cliff.

The floor of the passage wound back and forth like a twisting corridor, and sometimes Sithas could see no more than a dozen feet in front of him. At such times, he moved with extra caution, peering around the bend before proceeding ahead. Thus it was that he came upon the nest.

At first he thought it to be an eagle's eyrie. A huge circle of twigs sticks, and branches rested on a slight shoulder of the ravine. Steep cliffs dropped away below it. A hollow in the middle of the nest had obviously been smoothed out, creating a deep and sheltering lair that was nearly six feet across. Three small feathered creatures moved there, immediately turning to him with gaping beaks and sharp, demanding squawks.

The animals rose, spreading their wings and bleating with increased urgency. Their feathers, Sithas saw, were straggly and thin; they looked incapable of flight. Their actions seemed like those of fledglings, yet already the young griffons were the size of large hawks.

Sithas peeked carefully over the lip of a boulder. The tiny griffons, he saw, had collected themselves into a bundle of feathers and fur, talons and beaks. They hissed and spat, the feathers along the napes of their eagle necks bristling. At the same time, feline tails lashed back and forth in excitement and tension.

For several moments, the elf dared not draw a breath or even open his mouth. So powerful was the sense of triumph sweeping over him that he had to resist the temptation to shout his delight aloud.

He forced himself to keep still, hiding in the shadow of the huge rock, trying to restrain the pounding of his heart.

He had found the griffons! They lived!

Of course, these nestlings were not the proud creatures he sought, but the nearness of the flock was no longer a matter of doubt. It remained only a matter of time before he would discover the full-grown creatures. How many were there? When would they return? He watched and waited.

For perhaps half an hour, he remained immobile. He searched the skies above, even as he shrank against the wall of the ravine and tried to conceal himself from overhead view.

With sudden urgency, he pulled the ivory scroll tube from his backpack. Unrolling the parchment, he studied the symbols of enchantment. It would require concentration and discipline, he saw, in order to pronounce the old elvish script, which was full of archaic pronunciations and mystical terminology. He allowed his tongue to shape the unusual sounds, practicing silently.

"Keerin—silvartl . . . Thanthal ellish, Quirnost . . . Hothist kranthas, Karin Than-tanthas!"

Such a simple spell. Perhaps it was madness to expect success from it. It certainly seemed rash, now that he stood here, to face a multitude of savage carnivores with nothing more than these words to protect him.

Again his restlessness returned, and finally he had to move. With as much stealth as he could muster, Sithas worked his way up the slope of the ravine. He sought a place with a commanding view of the valley. His instincts told him that the events of the rest of this day would prove the worth of the entire quest. Indeed, they might measure the worth of his entire life.

He found a broad shoulder of the ridge, an open ledge that nevertheless lay in the shadow of an overhanging shelf of rock. From here, he believed, he could see all of the valley below him, but he could not be seen, or attacked, from above.

He settled down to wait. The sun seemed to hang motionless in the sky, mocking him.

He dozed for a while, lulled by the warmth of the sun and perhaps drained by his own tension. When he awoke, it was with abrupt alarm. He thought momentarily that he had entered a bizarre dream.

Blinking and shaking his head, Sithas saw a tiny spot of movement, no more than a speck of darkness against the clear sky. From the great distance, he knew that whatever he saw must be very large indeed. He saw a pair of broad wings supporting a body that seemed to grow with each passing moment. He stared, but could see nothing else beyond this lone scout.

The streamlined bird shape swooped into a low dive, settling toward the ridge across the valley. Even at this great distance, Sithas saw the leonine rear legs descend, supporting the griffon's weight on the ground while it used its wings to slowly settle its forefeet. He could plainly see the creature's size and sense its raw, contained power. Another flying beast hove into view, and then several more, all of them settling beside the first. From this far away, he might have been looking at a flock of blackbirds settling toward a farmer's field lush with ripening corn. But he knew that each of the griffons was larger than a horse.

The beasts returned to their valley, flying in a great flock and shrieking their delight at the homecoming. They sounded like great eagles, though louder and fiercer than even those proud birds. The flock spread across a mile or more, darkening the sky with their impressive presence.

They settled along the jagged ridge and gathered upon nearby summits, still miles away from Sithas. The many rocky knobs disappeared beneath slowly beating wings and smooth, powerful bodies seeking comfortable perches. For the first time, Sithas became aware of many nests, all along the ridges and slopes of his side of the valley, as dozens of fledglings squawked and squirmed in their nests. So splendidly were they camouflaged that he hadn't noticed the presence of several within a hundred feet of his vantage point.

Now several of the adults took to the air again, springing into the valley with long, graceful dives, allowing their hind legs to trail out behind them in sleek, streamlined efficiency. As they drew closer, Sithas could see long strips of red meat dangling from their mouths. Birdlike, they would tend to the feeding of their young.

The rest of the flock followed, once again filling the sky with the steady pulse of their wingbeats. They numbered in the hundreds, perhaps half a thousand, though Sithas did not take the time to count. Instead, he knew that he had to act boldly and promptly.

With quick, certain gestures, he unfurled the scroll and took a look at the bizarre, foreign-looking symbols. Gritting his teeth, he stepped boldly outward, to the lip of the precipice, raising the scroll before him. Now he felt totally naked and exposed.

His movement provoked a stunning and instant reaction. The valley rang with a chorus of shrill cries of alarm as the savage griffons spotted him and squalled their challenges. The ones in the lead, those carrying food for the young, immediately dove to the sides, away from the elven interloper. The rest tucked their wings and dove straight toward the Speaker of the Stars.

Terror choked in Sithas's throat. Never had he faced such a terrible onslaught. The griffons rocketed closer with astonishing speed. Huge talons reached toward him, eager to tear the flesh from his limbs.

He forced himself to look down at the scroll, thinking that his voice would never even be heard in this din!

But he read the words anyway. His voice came from somewhere deep within him, powerful and commanding. The sounds of the old elvish words seemed suddenly like the language he had known all his life. He spoke with great strength, his tone vibrant and compelling, betraying no sign of the fear that threatened to overwhelm him.

"Keerin-silvan!"

At this first phrase, a silence descended so suddenly that the absence of sound struck Sithas almost like a physical force, knocking him off his feet, He sensed that the griffons were still diving, still swooping toward him, but their shrill cries had been silenced by his first words. This enhanced his confidence.

"Thanthal ellish, Quimost."

The words seemed to flame on the scroll before him, each symbol erupting into life as he read it. He did not dare to look up.

"Hothist kranthas, Karin Than-tanthas!"

The last of the symbols flared and waned, and now the elf looked up, boldly seeking the griffons with his eyes. He would meet his death bravely or he would tame them.

The first thing he saw was the hate-filled visage of a diving griffon. The monstrous creature's beak gaped, and both the eagle claws of its front legs and the lion talons of its rear limbs reached toward Sithas, ready to tear him asunder.

But then suddenly it veered upward, spreading its broad wings and coming to rest upon the shelf of rock directly before the tall form of Sithas, Speaker of the Stars, scion of the House of Silvanos.

"Come to me, creatures of the sky!" Sithas cried. An awe-inspiring sense of power swept over him, and he raised his arms, his hands clenched into fists held skyward.

"Come, my griffons! Answer the call of your master!"

And come to him they did.

The flock, dramatically spellbound, swirled around him and settled toward places of vantage on the towering ridges nearby. One of these approached the elf, creeping along the crest of rock. Sithas saw a slash of white feathers across its brown breast, and his spirits soared in sudden recognition.

"Arcuballis!" he cried as the griffon's head rose in acknowledgment. The great creature lived and had somehow found a home with this flock of his kin!

The proud griffon sprang to Sithas, rearing before him and spreading his vast wings. The elf saw a gouge along one side of Arcuballis's head where the giant's club had cracked him. Sithas was surprised at the joy he felt at the discovery of his brother's lifelong steed, and that joy, he knew, would pale compared to Kith-Kanan's own delight.

The others, too, moved toward him—with pride and power, but no longer did they seem to be threatening. Indeed, curiosity seemed to be their dominant trait.

By the gods, he had done it! His quest had succeeded! Because of his elation, the distant war seemed already all but won.

That Day, Late Winter

18

The dire wolves attacked suddenly, bursting from the concealment of trees that grew within a hundred feet of the cave mouth. Kith-Kanan and One-Tooth had planned their defense, but nevertheless, the onslaught came with surprising speed.

"There! Hounds come!" shouted the giant, first to see the huge, shaggy brutes.

Kith-Kanan seized his bow and pulled himself to his feet, cursing the stiffness that still impaired the use of his leg.

The largest of the dire wolves led the charge. A nightmarish brute, with murderous yellow eyes and a great, bristling mane of black fur, the beast sprinted toward the cave, while others of its pack followed in its wake. It snarled, curling its black, drooling lips to reveal teeth as long as Kith's fingers. The dire wolves had the same narrow muzzles, alert, pointed ears, and fur-coated bodies and tails of normal wolves. However, they were much larger than their more common cousins, and of far more fearsome disposition. A dozen erupted from the trees in the first wave, and Kith saw more of the dim gray shapes lurking in the woods beyond.

The elf propped himself up against a wall. With mechanical precision, he launched an arrow, nocked another, and fired again. He released a dizzying barrage of missiles at the loping canines. The razor-sharp steel of the arrowheads cut through fur and sinew, gouging deep wounds into the bristling canines, but even the bloodiest cuts seemed only to enrage the formidable creatures.

One-Tooth lumbered forward, his club raised. The hill giant grunted and swung, but his target skipped to one side. Whirling, the dire wolf reached with hungry fangs for the giant's unprotected calf, but One-Tooth leaped away with surprising quickness, Instead of lunging after the giant, the monster darted toward Kith-Kanan as a snarling trio of its fellow wolves took up the assault on the hill giant.

The elf smoothly raised his bow and let fly another arrow. Though the missile scored a bloody gash on the beast's flank it didn't seem to appreciably affect its charge. One-Tooth whirled in a circle, clearing the menacing forms away from himself, and then swung desperately, knocking the rear legs of one large monster to the side. The wolf crashed to the ground and then sprang away.

The wolves began to circle One-Tooth. Kith-Kanan shot at yet another wolf, and another, dropping each with arrows to the throat. A wolf turned from the giant, loping toward the elf, and Kith brought it down—but not before driving three arrows into its chest, and even then the beast didn't stop until it had practically reached him.

Once again they came in a rush, a nightmarish image of snarling lips, glistening fangs, and gleaming, hate-filled eyes. The elf shot his arrows one after the other, scarcely noting the effect of one before the next was nocked. The giant bashed at the shaggy beasts, while they in turn tore at his legs, ripping gory wounds with their fangs.

The packed snow around the cave mouth was covered with gray bodies, and great patches of it were stained crimson by the spilled blood of the slain wolves. One-Tooth stumbled, nearly going down amid the viciously snarling attackers. A wolf leaped for the giant's neck, but the elven archer killed it in midair with a single arrow to the heart.

Then Kith-Kanan reached for another arrow and realized he had used them all. Grimly drawing his sword, he pushed himself away from the wall and limped toward the beleaguered giant. He felt terribly vulnerable without the rock wall behind him, but he couldn't leave the courageous hill giant to die by himself.

Then suddenly, before Kith reached the melee, the wolves sprang away from the giant and darted back to the shelter of the trees, leaving a dozen of their number behind, dead.

"Where go hounds?" demanded the hill giant, shaking his fist after the wolves.

I don't know," admitted the elf. "I don't think *I* scared them away."

"Good fight!" One-Tooth beamed at Kith-Kanan, wiping a trunk-like wrist below his running nose. "Big hounds—mean too!"

"Not so mean as we are, my friend," Kith noted, still puzzled by the sudden retreat of the wolves just when their victory had seemed assured.

Kith-Kanan was relieved to see that One-Tooth's wounds, while bloody, were not deep. He showed the giant how to clean them with snow, meanwhile keeping his eyes nervously on the surrounding pines.

He heard the disturbance in the air before One-Tooth did, but both of them instinctively looked up at the sky. They saw them coming from the east—a horizon full of great soaring shapes, with proudly spread wings and long, powerful bodies.

"The griffons!" Kith cried, whooping with glee. The giant stared at him as if he had lost his mind while he danced about the clearing, waving and shouting.

The great flock settled across the valley floor, squawking and growling over the best perches. Sithas came to earth, riding one of the griffons, and Kith-Kanan recognized his mount immediately.

"Arcuballis! Sithas!"

His brother, equally elated, leaped to the ground. The twins embraced, too full of emotion for words.

"Big lion-bird," grunted One-Tooth, eyeing Arcuballis carefully. "Rock-nose bring home."

"Bring home—to your village?" asked Kith.

"Yup. Lion-bird hurt. Rock-nose feed, him fly away."

"The giants must have taken him with them that night they first attacked us," Kith-Kanan guessed. "They nursed him back to health."

"And then he escaped, and found the flock in the wild. He was with them when I finally discovered their nests," Sithas concluded.

Sithas related the tale of his search and the discovery of the flock. "I left the nestlings and several dozen females who had been feeding them in the valley. The rest came with me."

"There are *hundreds,*" observed Kith-Kanan, amazed.

"More than four hundred, I think, though I haven't made an exact count,"

"And the spell? It worked like it was supposed to?"

"I thought they were going to tear me apart. My hands were shaking so much I could hardly hold the scroll," Sithas exaggerated, "I read the incantation, and the words seemed to flame off the page. I had just finished the spell when the first one attacked."

"And then what?"

"He just landed in front of me, as if he was waiting for instructions. They *all* settled down. That's when I saw Arcuballis. When I mounted him and he took to the air, the others followed."

"By the gods! Let's see the humans try to stand against us *now!*" Kith-Kanan practically crowed his excitement.

"How have you fared? Not without some trouble, I see." Sithas indicated the pile of dead wolves, and Kith told him about the attack.

"They must have heard you coming," Kith speculated.

"Let's get back to the city. A whole winter has passed!" Sithas urged.

Kith turned toward the cave, suddenly spotting One-Tooth. The giant had observed—at first with interest, but then with ill-concealed concern—the exchange between the brothers.

It surprised the elf to realize the depth of the bond that had developed between them.

"Three-Legs fly away?" One-Tooth looked at Kith, frowning quizzically.

Kith didn't try to explain. Instead, he clasped one of the giant's big hands in both of his own. "I'll miss you," he said quietly. "You saved my life today—and I'm grateful to have had your friendship and protection!"

"Good-bye, friend," said the giant sadly.

Then it was time for the elves to mount the griffons and to turn their thoughts toward the future . . . toward home.

PART III

Windriders

Early Spring, Year of the Bear
2213 (PC)

19

The forestlands of Silvanost stretched below like a shaggy green carpet, extending to the far horizons and beyond. Huge winged shadows flickered across the ground, marking the path of the griffons. The creatures flew in great **V**-shaped wedges, several dozen griffons in each wedge. These formations spread across more than a mile.

Kith-Kanan and Sithas rode the first two of the mighty beasts, flying side by side toward their home. The forest had stretched below them for two days, but now, in the far distance, a faint glimmer of ivory light appeared. They soared faster than the wind, and swiftly that speck became identifiable as the Tower of the Stars. Soon the lesser towers of Silvanost came into view, jutting above the treetops like a field of sharp spires.

As they left the wilderness behind, Kith-Kanan thought fondly of the giant they had grown to know. One-Tooth had waved to them from the snow-filled valley until the fliers had vanished from sight. Kith-Kanan still remembered his one tusklike tooth bobbing up and down in a forlorn gesture of farewell.

They followed the River Thon-Thalas toward the island that held the elven capital. The griffons streamed into a long line behind them, and several of them uttered squawks of anticipation as they descended. Five hundred feet over the river, they raced southward, and soon the whole city sprawled below them.

The creatures shrieked and squalled, alarming the good citizens of Silvanost so much that, for several minutes, there existed a state of general panic, during which time most elves assumed that the war had come home to roost via some arcane and potent human ensorcelment.

Only when the two blond-haired elves were spotted did the panic turn to curiosity and wonder. And by the time Sithas and Kith-Kanan had circled the palace grounds and then led their charges in a gradual downward spiral toward the Gardens of Astarin, the word had spread. The emotions of the Silvanesti elves exploded into a spontaneous outpouring of joy.

Nirakina was the first to meet the twins as the great creatures settled to the ground. Their mother's eyes flowed with tears, and at first she could not speak. She took turns kissing each of them and then holding them at arms length, as if making sure that they were alive and fit.

Beyond her, Sithas saw Tamanier Ambrodel, and his spirit was buoyed even higher. Lord Ambrodel had returned from his secret mission to Thorbardin. Loyally, he had stayed discreet about what he had learned. Now he might have decisive news about a dwarven alliance in the elven war.

"Welcome home, Your Highness," Ambrodel said sincerely as Sithas clasped the lord chamberlain's shoulders.

"It's good to see you here to greet me! We will talk as soon as I can break away." Ambrodel nodded, the elf's narrow face reflecting private delight.

Meanwhile, the griffons continued to descend into the gardens, and across the gaming fields, and even into many of the nearby vegetable plots. They shrieked and growled, and the good citizens of the city gave them wide berth. Nevertheless, each griffon remained well behaved once it landed, moving only to preen its feathers or to settle weary wings and legs. When they had all landed, they squatted comfortably on the ground and took little note of the intense excitement surrounding them.

Kith-Kanan, with a barely noticeable limp, took his mother's arm as Hermathya and a dozen courtiers emerged from the Hall of Audience. Lord Quimant walked, with a quick stride, at their bead.

"Excellency!" he cried in delight, racing forward to warmly embrace the Speaker of the Stars.

Hermathya approached a good deal more slowly, greeting her husband with a formal kiss. Her greeting was cool, though her relief was obvious even through her pretense of annoyance.

"My son!" Sithas said excitedly. "Where is Vanesti?"

A nursemaid stepped forward, offering the infant to his father.

"Can this be him? How much he's changed!" Sithas, with a sense of awe, took his son in his arms while the crowd quieted.

Indeed, the elfin child was much larger than when they had departed, nearly half a year earlier. His blond hair grew thick upon his scalp. As his tiny eyes looked toward his father, Vanesti's face broke into a brilliant smile.

For several moments, Sithas seemed unable to speak. Hermathya came to him and very gently took the child. Turning away from her husband, her gaze briefly met Kith-Kanan's. He was startled by the look he saw there. It was cool and vacant, as if he did not exist. It had been many weeks since he had thought of her, but this expression provoked a brief, angry flash of jealousy—and, at the same time, a reminder of his guilt.

"Come—to the palace, everyone!" Sithas shouted, throwing an arm around his brother's shoulders. "Tonight there will be feast for all the city! Let word be spread immediately! Summon the bards. We have a tale for them to hear and to spread across the nation!"

The news carried through the city as fast as the cry could pass from lips to ear, and all the elves of Silvanost prepared to celebrate the return of the royal heirs. Butchers slaughtered prime pigs, casks of wine rumbled forth from the cellars, and colorful lanterns swiftly sprouted, as if by magic, from every tree, lamppost, and gate in the city. The festivities began immediately, and the citizenry danced in the streets and sang the great songs of the elven nation.

Meanwhile, Sithas and Kith-Kanan joined Lord Regent Quimant and Lord Chamberlain Tarnanier Ambrodel in a small audience chamber. The regent looked at the chamberlain with some surprise and turned to Sithas with a questioning look. When the Speaker of the Stars said nothing, Quimant cleared his throat and spoke awkwardly.

"Excellency, perhaps the lord chamberlain should join us after the conclusion of this conference. After all, some of the items I have to report are of the most confidential nature." He paused, as if embarrassed to continue.

"Indeed, in this nearly half a year that you have been absent, I must report that the lord chamberlain has not in fact been present in the capital. He only returned recently, from his family estates. Apparently matters of his clan's business interests took precedence over affairs of state."

"Tamanier Ambrodel has my complete confidence. Indeed," Sithas replied, "we may find that he has reports to make as well."

"Of course, my lord," Quimant said quickly, with a deep bow.

Quimant immediately started to fill them in on the events that had occurred during their absence.

"First, Sithelbec still stands as strong as ever." The lord of Clan Oakleaf anticipated Kith-Kanan's most urgent question.

"A messenger from the fortress broke through the lines a few weeks past, bringing word that the defenders have repulsed every attempt to storm the walls."

"Good. It is as I hoped," Kith replied. Nevertheless he was relieved.

"However, the pressure is increasing. We have word of a team of dwarven engineers—Theiwar, apparently—aiding the humans in excavating siege works against the walls. Also, the number of wild elves throwing in their lot with Ergoth is increasing steadily. There are more than a thousand of them, and apparently they have been formed into a 'free elf' company."

"Fighting their own people?" Sithas was aghast at the notion. His face reddened with controlled fury.

"More and more of them have questioned the right of Silvanost to rule them. And an expedition of the wild elves of the Kagonesti arrived here shortly after you left to plead for an end to the bloodshed."

"The ignoble scum!" Sithas rose to his feet and stalked across the chamber before whirling to face Quimant. Vivid lines of anger marred his face. "What did you tell them?"

"Nothing," Quimant replied, his own face displaying a smug grin. "They have spent the winter in your dungeon. Perhaps you'd care to speak to them yourself!"

"Good." Sithas nodded approvingly. "We can't have this kind of demonstration. We'll make an example of them to discourage any further treachery."

Kith-Kanan faced his brother. "Don't you want to—at the very least—hear what they have to say?"

Sithas looked at him as if he spoke a different language. "Why? They're traitors, that's obvious! Why should we—"

"*Traitors?* They have come here to talk. The traitors are those who have joined the enemy out of hand! We *need* to ask questions!"

"I find it astonishing that *you*, of all of us, should take this approach," Sithas said softly. "You are the one who has to carry out our plans, the one whose life is most at risk! Can you not understand that these ... *elves*"—Sithas spat the word as if it were anathema—"should be dealt with quickly and ruthlessly?"

"If they are indeed traitors, of course! But you can take the trouble to hear them first, to find out if they are in fact treacherous or simply honest citizens living in danger and fear!"

Sithas and Kith-Kanan glowered at each other like fierce strangers. Tamanier Ambrodel quietly watched the exchange. He had offered no opinion on any topic as yet, and he felt that this was not the time to interject his view. Lord Quimant, however, was more forthright.

"General, Excellency, please . . . there are more details. Some of the news is urgent." The lord stood and raised his hands.

Sithas nodded and collapsed into his chair. Kith-Kanan remained standing, turning expectantly toward the lord regent.

"Word out of Thorbardin arrived barely a fortnight ago. The ambassador, Than-Kar of the Theiwar clan, reported it to me in a most unpleasant and arrogant tone. His king, he claims, has ruled this to be a war between the humans and elves. The dwarves are determined to remain neutral."

"*No* troops? They will send us *nothing*?" Kith-Kanan stared at Quimant, appalled. Just when he had begun to see a glimmer of hope on the military horizon, to get news like this! Nothing could be more disastrous. The general slowly slumped into his chair, trying unsuccessfully to fight a rising wave of nausea.

Shaking his head in shock, he looked at his brother, expecting to see the same sense of dismay written across Sithas's face. Instead, however, the speaker's eyes had narrowed in an inscrutable expression. Didn't he *understand?*

"This is catastrophic!" Kith-Kanan exclaimed, angry that the Speaker didn't seem to grasp this basic fact. "Without the dwarves, we are doomed to be terribly outnumbered in every battle. Even with the griffons, we can't prevail against a quarter of a million men!"

"Indeed," Sithas agreed calmly. Finally he spoke to Ambrodel. "And your own mission, my lord, does that bear this information out?"

Lord Quimant gave a start when he realized that Sithas was addressing Ambrodel.

"Rather dramatically not, Excellency," Ambrodel replied softly. Kith-Kanan and Lord Quimant both stared at the chamberlain in mixed astonishment.

"I regret the subterfuge, my lords. The Speaker of the Stars instructed me to reveal my mission to no one, to report only to him."

"There was no reason to say anything—not until now," Sithas said. Once again, the others felt that commanding tone in his voice that brought all discussion to an abrupt halt. "If the lord chamberlain will continue . . . ?"

"Of course, Your Excellency." Ambrodel turned to include them all in his explanation. "I have wintered in the dwarven kingdom of Thorbardin . . ."

"What?" Quimant's jaw dropped. Kith-Kanan remained silent, but his lips compressed into a tight smile as he began to appreciate his brother's wiliness.

"It had been the Speaker's assessment, very early on, that

Ambassador Than-Kar was not doing an appropriately thorough job of maintaining open and honest communication between our two realms."

"I see," Quimant said, with a formal nod.

"Indeed, as events have developed, our esteemed leader's assessment has been proven to be accurate."

"Than-Kar has deliberately sabotaged our negotiations?" demanded Kith.

"Blatantly. King Hal-Waith has long backed our cause, as it was presented to him by Dunbarth Ironthumb upon that ambassador's return home. Than-Kar's original mission had been to report to us the king's intent to send twenty-five thousand troops to aid our cause."

"But I saw no sign of these troops on the plain. There is no word of them now, is there?" Kith-Kanan probed.

Quimant shook his head. "No—and certainly reports would have reached Silvanost had they marched during the winter."

"They did *not* march, not then," continued Ambrodel. "The offer of aid came with several conditions attached, conditions which Than-Kar reported to his king that we were unwilling to accept."

"Conditions?" Now Kith was concerned. "What conditions?"

"Fairly reasonable, under the circumstances. The dwarves recognize you as overall commander of the army, but they will not allow their own units to be broken up into smaller detachments—and dwarven units will work only under dwarven leaders."

"Those commanders presumably answerable to me under battle conditions?" Kith-Kanan asked.

"Yes."Ambrodel nodded.

The elven general couldn't believe his ears. Dwarven fighting prowess and tactical mastery were legendary. And twenty-five thousand such warriors . . . why, if they fought alongside a griffon cavalry, the siege of Sithelbec might be lifted in a long afternoon of fighting!

"There were some other minor points, also very reasonable. Bodies to be shipped to Thorbardin for burial, dwarven holidays honored, a steady supply of ale maintained, and so on. I do not anticipate any objection on your part."

"Of course not!" Kith-Kanan sprang to his feet again, this time in excitement. Then he remembered the obstruction presented by Than-Kar, and his mood darkened. "Have you concluded the deal? Must we still work through the ambassador? How long—"

Arnbrodel smiled and held up his hands. "The army was mustering as I left. For all I know, they have already emerged from the underground realm. They would march, I was promised, when the snowmelt in the Kharolis Mountains allowed free

426

passage." The chamberlain shivered as he remembered the long, dark winter he spent there. "It *never* gets warm in Thorbardin! You're always damp and squinting through the dark. By the gods, who knows how the dwarves can stand living underground?"

"And the ambassador?" This time Sithas asked the question. Once again those lines of anger tightened his face as he pondered the extent of Than-Kar's duplicity.

"King Hal-Waith would consider it a personal favor if we were to place him under arrest, detaining him until such time as the next dwarven mission arrives. It should be here sometime during the summer."

"Any word on numbers? On their march route?" Tactics already swirled through Kith-Kanan's head.

Ambrodel pursed his lips and shook his head. "Only the name of the commander, whom I trust will meet with your approval."

"Dunbarth Ironthumb?" Kith-Kanan was hopeful.

"None other."

"That *is* good news!" That dignified statesman had been the brightest element of the otherwise frustrating councils between Thorbardin, Silvanesti, and Ergoth. The ambassador from the dwarven nation had retained a sense of humor and self-deprecating whimsy that had lightened many an otherwise tedious session of negotiation.

"Where am I to join him?" Kith-Kanan asked. "Shall I take Arcuballis and fly to Thorbardin itself?"

Ambrodel shook his head. "I don't think you could. The gates remain carefully hidden."

"But surely *you* could direct me! Didn't you say that you have been there?"

"Indeed," the chamberlain agreed with a nod. He coughed awkwardly. "But to tell you the truth, I never saw the gates, nor could I describe the approach to you or to anyone."

"How did you get in, then?"

"It's a trifle embarrassing, actually. I spent nearly a month floundering around in the mountains, seeking a trail or a road or any kind of sign of the gate. I found nothing. Finally, however, I was met in my camp by a small band of dwarven scouts. Apparently they keep an eye on the perimeter and were watching my hapless movements, wondering what I was up to."

"But you must have entered through the gate," Kith said.

"Indeed," nodded Ambrodel. "But I spent the two days of the approach—two very *long* days, I might add—stumbling along with a blindfold over my eyes."

"That's an outrage!" barked Quimant, stiffening in agitation. "An insult to our race!"

427

Sithas, too, scowled. Only Kith-Kanan reacted with a thin smile and a nod of understanding. "With treachery among their own people, it only seems a natural precaution," the elven general remarked. That lessened the tension, and Ambrodel nodded in reluctant agreement.

"Excellency," inquired Quimant, with careful formality. It was obvious that the lord regent was annoyed by not having been apprised of the secret negotiations. "This is indeed a most splendid development, but was it necessary to retain such a level of secrecy? Perhaps I could have aided the cause had I been kept informed."

"Indeed, quite true, my good cousin-in-law. There was no fear that the knowledge would have been misplaced in you—save this one: in your position as regent, you are the one who has spent the greatest amount of time with Than-Kar. It was essential that the ambassador not know of this plan, and I felt that the safest way to keep you from a revealing slip—inadvertent, of course—was to withhold the knowledge from you. The decision was mine alone."

"I cannot question the Speaker's wisdom," replied the noble humbly. "This is a most encouraging turn of events."

* * * * *

Kith left the meeting in order to arrange for the postings around the city. He wanted all Silvanost to quickly learn of the call for volunteers. He intended to personally interview and test all applicants for the griffon cavalry.

Sithas remained behind, with Quimant and Ambrodel, to attend to matters of government. "As to the city, how has it fared in our absence?"

Quimant informed him of other matters: Weapons production was splendid, with a great stockpile of arms gathered; refugees from the plains had stopped coming to Silvanost—a fact that had greatly eased the tensions and crowding within the city. The higher taxes that Sithas had decreed, in order to pay for the war, had been collected with only a few minor incidents.

"There has been some violence along the waterfront. The city guard has confronted Than-Kar's escorts on more than one occasion. We've had several elves badly injured and one killed during these brawls."

"The Theiwar?" guessed Sithas.

"Indeed. The primary troublemakers can be found among the officers of Than-Kar's guard, as if they *want* to create an incident." Quimant's disgust with the dwarves was apparent in his sarcastic tone.

"We'll deal with them . . . when the time is right. We'll wait till Kith-Kanan forms his cavalry and departs for the west."

"I'm certain he'll have no shortage of volunteers. There are many noble elves who had resisted the call to arms, as it applies to the infantry," said Lord Quimant. "They'll leap at the chance to form an elite unit, especially with the threat of conscription hanging over their heads!"

"We'll keep news of Thorbardin's commitment secret," Sithas added. "Not a word of it is to leave this room. In the meantime, tell me about the additional troops for the infantry. How fares the training of the new regiments?"

"We have five thousand elves under arms, ready to march when you give the command."

"I had hoped for more."

Quimant hemmed and hawed. "The sentiment in the city is not wholly in favor of the war. Our people do not seem to grasp the stakes here."

"We'll *make* them understand," growled Sithas, looking to the lord as if he expected Quimant to challenge him. His wife's cousin remained silent on that point, however.

Instead, Quimant hesitantly offered another suggestion. "We do have another source of troops," he ventured. "However, they may not meet with the Speaker's satisfaction."

"Another source? Where?" Sithas demanded.

"Humans—mercenaries. There are great bands of them in the plains north of here and over to the west. Many of them bear no great love for the emperor of Ergoth and would be willing to join our service—for a price, of course."

"Never!" Sithas leaped to his feet, livid. "How can you even suggest such an abomination! If we cannot preserve our nation with our own troops, we do not deserve victory!"

His voice rang from the walls of the small chamber, and he glared at Quimant and Ambrodel, as if daring a challenge. None was forthcoming, and slowly the Speaker of the Stars relaxed.

"Forgive my outburst," he said, with a nod to Quimant. "You were merely making a suggestion. That I understand."

"Consider the suggestion withdrawn." The lord bowed to his ruler.

* * * * *

The recruits for the griffon-mounted cavalry were sworn in during a sunny ceremony a week after the brothers had arrived in the city. The event was held on the gaming fields beyond the gardens, for no place else in the city provided enough open space for the great steeds and their proud newly appointed riders to assemble.

Thousands of elves turned out to watch, overflowing the large grandstands and lining the perimeter of the fields. Others gathered in the nearby towers, many of which rose a hundred feet or more into the air, providing splendid vantage.

"I welcome you, brave elves, to the ranks of an elite and decisive force, unique in our grand history!" Kith-Kanan addressed the recruits while the onlookers strained to hear his words.

"We shall take to the sky under a name that bespeaks our speed—henceforth we shall be known as the Windriders!"

A great cheer arose from the warriors and the spectators.

As Quimant had predicted, many scions of noble families had flocked to the call to arms once they learned of the nature of the elite unit. Kith-Kanan had disappointed and angered a great number of them by selecting his troops only after extensive combat tests and rigorous training procedures. Sons of masons, carpenters, and laborers were offered the same opportunities as the proud heirs of the noble houses. Those who were not truly desirous of the honor, or were unwilling or incapable of meeting the high standards established by Kith-Kanan, quickly fell away, consigned to the infantry. At the end of the brutal week of tests, the elven commander had been left with more than a thousand elves of proven courage, dedication, and skill.

"You will train in the use of the light lance, the elven longbow, and the steel-edged longsword. Lances will be wielded in the air or on the ground!"

He looked over the assembled elves. They stood, a pair flanking each griffon, wearing shiny steel helms with long plumes of horsehair. The Windriders wore supple leather boots and smooth torso armor of black leather. They were a formidable force, and the training to come would only enhance their abilities.

Brass trumpets blared the climax of the ceremony, and each of the Windriders received a steel-edged shortsword, which would be worn throughout the training. They would have to learn fast, Kith-Kanan had warned his new recruits, and he knew that they would.

He looked to the west, suddenly restless. It won't be long, now, he told himself.

Soon the siege of Sithelbec would be broken—and how long after that would it be before the war was won?

Midspring
2213 (PC)

20

Kith-Kanan couldn't sleep. He went for a walk in the gardens of Astarin, relieved that the griffons had all been moved to the sporting fields. There the creatures rested and enjoyed the fresh meat that the palace liverymen hastily had butchered and carted over to them.

For a time, the elf lost himself in the twists and turns of the elegant gardens. The soothing surroundings took him back to his youth, to untroubled days and, later, to passionate nights. How many times, he reflected, had he and Hermathya met among this secluded foliage?

Anxiously he tried to shrug off the memories. Soon he and Arcuballis would take to the air, leaving this city and its temptations behind. The mere sight of her was a source of deep guilt and discomfort to him.

As if circumstances mirrored his thoughts, he turned a corner and encountered his brother's wife, walking in quiet contemplation. Hermathya looked up, but if she was at all surprised to encounter him, her face didn't reveal anything.

"Hello, Kith-Kanan." Her smile was deep and warm—and suddenly, it seemed to Kith, reckless.

"Hello, Hermathya." He was certainly surprised to see her. The rest of the palace was dark, and the hour was quite late.

"I saw you come to the garden and came here to find you," she informed him.

Alarms bells went off in his mind as he gazed at her. By the gods, how beautiful she was! No woman he had ever known aroused him like Hermathya. Not even Anaya. He could tell, by the smoldering look in her eyes, that her thoughts were similar.

She took a step toward him.

The instinct to reach out and crush her to him, to pull her into his arms and touch her, was almost overpowering. But at the same time, he had sordid memories of their last tryst and her unfaithfulness to his brother. He wanted her, but he dare not weaken again—especially now, after all that he and Sithas had been through together.

Only with a great effort of will did Kith-Kanan step back, raising his hands to stop her approach.

"You are my brother's wife," he said, somewhat irrelevantly.

"I was his wife last autumn," she spat, suddenly venomous.

"Last autumn was a mistake. Hermathya, I loved you once. I think of you now more than I care to admit. But I will not betray my brother!" Again, he added silently. "Can you accept this? Can we be members of the same family and not torment each other with memories of a past that ought to be buried and forgotten?"

Hermathya suddenly clasped her hands over her face. Her body wracking with sobs, she turned and ran, swiftly disappearing from Kith-Kanan's sight.

For a long time afterward, he stared at the spot where she had stood. The image of her body, of her face, of her exquisite presence, remained vivid in his mind, almost as if she was still there.

* * * * *

Three days later, Kith was ready to embark. His plan of battle had been made, but there remained many things to be done. The Windriders wouldn't fly to the west for another six weeks. Under the tutelage of their new captain, Hallus, they had to train rigorously in the meantime.

"How long do you think it will take to find Dunbarth?" asked Sithas when he, his mother, and Tamanier Ambrodel came to see Kith-Kanan off.

Kith shrugged. "That's one reason I'm leaving right away. I have to hook up with the dwarves and fill them in on the timetable, then get to Sithelbec before the Windriders."

"Be careful," his mother urged. The color had come back into her face since the brothers' return, and for the past several weeks she had seemed as merry and robust as ever. Now she struggled not to weep.

"I will," Kith promised, holding her in his arms. They all hoped the war would end quickly but understood that it might be many months, even years, before he could return.

The door to the audience chamber burst open, and the elves whirled, surprised and then amused. Vanesti stood there.

Sithas's son, not yet a year old, toddled toward them with an unsteady gait and a broad smile across his elven features. In his hand, he brandished a wooden sword, slashing at imagined enemies to the right and left until his own momentum toppled him to the floor. The sword abandoned, he rose and approached Kith-Kanan unsteadily.

"Pa-pa!" cried the tiny elf, beaming.

Kith blushed and stepped aside. *"There's* your papa," he said, indicating Sithas.

Kith-Kanan noted how much Vanesti had changed during the course of their winter in the mountains. Conceivably the war could drag on for several more years. The toddler would be a young boy by the next time he saw him.

"Come to Uncle Kith, Vanesti. Say good-bye before I ride the griffon!"

Vanesti pouted briefly, but then he wrapped his uncle in a hug. Lifting the tiny fellow up and holding him Kith felt a pang of regret. Would he ever be able to settle down and have children of his own?

Once again Kith-Kanan and Arcuballis took off on an important mission. The vast forestlands of Silvanesti sprawled beneath them. Far to the south, Kith caught an occasional glimpse of the Courrain Ocean, which stretched past the horizon with a limitless expanse.

Soon he came to the plains, and they continued to soar high above the sea of grass that stretched to the limits of his vision. He knew that, northward, his embattled Wildrunners still held their fortress against the pressing human horde. Soon he would join them.

He spotted the snowy crests of the Kharolis Mountains jutting into the sky. For a full day, Kith watched the imposing heights grow closer, until at last he flew above the wooded valleys that extended from the heart of the range and he was encircled on all sides by great peaks.

Here he began his search in earnest. He knew that the kingdom of Thorbardin lay entirely underground, with great gates providing access from the north and south, The snowmelt had long passed from the forested valleys to the high slopes. The gate, he reasoned, would occupy a lower elevation, both for enhanced concealment and easier access.

He searched along these valleys every day from first to last light, seeking a sign of the passage of the dwarven army. The land consisted of almost entirely uninhabited wilderness, so he reckoned that the march of twenty thousand heavy-booted dwarves would leave some kind of obvious trail.

For days, his search was fruitless. He began to chafe at the lost time. Borne by his speedy griffon, he crossed the range two full times, but never did he find the evidence he sought. His search took him through all of the high valleys and much of the lower foothills. He decided in desperation that he would make his last sweep along the very northern fringe of the range, where the jagged foothills petered out into low slopes and finally the flat and expansive plains.

Frequent rainstorms, often accompanied by thunder and lightning, hampered his search. He spent many miserable afternoons huddled with Arcuballis under whatever shelter they could find while hail and rain battered the land. He wasn't surprised, for spring weather was notoriously violent on the plains, yet the forced delays were extremely dispiriting.

Nearly two weeks into his search, he was working his way to the north, following a broad zigzag from east to west. The sun was high that day, so much so that he could see his shadow directly below him. Finally the shadow ebbed away toward the east, matching the sun's descent in the west. Still he had seen no sign of his quarry.

It was near sunset when something caught his eye.

"Let's go, old boy—down there," he said, unconsciously voicing the command that he simultaneously relayed to Arcuballis through subtle pressure from his knees on the griffon's tawny flanks. The creature tucked his wings and swooped low, flying along a shallow stream that marked a broad, flat valley bottom.

At one place, however, the river spilled over a ten-foot shelf of rock, creating a bright and scenic waterfall. It wasn't the beauty of the scene that had caught Kith-Kanan's eye, however.

The elf noticed that the brush lining the streambanks was flattened and trampled; indeed, there was a swath some twenty feet wide. The matted brush and grass extended in an arc from the streambed above the falls to the waterway.

Kith-Kanan could see no other sign of passage anywhere in this broad, meadow-lined valley, nor were there any groves of trees that might have concealed a trail. Arcuballis came to rest on a large boulder near the streambank. Kith swiftly dismounted, leaving the griffon to preen his feathers and keep an eye alert for danger while the elf explored the terrain.

The first thing he noticed was the muddy streambank. Higher up, where the earth was slightly drier, he saw something that made his heart pound.

Bootprints! Heavy footgear had trod here, and in great numbers. The prints indicated their wearers were heading down the valley after emerging from the streambed. Of course! The dwarves had taken great pains to keep the entrance to their kingdom a secret, and now Kith understood why there had been no road, nor even a heavily used path, leading to the north gate of Thorbardin.

The dwarves had marched along the streambed!

"Come on—back into the sky!" he shouted, rousing Arcuballis.

The creature crouched low to allow Kith to leap into the wide, deep saddle. The elf lashed himself in with one smooth motion and kicked the griffon's flanks sharply.

Instantly Arcuballis sprang from the rock, his powerful wings driving downward to carry them through the air. As the griffon began to climb, Kith-Kanan nudged him with his knees, guiding him low above the stream.

They glided along the course of the stream while Kith-Kanan searched the ground along either bank for more signs. Thank the gods for that waterfall! Dusk soon cast long shadows across the valley, and Kith-Kanan realized that he would have to postpone his search until the morrow.

Nevertheless, it was with high spirits that he directed Arcuballis to land. They camped beneath an earthen overhang on the banks of the stream, and the griffon snatched nearly a dozen plump trout from the water with lighting grasps of his eagle-clawed forefeet. Kith-Kanan feasted on a pair of these while the griffon enjoyed his share.

The next morning Kith again beat the morning sun into the sky, and within an hour, he had left the foothills behind. The mountain stream he followed joined another gravel-bottomed watercourse, and here it became a placid brook, silt-bottomed and sluggish.

Here, too, there were signs that the dwarven column had emerged to march overland.

Now Kith-Kanan urged Arcuballis ahead, and the griffon's wings carried them to a lofty height. The trail became a wide rut of muddy earth, clearly visible even from a thousand feet in the air. The griffon followed the path below while the elf's eyes scanned the horizon. For much of the day, all he could see was the long brown trail vanishing into the haze of the north.

Kith-Kanan began to worry that the dwarves had already reached Sithelbec. Certainly they were tough and capable fighters, but even in their compact formations, they would be vulnerable to the sweeping charges of the human cavalry if they fought without the support of auxiliary forces.

It was late afternoon before he finally caught sight of his goal and knew that he was not too late. The marching column stretched as straight as a spear shaft across the plains, moving toward the north. Kith urged the griffon downward, picking up speed.

As he flew closer, he saw that the figures marched with military precision in a long column that was eight dwarves wide. How far into the distance the troops extended he could not be certain, though he flew overhead for several minutes after he had observed the tail of the column before he could even see its lead formations.

Now he was spotted from below. The tail of the column split and turned, while companies of short, stocky fighters broke to the right and left, quickly swinging into defensive postures. As Arcuballis dived lower, he saw the bearded faces, the metal helms with their plumes of feathers or hair, and, most significantly, the rank of heavy crossbows raised to fire!

He pulled back on the reins and brought Arcuballis into a sharp climb, hoping he was out of range and that the dwarves wouldn't, shoot without first identifying their target.

"Ho! Dwarves of Thorbardin!" he called, soaring about two hundred feet over the ranks of suspicious upturned faces.

"Who are you?" demanded one, a grizzled captain with a shiny helmet plumed by bright red feathers.

"Kith-Kanan! Is that you?" cried another gruff voice, one that the elf recognized.

"Dunbarth Ironthumb!" the elf shouted back, waving at the familiar figure.

Happy and relieved, he brought the griffon through a long, circling dive. Finally Arcuballis came to rest on the ground, though the griffon pranced and squawked nervously at the troops arrayed before him.

Dunbarth Ironthumb clumped toward him, a wide smile splitting his full, gray-flecked beard. Unlike the other officers of his column, the dwarf wore a plain, unadorned breastplate and a simple steel cap.

Kith sprang from the saddle and seized the stalwart dwarf in a bear hug. "By the gods, you old goat, I thought I'd never find you!" he declared.

"Humph!" snorted Dunbarth. "If we'd wanted to be found, we would have posted signs! Still, what with the storms we've been dodging—floods, lightning, even a black funnel cloud!—it's a lucky thing you did find us. Why were you looking?"

The grizzled dwarf raised his eyebrows in curiosity, waiting for Kith to speak.

"It's a long story," the elf explained. "I'll save it for the campfire tonight!"

"Good enough," grunted Dunbarth. "We'll be making camp after another mile." The dwarven commander paused then snapped his fingers in sudden decision.

"To the Abyss with it! We'll make camp here!"

Dunbarth made Kith-Kanan laugh easily. The elf commander ate the hardtack of the dwarves around the fire, and even took a draft of the cool, bitter ale that the dwarves hold so dear but which elves almost universally find to be unpleasant to the palate.

As the fire died into coals, he spoke with Dunbarth and a number of that dwarf's officers. He told them of the mission to capture the griffons and of the forming of the Windriders. His comrades took heart from the tale of the flying cavalry that would aid them in battle.

He also described, to mutters of indignation and anger, the complicity of Than-Kar and his brother's plans to arrest the ambassador and return him to King Hal-Waith in chains.

"Typical Theiwar treachery!" growled Dunbarth. "Never turn your back on 'em, I can tell you! He never should have been entrusted with a mission of such importance!"

"Why was he?" Kith inquired. "Don't let it go to your head, but you were always a splendid representative for your king and your people. Why did Hal-Waith send a replacement?"

Dunbarth Ironthumb shook his head and spat into the fire. "Part of it was my own fault, I admit. I *wanted* to go home. All that talking and diplomacy was getting on my nerves—plus, I'd never spent more than a few months on the surface at a time. I was in Silvanost for a full year, you'll remember, not counting time on the march."

"Indeed," Kith-Kanan said, nodding. He remembered Tamanier Ambrodel's remarks about that elf's long months underground. For the first time, he began to understand the adjustment these subterranean warriors must make in order to undertake an aboveground campaign. Growing up, working and training—all their lives were spent underground.

Surprising emotion choked his throat, for suddenly he realized the depth of the commitment that had brought forth the dwarven army. He looked at Dunbarth and hoped that the dwarf understood the strength of his appreciation.

Dunbarth Ironthumb gruffly cleared his throat and continued. "We have a tricky equilibrium in Thorbardin, I'm sure you appreciate. We of the Hylar Clan control the central realms, including the Life-Tree."

Kith-Kanan had heard of that massive structure, a cave city all of its own carved from the living stone of a monstrous stalagmite. He nodded his understanding.

"The other clans of Thorbardin all have their own realms—the Daergar, the Daewar, the Mar, and the Theiwar," continued Dunbarth. The old dwarf sighed. "We are a stubborn people, it is well known, and sometimes hasty to anger. In none of us are these traits so prevalent as among the Theiwar. But also there is a level of malevolence, of greed and scheming and ambition, among our paleskinned brethren that is not to be found among the higher dwarvert cultures. The Theiwar are much distrusted by the rest of the clans."

"Then why would the king appoint a Theiwar as ambassador to Silvanesti?" Kith-Kanan asked,

"Alas, they are all those things I said, but so too are the Theiwar numerous and powerful. They make up a large proportion of the kingdom's population, and they cannot be excluded from its politics. The king must select his ambassadors, his nobles, even his high clerics from the ranks of *all* the clans, including the Theiwar."

Dunbarth looked the elf squarely in the eye. "King Hal-Waith thought, mistakenly it would appear, that the crucial negotiations with the elves had been concluded with my departure from your capital. Therefore he took the chance of appointing a Theiwar to replace me, having in mind another important task for me and knowing that the Theiwar Clan would make a considerable disturbance if they were once again bypassed for such a prominent ambassadorship.

"I think you start to get the picture," Dunbarth continued. "But now to matters that lie before us, instead of behind. Do you have plans for a summer campaign?"

"The wheels are already in motion," Kith explained. "And now that I have caught up with you, we can put the final phase of the strategy into motion."

"Splendid!" Dunbarth beamed, all but licking his lips in anticipation.

Kith-Kanan went on to outline his battle plan, and the dwarven warrior's eyes lit up as every detail was described.

"If you can pull it off," he grunted in approval after Kith-Kanan had finished, "it will be a victory that the bards will sing about for years!"

They spent the rest of the evening making less momentous conversation, and around midnight, Kith-Kanan made his camp among the army of his allies. At dawn, he was up and saddling Arcuballis, preparing to leave. The dwarves were awake, too, ready to march.

"Less than three weeks to go," said Dunbarth, with a wink.

"Don't be late for the war!" chided Kith. Moments later, the sunlight flickered from the griffon's wing feathers a hundred feet above the dwarven column.

Arcuballis soared into the sky, higher and higher. Yet it was many hours before Kith saw it, a blocklike shape that looked tiny and insignificant from his tremendous height. He would reach it by dark. It was Sithelbec, and for now at least, it was home.

Late Spring in the Army of Ergoth

21

Long rows of makeshift litters filled the ten, and upon them, Suzine saw men with ghastly wounds—men who bled and suffered and died even before she could begin to treat them. She saw others with invisible hurts—warriors who lay still and unseeing, though often their eyes remained open and fixed. Oil lanterns sputtered from tent poles, while clerics and nurses moved among the wounded.

Men groaned and shrieked and sobbed pathetically. Others were delirious, madly babbling about pastoral surroundings they would in all likelihood never see again.

And the stench! There were the raw smells of filth, urine, and feces, and the sweltering cloud of too many men in too small an area. And there were the smells of blood, and of rotting meat. Above all, there remained an ever-pervasive odor of death.

For months, Suzine had done all that she could for the wounded, nursing them, tending their injuries, providing them what solace she could. For a time, there had been fewer and fewer wounded as those who had been injured in the battles of the winter had been healed or perished or were sent back to Ergoth.

But now it was a new season, and it seemed that the war had acquired a new ferocity. Just a few days earlier, Giarna had hurled tens of thousands of men at the walls of Sithelbec in a savage attempt to smash through the barricades. A group of the wild elves

440

had led the way, but the elves within the fortress had fallen upon their kin and the humans who followed with a furious vengeance. More than a thousand had perished in the fight, while these hundreds around her represented just a portion of those who had escaped with varying degrees of injuries.

Most of the suffering were humans, but there were a number of elves—those who fought against Silvanesti—and Theiwar dwarves as well. The Theiwar, under the stocky captain Kalawax, had spearheaded one assault, attempting to tunnel under the fortress walls. The elves had anticipated the maneuver and filled the tunnel, jammed tightly with dwarves, with barrels full of oil, which had then been set alight. Death had been fast and horrible.

Suzine went from cot to cot, offering water or a cool cloth upon a forehead. She was surrounded by filth and despair, but she herself bore hurts that could not be seen but which nevertheless cut deeply into her spirit.

So Suzine felt a kinship with these hapless souls and gained what little comfort she could by caring for them and tending their hurts. She remained throughout most of this long night, knowing that Giarna was tormented by the failure of his attack that he might seek her out. If he found her, he would hurt her as he always did, but here he would never come.

The hours of darkness passed, and gradually the camp fell into restless silence. Past midnight, even those men in the most severe pain collapsed into tentative slumber. Weary to the point of collapse, praying that Giarna already slept, she finally left the wounded to return to her own shelter.

Outside the hospital tent waited her two guards, the men-at-arms who escorted her when she moved about the camp. Actually they were a pair of the Kagonesti elves who had joined ranks with the army in the hope that it offered them a chance to gain independence for their people. Oddly, she had come to enjoy the presence of the soft-spoken, competent warriors in their face paint, feathers, and dark leather garb.

Suzine had wondered how such elves could rationalize their fight, since it was waged with great terror against their own people. Several times she had asked the Kagonesti about their reasons, but only once had she gotten an honest answer—from a young elf she was caring for, who had been wounded in one of the attempts to storm the fortress walls.

"My mother and father have been taken as slaves to work in the iron mines north of Silvanost," he had told her, his voice full of bitterness. "And my family's farm was seized by the Speaker's troops when my father was unable to pay his taxes."

"But to go to war against your own people," she had wondered.

"Many of my people have been hurt by the elves of Silvanost. *My* people are the Kagonesti and the elves of the plains! Those who live in that crystal city of towers are no more my kin than are the dwarves of Thorbardin!"

"Do you wish to see the elven nation destroyed?"

"I only wish for the wild elves to be left alone, to regain our freedom and to have nothing to do with the causes of governments that have made our lands a battleground!" The elf had gasped his beliefs with surprising vehemence, struggling to sit up until Suzine eased him back down.

"If the Emperor of Ergoth treats us ill after this war is won, then shall we struggle against him with the same fortitude! But until that time, the human army is our only hope of throwing off the yoke of Silvanesti oppression!"

She had been deeply disturbed by the elf's declarations, for it did not fit her idea of Kith-Kanan to hear such tales of injustice and discrimination. Surely he didn't know of the treatment accorded to Kagonesti by his own people!

Thus she had convinced herself of his innocence and looked upon the Kagonesti elves with pity. Those who had joined the human army she befriended and tried to ease their troubled hurts.

Now her two guards held open her tent flap for her and waited silently outside. They would stand there until dawn, when they would be relieved. As always, this knowledge gave her a sense of security, and she lay down, totally exhausted, to try to get some sleep.

But though she lay wearily upon her quilt, she couldn't sleep. An odd sense of excitement took hold of her emotions, and suddenly she sat up, aroused and intrigued.

Instinctively she went to her mirror. Holding the crystal on her dressing table, she saw her own image first, and then she concentrated on setting her mind free.

Immediately she espied that handsome elven face, the visage she had not looked upon for nearly eight months. Her heart leaped into her throat and she stifled a gasp. It was Kith-Kanan.

His hair flew back from his face, as though tossed by a strong wind. She remembered the griffon, only this time, instead of flying away from her, he was returning!

She stared at the mirror, breathless. She should report this to her general immediately. The elven general was returning to his fortress!

Yet at the same time, she sensed a decision deep within her. The return of Kith-Kanan stirred her emotions. He looked magnificent, proud and triumphant. How unlike General Giarna! She knew she would say nothing about what she had seen.

Swiftly, guiltily, she placed the mirror back inside of its velvet-lined case. Almost slamming the engraved ivory lid in her haste, she hid the object deep within her wardrobe trunk and returned to her bed.

Suzine had barely stretched out, still tense with excitement, when a gust of wind brushed across her face. She sensed that the flap of her tent had opened, though she could see nothing in the heavy darkness.

Instantly she felt fear. Her elven guards would stand firm against any illicit intruder, but there was one they would not stop—did not dare stop—for he held their fates in his hands.

Giarna came to her then and touched her. She felt his touch like a physical assault, a hurt that would leave no scar that could be seen.

How she hated him! She despised everything that he stood for. He was the master slayer. She hated the way he used her, used everyone around him,

But now she could bear her hatred because of the knowledge of a blond-haired elf and his proud flying steed—knowledge that, even as General Giarna took her, she found solace in, knowledge that was hers alone.

* * * * *

Kith-Kanan guided Arcuballis through the pitch-dark skies, seeking the lanterns of Sithelbec. He had passed over the thousands of campfires that marked the position of the human army, so he knew that the elven stronghold lay close before him. He needed to find the fortress before daylight so that the humans wouldn't learn of his return to the plains.

There! A light gleamed in the darkness. And another!

He urged Arcuballis downward, and the griffon swept into a shallow dive. They circled once and saw three lights arranged in a perfect triangle, glimmering on the rooftop, That was the sign, the signal he had ordered Parnigar to use to guide him back to the barracks.

Indeed, as the griffon spread his wings to set them gently atop the tower, he saw his trusted second-in-command holding one of the lights. The other lantern-bearers were his old teacher, Kencathedrus, and the steadfast Kagonesti elf known as White-lock.

The two officers saluted smartly and then clasped their commander warmly.

"By the gods, sir, it's good to see you again!" said Parnigar gruffly.

"It is a pleasure and a relief. We've been terribly worried!" Kencathedrus couldn't help but sound a little stem.

"I have a good excuse. Now let's get me and Arcuballis out

of sight before first light. I don't want the troops to know I've returned—not yet, in any event."

The officers looked at him curiously but held their questions in check while arrangements were made with a stablemaster to secure Arcuballis in an enclosed stall. Meanwhile, Kith-Kanan, concealed by a flowing, heavy robe, slipped into Kencathedrus's chamber and awaited the two elven warriors. They joined him just as dawn was beginning to lighten the eastern horizon.

Kith-Kanan told them of the quest for the griffons, describing the regiment of flying troops and the coming of the dwarves and detailing his battle plans.

"Two weeks, then?" asked Parnigar, scarcely able to contain his excitement.

"Indeed, my friend—after all this time." Kith-Kanan understood what these elves had been through. His own ordeals had been far from cheery. Yet how difficult it must have been for these dynamic warriors to spend the winter and the spring and the first few weeks of summer cooped up within the fortress.

"Fresh regiments are on the march to Sithelbec. The Windriders will leave in a few days, making their way westward. The dwarves of Thorbardin, too, are preparing to move into position."

"But you wish your own presence to remain secret?" asked Kencathedrus.

"Until we're ready to attack. I don't want the enemy to suspect any changes in our defenses. When the attack develops, I want it to be the biggest surprise they've ever had."

"Hopefully the *last* surprise," growled Parnigar.

"I'll stay here for a week, then fly west at night to arrange the rendezvous with the forces arriving from Silvanost. When I return, we'll attack. Until then, conduct your defenses as you have in the past. Just don't allow them to gain a breach."

"These old walls have held well," Parnigar noted. "The humans have tried to assault them several times and always we drove them back over the heaped bodies of their dead."

"The spring storms, in fact, did us more harm than all the human attacks." Kencathedrus added.

"I flew through some of them," Kith-Kanan said. "And I heard Dunbarth speak of them."

"Hail crushed two of the barns. We lost a lot of our livestock." Kencathedrus recounted the damage. "And a pair of tornadoes swept past, doing some damage to the outer wall."

Parnigar chuckled grimly. "*Some* damage to the wooden wall— and a lot of damage to the human tents!"

"True. The destruction outside the walls was even worse than within. I have never seen weather so violent."

"It happens every year, more or less," Parnigar, the more experienced plainsman, explained. "Though this spring was a little fiercer than most. Old elves tell of a storm three hundred years ago when a hundred cyclones came roaring in from the west and tore up every farm within a thousand miles."

Kith-Kanan shook his head, trying to imagine such a thing. It even dwarfed war! He turned his attention to other matters. "How about the size of the human army? Have they been able to replace their losses? Has it grown or diminished?"

"As near as we can tell—" Parnigar started to answer, but Kith-Kanan's former teacher cut him off.

"There's *one* addition they've had, it shames me to admit!" Kencathedrus barked. Parnigar nodded sorrowfully as the captain of the Silvanesti continued.

"Elves! From the woods! It seems they're content to serve an army of human invaders, caring naught that they wage war against their own kingdom!" The elf, born and bred amid the towers of Silvanost, couldn't understand such base treachery.

"I have heard this, to my surprise. Why are they party to this?" Kith-Kanan asked Parnigar.

The Wildrunner shrugged. "Some of them resent the taxes levied upon them by a far-off capital, with the debtors taken for servitude in the Clan Oakleaf mines. Others feel that trade with the humans is a good thing and opens opportunities for their children that they didn't have before. There are thousands of elves who feel little if any loyalty to the throne."

"Nevertheless, it is gravely disturbing," Kith-Kanan sighed. The problem vexed him, but he saw no solution at the present.

"You'll need some rest," noted Kencathedrus. "In the meantime, we'll tend to the details."

"Of course!" Parnigar echoed.

"I knew that I could count on you!" Kith-Kanan declared, feeling overwhelmed by a sense of gratitude. "May the future bring us the victory and the freedom that we have worked so hard for!"

He took the officers up on their offer of a private bunk and enjoyed the feel of a mattress beneath his body for the first time in several weeks. There was little more he could do at the moment, and he fell into a luxurious slumber that lasted for more than twelve hours.

Clan Oakleaf

22

The mouth of the coal mine gaped like the maw of some insatiable beast, hungry for the bodies of the sootblackened miners who trudged wearily between the shoring timbers to disappear into the darkness within. They marched in a long file, more than a hundred of them, guarded by a dozen whip-wielding overseers.

Sithas and Lord Quimant stood atop the steep slope that led down into the quarry. The noise from below pounded their ears. Immediately below them, a slave-powered conveyor belt carried chunks of crushed ore from a pit, where other slaves smashed the rock with picks and hammers, to the bellowing ovens of the smelting plant. There more laborers shoveled coal from huge black piles into the roaring heat of the furnace. Beyond the smelting sheds rose the smoke-spewing stacks of the weaponsmiths, where raw, hot steel was pounded into razor-edged armaments.

Some of the prisoners wore chain shackles at their ankles. "Those are the ones who have tried to escape," Lord Quimant explained. Most simply marched along, not needing any physical restraint, for they had been broken as slaves in a deeper, more permanent sense. Each of these trudged, eyes cast downward, almost tripping over the one ahead of him in the line.

"Most of them become quite docile," the lord continued, "after a year or two of labor. The guards encourage this. A slave who cooperates and works hard is generally left alone, while those who show rebelliousness or a reluctance to work are . . . disciplined."

One of the overseers cracked his whip against the back of a slave about to enter the mines. This fellow had lagged behind, opening a gap between himself and the worker in front of him. At the flick of the lash, he cried out in pain and stumbled forward. Even from his height, Sithas saw the red welt spread across the slave's back.

In his haste, the slave stumbled then crawled pathetically to his feet under another flurry of lashes from the guard.

"Watch now. The rest of them will step quite lively."

Indeed, the other slaves did hasten into the black abyss, but Sithas didn't think such cruelty was warranted.

"Is he a human or an elf?" wondered the Speaker.

"Who—oh, the tardy one?" Quimant shrugged. "They get so covered with dust that I can't really tell. Not that it makes much difference. We treat everybody the same here."

"Is that wise?" Sithas was more disturbed than he thought he would be about the brutality he saw here.

Lord Quimant had attempted to dissuade Sithas from visiting the Clan Oakleaf estates and mines, yet the Speaker had been determined to take the three-day coach ride to Quimant's family's holdings. Now he began to wonder if perhaps Lord Quimant had been right to want to spare him the sight. He had too many disturbing reservations about the Oakleaf mines. Yet at the same time, he had to admit he needed the steel that came from these mines and the blades that were cast by the nearby smithies.

"Actually, it's the humans who give us the most trouble. After all, the elves are here for ten or twenty years, whatever the sentence happens to be for their crime. They know they must suffer that time, and then they'll be free."

Indeed, the Speaker of the Stars had sentenced a number of citizens of Silvanost to such labor—for failure to pay taxes, violence or theft against a fellow elf, smuggling, and other serious transgessions. The whole issue had seemed a good deal simpler in the city, when he could simply dismiss the offending elf and rarely, if ever, think of him again.

"So this is their miserable fate," he said quietly.

Quimant continued. "The humans, you know, are here for life—of course, a foreshortened life, in any event. And you know how reckless they are anyway. Yes, indeed, humans are the ones who give us the most problems. The elves, if anything, help to keep them in line. We encourage their little acts of spying on one another."

"Where do all the humans come from?" inquired Sithas. "Surely they haven't all been sentenced by elven courts."

"Oh, of course not! These are mostly brigands and villains,

nomads who live to the north. They trouble the elves and kender of the settled lands, so we capture them and set them to work here."

Quimant shook his head, thinking before he continued. "Imagine—a paltry four or five decades to grow up, experience romance, try to make a success of your life, and leave children behind you! It's amazing they do so well, when you consider what little time they have to work with!"

"Let's go back to the manor," said Sithas, suddenly very weary of the harsh spectacle before him. Quimant had arranged for a splendid banquet after dark, and if they remained here any longer, Sithas was certain that he would lose his appetite.

* * * * *

The ride back to Silvanost seemed to Sithas to take much longer than the trip into the country. Still, he felt relieved to leave the Oakleaf estates behind.

The banquet had been a festive affair. Hermathya, the pride of Oakleaf, and her son Vanesti had been the stars of the evening. The affair lasted far into the night, yet Quimant and Sithas made an early start for the city on the following morning. Hermathya and the boy remained behind, intending to visit the clanhold for a month or two.

The first two days of the trip had seemed to drag on forever, and now they had reached the third and final day of the excursion. Sithas and Quimant traveled in the luxurious royal coach. Huge padded couches provided them with room to recline and stretch. Velvet draperies could be closed to block off dust and weather . . . or intrusive ears and eyes. Each of the huge wheels rested on its own spring mechanism, smoothing the potholes of the crushed gravel trail.

Eight magnificent horses, all large palominos, trotted at the head of the vehicle, their white manes and long fetlocks smoothly combed. Metal trim of pure gold outlined the shape of the enclosed cabin, which was large enough to hold eight passengers.

The two lords traveled with an escort of one hundred elven riders. Four archers, in addition to their driver, rode atop the cabin, out of sight and hearing of the pair of elves within.

Sithas sat shrouded in gloom. His mind would not focus. He considered all the progress that had been made toward a counterattack. The training of the Windriders was nearly complete. In a few days, they would fly west to begin their part in Kith-Kanan's great attack. The final rank of elven infantry—four thousand elves of Silvanost and the nearby clanholds—had already departed. They should reach the vicinity of Sithelbec at the same time as the Windriders.

Even these prospects did not brighten his mood. He imagined the satisfying picture of the dwarven ambassador Than-Kar captured and brought to the Speaker of the Stars in chains, but that prospect only reminded him of the prisoners of the Oak-leaf mines.

Slave pits! With *elven* slaves! He accepted the fact that the mines were necessary. Without them, the Silvanesti wouldn't be able to produce the vast supply of arms and weapons needed by Kith-Kanan's army. True, there were good stockpiles of weapons, but a few weeks of intensive fighting could deplete those reserves with shocking speed.

"I wonder," he said, surprising himself and Quimant by speaking aloud. "What if we found another source of labor?"

The lord blinked at the Speaker in surprise. "But how? Where?"

"Listen to this!" Sithas began to envision a solution, speaking his thoughts as they occurred to him. "Kith-Kanan still needs reinforcements on the ground. By Gilean, we were only able to send him four thousand troops this summer! And that left the capital practically empty of ablebodied males."

"If Your Majesty will remember, I cautioned against such a number. The city itself is laid bare. . . ."

"I still have my palace guard—a thousand elves of the House Protectorate, their lives pledged to the throne." Sithas continued. "We will form the slaves—the *elven* slaves—from your mines into a new company. Swear them to the Wildrunners for the duration of the war, their sentences commuted to military duty."

"They number a thousand or more," Quimant admitted cautiously. "They are hardened and tough. It's perhaps true that they would make a formidable force. But you can't close down the mines!"

"We will replace them with human prisoners captured on the battlefield!"

"We *have* no prisoners!"

"But Kith's counterattack begins in less than two weeks' time. He'll break the siege and rout the humans, and he's bound to take many of them as captives." Unless Kith's plan is a failure, he thought. Sithas wouldn't allow himself to consider that possibility.

"It may just work," Quimant noted, with a reluctant nod. "Indeed, if his attack is a great success, we might actually increase the number of, ah . . . laborers. Production could improve. We could open new mines!" He warmed to the potential of the plan.

"It's settled, then," Sithas agreed, feeling a great sense of relief.

"What about Than-Kar, Excellency?" inquired Quimant after several more miles of verdant woodlands slipped by.

"It will be time for retribution soon." Sithas paused. "You know that we intercepted his spy with a message detailing the formation of the Windriders."

"True, but we never discovered who the message was intended for."

"It was being carried west. It was sent to the Ergoth general, I'm certain." Sithas was convinced that the Theiwar had joined with the humans in a bid for dominance of the dwarven nation. "I'll keep Than-Kar in suspense until Kith is ready to attack, so he doesn't find out that we're onto his treachery until it's too late for him to send another warning to the west."

"A fine trap!" Quimant imagined the scene. "Surround the dwarves in their barracks with your guard, disarm them before they can organize, and like magic, you have *him* as your prisoner."

"It's too bad I promised to return him to King Hal-Waith," noted Sithas. "I'd like nothing better than to send *him* to your coal mines."

Suddenly they leaned toward the front of the cabin as the coach slowed. They heard the coachman calling out to the horses as he hauled back on the reins.

"Driver? What's the delay?" inquired the Speaker, leaning out the window. He saw a rider—an elf, wearing the breastplate of the House Protectorate—galloping toward them from the front of the column.

The elf wasn't a member of the escort, Sithas realized. He saw the foam-flecked state of the horse and the dusty, bedraggled condition of the rider, and knew that the fellow must have come a long way.

"Your Majesty!" cried the elven horseman, reining in and practically falling out of the saddle beside the speaker's carriage door. "The city—there's trouble! It's the dwarves!"

"What happened?"

"We kept a watch over them as you ordered. This morning, before dawn, they suddenly burst out of the inns where they were quartered. They took the guards by surprise, killed them, and headed for the docks!"

"Killed?" Sithas was appalled—and furious. "How many?"

"Two dozen of the House Protectorate," replied the messenger. "We've thrown every soldier in the city into the fray, but when I left six hours ago they were slowly fighting their way to the riverbank."

"They need boats," guessed Quimant. "They're making a break for the west."

"They sniffed out my trap," groaned Sithas. The prospect of Than-Kar escaping the city worried him, mostly because he feared the dwarf would somehow be able to warn the humans about the Windriders.

"Can the house guards hold until we get there?" demanded the Speaker.

"I don't know."

"Dwarves hate the water," observed Quimant. "They won't try a crossing at night."

"We can't take that chance. Come in here," he ordered the rider, throwing open the coach door. "Driver, to the city! As fast as you can get us there!"

The gilded carriage and its escort of a hundred mounted elves thundered toward distant Silvanost, raising a wide plume of dust.

*　*　*　*　*

"They've made it to the river, and even now they seize boats along the wharf!" Tamanier Ambrodel greeted Sithas on the Avenue of Commerce, the wide roadway that paralleled the city's riverfront.

"Open the royal arsenal. Have every elf who can wield a sword follow me to the river!"

"They're already there. The battle has continued all day." The royal procession had arrived in the city with perhaps two hours of light remaining.

Sithas leaped from the coach and took the reins of a horse that had been saddled for him on Tamanier's orders. He quickly donned a chain mail shirt and hefted the light steel shield that bore the crest symbolizing the House of Silvanos.

In the meantime, the riders from his escort had dismounted, readying for conflict.

"They've barricaded themselves into two blocks of warehouses and taverns, right at the waterfront. It seems they're having some difficulties getting their boats rigged," explained the lord chamberlain.

"How many have we lost?" asked the speaker.

"Nearly fifty killed, most in the first few hours of the fight. Since then we've been content to keep them bottled up until you got here."

"Good. Let's root them out now."

Surprisingly, that thought gave him a sense of grim satisfaction. "Follow me!" Sithas cried, turning the prancing stallion down the wide Avenue of Commerce. The elves of his guard followed him. He inspected detachments that held positions down several streets that led toward the wharf. Just beyond these companies, Sithas could see hastily erected wooden barricades. He imagined the white, wide eyes of Theiwar dwarves peering between the gaps of these crude defenses.

"They're there," a sergeant assured Sithas. "They don't show themselves until we attack. Then they give a good accounting of themselves. Our archers have picked off more than a few of them."

"Good. Attack when you hear the trumpets."

Sithas himself led the band of his personal guard toward White Rose Lane before leading them down a narrow thoroughfare that was the most direct route to the waterfront.

As he had suspected, the dwarves were prepared to meet them here as well. He saw several large fishing boats lashed to the wharf, while bands of dwarves wrestled several more into place. A sturdy line of dwarves blocked the street before him, a rank four deep, armed with crossbows, swords, and stubby dwarven pikes. A barrier of barrels, planks, and huge coils of rope stood before them.

Behind these, Sithas saw the dwarven ambassador himself. Than-Kar, squinting in the uncomfortable glow of afternoon sunlight, cursed and shouted at his guards as they tried to pull the largest of the boats against the quay.

"Charge!" Sithas cried, his voice hoarse. "Break them where they stand!" Three trumpeters blared his command. A roar arose from the elves gathered along the nearby streets and lanes. Sithas spurred his charger forward.

A piece of paving stone had worked its way loose over many winters of frost and springtimes of rain. Now it lay on White Rose Lane, looking for all the world like the rest of the securely cemented stones that made up the smooth surface of the street.

But when the right forehoof of Sithas's mount came to rest for a fraction of a second upon it, the treacherous stone skidded away, twisting the hoof of the charging horse. Bones snapped in the animal's leg, and it collapsed with a shriek of pain, hurling the Speaker of the Stars from the saddle. At the same time, a full volley of steel-tipped crossbow quarrels whistled through the air, whirring over Sithas's head. He took no note of the missiles as he crashed headlong into the roadway. His sword blade snapped in his hand, and his face exploded in pain. Groaning, he struggled to rise.

The elves of the royal guard, seeing their ruler collapse before them and not knowing that his fall had been caused by a loose paving stone, cried out in fury and rage. They charged forward, swords raised, and began to clash with the dwarves who blocked their path. Steel rang on steel, and shouts of agony and triumph echoed from the surrounding buildings.

Sithas felt gentle hands on his shoulders. Though he could barely move, someone turned him onto his back. With a shock, the Speaker of the Stars looked up to see that the sky had become a haze of red smoke. Then a kerchief dabbed at his head and cool water washed his brow. His eyes cleared, and he saw the anxious faces of several of his veteran guards. The red haze, he realized, had been caused by the blood that still spurted from the deep gashes on his forehead and cheeks.

"The fight," he gasped, forcing his lips and tongue to move. "How does the fight go?"

"The dwarves stand firm," grunted an elf, cold fury apparent in his voice. Sithas recognized the fellow as Lashio, a longtime sergeant-major who had been one of his father's guards.

"Go! I'll be all right! Break them! They must not escape!"

Lashio needed no urging. Seizing his sword, he sprang toward the melee. "Don't try to move, Excellency. I've sent for the clerics!" A nervous young trooper tried to dab at Sithas's wounds, but the Speaker angrily brushed the fellow's ministrations away.

Sitting up, Sithas tried to ignore the throbbing in his head. He looked at the hilt of his shattered weapon, still clutched in his bleeding hand. In fury, he tossed the rained piece away.

"Give me your sword!" he barked at the guardsman.

"B-but, Excellency . . . please, you're hurt!"

"Are you in the habit of disobeying orders?" Sithas snarled.

"No, sir!" The young elf bit his lip but passed his weapon, hilt first, to the Speaker of the Stars without further delay.

Unsteadily Sithas climbed to his feet. The throbbing in his head pounded into a crescendo, and he had to grit his teeth to prevent himself from crying out in pain. The din of the battle raging nearby was nothing compared to the pain inside his head.

His unfortunate horse lay beside him, moaning and kicking. From the grotesque angle of its foreleg, Sithas knew that the animal was beyond saving. Deliberately he cut its throat with the sword, watching sadly as its lifeblood spurted across the pavement, splattering his boots.

Slowly his head began to clear, as if the shock of the horse's death penetrated the haze of his own wounds. He looked down the narrow lane and saw the mass of his royal guard, still pressing against the line of Than-Kar's bodyguards. Sithas realized that he could do nothing in that direction.

Instead, he looked up the street and saw a nearby tavern, the Thorn of the White Rose. The melee in the street raged just beyond its doors. Sithas remembered the place. It was a large establishment, with sleeping rooms and kitchen as well as the typical great room of a riverfront tavern. Instinctively he knew that it would suit his purpose.

He started to hurry toward the door. Shouting to those members of his guard who were in the back of the fight, unable to reach the dwarves because of the press of their comrades and the narrow confines of the lane.

"Follow me!" he called, pushing open the door. Several dozen of his guardsmen, led by Lashio, turned to answer his call.

The startled patrons of the bar, all of whom were standing at the windows to watch the fight in the street, turned in astonishment as their blood-streaked ruler stumbled in. Sithas paid them no note, instead leading his small company past the startled bartender, through the kitchen, and out into the alley behind the place.

A lone dwarf stood several paces away, apparently guarding this route of approach. He raised his steel battleaxe and shouted a hoarse cry of alarm. It was the last sound he made as the Speaker of the Stars lunged at him, easily dodging the heavy blow of his axe to run him through.

Immediately Sithas and his small band raced from the alley onto the docks. The dwarves fought to reach their boats as bands of the royal guardsmen surged onto the waterfront from other nearby streets and alleys.

A black-bearded dwarf confronted Sithas. The elf saw that his attacker wore a breastplate and helm of black steel, but it was his eyes that caught Sithas's attention: wide and vacant, like the huge white circles of a madman, pure Theiwar.

Snarling his frustration—for he saw Than-Kar, behind this dwarf, scrambling into one of the boats—Sithas charged recklessly forward.

But this foe proved far more adept than the Speaker's previous opponent. The Theiwar's keen-edged battle-axe bashed Sithas's longsword aside, and only a desperate roll to the side saved the elf from losing his right forearm. He bounced to his feet in time to ward off a second blow, and for a few moments, the two combatants poked and stabbed ineffectively, each searching for an opening.

Sithas thrust again, grimly pleased to see panic flash in the Theiwar's otherwise emotionless eyes. Only a desperate twist to the side, one that dropped the dwarf to his knees for a moment, saved him from the elf's deadly steel. With surprising quickness, however, the dwarf sprang to his feet and parried Sithas's next blow.

Then the elf had to ward off several hard slashes as the dwarf drove him backward for several steps. Sithas caught his heel on a coil of rope and tripped, but recovered in time to parry a savage blow. Steel rang against steel, but his strong arm held firm.

Then, behind the black-armored warrior, the dwarven ambassador raised his head and gave a sharp call. The dwarves on the dock immediately fell back toward the boats, and this gave Sithas his opening.

The elf reached down and grasped the coil of rope. With a grunt of exertion, he hurled it at the carefully retreating Theiwar. The dwarf raised his axe to knock the snakelike strands aside, and Sithas darted forward.

His blade penetrated the dwarf's skin at the throat, just above his heavy breastplate. With a gurgling cry of pain, the warrior stumbled, his wildly staring eyes growing cold and vacant.

As his fallen foe slumped to the docks, Sithas leaped over the body, racing toward the boat where Than-Kar frantically gestured to his guards. The Speaker of the Stars reached the edge of the quay as the craft began to drift into the river. For a moment, he considered leaping after it.

A second look at the boat full of dwarves changed his mind. Such a leap would accomplish nothing but his own death. Instead, he could only watch in dismay as the Theiwar dwarf and his bodyguards, propelled by a timely breeze, made their way smoothly to the far bank of the Thon-Thalas River and the road to the west beyond.

A Week Later, Sithelbec

23

Kith-Kanan remained in Sithelbec for a week, keeping within the small officer's cabin for the whole time. He met with Parnigar, Kencathedrus, and other of his trusted officers. All were cautioned to secrecy on their leader's plan. Indeed, Kith made a point of asking Parnigar to keep the news from his wife, who was human.

Kith had plenty of time to rest as well, but his sleep was troubled by recurring dreams. Often in the past he had dreamed of Anaya, the lost love of his life, and more recently the alluring vision of Hermathya had haunted him, often banishing Anaya from his thoughts.

Now, since he had come to Sithelbec, a third woman intruded herself in his dreams—the human woman who had saved him from General Giarna when he had been captured. The trio of females waged a silent but forceful war in his subconscious. Consequently his periods of true sleep were few in number.

Finally the week was over, and in the middle of a dark night, he left the fortress upon the back of Arcuballis. This time his flight was short, a mere fifteen miles to the east. He made for the wide clearing, surrounded by a dense ring of forest, that he had established.

He was pleased when the Windriders, under the young, capable Captain Hallus, arrived on schedule. Four thousand elves of Silvanost had also camped here, providing him with substantial reinforcement. Kith-Kanan left fresh orders and flew back to the fortress before darkness broke. Few realized he had ever been gone.

It only remained to see whether Dunbarth and his dwarves would fulfill their part of the bargain, but Kith-Kanan had few worries on this score. One more day had to pass before their deadline.

* * * * *

Kencathedrus and Parnigar had done their work well. Kith-Kanan emerged from the captain's room at sunset to find the fortress of Sithelbec alive with tension and subdued excitement. Troops cleaned their weapons or oiled their armor. The elven horsemen fed and saddled their mounts, preparing for the sortie that was coming. Archers checked their bowstrings and gathered stores of extra arrows beside their positions.

Kith-Kanan walked among them, stopping to clap a warrior on the shoulder here or to ask a quiet question there. Word of his return spread through the fortress, and the activities of the Wildrunners took on a dramatic degree of purpose and determination.

Rumors spread like smoke on the wind. The Wildrunners would make a grand attack! An elven army gathered on the plains beyond the fortress! The morale of the human army had crumbled. They would be routed if faced with a vigorous sortie!

Kith-Kanan made no attempt to dispute these rumors. Indeed, his tight-lipped demeanor served to heighten the tension and anticipation among his troops. The long siege, barely a month short of a year, had brought the Wildrunners to a such state that they would willingly risk their lives to end the confinement.

The general made his way to the high tower of the fortress. Darkness still shrouded the plains, and the elves burned no lamps, even within the walls. Their nightvision allowed them to move around and organize without illumination.

At the base of the tall structure, Kith found Parnigar, waiting as he had been ordered to, with a young elf. The latter didn't wear the accoutrements of the warrior, but instead was wrapped in a soft cloth robe. He wore doeskin boots, no helmet, and his eyes were bright as Kith-Kanan approached.

"This is Anakardain," introduced Parnigar. The young elf saluted crisply, and Kith-Kanan acknowledged the gesture, signaling Anakardain to relax.

"Has Captain Parnigar informed you of my needs?" he inquired quickly.

"Indeed, General." Anakardain nodded enthusiastically. "I am honored to offer my humble skills in this task."

"Good. Let's get to the top of the tower. Captain?" Kith turned back to Parnigar.

"Yes, sir?"

"Have Arcuballis brought to the tower top. When I need to mount, I won't have time to come down to the stables."

"Of course!" Parnigar turned to get the griffon, while the two elves entered the base of the tower and made their way up the long, winding stairway to the top. Anakardain, Kith sensed, wanted to ask a hundred questions, but he remained silent, which Kith-Kanan greatly appreciated at this particular moment.

They emerged onto the high tower's parapet with the sky, still dark, looming overhead. They could see a red glow where the crimson moon, Lunitari, had just set over the western horizon. The white moon, Solinari, was a thin crescent in the east. The only other illumination above them came from millions of stars, while it seemed that an equal number of campfires burned in the great ring of the human army surrounding them.

The fortress of Sithelbec was a dark sprawl around them. The stars boded well, Kith-Kanan thought. It was important that they have a clear day for the implementation of his plan.

"This is where you desire my spell?" inquired Anakardain, finally breaking the silence.

"Yes—to the limits of your range!"

"It will be seen for twenty miles," promised the young mage.

A shape, rising through the air, emerged from the darkness, and Anakardain flinched backward nervously as Arcuballis came to rest on the parapet beside them. Kith chuckled, easing the young elf's tension as he took the griffon's bridle and led him onto the high platform.

Other elves, including Parnigar and a small detachment of archers, joined them. One of the troopers carried a shining trumpet, and even through the darkness, the instrument seemed to radiate a golden sheen. A faint glimmer of rosy sky marked the eastern horizon by now, and they watched as it gradually extended over their heads. One by one the stars winked out of sight, overtaken by the greater brightness of the sun.

Now Kith-Kanan could look down and see the fortress come alive around him. The Wildrunner cavalry, three hundred proud elves, gathered before the huge wooden gates that provided the main entrance and egress from the fort. Those gates had not been opened in eleven months.

Behind the riders, companies of elven infantry gathered in a long column. Some of these collected in the alleys and passages leading to the main avenue, for there wasn't enough open space for all of the troops, some ten thousand in number, to form up before the gates. The infantry included units of pike and longbow, plus many with sword and shield. The elves stood or paced restlessly.

The plans for the attack had been made carefully. Kencathedras himself rode a prancing charger before the gates. Though the proud veteran had wished to ride forth with the first wave of cavalry, Kith-Kanan had ordered him to remain behind until the infantry joined the fight.

This way, Kencathedrus would be able to direct each unit to begin its charge, and Kith hoped they would avoid a great traffic jam at the gates themselves.

The next hour was the longest of Kith-Kanan's life. All of the pieces were in place, all the plans had been laid. All that they could do now was to wait, and this was perhaps the most difficult task of all.

The sun, with agonizing slowness, reached the eastern horizon and slowly crept upward into the sky. The long shadow of the high tower stretched across the closest section of the human camp west of the fortress. As the sun climbed, it dazzled everyone—humans and elves alike—with its fiery brilliance.

The general studied the human camp. Wide, muddy avenues stretched among great blocks of tents. Huge pastures, beyond the fringes of the tents, held thousands of horses. Closer to the fortress walls, a ring of ditches, trenches and walls of wooden spikes had been erected. More piles of logs had been gathered at the fringes of the camp, dragged from the nearest forests, some ten miles away, and collected for a variety of uses.

These siege towers had been constructed over the winter. Though the humans preferred to let hunger and confinement do their work for them. Obviously their patience had begun to wear thin. These great wooden structures had many portals from which archers could shower their missiles over Sithelbec's walls. Huge wheels supported the towers, and Kith knew that eventually they would rumble forward to try to take the fortress by storm. Only the high cost of such an attack had stayed the human hand thus far.

Signs of activity began to dot the human camp as breakfast fires were lit and wagons of provisions, pulled by draft horses struggled along the muddy lanes. The sun crested the wall of the fortress. The elves could count on the fact that the humans to the west would be blinded by that bright orb.

The time, Kith-Kanan knew, had finally come.

"Now!"

The general barked that one word, and the trumpeter instantly raised his horn to his lips. The loud bray of the call rang from atop the tower, blaring stridently across the fortress and ringing harshly against the ears of the slowly awakening human army.

A deep rumble shook the fortress as gatesmen released the great stone counterweights and the massive fortress gates swung open with startling swiftness. Immediately the elven riders kicked their steeds, startling the horses into explosive bursts of speed. Shouts and cries of excitement and encouragement whooped through the air as the riders surged forth.

Still the trumpet brayed its command, and now the elven infantry rushed from the gates, emerging from the dust cloud raised by the stampeding horses. Kencathedrus, his lively mount prancing with excitement, indicated with his sword each company of foot soldiers, and, in turn, they followed but a pace or two behind the unit that rushed before.

In the camp of the humans, the surprise was almost palpable, jerking men from breakfast idylls, or for those who had had duty during the night, from sleep. Eleven months of placid siege-making had had the inevitable effect of lessening readiness and building complacency. Now the peace of a warm summer's morning exploded with the brash violence of war.

The cavalry led the elven charge while the companies of foot soldiers spread into lines and advanced behind the horsemen. The lead horses reached the ditch the humans had excavated around the fortress and charged through the obstacle. Properly manned, it would have been a formidable barrier, but the elven lances pierced the few humans who stood up to challenge them as the horses charged up the steep dirt sides.

The elven lancers thundered through the ditch and then smoothly spread their column into a broad line. Lances lowered, they charged into a block of tents, spearing and trampling any humans who dared oppose them.

Trumpet calls echoed from the companies of the Ergothian Army, but to the elven commander, the tones held a frantic, hysterical quality that accurately reflected the confusion sweeping through the vast body of men. A group of swordsmen gathered, advancing shield-to-shield into the face of the thundering cavalry.

The elven horses kicked and bucked. Riders stabbed with their lances. Some of the wooden shafts splintered as their tips met the hard steel of human shields, but others drove the sharp points between the shields into soft human flesh beyond. One powerful elf thrust his lance forward so hard that it penetrated a shield, sticking the soldier beyond into the ground like an insect might be pinned to a board for display.

That rider, like so many others, drew his sword following the loss of his lance. The tight ranks of horse, crowded in among the tangle of tents and supply wagons, inevitably broke into smaller bands, and a dozen skirmishes raged through the camp.

Elven riders hacked and chopped around them as the humans scrambled to put up a defense. A rider decapitated one foe while his horse trampled another. Three humans rushed at his shield side, and he bashed one of them to the ground. Whirling, the horse reared and kicked, knocking another of the men off his feet. As the steed's forefeet fell, the elf's sword, in a lightning stroke, caught the remaining footman in the throat. With a gurgling gasp, he fell, already forgotten as his killer looked for another target.

There was no shortage of victims amid that vast and teeming camp. Finally the humans started to gather with some sense of cohesion. Swordsmen collected in units of two or three hundred, giving the horsemen wide berth until they could face them in disciplined ranks. Other humans, the herdsmen, gathered the horses from the pastures and hastened to saddle them. It would be some minutes before human cavalry could respond to the attack, however.

Archers, in groups of a dozen or more, started to send their deadly missiles into the elven riders. Fortunately the horses moved so quickly and the camp around them was so disordered that this fire had little effect. Bucking, plunging horses trampled some of the canvas tents and kicked the coals from the numerous fires among the wreckage. Soon equipment, garb, and tents began to smolder, and yellow flames licked upward from much of the ruined camp.

* * * * *

"Where is that witch?" demanded General Giarna, practically spitting his anger. He spouted questions, orders, and demands at a panicked group of officers. "Quickly! Get the horses saddled! Organize archers north and south of the breach! Alert the knights! Gods curse your slowness!"

Beside him, Kalawax, the Theiwar commander, watched shrewdly. "This was unexpected," he murmured.

"Perhaps. It will also be a disaster for the elves. They have given me the opportunity I have so long desired, to meet them in the open field!"

Kalawax said nothing. He merely studied the human leader, his Theiwar eyes narrowed to slits. Even so, the whites showed abnormally large to either side of his pupils.

Suzine was forgotten for the moment.

"General! General!" A mud-splattered swordsman lurched through the crowd of officers and collapsed to his knees. "We attacked the elven line at the ditch, but they stopped us! My men, all killed! Only—"

Further words choked away as the general's black-gloved hand seized the gagging messenger. Giarna squeezed, and there was the sound of bones snapping.

Casting the corpse aside, General Giarna fixed each of his officers with a black, penetrating gaze. To a man, they were terrified to the core.

"Move!" barked the commander.

The officers scattered, each of them racing to obey.

*　*　*　*　*

More trumpets blared, and companies of humans swarmed from across the vast encampment, charging toward the elves who stood in a semicircle before the fortress gates. The companies of Wildrunner infantry, led by Kencathedrus, met the first of these attackers with shields and swords. The clash of metal and screaming of the wounded added to the cacophony.

The humans around the fort still outnumbered the elves by ten to one, and Kith-Kanan had only committed a quarter of the defenders to this initial sortie. Nevertheless, small bands of humans acquitted themselves well, hurling their bodies against the shredding blades of the elves.

"Stand firm there!" shouted Kencathedrus, urging his horse into a gap where two elves had just fallen.

The captain maneuvered his steed into the breach while his blade struck down two men who tried to force their way past him. Swords smashed against shields. Men and elves slipped in the mud and the blood. Now the ditch served as a defensive line for two of the elven companies. Cursing and slashing, the humans charged into the muddy trough, only to groan and bleed and die beneath the swords of the elves.

Elven archers showered the human troops with a deadly rain of steel-tipped hail. The ditch became a killing ground as panicked men turned to flee, tangling themselves among the fresh troops that the human commanders were casting into the fray.

Beyond the ditch, the elven cavalry of three hundred riders plunged and raced among thirty thousand humans. But more and more fires erupted, sending clouds of black smoke wafting across the field, choking noses and throats and blocking vision.

Greedy flames licked at the walls of one tent, and suddenly the blaze crackled upward. Wreckage fell inward, revealing several rows of neat casks, the cooking and lamp oil for this contingent of the human army. One of the casks began to blaze, and hot oil cascaded across the other barrels. A rush like a hot, dry wind surged from the tent, followed by a dull thud of sound. Instantly fiery oil sprayed outward. A cloud of hellfire mushroomed into the sky, wreathed in black smoke.

Instantly the inferno spread to neighboring tents. A hundred men, doused by the liquid death, screamed and shrieked for long moments before they dropped, looking like charred wood.

From his vantage on the tower, Kith-Kanan watched the battle rage through the camp. Though chaos reigned on the field, he could see that the sortie had affected only a relatively small portion of the human camp. The enemy had begun to recover from the surprise attack, and fresh regiments surged against the elven horsemen, threatening to cut them off from any possible retreat.

"Sound the recall—now!" Kith-Kanan barked.

The trumpeter blared the signal even as Kith finished his command. The notes rang across the field, and the elven riders immediately turned back toward the gates.

At the ditch, Kencathedrus and his men stood firm. A thousand human bodies filled the trench, and there wasn't an elven blade that didn't drip with gore. The infantry opened a gap in their line for the riders to thunder through as an increasing rain of arrows held the humans at bay.

Even as this was happening, Kith turned his eyes to the south, looking along the horizon for some sign that the next phase of his strategy could begin. The time was ripe.

There! He saw a row of banners fluttering above the grass, and soon he discerned movement.

"The dwarves of Thorbardin!" he cried, pointing.

The dwarves came on in a broad line, trotting as fast as their stocky legs could carry them. A throaty roar burst from their throats, and the legion of Thorbardin hastened into a charge.

The humans were pressing the elven forces at the gates of Sithelbec. From his vantage, Kith-Kanan watched with grim satisfaction as his Wildrunners managed to beat back attack after attack. To the south, some of the humans had now realized the threat lumbering forward against their backs.

* * * * *

"Dwarves!" The cry raced through the human camp, quicidy reaching General Giarna. Kalawax, beside him, gaped in astonishment, his already pallid complexion growing even paler.

"The dwarven legion! Hylar, from Thorbardin!" More reports, from the throats of hoarse messengers, were brought back to the general in his command tent. "They drive against the south!"

"I knew *nothing* of this!" squawked Kalawax, unconsciously backing away from Giarna. The dwarf's earlier aplomb had vanished with this new turn of events "My spies have been tricked. Our agents in Silvanost have worked hard to prevent this!"

"You have *failed!*"

Giarna's words carried with them a sentence of doom. His eyes, black and yawning, seemed to flare for a moment with a deep, parasitic fire.

His fist lashed out, pummeling the Theiwar on the side of his head. But this was no ordinary blow. It connected squarely, and the dwarf's thick skull erupted. The general's other hand seized the corpse by the neck. His face flushed, and his eyes flared with an insane pleasure. In another moment, he cast the Theiwar—now a dried and shriveled husk—to the side.

Kalawax was already forgotten as the general absently wiped his hand on his cloak, focusing on the problem of how to stem this most recent attack.

* * * * *

"For Thorbardin! For the king!"

A few human companies of swordsmen raced to block the surging waves of dwarves, but most of the Army of Ergoth was preoccupied with the elven sortie. Dunbarth Ironthumb led the way. A man raised a sword, holding his shield across his chest, and then chopped savagely downward at the dwarven commander. Dunbarth's battle-axe, held high, deflected the blow with a ringing clash. In the next instant, the dwarven veteran slashed his weapon through a vicious swing, cutting underneath the human's shield. The man shrieked in agony as the axe sliced open his belly.

"Charge! Full speed! To the tents!"

Dunbarth barked the commands, and the dwarves renewed their advance. Those humans who tried to stand in the way quickly perished, while others dropped their weapons and fled. Some of these escaped, while others fell beneath the volley of crossbow fire leveled by the dwarven missile troops.

Dunbarth led a detachment along a row of tents, chopping at the guy lines of each, watching the rude shelters collapse like wilting flowers. They came upon a supply compound, where great pots of stew had been abandoned, still simmering. Seizing everything flammable, they tossed weapons and harnesses, even carts and wagons, onto the coals. Quickly searing tongues of flame licked upward, igniting the equipment and marking the spot of the dwarven advance.

"Onward!" cried Dunbarth, and again the dwarves moved toward Sithelbec.

The human troops didn't react quickly to this new threat. Small bands perished as the stocky Hylar swept around them, and the waves of the attackers gave little time for the humans to muster a stand.

The sheer numbers of the defenders gave the humans an edge. Soon Dunbarth found some brave human contesting every forward step he tried to take. His axe rose and fell, and many an Ergothian veteran perished beneath that gory blade. But more and more of the humans stepped up.

"Stand firm!" cried Ironthumb.

Now the dwarves hacked and chopped in tight formation in the middle of a devastated human camp. A thousand men rushed against their left, met by the sharp clunk of crossbows and a volley of steel-tipped death. Hundreds fell, pierced by the missiles, and others turned to flee.

Swords met axes in five thousand duels to the death. The dwarves fought with courage and discipline, holding their ranks tight. They maimed and killed with brutal efficiency, but they were well matched by the courageous humans who pressed them in such great numbers.

But it was those numbers that would have to tell the tale. Slowly Dunbarth's force contracted into a great ring. Amid the cries and the clanging and the shouting and screaming, Dunbarth slowly realized the tactical situation.

The dwarven legion was surrounded.

Late Morning, Battle of Sithelbec

24

Kith-Kanan watched the courageous stand of the dwarves with a lump of admiration burning in his throat. Dunbarth's magnificent charge had taken the pressure off the elves at the gate, and now Kencathedrus's force could surge forward again, expanding their perimeter against the distracted humans.

Attacked from two sides, the Army of Ergoth wavered and twitched like a huge but indecisive beast set upon by a swarm of stinging pests. Great masses of human foot soldiers stood idle, waiting for orders while their comrades perished in desperate battles a few hundred yards away.

But now a sense of purpose seemed to settle across the humans. The tens of thousands of horses had been saddled. The riders, especially the light horsemen of General Giarna's northern wing, had reached their steeds and were ready for battle.

Unlike the humans on foot, however, the cavalry did not race piecemeal into the fray, setting themselves up for defeat. Instead, they collected into companies and regiments and finally into massive columns. The riders surged around the outside of the melee, gathering and positioning themselves for one crucial charge.

The elves of the sortie force could save themselves by a quick return to the fortress. The dwarves, however, were isolated amid the wreckage of the south camp and had no such fallback. Lacking pikes, they would be virtually helpless against the onslaught Giarna was almost ready to unleash.

Kith-Kanan turned to Anakardain, who had remained at his

side throughout the battle. "Now! Give the signal!" commanded the general.

The elven mage pointed a finger toward the sky. "*Exceriate! Pyros, lofti!*" he cried.

Instantly a crackling shaft of blue light erupted from his pointing hand, hissing upward amid a trail of sparks. Even in the bright sunlight, the bolt of magic stood out clearly, visible to all on the battlefield.

And, Kith devoutly hoped, to those who waited some twenty miles away—waited for this very signal.

For several minutes after the flare, the battle raged, unchecked. Nor was there any sign that might alter this, though Kith-Kanan kept his eyes glued to the eastern horizon. The sun hung midway between that horizon and the zenith of noon, though it seemed impossible that the battle had raged for barely three hours.

Now the human cavalry galloped from the pastures, an impressive mass of horsemen under the tight control of a skilled commander. They surged around the trampled encampment, veering toward the embattled dwarves.

Finally Kith-Kanan, still staring to the east, saw what he had been looking for: a line of tiny winged figures, a hundred feet above the ground and heading fast in this direction. Sunlight glinted from shiny steel helms and sparkled from deadly lance heads.

"The charge—sound it again!" barked the elven general to his trumpeter.

Another blare sounded across the field, and for a moment, the momentum of battle paused. Humans looked upward in surprise. Their officers, in particular, were puzzled by the command. The elven and dwarven troops, hard-pressed now, seemed to be in no position to execute an offensive.

"Again—the charge!"

Again and again the call brayed forth.

Kith-Kanan watched the Windriders as the soaring line approached nearer and nearer, within two or three miles of the field. The elven general picked up his shield and checked to see that his sword hung loosely in his scabbard.

"Take over the command," Kith told Parnigar, at the same time grabbing the reins of Arcuballis and stepping to the griffon's side.

The Wildrunner captain stared at his general. "Surely you're not going out there! We need you here. Your plan is working! Don't jeopardize it now!"

Kith shook his head, casting off the arguments. "The plan has a life of its own now. If it fails, sound the recall and bring the elves back into the fortress. Otherwise, continue to love them support from the archers on the walls—and be ready to bring the rest of them out if the humans start to break."

"But, General!" Parnigar's next objections died away as Kith-Kanan swung into his high leather saddle. Obviously he would not be deterred from his actions.

"Good luck to you," finished the captain, grimly looking over the field where thousands of humans still surged in attack.

"Luck has been with us so far," Kith replied. "May she stay with us just for a little longer."

Now the Windriders, still flying in their long, thin ranks, slowly nosed into shallow dives. They hadn't yet been sighted by the humans on the ground, who had no reason to expect attack from the air.

Again the bugler brayed his charge. Arcuballis sprang from the tower, his powerful wings carrying Kith-Kanan into line with the other Windriders. At this cue, the griffons shrieked their harsh challenge, a jarring noise that cut cleanly through the chaos of the battle. Talons extended, beaks gaping, they howled downward from the heavens.

The whole pulse of the battle ceased as the shocking vision swept lower. Men, elves, and dwarves alike gaped upward.

Cries of alarm and terror swept through the human ranks. Units of men who had until now maneuvered in tightly disciplined formations suddenly scattered into uncontrolled mobs. The shadows of the griffons passed across the field, and again the beasts shrilled their savage war cries.

If the reaction by the humans to the sudden attack was dramatic and pronounced, the effect upon the horses was profound. At the first sound of the approaching griffons, all cohesion vanished from the cavalry units. Horses bucked and pitched, whinnied and shrieked.

The Windriders passed over the entire battlefield a hundred feet above the ground. Occasionally a human archer had the presence of mind to launch an arrow upward, but these missiles always trailed their targets by great distances before arcing back to earth, to land as often as not among the human ranks.

Elven archers along the walls of Silthelbec showered their stunned opponents with renewed volleys as their captains sensed the battle's decisive moment.

"Again—once back, and we'll take to the ground!" Kith-Kanan cried, edging Arcuballis into a dive. The unit followed, and each griffon tucked its left wing, diving steeply and turning sharply to the left.

The creatures swung through a hundred-and-eighty-degree arc, losing about sixty feet of height. Now the cries of the elven riders joined those of the griffons as they raced over the human army. Bugles blared from the fortress walls and towers and from the ranks of the sortie force. Throaty dwarven cheers erupted from Dunbarth's veterans, and the legion of Thorbardin quickly broke its defensive position, charging into the panicked humans surrounding them.

The elves of the sortie force, too, charged through the ditch into the humans who had been pressing them with such intensity. Columns of elves burst from the open gates of Sithelbec, reinforcing their comrades.

Kith-Kanan selected a level field, a wide area of pasture between the western and southern human camps, for a landing site and brought the griffons to earth there. His first target would be the brigade of armored knights that were struggling to regain control of their mounts.

The griffons barely slowed as they tucked their wings and sprang forward, propelled by their powerful leonine hindquarters while their deadly foreclaws reached forward as if eager to shred the flesh of the foe.

The single line of griffons, their riders still holding their lances forward, ripped into the bucking, heaving mass of panicked horses. No charge of plate-mailed knights ever struck with such killing force. Lances punctured armor and horses fell, gored by the claws of the savage griffons, and then the elven swords struck home.

Kith-Kanan buried his lance in the chest of a black-armored knight as the human's horse bucked in terror. He couldn't see the man's face behind the closed shield of his dark helmet, but the steel tip of his weapon erupted from his victim's back in a shower of blood. Arcuballis sprang, his claws tearing away the saddle of the heavy war-horse as the terrified animal crashed to the ground.

His lance torn away by the force of the charge, Kith drew his sword. A knight plunged nearby, desperately struggling to control his mount; Kith-Kanan stabbed him in the back. Another armored warrior, on foot and wielding a massive morning star, swung the spiked ball at Arcuballis. The griffon reared back and then pounced on the man, tearing out his throat with a single powerful strike of his beak.

A chaotic jumble of shrieks and howls and moans surged around Kith, mingling with the pounding of hooves and the clash of sharp steel against plate mail. But even the superior armor of the humans couldn't save them. With no control over their mounts, they could do little more than hold on and try to escape the maelstrom of death. Very few of them made it.

"To the air!" Kith cried, spurring Arcuballis into a powerful upward leap. Shattered knights covered the ground below them while the thundering mass of their horses stampeded right through a line of human archers who couldn't get out of the way in time. All around Kith-Kanan, the other griffons sprang into the air, and with regal grace, the Windriders once again soared across the field. Slowly they climbed, forming again into a long line, flying abreast.

As the griffon's wings carried him upward, Kith looked across the field. In the distances rolled great clouds of dust. Some twenty thousand horses had already stampeded away from the battle, and these plumes marked their paths of flight. Human infantry fled from the tight ranks of the dwarven legion, while the elven reinforcements drove terrified humans into panic. Many of the enemy had dropped their weapons and thrown up their hands, pleading and begging for mercy.

Kith-Kanan veered toward the Ergothian foot soldiers, the line of Windriders following in precise formation. He took up his bow and carefully nocked an arrow. He let the missile fly, watching it dart downward and penetrate the shoulder of one of the foot soldiers. The fellow toppled forward, his helmet rolling in the mud, and Kith-Kanan got a jolt when he espied the long blond hair cascading around his body. Other arrows found targets among this company as the griffons passed overhead, and the general noticed with surprise these other men, too, all had blond hair.

One of them turned and launched an arrow upward, and a nearby griffon shrieked, pierced through the wing. The animal's limb collapsed, and the beast tipped suddenly to the side, plummeting to the earth among the Ergothian archers. The rider died from the force of the crash, but this didn't stop the soldiers from hacking and chopping at his body until only a gory mess remained.

Kith shot another arrow, and a third, watching grimly as each took the life of one of these blond savages. Only when the humans had been riddled with losses did the Windriders consider the death of their comrade avenged. As they soared away, Kith-Kanan was struck by the narrow face of one of his victims, lying faceup in the mud. Diving lower, he saw a pointed ear and blond hair.

Elves! His own people fighting for the Army of the Emperor of Ergoth! Growling in anger, he urged Arcuballis upward, the rest of his company following. With terrible purpose, he looked across the mud-and-blood-strewn field for an appropriate target.

He saw one group of horsemen, perhaps two thousand strong, that had rallied around a streaming silver banner—the ensign of General Giarna himself, Kith knew. Instantly he veered toward this unit as the general was urging his reluctant troops into a renewed charge. The griffons flew low, no more than ten feet off the ground, and the creatures shrilled their coming.

Unaffected by the curses of their commanding general, the human riders allowed their horses to turn and scatter, unwilling to face the griffon cavalry. Kith-Kanan urged Arcuballis onward, seeking the general himself, but the man had vanished, among the dusty, panicked ranks of his troops. He might already have been trampled to death, for all Kith-Kanan knew.

The Windriders flew across the field, landing and attacking here and there, wherever a pocket of the human army seemed willing to make a stand. Often the mere appearance of the savage creatures was enough to break a formation, while occasionally they crashed into the defending ranks and the griffons tore with talons and beaks while their elven riders chopped and hacked with their lethal weapons.

The elves on the ground and their dwarven allies raced across the field, encouraging the total rout of the human army. More and more of the humans held up their hands in surrender as they concluded that escape was impossible. Many of the horses were stampeded, riderless, away from the field, lost to the army for the forseeable future. A great, streaming column of refugees—once a proud army but now a mass of panicked, terrified, and defeated men—choked the few roads and scarred new trails across the prairie grasslands.

When the Windriders finally came to earth before the gates of Sithelbec, they landed only because there were no more enemies left to fight. Huge columns of human prisoners, guarded by the watchful eyes of elven archers and dwarven axemen, stood listlessly along the walls of the fortress. Amidst the smoke and chaos of the camps, detachments of the Wildrunners poked and searched, uncovering more prisoners and marking stockpiles of supplies.

"General, come quickly!" Kith-Kanan looked up at the cry, seeing a young captain approaching. The elf's face was pale, and he gestured toward a place on the field.

"What is it?" Sensing the urgency in the young soldier's request, Kith hurried behind him. In moments, he knew the reason for the officer's demeanor.

He found Kencathedrus lying among the bodies of a dozen humans. The old elf's body bled from numerous ugly wounds.

"We beat them today," gasped Kith-Kanan's former teacher and weaponmaster, managing a weak smile.

"Didn't we, though?" The general took his friend's head in his hands, looking toward the nearby officer. "Get the cleric!" he hissed.

"He's been here," objected Kencathedrus. Kith-Kanan could read the result in the wounded elf's eyes: there was nothing that even a cleric could do.

471

"I've lived to see this day. It makes my life as a warrior complete. The war is all but won. You must pursue them now. Don't let them escape!"

Kencathedrus gripped Kith's arm with surprising strength, nearly raising himself up from the ground. "Promise me," he gasped. "You will not let them escape!"

"I promise!" whispered the general. He cradled Kencathedrus's head for several minutes, even though he knew that he was dead.

A messenger—a Kagonesti scout in full face paint—trotted up to Kith-Kanan to make a report. "General, we have reports of enemy activity in the north camp."

That part of the huge circular human camp had seen the least fighting. Kith nodded at the scout and gently laid Kencathedrus's body on the ground. He rose and called to a nearby sergeant-major.

"Take three companies and sweep through the north camp," he ordered. He remembered, too, that General Giarna and his horsemen had escaped in that direction. He gestured to several of his Windriders. "Follow me."

Afternoon, Battle of Sithelbec

25

Suzine watched the battle in her glass. Here in her tent in the northern camp, she did not feel the brunt of battle so heavily. Though the men here had raced to the fight and suffered the same fate as the rest of the army, the camp itself had not yet experienced the wholesale destruction that marked the south and west camps of the humans.

She had seen the Windriders soaring from the east, had watched their inexorable and unsuspected approach against her general's army, and she had smiled. Her face and her body still burned from Giarna's assaults, and her loathing for him had crystallized into hatred.

Thus when the elf commander had led the attack that sundered the army around her, she had felt a sense of joy, not dismay, as if Kith-Kanan had flown with no other purpose than to effect her own personal rescue. Calmly she had watched the battle rage, following the elven general in her mirror.

When he led the charge against Giarna's remnant of the great cavalry brigades, she had held her breath, part of her hoping he might come upon the human general and strike him dead, another part wishing that Giarna would simply flee and leave the rewards of victory to the elven forces. Even when her elven guards fled from their posts, she had taken no note.

Now she heard marching outside her tent as the elves of the sortie force moved through the north camp looking for human survivors. Suzine heard some men surrender, pleading for their lives; she heard others attack with taunts and curses, and finally screams and moans as they fell.

The battle coursed around her, washing the tent city in smoke and flame and pain and blood. But still Suzine remained within her tent, her eyes fixed upon the golden-haired figure in her mirror. She watched Kith-Kanan, mounted upon the leaping, clawing figure of his great beast, slash and cut his way through the humans who tried to challenge him. She saw that the elven attack moved steadily closer to her. Now the Wildrunners fought a mere thousand yards to the south of her tent.

"Come to me, my warrior!" she breathed.

She willed him to come to her with all of her heart, watching in her glass as Kith-Kanan hacked the head from a burly human axeman.

"I am here!" Suzine desperately wanted Kith-Kanan to sense her presence, her desire, her—did she dare believe it?—love.

The opening of her tent flap interrupted her reverie. It was *him*! It *must* be! Her heart afire, she whirled, and only when she saw Giarna standing there did brutal reality shatter her illusion. As for Giarna, he looked past her violently, at the image of the elven commander in the mirror.

The human general stepped toward her, his face a mask of fury, more like a beast's than a man's. It sent an icy blade of fear into the pit of Suzine's stomach.

When Giarna reached her and seized her arms, each in one bone-crushing hand, that blade of fear twisted and slashed within her. She couldn't speak, couldn't think; she could only stare into those wide, maddened eyes, the lips flecked with spittle, stretched taut to reveal teeth that seemed to hunger for her soul.

"You betrayed me!" he snarled, throwing her roughly to the ground. "Where did these flying beasts come from? How long have they been waiting, ready to strike?" He knelt and punched her roughly, splitting her lip.

He glanced at the mirror on the table. Now, her concentration broken, the image of Kith-Kanan had faded, but the truth of her obsession had been revealed.

The general's black-gauntleted hand pulled a dagger from his belt, and he pressed it between her breasts, the point puncturing her gown and then brushing the skin beneath it.

"No," he said, at the very moment when she expected to die. "That would be too merciful, too cheap a price for your treachery."

He stood and glared down at her. Every instinct of her body told her to scramble to her feet, to fight him or to run! But his black eyes seemed to hypnotize her to the ground, and she couldn't bring herself to move.

"Up, slut!" he growled, kicking her sharply in the ribs and then reaching down to seize her long red hair. He pulled her to her knees, and she winced, closing her eyes, expecting another blow to her face.

Then she sensed a change within the small confines of the tent, a sudden wash of air against her face ... the increase in the sounds of battle beyond . . .

Giarna cast her aside, and she looked at the door to the tent. *There he was!*

Kith-Kanan stood in the opened tent flap. Beyond him lay bodies on the ground, and she caught a glimpse of men and elves hacking against each other with swords and axes. The tents in her line of view smoked and smoldered, some spewing orange flame.

The golden-haired elf stepped boldly into the darkened tent, his steel longsword extended before him. He spoke harshly, his blade and his words directed at the human general.

"Surrender, human, or die!" Kith-Kanan, obviously not recognizing the commander of the great human army in the semidarkness of the tent, took another step toward Giarna.

The human general, his dagger still in his hand and his body trembling with rage, stared soundlessly at the elf for a moment. Kith-Kanan squinted and crouched slightly, ready for close-quarter fighting. As he studied his opponent, recognition dawned, memories of that day of captivity a year before, when the battle had gone against the elves.

"It's *you*," the elf whispered.

"And it is fitting that *you* come to me now," replied the human general, his voice a strangled, triumphant snarl. "You will not live to enjoy the fruits of your victory!"

In a flash of motion, the man's hand whipped upward. In the same instant, he reversed his grip on the dagger, flipping its hilt from his hand and catching the tip of the foot-long blade in his fingertips.

"Look out!" Suzine screamed, suddenly finding her voice.

Giarna's hand lashed out, flinging the knife toward Kith's throat. Like a silver streak, the blade flashed through the air, true toward its mark.

Kith-Kanan couldn't evade the throw, but he could parry it. His wrist twitched, a barely perceptible movement that swung the tip of his sword through an arc of perhaps six inches. That was enough; the longsword hit the knife with a sharp clink of metal, and the smaller blade flipped over the elf's shoulder to strike the tent wall and fall harmlessly to the ground.

Suzine scrambled away from Giarna as the man drew his sword and rushed toward the elf. Kith-Kanan, eight inches shorter and perhaps a hundred pounds lighter than the human general, met the charge squarely. The two blades clashed with a force that rang like cymbals in the confines of the tent. The elf took one step back to absorb the momentum of the attack, but Giarna was stopped in his tracks.

The two combatants circled, each totally focused on the other, looking for the slightest hint, the twitch of an eye or a minute shifting of a shoulder, that would warn the other of an intended lunge.

They slashed at each other, then darted out of the way and just as quickly slashed again. Neither bore a shield. Consummate swordsmen both, they worked their way around the spacious tent. Kith-Kanan tipped a dressing screen in front of the human. The man leaped over it. Giarna drove the elf backward, hoping to trip him on Suzine's cot. Kith sensed the threat and sprang to the rear, clearing the obstacle and then darting to the side, driving against the human's flank.

Again the man parried, and the two warriors continued to circle, each conserving his strength, neither showing the weariness of the long day's battle. Where Giarna's face was a mask of twisted hatred, however, the elf's remained an image of cool, studied detachment. The man struck with power that the elf could not hope to match, so Kith-Kanan had to rely on skill and control for each parry, each lightning thrust of his own.

The woman glanced back and forth, her eyes wide with horror alternating with hope.

They were too equal in skill, she saw, and given this fact, Giarna's size and strength inevitably would vanquish the elf. An increasing sense of desperation marked Kith's parries and attacks. Once he stumbled and Suzine screamed. Only Giarna's heavy boot, as it caught in a fold of her rug, prevented his blade from tearing through the elf's heart.

Nevertheless, he managed to cut a slash in Kith's side, and the elf grunted in pain as he regained his balance. Suzine saw a tightness in his expression that hadn't been there before. It could be called the beginnings of fear. Once he glanced toward the door, as if he hoped for assistance from that quarter.

Only when he did that did Suzine notice the sudden quiet that seemed to have descended across the camp. The fight outside had moved beyond them. Kith-Kanan had been left behind.

She saw Giarna drive Kith backward with a series of ringing blows, and she knew she had to do something! Kith sprang forward, desperation apparent in each of his swinging slashes. Giarna ducked away from each blow, giving ground as he searched for the fatal opening.

There! The elf overreached himself, leaning too far forward in an attempt to draw blood from his elusive target.

Giarna's sword came up, its tip, glistening from Kith's moist blood, held for just a moment as the elf followed through with his reckless swing.

Kith tried to twist away, raising his left arm so that he would take the wound in his shoulder, but Giarna simply raised that deadly spike and drove it toward the elf's neck.

The sound of shattering glass was the next thing that Suzine knew. She didn't understand how she came to hold the frame of her mirror in her hands, didn't comprehend the shards of glass scattered across the rug. More glass, she saw, glinted upon Giarna's shoulders. Blood spurted from long slashes in his scalp.

The human leader staggered, reeling from the blow to his head, as Kith-Kanan twisted away. He looked at the woman, gratitude shining in his eyes—or was that something deeper, more profound, more lasting, that she wished to see there.

The elfs blade came up, poised to strike, as Giarna shook his head and cursed, wiping the blood from his eyes. His back to the door, he stared at the elf and the woman, his face once again distorted by his monstrous hatred.

Kith-Kanan stepped to Suzine's side, sensing the man's hatred and protecting her from any sudden attack.

But there would be no attack. Groggy, bleeding, surrounded by enemies, Giarna made a more pragmatic decision. With one last burning look at the pair, he turned and darted through the tent flap.

Kith-Kanan started forward but stopped when he felt Suzine's hand on his arm.

"Wait," she said softly. She touched the bloodstained tunic at his side, where Giarna's sword had cut him.

"You're hurt. Here, let me tend your wound."

The weariness of the great battle finally arose within Kith-Kanan as he lay upon the bed. For the first time in more months than he cared to remember, he felt a gentle sensation of peace.

* * * * *

The war almost ceased to exist for Kith-Kanan. It became distant and unreal. His wound wasn't serious, and the woman who tended him was not only beautiful but also had been haunting his dreams for weeks.

As the Army of Ergoth scattered, Parnigar took command of the pursuit, skillfully massing the Wildrunners to attack concentrations of the enemy wherever they could be found. Kith-Kanan was left to recuperate and paid little attention to his lieutenant's reports of progress.

They all knew the humans were beaten. It would be a matter of weeks, perhaps months now, before they were driven back across the border of their own empire. Windriders sailed over the plains, dwarves and elves marched, and elven cavalry galloped at will.

And back at the nearly abandoned fortress, the commander of this great army was falling in love.

Late Summer, Year of the Bear

26

Already the cool winds presaging autumn swirled northward from the Courrain Ocean, causing the trees of the great forestlands to discard their leaves and prepare for the long dormancy of winter. The elves of Silvanesti felt the winds, too, throughout the towns and estates and even in the great capital of Silvanost.

The city was alive with the great jubilation of victory. Word from the front told of the rout of the human army, Kith-Kanan's army was on the offensive. The elven general had sent columns of Wildrunners marching swiftly across the plains, fighting the pockets of human resistance.

The dwarven league did its part against the humans, while the Windriders swept down from the skies, shattering the once-proud Ergothian regiments, capturing or killing hundreds of humans, and scattering the rest to the four winds. Most bands of desperate survivors sought nothing more than flight back to the borders of Ergoth.

Great camps of human prisoners—tens of thousands—now littered the plains. Many of these Kith-Kanan sent to the east upon the orders of his brother, where the human prisoners were condemned to spend their lives in the Clan Oakleaf mines. Others were assigned to rebuild and strengthen the fortress of Sithelbec and repair the damage to settlements and villages ravaged by two years of war.

These should be the greatest days of my life! Sithas brooded over the reports from his great emerald throne. He was reluctant to leave the Hall of Audience for the brightness of the garden or the city despite the beautiful late afternoon sky.

An hour ago he had ordered his courtiers and nobles to leave him alone. He was disconsolate, despite the most recent missive from Kith-Kanan—borne by a Windrider courier, the news less than a week old—which had continued favorable reports of victory.

Perhaps he would have been relieved to talk to Lord Quimant—no one else seemed to understand the pressures of his office—but that nobleman had left the city more than a week earlier to assist in the administration of the new prisoner slaves at his family's mines in the north. He had no clear idea when he would return.

Sithas's mind ran over his brother's latest communication. Kith reported that the central wing of the Army of Ergoth, which had tried to march home by the shortest and most direct route, had since ceased to exist. The entire force had been eradicated when the Wildrunners gathered and attacked the central wing, causing massive casualties.

There was no longer much of a southern wing, either. Its soldiers had suffered the highest toll in the initial counterattack. And the smaller northern wing, with its thousands of light horsemen and fast-moving infantry under the shrewd General Giarna, had been scattered into fragments that desperately sought refuge among the clumps of forest and rough country that fringed the plains.

Why, then, could Sithas not share in the exultation of the Silvanost citizenry?

Perhaps because reports had been confirmed of Theiwar dwarves joining with the fleeing remnants of Giarna's force, even though their cousins, the Hylar, fought on the side of the elves, Sithas had no doubt that the Theiwar were led by the treacherous general and Ambassador Than-Kar. Such internecine dwarven politics served to further confuse the purposes of this war.

Neither was there any doubt now that large numbers of renegade elves fought on the side of Ergoth. Elves and dwarves and humans fighting against elves and dwarves! Quimant continued to advocate the hiring of human mercenaries to further reinforce Kith-Kanan's armies. This was a step that Sithas was not prepared to take. And yet . . .

The immediate victory didn't seem to offer an end to the differences among the elves. Would Silvanesti ever be pure again? Would involvement in this war break down the barriers that separated elvenkind from the rest of Krynn?

Even the name of the war itself, a name he had heard uttered in the streets of the city, even murmured from the lips of polite society, underscored his anguish. Following the summer's battles and the lists of the dead, it had become the universal sobriquet for the war, too commonly known to be changed even by the decree of the Speaker of the Stars.

The Kinslayer War.

The name left a bitter taste on his tongue, for to Sithas, it represented all that was wrong about the cause they fought against. Blind, misguided elves throwing in their lot with the human enemy—they forfeited their right to any kinship!

More serious to Sithas, in a personal sense, was the nasty rumor now making the rounds of the city, a preposterous allegation. The scurrilous gossip had it that Kith-Kanan himself had taken a human woman for a consort! No one, of course, dared present this news to Sithas directly, but he knew that the others believed and whispered the ludicrous tale.

He had ordered members of the House Protectorate to disguise themselves as workers and artisans and to enter the taverns and inns frequented by the citizens. They were to listen carefully, and if they overheard anyone passing this rumor, the culprit was to be immediately arrested and brought to the palace for questioning.

"Pa-pa?"

The voice brightened his mood as nothing else could. Sithas turned to see Vanesti toddling toward him, carrying—as always—the wooden sword Kith-Kanan had made for him before departing for Sithelbec.

"Come here, you," the Speaker of the Stars said, kneeling before the throne and throwing wide his arms.

"Pa-pa!" Vanesti, his beaming face framed by long golden curls, hastened his pace and immediately toppled forward, landing on his face.

Sithas scooped the tyke into his arms and held him, patting him on the back until his crying ceased. "There, there. It doesn't hurt so bad, does it?" he soothed.

"Ow!" objected the youth, rubbing his nose.

Sithas chuckled. Still carrying his son, he started toward the royal door that led to the Gardens of Astarin.

* * * * *

Quimant returned two days later and came to see Sithas as the Speaker sat alone in the Hall of Audience.

"Your plan has worked miracles!" reported the lord. If he noticed his ruler's melancholy air, he didn't call attention to it. "We have tripled the number of slaves and can work the mines around the clock now. In addition, the freed elves have marched off to the plains. They make a very formidable company indeed!"

"The war may be over by the time they reach the battlefield," sighed Sithas. "Perhaps I have simply freed a number of malefactors for nothing."

Quimant shook his head. "I've heard the reports. Even though the Wildrunners are pushing the humans westward, I wouldn't expect a complete end to the war before next summer."

"Surely you don't think the Army of Ergoth will reassemble now that the Windriders are pursuing them?"

"Not reassemble, no, but they will break into small bands. Kith-Kanan's army will find many of them, but not all. Yes, Excellency, I fear we will still have an enemy to contend with a year from now—perhaps even longer."

Sithas cast off the notion as unthinkable. Before the debate proceeded further, however, a guard appeared at the hall's door.

"What is it?" inquired the Speaker.

"Lashio has captured a fellow, a stonemason, in the city. He was spreading the—er, the tale about General Kith-Kanan."

Sithas bolted upright in his throne. "Bring him to me! And summon the stablemaster. Tell him to bring a whip!"

"Your Majesty?"

The words came from behind the guard, who stepped aside and let Tamanier Ambrodel enter. The noble elf approached and bowed formally. "May I have a private word with the Speaker?"

"Leave us," Sithas told the guard. When only Quimant and himself were present, he gestured Tamanier to speak.

"I wish to prevent you from allowing a grave injustice," Ambrodel began.

"*I* dispense the justice here. What business is it of yours?" demanded Sithas.

Ambrodel flinched at the Speaker's harsh tone but forged ahead. "I am here at your mother's request."

"What is the nature of this 'injustice'?"

"It concerns your punishment of this elf, this mason. Your mother, as you know, has received letters from Kith-Kanan separate from the official missives he sends to you. It seems that he communicates to her on matters that he does not care to discuss . . . with others."

Sithas scowled.

"Kith-Kanan *has* taken a human woman as his companion. He has written your mother about her. Apparently he is very much smitten."

Sithas sagged backward in the monstrous throne. He wanted to curse at Tamanier Ambrodel, to call him a liar. But he couldn't.

Instead, he had to accept the unthinkable, no matter how night-marish the knowledge.

He suddenly felt sick to his stomach.

* * * * *

Sithas labored for hours over the letter he tried to write to his brother. He attempted a number of beginnings.

Kith-Kanan, my brother,

I have word from mother of a woman you have taken from the enemy camp. She tells me that the human saved your life. We are grateful, of course.

He could go no further. He wanted to write, *Why?* Why? *Don't you understand what we're fighting for?* He wanted to ask why victory had come to smell like failure and defeat.

Sithas crumpled up the parchment and hurled it into the fireplace. The realization hit him brutally.

He no longer had anything to say to his brother.

Early Winter,
Last Day of 2213 (PC)

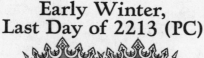

27

The blizzard swept over the iceberg-dotted ocean and around the snow-swept flanks of the Kharolis Mountains. It roared over the plains, making life a bitter and icy nightmare for the armies of both sides.

Those forces—human, elven, and dwarven—ceased all maneuvers and combat. Wherever the blast caught them, the brigades and regiments of the Wildrunners sought what little shelter they could and made quarters for the winter. Their Ergothian enemies, in even smaller bands, occupied towns, farm outposts, and wilderness camps in a desperate attempt to shelter themselves from nature's onslaught.

The Windriders, together with a large detachment of the dwarven legion, were more fortunate. Their camp occupied the barns and cabins of a huge farm, abandoned by its human tenants during the rout of the Ergothian Army. Here they found livestock for the griffons and bins of grain from which elven and dwarven cooks prepared a hard bread that, while bland and tough, would sustain the troops for several months.

The rest of Kith-Kanan's army occupied a multitude of camps, more than forty, across an arc of the plains stretching some five hundred miles.

On this brutally cold day, Kith made an inspection of the Windriders' camp. He pulled his woolen scarf closer about his face. It wouldn't entirely block the wind, but perhaps it would keep his ears from becoming frostbitten. In a few minutes, he would reach the shelter of the dwarven lodge, where he would meet with Dunbarth. After that, the warm fire of his own house . . . and Suzine.

The Wildrunners had succeeded in driving the remnants of the Ergothian Army hundreds of miles to the west. Throughout the campaign, Suzine had ridden with Kith on his griffon and lain with him in his tent. Zestful and hardy in a way that was unlike elven females, Suzine had adopted his life as her own and made no complaints about fighting conditions or the vicissitudes of weather.

The Army of Ergoth had left thousands of corpses behind on the plains. The bravest of the human warriors had taken shelter in tracts of forestland, where the Windriders couldn't pursue. Most of their fellows streamed home to Daltigoth. But these stubborn remnants, mostly light horsemen from the northern wing of the Ergothian Army, fought and held out.

Trapped within the forests, the horsemen couldn't use their strengths of speed and surprise. Out of necessity, the human army began waging a relentless campaign of guerrilla warfare, striking in small groups, then falling back to the woods. Ironically the elves among them had proven particularly adept at organizing and utilizing these scattershot tactics.

After months of hard pursuit and small victories in countless skirmishes, Kith-Kanan was preparing for a sweeping attack that might have expelled the hated enemy from the elven lands altogether. The Wildrunner infantry had assembled, ready to drive into the tracts of forest and expunge the Ergothian troops. Elven cavalry and the Windriders would fall upon them after they were forced into the open.

Then the early blows of winter had paralyzed military operations.

In his heart, the elven general felt scant disappointment that circumstances would force him to remain in the field at least until spring. He was content in the large, well-heated cottage that he had requisitioned, his due as commander. He was content in the arms of Suzine. How she had changed his life, revitalized him, given him a sense of being that extended beyond the present! It was ironic, he reflected, that it was war between their people that had brought them together.

The long, low shape of the dwarven lodge emerged before him, and he knocked on the heavy wooden door, setting aside thoughts of his woman until later. The portal swung open, and he stepped into the dim, cavelike log house that the dwarves had erected as their winter shelter. The temperature, while warmer than the outside air, was quite a bit cooler than that which was maintained in the elven shelters.

"Come in, General!" boomed Dunbarth, amid a crowd of his veterans gathered around a platform in the middle of the lodge.

Two nearly naked dwarves gasped for breath on the stage before hurling themselves at each other. One of them swiftly picked his opponent up and flipped him over his shoulder, whereupon the dwarven crowd erupted into cheers and boos. More than a few pouches, bulging with gold and silver coins, changed hands.

"At least you don't lack for diversion," remarked Kith-Kanan with a smile, settling beside the dwarf commander at a low bench that several other dwarves had swiftly vacated for him.

Dunbarth chuckled. "It'll do until we can get back to the *real* war. Here, I've had some wine heated for you."

"Thanks." Kith took the proffered mug while Dunbarth hefted a foaming tankard of ale. How the dwarves, who marched with a relatively small train of supplies, maintained a supply of the bitter draft was a mystery to Kith, yet every time he visited this winter shelter he found them drinking huge quantities of the stuff.

"And how do our elven comrades weather the storm?" inquired the dwarven commander.

"As well as could be expected. The griffons seem unaffected for the most part, while the Windriders and other elves have sufficient shelter. It could be a long winter."

"Aye. It could be a long war, too." Dunbarth made the remark in a lighthearted tone, but Kith-Kanan didn't think he was joking.

"I don't think so," the elf countered. "We have the remnants of the humans trapped to the west. Surely they can't move any more than we can in the midst of this storm!"

The dwarf nodded in silent agreement, so the elf continued. "As soon as the worst of the winter passes, we'll head into the attack. It shouldn't take more than two months to push the whole mass of them off the plains and back within the borders of Ergoth where they belong!"

"I hope you're right," replied the dwarven general sincerely. "Yet I'm worried about their commander, this Giarna. He's a resourceful devil!"

"I can handle Giarna!" Kith's voice was almost a growl, and Dunbarth looked at him in surprise.

"Any word from your brother?" inquired the dwarf after a moment's pause.

"Not since the storm set in."

"Thorbardin is disunited," reported his companion. "The Theiwar agitate for a withdrawal of dwarven troops, and it seems they might be winning the Daergar Clan over to their side.

"No wonder, with their own 'hero' joining ranks with the Army of Ergoth!" The reports had been confirmed in late autumn: After

Sithas had driven him from Silvanost, Than-Kar had delivered his battalion over to General Giarna. The Theiwar dwarves had helped protect the retreating army during the last weeks of the campaign before winter had stopped all action.

"A shameful business, that," agreed Dunbarth. "The lines of battle may be clear on the field, but in the minds of our people, they begin to grow very hazy indeed."

"Do you need anything here?" inquired Kith-Kanan.

"You wouldn't have a hundred bawdy dwarven wenches, would you?" asked Dunbarth with a sly grin. He winked at the elf. "Though perhaps they would merely sap our fighting spirits. One has to be careful, you know!"

Kith laughed, suddenly embarassed about his own circumstances. The presence of Suzine in his house was common knowledge throughout the camp. He felt no shame about that, and he knew his troops liked the human woman and that she returned their obvious affection. Still, the thought of her being regarded as his "bawdy wench" he found disturbing.

They talked for a while longer of the pleasures of homecomings and of adventures in more peaceful times. The storm continued unabated, and finally Kith-Kanan remembered that he needed to finish his rounds before returning to his own house. He bade his farewells and continued his inspection of the other elven positions before turning toward his cottage.

His heart rose at the prospect of seeing Suzine again, though he had been gone from her presence for mere hours. He couldn't bear the thought of this winter camp without her. But he wondered about the men. Did they see her as a "wench" as Dunbarth seemed to? As some sort of camp follower? The thought would not go away.

A bodyguard, an immaculate corporal in the armor of the House Protectorate, threw open the door of his house as he approached. Kith quickly went inside, enjoying the warmth that caressed him as he shook off his snow-covered garb.

He passed through the guardroom—once the parlor of the house, but now the garrison for a dozen men-at-arms, those trusted with the life of the army commander. He nodded at the elves, all of whom had snapped to attention, but he quickly passed through the room into the smaller chambers beyond, closing the interior door behind him.

A crackling blaze filled the fireplace before him, and the aroma of sizzling beef teased his nostrils. Suzine came into his arms and he felt completely alive. Everything would wait until the delights of reunion had run their course. Without speaking, they went to the hearth and lay down before the fire.

Only afterward did they slowly break the spell of their silence.

"Did you find Arcuballis in the pasture?" Suzine asked, lazily tracing a finger along Kith-Kanan's bare arm.

"Yes. He seems to prefer the open field to the barn," the elf replied. "I tried to coax him into a stall, but he stayed outside, weathering the storm."

"He's too much like his master," the human woman said tenderly. Finally she rose and fetched a jug of wine that she had warmed by the fireplace. Huddled together under a bearskin, they each enjoyed a glass.

"It's odd," said Kith-Kanan, his mood reflective. 'These are the most peaceful times I've ever spent, here beside the fire with you."

"It's not odd," replied the woman. "We were meant to know peace together. I've seen it, *known* it, for years."

Kith didn't dispute her. She had told him how she used to watch him in the mirror, the enchanted glass that she had crashed over Giarna's skull to save his life. She carried the broken shards of the glass in a soft leather box. He knew that she had seen the griffons before the battle yet hadn't told her commander about this crucial fact. Often he had wondered what could have made her take such a risk for one—an enemy!—she had met only once before.

Yet as the weeks became months, he had ceased to ask these questions, sensing—as did Suzine—the rightness of their lives together. She brought to him a comfort and serenity that he thought had been gone forever. With her, he felt a completeness that he had never before attained, not with Anaya nor Hermathya.

That she was a human seemed astonishingly irrelevant to Kith. He knew that the folk of the plains, be they elf or dwarf or human, had begun to see the war break the barriers of racial purity that had so long obsessed them. He wondered, for a brief moment, whether the elves of Silvanost would ever be able to appreciate the good humans, people like Suzine,

A schism was growing, he knew, among his folk. It divided the nation just as certainly as it would inevitably divide his brother and himself. Kith-Kanan had made up his mind which side he was on, and in that decision, he knew that he had crossed a line.

This woman with him now, her head resting so softly upon his shoulder, deserved more than to be considered a general's "bawdy wench." Perhaps the fumes from the fire wafted too thickly through the room, muddling his thoughts. Or perhaps their isolation here on the far frontiers of the kingdom brought home to Kith the truly important things in his life.

In any event, he made up his mind. Slowly he turned, feeling her stir against his side. Sleepily she opened an eye, brushing aside her red hair to smile at him.

"Will you become my wife?" asked the general of the army.

"Of course," replied his human woman.

PART IV

Kinslayer

From The River of Time, the Great Scroll of Astinus,
Master Historian of Krynn

28

The Kinslayer War spewed blood across the plainslands for nearly forty years. It was a period of long, protracted battles, of vast interludes of retrenchment, of starvation, disease, and death. Savage blizzards froze the armies camped in winter, while fierce storms—lightning, hail, and cyclonic winds—ripped capriciously through the ranks of both sides during the spring season.

From the historian's perspective, there is a dreary sameness to the war. Kith-Kanan's Wildrunners pursued the humans, attacked them, seemed to wipe them out, and then even more humans took the places of the slain.

General Giarna maintained complete control of the Ergothian troops, and though his losses were horrendous, he bore them without regret. The pressure of his sudden attacks chipped away at the elves, while reinforcements balanced out the general's losses. A stalemate evolved, with the forces of Silvanesti winning every battle, but with the humans always averting complete defeat.

Despite this monotonous pattern, the course of the war had several key junctures. The Siege of Sithelbec must be considered a decisive hour. It seemed the last chance for General Giarna to attain an undiluted victory. But the Battle of Sithelbec turned the tide and will always be ranked among the turning points of the history of Krynn.

Throughout, the life of one individual best illustrates the tragedy and the inevitability of the Kinslayer War. This is the human wife of Kith-Kanan, Suzine des Quivalin.

Relative of the great Emperor Quivalin V, as well as his heirs (a total of three Quivalin rulers presided over the war), her presence in the army of her nation's enemy served to solidify the human resolve. Disowned by her monarch, sentenced in absentia to hang by her former lover, General Giarna, she took to the elven cause with steadfast loyalty.

For over thirty-five years, the greater part of her life, she remained true to her husband, first as his lover and later as his companion and adviser, always as his wife. She was never accepted by the elves of Silvanesti; her husband's brother never even acknowledged her existence. She bore Kith-Kanan two children, and the half-elves were raised as elves among the clans of the Wildrunners.

Yet the elven army, like its society, changed over the years. Even as human blood entered the royal elven veins, the human presence came to be accepted as a part of the Wildrunner force. The pure racial lines of the eastern elves became irrelevant in the mixed culture of the west. Even as they fought for the cause of Silvanesti, Kith-Kanan's elves lost the distinction of the war's purpose as seen by Sithas.

And the battles raged on and seemingly built to an inevitable climax, only to have the elusive moment of decision once again slip out of reach.

Beyond these key moments, however, and certainly surpassing them in oddity, was the peculiar end of the war itself. . . .

Early Spring, Year of
the Cloud Giant, 2177 (PC)

29

The sprig that had once made such a proud sapling now towered over Kith-Kanan, a stalwart oak of some sixty feet in height. He gazed at it but could summon little emotion. He found that the memory of Anaya had faded over the distance of time. Nearly four decades of combat, of battles against the elusive armies of Ergoth, had worn away at his life. It seemed that treasured thoughts of a time before the war had been the first memories to disappear. Mackeli and Anaya might have been aquaintances of a friend, elves he had heard described and seen illustrated but had never actually met.

Even Suzine. He had a hard time now remembering her as she used to be. Her hair, in earlier days lush and fiery red, was now thin and white. Once supple grace had become slow and awkward movement, her once beautiful young body arthritic and stiff. Her sight and hearing had begun to fail. While he, with his elven longevity, was still a young adult, she had become an elderly woman.

He had flown here early this morning, partly in order to avoid her—to avoid all of those who gathered at the forest camp, an hour's flight by griffon from here, for the war conference. This was the eighth such council between himself and his brother. They met about once every five years. Most of the gatherings occurred, like this one, halfway between Silvanost and Silthelbec. Kith-Kanan couldn't bear the thought of returning to the elven capital, and Sithas preferred to avoid a journey all the way to the war zone.

These quintennial conferences had begun as grand outings, an opportunity for the general and his family, together with his most trusted captains, to embark on a journey away from the tedious rigors of war. By now, they were anathema to Kith, as predictable in their own way as the battlefield.

His brother's family and retinue had made an art out of shunning the human woman whom Kith-Kanan had married. Suzine was always invited to the banquets and feasts and celebrations. Once there, however, she was pointedly ignored. Some elves, such as his mother, Nirakina, had defied the trend, showing kindness and courtesy to Kith's wife. Nirakina's husband of the past thirty years, Tamanier Ambrodel, who came from the plainslands himself, tried to lessen the prejudice that fell upon her.

But Hermathya and Quimant and the others had shown her only contempt, and over the years, Suzine had tired of facing their antagonism. Now she avoided the large gatherings, though she still traveled with Kith-Kanan to the conference site.

Kith looked away from the tree, as if guilty about his thoughts, which now turned to his children. Suzine had borne him two half-elves, and he knew that they should bring him joy.

Ulvian, son of Kith-Kanan! That one, it would seem, was destined to rule some day. Was he not the eldest son of the elven hero who had led his army faithfully for all the years of the Kinslayer War? Despite the rapid growth to adulthood that was a mark of his half-human ancestry, how could he fail to show the wisdom and bravery that had been his father's traits of survival for all these years? So far, those traits hadn't been evident. The lad showed a lack of ambition bordering on indolence, and his arrogant and supercilious nature had alienated anyone who had tried to be his friend.

Or Verhanna, his daughter. Blessed image of her mother? She was in danger of becoming, with her constant tantrums and her litany of rude demands, a living reminder of the divisive war that had become a way of life for him and for all of the elven peoples.

The Kinslayer War. How many families had been divided by death or betrayal? No longer was this a war between elves and humans, if it had ever been that. The population of Silvanesti couldn't support the level of warfare, so now, in addition to the stalwart dwarves, huge companies of human mercenaries fought alongside his Wildrunners. They were well paid for serving the elven standards.

At the same time, many elves, especially the Kagonesti, driven from the nation by the demanding decrees of the Speaker of the Stars, had fled to the human banner. Dwarves, particularly of the Theiwar and Daewar clans, had also enlisted to serve the Emperor of Ergoth.

This was a strange admixture of alliances. How often had elf slain elf, human fought human, or dwarf butchered dwarf? Each battle brought new atrocities, as likely as not visited by fighters of one race against enemies of the same background.

The war, once fought along clear and precise lines, had become an endlessly feeding monster, for the numberless enemy seemed willing to pay any price to win, and the skilled and valiant troops of Kith-Kanan purchased victory after victory on scores of battle-fields with the precious coin of their own blood. Yet ultimate victory—a settlement of the war itself—remained elusive.

With a sigh, Kith-Kanan rose to his feet and crossed wearily to Arcuballis. He would have to get back to the camp, he knew. The conference was due to begin in an hour. The griffon leaped into the sky while the rider mused sadly about the time when his life had been shadowed by the growth of a tree in the forest.

* * * * *

"We have chased the humans across the plains every summer! We kill a thousand of them, and five thousand come to take their places!" Kith-Kanan loudly complained about the frustrating cycle of events.

Sithas, Lord Quimant, and Tamanier Ambrodel had come from the capital city to attend this council. For his part, Kith-Kanan had brought Parnigar and Dunbarth Ironthumb on his journey across the plains. Other members of their respective parties—including Hermathya, Nirakina, Suzine, and Mari, Parnigar's newest human wife—now enjoyed the shade of awnings and trees around the fringes of the great meadow where they camped.

Meanwhile, the two delegations engaged in heated discussion within an enclosed tent in the middle of the clearing. Two dozen guards stood, out of earshot, around the shelter.

The most savage of the spring storms were still some weeks away, but a steady drizzle soaked the tent and added to the gray futility of the mood.

"We crush an army in battle, and another army marches at us from another direction. They know they cannot defeat us, yet they keep trying! What kind of creatures are they? If they kill five of my Windriders at the cost of a thousand of their own soldiers, they hail it as a victory!"

Kith-Kanan shook his head, knowing that it was a human vic-tory whenever his griffon cavalry lost even one precious body. The Windriders numbered a bare hundred and fifty stalwart veterans now, scarcely a third of their original number. There were no more griffons to ride nor trained elven warriors to mount them.

497

Yet the tide of humans flowing across the plains seemed to grow thicker every year.

"What kind of beings *are* these that they could spill so much blood, lose so many lives and still carry forward their war?" Sithas demanded, exasperated. Even after forty years of warfare, the Speaker of the Stars couldn't fathom the motivations of the humans or their various allies.

"They breed like rabbits," observed Quimant. "We have no hope of matching their numbers, and our treasury runs dry simply to maintain the troops that we have."

"Knowing that this is true and doing something about it are two different things," Sithas retorted.

The council lapsed into glum silence. There was a depressing familiarity to their predicament. The national attrition caused by the war had become readily apparent thirty years earlier.

"The winter, at least, has been mild," suggested Parnigar, trying to improve their mood. "We lost very few casualties to cold or snow."

"Yes, but in the past, such winters have given us the heaviest spring storms!" answered Kith-Kanan. "And the summers are always bloody," he concluded.

"We could send peace feelers to the emperor," suggested Tarnanier Ambrodel. "It may be that Quivalin the Seventh is more amenable than his father or grandfather."

Parnigar snorted. "He's been ruler for four years. In that time, we've seen, if anything, an increase in the pace of Ergoth's attacks! They butcher their prisoners. This past summer, they began poisoning wells wherever they passed. No, Quivalin the Seventh is no peacemonger."

"Perhaps it is not the emperor's true will," suggested Quimant, drawing another snort from Parnigar. "General Giarna has made an empire for himself of the battlefield. He would be reluctant to relinquish it—and what better way to sustain his power than to ensure that the war continues?"

"There is the matter of General Giarna," grunted Dunbarth, with an uncharacteristic scowl. "He presses forward with every opportunity, more brutal than ever. I don't think he'd desist even if given the order. War has become his life! It *sustains* him!"

"Surely after all these years . . . ?" Tamanier wondered.

"The man doesn't *age!* Our spies tell us he looks the same as he did forty years ago, and he has the vitality of a young man! His own troops hate and fear him, but there are worse ways to insure the obedience of your subordinates."

"We have taken the extreme step of sending assassins after him, a brigade comprised of humans and elves both." Kith related the tale of the assassination attempt. "None survived. From what we have pieced together, they reached Giarna in his tent. His personal security seemed lax. They attacked with daggers and swords but couldn't even injure him!"

"Surely that's an exaggeration," suggested his brother. "If they got that close, how could they not have been successful?"

"General Giarna has survived before, under circumstances where I would have expected him to die. He has been showered with arrows. Though his horse may be slain beneath him, he gets away on foot. He has fought his way out of deadly ambushes, leaving dozens of dead Wildrunners behind him."

"Something unnatural is at work there," pronounced Quimant. "It's dangerous to think of peace with such a creature."

"It is dangerous to *fight* such a creature as well," remarked Parnigar pointedly. Quimant understood the intent of the remark. Parnigar had done nearly a half-century of fighting, after all, while Quimant's family had spent those years raking in a fortune in munitions profits. But the lord coolly ignored the warrior's provocation.

"We cannot talk of peace, yet," emphasized Sithas. He turned to his brother. "We need something that will allow us to bargain from a position of strength."

"Do you mean to suggest that you'd be willing to bargain?" asked Kith-Kanan, surprised.

Sithas sighed. "You're right. You've all been right, but for years, I've refused to believe you. But it has begun to seem inconceivable that we can win a complete victory over the humans. Still, we cannot maintain this costly war forever!"

"I must inform you," interjected Dunbarth, clearing his throat. "Though I have stalled my king for several years now, his patience will not last forever. Already many dwarves are agitating for us to return home. You must realize that King Pandelthain is not so suspicious of humans as was King Hal-Waith."

And you, old friend—you deserve the chance to go home, to rest and retire. Kith-Kanan kept that thought to himself. Nevertheless, the changes wrought by age in Dunbarth were more apparent than any that were manifest in the elves. The dwarf's beard and hair were the color of silver. His once husky shoulders had a frail look to them, as if his body was a mere shell of its former self. The skin of his face was mottled and wrinkled.

Yet his eyes still shone with a merry light and keen perceptiveness. Now, as if he followed Kith's thoughts, he turned to the elven general and chuckled. "Tell 'em, young fellow. Tell 'em what we've got up our sleeves."

Kith nodded. The time was right.

"We have word that the humans are planning a trap against the Windriders. They will lure the griffons into an archery ambush. We want to amass the Wildrunners, using all the mercenaries, garrison forces, and dwarves our entire army. We want to come at them from the north, east, and south. If we hit them hard and we keep the advantage of surprise, we'll achieve the kind of setback that will force them to the bargaining table."

"But Sithelbec—you'd leave the fortress unscreened?" Sithas asked. In the course of the Kinslayer War the siege of those high palisades had become an epic tale, and a bustling military city had blossomed around the walls. The place had a tremendous symbolic as well as practical importance to the Silvanesti cause, and a sizable proportion of the Wildrunners were permanently garrisoned there.

"It's a risk," Kith-Kanan admitted. "We will move quickly, striking before the humans can learn our intentions. Then the Windriders will act as the bait of the trap, and while the enemy is distracted, we will strike."

"It's worth a try," urged Parnigar, supporting his general's plan. "We can't keep chasing shadows year after year!"

"Some shadows are more easily caught," observed Quimant acidly. "The human women, for example."

Parnigar leaped to his feet, knocking his chair over backward and lunging toward the lord.

"Enough!" The Speaker of the Stars reached out and pushed the warrior back toward his chair. Even in his rage, Parnigar heeded his ruler.

"Your insulting remark was uncalled for!" barked Kith-Kanan, staring at Quimant.

"True," Sithas agreed. "But neither would it be invited if you and your officers kept your loyalties a little more clear in your own heads!"

Kith-Kanan flushed with anger and frustration. Why did it always come down to this? He glared at Sithas as if his twin was a stranger.

A noise at the tent flap pulled their attention away from the conference. Vanesti, Ulvian, and Verhanna, the children of the royal twins, erupted into the tent with impertinent boldness. Hermathya followed.

Kith-Kanan met her eyes and froze, suddenly numb. By the gods, he had forgotten how beautiful she was! Furious and guilty, he nonetheless watched her furtively. She cast him a sideways glance, and as always, he saw the beckoning in her eye. That only furthered his pain. Never again, he knew, would he betray his brother. And now there was the matter of his own wife.

"Uncle Kith!" Vanesti irritated his father by running directly to his uncle. The young elf stopped quickly and then pantomimed a formal bow.

"Come here. Stop acting like the court jester!" Kith swept his nephew into an embrace, keenly aware of the eyes of his own children upon him. Ulvian and Verhanna, though younger than Vanesti, had matured much more quickly because of their half-human blood. Already young adults, they looked disdainfully upon such adolescent outbursts of emotion.

Perhaps, too, they sensed the bitter contrast in their relationship with their own uncle. There had never been an "Uncle Sithas!" or a "Come here, children!" between them. They were half-human and consequently had no place in the Speaker's royal family.

Perhaps they understood, but they didn't forgive.

"This reminds me of a final matter for discussion," Sithas said stiffly. He relaxed when Vanesti left Kith's side to stand with Ulvian and Vehanna beside the open door flap of the tent.

"Vanesti is due to begin his training in the warrior arts. He has disdained the academies in the city and has prevailed upon me to make this request: will you take him as your squire?"

For a moment, Kith-Kanan sat back, acutely aware of Vanesti's hopeful gaze. He couldn't suppress a surge of affection and pride. He liked the young elf and felt that he would be a good warrior—good at whatever he attempted, for that matter. Yet he couldn't entirely ignore another feeling.

The proposition reminded him of Ulvian. Kith had sent his son to Parnigar, as squire to that most able soldier. The young half-elf had proven so intractable and shiftless that, with deep regret, Parnigar had been forced to send him back to his father. The failure had stung Kith-Kanan far more than it had disturbed Ulvian.

Yet when he looked at the young form of Vanesti, so much like a younger version of Kith-Kanan himself, he knew what his answer must be.

"It would be my honor," Kith replied seriously.

* * * * *

The aging woman watched the image of the elf in the mirror. The glass was cracked and patched, with several slivers, missing. It had, after all, been reconstructed from shards. Five years earlier, she had hired a legion of skilled elven artisans to take those broken pieces, guarded by Suzine for years, adding crafts of their own to restore the glass to some measure of its former power.

It seemed that, with the distance that had grown between herself and her husband, she had little left to do in life but observe the course of things around her. The mirror gave her the means to do so, without forcing her to leave her carriage and be exposed to the subtle humiliations of the Silvanesti elves.

Suzine flushed as she thought of Hermathya and Quimant, whose cutting remarks had hurt her decades earlier when she had allowed them to penetrate her emotions. Yet even those barbs had been easier to take than the aloof silence of Sithas, her own brother-in-law, who had barely acknowledged her existence!

Of course, there was goodness to be found in elvenkind, too. There was Nirakina, who had always treated her as a daughter, and Tamanier Ambrodel, who had offered friendship. But now age had impaired even those relationships. How could she feel like a daughter to Nirakina when the four-centuries-old elf-woman seemed like a spry young woman beside the aging Suzine? And her hearing made conversation difficult, so that even Tamanier Ambrodel had to shout his remarks, often repeating them two or three times. She found it less embarrassing to simply avoid these two good souls.

So she remained in this enclosed coach that Kith-Kanan had given her. The large vehicle was comfortably appointed, even to the point of containing a soft bed—a bed that was always hers alone.

For what must have been the millionth time, she wondered about the course her life had taken, about the love she had developed for an elf who would inevitably outlive her by centuries. She couldn't regret that decision. Her years of happiness with Kith-Kanan had been the finest of her life. But those years were gone, and if she didn't regret her choice of nearly four decades earlier, neither could she bury the unhappiness that was now her constant companion.

Her children were no comfort. Ulvian and Verhanna seemed embarrassed by their mother's humanness and shunned her, pretending to be full-blooded elves insofar as they could. But she felt pity for them as well, for their father had never shown them the affection that would have been due his proper heirs—as if he himself was secretly ashamed of their mixed racial heritage.

Now that she was too old to ride a horse, her husband carted her around in this carriage. She felt like so much baggage, a cargo that Kith-Kanan was determined to see properly delivered before he proceeded with the rest of his life. How long could she remain like this? What could she do to change her lot in her waning years?

Her mind drifted to the enemy—to her husband's enemy and her own. General Giarna frightened her now more than ever before. Often she had observed him in the repaired glass, shocked by the youthful appearance and vigor of the man. She sensed in him the power of something much deeper than she had first suspected.

Often she remembered the way Giarna had slain General Barnet. It was as if he had sucked the life out of him, she remembered thinking. That, she now knew, was exactly what he had done. How many more lives had the Boy General claimed over the years? What was the true cost of his youthfulness?

Her mind and her mirror drifted back to Kith-Kanan. She saw him in the conference. He was close enough to her that she could see him very clearly indeed. The elf's image grew large in her mirror, and then she looked into his eyes, through his eyes. She stared, as she had learned to do years before, into his subconscious.

She looked past the war, the constant fear that she found within him, to gentler things. She sought the image of his three women, for she was used to seeing the elfwomen Anaya and Hermathya there. Suzine sought the image of herself—herself as a young woman, alluring and sensual. That image had grown more difficult to find of late, and this added to her sorrow.

This time she could find no remembrance of herself. Even the spritely Anaya was gone, her image replaced by the picture of a tall, slender tree. Then she came upon Hermathya and sensed the desire in Kith's mind. It was a new sensation that suddenly caused the mirror to glow, until Suzine turned her face away. The mirror faded into darkness as tears filled her eyes.

Slowly, gently, she placed the mirror back into its case. Trying to stem the trembling of her hands, she looked about for her coachman. Kith-Kanan wouldn't return for several hours, she knew.

When he did, she would be gone.

Midspring
2177 (PC)

30

The lord-major-chieftain supreme of Hillrock stretched his brawny arms, acutely aware that his muscles were not so supple as they had once been. Placing a huge hand to his head, he stroked blunt fingers through hair that seemed to grow thinner by the week.

Squinting against the setting sun, he looked about his pastoral community of large one-room dwellings hewn from the rock of this sheltered valley. To the east towered the heights of the Khalkist Mountains, while to the west, the range settled into the flatlands of the Silvanesti plain.

For three decades, he had ruled as lord-major-chieftain supreme, and they had been good years for all of his people. Good years, but past now. Poking his broad tongue against the single tooth that jutted proudly from his lower gum, the lord-major exercised his mind by attempting to ponder the future.

A nagging urge tugged at him, desirous of pulling him away from peaceful Hillrock. He couldn't put his finger on the reasons, but the hill giant who had once been called One-Tooth now felt a need to leave, to strike out across those plains. He was reluctant to answer this compulsion, for he had the feeling that once he left, he would never return. He couldn't understand this compulsion, but it grew more persistent every day.

Finally the hill giant gathered his wives together, cuffing and cursing them until he had their attention.

"I go away!" he said loudly.

The formalities completed, he hefted his club and started down the valley. Whatever the nature of the longing that drew him to the plains, he knew that he would find its source in an elf who had once been his friend.

* * * * *

The conference broke up in awkward farewells. Only Hermathya displayed emotion, screaming and rebuking Sithas for his decision to send Vanesti to the battlefield. The Speaker of the Stars coolly ignored his wife, and she collapsed into spasms of weeping. She desperately hugged the young elf, to his acute embarrassment, and then retired to her coach for the long journey back to Silvanost.

Few had noted Suzine's departure late on the previous day. Kith-Kanan was puzzled by her leaving, though he assumed she had reason to return to Sithelbec. In truth, he was also a little relieved. The presence of his human wife put strain on any communication with Sithas, and Suzine's absence had made the subdued farewell banquet a little easier to endure.

Still, it was unlike her to depart so abruptly without advising him, so he couldn't totally banish his concern. This concern mounted to genuine anxiety when, ten days later, they finally arrived at the fortress and learned that the general's wife hadn't been seen. Nor had she sent any message.

He dispatched Windriders to comb the plains, seeking a sign of Suzine's grand coach. However, true to Kith's prediction, the spring storm season began early, and thunderstorms blanketed the grasslands with hail and torrential rains. Winds howled unchecked across hundreds of miles of prairie. The search became all but impossible and had to be suspended for all intents and purposes.

In the meantime, Kith-Kanan threw himself into the choreography of his great battle plan. The forces of the Wildrunners mustered at Sithelbec, preparing to march westward, where they would hit the human army before General Giarna even realized they had left the region of the fortress.

Intelligence about the enemy was scarce and unreliable. Finally Kith called upon the only scout he could count on to make a thorough reconnaissance: Parnigar.

"Take two dozen riders and get as close as you can," ordered Kith-Kanan, knowing full well that he was asking his old friend to place his life at grave risk. But he had no real alternative.

If the veteran resented the difficult order, he didn't let on. "I'll try to get out and back quickly," he replied. "We want to get the campaign off to an early start."

Agreed," Kith noted. "And be careful. I'd rather see you come back empty-handed than to not comeback at all!"

Parnigar grinned, then grew suddenly serious. "Has there been any word about—I should say 'from'—Suzine?"

Kith sighed. "Not a thing. It's as if the world gobbled her up. She slipped away from the conference that afternoon. I brought Vanesti back to the camp as my squire and found her gone."

"These damned storms will run their course in another few weeks," said the scout, "but I doubt you'll be able to send fliers out before then. No doubt she's holed up safe on some farmstead. . . ."

But his words lacked conviction. Indeed, Kith-Kanan had lost optimism and didn't know what to believe anymore. All indications were that Suzine had left the camp of her own free will. Why? And why wasn't he more upset?

"You mentioned your squire." Parnigar smoothly changed the subject. "How's the young fellow working out?"

"He's eager, I've got to grant him that. My armor hasn't gleamed like this in years!"

"When we march . . . ?"

"He'll have to come along," Kith replied. "But I'll keep him to the rear. He doesn't have enough experience to let him near the fighting."

"Aye," grunted the old warrior before disappearing into the storm.

* * * * *

'This will do, driver. I shall proceed on foot."

"Milady?" The coachman, as he opened the door for Suzine, looked at her in concern. "The Army of Ergoth has scouts all over here," he said. "They'll find you for sure."

I'm counting on that. Suzine didn't verbalize her reply. "Your dedication is touching, but, really, I'll be fine."

"I think the general would be—"

"The general will not be displeased," she said firmly.

"Very well." His reluctance was plain in his voice, but he assisted her in stepping to the ground. The carriage rested at the side of a muddy trail. Several wide pathways led into the woods around them.

She was grateful for the smoothness of the trail. Neither her eyes nor her legs were up to a rigorous hike. She turned toward the coachman who had carried her so faithfully across the plains for more than a week. Her mirror, now resting in the box on her belt, had shown her where to go, allowing her to guide them around outposts of human pickets. The only other possession she carried was in a pouch at her belt: a narrow-bladed knife. She wouldn't be coming back, but she couldn't tell the driver that.

"Wait here for two hours," she said. "I'll be back by then. I know these woods well. There are some old sights I would like to see."

Nodding and scowling, the driver climbed back onto his seat and watched until the woods swallowed her up. She hurried along the trail as fast as her aging legs would carry her, but even so, it took her more than an hour to cover two miles. She moved unerringly past many forks in the path, certain that the mirror had shown her the right way.

Shortly after she passed the end of her second mile, an armored crossbowman stepped into the path before her.

"Halt!" he cried, leveling his weapon. At the same time, he gaped in astonishment at the lone old woman who approached the headquarters of the Army of Ergoth.

"I'm glad you are here to greet me," she said pleasantly. "Take me to see General Giarna!"

"You want to see the general?"

"We're . . . old friends."

Shaking his head in amazement, the guard nevertheless led Suzine a short way farther down the trail, entering a small clearing. The top of the meadow was almost completely enclosed by a canopy of tall elms— protection against detection from the air, Suzine knew.

'The general's in there." The man gestured to a small cottage near the clearing's edge. Two men-at-arms flanked the doorway, and they snapped to attention as Suzine walked up to them.

"She wants to see the general," explained the crossbowman, with a shrug.

"Should we search her?" The question from a muscular halberdier sent a shiver down Suzine's stooped spine. She felt acutely conscious of the dagger in her pouch.

"That won't be necessary." Suzine recognized the deep voice from within the cottage. The watchmen stood aside, allowing Suzine to step through the door.

"You have come back to me."

For a moment, Suzine stood still, blinking and trying to see in the dim light. Then the large black-cloaked figure moved toward her, and she knew him—knew his sight, his smell, and his intimidating presence.

With a sense of dull wonder, she realized that the tales she had heard, the images of her mirror, were all true. General Giarna stood before her now. She knew that he must be at least seventy years old, but *he looked the same as he had forty years earlier!*

He stepped closer to her. She felt the revulsion and few she had known forty years earlier when he had approached her, had *used* her. Slowly her fingers closed around the weapon in her pouch. The man loomed over her, looking down with a slightly patronizing smile. She stared into his eyes and saw that same hollowness, the same sense of void, that she remembered with such vivid terror.

Then she pulled out the knife and threw back her arm. Why is he laughing? She wondered about that even as she drove the point of the weapon toward the unarmored spot at his throat. Giarna made no attempt to block her thrust.

The blade struck his skin but snapped as the weapon broke at the hilt. The useless shard of metal fell to the floor as Suzine blinked, incredulous.

General Giarna's throat showed not the tiniest hint of a wound.

* * * * *

It wasn't until Parnigar returned with his company of scouts that Kith-Kanan received any vital information regarding the enemy's positions. Wearing sodden trail clothes from the nine-day reconnaissance, the veteran captain reported to Kith-Kanan as soon as he returned to the fort.

"We pushed at the fringes of their position," he reported. "Their pickets were as thick as flies on a dead horse. They got two of my scouts, and the rest of us barely slipped out of their grasp."

Kith shook his head, wincing. Even after forty years of war, the death of each elf under his command struck him like a personal blow.

"We couldn't get into the main camp," explained Parnigar. "There were just too many guards. But judging by the density of their patrols, I have to conclude they were guarding the main body of Giarna's force."

"Thanks for taking the risk, my friend," said Kith-Kanan finally. "Too many times I have asked you."

Parnigar smiled wearily. "I'm in this fight to the end—one way or another!" The lanky warrior cleared his throat hesitatantly. "There's . . . something else."

"Yes?"

"We found the Lady Suzine's coachman on the outskirts of the human lines."

Kith-Kanan looked up in sudden fear. "Was he—is he alive?"

"Was." Parnigar shook his head. "He'd been taken by their pickets, then escaped after a fight. Badly wounded in the stomach, but he made it to the trail. We found him there."

"What did he tell you?"

"He didn't know where she was. He had dropped her beside the trail, and she followed a path into the woods. We checked out the area. Guards were thicker than ever there, so I think the headquarters must have been somewhere nearby."

Could she be heading back to Giarna? Kith-Kanan sensed Parnigar's unspoken question. Surely she wouldn't betray Kith-Kanan.

"Can you show me where this place is?" asked the elven commander urgently.

"Of course."

Kith sighed sympathetically. "I'm sorry that you must travel again so quickly, but perhaps . . . "

Parnigar waved off the explanation. "I'll be ready to ride when you need me."

"Go to your quarters now. Mari's been waiting for you for days," Kith-Kanan ordered, realizing that Parnigar still dripped from his drenched garments. "She's probably got dry clothes all ready to get you dressed."

"I doubt she wants to *dress* me!" Parnigar chuckled knowingly.

"Off to your wife now, before she grows old on you!" Kith's attempt at humor felt lame to both of them, though Parnigar forced a chuckle as he left.

Late Spring, Silvanost

31

Hermathya looked herself in the mirror. She was beautiful and she was young . . . yet for what purpose? She was alone.

Tears of bitterness welled in her eyes. She rose and whirled away from her table, only to be confronted by her bed. That canopied, quilted sleeping place mocked her every bit as harshly as did the mirror. For decades, it had been hers alone.

Now even her child had been sent away. Her anger throbbed as hot as ever, the same rage that had turned the two-week journey back to the city into a silent ordeal for Sithas. He endured her fury and didn't let it bother him, and Hermathya knew that he had won.

Vanesti was gone, serving beside his uncle on the front lines of danger! *How* could her husband have done this? What kind of perverse cruelty would cause him to torture his wife so? She thought of Sithas as a stranger. What little closeness they had once enjoyed had been worn thin by the stresses of war.

Her thoughts abruptly wandered to Kith-Kanan. How much like Sithas he looked—and yet how very different he was! Hermathya looked back upon the passion of their affair as one of the bright moments of her life. Before her name had been uttered as the prospective bride of the future Speaker of the Stars, her life had been a passionate whirl.

Then the announcement had come—Hermathya, daughter of the Oakleaf Clan, would wed Sithas of Silvanos! She remembered how Kith-Kanan had begged—he had *begged!*—her to accompany him, to run away. She had laughed at him as if he were mad.

Yet the madness, it now seemed, was hers. Prestige and station and comfort meant nothing, she knew, not when compared to the sense of happiness that she had thrown away.

The one time since then when Kith-Kanan and she had come together illicitly flared brightly in her mind. That episode had never been repeated because Kith-Kanan's guilt wouldn't allow it. He had avoided her for years and was awkward when they were brought together through necessity.

Shaking her head, she fought back the tears. Sithas was in the palace. Hermathya would go to him and make him bring their son back home!

She found her husband in his study, perusing a document with the Oakleaf stamp, in gold, at the top. He looked up when she entered, and blinked with surprise.

"You must call Vanesti back," she blurted, staring at him.

"I will not!"

"Can't you understand what he means to me?" Hermathya fought to keep her voice under control. *"I need* him here with me. He's all I've got"

"We've been over this. It will do the lad good to get out of the palace, to live among the troops! Besides, Kith will take good care of him. Don't you trust him?"

"Do *you*?" Hermathya uttered the insinuation without thinking.

"Why? What do you mean?" There had been something in her tone. Sithas leapt from his chair and stared at her accusingly.

She turned away, suddenly calm. She controlled the discussion now.

"What did you mean, do *I* trust him?" Sithas's voice was level and cold. "Of course I do!"

"You have been gullible before."

"I know that you loved him," the Speaker added. "I know of your affair before our marriage. I even know that he pleaded with you to go with him when he flew into exile."

"I should have gone!" she cried, whirling suddenly.

"Do you still love him?"

"No." She didn't know whether this was a lie or not. "But he loves me."

"That's nonsense!"

"He came to me in my bedroom long ago. He didn't leave until the morning." She lied about the room because it suited her purpose. Her husband wouldn't know that it was *she* who had gone to *him*.

Sithas stepped closer to her. "Why should I believe you?"

"Why should I lie?"

His open hand caught her across the cheek with a loud smack. The force of his blow sent her tumbling backward to the floor. With a burning face, she stood up, her eyes spitting fire at him.

"Vanesti will stay on the plains," Sithas declared as she turned and fled. He turned to the window, numb, and stared to the west. He wondered about, the stranger his brother had become.

* * * * *

"You believed that you could come here to *kill* me?" General Giarna looked at Suzine with mild amusement. The old woman backed against the closed door of his cottage. She had picked up the broken blade of her knife, but the weapon felt useless and futile, for it couldn't harm her enemy. Thunder rumbled outside as another storm swept across the camp.

"Your death would be the greatest thing that could happen to Krynn!" She spoke bravely, but her mind was locked by fear. How could she have been so stupid as to come here alone, thinking she could harm this brutal warrior? Instead, she had become his prisoner.

Her heart quailed as she remembered the man's dark tortures, his means of gaining information from his captives. And no captive had ever possessed such valuable information as the wife of his chief enemy.

Now the general laughed heartily, placing his hands on his hips and leaning backward like a young man. "My death, you should know, is not so easily attained."

Suzine stared at him.

"Do you remember the last night of General Barnet?"

She would never forget that awful, shriveled corpse, cast aside by General Giarna like an empty shell, drained of all its life.

"My powers come from places you cannot *begin* to understand!" He paced in agitation, looking at her.

"There are gods who care for people of power, gods whose names are only whispered in the dead of night, for fear of frightening the children!"

General Giarna whirled again, his brow furrowed in concentration. "There is Morgion, god of disease and decay. I tell you, he can be *bought*! I pay him in lives, and he saves his curse from my flesh! And there are others—Hiddukel, Sargonnas! And of course"— his voice dropped to a whisper; his body quivered, and he looked at Suzine—"the Queen of Darkness, Takhisis herself! They say that she is banished, but that's a lie. She is patient and she is generous. She bestows her powers on those who earn her favor!

"It is the power of *life,* in all its aspects! It allows me to be strong and young, while those around me grow old and die!"

Now he stared directly at her, and there seemed to be genuine anguish in his voice. "*You* might have shared this with me! You were a woman of power. You would have made a fitting partner for me! Who knows, one day we might have ruled Ergoth itself!"

"Your madness consumes you," Suzine replied.

"*It is not madness!*" he hissed. "*You* cannot kill me. No human can kill me! Nor a dwarf, nor an elf. *None* may slay me!"

General Giarna paced restlessly. A steady beat of rain suddenly began pounding on the roof, forcing him to raise his voice. "Not only do I remain young and vigorous, but I am also *invulnerable!*" He looked at, her sideways, slyly, "I even had my men capture a griffon so that I might devour it and take over its aura. Now not even one of those beasts—the bane of this long war!—can claim my blood.

"But enough of this talk," said Giarna, suddenly rough. He took her arm and pulled her to a chair, throwing her into it.

"My spies tell me that the Wildrunners prepare an attack. They will move on my headquarters here because they have learned of our plans to ambush the griffons."

Suzine looked at him dumbly.

"No doubt you know the route of march they will take when they come west. You will tell me. Be sure of this, you will tell me. I will simply move my ambush and consummate the victory that has eluded me for so long."

Fear pulsed hotly in Suzine's mind. She did know! Many nights she had been present during battle planning between Parnigar and Kith-Kanan. The other officers had ignored her, assuming that she wasn't listening, but out of curiosity, she had paid attention and absorbed most of the details.

"The only question is"—Giarna's voice was a deep bass warning—"will you tell me now or afterward?"

Her mind focused with exceptional clarity. She heard the rain beating steadily against the wooden frame of the house. She thought of her children and her husband, and then she knew.

There *was* a way—an escape for her! But she had to act fast, before she had second thoughts.

Her bleeding fingers, still clutching the knife blade, jerked upward. Giarna saw the movement, an expression of mild annoyance flickering across his face. The crone already knew she couldn't harm him!

Him. In that instant, he recognized his mistake as the keen edge sliced through Suzine's own neck. A shower of bright blood exploded from the torn artery, covering the general as the old woman slumped to the ground at his feet.

* * * * *

One-Tooth plodded through yet another thunderstorm. His march, already an epic by hill giant standards, had taken him through the foothills of his beloved mountains and across hundreds of miles of flatlands.

How did people ever *live* around here? He wondered at a life without the comforting rocky heights. He felt vulnerable and naked on these open prairies of grass.

Of course, his journey was made easier by the fact that such inhabitants as he encountered fled in panic at his approach, giving him a free sampling of whatever food had been bubbling on the stove or whatever milk might be chilling in the damp cellar.

The giant still didn't know why he had embarked upon this quest or what his ultimate destination would be. But his feet swung easily below him, and the miles continued to fall behind. He felt young again, more spry than he had in decades.

And he was propelled by an inchoate sense of destiny. When his march ended, that was where his destiny would be found.

One Week Later

32

Rain lashed at the griffon and its rider, but the pair pressed on through the storm. Though day was hours old, the horizon around them remained twilit and dim, so heavy was the gray blanket of clouds. Arcuballis flew low, seeking a place to land, cringing still closer to the earth against sudden blasts of lightning that seemed to warn them from the sky.

Finally Kith-Kanan found it—the small house in the center of the farmstead, down the trail where the coachman had seen Suzine disappear. Parnigar had showed him the trail two miles back, but he had flown past the clearing twice. So closely entwined were the overhanging branches that he hadn't even noticed it.

The trailhead was more than two miles away, and she couldn't have walked much farther than this. Yet there seemed to be nothing else besides anonymous woods for several miles in all directions. This *had* to be the place.

Arcuballis dived quickly to earth, dropping like a stone between the limbs of the broad elms. The griffon landed in a crouch, and Kith's sword was in his hand.

The door to the small house stood partially open, slamming and banging against its frame as the wind gusts shifted direction. The yard around the house was churned to mud, mired by the hooves of countless horses. Blackened pits showed where great cookfires had blazed, but now these were simply holes filled with sodden ash.

Cautiously Kith-Kanan dismounted and approached the house. He pushed the door fully open and saw that it consisted of one main room—and that room was now a shambles. Overturned tables, broken chairs, a pile of discarded uniforms, and a collection of miscellaneous debris all contributed to the disarray.

He began to pick through debris, kicking things with his boots and moving big pieces with his free hand, always holding his longsword at the ready. He found little of worth until, near the back corner, his persistence was rewarded.

A tingle of apprehension ran along his spine as he uncovered a wooden box he recognized instantly, for it was the one Suzine had used to store her mirror. Kneeling, he pulled it from beneath a moldy saddle blanket. He opened the top, and his reflection stared back at him. The mirror had remained intact.

Then as he looked, the image in the glass grew pale and wavery, and suddenly the picture became something else entirely.

He saw a black-cloaked human riding a dark horse, leading a column of men through the rain. The human army was on the march. He could recognize no landmarks, no signposts in the murky scene. But he knew that the humans were moving.

Obviously the planned ambush of the Windriders was suspected and now would have to be cancelled. But where did the humans march? Kith had a sickening flash of Sithelbec, practically defenseless since most of the garrison had marched into the field with the Wildrunners. Could General Giarna be that bold?

A more hideous thought occurred to him. Had Suzine betrayed him, revealing their battle plans to the human commander? Did the enemy march somewhere unknown to set up a *new* ambush? He couldn't bring himself to believe this, yet neither could he ignore the evidence that she had been here at the human command post.

Where was Suzine? In his heart, he knew the answer.

Grimly he mounted Arcuballis and took off. He made his way back to the east, toward the spearhead of his army, which he had ordered to march westward in an attempt to catch the human army in its camp. Now he knew that he had to make new plans—and quickly.

It took two days of searching before the proud griffon finally settled to earth in a damp clearing where Kith had spotted the elven banner.

Here he found Parnigar and Vanesti and the rest of the Wildrunner headquarters. This group marched with several dozen bodyguards, trying to remain in the approximate center of the farflung ripments. Because of the weather, the march columns were separated even more than usual, so that the small company camped this night in relative isolation.

"They've broken camp," announced Parnigar, without preamble.

"I know. Their base camp is abandoned. Have you discovered where they've gone?"

Kith's worst fears were confirmed by Parnigar's answer. "East, it looks like. There are tracks leading in every direction, as always, but it looks like they all swing toward the east a mile or two out of the camps."

Again Kith-Kanan thought of the ungarrisoned fortress rising from the plains a hundred miles to the east.

"Can we attack?" asked Vanesti, unable to restrain himself any longer.

"You'll stay here!" barked Kith-Kanan. He turned to Parnigar. "In the morning we'll have to find them."

"What? And leave me here alone? In the middle of nowhere?" Vanesti was indignant.

"You're right," Kith conceded with a sigh. "You'll have to come. But you'll also have to do what I tell you!"

"Don't I always?" inquired the youth, grinning impishly.

* * * * *

General Giarna slouched in his saddle, aware of the tens of thousands of marching soldiers surrounding him. The Army of Ergoth crept like a monstrous snake to the east, toward Sithelbec. Outriders spread across a thirty-mile arc before them, seeking signs of the Wildrunners. Giarna wanted to meet his foe in open battle while the weather was unchanged, hoping that the storm would neutralize the elves' flying cavalry. The Windriders had made his life very difficult over the years, and it would please him to fight a battle where the griffons wouldn't be a factor.

Even in his wildest hopes, he hadn't reckoned on weather as dismal as this. A day earlier, a tornado had swept through the supply train, killing more than a thousand men and destroying two weeks' worth of provisions. Now many columns of his army blundered through the featureless landscape, lost. Every day a few more men were struck by lightning, crippled or killed instantly.

The general didn't know that, even as he marched to the east, the elven army trudged westward, some twenty-five miles to the north. The Wildrunners sought the encampment of the human army. Both forces blundered forward in disarray, passing within striking range of each other, yet not knowing of their enemy's presence.

General Giarna looked to his left, to the north. There was something out there! He *sensed* it, though he saw nothing. His intuition informed him that the presence that drew him was many miles away.

"There!" he cried, suddenly raising a black-gloved hand and

pointing to the north. "We must strike northward! Now! With all haste!"

Some companies of his army heard the command. Ponderously, under the orders of their sergeants-major, they wheeled to the left, preparing to strike out toward the north, into the rain and the hail—and, soon, the darkness. Others didn't get the word. The ultimate effect of the maneuver spread the army across twice as much country as Giarna intended, opening huge gaps between the various brigades and adding chaos to an already muddled situation.

"Move, damn you!" the general cried, his voice taut. Lightning flashed over his head, streaks of fire lancing across the sky. Thunder crashed around them, sounding as if the world was coming apart.

Still the great formations continued their excruciating advance as the weary humans endeavored to obey Giarna's hysterical commands.

He couldn't wait. The scent drew him on like a hound to its prey. He wheeled his horse, kicking sharp spurs into the black steed's flanks. Breaking away from the column of his army, he started toward the north ahead of his men.

Alone.

* * * * *

Warm winds surged across the chill waters of the Turbidus Ocean, south of Ergoth, collecting moisture and carrying it aloft until the water droplets loomed as monumental columns of black clouds, billowing higher until they confounded the eyes of earthbound observers by vanishing into the limitless expanse of the sky.

Lightning flashed, beginning as an occasional explosion of brightness but increasing in fierceness and tempo until the clouds marched along to a staccato tempo, great sheets of hot fire slashing through them in continuous valleys. The waters below trembled under the fury of the storm.

The winds swirled, propelled by the rising pressure of steam. Whirlwinds grew tighter, shaping into slender funnels, until a front of cyclones roared forward, tossing the ocean into a chaotic maelstrom of foam. Great waves rolled outward from the storm, propelled by lashing torrents of rain.

And then the storm passed onto land.

The mass of clouds and power roared northward, skirting the Kharolis Mountains as it veered slightly toward the east. Before it lay the plains, hundreds of miles of flat, sodden country, already deluged by thunder and rain.

The new storm surged onto the flatlands, unleashing its winds as if it knew that nothing could stand in its path.

A soaking Wildrunner limped through the brush, raising his hand to ward off the hail and wipe rain away from his face. Finally he broke into a clearing and saw the vague outlines of the command post. Finding it had been sheer luck. He was one of two dozen men who had been sent with the report, in the hopes that one of them would reach Kith-Kanan.

"The Army of Ergoth!" he gasped, stumbling into the small house that served as the general's headquarters. "It approaches from the south!"

"Damn!" Kith-Kanan instantly saw the terrible vulnerability of his army, stretched as it was into a long column marching east to west. Wherever the humans hit him, he would be vulnerable.

"How far?" he asked quickly.

"Five miles, maybe less. I saw a company of horsemen—a thousand or so. I don't know how many other units are there."

"You did well to bring me the news immediately." Kith's mind whirled, "If Giarna is attacking us, he must have something in mind. Still, I can't believe he can execute an attack very well—not in this weather."

"Attack them, uncle!"

Kith turned to look at Vanesti. His fresh-faced nephew's eyes lit with enthusiasm. His first battle loomed.

"Your suggestion has merit," he said, pausing for a moment. "It's one thing that the enemy would never suspect. His grasp of the battle won't be much greater than mine, if I'm on the offensive. And furthermore, I have no way to organize any kind of defense in this weather. Better to have the troops moving forward and catch the enemy off balance."

"I'll dispatch the scouts," Parnigar noted. "We'll inform every company that we can. It won't be the whole army, you realize. There isn't enough time, and the weather is too treacherous."

"I know," Kith agreed. "The Windriders, for one, will have to stay on the ground." He looked at Arcuballis. The great creature rested nearby, his head tucked under one wing to protect himself from the rain.

"I'll take Kijo and leave Arcuballis here." The prospect made him feel somehow crippled, but as the storm increased around him, he knew that flight would be too dangerous a tactic.

He could only hope that his enemy's attack would be equally haphazard. In this wish, he was rewarded, for even as the fight began, it moved out of the control of its commanders.

* * * * *

The two armies blundered through the rain. Each stretched along a front of several dozen miles, and great gaps existed in their formations. The Army of Ergoth lumbered north, and where its companies met elves, they fought them in confusing skirmishes. As often as not, they passed right through the widely spaced formations of the Wildrunner Army, continuing into the nameless distance of the plains.

The Wildrunners and their allies struck south. Like the humans, they encountered their enemy occasionally, and at other times met no resistance.

Skirmishes raged along the entire distance, between whatever units happened to meet each other in the chaos. Human horsemen rode against elven swords. Dwarven battle-axes chopped at Ergothian archers. Because of the noise and the darkness, a company might not know that its sister battalion fought for its life three hundred yards away, or that a band of enemy warriors had passed across their front a bare five minutes earlier.

But it didn't matter. The real battle took shape in the clouds themselves.

Nightfall, Midsummer
Year of the Cloud Giant

33

Hail thundered through the woods, pounding trees into splinters and bruising exposed flesh. The balls of ice, as big across as gold pieces, quickly blanketed the ground. The roar of their impact drowned all attempts at communication.

Kith-Kanan, Vanesti, and Parnigar halted their plodding horses, seeking the minimal shelter provided by the overhanging boughs of a small grove of elms. They were grateful that the storm hadn't caught them on the open plains. Such a deluge could be extremely dangerous without shelter. Their two dozen bodyguards, all veterans of the House Protectorate, took shelter under neighboring trees. All the elves were silent, wet, and miserable.

They hadn't seen another company of Wildrunners in several hours, nor had they encountered any sign of the enemy. They had blundered through the storms for the whole day, lashed by wind and rain, soaked and chilled, fruitlessly seeking sign of friend or foe.

"Do you know where we are?" Kith asked Parnigar. Around them, the pebbly residue of the storm had covered the earth with round, white balls of ice.

"I'm afraid not," the veteran scout replied. "I *think* we've maintained a southerly heading, but it's hard to tell when you can't see more than two dozen feet ahead of you!"

All of a sudden Kith held up a hand. The hailstorm, with unsettling abruptness, had ceased.

"What is it?" hissed Vanesti, looking around them, his eyes wide.

521

"I don't know Kith admitted. "Something doesn't *feel* right."

The black horse exploded from the bushes with shocking speed, its dark rider leaning forward along the steed's lathered neck. Sharp hooves pounded the ice-coated earth, sending slivers of crushed hailstones flying with each step. The attacker charged past two guards, and Parnigar saw the glint of a sword. The blade moved with stunning speed, slaying both elven bodyguards with. quick chops.

"We're attacked!" Parnigar shouted. The veteran scout seized his sword and leaped into his saddle, spurring the steed forward.

Kith-Kanan, followed by Vanesti, ducked around the broad tree trunk just in time to see Parnigar collide with the attacker. The brutal impact sent the elf's mare reeling sideways and then tumbling to the ground. The horse screamed as the elven warrior sprang free, crouching to face the black-cloaked human on his dark war-horse.

"Giarna!" hissed Kith-Kanan, instantly recognizing the foe.

"Really?" gasped Vanesti, inching forward for a better look.

"Stay *back!*" growled the elven general.

The black steed abruptly reared, lashing out with its forehooves. One of them caught Parnigar on the skull, and the elf fell heavily to the ground.

Frantically Kith looked toward his bow, tied securely to his saddlebags on the other side of the broad tree. Cursing, he drew his sword and darted toward the fight.

With savage glee, the human rider leaped from his saddle, straddling Parnigar as the stunned elf struggled to move. As Kith ran toward them, the human thrust his sword through the scout's chest, pinning him to the ground with the keen blade.

Parnigar flopped on his back, stuck to the earth. Blood welled around the steel blade, and the icy pebbles of hail beneath him quickly took on a garish shade of red. In moments, his struggles faded to weak twitching, and then to nothing.

By that time, Kith had lunged at the black swordsman. The elf slashed with his sword but gaped in surprise as the quick blow darted *past* Giarna. The man's fist hammered into Kith-Kanan's belly, and the elf grunted in pain as he staggered backward, gasping for air.

With a sneer, the human pulled out his blade, turning to face two more Wildrunners, Kith's bodyguards, who charged recklessly forward. His sword flashed once, twice, and the two elves dropped, fatally slashed across their throats.

"Fight *me,* you bastard!" growled Kith-Kanan.

"That is a pleasure I have long anticipated!" General, Giarna's face broke into a savage grin. His teeth appeared to gleam as he threw his head back and laughed maniacally.

A quartet of veteran Wildrunners, all loyal and competent warriors of the House Protectorate, rushed General Giarna from behind. But the man whirled, his bloody sword cutting an arc through the air. Two of the guards fell, gutted, while the other two stumbled backward, horrified by their opponent's quickness. Kith-Kanan could only stare in shock. Never had he seen a weapon wielded with such deadly precision.

The retreating elves moved backward too slowly. Giarna sprang after them, leaping like a cat and stabbing one of them through the heart. The other elf rushed in wildly. His head sailed from his body following a swathlike cut that the human made with a casual flick of his wrist.

"You monster!" The youthful scream caught Kith-Kanan's attention. Vanesti had seized a sword from somewhere. Now he charged out from behind the elm trunk, lunging toward the murderous human general.

"No!" Kith-Kanan cried, out in alarm, rushing forward to try to reach his nephew. His boot caught on a treacherous vine and he sprawled headlong, looking up to see Vanesti swinging his sword wildly.

Kith scrambled to his feet. Each of his movements seemed grotesquely slow, exaggerated beyond all reason. He opened his mouth to shout again, but he could only watch in horror.

Vanesti lost his balance following his wild attack, stumbling to the side. He tried to deflect the human's straight-on stab, but the tip of General Giarna's blade struck Vanesti at the base of his rib cage, penetrating his gut and slicing through his spine as it emerged from his back. The youth gagged and choked, sliding backward off the blade. He lay on his back, his hands clutching at the air.

* * * * *

The lord-major-chieftain supreme of Hillrock pressed forward, trudging resolutely through weather the like of which he had never experienced before. Hailstones pummeled him, rain lashed his face, and the wind roared and growled in its futile efforts to penetrate the hill giant's heavy wolfskin cloak, a cloak he had worn proudly for forty years.

Yet One-Tooth plodded on, grimly determined to follow the compulsion that had drawn him here. He would see this trek through to its end. The burning drive that had led him this far seemed to grow more intense with each passing hour, until the giant broke into a lumbering trot, so anxious was his feeling that he neared his goal.

As he moved across the plains, a strange haze seemed to settle over his mind. He began to forget Hillrock, to forget the giantesses who were his wives, the small community that had always been his home. Instead, his mind drifted to the heights of his mountain range, to one snow-blanketed winter valley long age and a small, fire-warmed cave.

* * * * *

Later, elves who had lived for six hundred years swore that they had never before seen such a storm. The weather erupted across the plains with a violence that dwarfed the petty squabbles of the mortals on the ground.

The thunderheads grew in frenzy, an explosive, seething mass of power that transcended anything in human or elven memory. The storms lashed the plains, striking with wind and fire and hail.

At nightfall, when darkness gathered across the already sodden plains on the night of the summer solstice, Solinari gleamed fall and bright, high above the clouds, but no one on earth could see her.

Lightning erupted, hurling crackling bolts to the ground. Great cyclones of wind, miles across, whirled and roared. They spiraled and burst, a hundred angry funnel clouds that shrieked over the flat plains, leveling everything in their path.

The great battle of armies never occurred. Instead, a howling dervish of tornadoes formed in the west and roared across the plains, scattering the two forces before them, leaving tens of thousands of dead in their wake.

The most savage of the tornadoes swirled through the Anny of Ergoth, scattering food wagons, killing horses and men, and sending the remnants fleeing in all directions.

But if the human army suffered the bulk of the death toll, the Wildrunners suffered the greatest destruction. Huge columns of black clouds, mushrooming into the heights of the distant sky, gathered around the great stone block of Sithelbec. Dark and forboding, they collected in an awful ring about the city.

For hours, a dull stillness pervaded the air. Those who had sought shelter in Sithelbec fled, fearing the unnatural calm.

Then the lightning began anew. Bolts of energy lashed the city. They crackled into the stone towers of the fortress, exploding masonry and leaving the smell of scorched dust in the air. They seared the blocks of wooden buildings around the wall, and soon sheets of flame added to the destruction.

Like a cosmic bombardment, crackling spears of explosive electricity thundered into the stone walls and wooden roofs. Crushing and pounding, pummeling and bruising, the storm, maintained its pressure as the city slowly collapsed into ruin.

* * * * *

Kith realized that he was screaming, spitting his hatred and rage at this monstrous human who had dogged his life for forty years. He threw caution aside in a desperate series of slashes and attacks, but each lunge found Giarna's sword ready with a parry— and each moment of battle threatened to open a fatal gap in the elf's defenses.

Their blades clanged together with a force that matched the thunder. The two opponents hacked and chopped at each other, scrambling over deadfalls, pushing through soaking thornbushes, driving forward in savage attacks or careful retreats. The rest of the House Protectorate bodyguards rushed, in a group, to their leader's defense. The human's blade was a deadly scythe, and soon the elves bled the last of their lives into the icy, hail-strewn ground.

It became apparent to Kith that Giarna toyed with him. The man was unbeatable. He could have ended the fight at virtually any moment, and he seemed completely impervious to Kith's blows. Even when, in a lucky moment, the elf's blade slashed against the human's skin, no wound opened.

The man continued to allow Kith to rush forward, to expend himself on these desperate attacks, and then to stumble back, seemingly inches ahead of a mortal blow,

Finally he laughed, his voice a sharp, cruel bark.

"You see now that, for all your arrogance, you cannot live forever. Even elven lives must come to an end!"

Kith-Kanan stepped back, gasping for breath and staring at the hated enemy before him. He said nothing as his throat expanded, gulping air.

"Perhaps you will die with as much dignity as your wife," suggested Giarna, musing.

Kith froze. "What do you mean?"

"Merely that the whore thought she could do what all of your armies have been unable to do. She tried to kill me!"

The elf could only stare in shock. Suzine! By the gods, why would she attempt something so mad, so impossible?

"Of course, she paid the price for her stupidity, as you will do as well! My only regret was that she took her own life before I could draw the information I needed from her."

Kith-Kanan felt a sense of horror and guilt. Of course she had done this. He had left her no other way in which to aid him!

"She was braver and finer than we will ever be," he said, his voice firm despite his grief.

"Words!" Giarna snorted. "Use them wisely, elf. You have precious few left!"

Vanesti lay on the ground, so still and cold that he might have been a pale patch of mud. Near him, Parnigar lay equally still, his eyes staring sightlessly upward, his fingers curled reflexively into fists. His warm blood had melted the hailstones around him, so that he lay in an icy crimson pool.

Marshaling his determination, Kith charged, recklessly slashing at his opponent in a desperate bid to break his icy control. But Giarna stepped to the side, and Kith found himself on his back, looking up into gaping black holes, the deadened eyes of the man who would be his killer. The elf tried to scramble away, to spring to his feet, but his cloak snagged on a twisted limb beside him. Kith kicked out then fell back, helpless.

Trapped between two logs, Kith-Kanan couldn't move. Desperately, feeling a rage that was nonetheless overpowering for its helplessness, he glared at the blade that was about to end his life. Giarna stood over him, slowly raising the bloodstained weapon, as if the steel intended to savor the final, fatal thrust.

The crushing blow of a club knocked Giarna to the side before the killing blow could fall. Stuck behind the deadfall, Kith couldn't see where the blow had come from, but he saw the human stumble, watched the great weapon swing through his field of vision.

Snarling with rage, Giarna whirled, ready to slay whatever impertinent foe distracted him from his quarry. He felt no fear. Was he not impervious to the attack of elf, dwarf, or human?

But this was no elf. Instead, he stared upward at a creature that towered over his head. The last thing Giarna saw before the club crushed his skull and scattered his brains across the muddy ground was a lone white tooth, jutting proudly from the attacker's jaw.

* * * * *

"He's alive," whispered Kith-Kanan, scarcely daring to breathe. He kneeled beside Vanesti, noting the slow rise and fall of his nephew's chest. Steam wisped from his nostrils at terrifyingly long intervals.

"Help little guy?" inquired One-Tooth.

"Yes." Kith smiled through his tears, looking with affection at the huge creature who must have marched hundreds of miles to find him. He had asked him why, and the giant had merely shrugged.

526

One-Tooth reached down and grasped the bundle that was Vanesti. They wrapped him in a cloak, and now Kith rigged a small lean-to beneath the shelter of some leafy branches.

"I'll light a fire," said the elf. "Maybe that will draw some of the Wildrunners."

But the soaked wood refused to burn, and so the trio huddled and shivered through the long night. Then in the morning, they heard the sound of horses pushing along a forest trail.

Kith wormed his way through the bushes, discovering a column of Wildrunner scouts. Several veterans, recognizing their leader, quickly approached him, but they had to overcome their fear of the hill giant when they came upon the scene of the savage fight.

Gingerly they rigged a sling for the youth and prepared to make the grueling tide to Sithelbec.

"This time you'll come home with me," Kith told the giant. In the thinning mist, they started toward the east. Not for several days, until they met more survivors of his army—some who had had word from the fortress—did they learn that the home they marched to had been reduced to a smoldering pile of rubble.

Epilogue
Autumn, 2177 (PC)

Shapeless blocks of stone jutted into the sky, framed by the burned-out timbers that outlined walls, gates, and other structures of wood. Sithelbec lay in ruins. The tornadoes and lightning had razed the fortress more effectively than any human attack could have done. The surviving Wildrunners collected on the plains around the wreckage, nursing their wounded and trying to piece together the legacy of the disaster.

Only gradually did they become aware that the humans were gone. The Army of Ergoth had broken and fled, driven by nature to do what forty years of elven warfare had been unable to accomplish. The surviving humans streamed toward the lush farmlands of Daltigoth, the war forgotten.

The Theiwar dwarves—those who survived—fled back to Thorbardin. And the elves who had fought for the human cause returned to the woodlands, there to strive for survival in the ruins left by the storms of spring.

Dunbarth Ironthumb organized the ranks of his Hylar legion, most of whom had been fortunate enough to find riverbank caves that had sheltered them during the worst of the storm.

"It's back to good, old-fashioned rock walls and a stone ceiling over my head!" announced the gruff veteran, clasping Kith-Kanan's hand before he embarked on the long march.

"You've earned it," said the elf sincerely. For a long time, he watched the receding column of stocky figures until it disappeared into the mists to the south.

528

Sithas journeyed to the plains once more, two months after the great storm. He came to get his son, to bring him home. Vanesti would live, though, barring a miracle, he would never stand on his own legs.

The twins stood before the ruins of Sithelbec. The city was a blackened patch of earth, a chaotic jumble of charred timbers and broken, twisted stone.

The Speaker of the Stars met his brother's eyes.

"Tamanier Ambrodel has gone to Daltigoth. He, together with an ambassador from Thorbardin—a *Hylar* ambassador will arrange a treaty. We will see the swords sheathed once and for all."

"Those swords that remain," said Kith quietly. He thought of Parnigar and Kencathedrus—and Suzine—and all the others who had perished in the course of this war.

"This war has changed many things perhaps everything," observed Sithas quietly. Hermathya told me! his mind screamed silently. He wanted to accuse his brother, to set this discussion on the solid ground of truth, but he couldn't.

Kith nodded, silent.

These lands, Sithas thought, with a look at the wreckage around him. Were they worth clinging to? They had been held at a cost in lives that was beyond measuring. Yet what had they won?

Humans would never be totally banished from the western lands, the Speaker knew. Kith-Kanan would certainly allow those who had fought for his cause to remain. And the elves who had opposed them—what—would be their fate? Permanent banishment? Sithas didn't want to think of further strife, further suffering inflicted upon his people. Yet at the same time, he was opposed to further changes.

There was only one way now to preserve the purity of Silvanesti. Just as the infected limb of a diseased person must be removed to save the whole, so must the infected society of his nation be cut away to preserve the sanctity of Silvanesti.

"I'm granting you the lands extending from here to the west," announced Sithas firmly. "They are no longer part of Silvanesti; you may do with them as you like."

"I have thought about this," replied Kith, his voice a match for his brother's strength. His words surprised Sithas, for he had thought his announcement would be unanticipated. Yet Kith-Kanan, too, seemed to sense that they were no longer part of the same world.

"I will build my new capital to the west, among the forested hills." Qualinesti, he thought, though he didn't say the name aloud. To himself, he vowed that it would be a land of free elves, a place that would never go to war for the sake of some mistaken purity.

As the two brothers parted, the clouds remained leaden over the storm-lashed plains. The elves, once one nation, henceforth became two.

The Cornerstone
Prologue

Ten thousand footsteps rattled in the quiet mountain valley. It was early morning, just before sunrise, and mist still clung to the low places between the slopes. Five thousand elves, dwarves, and humans were assembling in this remote mountain pass. Many were warriors, resplendent in burnished armor and flowing capes, who had battled in the long years of the Kinslayer Wars, elf against man, man against dwarf, and elf against elf. So protracted had been the time of bloodshed that sons and daughters of warriors had grown up to bear arms alongside their parents.

This was an army of peace, gathered in the Kharolis Mountains. They had come from the kingdom of Thorbardin and the realm of Qualinesti to seal a bargain and to erect a fortress. Pax Tharkas, it was to be called; the name had already been agreed upon. In the elven tongue, it meant "Citadel of Peace."

From the southern end of the pass came the delegation of dwarves, led by their new king, Glenforth Sparkstriker. It was he who had led the doughty dwarven armies against the humans of Ergoth, checking their advance in the high mountain passes around Thorbardin. The Battle of Raven's Hook had cost Prince Glenforth an eye, but it had also put an end to the Emperor of Ergoth's plan to subjugate the dwarves. Now, with his eye patch of beaten gold and his magnificent coal-black beard rippling across his mailed chest, King Glenforth led his people in an even greater endeavor.

Behind the king came the most powerful thanes, those of Glenforth's own Clan Hylar. Richly dressed in crimson velvet and glittering with all the jewels they could possibly wear, the Hylar each bore a ceremonial hammer on his shoulder. Close behind the Hylar came the Daewar, for this great occasion wearing midnight blue tunics, yellow sashes, and great wide-brimmed hats of brown leather. The Daewar carried gilded rock chisels, as long as each dwarf was tall.

The thanes of the other clans, the Klar and the Neidar, less richly dressed but still proud, followed in the wake of their more powerful cousins. The Klar carried ceremonial trowels, and the Neidar picks.

Where the valley floor began to slope upward, King Glenforth raised a hand. The councilors and thanes halted and waited in respectful silence.

The delegation from Qualinesti approached the dwarves from the north end of the valley. Most of the delegation were formerly of Silvanesti, and had the chiseled features and light coloring of that ancient elven race. But sharp eyes could see the mingled characteristics of the Kagonesti, the elves of the forest, and even the broad features of humans. The new elven kingdom of Qualinesti had existed for just eighty years, and so far had proven the truth of its founder's dream: that elves and men and dwarves could live together in harmony, peace, and justice.

The founder himself led his nobles and notables to meet the Thorbardin thanes. In middle age now, as elves reckon time, the Speaker of the Sun was by far the most commanding figure in the valley. Age and toil had sent a few streaks of silver through his white-blond hair, but the clear, noble features of the House of Silvanos were unaltered by all the years of strife.

Kith-Kanan, the Speaker of the Sun, the founder of the nation of Qualinesti, stopped his entourage twenty paces or so from the dwarves. Alone, he went forward to meet King Glenforth of Thorbardin.

The elf met the dwarf near a large boulder that rose up in the center of the path. Glenforth extended his thick, powerful arms.

"Royal brother!" he said heartily. "I rejoice to see you!"

"And I you, Thane of Thanes!"

Tall elf and squat dwarf clasped hands about each other's forearms. "This is a great day for our nations," Kith-Kanan said, stepping back. "For all of Krynn."

"There were many times I didn't think I would live to see this day," Glenforth said frankly.

"I, too, have wondered if this new kingdom of ours could have been born without the blood and suffering of the war. My late wife used to say that all things are born that way—with blood and pain." Kith-Kanan nodded slowly, thinking of days gone by. "But we're here now, that's the important thing," he added, smiling.

"Praise the gods," said the dwarf sincerely.

Kith-Kanan turned back the folds of his emerald green cape to free his left hand. Looking to his waiting entourage, he smiled and lifted his arm, gesturing two figures forward. Glenforth squinted his good eye and saw that the two were children, a golden-haired boy and a brown-haired girl.

"King Glenforth, may I present my son, Prince Ulvian, and my daughter, Princess Verhanna," Kith-Kanan said, pushing the children forward. Ulvian dragged his feet and hung back from the unfamiliar dwarf. Verhanna, however, approached the king and bowed deeply to him.

"You do me honor," Glenforth said, a smile flashing amidst his black beard.

"No, sire. I am the honored one," Verhanna replied, her high voice ringing clear in the mountain air. Her large, dark brown eyes appraised the dwarf frankly, with no sign of fear. "I've heard the bards sing of your greatness in battle. Now that I've met you, I see the truth of their songs."

"Memories of battle are a poor comfort when one grows old and tired. I would trade all of mine for a child like you," he said gallantly. Verhanna flushed at this praise, stammered a thank-you, and withdrew to her father's side.

"Go on." Kith-Kanan said to his son. "Make your greetings to King Glenforth."

Prince Ulvian took a small step forward and bowed with a quick, bobbing motion. "Greetings, Great King," he said, running his words together in his haste to get them out. "I'm honored to meet you."

His duty done, Ulvian stepped back and hovered just behind his father.

With a fond pat on Verhanna's cheek, Kith-Kanan sent his children back to the ranks of nobles. Turning once more to the dwarf, he said softly, "Excuse my son. He hasn't been the same since his mother died. My daughter never really knew her mother; it's been easier for her."

Glenforth nodded politely. Practically everyone from Hylo to Silvanost knew the tale of Kith-Kanan and his human wife, Suzine. She had died many years before, in one of the last battles of the Kinslayer War. Her children matured at a much slower rate than human children, but not as slowly as full-blooded elven offspring. In human terms, both were still quite young.

The two monarchs exchanged more polite trivialities before returning to the reason for their meeting this morning. At a sign from Glenforth, an elderly dwarf came forward carrying an object covered by a red velvet cloth. It was obviously very heavy, and he held it firmly in both hands. Glenforth took the parcel, holding it easily. The elderly dwarf bowed to his king and was introduced as Chancellor Gendrin Dunbarth, senior thane of the Hylar clan.

"My lord," Kith-Kanan said, scrutinizing the chancellor, "I once knew a wise dwarf called Dunbarth of Dunbarth. Are you by chance related to him?"

Gendrin mopped his brow with a coarse-looking handkerchief. "Yes, Highness. Dunbarth of Dunbarth, ambassador to the court of Silvanesti, was my father," replied the dwarf, puffing from exertion.

Kith-Kanan smiled. "I met him in Silvanost many years ago and remember him with esteem. He was an honorable fellow."

Glenforth cleared his throat. Kith-Kanan returned his attention to the king. In loud, ringing tones, audible to the assembled thanes and Qualinesti, the dwarf king declared, "Great Speaker, on behalf of all the dwarves of Thorbardin, I present you with this special tool. I know you will wield it justly, for the benefit of your people and mine."

He passed the velvet-wrapped burden to Kith-Kanan. The Speaker of the Sun whisked the cover away, revealing a large iron hammer, wrought in traditional dwarven style but made larger to fit the hands of an elf. The octagonal iron handle was banded with silver, and the sides of the massive flat hammerhead were gilded.

"It is called Sunderer," Glenforth explained. "Our priests of Reorx forged it in a slow fire, and quenched it in dragon's blood to give it a worthy temper."

"It is magnificent," Kith-Kanan said in awed tones. He turned the great hammer in his hands. "This is the tool of a demigod, not a mortal such as I."

"Well, as long as it's good enough," the dwarf king said with a wry smile. He waved a beringed hand, and another Hylar thane came to him. This dwarf bore one of the long iron chisels banded with silver. He gave it to his king, then he and Gendrin Dunbarth withdrew.

Kith-Kanan and Glenforth walked in matched step to the boulder that lay in the center of the pass. As they proceeded with appropriate dignity, Kith-Kanan said softly, "Will you make the announcement, or shall I?"

"This was your idea." Glenforth replied in a low voice. "You do it."

"It's a joint project, Your Highness."

536

"Yes, but I'm no speechifier," said the dwarf. They stood by the boulder. "Besides, everyone knows elves are better talkers than dwarves."

"First I've heard of it," Kith-Kanan muttered.

The Speaker of the Sun turned to face the delegations. King Glenforth stood resolutely beside him, his hands resting on the long chisel as a warrior rests on his sword pommel.

Kith-Kanan listened for a moment to the stillness of the valley. The mist was vanishing, burned off by the rising sun. A flock of swifts darted and wheeled overhead. Somewhere in the distance, a dove made its mournful call.

"We have come here today," he began, "to erect a fortress. Not a stronghold for war, for we have too long followed that path. This fortress, which we of Qualinesti and our friends of Thorbardin shall build and occupy together, shall be a place of peace, a place where people of all races can seek haven and find protection and rest."

The Speaker paused as the first direct rays of the sun lanced over the mountain peaks into the valley. He was facing east, and the sunbeams warmed his face. A surge of resolution, of the rightness of what they were beginning here today, passed through Kith-Kanan.

"This boulder will be the cornerstone of Pax Tharkas, the Citadel of Peace. King Glenforth and I will carve it out ourselves, as a symbol of the cooperation and friendship between our countries."

He turned to the rock and set the great hammer Sunderer on his shoulder. Glenforth butted the chisel against the rock and steadied it with both of his thick, powerful hands.

"Swing true, Speaker," he said, half-jesting.

Kith-Kanan raised the hammer. Ulvian and Verhanna, standing with the Qualinesti nobles, stepped forward to get a better view of their father's work.

Sunderer came down on the chisel. A torrent of sparks fell across the boulder, spraying the dwarf king with fire. Glenforth laughed and urged Kith-Kanan to strike again. The third blow Kith-Kanan delivered was a mighty stroke indeed. It echoed through the valley like a roll of thunder and was quickly followed by the dry crack of cleaving rock. An entire side of the boulder fell away, leaving the rock with a face clean and straight. Cheers erupted from the onlookers.

Sweating in the cool mountain air, Kith-Kanan said to Glenforth, "Your hammer strikes nothing but true blows, Thane of Thanes."

"*Your* hammer, Great Speaker, like all tools, strikes only as its wielder aims," replied the dwarf thoughtfully. He blew on his hands and rubbed them together.

"What do you think of that, Ullie?" Kith-Kanan called, looking to his son. The boy had his head down, a hand pressed to his right cheek. The Speaker frowned. "What's wrong, son?"

Ulvian looked up slowly to meet his father's eyes. The boy's face showed pain. When he took his hands away, a small cut could be seen on his cheek. Gazing at the blood staining his fingers, Ulvian said softly, "I bleed."

"A rock chip hit you," Verhanna said matter-of-factly. "Some landed on me, too." She shook the folds of her boyish clothes and bits of stone and grit fell out.

Prince Ulvian's face twisted in anger. "I bleed!" he cried. He backed away from his father and bumped into a wall of courtiers and nobles. They parted for him, and the panicked prince fled into the crowd.

"Ulvian, come back!" Kith-Kanan shouted. The boy did not heed him.

"Want me to catch him?" Verhanna offered, sure in the knowledge that she was swifter than her brother.

"No, child. Stay here."

Kith-Kanan summoned his castellan, the elf in charge of his household, Tamanier Ambrodel. The elderly, gray-haired elf, dressed in a gray doublet and mauve cape, stepped out of the crowd.

"Find my son, Tam, and take him to a healer if he needs one," said the Speaker.

Tamanier bowed. "Yes, Highness."

Kith-Kanan watched his castellan disappear into the crowd. Hefting the great hammer, he said, "Ullie will be all right." Glenforth cleared his throat and pretended to be studying the boulder before him.

Verhanna and the rest of the crowd stood back as the Speaker of the Sun and the King of Thorbardin resumed their places at the stone. The valley rang with the sound of iron on rock.

In short order, the stone became a cube, square on four sides and rough on top. King Glenforth wasn't tall enough to bring the chisel to bear on the top of the boulder, so his thanes formed themselves into a living stair, that he might climb onto the rock. It was quite a sight, all the richly bedecked dwarves of Clans Hylar and Daewar, their thick arms locked together, bent over and braced against the cornerstone. Glenforth set aside the chisel and climbed up their backs. Once he was atop the stone, the thanes passed the chisel to him.

"Well, Great Speaker," said the dwarf from his lofty perch, "now I am higher than you! Will your councilors elevate you as mine did me?"

Kith-Kanan tossed the hammer to the top of the boulder, then faced his people. "You heard the Thane of Thanes! Will the nobles of Qualinesti stoop so that their Speaker can rise to the occasion?"

Half a hundred elves and men surged to the rock, ready to aid Kith-Kanan. Laughing, the Speaker ordered them back, then chose three elves and three humans. They looped their arms around each others' waists and bent to the rock. As the others cheered, Kith-Kanan climbed nimbly atop the boulder. He and Glenforth stood side by side, and the cheering continued. Finally Kith-Kanan raised his hands and waved for silence.

"My good and loyal friends!" he cried. "Many times in the recent past I have wondered if our coming to this new land was wise. Many times I have asked myself, should I have stayed in Silvanost? Should I have fought to establish in our old homeland the ideals we now share?"

There were shouts of "No! No!" from the crowd.

"And now—" Kith-Kanan again waved for quiet. "And now, I see us here today—men, elves, and dwarves—working together where once we fought, and I know I could have done nothing less than lead you to this new land, to make this new nation. You have all suffered and struggled and bled for Qualinesti. So have I. We did not fight to make a country like my father's, where tradition and age count for more than truth and justice. I do not want to rule for centuries and see all my ideals grow hoary with time. Therefore, on this rock, with this great hammer, Sunderer, in my hand, I will make you this pledge: the day this fortress is finished, I shall abdicate in favor of my successor."

A loud murmur of surprise spread through the assembly. The dwarves stroked their beards and looked concerned. Some of the Qualinesti elves cried out that Kith-Kanan should rule for life.

"No! Listen to me!" Kith-Kanan shouted. "This is what we fought for! The ruler and the ruled must be bound by a solemn pact that neither shall suffer the other unwanted. Once this fortress of peace is complete, let a younger, fresher mind lead Qualinesti forward to greater happiness and glory."

He nodded to King Glenforth. The dwarf placed the chisel against the surface of the rock. The gilded head of Sunderer flashed in the sun. Sparks flew as it smote Glenforth's chisel, and the blow Kith-Kanan struck reverberated down through the boulder into the stony ground of Krynn. Every elf, every dwarf, every human present felt the mighty stroke.

Shadow Talk

1

When Kith-Kanan led his followers west to found a new elven nation in the ancient woodland known first as Mithranhana, he had no goal, no plan in mind except that the mistakes of Silvanesti would not be repeated. By this he meant not only the autocratic, inflexible government of the first elven nation, but also the baroque, ornamental layout of the city of Silvanost itself.

The site of the first city in the new nation was chosen not by conscious thought, but by a lost deer. Kith-Kanan and his closest lieutenants were riding ahead of their column of settlers one afternoon when they spied a magnificent hart with ice-blue antlers and gray hide. Thinking the beast would make a fine trophy, as well as provide much needed meat, Kith-Kanan and his lieutenants gave chase. The hart bounded away with great leaps, and the elves on horseback were hard pressed to keep up. The deer led them farther and farther from their line of march, down a steep ravine. An arrow nocked, Kith-Kanan was about to try a desperate on-the-fly shot when the ravine ended at the precipitous edge of a river gorge. Kith-Kanan pulled his horse up sharply and gave a yell of surprise. The deer leapt straight off the cliff!

Astonished, the elves dismounted, hurried to the rim of the gorge, and looked down. There was no sign of the hart; no carcass lay smashed on the riverbank below. Kith-Kanan then knew the animal had been a magical one, but why had it deliberately crossed their path? Why had it brought them here?

The answer soon became obvious as the elves surveyed their surroundings. Across the wide gorge was a beautiful plateau, lightly wooded with hardwoods and conifers. After only a moment's reflection, Kith-Kanan knew this was to be the site of their new city, the capital of their new nation.

The plateau was bounded on the north, east, and west by two rivers, which converged at the north end of the plateau and became a tributary of the White Rage River. These two streams ran through deep, wide gorges. The south side of the roughly triangular escarpment was a labyrinth of steep, rocky ravines, and the land rose eventually to form the mountains of Thorbardin. From a natural point of view, the place was ideal, offering beauty and natural defenses. And as for the gray hart—well, the Bard King, Astarin, the god most revered by elves, is sometimes known as the Wandering Hart.

So the city of Qualinost was born. For a time, there was much sentiment to name the town after Kith-Kanan, as Silvanost had been named after the great Silvanos, august founder of the first elven nation. The Speaker of the Sun would not hear of it.

"This city is not to be a monument to me," he told his well-intentioned followers, "but a place for all people of good heart."

In the end, it was Kith-Kanan's friend and war companion, Anakardain, who named the city. That middle-aged warrior, who had fought beside Kith at the Battle of Sithelbec, remarked one night over dinner that the noblest person he'd ever heard of was Quinara, wife of Silvanos. The palace in Silvanost was called the Quinari, after her.

"You're right," Kith-Kanan declared. Though Quinara had died before he was born, Kith-Kanan knew well the stories of his grandmother's virtuous life. Thereafter, the budding city in the trees was known as Qualinost, which in Old Elven means "In Memory of Quinara."

The ranks of the immigrants were swelled daily by arrivals from Silvanesti. A vast camp grew up along the bank of the east river as more permanent dwellings sprouted among the evergreens on the plateau. The buildings of Qualinost, formed from the rose quartz that occurred naturally there, were domelike or conical in shape, reaching like leafless trees to the heavens.

Greatest effort was reserved for the Tower of the Sun, a tremendous golden spire that was to be the seat of the Speaker of the Sun's reign. In general design, it resembled Silvanost's Tower of the Stars, but in place of cold, white marble, this tower was covered with burnished gold. The metal reflected the warm, bright rays of the sun. The shape of the Tower of the Sun was the only likeness Qualinost bore to the old elven capital; when it was done, and Kith-Kanan had been formally installed as Speaker of the Sun, then the break between East and West was complete.

* * * * *

One spring morning in the two hundred and thirtieth year of the reign of Kith-Kanan, the calm of Qualinost was shattered by the tramping of massed hobnailed boots. City folk gathered outside their rose-hued homes, in the shade of the wide, spreading trees, and watched as nearly the entire Guard of the Sun, the army of Qualinesti, marched across the high-arched bridges that spanned the four corners of the city. Unlike human fortified towns, Qualinost had no walls; instead, four freestanding spans of wrought iron and bronze arched from tower keep to tower keep, enclosing the city in walls of air. The bridges were designed to aid in the protection of the city, yet not interfere with the free passage of traders and townsfolk. Not unimportantly, they were breathtakingly beautiful, as delicate as cobwebs but obviously strong enough to hold the troops that even now marched across them. The bronze of the cantilevered spans flashed fire in the sunlight, and at night, the black iron was silvered by the white moon, Solinari. The four keeps had been named by Kith-Kanan as Arcuballis, Sithel, Mackeli, and Suzine Towers.

That morning, the people stood with their faces turned upward as the companies of guards left the tower keeps and converged on Suzine Tower, at the southeast corner of the city. The elves had been at peace for over two centuries, and no such concentration of troops had been observed in all that time. Once the two thousand soldiers of the guard had gathered at the keep, quiet returned once more to the city. Though the curious Qualinesti watched for long minutes, nothing else seemed to be happening. The arched bridges were again empty. The people, their faith in their leaders and their troops strong, shrugged their shoulders and went back to their daily routines.

There were too many warriors to fit inside Suzine Tower, so many stood on the lower intersecting ends of the bridges. Rumors circulated through the ranks. What was happening? Why had they been summoned? The old enemy, Ergoth, had been quiet a long time. Tension existed with Silvanesti, and the frightening idea formed that the Speaker's twin brother, Sithas, Speaker of the Stars, was attacking from the east. This grim story gained momentum as it spread.

In ignorance, the troops waited as the sun passed its zenith and began its descent. When at last the shadow of the Tower of the Sun reached out and touched the eastern bridge, the keep's doors opened and Kith-Kanan emerged, along with a sizable contingent from the Thalas-Enthia, the Qualinesti senate.

The warriors clasped their hands to their armored chests and cried, "Hail, Great Speaker! Hail, Speaker of the Sun!" Kith-Kanan acknowledged their salutes, and the soldiers fell silent. The Speaker of the Sun looked tired and troubled. His mane of blond hair, heavily shot through with silver, was pulled back in a crude queue, and his sky-blue robes were wrinkled and dusty.

"Guards of the Sun," he said in a low, controlled voice, "I have summoned you here today with a heavy heart. A problem that has plagued our country for some years has grown so much worse that I am forced to use you, my brave warriors, to suppress it. I have consulted with the senators of the Thalas-Enthia and the priests of our gods, and they have agreed with my chosen course!"

Kith-Kanan paused, closing his eyes and sighing. The day was beginning to cool slightly, and a breeze wafted over the tired leader's face. "I am sending you out to destroy the slave traders who infest the confluence of the rivers that guard our city," he finished, his voice rising.

The guards broke out in subdued murmurs of surprise. Every resident of Qualinost knew that the Speaker had been trying to suppress slavery in his domain. The long Kinslayer War had, as one of its saddest consequences, created a large population of refugees, vagabonds, and lawless rovers. These were preyed upon by slavers, who sold them into bondage in Ergoth and Silvanesti. Since Qualinesti was a largely unsettled area between these two slave-holding countries, it was inevitable that the slavers would operate in Kith-Kanan's land. Slavers who drove their human and elven "goods" to market through Qualinesti territory frequently captured Qualinesti citizens as they went. Slavery was one of the principal evils Kith-Kanan and his followers had wanted to leave behind in Silvanesti, but the pernicious practice had insinuated itself into the new country. It was time for the Speaker of the Sun to put an end to it.

"Lord Anakardain will lead a column of a thousand guards up the eastern river to the confluence. Lord Ambrodel will command a second column of seven hundred and fifty mounted warriors, who will sweep the western branch and drive the slavers into Lord Anakardain's hands. As much as possible, I want these people taken alive for public trial. I doubt many of them will have the stomach to fight anyway, but I don't want them dealt with summarily. Is that clear?"

Most of the guards were former Wildrunners who had fought with Kith-Kanan against the Ergothians; they were the sons and daughters of Kagonesti elves who had been held in slavery in Silvanost for centuries. Slavers could expect little kindness from them.

Kith-Kanan stood back as Lord Anakardain began dividing the troops into the two forces, with the remaining two hundred fifty warriors to remain behind in the city. General Lord Kernian Ambrodel, son of Kith-Kanan's castellan, stood beside his sovereign.

"If you wish, sire, I can have Lady Verhanna assigned to the city guard," he said confidentially.

"No, no. She is a warrior the same as any other," Kith-Kanan said. "She would never want to be shown favoritism simply because she is my daughter."

Even in the crowd of two thousand troops, he could easily pick out Verhanna. Taller by almost a head than most of the Qualinesti warriors, her silver helm bore the red plume of an officer. A thick braid of light brown hair hung down her back to her waist. She was quite mature for a half-human. Never married, Verhanna was dedicated to her father and to the guards. Kith-Kanan was proud of his daughter's warrior skills, but some small fatherly portion of him wished to see her wedded and a mother before he died.

"I would prefer, however, that she go with you rather than Anakardain. I think she will be safer with the mounted troops," Kith-Kanan told Lord Ambrodel.

The handsome, fair-haired Silvanesti elf nodded gravely. "As you command, sire."

Lord Anakardain called his young subordinate to his side. Kith-Kanan watched Lord Ambrodel hurry away, and he was once more struck by the strong resemblance the young general bore to his elderly father.

As the guards broke up into their two units, the Speaker reentered Suzine Tower, trailed by several members of the Thalas-Enthia. With a notable lack of protocol, Kith-Kanan went to a table set beside the curved wall and poured himself a large cup of potent nectar.

The senators ringed round him. Clovanos, who was of an old, noble Silvanesti clan, said, "Great One, this act will cause great dismay to the Speaker of the Stars."

Kith-Kanan set down his cup. "My brother must deal with his own conscience," he said flatly. "I will not tolerate slavery in my realm."

Senator Clovanos waved a dismissive hand. "It is a minor problem, Great Speaker," he said.

"Minor? The buying and selling of people as if they were

chickens or glass beads? Do you honestly consider that a minor problem, my lord?"

Senator Xixis, who was half Kagonesti, put in, "We only fear retribution by the Speaker of the Stars or the Emperor of Ergoth if we mistreat those slavers who happen to be their subjects. Our country is still very new, Highness. If we were attacked by one or both of those countries, Qualinesti would not survive."

"I think you gravely underestimate our strength," said a human senator, Malvic Pathfinder, "and overestimate the concern of two monarchs for some of the worst scum to walk this world."

"There are deeper roots to this business than you know," Clovanos said darkly. "Even within Qualinost; there are those who profit by this trade in flesh."

Kith-Kanan snapped around, his robes swirling about his feet. "Who would dare," he demanded, "in defiance of my edicts?"

Clovanos paled before the Speaker's sudden wrath. He backed up a step and stammered, "G-great Majesty, one hears things in taverns, in temples. Shadow talk. Dark things without substance."

Xixis and Irthenie, a Kagonesti senator who still proudly wore the face paint popular with her wilder cousins, stepped between Kith-Kanan and the chastened Clovanos. Irthenie, whose intelligence and strong antislavery stance made her a confidant of the Speaker, declared, "Clovanos speaks the truth, Majesty. There are places in the city where money changes hands for influence and for slaves sold in other lands."

Kith-Kanan released the gold clasp from his long hair and combed through the pale strands with his fingers. "It never ends, does it?" he said tiredly. "I try to give the people a new life, and all the old vices come back to haunt us."

His gloomy observation hung in the air like dark smoke. Embarrassed, Clovanos and Xixis were the first to leave. Malvic followed, after offering words of support for the Speaker's stand. The half-human Senator Harplen, who seldom spoke, left with Malvic. Only Irthenie remained.

With much tramping and shouting, the two units of the Guards of the Sun dispersed. Kith-Kanan watched from the window as his warriors streamed over the bridges to the tower keeps and down into the city. He looked for, but didn't see, Verhanna.

"My daughter is going out with the guard," he said, his back to the Kagonesti woman. "This will be her first taste of conflict."

"I doubt that," said Irthenie flatly. "No one close to you can be unfamiliar with conflict, Kith. What I don't understand is why you don't send your son along, too. He could use some hard lessons, that boy."

Kith-Kanan rolled the brass cup back and forth in his hands, warming the nectar within. "Ulvian has gone off with his friends again. I don't know where. Probably drinking himself sick, or gambling his shirt on a roll of the bones." The Speaker's tone was bitter. A frown pulled at the corners of Kith-Kanan's mouth. He set his cup aside. "Ullie has never been the same since Suzine died. He was very close to his mother."

"Give him to me for six months and I'll straighten him out!"

Kith-Kanan had to smile at her declaration. Irthenie had four sons, all of whom were vigorous, opinionated, and successful. If Ulvian were younger, he might take Irthenie up on her offer. "My good friend," he said instead, taking her dark, age-worn hands in his, "of all the problems that face me today, Ulvian is not the worst."

She looked up at him, studying him closely. "You're wrong, Speaker," she said. "The fortress of Pax Tharkas is nearing completion, and the time is fast approaching when you vowed to abdicate. Can you in good conscience appoint a good-for-nothing idler like Ulvian the next Speaker of the Sun? I think not."

He dropped her hands and turned away, his face shadowed by concern. "I can't go back on my word. I swore I would abdicate once Pax Tharkas was finished." He sighed heavily. "I wish to pass on the mantle of leadership. After the war, and after building a new nation, I am tired."

"Then I tell you this, Kith-Kanan. Take your rest and give over the title to another, as long as it is anyone but your son," Irthenie said firmly.

The Speaker did not reply. Irthenie waited for several minutes, then bowed and left the tower.

Kith-Kanan sat down on a hard barrack chair and let the sunshine wash over his face. Closing his eyes, he gave himself over to deep and difficult thoughts.

* * * * *

"Ho there, trooper! Close up your ranks."

Sullenly the guards reined their horses about. They weren't usually so glum, but they happened to have been assigned to the strictest, most particular captain in the Guards of the Sun. Verhanna Kanan did not spare herself, or anyone in her command.

Verhanna's troop was moving northward, patrolling the western slopes of the Magnet Mountains, a small but steep range of peaks west of Qualinost. The stream that flowed past the western side of the city originated in these mountains. The land was sparsely wooded this close to the range of hills. Lord Ambrodel had given

Verhanna's troop the task of searching closest to the foot of the peaks, where the guards were vulnerable to ambush from above.

The captain kept her warriors close together. She didn't want any stragglers getting picked off. Her eyes never left the hillside. The red rock and brown soil were streaked with veins of black. These were deposits of lodestone, the natural magnets that gave the mountains their name. Kender shamans came from all across Ansalon to dig up the lodestone for protective amulets. So far on this sortie, the only living things Verhanna had seen were a few of the small kender race, working at the outcroppings of lodestone with deer antler picks.

Her second-in-command, a former Silvanesti named Merithynos, Merith for short, kept by her side as their horses picked their way slowly over the stony ground. The slopes were in shadow all morning.

"A futile task," Merith said, sighing loudly. "What are we doing here?"

"Carrying out the Speaker's command," Verhanna replied firmly. Her gaze rested on a dark figure nestled in a fold in the ground. She stared hard at it but soon realized it was only a holly bush.

Merith yawned, one hand pressed against his mouth. "But it's such a bore."

"Yes, I know. You'd rather be in Qualinost, strutting down the street, impressing the maids with your sword and armor," Verhanna, said dryly. "At least out here you're earning your pay."

"Captain! You wound me." Merith clutched his chest and swayed as if shot by an arrow.

She scowled at him, a mock frown on her face. "Fool! How did a dandy like you ever get in the guards?" she asked.

"Actually, it was my father's idea. Priesthood or warriorhood, that's what he told me. 'There's no room in Clan Silver Moon for wastrels', he said."

Verhanna stiffened and reined her horse up short. "Quiet," she hissed. "I saw something."

With hand signals, the captain divided her troop of twenty in half, with ten warriors, including herself, dismounting. Sword and buckler at the ready, she led the guards up the gravelly slope. Their booted feet slid in the loose dirt. The climb was a slow one.

Suddenly a shape rose up in front of Verhanna and scampered away, like a partridge flushed by a spaniel.

"Get him!" the captain shouted. The small creature, which seemed to be wrapped in a white cloth, darted away but lost its footing and rolled downhill. It came to rest with a bump against Merith's booted feet.

He put the tip of his slender elven blade against the sheeted mound, pricking the creature until it lay still. "Captain," Merith called coolly, "I have him."

The guards closed around the captive. Verhanna took one edge of the white sheet and pulled hard, spinning the occupant around. Out popped a small, sinewy figure with flaming red hair and a face to match.

"Stinkin', poxy, rancid, dirty, lice-ridden—" he sputtered, rubbing his backside. "Who poked me?"

"I did," Merith said. "And I'll do it again if you don't hold your tongue, kender."

"That's enough, Lieutenant," Verhanna said sharply. Merith shrugged and gave the outraged fellow an insolent smile. The captain turned to her captive and demanded, "Who are you? Why did you run from us?"

"Wrinklecap is who I am, and you'd run, too, if you woke from a nap to see a dozen swords over you!" The kender stopped rubbing his backside and twisted around to look at it. An almost comical expression of outrage widened his pale blue eyes. "You made a hole in my trousers!" he said, glaring at them. "Someone's gonna pay for this!"

"Be still," Verhanna said. She shook out the sheet Wrinklecap had been sleeping in. A double handful of black pebbles fell from its folds. "A lodestone gatherer," she said. The disappointment in her voice was obvious.

"*The* lodestone gatherer," intoned the tiny fellow, tapping his chest with one finger. "Rufus Wrinklecap of Balifor, that's me."

The guards who were waiting below on horseback called out to their captain. Verhanna shouted back that all was well. Sheathing her sword, she said to the kender, "You'd better come along with us."

"Why?" piped Rufus.

Verhanna was tired of bandying words with the noisy kender, so she pushed him ahead. Rufus snatched his sheet from the elven captain and rolled it up as he walked.

"Not fair—big bunch of bullies—creepin', pointyheaded elves—" he grumbled all the way down the slope.

Verhanna halted and ordered her troopers to remount. She sat down on a handy boulder and waved the kender over. "How long have you been in these parts?" she asked him.

After a few seconds of hesitation, the kender took a deep breath and said, "Well, after Uncle Trapspringer escaped from the walrus men and was eaten by the great ice bear—"

The captain quickly clamped a hand over the kender's open mouth. "No," she said firmly. "I do not want your entire life history.

Simply answer my questions, or I'll let Lieutenant Merith poke you again."

His long red topknot bobbled as Rufus swallowed hard. Verhanna was easily twice his size. Merith, from his mounted position next to them, was tapping the pommel of his sword meaningfully. The kender nodded. Verhanna released her hold on him.

"I've been here going on two months," Rufus said sulkily.

Verhanna remembered the loose stones he'd had. "You don't have much to show for two month's work," she commented.

Rufus puffed out his thin chest. "I only take the best stones," he said proudly. "I don't fill my pockets with trash like all them others do."

Ignoring for the moment the little fellow's last remark, Verhanna asked, "How do you live? I don't see any camp gear, cooking pot, or waterskin."

The kender turned innocent azure eyes on her and said, "I find what I need."

Merith snorted loudly. A smile touched Verhanna's lips. "Find, eh? Kender are good at that. Who have you 'found' things from?" she asked.

"Different people."

Verhanna drew a long, double-edged dagger from her belt and began to strop it slowly against her boot. "We're looking for some different people," she said carefully, making sure the kender followed every stroke of the bright blade. "Humans. Maybe some elves." The dagger paused. "Slavers."

Rufus let out his breath with a whoosh. "Oh!" he exclaimed, his high-pitched voice descending the scale. "Is that who you're after? Well, why didn't you say so?"

The kender launched into a typically random account of his activities of the past few days—caves he'd explored, wonders he'd beheld, and a secret camp he'd found over the mountains. In this camp, he claimed there were humans and elves holding other humans and elves in chains. Rufus had seen the camp just two days before.

"On the other side of the mountains?" Verhanna said sharply. "The eastern slope?"

"Yup. Right by the river. Are you going to attack them?" The kender's eagerness was unmistakable. His darting gaze took in their armor and weapons, and he added, "Well, of course you are. Want me to show you where I saw them?"

Verhanna did indeed. She ordered food and water for Rufus while she conferred with Merith about this new intelligence.

The kender wolfed down chunks of *quith-pa*, a rich elven bread, and bites of a winesap apple. "This little fellow may be a great help to us," she said confidentially to Merith. "Send a message to Lord Ambrodel informing him of what we've learned."

Merith saluted. "Yes, Captain." His expression turned grim as he added, "You realize what this means, don't you? If the slavers are on the other side of the mountain, then they are operating within sight of the city."

He turned on one heel and strode away to send the dispatch to Lord Ambrodel. Verhanna watched him for a moment, then pulled on her gauntlets and said to Rufus, "Can you ride pillion?"

The kender hastily lowered a water bottle from his lips, dribbling sweet spring water down his sunbrowned cheeks. "Ride a what?" he asked suspiciously.

Not pausing to explain, Verhanna swung onto her black horse and grabbed the kender by the hood attached to the back of his deerhide tunic. Yelping, Rufus felt himself lifted into the air and settled on the short leather tail of her saddle.

"That's a pillion," she said. "Now hold on!"

The Raid

2

The kender led Verhanna's troops across the mountains to a bluff overlooking the River of Hope, which formed Qualinost's western boundary. The towers and bridges of the city rose up to the northeast not three miles away. The sun was setting behind the mountains at the warriors' backs. Its light washed the capital, and the arched bridges glowed like golden tiaras. Nestled in the light green of spring leaves, thousands of windows reflected the crimson sun. Brightest of all, the Tower of the Sun mirrored the fiery glow with a vigor that nearly burned Verhanna's eyes.

Verhanna gazed over the city her father had founded, and a deep sense of peace filled her. Her home was beautiful; the thought that dealers in elven and human misery operated within sight of Qualinost's beauty sent a wave of resolute anger washing over her.

Rufus broke her reverie. "Captain," he whispered, "I smell smoke."

Verhanna strained until she caught a faint tang of wood smoke on the gentle breeze. It was coming from below, from the base of the bluff. "Is there a way down there?" she queried.

"Not on horseback. The path's too narrow," Rufus replied.

Quietly Verhanna ordered her troops to dismount. The horses were tethered among the rocks, and a group of five warriors was set to watch them. The remaining fifteen followed Verhanna to the path. She, in turn, followed Rufus Wrinklecap.

It was obvious that others had been using this path. Sand from the riverbank had been spread over the rocky ground, no doubt to soften footfalls. Now the sand served the guards as they crept down the path two abreast. They were careful to keep their shields from banging against anything. The smell of wood smoke grew stronger.

The base of the bluff was some thirty yards from the river's edge. Scrub pines dotted the landscape, and halfway out from the cliff, there was nothing but sand deposited by the river during spring floods. Verhanna caught Rufus by the shoulder and stopped him. The warriors crouched silently behind their captain, shielded from the camp by the small trees.

Voices drifted to them—voices and sounds of movement.

"Can't see how many there are," Verhanna said in a tense whisper.

"I can find out," Rufus said confidently, and before she could stop him, he had eased out from under her hand and started forward.

"No! Come back!" the captain hissed.

It was too late. With the fearlessness, some might say foolishness, of his race, the kender scrambled forward a few paces, stood, and dusted the sand from his knees. Then, whistling a cheery air, he marched into the unseen slavers' camp.

Merith crawled to his captain. "The little thief will give us away," he murmured.

"I don't think so," she replied. "By the gods, he's a brave little mite."

Moments later, rough laughter filled the air. Rufus's treble voice, saying something unintelligible, followed, then more laughter. To Verhanna's surprise, the kender came rolling through the scrub pines, knees tucked under his chin. He made a graceful flip onto his feet and flung out his arms. There was more laughter, and a spattering of applause. Verhanna understood; the kender was playing the fool, doing acrobatic tricks to amuse the slavers.

Rufus scuffed his feet on the sand and dove headfirst into a somersault. From her hiding place, Verhanna could just make out what he'd marked in the dirt. A one and a zero. There were ten slavers in the camp.

"Good fellow," she whispered fiercely. "We'll rush them. Spread out along the riverbank. I don't want any of them jumping in the water and swimming away." Burdened by armor, her guards wouldn't be able to pursue the slavers in the river.

Swords whisked out of scabbards. Verhanna stood, silently thrusting her blade in the air. The last rays of daylight fell across her face, highlighting its mix of human and elven features.

Almond-shaped elven eyes, rather broad human cheeks, and a sharp Silvanesti chin proclaimed the captain's ancestry. Her braid of light brown hair hung forward across her chest, and she flicked it behind her. She nodded curtly to her warriors. The guards swept forward.

As Verhanna hurried through the screen of scrawny trees, she took in the slavers' camp in a quick glance. At the foot of the cliff stood several huts made of beach stone chinked with moss. They blended in so well with their surroundings that from a distance no one would have recognized them as dwellings. Two small campfires burned on the open ground in front of the huts. The slavers stood in a ragged group between the fires. Rufus, his red topknot dripping perspiration and his blizzard of freckles lost on his flushed face, was standing on his hands before them.

The astonished slavers shouted when they saw the guards crashing toward them. A few reached for weapons, but most elected to flee. Verhanna pounded across the sand, straight at the nearest armed slaver. He appeared to be a Kagonesti, with dark braided hair and red triangles painted on his cheeks. In his hands he held a short spear with a wicked barbed head. Verhanna fended off the spear point with her shield and hacked at the shaft with her sword, lopping off the spearhead. The Kagonesti cursed, flung the wooden shaft at her, and turned to run. She was on him in a heartbeat, her long legs far swifter than his. The captain lowered her sword and slashed the fleeing slaver on the back of his leg. He fell, clutching his wounded limb. Verhanna hopped over him and kept going.

The slavers fell back, driven in toward the cliff base by the swords of the guards. Some chose to fight the Qualinesti, and these died in a brief, bloody skirmish. The ragged band was poorly armed and outnumbered, and soon they were on their knees, crying out for quarter.

"Down on your bellies!" Verhanna shouted. "Put your hands out flat on the ground."

She heard a warning shout from her left and turned in time to see one of the slavers sprinting for the river. He had too much of a head start for any of the guards to catch him, but he hadn't reckoned on Rufus Wrinklecap. The kender whipped out a sling and quickly loosed a pellet. With a thunk, the stone hit the back of the slaver's head, and the escaping human fell and lay still. Rufus trotted over to him, and his hands began moving through the fellow's clothing.

The fight was over. The slavers were searched and bound hand and foot. Of the ten in the camp, four were human men, four were Kagonesti, and two were half-humans. Merith remarked on the fact that the three who died fighting were all Kagonesti.

"They're not inclined to submit," Verhanna replied grudgingly. "Have those huts searched, Merith."

Rufus came sauntering up, swinging his sling jauntily. "Pretty good fight, eh, Captain?" he said cheerfully.

"More a pigeon shoot than a fight, thanks to you."

The kender beamed. Verhanna dug into her belt pouch and found a gold piece. Her father's graven image stared up from the coin. She tossed it to Rufus.

"That's for your help, kender," she said.

He caressed the heavy gold piece. "Thank you, my captain."

Just then Merith shouted, "Captain! Over here!" He stood by one of the huts.

"What is it?" she asked sharply when she reached him. "What's wrong?"

Ashen-faced, he nodded toward the hut. "You—you'd best go inside and see."

Verhanna frowned and pushed by him. The door of the crude stone house was nothing but a flap of leather. She thrust a hand through and stepped inside. A candle burned on the small table in the center of the one-room dwelling. Someone was seated at the table. His face was in shadow, but Verhanna saw numerous rings on the hand that rested on the table, including a familiar silver signet ring. A ring that belonged to—

"Really, sister, you have the most appalling timing in the world," said the seated figure. He leaned forward into the candlelight, and the hazel eyes of the line of Silvanos sparkled.

"Ulvian! What are you doing here?" Verhanna asked, shock reducing her voice to a whisper.

Kith-Kanan's son pushed the candle aside and clasped his hands lightly on the tabletop. "Conducting some very profitable business, till you so rudely disrupted it."

"Business?" For a long moment, his sister couldn't take it in. The crude plates and utensils, the worn wooden table, the rough pallet of blankets in one corner, even the sputtering candle—all claimed her roving gaze before her eyes once more rested on the person before her. Then, with the force of a summer storm, she exploded, "Business! Slavery!"

Ulvian's handsome face, so like his mother Suzine's, twitched slightly. Full-blooded elven males couldn't grow beards or mustaches, but Ulvian kept a modest stubble as a sign of his half-human heritage. With a quick, distracted motion, he stroked the fine golden hair.

"What I do is none of your affair," he said, annoyed. "Nor anyone else's, for that matter."

Her own brother a trafficker in slaves! Eldest son of the House of Silvanos and the supposed heir to the throne of Qualinesti.

Verhanna's face flamed with her disgrace and the knowledge of the shame and pain this would cause their father. How could Ulvian do such a thing? Then her mortification was replaced by anger. Cold rage filled the Speaker's daughter. Grabbing Ulvian by the front of his crimson silk doublet, Verhanna dragged him from behind the table and out of the hut. Merith was still waiting outside.

"Where are the slaves?" she rasped. Mutely Merith pointed to the larger of the two remaining huts.

"Come on, Brother," growled Verhanna, shoving Ulvian ahead of' her. Other guards saw the Speaker's son and gaped. Merith stormed at them.

"What are you gawking at? Mind those prisoners!" he ordered.

Verhanna propelled Ulvian into the slave hut. Within, a guard was removing a young, emaciated female elf's chains with a hammer and chisel. Other slaves slumped against the walls of the hut. Even with their deliverance at hand, they were broken in spirit, listless and passive. There were some half-human males, and to Verhanna's horror, two dark-haired human children who couldn't have been more than nine or ten years old. All the captives were caked with filth. The hut reeked of stale sweat, urine, and despair.

The guard hacked the elf woman's chain in two and helped her stand. Her thin, frail legs wouldn't support her. With only the faintest of sighs, she crumpled. The guard lifted her starved body in his arms and carried her out.

Verhanna knew she must get control of her emotions. Closing her eyes, she willed herself to be calm, willed her heart to slow its frenzied beating. Opening her eyes once more, she said with certainty, "Ulvian, Father will have your head for this. If he favors me, I'll gladly swing the axe."

One pale hand adjusting the lace at his throat, Ulvian smiled. "I don't think so, sweet Sister. After all, it wouldn't look good for the Speaker's heir to go around without a head, now would it?"

The captain slapped her brother. Ulvian's head snapped back. Slowly he turned to face his sister. She was four inches taller than he, and the prince tilted his head back slightly to stare directly into her eyes. The smirk was gone from his lips, replaced by cold-blooded fury.

"You will never be Speaker if I have anything to say about it," Verhanna swore. "You are unfit to utter our father's name, let alone inherit his title."

A single bead of blood hung from the corner of Prince Ulvian's mouth. He dabbed at it and said softly, "You always were Father's lapdog."

Sweeping the door flap aside, Verhanna called, "Lieutenant Merith! Come here!" The elegant elf hustled in, scabbard jangling against his armored thigh.

"Put Prince Ulvian in chains," she ordered. "And if he utters one word of protest, gag him as well."

Merith stared. "Captain, are you sure? Chain the prince?"

"Yes!" she thundered.

Merith searched among the heaps of chain in the slave hut and found a set of manacles to fit Prince Ulvian. Abashed, he stood before Kith-Kanan's son and held open the cold iron bonds.

"Highness," Merith said tightly. "Your hands, please."

Ulvian did not resist. He presented his slim arms, and Merith snapped the bands around his wrists. A hole in the latch would take a soft iron rivet.

"You will regret this, Hanna," the prince said in a barely audible voice as he stared at his manacled wrists.

* * * * *

By the time Verhanna's warriors had the slavers' camp sorted out, Lord Ambrodel and his personal escort of thirty riders had come thundering up the riverbank, summoned by fast dispatch. The elves set up a double row of torches in the sand to light the riders' way. By the same light, they had sorted the wretched captives by race and gender. The slavers were chained together in one large band, and a guard of bow-armed warriors set to watch them.

Lord Ambrodel rode up, sand flying beneath his horse's hooves. He called out loudly for Verhanna. The Speaker's daughter came forward and saluted the younger Ambrodel.

"Give me your report," he ordered before dismounting.

Verhanna handed him a tally showing eight slaves found and freed, and seven slavers captured. "Three chose to fight and were killed," she added. Lord Ambrodel slipped the parchment under his breastplate.

"How were they moving the slaves?" he asked, surveying the cunningly concealed camp.

"By river, sir."

Lord Ambrodel glanced back at the moonlit water.

"My lord," Verhanna continued, "we found signs that more slaves were sent on from this camp. The ones we found here were too sick to travel. I'd like to take my troop on and try to intercept the rest before they reach the Ergoth border."

"You're far too late for that, I'm sure," Lord Ambrodel replied. "I want to question the leader of the slavers. Did you take him alive?" Verhanna nodded curtly. The warrior lord tugged off his leather gauntlets and slapped the sand from his mailed thighs. "Well, Captain, show him to me," he said impatiently.

Without a word, Verhanna turned on one heel and led her commander toward the huts. The slavers lay on the ground, their heads buried in their arms in despair or else staring with hatred at their captors. Verhanna yanked a torch from the sand and held it high. She held the door flap open for Lord Ambrodel and thrust the torch inside. The face of the figure seated before them leapt into clarity.

Lord Ambrodel recoiled sharply. "It cannot be!" he gasped. "Prince Ulvian!"

"Kemian, my friend," the prince said to the general, "you'd best have these fetters removed. I am not a common criminal, though my hysterical sister insists on treating me like one."

"Release him," said Lord Ambrodel. His face was white.

"My lord, Prince Ulvian was caught engaging in the forbidden commerce of slavery," Verhanna put in quickly. "Both my father's edicts and the laws of the Thalas-Enthia demand—"

"Don't quote the law to me!" Lord Ambrodel snapped. "I shall bring this matter to the attention of the Speaker at once, but I will not drag a member of the royal family through the streets of Qualinost in chains! I cannot disgrace the Speaker so!"

Before she could order it, Merith was at Verhanna's side, chisel in hand. She shoved her lieutenant's hands aside and grasped the cold iron clamps in her own bare hands. With the strength bestowed upon her by her elven heritage, Verhanna pried the manacles apart just enough so that Ulvian could slip his arms out. Impudently he handed the empty chains to his sister.

"Captain," Lord Ambrodel said, "return to your troop. Muster them for marching."

"My lord! To what destination?" she answered tersely.

"Southeast—to the forest. I want you to search for other slaver camps there. Lieutenant Merithynos will remain to report on the finding of the slavers."

Verhanna's gaze flickered to her brother, to Merith, and back to Lord Ambrodel. She was too disciplined in the ways of the warrior to disobey her commander, but she knew Lord Ambrodel was sending her away so he could handle the delicate business of Ulvian's crime and punishment. Kemian would not let the prince escape; he was too honest for that. But he would grant her brother every privilege, up to the moment he turned Ulvian over to Kith-Kanan himself.

"Very good, sir," Verhanna finally responded. With a curt nod, she departed, spurs ringing as her heels struck the packed sand.

Ulvian rubbed his wrists and smiled. "Thank you, my lord," he said. "I shall remember this."

"Save your gratitude, my prince. I meant what I said; you will be given over to your father's judgment."

Ulvian maintained his smile. The ruddy light of the torch made his blond beard and hair look like copper. "I'm not afraid," he said lightly. Indeed he wasn't. His father had never punished Ulvian for his errant ways in the past.

As Verhanna gathered her warriors together with hoarsely shouted commands, the kender reappeared. His pockets were bulging with plunder from the slavers' camp: knives, string, flints, clay pipes, brass-studded wristbands.

"Hail, Captain," Rufus called. "Where to now?"

Verhanna looped her reins around her left hand. "So you came back! I thought I'd seen the last of you."

"You paid me. I'm your scout now," Rufus announced. "I can lead you anywhere. From which horizon will we next see the sun?"

Verhanna swung into the saddle. Her eyes rested on the hut where her brother and Lord Ambrodel still tarried. Her brother, the slaver.

"South," she said, biting off the word as it left her tightly drawn lips.

* * * * *

The Speaker's house was quite large, though far less grand than the Quinari Palace in Silvanost where Kith-Kanan had grown up. Built entirely of wood, it had a warmth and naturalness he felt was missing from the great crystal residence of his brother, the Speaker of the Stars. The house was more or less rectangular in shape, with two small wings radiating to the west. The main entrance was on the east side, facing the courtyard of the Tower of the Sun.

Lord Ambrodel, Lieutenant Merith, and Prince Ulvian stood in the lamplit antechamber where Kith-Kanan usually greeted his guests. As it was well past midnight, the bright moons of Krynn had already set.

Despite the late hour, the Speaker looked alert and carefully groomed as he and Tamanier Ambrodel descended the polished cherrywood staircase to the antechamber. His fur-trimmed robe swept the floor. The toes of his yellow felt slippers protruded from under the green velvet hem.

"What has happened?" he asked gently.

As senior officer present, it fell to Kemian Ambrodel to explain. When he reached the point in his story where Verhanna had discovered Prince Ulvian in the slavers' camp, Kemian's father Tamanier gasped in astonishment. Kith-Kanan's gaze shifted to Ulvian, who pursed his lips and rocked on his heels in an obvious display of arrogance.

"Were the slaves you found badly treated?" asked the Speaker in clipped tones.

"They were sick, filthy, and ill-fed, Majesty. From what they told us, they were held back from a larger group of slaves sent on by river to Ergoth because they were deemed too feeble for hard work." Kemian fought down his disgust. "A few had been whipped, Speaker."

"I see. Thank you, my lord."

Kith-Kanan clasped his hands behind his back and studied the floor. The maple had a beautiful grain pattern that resembled the dancing flames of a fire. Suddenly, he lifted his head and said, "I want you all to swear to keep what happens here tonight strictly secret. No one is to know of it—not even your families. Is that clear?" The assembled elves nodded solemnly, except Ulvian. "This is a delicate matter. There are those in Qualinost who would try to profit from my son's actions. For the safety of the nation, this must remain a secret."

Stepping down from the last stair, the Speaker stood nose-to-nose with his son. "Ullie," he said quietly, "why did you do it?"

The prince quivered with suppressed anger tinged with fear. "Do you really want to know?" he burst out. "Because you preach about justice and mercy instead of strength and greatness! Because you waste money on beggars and useless temples instead of a proper palace! Because you were the most famous warrior of the age, and you've thrown all your glory away to idle in gardens instead of fighting your way to the gates of Silvanost, our rightful home!" His voice choked off.

Kith-Kanan looked his son up and down. The grief on his face was visible to all. The Speaker's great dignity asserted itself, however, and he said, "The war and the great march west left Silvanesti with an acute shortage of farmers, crafters, and laborers. To appease the nobles and clerics, my brother, the Speaker of the Stars, has sanctioned slavery throughout his realm. A similar condition exists in Ergoth, with similar results. But no amount of inconvenience justifies the bondage of living, thinking beings by others. I have made it my life's goal to stamp out the evil traffic in servitude in Qualinesti, and yet my own son—" Kith-Kanan folded his arms, gripping his biceps hard through the plush velvet of his robe. "Ulvian, you will be held under close confinement in Arcuballis Tower until—until I can think of a proper punishment for you," he declared.

"You don't dare." The prince sneered. "I am your son, your only legitimate heir! Where will your precious dynasty be without me? I know you, Father. You'll forgive me anything to keep from being the first and last Speaker of the Sun from the House of Silvanos!"

The aged Tamanier Ambrodel could contain himself no longer. He had been friend to Kith-Kanan ever since the Speaker was a young prince in Silvanost. To listen to this spoiled pup jeering at his father was more than mortal flesh could bear. The gray-haired castellan stepped forward and struck Ulvian with his open hand. The prince rounded on him, but Kith-Kanan moved swiftly, placing himself between his son and castellan.

"No, Tam. Stop," he said, his voice shaking. "Don't justify his hatred." To Ulvian, he added, "Fifty years ago you might have earned a beating for your insolence, but now I will not ease your conscience so readily."

Tamanier stepped back. Kith-Kanan beckoned to Merith, standing quietly behind Kernian Ambrodel.

"I have a charge for you, Lieutenant," Kith-Kanan said gravely. The Speaker's gaze unnerved the anxious young elf. "You will be my son's keeper. Take him to Arcuballis. Stay with him. He must see and speak to no one—no one at all. Do you understand?"

"Yes, Great Speaker." Merith saluted stiffly.

"Go now, while it is still dark."

Merith drew his sword and stood beside Ulvian. The prince glared sullenly at the naked blade. Speaker, castellan, and general watched the two leave for the tower keep that guarded the city's northeastern corner. When the great doors of the house closed behind them, Kith-Kanan asked Kernian where Verhanna was. Lord Ambrodel explained how he'd thought it best to separate brother and sister at such a crisis.

"A wise decision," Kith-Kanan said ruefully. "Hanna would wring Ullie's neck."

The Speaker bade Kemian return to the field and continue the hunt for slavers. The general bowed low, first to his sovereign and then to his father, and swept out of the hall. Once he was gone, Kith-Kanan sank shakily to the steps. Tamanier swiftly knelt beside him.

"Majesty! Are you ill?"

Tears glistened in Kith-Kanan's brown eyes. "I am all right," he murmured. "Leave me, Tam."

"May I escort Your Majesty to his room?"

"No, I want to sit a while. On your way now, old friend."

Tamanier rose and bowed. The scuff of his sandals faded in the dimly lit corridor. Kith-Kanan was alone.

He realized his hands were clenched into fists, and he relaxed them. Five hundred years was not a long time to live, by elven standards, yet at that moment, Kith-Kanan felt very aged indeed. What was he to do with Ulvian? The boy's motives were a mystery to him. Did he need money so badly? Was it the thrill of doing something forbidden? No reason could excuse his conduct this time.

Once, after Ulvian had returned home half-naked and filthy after literally losing his shirt gambling, Verhanna had cornered her father. "He's no good," she had said.

"Isn't he? Who made him so?" Kith-Kanan had wondered aloud. "Can I blame anyone but myself? I hardly ever saw him till he was twelve. The war was going badly, and I was needed in the field."

"Mother spoiled him. She filled his head with a lot of nonsense," Verhanna said bitterly. "I can't count the times he's told me you were responsible for her death."

Kith-Kanan drew a hand across his brow. He couldn't count the times he'd told Ulvian the truth about Suzine, that she had sacrificed her life for her husband and his cause, but Ulvian never believed it.

What could he do? Ulvian was right; Kith-Kanan couldn't have his own son executed or banished. He was the Speaker's heir. After working so hard, sacrificing so much, to build this great nation, Kith-Kanan wondered, was it all to be lost?

A bell tolled somewhere far off. The priests of Mantis, called Matheri in old Silvanost, were ringing the great bronze temple bell, signaling the imminent dawn. Kith-Kanan raised his weary head from his hands. The sound of the bell was like a voice, calling to him. Come, come, it said.

Yes, he thought. I will meditate and ask the gods. They will help me.

The Balance of Justice

3

The domed ceiling of the Tower of the Sun was decorated with an elaborate mosaic symbolizing the passage of time and the forces of good and evil. One half of the dome was blue sky, made up of thousands of chips of turquoise, and a brilliant sun made from gold and diamonds. The opposite half was tiled with the blackest onyx and sprinkled with diamond stars. The three moons of Krynn were represented by discs of ruby for Lunitari, silver for Solinari, and oxblood garnet for Nuitari. Dividing these hemispheres was a rainbow band set with crimsonite, topazes, peridots, sapphires, and amethysts. The rainbow was a barrier and bridge between the worlds of night and day, a symbol of the intervention of the gods in mortal affairs.

Kith-Kanan meditated on the symbolism of the dome as he lay on his back on the rostrum in the center of the tower floor. Unlike its counterpart in Silvanost, this tower was not used as the throne room. The Tower of the Sun was mainly used when Kith-Kanan wanted to, as Verhanna put it, "impress the boots off a visitor."

Kith-Kanan pillowed his head on one hand. His silver-blond hair was loose and spread out around his head like a halo. Fixing his gaze on the ceiling of the tower, he opened his mind. The peace and balanced beauty of the Tower of the Sun calmed him, allowing him to consider difficult matters.

Rows of windows and mirrors spiraled up the height of the tower, letting in the sun and reflecting it in endless cascades. No matter where the sun was in the sky, the Tower of the Sun would always be brightly lit. The Speaker draped his free arm over his face. A cool breeze played over his arms as it whistled through the tower windows. Even that was soothing. On this day, the Speaker of the Sun needed every bit of peace he could find as he wrestled with the problem of succession.

Qualinesti must have an heir. Kith-Kanan had sworn, before the gods and the assembly at Pax Tharkas, that he would step aside when the fortress was complete. Weekly dispatches from the chief architect and master builder, the dwarf Feldrin Feldspar, kept him informed of the progress there. Pax Tharkas was ninety percent done; with good weather and no delays, the citadel would be finished in another two or three years. Kith-Kanan must name his successor soon.

For too long, the Speaker had consoled himself with the thought that his only son was merely wayward, but now there was no denying that the problems ran much deeper. His own son involved in the slave trade. . . .

With Ulvian obviously unworthy for the position of Speaker of the Sun, Kith-Kanan pondered other candidates. Verhanna? Not a good choice. She was brave, intelligent, and as honorable as any highborn Silvanesti, but also temperamental and sometimes prone to harshness. In spite of Kith-Kanan's dreams of equality in his kingdom, the fact that Verhanna was half-human would also weigh against her in the minds of some of his full-blooded elven subjects. These prejudices were kept carefully tucked away, out of plain sight, but the Speaker knew they existed still. Coupled with the fact that Verhanna was female, that bias would be too much to overcome.

"You could marry again," said a quiet voice.

Kith-Kanan descended the rostrum and looked around. The tower was pitch-dark, though he knew it wasn't yet midday. Standing to his left, between two of the pillars that ringed the chamber, was a strange elf, wreathed in yellow light.

"Who are you?" demanded Kith-Kanan.

The halo of light followed the stranger as he approached the rostrum, though the elf carried no lamp or candle. He was clad entirely in a suit of close-fitting red leather. A scarlet cape hung from one shoulder and brushed the floor. The stranger's ears were unusually tall and pointed, even for an elf, and his long hair was a vivid ruby red.

"I am one who can help you," the intruder said. He spoke with an air of supreme self-assurance. Now that he was closer, Kith-Kanan saw that his eyes were black and glittering, set in a face as dead white as dry bones. No lines at all touched the face; it might have been carved from purest alabaster.

"Begone from here," Kith-Kanan said sharply. "You intrude on my privacy." He faced the stranger, his muscles tensed for fight or flight.

"Come, come! You're in a quandary about your son, aren't you? I can help. I have considerable power."

Kith-Kanan knew this elf must be, at the very least, a powerful sorcerer. The tower was wrapped in protective spells, and for any malign being to enter would require great mastery of magic. "What is your name?"

The red elf shrugged, and his cape rippled like waves in a scarlet sea. "I have many names. You may call me Dru if you like." With one hand at his slim waist and the other held out before him, Dru made a graceful, mocking bow. "You came here seeking help from higher powers, Great Speaker, so I have answered your call."

Kith-Kanan's brows arched. "Are you mortal?"

"Does it matter? I can help you. Your son has offended you, and you want to know what to do about it . . . yes? You are Speaker of the Sun. Condemn him," Dru said smoothly.

"He is my only son."

"And yet you might have another, if you marry again. For a slight fee, I can procure for you the mate of your heart's desire!" He smiled, revealing teeth as red as his hair. Kith-Kanan recoiled and moved quickly back to the rostrum, where the potent magic symbols set in the floor mosaic would protect him from evil spells.

"I will not bargain with an evil spirit," he exclaimed. "Begone! Trouble me no more!"

The red elf laughed, the loud peals echoing weirdly in the black, empty tower. "Our bargain has already commenced, Great Speaker."

Kith-Kanan was confused. Already commenced? Had he somehow summoned this odd being from the netherworld?

"Of course you did," Dru said, reading his thoughts. "I'm a busy fellow. I don't waste my valuable time appearing to just anyone. Here, son of Sithel. Let me demonstrate what I can do."

Dru brought his white hands together with a loud clap. Kith-Kanan felt a breeze rush by him, as if all the air in the tower gusted toward the strange elf. With a crackling hiss, a ball of fire appeared suddenly between Dru's palms, and he flung it to the floor, where it burst. The loud crack and blinding flash caused Kith-Kanan to stagger back. When his vision cleared, he beheld a transformed scene.

Kith-Kanan no longer stood in the Tower of the Sun, though its rostrum was still solid beneath his feet. His surroundings were those of a smaller tower. By the stonework and the shape of the windows, he knew that it was in Silvanost. Tapestries in shades of pale green and blue hung on the walls, depicting woodland scenes and elegantly clad ladies. Sunlight filled the room.

A sigh caught his ears. He turned and saw a large, heavy wooden chair, its back to him, facing an open window. Someone was sitting in the chair. Kith-Kanan couldn't see who.

Suddenly the someone stood. Kith-Kanan glimpsed her beautiful red hair and his breath caught.

"Hermathya," he whispered.

"She cannot see or hear us," Dru informed him. "You see how she languishes in Silvanost, unloved and unloving. I can have her at your side in the blink of any eye."

Hermathya . . . the love of his youth. For many years the wife of his twin brother, Sithas. She stared straight through the spot where Kith-Kanan stood, piercing him unknowingly with her deep blue eyes. Her red-gold hair was piled up on her head in elaborate braids, showing the elegant shape of her upswept ears, and she wore a gown of the finest spider's web gold, thin and clinging. Once he had proposed marriage to her, but his father, not knowing of their love, had betrothed her to Kith-Kanan's twin, Sithas. So much time had passed since that distant day. Now Sithas was leader of the Silvanesti elves, as Kith-Kanan ruled the Qualinesti.

Lonely and a bit self-pitying, Kith-Kanan felt himself sorely tempted. Always Hermathya's great beauty had been able to arouse him. An elf would have to be made of stone not to feel something in her presence.

Just as he was about to ask Dru his terms, Hermathya turned away. She lunged at the open window before her chair. Kith-Kanan cried out and reached for her.

Before she could hurtle through the high window, Hermathya was brought up short. The harsh clank of metal shocked Kith-Kanan. Beneath the hem of her golden gown, he spied an iron fetter, locked about her right ankle and attached by a chain to the heavy chair. The chair was fastened to the floor. Though the fetter was lined with padded cloth, it gripped Hermathya's slender ankle tightly.

"What does this mean?" demanded Kith-Kanan.

Dru seemed vexed. "A minor problem, Great Speaker. The lady Hermathya suffers from despondency over the crippling of her son during the war and, I might add, over the loss of your love. The Speaker of the Stars has ordered her chained so that she won't harm herself."

Hermathya had been staring with palpable longing at the open window. Her face was as exquisitely lovely as Kith-Kanan remembered it. The high cheekbones, the delicately slender nose, and skin as smooth as the finest silk. Time hadn't marked her at all. Once more her faint sigh came to him, a sound full of sorrow and yearning. Kith-Kanan squeezed his eyes shut. "Take me away," he hissed. "I cannot bear to see this."

"As you wish."

The dark embrace of the Tower of the Sun in Qualinost returned.

Kith-Kanan shuddered. Hermathya had been out of his thoughts, and out of his heart, for centuries. The break between him and his twin brother had been widened by the passion Kith-Kanan had felt for Hermathya. Time and other loves had practically extinguished the old fire. Why did he feel such longing for her now?

"Old wounds are the deepest and the hardest to heal," said Dru, once more answering Kith's thoughts.

"I don't believe any of this," the Speaker snapped. "You created that scene with your magic to deceive me."

Dru sighed loudly and circled the rostrum, his yellow aura moving with him. "Ah, such lack of faith," Dru said sardonically. "All I offered was true. The lady can be yours again if you meet my terms."

Kith-Kanan folded his arms. "Which are what?"

The red elf pressed his hands together prayerfully, but the expression on his face was anything but pious. "Permit the passage of slave caravans from Ergoth and Silvanesti through your realm," he said quickly.

"Never!" Kith-Kanan strode toward Dru, who did not retreat. The strange elf's yellow aura stopped the Speaker's advance. When he reached out to touch the golden shell, he snatched his fingers back as if they'd been burned. But the glow was bizarrely, intensely cold.

"You are brave," Dru mused, "but do not try to lay hands on me again."

At that moment, Kith-Kanan realized who Dru really was, and for one of the few times in his life, he was truly frightened.

"I know you," he said in a voice that wavered, though he fought to keep it steady. "You are the one who corrupts those beset by adversity." Almost too softly to be heard, he added, "Hiddukel."

The God of Evil Bargains, whose sacred color was red, bowed. "You are tiresome in your virtues," he remarked. "Is there nothing you want? I can fill this tower twenty times with gold or silver or jewels. What do you say to that?" His red eyebrows rose questioningly.

"Treasure will not solve my problems."

"Think of the good you could do with it all." Hiddukel's voice dripped with malicious sarcasm. "You could buy all the slaves in the world and set them free."

Kith-Kanan backed away toward the rostrum. It was his safe haven, where not even the evil god's magic could reach him. "Why do you concern yourself with the slave trade, Lord of the Broken Scales?" he asked.

The god's elven form shrugged. "I concern myself with all such commerce. I am the patron deity of slavers."

The stone of the rostrum bumped against Kith-Kanan's heels. Confidently he climbed backward onto it. "I refuse all your offers, Hiddukel," he declared. "Go away, and trouble me no further."

The look of malign enjoyment left the red-garbed elf's face. Addressed by his true name, he had no choice but to depart. His pointed features twisted into a hateful grimace.

"Your troubles will increase, Speaker of the Sun," the God of Demons spat. "That which you have created will come forth to strike you down. The hammer shall break the anvil. Lightning shall cleave the rock!"

"Go!" Kith-Kanan cried, his heart pounding in his throat. The single syllable reverberated in the air.

Hiddukel backed away a pace and spun on one toe. His cape swirled around like a flame. Faster and faster the god whirled, until his elven form vanished, replaced by a whirling column of red smoke and fire. Kith-Kanan threw up an arm to shield his face from the virulent display. The voice of Hiddukel boomed in his head.

"The time of wonders is at hand, foolish king! Forces older than the gods surround you! Only the power of the Queen of Darkness can withstand them! Beware!"

The fiery specter of Hiddukel flew apart, and in two heartbeats, the Tower of the Sun was quiet once more. The deep darkness that filled it remained, however. Sweating and shaking from his near escape from the Collector of Souls, Kith-Kanan sank to the floor. His body was wracked with spasms he could not control. A jumble of thoughts and images warred inside his brain—Ulvian, Hermathya, Suzine, Verhanna, his brother Sithas—all surmounted by the leering visage of Hiddukel. He felt as if his soul was the object of a deadly tug-of-war.

Kith-Kanan's entire body ached. He was limp, worn out, exhausted. Rest was what he craved. He must rest. His eyelids fluttered closed.

*　*　*　*　*

"Sire? Speaker?" called a faint voice.

Kith-Kanan pushed himself up on his hands. "Who is it?" he replied hoarsely, brushing hair from his eyes.

A glow appeared from the entry hall. This time it was the mundane light of a lamp in the hands of his castellan.

"I'm here, Tam."

"Great Speaker, are you well? We could not reach you, and— and the whole city has been plunged into darkness! The people are terrified!"

Concentrating his strength, Kith-Kanan struggled to his feet. Behind the agitated Tamanier were several silent Guards of the Sun. Their usual jaunty posture was gone, replaced by an attitude of tense fear.

"What do you mean?" the Speaker demanded shakily. "How long have I been in here? Is it night?"

Tamanier came closer. His face was white and drawn. "Sire, it is barely noon! Not long after you entered the tower to meditate, a curtain of blackness descended on the city. I came at once to inform you, but the tower doors were barred by invisible forces! We were frantic. Suddenly, only a few moments ago, they swung wide."

Kith-Kanan adjusted his rumpled clothing and combed his hair back with his fingers. His mind was racing. The tower seemed normal, except for the darkness cloaking it. There was no trace of Hiddukel. He took a deep, restoring breath and said, "Come. We will see what the situation is and then calm the people."

They went to the entrance, Kith-Kanan striding as purposefully as his nerves and throbbing muscles would allow. Tamanier hurried along with the lamp. The guards at the door presented arms and waited dutifully for the Speaker to pass. The great doors stood open.

Kith-Kanan paused, his feet on the broad granite sill. The gloom beyond was intense, far denser than ordinary night. In spite of the torches carried by Tamanier Ambrodel and several warriors, Kith-Kanan could barely see to the bottom of the tower steps. The torchlight seemed muffled by the jet-black fog. There were no lights to be seen in the gloom, though from this high vantage point, all of Qualinost should be spread out before him. Overhead, no stars or moons were visible.

"You say this happened just after I entered the tower?" he asked tensely.

"Yes, sire," replied the castellan.

Kith-Kanan nodded. Was this some spell of Hiddukel's, to coerce him into accepting the god's vile bargain? No, not likely. The Lord of the Broken Scales was a deceiver, not an extorter.

Hiddukel's victims damned themselves. Their torment was thus sweeter to the wicked god.

"It's very strange," Kith-Kanan said in his best royal manner. "Still, it doesn't seem dangerous, merely frightening. Is the prisoner still in Arcuballis Tower?" No need to bandy the prince's name about.

One of the guards stepped forward. "I can answer that, sire. I was at the tower myself when the blackness fell. Lieutenant Merithynos thought it might be part of a plot to free his prisoner. No such attempt was made, however, Highness."

"This is no mortal's spell," remarked Kith-Kanan. He swept a hand. through the murk, half expecting it to stain his skin. It didn't. The gloom that looked so solid felt completely insubstantial, not even damp like a normal fog.

"Tell Merithynos to bring his prisoner to my house," Kith-Kanan ordered briskly. "Keep him sequestered there until I return."

"Where are you going, sire?" asked Tamanier, confused and unsure.

"Among my people, to reassure them."

With no escort and bearing his own torch, Kith-Kanan left the Tower of the Sun. For the next several hours, he walked the streets of his capital, meeting common folk and nobles alike. Fear had thickened the air as surely as the weird gloom. When word spread that Kith-Kanan was in the streets, the people came out of the towers and temples to see him and to hear his calming words.

"Oh, Great Speaker," lamented a young elf woman. "The blackness smothers me. I cannot breathe!"

He put a hand on her shoulder. "It's good air," he assured her. "Can't you smell the flowers in the gardens of Mantis?" His temple was close by. The aroma of the hundreds of blooming roses that surrounded it scented the still air.

The elf woman inhaled with effort, but her face cleared somewhat as she did. "Yes, sire," she said more calmly. "Yes . . . I can smell them."

"Mantis would not waste his perfume in suffocating air," said the Speaker kindly. "It's fear that chokes you. Stay here by the gardens until you feel better."

He left her and moved on, trailed by a large crowd of worried citizens. Their pale faces moved in and out of the gloom, barely lit by the scores of blazing brands that had sprouted from every window and in every hand. Where the avenue from the Tower of the Sun joined the street that curved northwest to the tower keep called Sithel, Kith-Kanan found a band of crafters and temple acolytes debating in loud, angry voices. He stepped between the factions and asked them why they were arguing.

"It's the end of the world!" declared a human man, a coppersmith by the look of the snips and pliers dangling from his oily leather vest. "The gods have abandoned us."

"Nonsense!" spat an acolyte of Astra, the patron god of the elves. "This is merely some strange quirk of the weather. It will pass."

"Weather? Black as pitch at noon?" exclaimed the coppersmith. His companions—a mix of elves and humans, all metal crafters—loudly supported him.

"You should heed the learned priest," Kith-Kanan said firmly. "He is versed in these matters. If the gods wanted to destroy the world, they wouldn't wrap us in a blanket of night. They'd use fire and flood and shake the ground. Don't you agree?"

The smith hardly wanted to contradict his sovereign, but he said sullenly, "Then why don't they do something about it?" He gestured to the half-dozen young clerics facing him.

"Have you tried?" Kith-Kanan asked the acolyte of Astra.

The cleric frowned. "None of our banishing spells worked, Highness. The darkness is not caused by mortal or divine magic," he said. The other clerics behind him murmured their agreement.

"How long do you think it will last?"

The young elf could only shrug helplessly.

The coppersmith snorted, and Kith-Kanan turned to him. "You ought to be grateful, my friend, for this darkness."

That caught the fellow off guard. "Grateful, Majesty?"

"It's pitch-black on a working day. I'd say you have a holiday." The crafters laughed nervously. "If I were you, I'd hie on over to the nearest tavern and celebrate your good fortune!" A broad grin brightened the coppersmith's face, and the disputants began to disperse.

Kith-Kanan continued on his way. Passing a side street on his right, he halted when he heard weeping coming from the dim alley.

The Speaker turned into the side street, following the sound of sobbing. Suddenly a hand reached out of the dark and pressed against his chest, stopping him.

"Who are you?" he said sharply, thrusting the torch toward the one who'd halted him.

"I live here. Gusar is my name."

The weak torchlight showed Kith-Kanan an old human, bald and white-browed. Gusar's eyes were white, too. Cataracts had taken his sight.

"Someone is in trouble down there," said the Speaker, relieved. An old blind man was hardly a threat.

"I know. I was going to help when you blundered up behind me."

Kith-Kanan bristled at the man's bluntness. "Get that brand out of my face, and I'll be on my way," the blind man continued.

The monarch of Qualinesti drew his torch back. Gusar moved off with the easy confidence of one used to darkness. Kith-Kanan trailed silently behind the blind man. In short order, they came upon a trio of elf children huddled by the closed door of a tower home.

"Hello," Gusar said cheerfully. "Is someone crying?"

"We can't find our house," wailed an elf girl. "We looked and looked, but we couldn't see the daisies that grow by our door!"

"Daisies, eh? I know that house. It's only a few steps more. I'll take you there." Gusar extended a gnarled hand. The elf children regarded him with misgiving.

"Are you a troll?" asked the smallest boy, his blue eyes huge in his tiny face.

Gusar cackled. "No. I'm just an old, blind man." He pointed a thumb over his shoulder. "My friend has a torch to help light your way."

Kith-Kanan was surprised. He hadn't realized the old man knew he was still there.

The girl who'd spoken got up first and took the human's hand. The two boys followed their sister, and together the children and the old human wandered down the lane. Kith-Kanan followed at a distance, until the little girl turned and announced, "We don't need you, sir. The old one can see us home."

"Fare you well, then," Kith-Kanan called. The bowed back of the aged human and the flaxen hair of the elf children quickly vanished in the inky air.

For the first time in days, the Speaker smiled. His dream of a nation where all races could live in peace was truly taking hold when three children of pure Silvanesti blood could fearlessly take the hand of a gnarled old human and let him lead them home.

The Lightning and the Rock

4

On the morning of what would have been the fourth day of darkness, a ball of red fire appeared in the eastern sky. The people of Qualinost swarmed into the streets, fearfully pointing at the dangerous-looking orb. Within minutes, dread turned to relief when they realized that what they were seeing was the sun, burning through the gloom. The darkness lifted steadily, and the day dawned bright and cloudless.

Kith-Kanan looked out over his city from the window of his private rooms. The rose-quartz towers sparkled cleanly in the newborn sunlight, and the trees seemed to bask in the warmth. All over Qualinost, in every window and every gracefully curving street, faces were upturned to the luxurious heat and light. As the Speaker looked south across his city, the songs and laughter of spontaneous revelry reached his ears.

The return of light was a great relief to Kith-Kanan. For the past three days, he had done nothing but try to hold his people together, reassuring them that the end of the world was not nigh. After two days of darkness, emissaries had arrived in Qualinost from Ergoth and Thorbardin, seeking answers from the Speaker of the Sun as to the cause of the fearful gloom. Kith-Kanan had his own ideas, but didn't share them with the emissaries. Some new power was rising from a long sleep. Hiddukel had said it was a power older even than the gods. The Speaker did not yet know what its purpose was, and he didn't want to spread alarms through the world based on his own flimsy theories.

From all over his realm, people poured into Qualinost, clogging the bridges and straining the resources of the city. Everyone was afraid of the unknown darkness. Fear made allies of the oldest enemies, too. From outside Kith-Kanan's enlightened kingdom came humans and elves who had fought each other in the Kinslayer Wars. During the darkness, they had huddled together around bonfires, praying for deliverance.

From his window overlooking the sunlit city, Kith-Kanan mused. Perhaps that was the reason for it—to bring us all together.

There was a soft, firm knock at the door. Kith-Kanan turned his back on the city and called, "Enter." Tamanier Ambrodel appeared in the doorway and bowed.

"The emissaries of Ergoth and Thorbardin have departed," the castellan reported, hands folded in front of him. "In better spirits than when they arrived, I might add, sire."

"Good. Now perhaps I can deal with other weighty matters. Send Prince Ulvian and the warrior Merithynos to me at once."

"At once, Majesty," was Tamanier's quiet reply.

As soon as the castellan had departed, Kith-Kanan moved to his writing table and sat down. He took out a fresh sheet of foolscap. Dipping the end of a fine stylus into a jar of ink, he began to write. He was still writing when Ulvian and Merith presented themselves.

"Well, Father, I hope this ridiculous business is over," Ulvian said with affected injury. He was still clad in the crimson doublet and silver-gray trousers he'd been captured in. "I've been bored silly, with no one to talk to but this tiresome warrior of yours."

Merith's hand tightened on the pommel of his sword. His cobalt-blue eyes stared daggers at the prince. Kith-Kanan forestalled the lieutenant's offended retort.

"That's enough," the Speaker said firmly. He finished writing, melted a bit of sealing wax on the bottom of the sheet, and pressed his signet ring into the soft blue substance. When the seal was cool, he rolled the foolscap into a scroll and tied it with a thin blue ribbon. This he likewise sealed with wax.

"Lieutenant Merithynos, you will convey this message to Feldrin Feldspar, the master builder who directs the work at Pax Tharkas," said the Speaker, rising and holding out the scroll. Merith accepted it, though he looked perplexed.

"Am I to give up guarding the prince, Majesty?" he asked.

"Not at all. The prince is to accompany you to Pax Tharkas." Kith-Kanan's eyes met his son's. Ulvian frowned.

"What's in Pax Tharkas for me?" he asked suspiciously.

"I am sending you to school," his father replied. "Master Feldrin is to be your schoolmaster."

Ulvian laughed. "You mean to make an architect out of me?"

573

"I am putting you in Feldrin's hands as a common laborer—a slave, in fact. You will work every day for no wage and receive only the meanest provender. At night, you will be locked in your hut and guarded by Lieutenant Merithynos."

Ulvian's confident smirk vanished. Hazel eyes wide, he backed away a few steps, falling to one of the Speaker's couches. His face was pale with shock.

"You can't mean it," he whispered. More loudly, he added, "You can't do this."

"I am the Speaker of the Sun," Kith-Kanan said. Though his heart was breaking with the punishment he was visiting on his only son, the Speaker's demeanor was firm and unyielding.

The prince's head shook back and forth, as if denying what he was hearing. "You can't make me a slave." He leapt to his feet and his voice became a shout. "I am your son! I am Prince of Qualinesti!"

"Yes, you are, and you have broken my law. I'm not doing this on a whim, Ullie. I hope it will teach you the true meaning of slavery—the cruelty, the degradation, the pain and suffering. Maybe then you will understand the horror of what you've done. Maybe then you'll know why I hate it, and why you should hate it, too."

Ulvian's outrage wilted. "How—how long will I be there?" he asked haltingly.

"As long as necessary. I'll visit you, and if I'm convinced you've learned your lesson, I'll release you. What's more, I will forgive you and publicly declare you my successor."

That seemed to restore the prince somewhat. His gaze flickered toward Merith, who was standing at rigid attention, though his expression reflected frank astonishment. Ulvian said, "What if I run away?"

"Then you will lose everything and be declared outlaw in your own country," Kith-Kanan said evenly.

Ulvian advanced on his father. There was betrayal and disbelief in his eyes, and rage as well. Merith tensed and prepared to subdue the prince if he attacked the Speaker, but Ulvian stopped a pace short of his father.

"When do I go?" he asked through clenched teeth.

"Now."

A roll of thunder punctuated Kith-Kanan's pronouncement. Merith stepped forward and took hold of the prince's arm, but Ulvian twisted out of his grasp.

"I'll come back, Father. I will be the Speaker of the Sun!" the prince vowed in ringing tones.

"I hope you will, Son. I hope you will."

A second crash of thunder finished the confrontation. Merith led the prince reluctantly away.

Hands clasped tightly behind his back, Kith-Kanan returned to his window. Melancholy washed over him in slow, steady waves as he gazed up at the cloudless sky. Then, even as his mind was far away, from the corner of one eye, he spied a bolt of lightning. It flashed out of the blue vault and dove at the ground, striking somewhere in the southwestern district of Qualinost. A deep boom reverberated over the city, rattling the shutters on the Speaker's house.

Thunder and lightning from a clear sky? Kith-Kanan's inner torment was pushed aside for a moment as he digested this remarkable occurrence.

The time of wonders was indeed at hand.

*   *   *   *   *

Twenty riders followed the dusty trail through the sparse forest of maple saplings, most no taller than the horses. Twenty elven warriors, under Varhanna's command and guided by their new kender scout, Rufus Wrinklecap, rode slowly in single file. No one spoke. The muggy morning air oppressed them—that, and the cold trail they were trying to follow. Four days out of Qualinost, and this was the only sign of slavers they'd found. It hadn't helped that they'd had to flounder on in three days of total darkness. Rufus warned the captain that the tracks they were tracing were many weeks old and might lead to nothing.

"Never mind," she grumbled. "Keep at it. Lord Ambrodel sent us here for a reason."

"Yes, my captain."

The kender eased his big horse a little farther away from the ill-tempered Verhanna. Rufus was a comic sight on horseback; with his shocking red topknot and less than four feet of height, he hardly looked like a valiant elven warrior. Perched on a chestnut charger that was bigger than any other animal in the troop, he resembled a small child astride a bullock.

During their brief stopover in Qualinost, while the troops were reprovisioned and a horse was secured for him, the kender had bought himself some fancy clothes. His blue velvet breeches, vest, and white silk shirt beneath a vivid red cape made quite a contrast to the armor-clad elves. Atop his head perched an enormous broad-brimmed blue hat, complete with a white plume and a hole in the crown to allow his long topknot to trail behind.

They had passed through the easternmost fringe of the Kharolis Mountains onto the great central plain, the scene of so many battles during the Kinslayer War. Now and then the troop saw silent reminders of that awful conflict: a burned village, abandoned to weeds and carrion birds; a cairn of stones, under which were buried the bodies of fallen soldiers of Ergoth in a mass grave. Occasionally their horses' hooves turned up battered, rusting helmets lodged in the soil. The skulls of horses and the bones of elves shone in the tall grass like ivory talismans, warning of the folly of kings.

Once every hour Verhanna halted her warriors and ordered Rufus to check the trail. The nimble kender leaped from his horse's back or slid off its wide rump and scrambled through the grass and saplings, sniffing and peering for telltale signs.

During the third such halt of the morning, Verhanna guided her mount to where Rufus squatted, busily rubbing blades of grass between his fingers.

"Well, Wart, what do you find? Have the slavers come this way?" she asked, leaning over her animal's glossy neck.

"Difficult to say, Captain. Very difficult. Other tall folk have passed this way since the slavers. The trails are muddled," muttered Rufus. He put a green stem in his mouth and nibbled it. "The grass is still sweet," he observed. "Others came from the east and passed through during the days of darkness."

"What others?" she said, frowning.

The kender hopped up, dropping the grass and dusting off his fancy blue pants. "Travelers. Going that way," he said, pointing to the direction they'd come from Qualinost. "They were in deeply laden, two-wheeled carts."

Verhanna regarded her scout sourly. "We didn't pass anyone."

"In that darkness, who knows what we passed? The Dragonqueen herself could've ridden by clad in cloth o' gold and we wouldn't have seen her."

She straightened in the saddle and replied, "What about our quarry?"

Rufus rubbed his flat, sunburned nose. "They split up."

"What?" Verhanna's shout brought the other troopers to attention. Her second-in-command, a Kagonesti named Tremellan, hurried to her side. She waved him off and dismounted, slashing through the tall grass to Rufus. Planting her mailed hands on her hips, the captain demanded, "Where did they split up?"

Rufus took two steps forward and one sideways.

"Here," he said, pointing at the trodden turf. "Six riders, the same ones we've been chasing all along. Two went east. They were elder folk, like the Speaker." By this, the kender meant the two were Silvanesti. "Two others went north. They smelled of fur and had thick shoes. Humans, I'd say. The last two continued south, and they're tricky. Barefoot, they are, and they smell just like the wind. Dark elders, and wise in the ways of the chase."

"What does he mean?" Verhanna muttered to Tremellan.

"Dark elders are my people," offered the Kagonesti officer. "They probably work as scouts for the other four. They find travelers, or a lonely farm, and lead the slavers there."

Verhanna slapped her palms together with a metallic clink. "All right. Gather the troop around! I want to speak to them."

The elven warriors made a circle around their captain and the kender scout. Verhanna grinned at them, arms folded across her chest.

"The enemy has made a mistake," she declared, rocking on her heels. "They've split themselves into three groups. The humans and Silvanesti are headed for their homelands, probably carrying the gold they made selling slaves. Without their Kagonesti scouts, they don't stand a chance against us. Sergeant Tremellan, I want you to take a contingent of ten and ride after the Silvanesti. Take them alive if you can. Corporal Zilaris, you take five troopers and follow the humans. They shouldn't give you much trouble. Four warriors will come with me to find the Kagonesti."

"Excuse me, Captain, but I don't think that's wise," Tremellan said. "I don't need ten warriors to catch the Silvanesti slavers. You should take more with you. The dark elders will be the hardest to catch."

"He's right." chimed in Rufus. His topknot bobbed as he nodded vigorously.

"Who's captain here?" Verhanna demanded. "Don't question my orders, Sergeant. You don't imagine I need numbers to track the woods-wise Kagonesti, do you? No, of course not! Stealth is what's needed, Sergeant. My orders stand."

A rumble of thunder rolled across the plain and was ignored. Without further discussion, Tremellan collected half the warriors and redistributed food and water among them. He formed his group around him while Verhanna gave him final orders.

"Pursue them hard, Sergeant," she urged. Her blood was up, and her brown eyes were brilliant. "They've a week's head start, but they might not yet know anyone is after them, so they won't be moving fast."

"And the border, Captain?" asked Tremellan.

"Don't talk to me about borders," snapped the captain. "Get those damned slavers! This is no time for faint hearts or half measures!"

Tremellan suppressed his irritation, saluted, and spurred his horse. The troop rode off through the maple saplings as thunder boomed at their backs.

Verhanna felt a tug on her haqueton. She turned and looked down, seeing Rufus standing close beside her. "What is it?"

"Look up. There are no clouds, " he said, turning his small face heavenward. "Thunder, but no clouds."

"So the storm is over the horizon," Verhanna replied briskly. She left the kender still staring at the clear-blue sky. Corporal Zilaris took his detachment and headed north after the human slavers. Verhanna was watching them recede in the distance when suddenly a bolt of lightning lanced down a scant mile away. Dirt flew up in the air, and the crack of thunder was like a blow from a mace.

"By Astra!" she exclaimed. "That was close!"

The next one was closer still. With no warning, a column of blue-white fire slammed into the ground less than fifty paces from Verhanna, Rufus, and the remaining warriors. The horses screamed and reared, some falling back on their startled riders. Verhanna, still on the ground, kept a tight hand on her straining mount's bridle. Rufus had just remounted, and when his horse began to snort and dance, the kender climbed onto its neck to get a better hold. His cape flopped over the horse's eyes, a fortuitous accident, and the beast calmed.

The shock of the lightning strike passed, and the elves slowly recovered. One warrior lay moaning on the ground, his leg broken when his horse fell on him. Verhanna and the others set to binding his shattered limb. Rufus, not being needed, wandered over to the crater gouged by the lightning.

The hole was twenty feet across and nearly as deep. The sides of the pit were black and steaming. Tiny flames licked the dry prairie grass around the rim of the hole. Rufus stamped on the fires he saw and gazed with awe at the gaping pit. A shadow fell over him. He turned to see that Verhanna had joined him.

"Someone's hurling thunderbolts at us, my captain," he said seriously.

"Rot," was her reply, though her tone was uncertain. "It was just an act of nature." The next flash of lightning came in an instant. Verhanna uttered a brief warning cry and threw herself down. The bolt struck some distance away, and she sheepishly raised her head. Rufus was shading his eyes, staring at the southern horizon.

"It's moving that way," he announced.

Verhanna stood up and brushed dirt and grass from her haqueton. Her cheeks were stained crimson with embarrassment, and she was grateful that the kender ignored her nervous dive for cover. "What's moving away?" she asked quickly.

"The lightning," he replied. "Three strikes we've seen, each one farther south than the last."

"That's crazy," said Verhanna dismissively. "Lightning is random."

"Ain't no ordinary lightning," the kender insisted.

The warriors made their injured comrade comfortable, and when

Verhanna and Rufus rejoined them, she ordered one of the warriors to remain with the injured elf to help him back to Qualinost.

"Now we are four," she remarked as they formed up to resume their hunt. A glance at Rufus caused her to amend her statement. "Four and a half, I mean."

"Not good odds, captain," one of the warriors said.

"Even if I were alone, I'd go on," stated Verhanna firmly. "These criminals must be caught, and they will be."

To the south, where the plain seemed to stretch on endlessly, the flash and crack of lightning continued. It was in that direction the little band rode.

* * * * *

The audience hall of the Speaker's house was crammed with Qualinesti, all talking at once. The breeze stirred up by the roiling crowd had set the banners hanging from the high ceiling to waving gently. The scarlet flags were embroidered in gold, hand-worked by hundreds of elven and human girls. The crest of Kith-Kanan's family—the royal family of Qualinesti, not the old line in Silvanost—was a composite of the sun and the Tree of Life.

In the midst of this maelstrom, the Speaker of the Sun sat calmly on his throne while his aides tried to sort out the confusion. However, his inner conflict showed in the small circular movements of his thumbs on the creamy wooden arm of his throne. The wood was rare, a gift from an Ergothian trader who called it vallenwood and said it came from trees that grew to enormous size. Once polished, the vallenwood seemed to glow with an inner light. Kith-Kanan thought it the most beautiful wood in the world. It felt smooth and comforting under his nervously moving fingers.

Tamanier Ambrodel was arguing heatedly with Senators Clovanos and Xixis. "Four towers have been toppled by lightning strikes!" Clovanos said, his voice becoming shrill. "A dozen of my tenants were hurt. I want to know what's being done to stop all this!"

"The Speaker is attending to the problem," Tamanier said, exasperated. His white hair stood out from his head as he ran his hand through it in distraction. "Go home! You are only adding to the problem by being hysterical."

"We are senators of the Thalas-Enthia!" Xixis snapped. "We have a right to be heard!"

All through this mayhem, thunder boomed outside and flashes of lightning, mixed with the bright morning sun, gave the hall eerie illumination. Kith-Kanan glanced out a nearby window. Three columns of smoke were visible, rising from spots where trees had been set afire by lightning. After two days of lightning, the damage was mounting.

Kith-Kanan slowly rose to his feet. The crowd quickly fell silent and ceased its nervous shuffling.

"Good people," began the Speaker, "I understand your fear. First the darkness came, weakening the crops and frightening the children. Yet the darkness left after causing no real harm, as I promised it would. Today begins our third day of lightning—"

"Cannot the priests deflect this plague of fire?" shouted a voice from the crowd. Others took up the cry. "Is there no magic to defend us?"

Kith-Kanan held up his hands. "There is no need to panic," he said loudly. "And the answer is no. None of the clerics of the great temples has been able to dispel or deflect any of the lightning."

A low murmur of worry went through the assembly. "But there is no threat to the city, I assure you!"

"What about the towers that were knocked down?" demanded Clovanos. His graying blond hair was coming loose from its confining ribbon, and small tendrils curled around his angry face.

From the rear of the hall, someone called out, "Those calamities are your fault, Senator!"

The mass of elves and humans parted to let Senator Irthenie approach the throne. Dressed, as was her custom, in dyed leather and Kagonesti face paint, Irthenie cut an arresting figure among the more conservatively attired senators and townsfolk.

"I visited one of the fallen towers, Great Speaker. The lightning struck the open ground nearby. The shock caused the tower to fall," announced Irthenie.

"Mind your business, Kagonesti!" Clovanos growled.

"She is minding her business as a senator," Kith-Kanan cut in sharply. "I know very well you expect compensation for your lost property, Master Clovanos. But let Irthenie finish what she has to say first."

A flash of lightning highlighted the Speaker's face for a second, then passed away. Chill winds blew through the audience hall. The banners suspended above the assemblage flapped and rippled.

More calmly, Irthenie said, "The soil near Mackeli Tower is very sandy, Your Majesty. I recall when Feldrin Feldspar erected that great tower keep. He had to sink a foundation many, many feet in the ground until he struck bedrock."

She turned to the fuming Senator Clovanos, eyeing him with disdain. "The good senator's towers are in the southwestern district, next to Mackeli, and they had no such deep foundations. It's a wonder they've stood this long."

"Are you an architect?" Clovanos spat back. "What do you know of building?"

"Is Senator Irthenie correct?" asked Kith-Kanan angrily. Before the fire in his monarch's eyes and the dawning disgust evident in the faces around him, Clovanos reluctantly admitted the accuracy of Irthenie's words. "I see," the Speaker concluded. "In that case, the unhappy folk who lived in those unsafe towers shall receive compensation from the royal treasury. You, Clovanos, shall get none. And be thankful I don't charge you with endangering the lives of your tenants."

With Clovanos thus humbled, the other complainants fell back, unwilling to risk the Speaker's wrath. Sensing their honest fear, Kith-Kanan tried to raise their spirits.

"Some of you may have heard of my contact with the gods just before the darkness set in. I was told that there would appear wonders in the world, portents of some great event to come. What the great event will be, I do not know, but I can assure you that these wonders, while frightening, are not dangerous themselves. The darkness came and went, and so shall the lightning. Our greatest enemy is fear, which drives many to hasty, ill-conceived acts.

"So I urge you again: be of stout heart! We have all faced terror and death during the great Kinslayer War. Can't we bear a little gloom and lightning? We are not children, to cower before every crack of thunder. I will use all the wisdom and power at my command to protect you, but if you all go home and reflect a bit, you'll soon realize there is no real danger."

"Unless you have Clovanos for a landlord," muttered Irthenie.

Laughter rippled in the ranks around her. The Kagonesti woman's soft words were repeated through the ranks until everyone in the hall was chortling in appreciation. Clovanos's face turned beet red, and he stalked angrily out, with Xixis on his heels. Once the two senators were gone, the laughter increased, and Kith-Kanan could afford to join in. Much of the tension and anxiety of the past few days slipped away.

Kith-Kanan sat back down on his throne. "Now," he said, stilling the mirth swelling across the hall, "if you are here to petition for help due to damage caused by the darkness or the lightning, please go to the antechamber, where my castellan and scribes will take down your names and claims. Good day and good morrow, my people."

The Qualinesti filed out of the hall. The last ones out were the royal guards, whom Kith-Kanan dismissed. Irthenie remained behind. The aged elf woman walked with quick strides to the window. Kith-Kanan joined her.

"The merchants in the city squares say the lightning isn't in every country as the darkness was," Irthenie informed him. "To the north, they haven't had any at all. To the south, it's worse than here. I've heard tales of ships being blasted and sunk, and fires in the southern forests all the way to Silvanesti."

"We seem to be spared the worst," Kith-Kanan mused. He clasped his hands behind his back.

"Do you know what it all means?" the senator asked. "Old forest elves are incurably curious. We want to know everything."

He smiled. "You know as much as I do, old fox."

"I may know a deal more, Kith. There's talk in the city about Ulvian. He's missed, you know. His wastrel friends are asking for him, and rumors are rampant."

The Speaker's good humor vanished. "What's being said?"

"Almost the truth—that the prince committed some crime and you have exiled him for a time," Irthenie replied. A sizzling lightning bolt hit the peak of the Tower of the Sun, just across the square from the Speaker's house. Since the strange weather had begun, the tower had been struck numerous times without effect. "His exact crime and place of exile remain a secret," she added.

Kith-Kanan nodded a slow affirmation. Irthenie pursed her thin lips. The yellow and red lines on her face stood out starkly with the next lightning blast.

"Why do you keep Ulvian's fate a secret?" she inquired. "His example would be a good lesson to many other young scoundrels in Qualinost."

"No. I will not humiliate him in public."

Kith-Kanan turned his back to the display of heavenly fire and looked directly into Irthenie's hazel eyes. "If Ulvian is to be Speaker after me, I wouldn't want his youthful transgressions to hamper him for the rest of his life."

The senator shrugged. "I understand, though it isn't how I would handle him. Perhaps that's why you are the Speaker of the Sun and I am a harmless old widow you keep around for gossip and advice."

He chuckled in spite of himself. "You are many things, old friend, but a harmless old widow is not one of them. That's like saying my grandfather Silvanos was a pretty good warrior."

The Speaker yawned and stretched his arms. Irthenie noticed the dark smudges under his eyes and asked, "Are you sleeping well?" He admitted he was not.

"Too many burdens and too many anxious dreams," Kith-Kanan said. "I wish I could get away from the city for a while."

"There is your grove."

Kith-Kanan clapped his hands together softly. "You're right! You see? Your wits are more than a little sharp. My mind is so muddled that I never even thought of that. I'll leave word with Tam that I'm spending the day there. Perhaps the gods will favor me again, and I'll discover the reason behind all these marvels."

Kith-Kanan hurried to his private exit behind the Qualinesti throne. Irthenie went to the main doors of the audience hall. She paused and looked back as Kith-Kanan disappeared through the dark doorway. Thunder vibrated through the polished wooden floor. Irthenie opened the doors and plunged into the crowd still milling in the Speaker's antechamber.

* * * * *

There were no straight streets in Qualinost. The boundary of the city, laid out by Kith-Kanan himself, was shaped like the keystone of an arch. The narrow north end of the city faced the confluence of the two rivers that protected it. The Tower of the Sun and the Speaker's house were at that end. The wide portion of the city, the southern end, faced the high ground that eventually swelled into the Thorbardin peaks. Most of the common folk lived there.

In the very heart of Qualinost was the city's tallest hill. It boasted two important features. First, the top of the hill was a huge flat plaza known as the Hall of the Sky, a unique "building" without walls or roof. Here sacred ceremonies honoring the gods were held. Convocations of the great and notable Qualinesti met, and festivals of the seasons were celebrated. The huge open square was paved with a mosaic of thousands of hand-set stones. The mosaic formed a map of Qualinesti.

The second feature of this tall hill, lying on its north slope, was the last bit of natural forest remaining within Qualinost. Kith-Kanan had taken great care to preserve this grove of aspens when the rest of the plateau was shaped by elven spades and magic. More than a park, the aspen grove had become the Speaker's retreat, his haven from the pressures of ruling. He treasured the grove above all features in his capital because the densely wooded enclave reminded him of days long past, of the time when he had dwelt in the primeval forest of Silvanesti with his first wife, the Kagonesti woman Anaya, and her brother Mackeli.

His time with Anaya had been long ago . . . four hundred years and more. Since then he had struggled and loved, fought, killed, ruled. The people of Qualinost were afraid of the darkness and lightning that had fallen upon them. Kith-Kanan, however, was troubled by the impending crisis of his succession. The future of the nation of Qualinesti depended on whom he chose to rule after him. He had to keep his word and step aside. More than that, he really wished to step aside, to pass the burden of command on to younger shoulders. But to whom? And when? When would Pax Tharkas be officially completed?

The grove had no formal entrance, no marked path or gate. Kith-Kanan slowed his pace. The sight of the closely growing trees already calmed him. No lightning at all had touched the grove. The aspen trees stood bright white in the morning sun, their triangular leaves shivering in the breeze and displaying their silvery backs.

The Speaker slipped the hood back from his head. Carefully he lifted the gold circlet from his brow. This simple ring of metal was all the crown Qualinesti had, but for his time in the grove, Kith-Kanan did not want even its small burden.

He dropped the crown into one of the voluminous pockets on the front of his monkish robe. As he passed between the tree trunks, the sounds of the city faded behind him. The deeper he went into the trees, the less the outside world could intrude. Here and there among the aspens were apple, peach, and pear trees. On this spring day, the fruit trees were riotous with blossoms. Overhead, in the breaks between the treetops, he saw fleecy clouds sailing the sky like argosies bound for some distant land.

Crossing the small brook that meandered through the grove, Kith-Kanan came at last to a boulder patched with green lichen. He himself had flattened the top of the rock with the great hammer Sunderer, given to him decades before by the dwarf king Glenforth. The Speaker climbed atop the boulder and sat, sighing, as he drank in the peace of the grove.

A few paces to his right, the brook chuckled and splashed over the rocks in its path. Kith-Kanan cleared his mind of everything but the sounds around him, the gently stirring air, the swaying trees, and the play of the water, It was a technique he'd learned from the priests of Astra, who often meditated in closed groves like this. During the hard years of the Kinslayer Wars, it had been moments like this that preserved Kith-Kanan's sanity and strengthened his will to persevere.

Peace. Calm. The Speaker of the Sun seemed to sleep, though he was sitting upright on the rock.

Rest. Tranquility. The best answers to hard questions came when the mind and the body were not fighting each other for control.

A streak of heat warmed his face. Dreamily he opened his eyes. The wind sighed, and white clouds obscured the sun. Yet the sensation of heat had been intense. He lifted his gaze to the sky. Above him, burning like a second sun, was an orb of blue-white light. It took him only half a heartbeat to realize he was staring at a lightning bolt *that was falling directly toward him.*

Shocked into motion, Kith-Kanan sprang from the boulder. His feet had hardly left its surface when the lightning bolt slammed into the rock. All was blinding flash and splintered stone. Kith-Kanan fell face down by the brook, and broken rock pelted his back. The light and sound of the bolt passed away, but the Speaker of the Sun did not move.

*　*　*　*　*

It was after sunset before Kith-Kanan was missed. When the Speaker was late for dinner, Tamanier Ambrodel sent warriors to the grove to find him. Kemian Ambrodel and his four comrades searched through the dense forest of trees for quite a while before they found the Speaker lying unconscious near the brook.

With great care, Kemian turned Kith-Kanan over. To his shock and surprise, the Speaker's brown eyes were wide open, staring at nothing. For one dreadful instant, Lord Ambrodel thought the monarch of Qualinesti was dead.

"He breathes, my lord," said one of the warriors, vastly relieved.

Eyelids dipped closed, fluttered, then sprang open again. Kith-Kanan sighed.

"Great Speaker," said Kemian softly, "are you well?"

There was a pause while the Speaker's eyes darted around, taking in his surroundings. Finally he said hoarsely, "As well as any elf who was nearly struck by lightning."

Two warriors braced Kith-Kanan as he got to his feet. His gaze went to the blasted remains of the boulder. Almost as if he was talking to himself, the Speaker said softly, "Some ancient power is at work in the world, a power not connected with the gods we know. The priests and sorcerers can discern nothing, and yet . . ."

Something fluttered overhead. The elves flinched, their nerves on edge. A bird's sharp cry cut through the quiet of the aspen grove, and Kith-Kanan laughed.

"A crow! What a stalwart band we are, frightened out of our skins by a black bird!" he said. His stomach rumbled loudly, and Kith-Kanan rubbed it. There were holes burned through his clothing by bits of burned rock. "Well, I'm famished. Let's go *home*."

The Speaker of the Sun set off at a brisk pace. Lord Ambrodel and his warriors fell in behind him and trailed him back to the Speaker's house, where a warm hearth and a hearty supper awaited.

The Citadel of Peace

5

The blazing sun provided little heat in the thin air of the Kharolis Mountains. Under that dazzling orb, twenty thousand workers labored, carving the citadel of Pax Tharkas out of the living rock. Dwarves, elves, and humans worked side by side on the great project. Most of them were free craftsmen—stonecutters, masons, and artisans. Out of the twenty thousand, only two thousand were prisoners. Those with useful skills worked alongside their free comrades, and they worked well. The Speaker of the Sun had made them this bargain: if the prisoners performed their duties and kept out of trouble, they would have their sentences reduced by half. Outdoor work at Pax Tharkas was far preferable to languishing in a tower dungeon for years on end.

Not all the convicts were so fortunate. Some simply would not conform, so Feldrin Feldspar, the dwarf who was master builder in charge of creating the fortress, collected the idle, the arrogant, and the violent prisoners into a "grunt gang." Their only task was brute labor. Alone of all the workers at Pax Tharkas, the grunt gang was locked into its hut at night and closely watched by overseers during the day. It was to the grunt gang that Prince Ulvian was sent. He had no skill at stonecarving or bricklaying, and the Speaker had decreed that he should be treated as a slave. That meant he must take his place with the other surly prisoners in the grunt gang, pushing and dragging massive stone blocks from the quarry to the site of the citadel.

Ulvian's one meeting with Feldrin had not gone well. The chained prince, now dressed in the green and brown leathers of a

586

forester, had been led by Merith to the canvas hut where the master builder lived. The dwarf came out to see them, setting aside an armful of scrolls covered with lines and numbers. These were the plans for the fortress.

"Remove his chains," Feldrin rumbled. Without a word, Merith took Ulvian's shackles off. Ulvian sniffed and thanked the dwarf casually.

"Save your thanks," replied Feldrin. His thick black beard was liberally sprinkled with white, and his long stay in the heights of the Kharolis had deeply tanned his face and arms. He planted brick-hard fists on his squat hips and skewered the prince with his blue eyes. "Chains are not needed here. We are miles from the nearest settlement, and the mountains are barren and dry. You will work hard. If you try to run away, you will perish from hunger and thirst," the dwarf said darkly. "That is, if my people don't hunt you down first. Is that clear?"

Ulvian rolled his eyes and didn't answer. Feldrin roared, "Is that clear?" The prince flinched and nodded quickly. "Good."

He assigned Ulvian to the grunt gang, and a burly, bearded human came to escort the prince to his new quarters.

When they were gone, Merith's shoulders sagged. "I must confess, Master Feldrin, I am exhausted," he said, sighing. "For ten days, I have had the prince in my keeping, and I haven't had a moment's rest!"

"Why so, Lieutenant? He doesn't look so dangerous."

Feldrin stooped to retrieve his plans. Merith squatted to help.

"It wasn't fear that spoiled my sleep," the warrior confided, "but the prince's constant talk! By holy Mantis, that boy can talk, talk, talk. He tried to convert me, make me his friend, so that I wouldn't deliver him to you. He's engaging when he wants to be, and clever, too. You may have trouble with him."

Feldrin pushed back the front flap of his hut with one broad, blunt hand. "Oh, I doubt it, Master Merithynos. A few days dragging stone blocks will take the stiffness out of the prince's neck."

Merith ducked under the low doorframe and entered the hut. Though the walls and roof were canvas, like a tent, Feldrin's hut had a wooden frame and floor, sturdier than a tent. The mountains were sometimes wracked by fierce winds, blizzards, and landslides.

Feldrin clomped across the bare board floor and dropped his scrolls on a low trestle table in the center of the room. He turned up the wick on a brass oil lamp and settled himself on a thick-legged stool, then proceeded to rummage through the loose assortment of parchment until he found a scrap.

"I shall send a note back to the Speaker," he said, "so that he will know you and the prince arrived safely."

The lieutenant glanced back at the door flap hanging loosely in the still, cool air. "What shall I do, Master Feldrin? I'm supposed to guard the prince, but it seems you don't really need me."

"No, he won't be any trouble," muttered the dwarf, finishing his brief missive with a flourish. He shook sand over the wet ink to dry it. "But I may have another use for you."

Merith drew himself up straight, expecting an official order. "Yes, master builder?"

Stroking his thick beard, Feldrin regarded the tall elf speculatively. "Do you play checkers?" he asked.

* * * * *

Bells and gongs rang through the camp, and all over Pax Tharkas workers set down their tools. The sun had just begun to set behind Mount Thak, which meant only an hour of daylight remained. It was quitting time.

Ulvian dragged along at the rear of the ragged column of laborers known as the grunt gang. His arms and legs ached, his palms were blistered, and despite the cool temperature, the stronger sun at this high elevation had burned his face and arms cherry red. The overseers—the mute, bearded human Ulvian had met his first day in camp and an ill-tempered dwarf named Lugrim—stood on each side of the barracks door, urging the exhausted workers to hurry inside.

The long, ramshackle building was made from slabs of shale and mud, and the rear wall was sunk in the mountainside. There were two windows and only one door. The roof was made of green splits of wood and moss, and the whole barrack was drafty, dusty, and cold, despite the fires kept burning in baked-clay fireplaces at each end.

Inside the dim structure, the grunt gang members headed straight for their rude beds. Ulvian's was near the center of the single large room, as far from either fire as it could be. Still, he was so tired that he was about to fall on his bunk when he noticed the man who slept on his right was already in bed, where he had apparently lazed all day. Ulvian opened his mouth to protest.

The prince froze two paces from the bed. The human's head and right leg were swathed in loose, bloodstained bandages. His hands hung limply over the sides of the narrow bunk.

"Poor wretch won't live the night," rasped a voice behind the prince. Ulvian whirled. A filthy, rag-clad elf stood close to him, staring at him with burning gray eyes. "He was taking a load of bricks up the tower, and the scaffold broke. Broke his leg and cracked his skull."

"Aren't—aren't there healers to take care of him?" Ulvian exclaimed.

A dry rattle of laughter issued from the throat of the sun-baked elf. He was nearly as tall as Ulvian, and very thin. When he looked down at the human on the bed, dust fell from his blond eyebrows and matted hair. "Healers?" he chortled. "Healers are for the masters. We get a swig of wine, a damp cloth, and a lot of prayers!"

Ulvian recoiled from the loud elf. "Who are you?"

"Name's Drulethen," said the elf, "but everyone calls me Dru."

"That's a Silvanesti name," Ulvian said, surprised. "How did you come to be here?"

"I was once a wandering scholar who sought knowledge in the farthest comers of the world. Unfortunately when the war started, I was in Silvanesti, and the Speaker of the Stars needed able-bodied elves for his army. I didn't want to fight, but they forced me to take up arms. Once out in the wilderness, I ran away."

"So you're a deserter," said Ulvian, understanding dawning.

Dru shrugged. "That's not a crime in Qualinesti," he said idly and sat down on the nearest bed. "While I wandered the great plain, I found it was easier to take what I wanted than work for it, so I became a bandit. The Wildrunners caught up to me, and the Speaker of the Sun graciously allowed me to work here rather than rot in a Qualinost dungeon." He held out his slender hands palms up. "So it goes."

No one had spoken at such length to Ulvian since his arrival at Pax Tharkas. Dru might be a coward and a thief, but it was obvious he had a certain amount of education, which was as rare as diamonds in the grunt gang. Sitting down on his own bed, the prince asked Dru a question that had been bothering him. "Why can't we get closer to the fires?" he said in a low voice. Dru laughed nastily.

"Only the strongest ones get a place by the chimneys," he said. "Weaklings and newcomers get stuck in the middle. Unless you want a beating, I suggest you don't dispute the order of things."

Before Ulvian could broach another question, Dru moved to his own bunk. Dropping down on the bed, he turned his back to the prince and in seconds began to snore lightly with each intake of breath. Ulvian threw himself across his own bed, which consisted of strips of cloth nailed to a rough wooden frame. It stank of sweat and dirt even more strongly than the barracks as a whole. The prince locked his hands together behind his head and stared at the crude ceiling overhead. The orange-tinged sunlight filtered in through the chinks in the roof slats. While he pondered his fate, he dozed fitfully.

Something thumped against the prince's feet, which hung over the end of his short bunk. Ulvian snapped to a sitting position. Dru had bumped him on his way to the injured human's bed, where he now stood. Skinning back the man's eyelid with his thumb, Dru shook his head and made clucking sounds in his throat.

"Frell's gone," he announced loudly.

An especially tall human came to the dead man's bed and hoisted the body easily over his shoulder. He strode across the room and kicked the front door open. The red wash of sunset flowed into the gloomy barracks. The tall human dumped the corpse unceremoniously on the ground outside. Before he could close the door again, a dozen gang members were already picking the dead man's bed clean. They took everything, from his scrap of blanket to the few personal items he'd stowed under the bunk. The press was so great that Ulvian was forced to move away. He spied Dru leaning against the wall near the water barrel. Slipping through the crowd, he finally faced the Silvanesti.

"Is that it?" he asked sharply. "A man dies and he gets dumped outside?"

"That's it. The dwarves will take the body away," Dru replied, unconcerned.

"What about his friends? His family?" insisted the prince.

Dru took a small stone from his pocket. It was a four-inch cylinder of onyx the thickness of his thumb. "Nobody has friends here," he said. "As to family—" He shrugged and didn't finish. His fingers rubbed back and forth over the piece of black crystal.

Just as night was claiming the mountain pass, the sound of metal against metal sent the grunt gang storming toward the door. Outside was a huge iron cart wheeled by four dwarves. The cart bore a great kettle, and when one of the dwarves removed its lid, steam poured out. Ulvian let the rest of the gang press ahead of him, having no desire to be trampled for a dish of stew.

When he got outside, he shivered. A raw wind whistled down the pass, knifing through the clothing the prince wore. He watched the laborers, clay bowls in hand, mill around the food wagon while the dwarves served the steaming stew and doled out formidable loaves of bread to each worker. The aroma of roasted meat and savory spices drifted to Ulvian's nose. It drew him toward the wagon.

He was promptly shoved away by a Kagonesti with a shaved head and two scalp locks that hung down his back. Ulvian bristled and started to challenge the wild elf, but the hard muscles in the fellow's arms and the definite air of danger in his manner held the prince back. Ulvian slinked to the rear of the poorly formed line and waited his turn.

By the time he reached the wagon, the dwarves were scraping the bottom of the kettle. The ladle-bearing dwarf, warmly dressed in fur and leather, squinted down from the cart at Ulvian.

"Where's your bowl?" he growled.

"I don't know."

"Idiot!" He swung the ladle idly at the prince, who ducked. The copper dipper was as big as his hand and stoutly formed. The dwarf barked, "Get back inside and find yourself a bowl!"

Chastened, Ulvian did so. He searched the room until he saw Dru, who was leaning against the wall by the water barrel, eating his stew.

"Dru," he called, "I need a bowl. Where can I get one?"

The Silvanesti pointed to the fireplace at the south end of the room. Ulvian thanked him and wended his way through the crowd to the fireplace. Up close, he saw that the hearth was dominated by the same Kagonesti who had shoved him away from the food cart.

"What do you want, city boy?" he snarled.

"I need a bowl," replied Ulvian warily.

The Kagonesti, who was called Splint, set down his bowl. Glaring at the prince, he said, "I'm no charity, city boy. You want a bowl, you got to buy it."

The Speaker's son was perplexed. He had nothing to trade. All his valuables had been taken from him before he left Qualinost.

"I don't have any money," he said lamely.

Harsh laughter rang out around him. Ulvian flushed furiously. Splint wiped his mouth with the end of one of his long scalp locks.

"You got a good pair of boots, I see."

Ulvian looked at his feet. These were his oldest pair of boots, scuffed and dirty, but there were no holes in them and the soles were sound. They were also the only shoes he had.

"My boots are worth a lot more than a clay dish," Ulvian said stiffly.

Splint made no reply. Instead, he picked up his bowl and started eating again. He studiously ignored Ulvian, who stood directly in front of him.

The prince fumed. Who did this wild elf think he was? He was about to denounce him and tell everyone in earshot that he was the son of the Speaker of the Sun, but the words died in his throat. Who would believe him? They would only laugh at him. Hopelessness welled up inside him. No one cared what happened to him. No one would notice if he lived or died. For a horrible instant, he felt like crying.

Ulvian's stomach rumbled loudly. A few of the gang around him chuckled. He bit his lip and blurted out, "All right! The boots for a bowl!"

Languidly Splint stood up. He was the same height as Ulvian, but his powerful physique and menacing presence made him seem

591

much larger. The prince shucked off his boots and was soon standing on the cold dirt floor in his stockings. The Kagonesti slipped his ragged sandals off and pulled on the boots. After much stamping of his feet to settle them into the unfamiliar footwear, he pronounced them a good fit.

"What about my bowl?" Ulvian reminded him angrily.

Splint reached under his bunk next to the fireplace and brought out a chipped ceramic bowl, enameled in blue. Ulvian snatched the dish and ran to the door, leaving gales of coarse guffaws in his wake. By the time he threw open the door and dashed out, the dwarves and the food wagon were gone.

The grunt gang was still laughing when he returned moments later. He stalked through them to the crackling fire, where Splint sat warming himself.

"You tricked me." Ulvian said in a scant whisper. He was afraid to raise his voice, afraid he would start shrieking. "I want my boots back."

"I'm not a merchant, city boy. I don't make any exchanges."

The barracks were quiet now. Confrontation was as thick in the air as smoke.

"Give them back," demanded the prince, "or I'll take them back!"

"You truly are an idiot, pest. Go to sleep, city boy, and thank the gods I don't beat you senseless," Splint said.

Ulvian's pent-up rage exploded, and he did a rash thing. He raised a hand high and smashed the empty bowl against the Kagonesti's head. A collective gasp went up from the workers. Splint rocked sideways with the blow, but in a flash, he had shaken it off and leapt to his feet.

"Now you got no boots and no bowl!" he spat. His fist caught Ulvian low in the chest. The prince groaned and fell against one of the spectators who had gathered, who promptly flung him back to Splint. The Kagonesti delivered a rolling punch to Ulvian's jaw, sending him spinning into the wall. Splint followed the reeling prince.

Ulvian's world swam in a sea of red fog. He felt strong hands grasp his shirt and drag him away from the support of the wall. More blows rained on his head and chest. Every time he was knocked down, someone picked him up and tossed him back to receive more abuse. Vainly he tried to grapple with Splint. The wild elf broke his feeble grip with little more than a shrug, kicking him in the stomach.

"He's had enough, Splint," Dru said, stepping between the prostrate Ulvian and the raging Kagonesti.

"I ought to kill him!" Splint retorted.

"He's new and stupid. Let him be," countered Dru.

"Bah!" Splint spat on Ulvian's back. He rubbed his throbbing knuckles and returned to his place by the fire.

Dru dragged the semiconscious prince to his bed and rolled him into it. Ulvian's face was bruised and battered. His left eye would soon be invisible behind a rapidly swelling lid. Eventually the pain of his injuries gave way to sleep. Hungry and beaten, Ulvian sank into forgiving darkness.

During the night, someone stole his stockings.

Bards and Liars

6

The lightning lasted three days, then suddenly ceased. The next day, exactly one week after the darkness had fallen across the world, the sky filled with clouds. No one thought much of it, for they were ordinary-looking gray rain clouds. They covered the sky from horizon to horizon and lowered until it seemed they would touch the lofty towers of Qualinost. And then it began to rain—brilliant, scarlet rain.

It filled the gutters and dripped off leaves, a torrent that drove everyone indoors. Though the crimson rain had no effect on anyone save to make him wet, the universal reaction to the downpour was to regard it as unnatural.

"At least I am spared the hordes of petitioners who sought an audience during the darkness and lightning," Kith-Kanan observed. He was standing on the covered verandah of the Speaker's house, looking south across the city. Tamanier Ambrodel was with him, as was Tamanier's son, Kemian. The younger Ambrodel was in his best warrior's garb—glittering breastplate and helm, white plume, pigskin boots, and a yellow cape so long it brushed the ground. He stood well back from the eaves so as not to get rain on his finery.

"You don't seem upset by this new marvel, sire," Tamanier said.

"It's just another phase we must pass through," Kith-Kanan replied stoically.

"Ugh," grunted Kemian. "How long do you think it will last,

Great Speaker?" Scarlet rivulets were beginning to creep over the flagstone path. Lord Ambrodel shifted his boots back, avoiding the strange fluid.

"Unless I am mistaken, exactly three days," said the Speaker. "The darkness lasted three days, and so did the lightning. There's a message in this, if we are just wise enough to perceive it."

"The message is 'the world's gone mad,' " Kemian breathed. His father didn't share his concern. Tamanier had lived too long, had served Kith-Kanan for too many centuries, not to trust the Speaker's intuition. At first he'd been frightened, but as his sovereign seemed so unconcerned, the elderly elf quickly mastered his own fear.

Restless, Kemian paced up and down, his slate-blue eyes stormy. "I wish whatever's going to happen would go ahead and happen!" he exclaimed, slamming his sword hilt against his scabbard. "This waiting will drive me mad!"

"Calm yourself, Kem. A good warrior should be cool in the face of trial, not coiled up like an irritated serpent," his father counseled.

"I need action," Kemian said, halting in midstride. "Give me something to do, Your Majesty!"

Kith-Kanan thought for a moment. Then he said, "Go to Mackeli Tower and see if any foreigners have arrived since the rain started. I'd like to know if the rain is also falling outside my realm."

Grateful to have a task to perform, Kemian bowed, saying, "Yes, sire. I'll go at once."

He hurried away.

* * * * *

Red rain trickled down Verhanna's arms, dripping off her motionless fingertips. Beside her, Rufus Wrinklecap squirmed. She glared at him, a silent order to keep still.

Ahead, some thirty feet away, two dark figures huddled by a feeble, smoky campfire. Rufus had smelled the smoke from quite a distance off, so Verhanna and her two remaining warriors had dismounted and crept up to the camp on foot. Verhanna grabbed the kender by his collar and hissed, "Are these the Kagonesti slavers?"

"They are, my captain," he said solemnly.

"Then we'll take them."

Rufus shook his head, sending streams of red liquid flying. "Something's not right, my captain. These fellows wouldn't sit in the open by a campfire where anyone could find them. They're too smart for that." The kender's voice was nearly inaudible.

"How do you know? They just don't realize we're on their trail," Verhanna said just as softly. She sent one of her warriors off to the left and the other to the right to surround the little clearing where the slavers had camped. Rufus fidgeted, his sodden, wilting plume bobbing in front of Verhanna's face.

"Be still!" she said fiercely. "They're almost in position." She caught a dull glint of armor as the two elf warriors worked their way into position. Carefully the captain drew her sword. Muttering unhappily, Rufus pulled out his shortsword.

"Hail Qualinesti!" shouted Verhanna, and bolted into the clearing. Her two comrades charged also, swords high, shouting the battle cry. The slavers never stirred.

Verhanna reached them first and swatted at the nearest one with the flat of her blade. To her dismay, her blow completely demolished the seated figure. It was nothing but a cloak propped up by tree limbs.

"What's this?" she cried. One of her warriors batted at the second figure. It, too, was a fake.

"A trick!" declared the warrior. "It's a trick!" A heartbeat later, an arrow sprouted from his throat. He gave a cry and fell onto his face.

"Run for it!" squealed Rufus.

Another missile whistled past Verhanna as she sprinted for the trees. Rufus hit the leaf-covered ground and rolled, bounced, and dodged his way to cover. The last warrior made the mistake of following his captain rather than making for the edge of the clearing nearest him. He ran a half-dozen steps before an arrow hit him in the thigh. He staggered and fell, calling out to Verhanna.

The captain crashed into the line of trees, blundering noisily through the undergrowth. When she reached her original hiding place, she stopped. The wounded elf warrior called to her again.

Breathing hard, Verhanna sheathed her sword and put her back against a tree. The red rain coursed down her cheeks as she gasped for breath.

"Psst!"

She jumped at the sound and whirled. Rufus was on his hands and knees behind her.

"What are you doing?" she hissed.

"Trying to keep from getting an arrow in the head," said the kender. "They was waitin' for us."

"So they were!" Furious with herself for walking into the trap, she said, "I've got to go back for Rikkinian."

Rufus grabbed her ankle. "You can't!"

Verhanna kicked free of his grasp. "I won't abandon a comrade!" she said emphatically. Shrugging off her cloak, Verhanna soon stood in her bare armor. She drew a thick-bladed dagger from her belt and crouched down, almost on all fours.

"Wait, I'll come with you," said the kender in a loud whisper. He scampered through the brush behind her.

Verhanna reached the edge of the clearing. Rikkinian, the wounded elf, was now silent and unmoving, lying face down in the mud. The other warrior sprawled near the phony slavers. Curiously, the stick figures and cloaks had been re-erected.

"Come here, Wart," the captain muttered. Rufus crawled to her. "What do you think?"

"They're both dead, my captain."

Verhanna's gaze rested on Rikkinian. Her brisk demeanor was gone; two warriors had paid for her mistake. Plaintively she asked, "Are you certain?"

"No one lies with his nose in the mud if he's still breathing," Rufus said gently. He squinted at the propped-up cloaks. "The archers are gone," he announced. Again Verhanna asked him if he was sure. He pointed. "There are two sets of footprints crossing the clearing over there. The dark elders have fled."

To demonstrate the truth of his words, Rufus stood up. He walked slowly past the fallen elves toward the smoldering fire. Verhanna went to Rikkinian and gently turned him over. The arrow wound in his leg hadn't killed him. Someone had dispatched him with a single thrust of a narrow-bladed knife through the heart. Burning with anger, she rose and headed for her other fallen comrade. Before she reached him, she was shocked to see Rufus raise his little sword and fall on the back of one of the propped-up cloaks. This time the cloak didn't collapse into a pile of tree limbs. Arms and legs appeared beneath it, and a figure leapt up.

"Captain!" Rufus shouted. "It's one of them!"

Verhanna fumbled for her sword as she ran toward the campfire. The kender stabbed over and over again at the cloaked figure's back. Though not muscular, Rufus possessed a wiry strength, but his attack appeared to have no effect. The cloaked one spun around, trying to throw the pesky kender off. When the front of the hood swung past Verhanna, she froze in her tracks and gasped.

"Rufus! It has no face!" she shouted.

With one last prodigious shake, the cloaked thing hurled Rufus to the ground. The kender's small sword flew into the woods as Rufus landed with a thud. He groaned and lay still, crimson rain beating down on his pallid face.

Verhanna gave a cry and slashed at the faceless figure, her slim elven blade slicing through the cloth with ease. She felt resistance as the blade passed through whatever lay beneath the cloak, but no blood flowed. Under the hood, where a face should have been, there was only a ball of grayish smoke, as if someone had stuffed the hood with dirty cotton.

Cutting and thrusting and hacking, Verhanna soon reduced the cloak to a tattered mass on the muddy ground. Shorn of its garment, the thing was revealed to be a vaguely elf-shaped column of dove-colored smoke. Two arms, two legs, a head, and torso were visible, but nothing else—only featureless vapor. Realizing she was exhausting herself to no avail, Verhanna stood back to catch her breath.

Rufus sat up slowly and clutched his head. He shook the pain aside and looked up at the smoky apparition standing between him and his captain. His hat had been trodden in the mud, and rain streamed from his long hair. Rufus glanced from the wispy figure to the dying campfire. Only a single coil of vapor, as thick as his wrist, snaked upward from the damp wood, and it twisted and writhed oddly in the still air.

Suddenly the kender had an inspiration. He dragged the other, unoccupied cloak to the fire and threw it over the smoldering wood. The sodden material soon extinguished the last of the sparks, and the fire died. As it did, the smoky figure thinned and finally vanished.

There was a long moment of silence, broken only by Rufus's and Verhanna's heavy breathing. At last Verhanna demanded, "What in Astra's name was that infernal thing?"

"Magic," Rufus replied simply. His attention was centered on retrieving his hat from the mud. Sorrowfully he tried to straighten the long, crimson-stained plume. It was hopeless; the feather was broken in two places and hung limply.

"I know it was magic," Verhanna said, annoyed. "But why? And whose?"

"I told you those elves were clever. One of them knows magic. He made the ghost as a diversion, I'll bet, to keep us busy while they escaped."

Verhanna slapped the flat of her blade against her mailed thigh. "E'li blast them! My two soldiers killed and we're diverted by magic smoke!" She stamped her foot, splashing blood-colored puddles over Rufus. "I'd give my right arm for another crack at those two! I never even saw them!"

"They're very dangerous," said Rufus sagely. "Maybe we should get more soldiers to hunt them down."

The Speaker's daughter was not about to admit defeat. She slammed her sword home in its scabbard. "No, by the gods! We'll take them ourselves!"

The kender jammed his soggy blue hat down on his head. His new clothes were ruined. "You don't pay me enough for this," he said under his breath.

* * * * *

How empty the great house seemed with Verhanna gone and Ulvian sent off to toil in the quarries of Pax Tharkas. Lord Anakardain was away from the city, with the lion's share of the Guards of the Sun chasing down the last stubborn bands of slavers. Kemian Ambrodel was out questioning new arrivals in Qualinost about the red rain and other marvels of days past.

So many friends and familiar faces gone. Only he, Kith-Kanan, had remained behind. He had given up his freedom to roam when he accepted the throne of Qualinesti. After all these centuries, he finally understood how his father, Sithel, had felt before him. Bound up in chains like a prisoner. Only a Speaker's chains weren't made of iron, but of the coils of responsibility, duty, protocol.

It was hard, very hard, to remain inside the arched bridges of Qualinost, just as it was hard to keep inside the walls of the increasingly lonely Speaker's house. Sometimes his thoughts were with Ulvian. Had he done right by his son? The prince's crime was heinous, but did it justify Kith-Kanan's harsh sentence?

Then he thought of Verhanna, probing every glade and clearing from Thorbardin to the Thon-Thalas River, seeking those whose crimes were the same as her brother's. Loyal, brave, serious Hanna, who never swerved from following an order.

Kith-Kanan rose from his bed and threw back the curtains from his window. It was long after midnight, by the water clock on the mantle, and the world outside was as dark as pitch. He could hear the bloody rain still falling. It seeped under window-sills and doors.

A name, long buried in his thoughts, surfaced. It was a name not spoken aloud for hundreds of years: "Anaya!"

Into the quiet darkness, he whispered the name of the Kagonesti woman who had been his first wife. It was as if she was in the room with him.

He knew she was not dead. No, Anaya lived on, might even manage to outlive Kith-Kanan. As her life's blood had flowed out of a terrible sword wound, Anaya's body had indeed died. But undergoing a mysterious, sublime transformation, Anaya the elf woman had become a fine young oak tree, rooted in the soil of the ancient Silvanesti forest she had lived in and guarded all her life. The forest was but a small manifestation of a larger, primeval force, the power of life itself.

The power—he could think of nothing else to call it—had come into existence out of the First Chaos. The sages of Silvanost, Thorbardin, and Daltigoth all agreed that the First Chaos, by its very randomness, accidentally gave birth to order, the Not-Chaos.

Only order makes life possible.

These things Kith-Kanan had learned through decades of studying side by side with the wisest thinkers of Krynn. Anaya had been a servant of the power, the only force older than the gods, protecting the last of the ancient forests remaining on the continent. When her time as guardian was ended, Anaya had become one with the forest. She had been carrying Kith-Kanan's child at the time.

Kith-Kanan's head hurt. He kneaded his temples with strong fingers, trying to dull the ache. His and Anaya's unborn son was a subject he could seldom bear to think about. Four hundred years had passed since last he'd heard Anaya's voice, and yet at times the pain of their parting was as fresh as it had been that golden spring day when he'd watched her warm skin roughen into bark, when he'd heard her speak for the final time.

The rain ended abruptly. Its cessation was so sudden and complete it jarred Kith-Kanan out of his deep thoughts. The last drop fell from the water clock. Three days of scarlet rain were over.

His sigh echoed in the bedchamber. What would be next? He wondered.

* * * * *

"Thank Astra that foul mess has stopped!" exclaimed Rufus. "I feel like the floor of a slaughterhouse, soaked in blood!"

"Oh, shut up. It wasn't real blood, just colored water," Verhanna retorted. For two days, in constant rain, they had tracked the elusive Kagonesti slavers with little result. The Kagonesti's trail had led west for a time, but suddenly it seemed to vanish completely. The crimson rain had ceased overnight, and the new day was bright and sunny, but Kith-Kanan's daughter was weary and saddle sore. The last thing she wanted to listen to was the kender complaining about his soggy clothes.

Rufus prowled ahead on foot, leading his oversized horse by the reins. He peered at every clump of grass, every fallen twig. "Nothing," he fumed. "It's as if they sprouted wings and flew away."

The sun was setting almost directly ahead of them, and Verhanna suggested they stop for the night.

Rufus dropped his horse's reins. "I'm for that! What's for dinner?"

She poked a hand into the haversack hung from the pommel of her saddle. "Dried apples, quith-pa, and hard-boiled eggs," Verhanna recited without enthusiasm. She tossed a cold, hard-boiled egg to her scout. He caught it with one hand, though he grumbled and screwed his face into a mask of disgust. She heard him mutter something about "the same eats, three times a day, forever" as he tapped the eggshell against his knee to crack it—then suddenly let it fall to the ground.

"Hey!" called Verhanna. "If you don't want it, say so. Don't throw it in the mud!"

"I smell roast pig!" he exulted, eyes narrow with concentration. "Not far away, either!" He vaulted onto his horse and turned the animal.

Verhanna flopped back the wet hood of her woolen cape and called, "Wait, Rufus! Stop!"

The reckless, hungry kender was not to be denied, however. With thumps of his spurless heels, he urged his horse through a line of silver-green holly, ignoring the jabs and scratches of the barbed leaves. Disgusted, Verhanna rode down the row of bushes, trying to find an opening. When she couldn't, she pulled her horse around and also plunged through the holly. Sharp leaf edges raked her unprotected face and hands.

"Ow!" she cried. "Rufus, you worthless toad! Where are you?"

Ahead, beyond some wind-tossed dogwoods, she spied the flicker of a campfire. Cursing the kender soundly, Verhanna rode toward the fire. The foolish kender didn't even have his short sword anymore. In the fight with the smoke creature, Rufus's blade had been broken.

Serve him right if it was a bandit camp, she thought angrily. Forty, no, fifty bloodthirsty villains, armed to the teeth, luring innocent victims in with their cooking smoke. Sixty bandits, yes, all of whom liked to eat stupid kender.

In spite of her ire, the captain kept her head and freed her sword from the leather loop that held it in its scabbard. No use barging in unprepared. Approaching the campfire obliquely, she saw shadowy figures moving around it. A horse whinnied. Clutching her reins tightly, Verhanna rode in, ready for a fight.

The first thing she saw was Rufus wolfing down chunks of steaming roast pork. Four elves dressed in rags and pieces of old blankets stood around the fire. By their light hair and chiseled features, she identified them as Silvanesti.

"Good morrow to you, warrior," said the male elf nearest Rufus. His accent and manner were refined, city-bred.

"May your way be green and golden," Verhanna replied. The

travelers didn't appear to be armed, but she remained on her horse just in case. "If I may ask, who are you, good traveler?"

"Diviros Chanderell, bard, at your service, Captain." The elf bowed low, so low that his sand-colored hair brushed the ground. Sweeping an arm around the assembled group, he added, "And this is my family."

Verhanna nodded to each of the others. The older, brown-haired female was Diviros's sister, Deramani. Sitting by the fire was a younger woman, the bard's wife, Selenara. Her thick hair, unbound, hung past her waist, and peeking shyly out from behind the honey-golden cascade was a fair-haired child. Diviros introduced him as Kivinellis, his son.

"We have come hither from Silvanost, city of a thousand white towers," said the bard with a flourish, "our fortunes to win in the new realm of the west."

"Well, you've a long way to go if Qualinost is your goal," Verhanna said.

"It is, noble warrior. Will you share meat with us? Your partner precedes you."

She dismounted, shaking her head at Rufus. He winked at her as Diviros's sister handed Verhanna a trencher of savory pork. The captain stabbed the cutlet with her knife and bit off a mouthful. It was good, sweet flesh, as only the Silvanesti could raise.

"What sets you wandering the lonely fields by night, Captain?" asked Diviros, once they were all comfortable around the campfire. He had a thin, expressive face and large amber eyes, which gave emphasis to his words.

"We're on an elf hunt," blurted Rufus between mouthfuls.

The bard's pale brows flew up. "Are you, indeed? Some dire brigand is haunting these environs?"

"Naw. They're a couple of woods elves wanted for slaving." Food had restored the kender's natural garrulousness. "They ambushed some of our warriors, then used magic to get away."

"Slavers? Magic? How strange!"

Rufus launched into an animated account of their adventures. Verhanna rolled her eyes, but only when Rufus nearly revealed Verhanna as the daughter of the Speaker of the Sun did she object.

"Mind your tongue," she snapped. She didn't want her parentage widely known. After all, traveling across the wild country with only a chatty kender for company, the princess of Qualinesti would make an excellent hostage for any bandit.

Planting his hands on his knees and glancing at his family, Diviros told his story in turn. "We, too, have seen wondrous things since leaving our homeland."

Rufus burped loudly. "Good! Tell us a story!"

Diviros beamed. He was in his element. His family sat completely still as all eyes fastened on him. He began softly. "Strange has been the path we have followed, my friends, strange and wonderful. On the day we left the City of a Thousand White Towers, a pall of darkness fell over the land. My beautiful Selenara was sore afraid."

The bard's wife blushed crimson, and she looked down at the tortoiseshell comb in her hand.

Diviros went on. "But I reasoned that the gods had draped this cloak of night over us for a purpose. And lo, the purpose was soon apparent. Warriors of the Speaker of the Stars had been turning back those who wished to leave the country. His Majesty feared the nation was losing too many of her sons and daughters to the westward migration, and he—but I digress. In any event, the strange darkness allowed us to slip by the warriors unseen."

"That was lucky," Verhanna said matter-of-factly.

"Lucky, noble warrior? 'Twas the will of the gods!" Diviros said ringingly, lifting a hand to heaven. "That it was so was shown five days later as we traversed the great southern forest amid a tempest of thunderbolts, for there we beheld a sight so strange the gods must have preserved us that we might be witness to it!"

Verhanna was growing weary of the bard's elaborate storytelling and showed it by sighing loudly. Rufus, however, was in awe of so spellbinding a speaker. "Go on, please!" he urged, a forkful of pork halted midway to his mouth.

Diviros warmed under the kender's intense regard. "We had stopped by a large pool of water to refresh ourselves. Such a beautiful spot, my little friend! Crystalline water in a green bower, surrounded by a snowy riot of blooming buds. Well, as we were all partaking of the icy cold liquid, a monstrously large bolt of lightning struck not a score of paces from us! The flash was brighter than the sun, and we were all knocked completely senseless.

"It was Selenara who roused first. She knows well the sound of a child in distress, and it was just such a sound that brought her awake—a mewling noise, a crying. My good wife wandered up the wooded hillside into a large meadow, and lo! there a great oak tree had been hit by the lightning, blasted into more splinters than there are stars in the heavens! Where the broad trunk had split open, she found the one who cried so piteously."

Diviros paused dramatically, gazing directly into Verhanna's impatient eyes. "It was a fully grown male elf!"

Rufus and his captain exchanged a look. Verhanna set aside her empty trencher and asked, "Who was it—some traveler sleeping under the tree when it was hit?"

The bard shook his head solemnly, and once more his voice was low and serious as he replied, "No, good warrior. It was clear that the fellow had been inside the tree and that the lightning had released him."

"Bleedin' dragons!" sighed the kender.

"My good spouse ran back to the pool and raised us from our stupor. I hurried to the shattered tree and beheld the strange elf. He was slick with blood, yet as my wife and sister washed him, there was not a cut, not even a scratch, anywhere on him. Moreover, there was an oval hollow in the tree, just large enough for him to have fitted in with his legs drawn up."

Verhanna snorted and waved a hand dismissively. "Look here," she said kindly, "that's quite a tall tale you've spun, bard, but don't carry on so hard that you begin to believe it yourself! You are a tale-spinner, after all, and a very good one. You almost had yourself convinced."

Diviros's mobile face showed only the briefest flash of annoyance. "Forgive me. I did not intend to deceive, only to relate to you the marvel we encountered in this elf who seemed born from a tree. If I offended, I apologize." He bowed again, but Kivinellis blurted, "Tell them about his hands!" Everyone stared at the child, and he retreated once more behind his mother's back. Rufus hopped up from the log he'd been sitting on.

"What about his hands?" asked the kender.

"They were discolored," Diviros said casually. "The elf's fingers, including his nails, were the color of summer grass." His tawny eyes darted to his son, and the quick look was not kind.

"What happened to the green-fingered elf?" Rufus wondered aloud.

"We cared for him a day or two, and then he wandered off on his own."

Verhanna detected a note of resistance in his voice. In spite of Rufus's obvious enjoyment of the story, the bard was suddenly reluctant to speak. The captain had never known a bard to be reticent before an attentive audience. She decided to press him. "Which way did this odd, green-fingered fellow go?"

There was a momentary hesitation, barely discernible, before Diviros answered, "South by west. We have not seen him since."

The Speaker's daughter stood. "Well, we thank you, good bard, for your tale. And for our dinner. We must be off now."

She tugged Rufus to his feet.

"But I haven't finished eating!" protested the kender.

"Yes, you have."

Verhanna hustled him to his horse and sprang to her own saddle. "Good luck to you!" she called to the family. "May your way be green and golden!"

In a moment, they'd left the group of elves staring in surprise after them.

Back on the trail, cloaked by the robe of night, Verhanna brought her horse to a stop. Rufus bounced up beside her. The kender was still babbling about their abrupt departure and the premature end of his meal.

"Forget your stomach," Verhanna ordered. "What did you make of that strange encounter?"

"They had good food," he said pointedly. When she raised a warning eyebrow, Rufus added hastily, "I thought the bard was all right, but the others were a little snooty. Of course, a lot of the elder folk are like that—your noble father excluded, my captain." He flashed an ingratiating smile.

"They were afraid of something," Verhanna said, lowering her voice and tapping her chin thoughtfully. "At first I thought it was us, but now I think they were afraid of Diviros."

The kender crinkled his nose. "Why would they be afraid of him?"

Verhanna wrapped her reins tightly around her fist. "I have an idea."

She turned her horse back toward the bard's campfire. "Get your knife out and follow me!" she ordered, putting her spurs to work.

Her ebony mount bolted through the underbrush, its heavy hooves thrashing loudly. Puzzled, Rufus turned his unwieldy animal after his captain, his heart pounding in excitement.

Verhanna burst into the little clearing in time to see Diviros shoving his small son into the back of one of their carts. The bard whirled, eyes wide in alarm. He reached under the cart and brought out a leaf-headed spear—hardly bardic equipment. Verhanna shifted her round buckler to catch the spear point and deflect it away. Diviros planted the heel of the spear shaft against his foot like an experienced soldier and stood while the mounted warrior charged toward him.

"Circle around them, Wart!" the captain cried before ducking her face behind the rim of her shield. Verhanna and Diviros were seconds from collision when the young elf boy stood up in the cart and hurled an earthenware pot at his father. The thick clay vessel thudded against Diviros's back. He dropped his spear and fell to his knees, gasping for air. Verhanna reined in her mount and presented the tip of her sword at his throat.

"Yield, in the name of the Speaker of the Sun!" she declared.

Diviros's head dropped down in dejection, and he spread his hands wide on the ground.

Rufus clattered up to the cart. The boy scrambled over the baggage and bounced up and down in front of the kender.

"You've saved us!" he cried joyously.

"What's going on here?" Rufus asked, his confusion evident. He looked up at Verhanna. "Captain, what in darkness is going on?"

"Our friend Diviros is a slaver." Verhanna prodded Diviros with her sword tip. "Aren't you?" The elf didn't answer.

"Yes!" the boy said. "He was taking us all to Ergoth to be sold into slavery!"

The two elf women were released from their cart, where Diviros had bound and gagged them. Gradually the whole story came out.

The Guards of the Sun, under Kith-Kanan's orders, had so disrupted the traffic of slaves from Silvanesti to Ergoth that slave dealers in both lands were resorting to ruses like this one. Small groups of slaves, disguised as settlers and held by one or two experienced drivers, were being sent on many different routes.

Verhanna ordered Diviros bound. The elf women did her bidding eagerly. Once the erstwhile bard was secured, Rufus approached her and said, "What do we do now, Captain? We can't keep trailing the Kagonesti with a prisoner and three civilians in tow."

Disappointment was written on Verhanna's face. She knew the kender was right, yet she burned to bring the crafty Kagonesti slavers to justice.

"We can resume the hunt," she said firmly. "Their trail was leading west, and we'll continue in that direction."

"What's in the west?"

"Pax Tharkas. We can turn Diviros over to my father's guards there. The captives will be taken care of, too."

She looked up into the starry sky. "I want those elves, Wart. They ambushed my soldiers and made a fool of me with their smoke phantom. I want them brought to justice!" She drove her mailed fist into her palm.

They bundled Diviros into one of the carts and set Deramani, the older elf woman, to watch him. The younger woman, Selenara, volunteered to drive their wagon. Rufus tied Diviros's horse to the other cart and climbed in beside Kivinellis. Once Verhanna was mounted, she led the caravan out of the clearing and headed west.

The elf boy told Rufus and Verhanna that he was actually an orphan from the streets of Silvanost. Then he proceeded to shower them with questions about Qualinesti, Qualinost, and the Speaker of the Sun. He'd heard tales of Kith-Kanan's exploits in the Kinslayer War, but since the schism between East and West, even the mention of Kith-Kanan's name was frowned upon in Silvanesti.

Verhanna told him all he wanted to know—except that she was the daughter of the famous Speaker.

Then Rufus posed a question to Kivinellis. "Hey, was that story about the elf coming out of the tree true?" he asked.

"Don't be ridiculous," put in Verhanna. "Diviros was lying, playing the part of a bard."

"Oh, no, no!" said the boy urgently. "It was true! The green-fingered elf appeared just as he said!"

"Well, what happened to him?" queried the kender.

"Diviros tried to feed him a potion in order to steal his will so he could sell him in Ergoth as a slave. But the potion had no effect on him! In the night, while we all slept, the green-fingered one vanished!"

Verhanna shrugged. "I don't believe it," she muttered.

The red moon, Lunitari, set at midnight. The freed slaves slept in the carts, but Verhanna and Rufus remained awake, and the caravan continued to move west through the night.

The Black Amulet

7

"Clear away, clear away there! Do you want to be mashed to jelly? Get out!" The dwarf overseer, Lugrim, bellowed down at one of the workers pushing a granite block ten feet long, eight feet wide, and six feet high. It didn't help the grunt gang that the rotund dwarf stood on top of the block, adding his own weight to their overall burden. The block was sliding slowly down an earthen ramp. Other workers, human and half-human boys, skipped back and forth in front of the stone, sweeping the wave of displaced dirt out of the way with shovels and rakes. Theirs was a dangerous job; the block could not be stopped once in motion, and if the boys got caught or fell while sweeping, the stone would crush them. Only the most nimble worked as sweepers. Ulvian was embedded in a mass of sweating, straining bodies, his hands flat on the block and his bare toes dug into the dirt. The red rain had stopped just two days before. Its remains were evident all over Pax Tharkas in the form of crimson puddles, and now the damp soil gripped like glue. Five days he had been at Pax Tharkas. Five days of exhaustion, toil, and fear.

"Push, you laggards!" Lugrim exhorted. "My old mother could push harder than you!"

"I knew your mother," Dru shot back quickly, face to the ground as he strained. "Her breath could move solid rock!"

The overseer turned and glared in the direction from which the voice had come. A squat fellow, even by dwarven standards, he could barely see over his thick, fur-wrapped belly. "Who said that?" he demanded, his eyes darting over the gang.

"All together, lads," grunted Splint. As one, the convicts gave a hard, sudden shove. The block slid forward, skewing to the left. The dwarf atop the stone lost his footing and toppled over the side. He let out a loud "oof!" and lay stunned. The block ground inexorably onward.

Merith appeared, elegantly clad in burnished armor and a fur mantle, his fair hair clean and neatly combed. Helping the fallen dwarf to his feet, he asked, "Are you all right?"

"Aye." Lugrim braced his arms against his back and winced, then turned ponderously to face the grunt gang, who were watching him. "You think you're clever, don't you, scum?"

"Yes, Master Lugrim," they replied in unison, sing-songing their words like naughty children.

Merith easily picked out Ulvian in the crowd of twenty convicts. The prince didn't meet his glance but kept his legs driving forward in the blood-colored mud. In spite of his growing blond beard, the marks of his beating by Splint still showed. Gossip had told Merith what happened, but the warrior refused to intervene. Kith-Kanan's son had hard lessons to learn if he was to survive.

Below the pinnacle where Merith stood, the two square tower keeps that were the innermost defense of the fortress rose to unequal heights. Construction on the west tower was farther along than on the east. Its parapets were already in place. From this distance, Merith could see tiny figures walking on them and on the great wall that connected the two towers.

The camp was situated in the valley behind the fortress. In front of the citadel, farther down the pass, two curtain walls had been erected as the first lines of defense against any attacker. Tall, single gates of hammered bronze were the only openings in the walls. They stood open now, propped apart by huge timber balks. Workers and artisans poured in and out like streams of ants around a bowl of fruit.

Looking down on all this, Merith could well believe the completion of Pax Tharkas was not far away. A year, perhaps less. Feldrin Feldspar had done a magnificent job, building the citadel not only quickly but also well.

The night before, the master builder had shown him detailed drawings of the underground galleries that were being hollowed out of the mountainside beneath each tower. Enough food and water to last for years could be stored there, making Pax Tharkas resistant to any siege. An elaborate throne room, suitable for either the King of Thorbardin or the Speaker of the Sun, was also being constructed. Details such as these might take a few more years to finish, but the basic fortress would be ready to occupy much sooner than that.

A shadow fell across Merith; a cloud had covered the sun. As he turned from his study of the fortress, tiny particles peppered his face, and he inhaled grit. Vibrations tingled the soles of his shoes. It was an odd, tickling sensation, and Merith shifted his weight, looking down at his boots. Then he became aware of a deep humming sound, like the bass drums the priests of E'li sometimes played during festivals. The dust cloud was thickening. Below, workers scrambled in confusion.

"Landslide!" someone shouted.

Merith whirled and saw behind and to his left what he had only felt before. Boulders and rain-soaked chunks of wet soil were rolling down the east face of the mountain. Paralyzed, the elf warrior could only stare in amazement as tons of rock and dirt hurtled toward the quarries in the high pass. The noise increased to a deafening roar, and the ground shook so that he lost his footing and fell.

Screams filled the air, piercing the thunder of the avalanche. Merith rolled about like a pea shaken in its pod. He clawed at the stony earth, trying to keep his balance.

The landslide hit the pass. Rock chips and boulders flew, crushing everything they hit. Merith watched helplessly as a huge stone bowled over half a dozen quarry workers. A pall of reddish dust descended over the scene. The roar faded. The sobbing of the terrified and injured was everywhere.

"Help!" A loud cry sliced through the moans of the injured and dying. "Help, somebody! Help me!"

Merith stumbled to his feet and ran down the earthen ramp. The overseer was lying on the path on this side of the block. The convicts had scattered, as had the sweeper boys. Merith knelt beside the dwarf. Lugrim had an ugly, bleeding gash on his forehead. His heart beat strongly, however, so the elf warrior knew he was only knocked unconscious.

"Help, in the names of the gods! The stone is moving!" The shout came again, nearer this time. Merith looked up and caught his breath in a gasp. The severe vibrations from the landslide had twisted the path of the granite block. It was teetering on the edge of the ramp, and people lay prostrate in the very shadow of the rock.

Merith left the dwarf where he lay. A few paces closer, he saw two gang members close to the block. One was a Silvanesti he didn't know; the other was Prince Ulvian. The prince's pant leg was caught under the block! The granite had run over his trailing hem and was dragging him along. Only one of his comrades remained behind to help him.

"Merithynos! Help me!" screamed Ulvian. He kicked vainly at the huge stone with his left leg. His other was hard against the

610

rock. The block crept forward on its own, driven by the slope of the ramp and its skewed position. In another yard or two, it would be far enough off the ramp that it would topple over on its side. Anything or anyone in its way would be crushed.

Merith and the Silvanesti pulled on Ulvian's arms, trying to tear him free. The prince's forester clothing was made of deerhide and was very tough. The warrior drew his knife and sawed at the leather. Too slow, too slow!

"Do something!" Ulvian pleaded, tears streaking his face.

"I'm trying, Your Highness!" Merith replied. The other elf stiffened for a moment, staring at Merith.

The lieutenant sawed harder at the deerhide and finally succeeded in making a small slit.

The block ground a sweeper's broom into the stony ramp. The crushing sound of the wooden handle being pulverized sent fresh paroxysms of terror through the prince. "Please don't let me die!" he groaned piteously. "Save me, Merith, Dru!"

The enormous cube of granite wobbled on the edge of the ramp. Merith cursed and tore at the leather pants with his hands. Ulvian's lower body already hung over the rim of the ramp, while he was pinned on his back.

The Silvanesti, Dru, grabbed Merith by his cloak and dragged him away. "Go to the tent of Feldrin Feldspar," he shouted at the warrior's horrified face. "Get the onyx ring he keeps on a thong around his neck!" When Merith continued to regard him with utter incomprehension, Dru shook him and roared, "Go now, if you hope to save your royal charge!"

Merith scrambled up the ramp and sprinted toward the master builder's tent. Mobs of dazed workers clustered around it, seeking Feldrin's attention. Merith had to whip out his sword in order to convince them to part to let him through.

Feldrin stood at the door of his hut, a cold wet cloth pressed to his head. He took it away and dipped it in a bowl of fresh water. There was a goose-egg-size bruise over his left eye.

"Quick! Give me the ring!" Merith demanded.

"What?" rumbled Feldrin. Merith thrust a hand into the dwarf's collar and found the onyx ring on a thong, just as Dru had said. It was made of black crystal, slightly larger than a finger ring, square cut, with odd glyphs engraved around the edge. Just then a shriek pierced the air. Merith yanked the ring from Feldrin's neck and took off at a run. The master builder bellowed for him to stop.

If the prince dies, it will be my fault, Merith thought desperately. Not only Ulvian, but also perhaps the entire dynasty of the House of Silvanos might come to an end under that block of gray stone. Dru was a few feet from the block, kneeling, his eyes mere slits, his hands clasped around the four-inch-long cylinder of onyx he constantly carried with him. Ulvian was calling out to the gods, begging for a merciful, quick death. As Merith approached, he saw the near end of the stone begin to lift off the ramp, about to topple over.

"Here!" he cried, thrusting the black crystal ring into Dru's fingers. The elf's eyes snapped open. Not even the terror of the moment could overcome Merith's shock at seeing the Silvanesti's eyes. They were solid black, with no white at all.

Dru took the ring from the thong and fitted the cylinder of onyx into its center hole. The result was an object that looked very much like a child's top-indeed, Dru balanced the two onyx pieces on the tip of the cylinder and removed his hand. The piece didn't topple over, but instead began to spin. All by itself.

A roaring filled Merith's ears. The air above the spinning top coalesced into a tight vortex, like a miniature whirlwind. Dust whirled and spun, caught up by the racing air. Dru rose to his feet and walked straight into the vortex. Merith, trying vainly to shield his face from the flying grit, was pressed backward. Invisible hands shoved him to his knees and then onto his back. It was as if lumps of stone had been laid across his chest. He could barely move his head, and his breath came in ragged gasps.

Through a haze of flying dirt, Merith saw Dru step up to the granite block and, with his bare hands, turn it over! The black-eyed elf simply grasped the lower edge of the stone and lifted it, with no more strain than shifting an empty barrel. The block slammed down on the ramp. Ulvian was saved!

Dimly Merith saw figures move past him. Feldrin Feldspar, walking jerkily, slowly, went straight to where the onyx top still rotated. The dwarf pulled a sparkling silver cloth from a small leather pouch and dropped it on the top.

Instantly the tremendous magical force dissipated. Blessed air filled Merith's lungs with a rush. His straining muscles, freed from the terrible force, slackened, and he lay limply on the ground. Through a pounding headache, he discovered a dampness on his face that proved to be a nosebleed. Painfully he sat up.

Armed overseers seized Dru and shoved him to the ground. A large wooden fork was thrust around his neck, pinning him to the dirt. Ulvian dragged himself to the elf who had saved his life and demanded in a weak voice that Dru be released.

"That cannot be done," Feldrin said, grimly surveying the area. "He could slay us all."

Workers and artisans had gathered in a crowd around the scene. Feldrin bent down and scooped up the silver cloth and onyx top, being careful to keep the black crystals wrapped in the shiny covering. Merith hauled himself to his feet and stood swaying.

"Come with me" Feldrin told him. "The rest of you, return to your tents! The healers will come and tend to your injuries!"

Feeling quite battered, Merith sluggishly followed Feldrin back to his tent. The master builder put the onyx pieces and silver cloth in a small golden box and locked it. Then he poured the grateful lieutenant a mug of Qualinesti nectar. Merith gulped it down.

"That was a very dangerous thing you did," Feldrin said, crossing his powerful arms over his broad chest.

The room still seemed to Merith to be spinning like the magical onyx top, and he put a hand to his head. "I don't understand," he protested.

"That elf is Drulethen, the infamous sorcerer. For fifty years, he ruled a portion of the Kharolis Mountains from his hidden keep, and he used his terrible magic to kill and enslave anyone who passed by. Finally, the King of Thorbardin led an expedition of elves and dwarves against him. The clerics managed to defeat his spells only with great difficulty, but the warriors were finally able to storm the keep and take him prisoner."

Merith's mug was empty, and Feldrin refilled it. "It was discovered that his power was chiefly invested in a simple onyx amulet. When that was taken away, he was powerless. We didn't know about the other piece of onyx. Drulethen must've kept it hidden for just such an occasion."

The nectar was sweet and strong. It sent strength coursing through Merith's veins as his head cleared. "But—he saved the prince!"

Feldrin sighed gustily. "Yes, thank Reorx! I don't know why he did it, but I can't fault his deed."

"Why don't you destroy the amulet? Or send it to Thorbardin, or somewhere else where Dru can't possibly get at it?"

Feldrin smote the table top with his fist. "That's the trouble! We can't! My king originally took the ring to his palace in Thorbardin. While it was in his possession, he was so wracked by illness and his sleep so tormented by dreadful nightmares that in desperation he sent it back to me." The master builder lowered his voice, though they were alone in the tent. "You see, my friend, the amulet is alive. It sometimes talks to mortals, and indeed there are those who say it was fashioned by the Queen of Darkness herself. It cannot be destroyed. Only the silver cloth can confine it once its power has been unleashed."

Merith asked about the cloth. "One of the most sacred relics of my people," Feldrin informed him. "No less than a scrap of hide from the Silver Dragon, the same one who loved and fought with the great human warrior Huma Dragonsbane."

This revelation stunned the already woozy Merith. "By the gods," he breathed. "I had no idea who or what I was dealing with! My only thought was to save the prince!"

"No harm done, young warrior." Feldrin put a hand on Merith's shoulder. "The Speaker of the Sun and the King of Thorbardin made a bargain to put the evil Drulethen to work. Personally, I would have struck his head off, but my royal master believes he can use the sorcerer's knowledge for his own benefit, and the great and wise Kith-Kanan thinks he can actually reform Drulethen!" Feldrin shook his head. "The Speaker is always trying to improve his enemies."

"Aye," Merith agreed. "Ofttimes I have heard him say, 'I used to kill my foes; now I make them my friends. A warrior needs as few enemies as possible, but a Speaker needs as many friends as he can make.' "

* * * * *

The barracks were quiet, save for the coughs of sleeping grunt gang members trying to expel the dust they'd breathed all day. Ulvian lay on his side, wide awake. Aside from some scrapes and an aching right leg, he was essentially unharmed by his brush with death, yet he could not sleep. Over and over he replayed the scene—the block teetering above him, Dru pushing it aside with his bare hands, the awesome presence of the power in the black crystal.

The prince sat up, wincing as his wrenched muscles protested. He padded on bare feet to Dru's bed. Peering through the darkness, the prince realized his savior was not lying down but sitting with his knees drawn up to his smooth chin.

"Dru?" he whispered. "I need to talk to you."

"If you answer one question for me. Are you in truth the son of Speaker Kith-Kanan?" Ulvian admitted he was. "I knew the Speaker had some half-human children," Dru, said softly. A gruff voice nearby rumbled a demand for silence. The sorcerer rose and took Ulvian by the arm. He led the prince to the relatively open area by the water barrel, where they could talk more freely.

"I won't forget your deed," Ulvian began.

"I should hope not." Dru said dryly. He smiled, his teeth showing white in the darkness. "We are a natural pair of allies, are we not? A prince and a sorcerer, both sentenced to labor on this ridiculous mausoleum, both required to hide their true identities."

Dru lifted a dipperful of water to his lips. Once he'd taken a long drink, he asked, "What did you do to end up in such a place,

Your Highness? Why did your infamously just father send you here to work like a dog?"

With some hemming and hawing, Ulvian explained his activities as a slave trader.

"It was a harmless diversion," he insisted. "A few wealthy traders approached me and asked for my patronage. I had influence and knew warriors who could be bribed to look the other way. It was a mere lark, an adventure to keep boredom at bay, but my enemies in Qualinost used my capture as an excuse to exile me!" His voice rose until Dru had to quiet him. "I will reclaim what is rightfully mine," the prince finished darkly. "I will fulfill my destiny!"

Dru squatted and began to idly trace elaborate designs in the dirt floor. Curving lines, loops, and squares took shape. "What enemies do you have, my prince? Who are they?"

Ulvian hunkered down across from his friend and said, "There is my sister, Verhanna, for one. The old castellan, Tamanier Ambrodel, thinks I'm immoral and wicked, and his son, General Lord Kemian Ambrodel, believes he is better suited to be Speaker than I. There is an old Kagonesti senator, Irthenie by name, who—"

"I see."

Dru brushed the designs away with his hand. "I think we should make common cause, Your Highness. Your father and the king of the dwarves put me here. I've had to keep my true identity hidden because some of the elves and dwarves we work alongside would kill me if they knew who I really was." The sorcerer thrust his face close to Ulvian's. "Together we can escape this place and regain the power and position we are destined to have."

"Escape?" Ulvian echoed weakly. "I—I can't. My father will declare me an outlaw if I flee the country."

"Who said anything about fleeing the country? You and I will go to Qualinost. There must be nobles, senators, and clerics who favor you, my prince. We'll rally them round you and demand a pardon. What do you say?"

Ulvian rubbed his palms together. Despite the cool mountain air, his hands were damp with sweat. "I—I don't know," he said faintly. Much as he loathed his current situation, the prince realized that such a plan was risky at best. "When would we leave?" Ulvian asked hesitantly.

"This very night," Dru said, and Ulvian actually started at the abrupt words. "Both parts of my amulet are in camp. We can break into Feldrin's tent and get them. Then no power within a hundred miles can stop us."

The prince sank back slowly on his haunches. Bracing himself with his hands, he said, "Feldrin won't just hand—"

"With your help, I'll kill the old stonebreaker," the sorcerer snapped.

"No." Ulvian stood up, looking around nervously. "I can't do that. I can't murder Feldrin. I plan to be vindicated and pardoned. I won't murder my way to freedom."

Dru stood and shrugged expressively. "As you wish, my prince. I've been here for many years, you only a short time. After you've broken your back working on this damn fortress for a while longer, perhaps you'll change your mind."

Ulvian was about to reply when Dru's head suddenly snapped around, as if he'd heard a strange noise. He held up one hand to forestall Ulvian's words. "Wait," he said. "Something's amiss."

Ulvian followed the sorcerer to one of the two windows in the barracks. It seemed brighter outside than it should be this late at night. As they watched, it grew brighter still. The outline of the camp became clearer. Silhouetted tents gained distinct features. To Ulvian's astonishment, the sun appeared in the sky directly overhead. At first, only a faint red glow was visible, but then it blazed more and more brilliantly until the mountain pass was bathed in the full light of noon.

"What—what's happening?" Ulvian cried, shading his squinting eyes from the sudden glare.

Dru stroked his dirty, pointed chin. "Someone is tampering with the balance of nature," he said coolly. "Someone—or something—very powerful."

Men and dwarves emerged from their huts to stare at the bright sky and scratch their heads in wonderment. By the water clocks, it was still two hours till sunrise, yet sunlight flooded the tents.

* * * * *

Dust from the landslide tinted the sky over the Kharolis Mountains rusty red. The gritty fog hung in the still air, unmoving. The day after the avalanche, the sun burned like an orange ball through the haze. It hung fixed at the peak of the heavens. As measured by notched candles and water clocks, several hours had passed, yet the sun had never budged.

"Master Lugrim, what o'clock is it?" called Ulvian to the overseer, whose face was hidden by a dripping dipper of cool water.

Lugrim poured the last few drops on his brow, which was already wet with sweat. "Nigh time to work again," he growled. "Are you men or camels? How much do you plan to drink?"

"I'm no man," Splint said acidly, "and I'll drink how I please."

" 'Tis fearful hot," added a human named Brunnar in a thick Ergothic accent.

Six hours had passed since the sun's abrupt appearance, and the temperature had been growing steadily warmer. The air was unusually dead; no breeze wafted through the pass, and no clouds shielded the workers from the sun. Only the ever-present dust diffused the sunlight, coating the workers' sweltering bodies.

At Feldrin Feldspar's hut, a crowd of overseers and guild masters had formed. There was much debate over the strange sunrise. Some in the group insisted that work be halted until the heat abated, while others argued that work should continue.

"Our covenant with the Speaker of the Sun calls for us to work till sunset," the chief mason complained. "We must honor our pledge."

"Our people can't work forever," objected the leader of the carpenters' guild.

"Quiet, you shortsighted fools!" rumbled Feldrin, waving his hands over his head. "The sun hasn't moved for hours. Merciful Reorx! A calamity is upon us, and you quibble about schedules and quotas!"

The overseers and masters lapsed into embarrassed silence. Merith appeared and stood on the fringe of the crowd. He'd shed his armor in the heat and wore a lightweight white tunic and baggy gray trousers.

"This must be yet another of the wonders," said the elf warrior. "Like the darkness, the lightning, and the scarlet rain."

That set off a fresh wave of contention in the group. Feldrin let them argue a while, then shouted for quiet again.

The chief mason wailed, "What are we to do!"

"Collect all the fresh water you can," ordered Feldrin. "Fill every pot and jar in Pax Tharkas. Tell the sewing women to make canopies—very large canopies. We will erect them over the quarry walls to shade the workers."

The master builder loosened his fur mantle and let it fall to the ground. "Let it be done. And tell everyone to get rid of his heavy garments!"

"Do we resume work?" asked Lugrim.

"In two hours, by the water clock."

Feldrin's assistants dispersed to carry out his bidding. The trumpets blew, signaling an end to work, and every worker in the pass hurried indoors, out of the broiling sun. Feldrin and Merith watched the teeming site become a ghost fortress in a matter of minutes. The last people in sight were the dwarves who had been working on the parapet of the west tower. They secured their hoist and winch, then ducked inside the massive stone structure. For some time after that, the hoist swung to and fro, the block and tackle creaking loudly.

The sight of the sun-baked, lifeless fortress bothered the master builder. It was unnerving. In a gloomy tone, he said as much to the lieutenant.

"Why so, my lord?" asked Merith, surprised.

"The other marvels were like conjurer's tricks—they seemed mysterious and impressive, but they were essentially harmless. This is different. A few days of unrelieved sun could be the end of us all."

Feldrin dabbed sweat from his brow with the sleeve of his yellow linen shirt. "I can't help but wonder who has the power to do this. Who can stop the course of the sun itself through the sky?"

"Drulethen?" the lieutenant suggested.

"Certainly not," Feldrin said firmly. "Even if he possessed both halves of his evil talisman, he could never do such a thing." The dwarf shook his head. "I wonder if even the gods themselves . . ."

"Nothing is beyond the gods," Merith replied reverently.

"Perhaps. Perhaps."

The dwarf picked up his discarded cloak and draped it over one arm. Already his salt-and-pepper hair was clinging to his damp face. With a sigh, he said, "I shall retire indoors now. Can't have my brain getting scrambled in this blasted sun."

"A wise notion, master. I shall do likewise."

Elf and dwarf parted company. Merith crossed the winding road to the fortress site alone, the only living thing moving through the entire construction site. Overhead, the hoist continued to sway and creak. The lieutenant thought it a mournful, lonely sound.

Greenhands

8

Midnight in Qualinost was as bright as any noon. There had been no night at all for two days, and the heat was appalling. Half the public fountains in the city had dried up during the first twenty-four-hour period of the strange daylight. The people of Qualinost filled the courtyards of the great temples, begging the priests and priestesses to intercede on their behalf with the gods. Incense burned and chants rose to the heavens, but the sun burned mercilessly on.

The water clock in the chamber of the Thalas-Enthia showed it was midnight, yet the senators of Qualinesti were all present. Seated in his place of honor on the north side of the circular room, Kith-Kanan listened to the representatives of the people debate the series of marvels they had experienced, including the current dangerous manifestation. Many of the senators bore the signs of lack of slumber; not only were their duties pressing in this time of crisis, but the lack of night made it difficult for many in Qualinost to sleep.

"Clearly we have offended the gods," Senator Xixis said, "though I have no knowledge of what the offense could have been. I propose that offerings be made at once, and that they be continued until these plagues cease."

"Hear! Hear!" murmured a group of senators sitting on the western side of the chamber. These were known as the Loyalists, because they were loyal to the old traditions of Silvanesti, especially in matters of religion and royalty. Most of the full-blooded elven senators were members of this extremely conservative faction.

Clovanos, senior senator of the Loyalists, descended from his seat to the floor. The Thalas-Enthia met in a squat, round tower, larger in diameter than even the Tower of the Sun, though far less tall. The floor of the meeting chamber was covered with a mosaic map of the country, exactly like the more famous and larger map in the Hall of the Sky. High on the wall, near the ceiling, more mosaics ringed the chamber. These were the crests of all the great clans of Qualinesti.

Clovanos held out his hand to his friend Xixis, and the latter handed him the speaking baton. A rod twenty inches long made of ivory and gold, the baton was passed to whomever was addressing the Thalas-Enthia.

Resting the baton in the crook of his left arm, a signal that he intended to speak at length, Senator Clovanos scanned the assembly. The so-called New Landers sat on the east side of the chamber. They were a loose association of humans, half-humans, Kagonesti, and dwarves who favored new traditions, ones that reflected their mixed society. On the south wall was the middle-of-the-road group that had come to be known as the Speaker's Friends, people like Senator Irthenie, who preferred to follow the personal leadership of Kith-Kanan.

"My friends," Clovanos finally began, "I must agree with the learned Xixis. From the strange and terrifying wonders that have been visited upon our helpless world, it is quite obvious that a grave offense has been committed, an offense against the natural order of life, against the gods themselves. Now they seek to punish us. Our priests have divined and meditated; our people have prayed; we ourselves have debated continuously. All to no avail. No one can determine why this should be so. However, very recently I received some information—information that enabled me to ascertain what the dreadful sacrilege was."

A buzz of speculation swept the chamber in the wake of Clovanos's words. The senator allowed it to continue for a moment, then said, "The knowledge came to me from a strange place—a place close to the hearts of the Speaker's Friends."

"Speak up. I can't hear you," Irthenie droned mockingly. A scattering of laughter among the New Landers and Friends made Clovanos's heat-reddened face grow even more florid.

"My information came from Pax Tharkas," he said loudly, facing the calm Kagonesti woman, "that folly of a fortress the Speaker puts so much faith in."

"Get on with it! Tell us what you know!" chorused several impatient senators.

Clovanos brandished the baton. The cries declined. "I received a letter from a friend and fellow Loyalist," he said with heavy emphasis, "who happens to be at the site of the fortress. He wrote, 'Imagine my surprise when I saw the Speaker's son, Prince Ulvian, working as a common laborer in the crudest and most dangerous of jobs.' "

Having thus spoken, Clovanos turned quickly to face Kith-Kanan. The chamber erupted. New Landers and Loyalists stood and shouted at each other. Denunciations flew in the thick, hot air. Only the Speaker's Friends sat quietly, waiting for Kith-Kanan to deny the report.

Slowly, with great deliberation, the Speaker rose and crossed the floor to where Clovanos had turned to hurl retorts at the ranks of New Landers seated above him. He tapped on the senator's shoulder and asked for the baton. Clovanos had no choice but to surrender the speaking symbol to Kith-Kanan. Stiffly, his face sheened with sweat, the Silvanesti senator climbed the marble steps to his place among the Loyalists.

Kith-Kanan held the baton over his head until the room grew still. Bare to the waist in the dreadful heat, his tanned chest bore pale scars from wounds he'd received in the great Kinslayer War. A simple white kilt, a wide golden belt, and leather sandals were all he wore, save for the circlet of Qualinost atop his head. Though past midlife, his face growing more lined, the white blond of his hair now more than half silver, the Speaker of the Sun was still as vibrant and handsome as he had been centuries earlier when he led his people out of Silvanesti.

"My lords," Kith-Kanan said in a firm voice, "what Senator Clovanos tells you is true."

The chamber grew so quiet that a falling feather would have rung out like a gong. After Clovanos's longwinded oration, the Speaker's simple statement seemed blunt and harsh. "My son is indeed working as a slave at Pax Tharkas."

Xixis leapt to his feet. "Why?" he shouted.

Kith-Kanan turned slowly to face the senator. "Because he was taken during the campaign to stamp out slave-trading and found guilty of helping such traders cross Qualinesti territory."

Malvic Pathfinder, a human and a New Lander, called out, "I thought the penalty for slave-trading was death."

A dozen Loyalists booed him.

"No father wishes to sentence his own son to the block," Kith-Kanan replied frankly. "Ulvian's guilt was plain, but instead of a useless death, I decided to teach him a lesson in compassion. I believed, and still believe, that once he had experienced the wretched life of a slave, he would never again be able to look upon people as cattle that can be bought and sold."

Kith-Kanan's well-muscled frame might have been carved from

wood or marble. His proud and noble countenance was so over-powering that no one spoke for some time.

Finally Irthenie broke the silence. "Great Speaker, how long will Prince Ulvian be held at Pax Tharkas?" she asked. Her words, spoken with quiet force, carried to every bench in the chamber.

"He remains at my discretion," Kith-Kanan replied, facing her.

"It is wrong!" Clovanos countered. "A prince of the blood should not be forced to work as a slave by his own father! This is the offense the gods are punishing us for!" The other Loyalists took up his refrain. The chamber echoed with their outraged cries.

"Your Majesty, will you recall the prince?" asked Xixis.

"I will not. He has been there only a few weeks," Kith-Kanan answered. "If I freed him now, the only lesson he would have learned is that influence is stronger than virtue."

"But he is your heir!" insisted Clovanos.

Kith-Kanan gripped the speaking baton tightly, his other hand clenched into a fist. "It is my decision!" he replied, his voice ringing through the chamber. "Not yours!"

All the arguments and accusations ceased abruptly. Kith-Kanan's blazing gaze was fastened on the unfortunate Clovanos. The senator, his body quivering with anger, stared balefully down at his sovereign. Breaking the tense silence, Xixis said unctuously, "We are naturally concerned for the safety and future of the royal house. Your Majesty has no other heir."

"Your time, my lords, would be better spent finding ways to soothe the troubles of the common folk, and not interfering with the manner in which I discipline my son!" Kith-Kanan turned on his heel, strode to the door, and departed.

Since the Speaker had taken the baton with him, that meant the Thalas-Enthia session was over. The senators filled the aisles, clustering in small groups to discuss Kith-Kanan's stand.

There was no debate between Clovanos and Xixis. The two elves were in complete agreement.

"The Speaker will ruin the country," breathed Xixis anxiously. "His stubbornness has already offended the gods. Does he think he can stand against their will? It will mean the end of us all!"

"He has already cost me plenty," Clovanos agreed. He couldn't forget the loss of his towers during the siege of lightning. "If only we could come up with some alternate plan."

The din in the chamber was considerable. Xixis leaned closer to his ally. "What do you mean?" he asked.

"I can't speak in certainties," Clovanos replied, his words barely audible, "but suppose the fortress is finished before the Speaker decides the prince has been rehabilitated? Kith-Kanan has sworn to retire once Pax Tharkas is done; if Prince Ulvian is still under a cloud, another candidate must be found."

Xixis's mouse-colored hair was limp with perspiration, and his flowing robe clung to his clammy skin. Blotting his face with one sleeve, his eyes darted around. No one was listening to them.

"Who, then?" he hissed. "Not that dragon of a daughter!"

Clovanos sneered. "Even the open-minded people of Qualinesti would balk at having a half-human female as Speaker of the Sun! No, listen. You are familiar with the name Lord Kemian Ambrodel?" Xixis nodded. Lord Ambrodel was a prominent figure. "He is pure Silvanesti in heritage and a notable warrior."

"But he is not of House Silvanos!" Xixis cried, and Clovanos shushed him.

"That's the beauty of my plan, my friend. If we begin a campaign to have Lord Ambrodel named as the Speaker's heir, then His Majesty will feel compelled to recall Prince Ulvian from Pax Tharkas."

Xixis regarded his companion blankly.

"Don't you see?" Clovanos went on. "Publicly the Speaker may denounce his son as a failure, a weak and cruel rogue who deals in slaves. However, Kith-Kanan won't deny his own family. He cannot, any more than he could have had Ulvian executed. No, the Speaker, for all his harsh words, wants only his own son, the direct descendant of the great Silvanos, to ascend the throne of Qualinesti. If we agitate for another heir, it will force the Speaker's hand. He must recall the prince!"

Xixis didn't seem convinced. "I have known the Speaker for two hundred years," he said. "I fought with him in the great war. Kith-Kanan will do what he thinks is right, not what's best for his family."

Clovanos rose to go, smoothing his pale hair back from his face. Xixis stood also. Linking his arm in the arm of Xixis, Clovanos murmured sagely, "We'll see, my friend. We'll see."

* * * * *

"This air is like dragon's breath!" complained Rufus, sagging on the seat of the cart. Beside him rode Verhanna on her coal-black horse, and behind the kender creaked the other cart containing the freed slaves. Two days had passed, and the sun had burned continuously for a day and a half now.

"Have some water," Verhanna suggested, licking her dry lips. She passed her waterskin to the kender. He put the spout to his lips and drank deeply. "How far do you think we've ridden?" she asked. Without the moons or stars to go by, or even the passage of the sun across the sky, they'd lost track of what hour or day it was.

Rufus pondered her question. His scouting skills had grown fuzzy in the constant daylight and mounting heat. "A horse can walk forty miles a day," he said slowly. His freckled face screwed itself into a fearsome frown. "But how long is a day when the sun doesn't shift and the stars don't shine?" He shook his small head, lashing his damp topknot from side to side. "I don't know! Is there anything more to drink?" The waterskin was drained.

Verhanna sighed and admitted there was no more water. She'd shed her armor and cloak and was down to wearing a thin white shirt and divided kilt. Her elven heritage was ever more apparent in her long limbs and pale skin. The subtle influence of her human blood showed in her figure, more muscular than any elven woman.

"Any problems back there?" she called over her shoulder. The boy, Kivinellis, and the elf woman, Deramani, sprawled atop a mound of loose baggage in the second cart, waved listlessly from their perch. Selenara, driving the cart, was too weary even to acknowledge Verhanna's call. Diviros himself was propped up in the first cart, driven by Rufus, and his hands and feet were still tied, a gag in his mouth.

No trace of the Kagonesti slavers had turned up during their drive west. Verhanna had resigned herself to the fact that they had lost the slavers. Nevertheless, she felt a strong sense of responsibility for the former slaves in her care. Rufus, however, insisted he might still recover their trail. Ahead lay the Astradine River, and the Kagonesti would have to cross it. There was no bridge, the kender recalled, just privately owned ferries. Someone would have seen the Kagonesti. Someone would remember them.

They rode on, their heads nodding as they drifted in and out of heat-fogged sleep. The forest around them was unnaturally quiet. Even the birds and beasts were oppressed by the heat.

As he bobbed along, the kender dreamed he was back in the snow-capped peaks of the Magnet Mountains, where the captain had first found him. In his mind, he climbed the highest slopes and threw himself down into the drifted snow. How good it felt! How sweet the wind was, how fresh the clear, cold air! The gods themselves knew no kinder home than the peaks of the Magnets.

No one had any business screaming in such a peaceful place.

A drop of sweat slid down Rufus's nose. He batted it away. Ah, to shiver as the chill air brought gooseflesh to his bare arms! The brilliance of the valley below . . . Screaming?

He forced his eyes open as the sound came again. Verhanna was also drowsing, and it took several tugs on her arm before Rufus could get her to open her eyes.

"What—what is it"" she asked languidly.

"Trouble," was his matter-of-fact reply. As if on cue, the scream rang out a third time. Verhanna sat up and pulled in her reins.

"By Astra!" she exclaimed, "I thought I'd dreamed that!"

Kivinellis ran up beside Verhanna's horse. Damp with sweat, his blond hair gleamed in the brilliant sunlight. "It sounds like a lady in distress!" he announced.

"So it does. Can you tell which direction, Wart?" Verhanna nervously drew her sword.

Rufus stood on the cart seat and slowly craned his head in a circle, trying to catch the source of the sound. His pointed, elf-like ears were infallible. "Ha!" he crowed at last and bounced on his toes.

Verhanna listened hard. Sure enough, she heard a faint crashing sound, the sort of noise a person might make if he were running pell-mell through the woods. She thrust her dagger and shield at Kivinellis.

"Defend the carts!" she cried. The shrill scream split the air once more. "Grab your horse, Wart. We're off!" Rufus was off the cart and on his chestnut mount before the words had scarcely left his captain's mouth. They turned their horses south, off the narrow track they'd been following, and plunged into the forest proper. Saplings and tree limbs raked at their faces. Verhanna had her sword, but the kender was poorly armed for a fight. Aside from a sheath knife, his only weapon was a kender sling. It was a light, handy missile thrower, which he'd used to good effect in the fight at the slavers' camp, but it would be hard to use in the close-growing trees.

Indistinct shouts came from ahead, off to their left. Verhanna halted her horse and waited. Someone was running.

A black-haired human woman, clutching a baby to her breast, came stumbling through the undergrowth. Tears streaked her face. Now and again, she looked back over her shoulder and screeched in terror. Verhanna dug in her spurs and rode hard toward her. The woman saw the warrior maid on horseback, sword drawn, and screamed again—this time for pure joy. She threw herself at the horse's feet.

"Noble lady, save us!" she whimpered. The baby in her arms was bawling loudly, nearly drowning out her words.

Rufus rode up beside his mistress. "Who's after you?" he asked the frightened woman.

"Terrible creatures—monsters. They want to eat my child!"

Hardly had she finished this declaration when a trio of hideous, gnarled creatures appeared in the undergrowth, obviously following the woman's trail. Verhanna's lip curled in disgust.

"Goblins," she said with distaste. "I'll settle with them."

They were indeed goblins, but of the most backward and gruesome sort. All wore necklaces of human or elven teeth and bones, and one wore a sort of helmet made from a human skull. Their long fangs protruded over their bottom lips. Even from ten yards away, it was impossible not to smell their rank odor. The goblins were armed with crude maces made from lumps of rounded stone tied to thick ironwood handles. The sight of Verhanna, sword in hand, did not seem to upset the angry creatures. They must be desperately hungry, the captain decided, or driven mad by the suffocating heat.

Verhanna rode straight at them while the kender fitted a pellet into his sling. Clutching her baby tightly, the human woman crawled through the dead leaves until Rufus's broad horse was between her and the goblins.

Leaning forward, Verhanna smote the nearest creature with her keen Qualinesti blade. The goblin gave an inarticulate gurgle and dropped his club, his chest split open from shoulder to breastbone. The captain planted a foot on his chest and withdrew her blade. The goblin was dead before he hit the ground.

The other two monsters separated, one on each side of the warrior woman's horse. They swept their maces back and forth, warding off her sword. The goblin on Verhanna's left tried to get by to reach the woman cowering in the leaves. Before the captain could turn to cut him off, Rufus had put a pellet in the center of the goblin's forehead. Stunned, the cannibal creature fell facedown.

"Nice shot!" Verhanna cried.

"Look out!" yelled the kender at the same time.

His warning came too late. Verhanna had been distracted by the first goblin and had turned her back on the other. The second creature, who wore the human skull on its pointed head, dropped its mace in favor of using its teeth and claws. Grabbing her with its taloned hands, he yanked the captain off her horse.

Rufus drew his knife and half fell from his mount. The goblin sank its fangs into Verhanna's shoulder. She yelled loudly enough to rattle the leaves on the trees, and together she and the goblin toppled to the ground. The creature wrapped its arms and legs around her, entwining its rubbery black toes together. As Verhanna tried to pry it off, they rolled over and over in the leaves, locked in deadly embrace.

When the goblin presented its back to him, Rufus rammed his iron blade into its body—once, twice, thrice. The ferocious creature howled and let go of Verhanna. It turned on the little kender, murder in its bulging red eyes. Rufus held out his short blade and looked startled. How would it feel to be torn to bits by a filthy, heat-crazed goblin?

Wounded but not out of the fight, the captain flung herself at her sword where it lay in the dead leaves. As the wounded goblin gathered itself to leap on the kender, Verhanna beheaded it with one two-handed blow. Then the blade fell from her hands and she collapsed.

Just then the goblin that Rufus had knocked out with a pellet stirred noisily in the leaves. The kender quickly dispatched it by cutting its throat, then rushed to Verhanna.

"Captain, can you hear me?" he shouted.

"Of course I can hear you, Wart," she muttered. "I'm not deaf."

Indignation spread over the kender's mobile face. "I thought you were dead!"

"Not yet. Help me up."

Rufus pulled on her arm until Verhanna was able to sit up. Aside from the bite wound on her right shoulder and a few cuts and bruises, she didn't seem to be seriously injured.

"Where's the woman and her baby?" she asked, pushing her tumbled brown hair out of her eyes. Rufus looked toward his horse; there was no sign of the woman. In the confusion of battle, she must have fled. He didn't blame her. For a moment, it had looked like the goblins were going to get the best of them.

"She skedaddled," he reported, wiping the noxious goblin blood from his knife blade. "No sign of her or the baby."

"That's gratitude for you," grumbled Verhanna, wobbling to her knees. "Ugh! These goblins are the filthiest creatures I know."

Studying her shoulder dispassionately, the kender said, "Your wounds should be washed, but we haven't any water."

"Never mind. We'll be at the Astradine soon."

The captain put a hand on her scout's shoulder and heaved herself to her feet. The two of them remounted their horses, and Verhanna took one last look at the bloody scene before they moved on. Her shoulder burned as if a glowing coal had been set under the skin. Verhanna held her reins limply in her left hand, favoring her injured side.

"Wait a minute," said Rufus. "This isn't the way we came in."

"Are you sure?"

He scratched his head and looked all around. There was nothing but trees and brush in all directions. "Blind me with beeswax! Which way do we go?" Shielding his eyes with his hands, the kender squinted into the hazy sky. The immobile sun gave no clue which direction they should take.

627

"Can't you find the trail?" Verhanna asked hoarsely. "That's what I pay you for, to be a scout."

Rufus leapt to the ground. He sniffed the dead leaves and dry moss. He turned his head, straining for any sound. Finally, in desperation, he shouted, "Ho, Kivinellis! Can you hear me? Where are you?" In spite of repeated calls, there was no answer. At last the kender turned to Verhanna and shrugged helplessly.

"Wart," she said weakly, "you're fired."

Verhanna's eyes rolled up until only the white showed. Without another sound, she toppled from her saddle and landed squarely on the kender.

Mashed flat on his back, with only his head showing under the prostrate warrior maiden, Rufus groaned loudly. "Ow! Feels like a bear fell on me!"

There was no response from his captain. Finally he managed to haul himself out from under her and rolled her over. Verhanna was still breathing, but her face was deathly pale and her skin blazed hotter than the calm, radiant air.

* * * * *

Rufus set to work. He hadn't lived so long by his own wits without learning a thing or two about sickness. His captain had been poisoned by the filthy goblin's fangs, and unless he could cool her off, the raging fever would be the death of her.

Among their camp gear was a short-handled spade. The kender used it to rake away the layers of leaves that covered the forest floor. Within seconds, he was down to black soil. Below the dry top layer, he knew the earth would be moist and cool. Disregarding his parched throat and sweat-stung eyes, Rufus dug a shallow hole six feet long, two feet wide, and eight inches deep. It was hard going. The forest soil was a tangle of roots, rocks, and chunks of decayed wood. The captain was his friend though, and Rufus intended to do everything he could to save her. An hour after she'd fallen from her horse, the hole was ready for her.

Dropping his shovel, the kender dragged the much larger half-elf woman to the shallow pit and rolled her in so she lay on her back. Collapsing over her unmoving form, he panted and puffed with the exertion. This was hard work, especially since it was like toiling in a blast furnace. Not, of course, that Rufus had ever toiled in a blast furnace . . .

After a bit, he set about heaping damp dirt around her and scattering leaves on top of her. Her face he left uncovered. Steam rose from the ground, drawn out either by the hot, dry air or

Verhanna's fever. Finished at last, Rufus sat down near his captain's head and waited.

He prayed to the Blue Lady to heal Verhanna; to be fair, he also addressed the goddess of healing by her Qualinesti name, Quen. Perhaps if he prayed to both her incarnations, she would be more likely to heal his captain.

Verhanna shifted restlessly under her covering of leaves and moist soil. The kender patted her forehead distractedly and pondered his situation. If Verhanna died, should he return to Qualinost with the news, or go on with the hunt for the Kagonesti slavers? And if she lived, how could they go on? How could anyone find his way cross-country without the sun or moons or stars to guide him?

The kender chewed his lip while his mind raced. Briefly he wished that he was back in the Magnet Mountains. At least there he knew his way around. Of course, life there hadn't been nearly so exciting. Since meeting his captain, he had fought slave-traders and goblins, met the Speaker of the Sun, and had a chance to investigate the city of Qualinost. Unbidden, his hands explored the multitudinous pockets of his tunic and vest for all the trinkets he'd collected. Instead of rings or beads or writing styluses, Rufus's nimble fingers brought out a walnut-sized piece of lodestone. Surprise lifted his eyebrows. He'd forgotten he had that.

Something about lodestones made his nose itch. Rufus scratched. No, that wasn't it. Something about lodestones made his brain itch. Yes, there was something important about the little rock. Lodestones, mountains, and mines. What about mines? He'd once sold some stones to a band of dwarf miners. In Thorbardin, the dwarves had mines that ran for miles under the ground, where the tunnels and shafts and galleries were quite confusing. How did they navigate? They never saw the sun or stars down there.

Now the kender's ear itched. He swiped at it with one hand; then both ears started itching. It grew unbearable.

Grabbing the wide brim of his blue hat, Rufus yanked it from his head. Two ravelings from the sewn headband were hanging down and tickling his ears. He started to break off the annoying threads.

Threads!

In an instant, he remembered what he'd been trying to remember about lodestones. A dwarf had told him once, "To find your direction underground, hang a sliver of lodestone from a thread. It will always point north and south." Rufus had scoffed at the dwarf's tale. After all, how could a dumb piece of rock know directions?

Verhanna moaned loudly, interrupting the kender's darting thoughts. Recalling again what he had finally remembered before about the lodestone, Rufus brought out his knife and whittled the small stone, trying to get it long and narrow, like a pointer should be. His blade grew dull and several fresh nicks appeared, but before long, he had the stone roughly spindle-shaped.

Carefully he pulled a long raveling from his hatband. The woolen strand was about six inches long. He tied it around the center of the stone and let the black rock dangle from his fingers. The whittled stone turned round and round, then gradually slowed and stopped.

The kender realized he didn't know which way was north and which was south. And he wasn't entirely certain he could trust such a silly trick.

"What choice have you got?" Rufus asked himself aloud. None, he answered himself silently.

He tied Verhanna's horse's reins to his saddle. Then he set about uncovering his captain. She was noticeably cooler, thanks to his treatment, but still gravely ill. He had a dragon's own time getting the unconscious woman out of the hole. Grunting with effort, he braced her up in a sitting position on the ground.

Verhanna's fever-fogged eyes opened. "Wart," she muttered. "I thought I fired you."

"You haven't paid me yet, my captain. I can't leave till I get my gold!"

With much wobbling, Verhanna rose to her feet. Rufus boosted her into her saddle, his head and both hands pushing on her backside. In another time and place, it might have been a comical scene, but now Verhanna's life was literally hanging by a thread—a woolen thread from a kender's hat.

The warrior maid drooped over her horse's neck. Leaving her mount tied to his saddle, Rufus took his horse's reins in hand and began to lead them out. The track they'd been on with the carts lay to the north, so he chose a direction and hoped it was right. His eyes were glued to the sliver of lodestone he held in his other hand. He walked and walked and walked. So intent was he on keeping to his course that it was some time before he noticed it was getting harder and harder to see.

"Just my luck!" the kender exclaimed. "I'm going blind!"

But Rufus was not going blind. The sun, so long fixed overhead, was finally moving. Already it was low in the sky off to his left, sinking through the trees and confirming his route as northerly. Never unhappy for very long, the kender found himself feeling rather satisfied. He had chosen the right path. His lodestone pointer worked.

A few minutes later, he came to the track through the forest they'd left earlier. Rufus danced with joy. He was the best scout in the whole world! He climbed onto his mount and thumped his heels cheerily against its sides, turning its face toward the setting sun. There was no sign of the two carts or the former slaves, but Rufus was immensely relieved to be on the path again.

Crickets and birds, silent during the three days of noon, sang again as shadows lengthened on the trail. Rufus stopped now and then to see how his captain was doing. Her breathing was shallow and quick, and her face was too warm again. That was bad. How he wished he was in Balifor, where he knew several healing shamans! There was one on Peacock Street who had—

Water. The kender's button nose twitched. He smelled water. In a few seconds, the horses detected it, too. The tired, parched animals shambled faster, eager for a refreshing drink. Agreeing with them completely, Rufus let them have their heads.

The trees thinned and finally disappeared. In the last of the daylight, the kender saw that a wide bed of mud lay before him. The horses walked laboriously across the mud, pulling their hooves free with loud sucking noises. Evidently the river had shrunk during the long heat wave. Rufus wondered if there was any water left. If so, he couldn't see it. A thick scroll of fog shrouded the center of the river.

As they entered the fog, Rufus heard a splashing sound. He looked down. The horses had found the water. They waded in up to their bellies. Rufus leaned over and drank some of the sweet liquid from his cupped hand. Then he stood in his saddle and clambered over to Verhanna's mount.

Her hands and feet trailed in the cool stream. Standing with one foot in her stirrup, the kender scooped up a hatful of water and held it to her lips. Only partly conscious, she drank.

Sounds from the opposite shore caught Rufus's attention— voices, axles creaking, horses whinnying, Incapable of ignoring something that sounded so interesting, Rufus slipped into the water and swam quietly toward the noises.

As the kender rose out of the river, his soaked topknot fell across his face. He pushed it aside. Only his head showed above water, and the fog hung close around him. When he felt the oozy bottom under his toes, he walked slowly to shore.

The figures in the fog resolved themselves into tall people, elves or humans, who were trying to push a heavily loaded wagon out of the mud. They had foolishly steered the conveyance too close to the water's edge, and now it was held fast by the thick muck. As far as Rufus could see by the light of their torches, they were unarmed. Mostly they were muddy, and from the sounds they were making, disgusted with their plight.

He decided they must be immigrants bound for Qualinesti.

Perhaps there would be a healer among them. He'd have to go back and get his captain.

When he returned to his horses, he remounted and started for the far shore, toward the immigrants. The very center of the stream was too deep for the animals to walk, but the Thoradin-bred chargers swam the short distance easily. Kender, horses, and the unconscious warrior maiden splashed ashore.

"Hullo there! Rufus! Rufus Wrinklecap!" called a high voice. The startled kender saw a small fellow break away from the others.

"Kivinellis? Is that you?" The elf boy yelped with delight and waved Verhanna's dagger over his head. The other elves froze in their tracks.

Rufus clapped the boy on the back, saying, "Good to see you! My captain's wounded. We had a fight with some goblins, then got lost in the woods."

He peered over the boy's head at the people beside the wagon. None of them looked familiar.

"Where're Diviros and the women?" he asked quickly. "Who are these folk?" The Kagonesti at the wagon broke ranks and came toward him.

"Oh, these are my friends," said Kivinellis. "When you and the warrior lady rode off, Diviros got his legs untied and jumped down from the cart. I chased him, but he ran into the woods and I was afraid to follow. Me and the womenfolk came to the river 'cause you didn't come back."

The Kagonesti settlers were close now, so Rufus hailed them. "Hello! My captain is sick with a goblin's bite. Is there a healer among you?"

One Kagonesti male, his face painted with a host of black and white dots, turned away from the kender and called over his shoulder, "They have come, just as you said!"

Puzzled, Rufus said to Kivinellis, "Who's he talking to?" The fair-haired elf boy merely shrugged.

A soft yet penetrating voice pierced the night. "Bring the woman to me."

A male voice, Rufus decided. A little farther up the riverbank.

Two sinewy Kagonesti lifted Verhanna from her horse and carried her ashore. Rufus and Kivinellis followed, and the boy explained that his female companions had gone on to Qualinost with another group of wagons. He had decided to wait at the river ford for a while to see if Verhanna and the kender turned up.

"Where are they taking my captain?" asked Rufus, loud enough for the elves to hear.

His answer came striding out of the dark. A head taller than the Kagonesti, the newcomer was also an elf, though fairer in complexion. His face wasn't painted. Yellow hair hung loose around his wide shoulders. A rough horsehair blanket, with a hole cut in the center for his head, covered his chest and arms. His legs were sheathed in leather trews.

He stopped where the grassy shore met the mud flats. "I can help you," said the stranger. His words were softly spoken, yet carried easily to Rufus.

"Are you a healer?" asked Rufus.

"I can help you," he repeated.

The tall, yellow-haired elf went to the Kagonesti and took Verhanna from their arms. He carried the strapping warrior woman effortlessly, but with great gentleness. He turned and started away from the river.

"Where are you going?" called the kender. He pushed between the Kagonesti and splashed through the mud till he was dogging the tall elf's heels. Kivinellis remained with the Kagonesti, conversing with the wild elves. Where a line of locust trees bordered the grassy bank, the stranger lowered Verhanna to the ground.

"A goblin bit her," Rufus said, panting. "The wound's poisoned."

The stranger's long fingers probed Verhanna's shoulder. She gasped when he touched the wound itself. Sitting back on his haunches, the tall elf regarded her with rapt attention.

"What're you waiting for? Make a poultice. Work a spell!" The kender wondered if this fellow was really a healer.

The stranger held up a hand to quell the impatient Rufus. By the light of Krynn's stars and two bright moons, the kender could see that his fingers were dark, as if stained with dye. Rufus's penetrating vision could just make out that the stain was green.

Green. Green fingers. In a flash, Rufus remembered Diviros's queer tale of the lightning splitting the oak and a fully grown elf falling from the broken tree—a fully grown elf whose hands were green.

"It's you!" the kender exclaimed. "The one from the shattered tree! Greenhands!"

"I have been waiting for you," said Greenhands. "Through days of red rain and endless sun."

He bent down and slipped his arms around Verhanna. Taking her limp form into his embrace, Greenhands closed his right hand over the ugly, swollen wound on her shoulder. Rufus could see the muscles in the tall elf's neck tighten as he drew Verhanna closer to him, as if he were embracing a lover.

"What're you—?"

She groaned once, then cried out in torment as the stranger dug his odd, grass-colored fingers into her wound. Verhanna's eyes flew wide. She stared over the strange elf's shoulder at Rufus. What was in her eyes? Terror? Wonder? The kender couldn't tell. She uttered a long, tearing wail, and Greenhands suddenly joined his voice with hers. The combined scream hammered painfully at the listeners, wrenching their hearts as it agonized their ears.

Kith-Kanan's daughter closed her eyes with a slow flutter. Greenhands lowered her carefully to the ground, straightened up, and walked away. Rufus went to his captain.

Her breast rose and fell evenly. She was asleep. Beneath the filthy shreds of her linen shirt, Verhanna's right shoulder was as smooth and unscarred as a baby's cheek.

The kender yelped in astonishment. He jumped up and stared after Greenhands, who was still walking away. "Wait, you!" he yelled. Not ten paces from where Verhanna lay, Greenhands sank to the ground. The kender and elves ran to him.

"Are you all right?" Rufus asked as he reached the elf. Kivinellis already knelt by the stranger. It was he who noticed the change.

"Look at his hand!" the boy gasped.

The tall elf's right hand, the one he'd healed Verhanna's wound with, was split open. A long, deep gash, from which blood oozed, ran across his palm. Black blood caked his green fingers, and the smell of the suppurating goblin bite rose up like foul smoke.

"He is *thalmaat*," said one of the Kagonesti in deeply reverent tones.

"What's that?" asked Kivinellis, unfamiliar with the old dialect.

Rufus glanced from the bloody green hand of the tall stranger to his captain, now peacefully resting. "It means 'godsent'," the kender said slowly. "One who is actually sent by the gods."

The Pact

9

Rain pattered on the dry streets of Qualinost. After three days of continuous sunshine, the rain was a blessing. The city dwellers, who had so fastidiously avoided the crimson downpour, stayed outside, luxuriating in the refreshing, clean liquid. The wide, curving streets were full of people.

Once the rain had abated to a soft shower and cool breezes flowed across his capital, Kith-Kanan rode with Senator Irthenie and Kemian Ambrodel through the busy streets. The Speaker of the Sun was surveying the city to see how much it had suffered in the three days of heat. Qualinost, he was relieved to see, didn't seem to have been much damaged by the burning sun.

His subjects noticed the Speaker riding among them. They tipped their hats or bowed as he passed. Here and there, Kith-Kanan came upon a gang of gardeners removing some tree or bush that had succumbed to the relentless heat. At the right hand of each of these groups waited a priest of Astra, ready to plant a new tree in place of the old. No, Qualinost had not suffered very much.

The market square was less cheerful. Kith-Kanan rode ahead of his two companions across the almost deserted plaza and saw all the empty stalls and ruined produce lying trodden on the cobblestones. One merchant, a burly human with a leather apron, was sweeping up some spoiled potatoes when Kith-Kanan reined in to speak with him.

"Hello there, my good fellow," called the Speaker. "How goes it with you?"

The man didn't look up from his work. "Rotten! All of it rotten! What's a man supposed to do with five bushels of dried-out, split-open, rotten vegetables?"

Irthenie and Kemian drew alongside Kith-Kanan. "So the sun ruined your crop?" asked the Speaker sympathetically.

"Aye, the sun or the darkness or the lightnin' or the flood of bloody rain. Makes no never-mind to me which it was. It happened." The man spat on the damp stones.

An elf woman with a basket of withered flowers under one arm heard their conversation. With a quick curtsy to her sovereign, she asked, "Why do the gods punish us so? What sin have we committed?"

"How do you know the gods are punishing anyone? These strange things might all be signs of some great wonder to come," Kith-Kanan suggested.

The human, squatting on the ground to gather his ruined potatoes into baskets, grumbled, "They say it's because Kith-Kanan has put his own son in chains to help build the fortress at Pax Tharkas." He still didn't realize to whom he was conversing. At his harsh words, the elf woman blushed, and Kemian Ambrodel cleared his throat loudly. The human lifted his head.

Even though the Speaker didn't wear the glitter and gold of state robes, the man recognized him. "Mercy, Your Worship, I'm sorry!" the man gasped. "I didn't know it was you!"

Grimly Kith-Kanan replied, "Have no fear. I would hear everything my people think of me."

"Is it true, Majesty?" asked the elf woman meekly. "Did you sell your own son into slavery just to finish that big castle?"

Kemian and Irthenie started to remonstrate with the woman for her blunt query. The Speaker held up his hands to silence them. Patiently he explained what Ulvian had done, and why he had sent him to Pax Tharkas. His earlier wish to keep Ulvian's crime from public gossip seemed hopeless. Now he felt it was more important for his people to know the truth and not entertain wild imaginings.

While he spoke, more people gathered—peddlers, tinkers, farmers, potters. All came to hear Kith-Kanan's story of the trouble he was having with his son. To his amazement, they all believed that Ulvian's exile and the twelve days of marvels were related.

"Where did you get these ideas?" Irthenie asked sharply.

The potato man shrugged. "Talk. Just talk . . . you know."

"Shadow talk," said Kith-Kanan, too faintly for most to hear. Kemian heard, and he glanced at the Speaker.

"Is Lord Kemian Ambrodel to be your son now?" shouted a voice from the crowd. The three mounted elves turned their heads to and fro, trying to spot the one who'd spoken.

"Will Lord Ambrodel be the next Speaker of the Sun?" the same voice demanded.

"Who said that?" muttered Irthenie. No one answered, but others in the crowd took up the cry. Keeping a steady hand on his fractious mount's reins, Kith-Kanan let the shouting grow a while. He wanted to measure the sentiment of his people.

Kemian, however, could not remain calm. "Silence!" the general roared. "Show respect for the Speaker!"

"Silvanesti!" someone shouted back at him, and it was like a curse. The young warrior, in an agony of embarrassment and anger, looked to his sovereign. Kith-Kanan seemed thoughtful.

"Sire," said Kemian desperately, "I think you'd best assure them I am not to be your successor!" His voice was tight but earnest.

"Say something," Irthenie urged from the side of her mouth.

At last the Speaker held up a hand. "Good people," he said. "The crowd instantly fell silent, awaiting his response. "I understand your concern for the throne. Lord Ambrodel is a faithful and valiant servant. He would make an excellent Speaker—"

"No! No!" the crowd erupted. "No Silvanesti! No Silvanesti!" they chanted. In his own shock at the Speaker's words, Kemian barely heard their insults.

"Have you forgotten that I am of the royal house of Silvanos?" Kith-Kanan said icily. "No one is more Silvanesti than I!"

"You are the Speaker of the Sun! The father of our country!" a male voice answered. "We don't want some Silvanesti courtier's boy to rule us. We want a ruler of your blood or none!"

"Your blood or none!" echoed a large segment of the crowd.

Kemian snatched at his reins, ready to charge into the mass of unarmed Qualinesti and put an end to these insults. Kith-Kanan leaned over and laid a hand on the warrior's arm. Eyes blazing, Kemian stared angrily at the Speaker, but he didn't try to evade his grasp. Reluctantly he relaxed, and Kith-Kanan let go of his mailed arm.

"Go back to the Speaker's house, General," Kith-Kanan said coolly. "I shall return shortly."

"Sire!" Kemian saluted and wheeled his prancing horse in a tight half-circle. The traders and farmers scattered from his path. The general let out a yell and spurred his mount. With a loud clatter of hooves, horse and rider tore across the market square and vanished down a curving street.

The people cheered his abrupt departure. Disgusted with them, Kith-Kanan was about to follow Kemian's exit when Irthenie abruptly got down off her horse.

"I'm too old to stay up that high for so long," she proclaimed loudly, rubbing her backside with exaggerated care. "For seven hundred and ninety-four years, I walked everywhere I needed to go. Now that I'm a senator, I'm not supposed to walk anywhere." Those nearest the Kagonesti woman chuckled. "One pays a price to sit in the Thalas-Enthia," she said gruffly. More people laughed.

Kith-Kanan slackened his reins and sat still, waiting to see what the foxy senator was up to. "You people," she said loud enough to carry to the fringes of the mob, "you stand here and say you don't want Kemian Ambrodel as the next Speaker of the Sun. I say, who told you he would be? It's the first I've heard of it." She stepped away from her dapple-gray horse, deeper into the crowd.

"He's a fine general, that elf, but you're right about one thing: we don't want a bunch of Silvanesti nobles ruling us, telling us we're not as good as they are. That's one reason we left the old country, to get away from so many lords and masters."

Irthenie's Kagonesti garb blended in well with the crowd, her leather and raw linen against their homespun wool and drab cotton. She literally rubbed shoulders with the people in the square. Irthenie was one of them.

"When I was younger and better-looking"—laughter rippled across the plaza—"I was taken from the forest by warriors. They were looking for wives, and their idea of catching one was to drag a net through the bushes and see what they flushed out." The senator stopped walking when she reached the center of the crowd. Every eye was on her. Kith-Kanan experienced a moment of nervousness at the sight of her small figure hemmed in on all sides by the mob. "I didn't much want to be a warrior's woman, so I ran away the first chance I got. They caught me, and this time, they broke my leg so I couldn't run again. Vernax Kollontine was hardly a loving husband. After he beat me for not washing his clothes often enough and not cooking his supper fast enough, I killed him with a bread knife."

There was a concerted gasp at this revelation. The Speaker of the Sun seemed just as surprised as his subjects, and he listened to the senator's tale just as intently. Irthenie held up a hand to calm the crowd, insisting, "No, no, it was a fair fight." Kith-Kanan smiled.

"The point of this long and boring story is that the Speaker of the Stars at that time, Sithel, ordered me sold into slavery as punishment for my crime. I lived as a slave for thirty-eight years. The great war freed me, and I was in the first band of settlers who came with Kith-Kanan to found Qualinost. This city, this country, is like no other in the world. Here every race can live and work, can worship, and can prosper or not as they please. That's freedom. That you and I enjoy it is mostly due to that fellow on horseback you see over there. It was his wisdom and judgment that got us here. If you're pleased with that, then you ought not doubt his wisdom regarding either his son or his successor."

The square remained quiet after she finished speaking. Only the soft patter of rain accompanied Irthenie's final words.

"Slavery is an evil, ugly thing," she concluded. "It degrades not only the slave, but the master as well. Like any good father, the Speaker is trying to save his son from a terrible mistake. You should pray for him as I often do."

Irthenie walked back through the calmed crowd to her horse. Kith-Kanan handed her the reins, and she climbed into the saddle with a grunt. "Damn leg," she muttered. "It always gets stiff when it rains."

The Speaker and the senator rode on across the square. The people parted, making way for them. Hats were doffed. Wool tams and felt hoods were removed in respect.

Kith-Kanan kept his gaze serenely ahead. What had been a potentially dangerous situation had been reversed by the words of his old friend.

The cool rain felt good on his face. The air smelled sweet. Though nothing had been decided or changed, Kith-Kanan felt a sudden rush of confidence. Whatever forces were at work, he felt sure they were in his favor. Hiddukel's dire prophecies in the Tower of the Sun seemed like remote threats now.

"A question," he said as they rode on. "Was that story you told the crowd true?"

Irthenie kicked her heels against her horse's sides. The gelding broke into a trot.

"Some of it was," she replied.

*　*　*　*　*

Steam hung in the air where the cold rain hit the baked stones of Pax Tharkas. All outside work had ceased, as it was too danger-ous to cut stone or move blocks when the ground was wet. The grunt gang was not allowed to lie idle, though. Feldrin Feldspar was anxious about his rate of progress, so he put the convicts to work enlarging the tunnels being sunk into the mountainside beneath the towering citadel.

Ulvian hobbled about on a makeshift crutch. His right leg, the one that had been caught by the runaway granite block, had stiffened to the point where he needed a crutch to get around. He wasn't excused from work however, so he limped through the dim, limestone tun-nels, carrying waterskins to the other grunt gang members.

Near the end of one long gallery, barely wider than his shoul-ders, he came upon Dru. Ulvian paused a few feet away from the laboring elf. A small lamp burned on the tunnel floor. In its brassy light, Dru's chalk-covered body appeared ghostly.

"Here, friend," said the prince. "Drink while the water's still cool."

Dru set aside his pick and took the skin. He pointed the spout at his lips and let a stream of cold water flow into his mouth.

"Don't take it all. There are others who will want a drink."

Dru let the prince take the nearly drained skin. "You puzzle me," the Silvanesti said, leaning against the wall. The lamp threw weird highlights from below, making the elf's lean, angular face look like a mask. "You are a prince, the son of a monarch, and yet you fetch and carry water like any base-born serf."

"Hold your tongue! You may have saved my life, but I don't have to endure a lecture from you!" snapped Ulvian, more like his arrogant, proud, former self.

Dru smiled thinly. "That's better. That's what I want to hear." Clasping his pick, the sorcerer stepped over the lamp and stood nose to nose with the son of Kith-Kanan. "If you can behave like a prince and not a serf, we can be gone from this miserable prison. Are you with me?"

"In what?" was Ulvian's derisive reply. "Shall we run away to the mountains, just so Feldrin's watchdogs can hunt us down? I'm on my good behavior here. If I sacrifice that, I have no hope of gaining my father's throne."

"We have only to cause a little excitement. That will distract the camp long enough for us to get inside Feldrin's tent and get my amulet."

So they were back to that. Ulvian folded his arms, disgust evident on his face. "I won't murder Feldrin. He's a thickheaded old bore, but he's honest."

Dru's smile was nasty. He turned and went to the low niche he'd already hollowed out in the soft rock. He tossed his pick aside. It rang dully on the dusty floor. Slumping against the wall, Dru said, "When are you going to wake up, Highness?" His tone dripped irony. "I have waited a long time for someone with whom I could ally myself. No one else in the grunt gang has any wit or breeding. But you and I, my friend, can go far together. You spoke of enemies. I can help you defeat them. The throne of your father can be yours, not in ten years or a hundred, but in two months. Perhaps sooner. With your leadership and my magic, we can make Qualinesti the most powerful empire in the world!"

His words held the prince's attention. Without realizing it, Ulvian let the waterskin drop from his fingers. It sloshed to the ground.

"I've dreamed of the day I would see Verhanna and the Ambrodels groveling at my feet," Ulvian whispered. "And the Crown of the Sun on my head." The prince's eyes were distant, beholding future glory. Visions of the empire he would rule, of the grand and opulent palace he would build, filled Ulvian's mind. Power and glory, comfort and ease, riches beyond dreaming. His word would be law. The people would worship him as they now worshiped his father.

Cutting through Ulvian's golden dreams, a rough voice from farther back in the tunnel called faintly, "Waterboy! Where's that waterboy?"

Abruptly Ulvian focused once more on Dru. "If we can accomplish this without bloodshed, count me in," he said grimly.

Dru bowed his head. "As Your Highness wishes. I shall be very careful." Then he quickly gave Ulvian a precise list of the things he'd need. It was a short list, but a puzzling one.

"What on Krynn can you do with a pound of white clay, some chips of coal, a span of leather thong, and a copper brazier?" the prince asked, confused. "None of them is rare or guarded. Why don't you collect them yourself?"

The sorcerer's gray eyes glittered like diamonds in the half-light. "You may not realize it, my prince, but I am closely watched. No one dares kill me, but I dare not do anything to cause suspicion, or my limbs would be fettered and I would be consigned to a deep, dark hole." He gestured at the rough limestone walls. "Like this."

Ulvian left him there. As he wended his way to the main tunnel under the central citadel, he mulled over the possibilities. Dru was dangerous, but a potentially powerful ally. Ulvian smiled in the dark tunnel as he limped along. Let Dru believe he was a vainglorious fool. That was a useful illusion. The time might come when Ulvian would no longer require Dru's services. . . .

Rough hands seized his shirt front. "Here!" bellowed a harsh voice. "Here he is, lads!"

Ulvian was dragged into a side tunnel and flung to the floor. His bruised leg knifed with pain. Through the gloom, he saw three grunt gangers standing over him. Two he knew well—the Kagonesti Splint, and a human called Brunnar. The third was another Kagonesti he knew only as Thrit.

"We been waiting an awful long time for our water," snarled Splint. "The damn dust down here is thicker than soup." He planted a foot on Ulvian's back. "So where's the water?"

Painfully the prince dragged the waterskin from beneath him. It was snatched from his grasp by Thrit, who reported that it was empty.

"I think our little waterboy needs a lesson," Splint growled, and kicked the prince in the ribs. The three tall figures closed in.

Dru swung his pick energetically at the limestone around him. He had no interest in working hard for his captors; the physical activity was simply a reflection of the state of fevered excitement in his mind. His time in this unnatural prison could be measured in days, perhaps only hours. Soon he would be free! Surely his patron god had sent that fool of a prince to be the instrument of his deliverance.

A sound in the passage behind him made him pause. Pick in hand, Dru whirled. The feeble glow of the fat-burning lamp didn't penetrate beyond the bend in the tunnel some six feet away. He waited. The noise came again, a scraping, dragging sound. Carefully the sorcerer bent down to take up the lamp, his eyes never leaving the black passage.

A hand, pale and slim, came into view on the dusty floor. Dru crept forward until the lamplight fell across the form of Prince Ulvian, sprawled on the ground. Blood matted his unkempt beard, and one eye was swollen shut.

Dru knelt. "Your Highness! What happened?"

"Splint . . . Brunnar . . . Thrit . . . beat me." Ulvian's lips were swelling, making speech difficult.

Dru dragged the prince to the far end of the tunnel and propped him against the wall. After making certain no one was around, the sorcerer reached under the waist of his baggy trousers and brought out a small hide drawstring bag. He poured a little of its contents into his hand. A pungent, sweet smell filled the air.

"Take this," murmured Dru, putting his hand to Ulvian's purple lips. "It's an herbal mixture of my own. It will restore you."

The prince managed to swallow some of the ground herbs. In a few minutes, the swelling in his eye and lips began to subside. A modicum of strength flowed into his body. Though the pain of his injured leg eased, his ribs still ached from his beating.

Ulvian lifted clouded eyes to the sorcerer's face and struggled to his feet.

"Rest a bit longer, Highness."

"No." Ulvian struggled to his feet. The magic herbs hadn't healed all his pains, but he felt considerably better. "I want to proceed with our plans as quickly as possible," he informed Dru. "And I've added a condition of my own."

Dru tucked his herb bag away. "What's that?"

"Twice Splint has laid hands on me. I want revenge!"

"Easily done, Highness. Just get the items I need."

Ulvian pushed Dru aside and hobbled off down the tunnel. His voice echoed back to the pleased sorcerer. "I'll have it all for you tonight!" he declared grimly.

The Knowing Child

10

Verhanna slept deeply for the rest of the night and well into the next day. When at last she stirred and sat up, she saw Rufus sitting on the ground beside her. A cool compress of damp moss fell away from her forehead when she moved. "What—what is this? Where are we?"

"The west bank of the Astradine River," said the kender.

Rufus gave her a strand of venison jerky he'd bought from the Kagonesti settlers. Verhanna gnawed on the tough meat in silence for a while, then finally said, "Now I remember. The goblins! That rotten scab of a creature bit me. The wound festered." Suddenly she twisted around and lifted the horsehair poncho draped over her. "It's gone!" she shouted. Verhanna lowered the piece of blanket. "Who healed me? My muscles aren't even sore!"

The kender pointed away from their campsite. "Him," Rufus said simply.

Seated on a fallen log a dozen paces distant was Greenhands, bare-chested now since Verhanna was using his poncho. His hair, which had appeared yellow by torchlight, was revealed by the light of day to be of purest white. Kith-Kanan's daughter picked her way down the mossy riverbank toward him. The strange elf was gazing placidly across the sluggish stream, which was still depleted by the three-day onslaught of the sun.

Verhanna opened her mouth—to demand, question, challenge—but she closed it again without speaking. There was something unsettling about this elf, something compelling. He was not handsome by elven standards. His cheeks were broad, but not high; his chin and nose were not fashionably narrow; his lips were full, not thin; and his forehead was massive, almost human in proportion. However, he was unmistakably elven, with almond-shaped eyes, elegantly pointed ears, and exquisitely long, tapering fingers. The expression on his face was serene.

"Hello," the Qualinesti princess finally said. His green eyes left off their study of the river and found her. A chill passed through Verhanna. She'd never seen any elf with eyes that color, and his gaze was direct—unwavering and unnerving. "Can you speak?"

"I speak."

"Thank Astra." She paused, embarrassed at the debt she owed him and unsure what to say. After a long moment, during which the elf's eyes never left her, she added rather hastily, "Rufus tells me you healed me. I—I wanted to thank you."

"It needed to be done," replied Greenhands. The wild elves whose wagon had been stuck in the mud hailed them, and the elder Kagonesti male called for Greenhands to join them.

"Come along," the Kagonesti said. "We're bound for Qualinost."

The strange elf replied, "I cannot go." Still his eyes remained on Verhanna.

The Kagonesti father tied off his reins and jumped down from the wagon. "What's that? Is this warrior holding you back?" he asked, glaring at the warrior maiden.

"I am not," she replied tartly.

"I must go to the west," Greenhands said. He rose and faced in that direction. "To the High Place. They must come with me." He indicated Verhanna and Rufus, who had managed to join them quietly for a change. Kivinellis, riding in the wagon with the Kagonesti's family, jumped off and ran to Verhanna.

"I want to go, too!" he declared. The father protested strongly. A young boy couldn't wander around with a kender, a warrior, and a simpleminded elf.

Verhanna ignored the Kagonesti and turned to Greenhands. "Why do you have to go west with us?" she wanted to know.

His brow furrowed in thought. "I have to find my father," he said.

"Who is your father?"

"I do not know. I have never seen him."

In spite of these vague replies, Greenhands was obstinate. He must go west, and Verhanna and Rufus must go with him. Defeated, the Kagonesti returned to his wagon, propelling Kivinellis ahead of him. The elf boy complained all the way.

"Poor little fellow," said Rufus. "Couldn't we keep him, my captain?"

Verhanna's attention was all on Greenhands. "No, he's better off with a family," she said distantly. "Astra only knows where we're headed—" The creak of wheels interrupted her. The loaded wagon lurched onto level ground and pulled away. Kivinellis, his blond head shining among the dark elves, waved forlornly from the back of the wagon. He was securely held by the Kagonesti's wife. Verhanna returned the wave, then turned back to Greenhands.

"I need some answers," Verhanna declared. "Who are you?"

"I have no name," was the mild answer.

"Greenhands, that's your name," said the kender. He clasped the elf's grass-hued hand in both of his small ones. "Pleased to meetcha. I'm Rufus Wrinklecap, forester and scout. And that's my captain, Verhanna. Her father is Kith-Kanan, the Speaker of the Sun."

Greenhands seemed startled, even bewildered, by this flood of information.

"Never mind," said Verhanna, shaking her head. Awkwardly she put a hand on the elf's bare shoulder. His skin was warm and smooth. When she touched him, Verhanna felt a tingle shoot up her arm. She didn't know if it was due to some force passing between them or if it was simply her own nervousness. Greenhands didn't seem to notice anything odd.

Looking him directly in the eyes, Verhanna asked firmly, "Who are you? Really?"

He shrugged. "Greenhands."

A flush of irritation washed over the warrior maiden. She was intrigued by this odd fellow and deeply grateful that he'd saved her life, but his naive and evasive replies were getting under her skin.

"I guess you'd better come with us," she stated. "My father would want me to bring you to Qualinost."

"What about the slavers?" asked Rufus.

"This is more important."

Greenhands shook his head. "I cannot go with you. I must go to the High Place." He pointed west, toward the Kharolis Mountains. "There. To find my father."

Verhanna's eyes narrowed, and her jaw clenched. Rufus intervened quickly. "It's not so far off the track to Qualinost, my captain. We could swing by the mountains first. You know," he said, changing the subject completely, "my father was a famous pot thrower."

Suitably distracted, Verhanna hitched the horse blanket up on her shoulders and looked at her scout. "You mean he made pots—threw them—on a wheel?" she asked.

"No, he threw them at my Uncle Four-Thumbs. In the carnival."

Suddenly Verhanna realized Greenhands was no longer with them. He was twenty paces away, loping along with the morning sun at his back. She called out for him to stop.

"You must stay with us!" she shouted.

Wind stirred his long, loose hair. He stopped, eyes fixed on the western horizon, while Verhanna retired to a stand of trees to dress. Now that the perishing heat was over, she donned her breastplate, childrons, and greaves over a fresh haqueton. Rufus did one of his usual vaults to reach the broad back of his red-coated Thoradin mount, and together they rode to where Greenhands waited.

"Do you ride?" Verhanna asked, returning the poncho to Greenhands. "There's room behind Wart if you do."

"There's room for most of Balifor up here," opined Rufus.

Greenhands pulled the poncho on over his head. "I'll walk," he said.

"It's a long way to the mountains," she warned, leaning on the pommel of her saddle. "You'll never be able to keep pace with the horses."

"I'll walk," he repeated, with exactly the same intonation.

She shook her head. "Suit yourself."

They topped a low rise and were out of the shallow valley cut by the river and back on the grass-covered plain. To the south, the blue humps of the Kharolis foothills were plainly visible in the clear morning sky, but Greenhands went resolutely west.

So intent were Verhanna and Rufus on keeping their eyes on Greenhands that neither bothered to look back at the riverbank. What had been a mud flat the night before was now a blossoming meadow. Grass had sprung up knee high in a few short hours, and a thousand colors of wild flowers bloomed where once there had been nothing but mud and cattails. Moreover, this strange growth narrowed as it entered the upland. Eventually it thinned to a point—the exact trail where Greenhands trod.

* * * * *

The day wore on, and Greenhands showed no signs of tiring.

Verhanna and Rufus ate in the saddle, passing a water bottle back and forth between them. Greenhands plucked a few stems of grass from the turf to nibble. He ate and drank nothing else.

By mid-afternoon the novelty of watching the strange elf had worn off. Rufus lay down on his horse's back, clasping his hands behind his head and shading his face with his travel-worn hat. He gave his reins to his captain, and soon high-pitched snores whistled from his lips. Verhanna nodded a bit, but she was too conscious of her duty to falter and fought the sleep that tried to claim her.

Fatigue and the lingering shock of her healed goblin bite proved too strong, though, and she, too, eventually nodded off. When her charger stumbled slightly over a gopher mound, Verhanna jolted awake. Greenhands was no longer forging ahead on foot. The warrior maiden reined in and looked back. In the high grass fifteen yards behind them, the tall elf was kneeling.

"Wake up, Wart," she called to the kender. Yawning, Rufus sat up and caught his reins as she tossed them.

"Hey," the kender said sleepily, "where'd all the flowers come from?"

Verhanna looked past Greenhands and saw the vast trail of blooms that widened as it stretched out behind him. Not only flowers, but the dry prairie grass in the area had grown a foot taller.

"Look you," she said, leaning down from the saddle. "What sort of magic is this?"

"Quiet," he murmured. "The children call me."

She bristled at his abrupt command. "I'll speak when I like!"

The strange elf's tense, prayerful posture suddenly relaxed. He inhaled deeply and said, "They come."

Verhanna was about to make a rejoinder when a faint rumbling sound reached her ears. Heavy vibrations in the ground caused her mount to shift his feet and stamp nervously. Rufus sat up and called, "Captain, look!"

To the south, a dark brown line appeared on the horizon. It bulked larger and higher, and the rumbling grew louder. Swiftly the brown mass resolved into elk—thousands of them. A gigantic herd, stretching far to the left and right, was coming straight toward them.

"By Astra, it's a stampede!" Verhanna cried. She twisted her horse around to ride hard in the same direction the elk were moving. Their only chance was to go with the flow and not fall under those churning hooves.

"Give me your hand!" she shouted to Greenhands. "We must flee!"

The elk were only a couple hundred paces off and gathering speed. Rufus turned his mount and urged it next to his captain's. Bouncing to his feet in the saddle, he crowed with delight, "What a sight! Have you ever seen so many deer? If only I had a bow, we'd have venison for dinner forever!"

"You idiot, we're going to be trampled!"

Then the elk herd was upon them like a living wall of hide, antlers, and sharp hooves. The musky smell of the animals mingled with the dry odor of trampled grass. Thinking first of her decision to bring Greenhands to Qualinost, Verhanna threw herself on top of the elf to shield him from harm. Only after an eternal, terrifying second did the realization sink in that the herd had split and was flowing around them. The patch of ground with Verhanna, Greenhands, Rufus, and the two horses had been spared.

Thousands of elk, with liquid brown eyes and gaping mouths, rushed past them, nose to flank, shoulder to hip. The noise of their passage was deafening. Verhanna raised her head just enough to see the kender, still standing on his quiescent horse, hands clamped over his ears. With great astonishment, the warrior maid discovered that the stupid fellow was grinning. His carroty topknot was whipped back by the wind of the herd's passage, and a huge smile lit his pale eyes.

It seemed hours before the herd thinned. Alone or in pairs, the last few animals bounded in wide zigzags. In minutes more, the receding herd was again a brown line on the horizon. Then there was nothing but flying dust and the fading rumble of ten thousand hooves.

"E'li be merciful!" Verhanna breathed. "We are truly blessed!"

"Move away," Greenhands grumbled from beneath her. "You smell terrible."

She rolled smartly aside, and he sat up. Verhanna slipped the mail mitten back from her hand and slapped the elf across the jaw. She was instantly sorry, because tears formed in his vivid green eyes and his lips quivered.

"It's the metal you wear," he sniffled. One tear traced a shining path down his cheek. "It smells like death."

"Yippee!"

The two of them turned to look up at Rufus. The kender was capering atop his horse. "What a sight!" he caroled gleefully. "That must be the biggest herd of elk in the world! Did you feel the wind they kicked up? The ground shook like a jelly pudding! What do you suppose made them run like that?"

"Thirst," Greenhands said. He sniffed and touched a hand to his wet cheek. The sight of his own tears seemed to confound him. "The heat of days past made them mad with thirst."

"How do you know?" Verhanna demanded.

"They called out to me. I told them how to get to the river."

"You told them? I suppose you told them not to trample us, too?"

"Yes. I told the horses to stand still, and the elk would go around us."

The tall elf rubbed his fingertips together till the tears were gone. Then he stood and walked slowly away, not west as they had been going, but veering south. Exasperated beyond words, Verhanna swung into her saddle and followed him. Rufus fell in beside her. He could hear her grumbling and grinding her teeth.

"Why so angry, my captain?" the kender asked, his eyes still bright at their encounter with the elk herd.

"We spend our time trailing after him like body servants!" She slapped her armored thigh. "And the lies he tells! He knows more than he's telling, mark my words."

The kender turned down his hat brim to shade his eyes from the lowering sun. "I don't think he knows how to lie," he said quietly. "The elk herd might've split by coincidence, but my horse just stood like a statue. It wasn't even quivering. If you ask me my opinion, Greenhands did talk to the elk."

Rising Son

11

Kith-Kanan watched the sun set from the Hall of the Sky. He'd been alone there for hours, thinking. Since the day Irthenie had calmed the crowd in the market square, there had been other demonstrations in the streets in favor of Ulvian. Kemian Ambrodel, who sought no higher office than the one he held, was berated everywhere he went. Once he was even pelted with overripe fruit. The Speaker had to order him to remain in the Speaker's house to protect the proud warrior from further humiliation or worse.

Clovanos and the Loyalists were discreet enough not to be seen leading the activities, but within the hall of the Thalas-Enthia, they trumpeted the popular sentiment and demanded the return of Prince Ulvian. Lengthy petitions, inscribed on parchment scrolls three feet long, arrived at the Speaker's house daily. The signatures on the petitions grew more numerous each time, with many of the New Landers joining the Loyalists in seeking Ulvian's confirmation as Kith-Kanan's heir. Disgusted with the senate's shortsightedness, Kith-Kanan repaired to the Hall of the Sky to ponder his choices. He half hoped that the gods would choose for him, that some meaningful sign would show him what to do. However, nothing so mystical happened. He remained in the great plaza, watching his city through the waving treetops, until at last Tamanier Ambrodel came from the Speaker's house.

The Speaker got up from his knees and crossed the vast mosaic map to greet his faithful castellan. In spite of the worries that clouded his mind, his step was springy; no one viewing the beauty of the sunset and the great elven city from this vantage point could fail to be moved, and some small measure of his strength had been renewed by his meditation.

"Good health to you, Majesty," Tamanier said, bowing and presenting Kith-Kanan with an embossed dispatch case.

By the seal pressed in the wax of the lid, Kith knew the dispatch case was from Feldrin Feldspar. He broke the seal with his knife tip, and while Tamanier held the box, the Speaker raised the lid and drew out the papers inside.

"Hmm . . . Master Feldrin's report on the progress at Pax Tharkas . . . the usual requests for food, clothing, and other supplies . . . and what's this?" From between the sheets of official correspondence, the Speaker pulled a small folded letter on fine vellum, sealed carefully with a ribbon and a drop of blue wax.

He returned the other documents to the box and opened the sealed letter. "It's from Merithynos," he said, surprised.

"Good news, sire?"

"I'm not sure." Frowning, Kith-Kanan read the brief letter, then handed the vellum to his castellan. Tamanier read Merith's account of Ulvian's near death, his salvation at the hands of the sorcerer Drulethen, and the friendship that Merith had observed growing between the prince and Dru.

"Drulethen—isn't he the monster who ruled the high pass to Thorbardin during the Kinslayer War?" asked Tamanier.

"Your memory is still sharp. I'd forgotten the sorcerer was at Pax Tharkas. He shouldn't be allowed to cultivate my son's friendship; he's far too dangerous." The memory of another voice suddenly flashed into Kith-Kanan's mind. What was it the god Hiddukel had said when he'd manifested himself in the Tower of the Sun?

You may call me Dru. It couldn't be coincidence that the god had chosen the name of the evil sorcerer. Where the gods were concerned, little was left to chance.

Tamanier continued to stand holding the dispatch box. After a long moment of silence, Kith-Kanan's eyes focused once more on the old castellan. "Return to the house, Tam," he said briskly. "Prepare for a trip. Small entourage, with a light, mounted escort. I want to move quickly."

The castellan's brows lifted. "Where are you going, Great Speaker?"

"To Pax Tharkas, my friend. I'll leave as soon as Lord Anakardain can get back to Qualinost. I want him to keep order here while I'm gone."

Tamanier bowed and withdrew, head buzzing with the speed of events. Kith-Kanan remained in the Hall of the Sky a while longer. Standing at the edge of the artificial plateau, he looked out over his city. One by one, lamps were being lit in towers and on street corners, until it seemed the star-salted sky was mirrored on the ground. As the Speaker watched, lights illuminated the sweeping arch of the northern bridge directly ahead of him, behind the Tower of the Sun. Kith-Kanan turned slowly to each point of the compass to see the other three bridges similarly lighted. They surrounded Qualinost in a sparkling embrace.

Despite this glorious vista, something gnawed at Kith-Kanan. The great forces he'd sensed behind the marvels of the past days now seemed overshadowed by evil. He'd believed the wonders to be portents of some great event; perhaps they were indeed portents, but of a darker nature.

* * * * *

The bells clanged, signaling the end of another day of toil at Pax Tharkas. Ropes were tied off or dropped, tools piled on carts to be taken back to storage sheds, and cook fires blazed in the twilight. From the parapet of the west tower, Feldrin Feldspar surveyed the site as Merith stood close by.

"It will stand ten times a thousand years," declared the dwarf, clasping his stout arms behind his back. "An eternal bridge between Thorbardin and Qualinesti."

In the ruby glow of sunset, the stones of the citadel shone a soft pink. It was a magnificent yet lonely sight, the great gateway wedged between the slopes of the wide pass. Merith, who didn't care for heights, kept back from the unwalled edge of the tower top. Feldrin stood with his toes hanging over the edge, completely unconcerned about the long drop before him.

"How long until it's finished?" asked Merith.

"Barring strange quirks of weather and landslides, the east tower can be completed in six months. The fortress will be habitable then, though the inside details may take another year to dress out." Feldrin sighed, and it was like the grunt of an old bear.

He raised a hand to shade his eyes from the sun, setting behind the mountains to their left. Below, the pass was a narrow valley stretching away to the north. A small stream wended its way through the pass, shadowed now that the sun was nearly down. Staring up into the dark hollows of the high pass, the dwarf said, "Dust. Hmm . . . could be riders coming."

Merith moved as close as he dared to the edge of the parapet and looked up the valley. "From the north?" he queried. That meant Qualinost.

"Probably some dandified courtier or senator from the city who expects a guided tour of the fortress," growled Feldrin. "I guess this means I have to wash my hands and beard and put on a clean vest." He sniffed.

"It could be a courier from the Speaker," Merith suggested, "in which case you'll only have to wash your hands."

Feldrin caught the small smile on the fair-haired warrior's lips. "Very well! A compromise, lieutenant. I'll wash my hands and beard, but I won't change my vest!"

Chuckling, the two entered the stairwell sunk into the roof of the tower and descended the long set of steps. By the time they reached ground level and made their way outside, the rising plume of dust in the pass had been dispersed by the ever-present wind. There was no further sign of riders.

"Maybe they changed their minds and went home," joked Feldrin. He shrugged and added, "The dust must have come from a rockslide. All the better. Let's see what rubbish the cook has inflicted on us tonight."

In fact, Feldrin's cook was excellent. He did amazing things with the simple fare provided for the master builder's table. Dwarven food was usually too heavy for elves, but Feldrin's cook managed to prepare lighter dishes that Merith found quite delicious.

The lieutenant trailed after the fast-moving dwarf. Once more he looked up into the pass, where they had spotted the dust cloud.

"I wonder," he said softly. "Were they riders, or—"

"Come, Merith! Why are you lagging?"

There were no sentinels in Pax Tharkas. No night watch patrolled the sleeping complex of tent, huts, and sheds. None had ever been needed. Not even the grunt gang barracks were guarded once its single door was locked for the night. Thus it was that Ulvian slipped unseen out a window of the barracks and worked his way around the camp, collecting the items Dru had requested. From the plasterers' mixing shed, he got more than a pound of dry white clay, as fine and pure as cake flour. The prince dumped it in a wide-mouthed pottery jar and hurried on. He made for the long row of blacksmiths' sheds. Coal by the peck was available there, hard black coal from Thorbardin, which the dwarf smiths used to forge some of the hardest iron in the world. Ulvian crept up to the closest furnace. It still glowed dull orange from the day's fire. Squatting on the dirt floor, he picked through the rubbish that lay scattered around the hearth doors. He dropped several pieces of coal into the jar containing the clay.

The tanner's shed yielded a length of thong. Now . . . where to find a copper brazier? Dru had been quite specific; only copper would do. Hugging the pot of dry clay and coal to his chest, Ulvian ran across the open compound to the coppersmith's hut. Inside, he found an abundance of copper plates, nails, and ingots, but no brazier.

Outside once more, Ulvian huddled under the eaves of the hut for a moment, pondering where he might find what he needed. Only two kinds of people used copper fire pans: priests and cooks. There were no clerics at Pax Tharkas, but there were certainly cooks.

Half an hour later, Ulvian was back at the grunt gang barracks. He knelt by Dru's bed and reached a hand out to awaken the sorcerer.

Before Ulvian touched him, Dru said quietly, "Do you have it all?"

"Yes—and it wasn't easy."

"Good. Put it under my bed and go to sleep."

Ulvian was taken aback. "Aren't you going to do anything now?"

"At this hour? No indeed. Morning will be soon enough. Go to bed, my prince. Tomorrow will be a busy day, and you'll wish you had slept tonight." So saying, Dru rolled over and closed his eyes. Ulvian stared, mouth agape, at the sorcerer's back. With no other recourse, the prince shoved the pot, the cooking brazier, and the leather strap under Dru's bed and lay down on his own sagging, dirty cot. In spite of the excitement of the night's foray, he was asleep in a few minutes.

*　*　*　*　*

The soft sound of rattling chains caused Ulvian to open his eyes. A pair of scales was hanging in the air over his bed. The fulcrum of the scales was broken, and one of the golden pans was tilted, its chains sagging loosely. From the tilted pan, white powder fell, landing on Ulvian's chest. It looked like the clay powder he'd gotten for Dru.

"What's this?" he muttered, trying to sit up. Strangely he could not. A great weight seemed to settle on his chest, just where the powdered clay rested. But it was only a small heap of dust, his mind protested. It couldn't hold him pinioned in his bed.

The pressure grew and grew until the prince found it difficult to draw breath. He lifted a weak hand to deflect the stream of powder cascading down. When his fingers touched the golden scale pan, he snatched them back quickly. The pan was red hot!

"Help!" he gasped, continuing his efforts to rise. "I'm suffocating! Help!"

"Be still," said a soft, chiding voice. Ulvian opened his eyes and encountered blackness. He was lying facedown on his bunk, his nose and mouth buried in his dirty scrap of blanket. The prince bolted to his feet, flinging the blanket aside.

A wild glance around showed Dru sitting cross-legged on his own bed, mixing something in a wooden bowl. The grunt gang barracks were otherwise empty.

"What's the matter?" Dru asked, not looking up from his task.

"I—I had a bad dream," stammered the prince. "Where is everybody?"

"It's the half-day of rest," replied the sorcerer. "They're all at breakfast." He set aside his stirring stick and poured a bit more water into the bowl. The stick was thickly coated with gluey white clay.

Ulvian's breathing returned to normal, and he ran his fingers through his tousled hair. When he was calm, he went to see what Dru was doing. The sorcerer had made a ball of clay the size of two fists. He wet his hands and picked up the mass. The thong and copper brazier sat on the floor by his bed.

"One of the simplest kinds of spells is image magic," said Dru, sounding like some sort of schoolmaster. "The sorcerer makes an image and consecrates it as the double of a living person. Then whatever he does to the image happens to the living person." He rolled the clay into a long cylinder and tore off smaller bits, which he dropped into the bowl. "A more advanced spell creates an image that has no connection to the living. From that image, another double can be born."

Fascinated, Ulvian knelt on one knee. "Is that what you're doing?"

Dru nodded. "With this small figure, I will generate a much larger double that will do my bidding. Such clay creatures are called golems."

He had molded the rough form of a stocky body. To it, he attached clay arms and legs, and a round ball for a head. With chips of coal, Dru made eyes for the image. Laying the clay doll on the bed, he dipped the leather thong in the damp bowl.

The sorcerer tied the wet thong around the waist of the clay figure. Then he sent Ulvian to get some live coals and kindling from the fireplace. With a crackling fire laid in the brazier, Dru began dangling the clay figure over the flames.

"Rise up, O golem. Gather yourself from the dust and arise! I, Drulethen, command you! The fire is in you, the dust of the mountains! Gather yourself and do my will!" Unlike his usual soft tone, the sorcerer's voice was changing, deepening, strengthening.

Wind whistled through the chinks in the crude barracks walls. Outside, the grunt gang members lounging around the breakfast wagon grumbled loudly about the dust being whirled into their eyes. In the barracks, Dru twisted the thong in his fingers, making the clay doll spin, first left, then right.

"Rise up, O golem! Your form is here! Take the fire I give you and arise!" Dru shouted. Ulvian felt his skin crawl as the sorcerer's voice boomed through the room. The rafters of the poorly built barracks rattled, and bits of dried moss fell through the cracks.

Steam began to rise from the white clay doll. The smell of burning hide filled the prince's nostrils, threatening to gag him. The air vibrated, sending a tingling all along the surface of Ulvian's skin. The walls of the building groaned, and suddenly the complaints of the workers outside ceased. In seconds, hoarse shouts replaced the muttered grumblings.

"What's happening?" whispered Ulvian.

Breathing heavily, Dru never ceased his turning of the clay figure in the flames. "Go and see, my prince!" he gasped.

Ulvian went to the door and threw it open. The astonished faces of the grunt gang were looking off to the left, toward the quarries and the tent city. When he turned his face in that direction, the prince saw that a whirlwind of white dust writhed heavenward near the open pits where the limestone was cut. Elves, men, and dwarves ran from the area, shouting things Ulvian couldn't understand.

As Dru's invocation continued, the whirlwind coalesced into a thick, white body, twice as tall as the tallest tents. The black eyes on the featureless face mimicked the coal chips on the sorcerer's doll.

"By the gods!" Ulvian exclaimed, turning to Dru. "You've done it! It's as big as a watchtower!"

The sorcerer's hand was nearly invisible, shrouded by the steam rising from the baking clay figure. "Go!" he hissed. "The confusion will cover you. Get my black amulet!" Dru clenched his eyes shut, and tears trickled down his cheeks. The steam was scalding his hand. "Go! Hurry!"

"I will, but remember our bargain. You know who I want punished!" As he left, Ulvian closed the barracks door behind him. The grunt gang were all gone, and the dwarves who managed the food wagon had taken refuge underneath it. The clay giant was moving, striding stiffly across the camp, smashing through tents and huts as it went. The ground shook each time it took a step. No one tried to stop it. The workers weren't soldiers, and what arms there were in camp were of little avail against a twenty-foot-tall golem.

Feldrin Feldspar was in the west tower when the giant appeared. He heard the commotion and came outside in time to see the monster plowing through his workers' homes.

"By Reorx!" he shouted. "What is that thing?" No one stopped to answer his question, though he bellowed at his scattering people to stand and fight. The dwarf stood at the base of the west tower, shouting, until Merith appeared, mounted and in full battle armor.

"What do you propose, warrior?" Feldrin said, yelling above the uproar.

"Repel the monster," Merith replied simply. He drew his long elven blade. His buckskin horse pranced nervously, upset by the tumult around them.

"That's no natural beast!" Feldrin cried. "You'd be better off to find Drulethen. He's got to be behind this!"

"You find him," replied Merith. His horse turned a full circle. Touching his spurs to his mount's side, Merith was off, moving against the flow of terrified workers. All the artisans and laborers streamed toward the finished section of the citadel, seeking shelter from the rampaging giant.

Once clear of the panicked workers, Merith reined in and studied the monster as it tramped on. As nearly as he could tell, it hadn't injured anyone yet, but it had smashed about half a dozen huts with its thick feet and legs. It zigzagged around the camp as if it were looking for something.

Merith urged his horse forward, but the animal wanted no part of the giant. It reared and danced, trying to unseat its rider. The elf warrior held on and drew a yellow silk handkerchief from beneath his breastplate. It was a gift from a female admirer in Qualinost, but it served to cover his horse's eyes and quieted the animal somewhat. Merith wrapped the reins around his mailed fist and spurred ahead.

The golem halted and bent stiffly at the waist. Bits of dried clay the size of an elf's palm flaked off the giant's joints and fell to the ground.

Merith watched, fascinated, as the monster's hand split apart into five thick fingers. It plunged the hand into the ruins of a row of huts, and when it stood erect again, there was someone struggling in its grasp. The giant had the fellow by the throat. Merith saw that he was a Kagonesti elf.

Snapping down the visor on his helm, he charged at the monster. It paid no attention to him at all, even when Merith struck it full force with his sword. A wedge of hard white clay flew from the wound, but the giant was uninjured. The impact of the blow stung the elf warrior's arm. Grimacing, he struck again. Another chip of clay flew, but to no avail; the poor wretch in the monster's hand ceased kicking. The giant's black eyes never blinked. Opening its fingers, it allowed the Kagonesti to drop to the ground close to Merith.

657

Crouched under the awning of a hut, Prince Ulvian took in the scene with satisfaction. The death of his tormentor, Splint, pleased him immensely. He also saw the warrior, Merithynos, trying to subdue the clay giant with his sword. The prince laughed out loud at the lieutenant's antics, chopping at the mass of hard clay with comic futility.

Ulvian dashed down the lane, behind the busy Merith, up the hill toward Feldrin's hut. The golem had stomped flat nearly every other structure around the master builder's home. Ulvian burst through the door flap.

The outer room was empty. He searched every box and chest, with no result. The structure was divided by a canvas wall, the other half being Feldrin's bedchamber. Ulvian bolted in and pulled up sharply. Feldrin himself stood guard over a small golden casket.

"So," said the dwarf coolly, "you have joined forces with Drulethen."

"Give me the amulet," Ulvian said in a commanding tone.

"Don't be a fool, boy! He's using you. Can't you see that? He'd promise anything to get his hands on that amulet again—and break every promise once he had it. He has no honor, Highness. He will destroy you if he has the chance."

"Save your entreaties for someone else!" Ulvian's voice was a harsh, angry rasp. "My father sent me here to suffer, and I've suffered enough. Drulethen has sworn to serve me, and serve me he will. You all think I'm a fool, but you'll find out differently." There was a loud crash nearby, and Ulvian added impatiently, "Now surrender the amulet, or the golem will crush you to jelly!"

Feldrin drew a jeweled shortsword from behind his back. "You will get it from me only after I'm dead," he said solemnly.

Ulvian was unarmed. Feldrin's keen sword and the steely look of determination in the dwarf's eyes discouraged any rash action.

"You'll regret this!" the prince declared, edging back toward the doorway in the canvas wall. "The golem won't stand and argue with you. Once he comes, you will die!"

"Then it is by Reorx's will."

Furious, Ulvian dashed out of the tent. He nearly bowled over Dru, who was coming in his direction. The sorcerer cradled his left hand to his chest, and his ragged robes were soaked with sweat.

"Did you get it?" he cried, desperation glazing his eyes.

"No, Feldrin is guarding it. Why aren't you with the brazier? Is the spell over?"

Dru mustered his strength; his spell had exhausted him. "I hung the doll over the brazier. The thong is almost burned in two. When it severs, the magic will end."

The giant figure of the golem came into view over Dru's shoulder. It had nearly reached the citadel. The parapets were lined with workers, many of whom were hurling stones at the unheeding monster.

"Can you control it?" asked Ulvian quickly. "If you can, then bring it here. It's the only way to scare Feldrin into giving up the amulet!"

Wordlessly the sorcerer slid to his knees. His eyelids fluttered closed. Ulvian thought he had fainted, but Dru's lips were moving slightly.

Abruptly the golem did a jerky about-face and came marching toward Feldrin's hut. Merith dogged its heels, no longer slashing with his sword, but keeping it in view. When the elf warrior spied Ulvian and Dru, he put his head down and rode hard toward them.

"Merith is coming!" shouted the prince.

Still the sorcerer chanted. The golem's wide, round head swiveled down to look at the mounted warrior. An arm the thickness of a mature oak limb swept down, knocking horse and rider to the ground. The horse let out a shriek and lay still. Merith struggled vainly but was pinned under his dead mount.

"That got him!" Ulvian cried, leaping into the air in his excitement.

"And I've got you," said Feldrin from the door of his hut. Startled, the prince stepped back.

The dwarf had been a fighter of some note in his youth, and he knew how to handle a sword. Raising the jeweled blade high, he advanced toward Dru. The sorcerer never flinched, so complete was his concentration. Ulvian flung himself at the dwarf and grappled with him. The golem was only a score of yards away, and its long stride ate up the distance rapidly.

"Let go!" roared Feldrin. "I've no wish to harm you, Prince Ulvian, but I must—"

His muscled arms pushed steadily against Ulvian's lighter strength. The prince's grip was slipping. Gleaming in the morning sun, Feldrin's sword was only inches from the sorcerer's skull.

A wall of white fell on the prince and the dwarf. Ulvian was knocked backward through the air, landing hard on a pile of torn canvas and broken tent stakes. The breath was driven from his body, and the world vanished in a red, roaring haze.

Hands propped the prince up. He gasped and fought for air, and at last breath whooshed into his lungs. His vision cleared, and he saw Dru kneeling beside him. Ulvian shook his head to clear it, for he saw a remarkable thing: The spell animating the golem had obviously ended and the giant had fallen on Feldrin's hut, breaking into several large clay pieces. From under a barrel-sized portion of the monster's torso, Feldrin's fur-wrapped legs protruded. His feet twitched slightly. A groan sounded from under the mass of clay.

Dru was shaking and drenched with sweat, but his voice was triumphant as he said, "Where's the amulet?" Ulvian stammered that Feldrin kept the onyx talisman in a golden box. The sorcerer dashed into the ruins of the master builder's hut.

A profound silence had fallen over the construction camp. Ulvian blinked and gazed across the wrecked site. The walls of the citadel were lined with workers, all staring at him. Already some were leaving the parapet, no doubt to hurry to Feldrin's rescue.

Dru was tearing through the broken bits of hut, muttering. Ulvian called out, "We must flee! The workers are coming!"

The sorcerer didn't even respond, but kept up his frantic digging. Feldrin groaned once more, louder. Ulvian picked his way through the chunks of lifeless golem. He pushed a heavy slab of clay off the dwarf and knelt beside him.

"I regret this, Master Feldrin, " said the prince. "But injustice requires strong deeds."

The dwarf coughed, and blood appeared on his lips. "Don't go with Drulethen, my prince. With him lies only ruin and death. . . ."

"Aha!" shouted the sorcerer, falling to his knees. He flung aside a bit of canvas, revealing the gilded box. No sooner did Dru stoop to pick it up than he shrieked in pain and dropped it again.

"You filthy worm!" he howled at Feldrin. "You put my amulet in a charmed case!" But Feldrin had lost consciousness and was beyond Dru's maledictions.

"Come here!" the sorcerer barked peremptorily. "Pick up the box."

Ulvian glared at him. "I'm not your servant," he retorted.

The first band of workers from the citadel appeared at the end of the wrecked street. They were armed with hammers, staves, and mason's tools. Eight men went to lift the dead horse off the fallen Merith. The warrior got stiffly to his feet and pointed expressively toward Feldrin's tent.

"There's no time for false pride now!" Dru spat. "Do you think those fools are going to pat us on the back for what we've done? It's time to flee, and I can't touch that wretched box. Pick it up, I say!"

Reluctantly Ulvian did so. Then he and the shaken sorcerer ran for the corral near the foot of the eastern slope. The prince snared two horses, short-legged mountain ponies, and boosted the weakened Dru onto one of them. Bareback, the pair rode hell-for-leather out the gate, scattering the other animals as they went. By the time the outraged workers reached the corral, not a single horse remained, and the only sign of the fugitives was a rapidly rising cloud of dust.

* * * * *

Merith stood by a crackling fire, which blazed in a wide stone urn outside Feldrin Feldspar's hut. In spite of his badly bruised left leg, he had insisted on standing guard personally outside the master builder's home. The entire camp was silent, and nothing stirred but the wavering flames before him. The lieutenant kept his cloak close around his throat to ward off a persistent chill.

The clip-clop of horse's hooves alerted him. Quickly he stepped back from the fire, back into the deep shadows cast by the hut's overhanging roof. Drawing his sword, he set his shield tightly on his forearm. The hoofbeats drew nearer.

A tall figure, mounted on a rather tired-looking sorrel, emerged from the night. The newcomer's face and figure were obscured by a long, monkish robe with a deep hood. The rider approached the fire and dismounted. He peeled off a pair of deerskin gloves and held his long, tapered fingers to the heat. Merith watched carefully. Short plumes of warm breath issued from the stranger's hood. Though he waited long minutes, the newcomer made no threatening moves. Warming his icy hands and body seemed to be his greatest concern. The lieutenant stepped out of the shadows and faced the robed figure.

"Who goes there?" he demanded.

"A weary traveler," answered the stranger. He spoke through the lower edge of the hood, and his words were muffled. "I saw your fire from a distance and stopped to warm myself."

"You are welcome, traveler," Merith said warily.

"A naked sword is a strange welcome. Are you troubled by bandits hereabouts?"

"Not bandits. A single elf did all this. A sorcerer."

The hooded one jerked his hands back from the fire. "A sorcerer! Why would a sorcerer trouble a lonely outpost such as this?"

"The evil one was a captive here, a prisoner of the King of Thorbardin and the Speaker of the Sun," Merith explained. "Through treachery, he regained his powers, wrecked the camp, and escaped."

The visitor passed a hand across his hidden brow. Merith caught the glint of metal at the fellow's throat. Armor? Or just a decorative torc?

The stranger asked how the sorcerer had escaped. The elf warrior told him briefly about the golem, though he didn't mention Ulvian's part in the affair. The visitor asked endless questions, and Merith found the late-night conversation tired him. His leg ached unmercifully, and his heart was heavy with the news he must send to his sovereign. The hooded stranger must be a cleric, he decided. Only they were so talky and inquisitive.

Weariness was banished instantly when Merith saw a pair of horses appear at the far end of the path. One of the riders was wearing armor. Merith lifted his sword and shield. The hooded stranger waved at him soothingly.

"Put down your weapons, noble warrior. These are friends of mine," he said. In a swirl of dark robes, the hooded one turned and hailed the two mounted fellows.

"Is something the matter, sire?" called the armored rider.

"Sire?" wondered Merith.

The stranger faced Merith and tossed back his hood. Pale hair gleamed in the firelight. It was Kith-Kanan himself.

"Great Speaker!" Merith cried. "Forgive me! I had no idea—"

"Be at ease." Kith-Kanan waved, and Kemian Ambrodel and his father, Tamanier, rode up to the crackling fire.

"Are there just the three of you, Majesty?" asked Merith, scanning the path for more riders. "Where is your entourage?"

"I have a small party at the high end of the pass," Kith-Kanan explained. "I came down with the Ambrodels to find out what had happened. Even in the dark, the camp looks like a cyclone hit it."

Merith told the story of Drulethen, Ulvian, and the golem in detail, this time leaving out nothing. "I led a band of fifty trusted workers along the trail Prince Ulvian and Drulethen made," he finished, "but we couldn't hope to catch up on foot."

"Never mind, Lieutenant. Is Feldrin Feldspar well?" asked the Speaker.

"He has some broken ribs, but he will survive, sire." Merith managed a smile.

Kemian relieved the younger warrior and sent Merith to bed. Once the lieutenant was gone, Kith-Kanan shed his monkish habit, revealing full battle armor.

"I had a premonition something evil would happen," Kith-Kanan said grimly. "Now it is up to me to set things right. Tomorrow Lord Kemian and I will take the escort cavalry and go after Drulethen."

Tamanier said, "And Prince Ulvian?"

The silence in the camp was unbroken except by the soft snapping of the fire in the urn before them. The Speaker stared into the flames, the light giving his face and hair a ruddy glow. When the castellan was certain his sovereign wasn't going to answer, Kith-Kanan looked up and said evenly, "My son will face the consequences of his deeds."

The Green and Golden Way

12

The high plains in summer were a harsh place. Dry and barren, they were frequently swept by grass fires that would burn right up to the stony bases of the Kharolis Mountains before dying out from lack of tinder. Yet as Verhanna, Rufus, and Greenhands ascended the sloping plain toward the distant blue peaks, the grassland was not only green, but also covered with flowers.

"Aashoo!" The kender sneezed loudly. "Where did all dese flowers come fum?" he muttered through a clogged nose. The air was thick with blowing pollen, released by the thousands of wild flowers. Verhanna wasn't much bothered by it, though she was startled by the vigor and variety of the flowers around them. The plain was an ocean of crimson, yellow, blue, and purple blossoms, all nodding gently in the breeze.

"You know, I've been this way before, on the way to Pax Tharkas," she said. "But I've never seen the grasslands bloom like this. And in the heat of midsummer!"

Ahead of them, his rough horsehair poncho coated with yellow dust, Greenhands walked steadily onward. His simple, sturdy features took on a special nobility in the warm light of day, and Verhanna found herself studying him more and more as they traveled.

"Ushwah!" barked Rufus. "Dis is tewwibuh! I cand bweathe!"

The warrior maiden dug deep into her saddlebag. In a moment, she brought out a thin red pod, shriveled into a curl. "Here," she said, tossing it to her scout. "Chew on that. It'll clear your head."

Rufus sniffed the tiny pod, but to no avail; nothing could penetrate his stuffy nose. "Whad is id?" he asked suspiciously.

"Give it back, then, if you don't want it," Verhanna said airily.

"Oh, all wide." The kender stuck the stem end of the seed pod in his mouth and chewed. In seconds, his look of curiosity was replaced by one of horror.

"Ye-ow!" Rufus's shriek rent the calm, flower-scented air. Greenhands halted and looked back, startled out of his unvarying gait. "Dat's hot!" protested the kender, his small face purpling in distress.

"It's a dragonseed pod," Verhanna replied. "Of course it's hot. But it will clear your head." Despite its fearsome name, dragonseed was a common spice plant grown in the river delta region of Silvanesti. It was used to make the famous vantrea, a hot, spicy dried fish that was beloved by southern elves.

Their horses overtook Greenhands. Verhanna reined in and said, "Don't worry. Wart was complaining about the pollen, so I did a little healing of my own."

Tears running down his cheeks, Rufus sluiced his tingling mouth out with water. Then he sniffed, and a pleased expression spread across his florid features. "What do you know! I can breathe!" he declared.

Greenhands had been standing between their two horses. Now he headed out once more, and they rode after him.

Verhanna urged her mount forward until she was alongside the silver-haired elf. The day was quite warm, and he had flipped back the front edges of his makeshift poncho, exposing his chest to the sun. In secret, sidelong glances, the warrior maiden admired his physique. With a little training, perhaps he could become a formidable warrior.

"Why do you stare at me?" asked Greenhands, intruding on the captain's thoughts.

"Tell me the truth, Greenhands," she said in a low voice. "How is it you're able to do the things you do? How did you heal my shoulder? How did you turn aside a herd of wild elk? Raise flowers out of dry soil?"

There was a long pause before he replied. Finally he said, "I've been thinking about those things. There seems to be something with me. Something I carry . . . like this garment." He passed a hand over the coarse fabric of the blanket he wore. "I feel it around me and inside me, but I can't set it aside. I can't separate myself from it."

Intrigued, Verhanna asked, "What does it feel like?"

Shutting his eyes, he lifted his face to the golden sunlight. "It's like the heat of the sun," he murmured. "I feel it, yet I can't touch it. I carry it with me, but I can't take it off." He opened his eyes and regarded her. "Am I mad, Captain?"

"No," she said, and her voice was soft. "You're not mad."

A piercing whistle cut her off. "Hey!" Rufus called from behind them. "Are you two going to walk right off the edge?"

Greenhands and Verhanna halted, taking in their surroundings. Not five paces in front of them was a deep ravine, cut through the grassy sod by some winter flood. They had been so absorbed in their conversation, neither had noticed the danger.

They turned and paralleled the rift for a dozen yards. Behind them, Rufus rode up to the lip of the ravine and gazed across. On the other side, the sere plain was covered with dry brown grass. At the kender's back, the landscape was carpeted with lush green grass and a riot of blooming flowers.

"Wha—how!" A neck-snapping sneeze wrenched the kender. His nose felt like it was filling even as he sat. Kicking his heels against his horse's red flanks, Rufus hastened after his captain. He hoped she could discover another dragonseed pod in her saddlebag.

* * * * *

Late in the afternoon, the trio was well into the shadowed presence of the Kharolis Mountains. Peaks welled up on three sides, and the open ground was ever steeper in grade. Hereabouts there was only one path through the mountains wide enough for horses, and it funneled directly to Pax Tharkas.

Once the carpet of grass and flowers thinned, Rufus found his head much clearer. He occupied his time by tootling discordantly on a reed pipe he'd made back at the Astradine River. The shrill cacophony got on Verhanna's nerves, and finally she snatched the reed from the kender's lips.

"Are you trying to drive me mad?" she snapped.

He bristled. "That was a kender ballad, 'You Took My Heart While I Took Your Rings.' "

"Ha! Trust a wart like you to know a love song with theft in it." Verhanna tossed the reed flute away, but Greenhands detoured from his path to retrieve it. The warrior maiden sighed. "Don't you plague me with that thing either," she warned.

Unheeding, the elf put the flute to his mouth and blew a few experimental notes. His fingers ran up and down the scale, and the instrument trilled melodically. Rufus raised his head and peered down at Greenhands.

"How did you do that?" he asked. Greenhands shrugged, a gesture he'd only lately acquired from Verhanna. Rufus asked for his flute back. When he had it, he piped several notes. Verhanna grimaced; it still sounded like the death throes of a crow.

Before she could voice her protest again, Rufus thrust the reed flute back at Greenhands. "You keep it," he said generously. "It's not refined enough for kender music."

His captain snorted. The elf accepted the instrument gravely and walked along slowly, playing random notes. Without warning, a red-breasted songbird settled on his shoulder. The tiny bird regarded Greenhands curiously, its beady black eyes almost intelligent.

"Hello," Greenhands said calmly. Verhanna and Rufus stared. The strange elf put the flute to his lips and played a fluttering trill. Much to his companions' astonishment, his feathered friend imitated the sound perfectly.

"Very good. Now this." He sounded a slightly more complex series of notes. The redbreast repeated the notes exactly.

A second bird, slightly larger and duller in color, circled the elf's head and settled on the opposite shoulder. A funny sort of musical trio began, as Greenhands and the little songbird exchanged perfectly pitched notes, while the brown thrush added off-key harmonics.

"The big bird sounds like you," Verhanna commented to the kender. Rufus answered her with a rude noise.

The captain's mount danced in a circle. The greenfingered elf had attracted more and more birds; in seconds, he was wrapped in a cloud of wildly singing creatures. He seemed unworried by them, continuing to walk steadily forward as his flute trilled. However, the birds were unnerving the horses.

"Stop it!" Verhanna called to Greenhands. "Send them away!" He couldn't hear her over the shrill sound of birdsongs. More and more birds appeared, zooming around the group, dipping, soaring, diving. Wing tips and tails grazed their faces. Their mounts bucked and danced.

"Yow!"

A sizable starling thudded into the kender's back. He yanked off his hat and began swinging it at the darting creatures without success. A careening purple martin flew too close to Verhanna and smacked solidly into her neck. She quickly pulled her visor down to protect her eyes. Though her hands were full trying to calm her frantic horse, she managed to draw her sword.

With a loud war cry, the captain drove her nervous mount hard at Greenhands. Birds thumped off her armored head and against her horse. Verhanna pushed through the swarm. Completely unaware of the havoc he was causing, the elf was walking along in the center of an avian maelstrom, playing Rufus's flute.

Verhanna struck the pipe from the elf's hands with the flat of her blade. The instant the notes ceased, the birds stopped their mad whirling and dispersed quickly in all directions.

Greenhands stared at the broken flute lying in the grass. He picked up the two halves and then turned accusing eyes upon Verhanna.

"Your playing drove those birds mad," she explained, panting. He clearly had no idea what she was talking about. "We could've been killed!"

Understanding dawned on his face, and he apologized. "I'm sorry. I didn't mean to make trouble."

Rufus rode up, brushing feathers from his topknot. "Blind me with beeswax! What was that all about?"

Verhanna pointed to the chastened Greenhands. "Our friend here doesn't understand the power he has."

Humbly he repeated, "I'm sorry."

They resumed their march, guided by Greenhands. Though he honestly disavowed any knowledge of the fortress, it was obviously their destination.

The flowering grassland gave way to piles of boulders spotted by patches of dark green lichen. Coolness crept into the warm air of daytime, promising a brisk night. The sun sank behind the mountain peaks, washing the sky in gold, crimson, and finally deepest burgundy. As the last of the light was dying from the day, Verhanna dismounted. They had come to a wide spot in the pass, only a few hundred paces from the entrance. "We can camp here for the night," she decided.

The kender and the elf were agreeable. They tethered their horses and built a campfire. Rufus did the cooking for the little band. Considering a kender's ideas about dinner, things weren't bad. He busied himself warming a soup of dried vegetables, bread crumbs, and water while his captain curried their animals.

Greenhands settled down by the fire, staring unblinking into the flames. The yellow light made his green eyes and fingers stand out against the dark background of his poncho. Verhanna found herself peering at him over the back of her horse. Her right hand, wielding the curry comb, slowed and stopped in its motion as her scrutiny of the elf intensified. The light tan of his skin was deepened by the golden glow of the firelight. Though at rest, his well-formed body showed a lithe grace and beauty she found arresting. His profile was somehow quite attractive. Strong brow, rather a long nose, firm lips, a good chin. . . .

She brought herself up short. What was she doing? So many unfamiliar thoughts tumbled in her head. But one, quite odd, idea took precedence.

Could Greenhands be the husband she never thought she'd find?

A smile tugged the corners of her mouth upward. Wouldn't her father be surprised? He'd wanted her to marry for a long time. Though he never pushed openly, the warrior maiden knew he longed for her to be wife and mother. As quickly as this thought occurred to her, a sharp chill set her to shuddering. The mountain air had cooled rapidly with the setting of the sun.

When she'd finished with the horses, Verhanna wrapped her bedroll around her shoulders and settled by the fire. The kender was just downing the last of his soup. He handed her a bowl and, while she ate, he skipped around the campsite, humming his tuneless kender songs.

"What are you so happy about?" Verhanna asked him with a smile.

"I like the mountains," he said. "When the air is thin and the nights are cold, then Rufus Wrinklecap is at home!"

Verhanna laughed, but Greenhands' eyes were closed, and gentle snores issued from his mouth. Though still sitting upright, the elf had fallen fast asleep.

The kender scaled a pile of boulders resting against the sheer wall of the mountain behind the warrior maiden. When she asked what he was doing, Rufus replied, "In these parts, it's not wise to lie on low ground."

Her brow wrinkled in thought. "Why not?"

"Falling rocks, sudden floods, prowling wolves, poisonous snakes. . . ." The kender spoke a cheerful litany of disaster. He stopped and added a blithe "Good night, my captain. Sleep well!"

How well could she sleep after his listing of all those dangers? Her brown eyes searched the darkness beyond their dying fire. Moonlight and starlight washed the mountain pass, and the air was filled with the faint but normal sounds of night. The warrior maiden set her empty soup bowl down and sidled around the fire until she was close to Greenhands. Laying her head down by his crossed legs, she reasoned that since he seemed so connected to the wild, then he was probably safe from any natural disasters or creatures of the night.

The strange elf still slept upright, his head drooping toward the embers. The white light of Solinari washed his hair in silver. The dying firelight tinged the silver with rose. A single coral-hued strand had fallen across his closed eyes. Verhanna put up a hand to brush it away, but as her finger drew near, she shivered violently. It wasn't the cold of the night, for under her bedroll, by the fire, she was quite warm.

It must be tiredness, she decided, and the lingering effects of the goblin bite. The Qualinesti princess withdrew her hand and put her head down to sleep.

Verhanna's rest was troubled. She wasn't usually prone to disturbing dreams, but on this occasion, visions appeared in her mind, images of magic and power in a dark forest peopled by her father, Ulvian, Greenhands, and some others she didn't recognize. One countenance appeared frequently—a Kagonesti woman unknown to her. The wild elf woman had eyes the same brilliant green as Greenhands, and her face was painted with yellow and red lines. Her expression was ineffably sad, but in spite of the barbaric face paint, it was also regal and proud.

A faint noise intruded on Verhanna's visions. The warrior maiden's trained senses brought her fully awake. Only her eyes shifted as she tried to discover what had disturbed her. The fire was out, though a thin ribbon of white smoke rose from the bed of cinders. Her half-human eyes weren't as sharp as those of her fullblooded elf kin, but they were better than any human's. The moons had set, but the light of the stars was enough for her to make out a dark shape hovering over their pile of baggage, only a few yards from where she lay.

Kender, if you're trying to scare me, I'll have your topknot for a feather duster, she vowed silently. The black shape rose from its crouch. It was far too tall to be Rufus Wrinklecap.

In a flash, Verhanna rolled to her feet and drew her sword. She'd been lying on it, just in case Rufus was right about wolves. The intruder flinched and backed away. She heard hooves striking the stony ground. Her opponent must be mounted.

"Who are you?" Verhanna demanded. A strong animal smell invaded her nostrils.

More hoofbeats thumped in the shadows beyond Verhanna's line of sight. She was getting worried; there was no telling how many foes she faced. Advancing to the firepit, she kicked some of the kindling Rufus had piled up onto the coals. The dry bark caught quickly and blazed up.

"Kothlolo!" With a loud bass cry, the thing near their baggage threw up an arm to shield its eyes. Verhanna gasped when she saw it clearly—it had the head, arms, and torso of a man, but four legs and a swishing horse's tail. A centaur!

"Kothlolo!" shouted the centaur again. The circle of firelight caught the movement of other centaurs a few paces away. Verhanna shouted to Rufus and Greenhands to wake up.

"Rufus! Rufus, you dung beetle! Where are you?" she called.

"Here, my captain." He was just behind her. She wrenched her gaze from the nearest centaur long enough to spy the kender sitting atop a large boulder. "Who are your new friends?" he asked innocently.

"Idiot! Centaurs murder travelers! Some of them are cannibals!"

"Ho," rumbled the nearest centaur. "Only eat ugly two-legs."

She almost dropped her sword in surprise. "You speak Elven?"

"Some." On Verhanna's left and right, half-man, half-horse creatures pressed in toward the fire. She counted seven of them, five brown and two black. They carried rusty iron swords and spears or crude clubs made from small tree trunks. The one who had spoken to Verhanna carried a bow and quiver of arrows slung across his body.

"You do not fight, we do not fight," he said, cocking his brown head at her. Verhanna put her back against the boulder and kept her sword ready. Above her, Rufus loaded his sling.

"What do you want?" asked the warrior maiden.

"I am Koth, leader of this band. We follow the *jerda*, we hunt them," said the centaur. He held up hairy brown fingers to his forehead to imitate horns. Understanding dawned on Verhanna. He meant the elk herd. "Jerda ran hard, and we lost them. Kothlolo are very hungry."

Kothlolo must be the centaur word for "centaur," Verhanna decided. "We haven't much food ourselves," she said. "We did see the elk herd. It was heading toward the Astradine River."

A black-coated centaur picked up her saddlebags and pawed through them. He found a lump of bacon and shoved it in his mouth. Immediately those nearest him swarmed over him, trying to snatch the smoked meat from his lips. The centaurs dissolved into a bucking, scrabbling fight, with only the bass-voiced Koth remaining aloof.

"They are pretty hungry," Rufus observed.

"And numerous," mumbled Verhanna. She couldn't very well start a fight with so many centaurs. She and Rufus might well end up as the main course at a losers' banquet.

"Where's Greenhands?" she said softly, looking around.

Through all the talking and squabbling over food, Greenhands had sat unmoving, lost in slumber. So complete was his sleep, Verhanna felt obliged to see if he was breathing. He was.

"By Astra, when he sleeps, he sleeps," she muttered.

A centaur found Rufus's store of walnuts in his ration bag. The others tore at his hand, scattering the nuts over the campsite. A few landed on Greenhands' head, and he finally stirred.

"You're alive," Verhanna said caustically. "I thought I was going to have to beat a gong."

The elf's face was blank. He licked his dry lips and said, "I've been away. Far away. I saw my mother and spoke to her." Looking up at Verhanna, he added, "You were with me for a time. In the forest, with others I did not know."

Had they been sharing the same dream? At another time, Verhanna might have been curious, but just now she had other worries. "Never mind that now," she said to the elf. "We've got a camp full of wild, starving centaurs."

Greenhands started in surprise. He jumped to his feet and walked right up to the centaur leader.

"Greetings, uncle," he said. "How fare you?"

As Rufus and Verhanna exchanged looks of consternation, Koth bowed and replied, "I am a dried gourd, my cousin. And my cousins here are likewise empty."

"My friends have little to eat, uncle. May I show you to a stand of mountain apples? They are nearby and very sweet."

The centaur laughed, showing fearsome yellow teeth. "Ho, little cousin! I am not so young in the world that I think there are apples in early summer!"

Greenhands pressed a hand to his heart. "They are there, uncle. Will you come?"

The sincerity of his manner won over the centaur's natural skepticism. He snapped an order to his squabbling comrades, and the band of centaurs formed behind Greenhands. Then, without a brand to light the way, he stepped into the darkness, up the far slope. The centaurs followed, their small, worn hooves fitting deftly into the clefts in the rocks.

Rufus jumped off his boulder and started after them. "You too?" snorted the warrior woman.

"My captain, I doubt nothing about that elf."

Sheathing her sword, Verhanna found herself alone by the campfire. With a long-suffering sigh, she reluctantly followed the troop. Rufus made his way easily up the slope; the going was less easy for her, being larger and burdened with armor. Soon Rufus pulled away from her, and the only sign she had of him was the steady trickle of pebbles he dislodged on his way up.

The slope ended suddenly. A ravine plunged down in front of Verhanna, and she almost fell face first into it. She flung her hands wide on the crumbling, gravelly soil and cursed herself for following Greenhands in the middle of the night. Once she'd gotten to her feet and dusted the dirt from her palms, Verhanna looked down into the shallow ravine. She was amazed by what she saw. There, nestled close to the sheer wall of the rising mountain, was a stand of apple trees, heavy with fruit. The Qualinesti princess moved down for a closer look.

The ground around the trees was littered with fallen apples, some rotten-soft, and the air was spiced by their fermented odor. The centaurs appeared to esteem these, for they galloped up and down the ravine, filling their arms with the fallen fruit. Greenhands, Rufus, and Koth, the centaur leader, were standing together under the largest apple tree. The ancient tree was warped by wind and frost, yet its gnarled roots gripped the stony earth tenaciously.

"How did you know these were here?" Verhanna asked.

Greenhands looked at the laden branches close to his head. "I heard them. Old trees have loud voices," he said.

Verhanna was speechless. His words seemed completely ridiculous to her, yet she couldn't dispute the find.

Rufus went to the tree and climbed up to a triple fork of branches. He inched out on a branch until he could just reach a ripe fruit still hanging from the tree. Before his fingers could close on it, Greenhands was there, his moss-colored fingers wrapping tightly around the kender's wrist.

"No, little friend," he chided. "You mustn't take what the tree has not offered!"

Koth popped a whole apple in his mouth and chewed it up—stem, seeds, skin, and all. He grinned at Verhanna. "Your cousin with the green fingers is one of the old ones," he said.

"Old ones" was a common epithet given to members of the elven race. Verhanna, still ill-at-ease around the centaur band, said, "He's not my cousin."

"All peoples are cousins," answered Koth. Bits of overripe apple flew from his mouth. The other centaurs were racing around the ravine, yelling and dancing. Verhanna realized that the fermented fruit was making them tipsy. Soon the centaurs were singing, arms looped around their fellows' shoulders. Their bass and baritone voices sounded surprisingly harmonious.

Koth sang:

> *"Child of oak, newly born,*
> *Walks among the mortals mild,*
> *By lightning from his mother torn.*
> *Who knows the father of this child?*
> *Who hears music in the flowers' way*
> *And fears no creature in the wild*
> *Shall wear a crown made far away*
> *And dwell within a tower tiled."*

"You made up a song about Greenhands," Rufus said admiringly. "That part about crowns, though—"

"It is a very sad song," Koth interrupted. "My grand-father's grandfather sang it, and 'twas ancient then."

Verhanna was growing tired of the drunken, bumptious centaurs. When one thumped into her for the second time, she announced she was going back to get some sleep. She strongly hinted that Rufus and Greenhands should do likewise.

"Cousin," said Koth to Greenhands, "You travel far?"

The centaurs quieted down and gathered around the green-fingered elf. "Yes, uncle. My father awaits me in a high place of stone," replied Greenhands.

"Then take this with you, gentle cousin." Koth took a ram's horn that hung by a strap around his neck and gave it to the elf. "If ever you need the Sons of the Wind, blow hard on this horn and we shall come."

"Thank you, uncle, and all my cousins," Greenhands said, looping the strap around his neck.

He led the warrior maiden and the kender back to their camp. No one spoke. The shouts of the centaurs echoed once more through the peaks, slurred now as they continued to eat the fermented apples. Greenhands returned to the same boulder he'd sat by before, and he was asleep nearly as soon as he sat down. Rufus climbed back up to his safe perch, and Verhanna curled up by the dying fire. The smell of the centaurs lingered in her nostrils a long time. So did the words to Koth's ancient song.

The Great Stone House

13

Dru and Ulvian rode all day without stopping. The rugged mountain ponies were hardy beasts, but even they rebelled at such treatment. By evening, they were panting and balking. In a fury, Dru lashed at his mount with a cut sapling switch. The pony responded by throwing the short-tempered sorcerer to the ground and galloping away.

Ulvian, sitting calmly on his own mount, watched Dru's fall and the flight of the abused pony. Dru scrambled to his feet and shouted, "After him! Worthless nag! I'll flay him if I ever get my hands on him!"

"Seems unlikely, from where I sit," remarked the prince. He slid off his horse, wincing. Riding bareback through the mountains for six hours had taken its toll on his aching backside.

Dru scowled and threw the hair back from his eyes. His manner had changed considerably since they left Pax Tharkas; his respectfulness, never sincere, had vanished completely. Sitting on a convenient boulder, he stared daggers in the direction of the fleeing pony.

All anger at the horse was forgotten, though, when Ulvian pulled the golden box out of his ragged cloak. The gilt flashed in the failing daylight. Dru licked his thin lips expectantly as Ulvian set the box on the ground between his feet. The prince produced the only tool he had, a mason's trowel he'd picked up near Feldrin's tent. He poked and scraped at the box. The gilt covering was supple, like leather, but the hard dwarven iron of the trowel didn't even scratch it. A charmed box indeed. Ulvian examined the hinges, the hasp in front, and the seal that held the box closed.

"Well?" Dru demanded peevishly. "What are you waiting for? Open it!"

"I shall. There's no sense blundering into it, though." The sorcerer slapped his thigh in frustration.

Ulvian lifted the seal on its silken string. He guessed that Feldrin wouldn't rely on a flimsy wax seal alone to protect the black amulet. Hooking the tip of the trowel inside the loop of silk, he broke the seal. Dru inhaled sharply.

"Now," he breathed. "Open it!"

The prince set the box down. The hasp was loose. Very gently he inserted the tip of the trowel under the lid and, with a sudden jerk, flipped the lid up. Something moved with blinding speed toward his hand. Ulvian recoiled and drove the trowel like a knife into the yellowgreen thing that had leapt at him.

Dru peered over his shoulder. "What is it?"

Skewered neatly on the tool was a large spider with a red rectangle on its belly.

"A headstone spider," Dru said. His tone was admiring. "One bite means certain death. Old Feldrin wasn't such a fool after all."

The prince flung the dead spider aside. Inside the box was a folded piece of silver cloth. Though there was little light remaining, the silver material threw off scintillas of light. When Ulvian touched it, its surface rippled with iridescent colors. The lumpy shape of the onyx amulet was obvious beneath the supple material. Without removing the cloth, he surreptitiously pushed the cylinder out of the ring, separating the halves of the magic talisman.

"Give it to me," Dru ordered imperiously. "Why are you so slow? Give me my amulet!"

Ulvian's hazel eyes glittered like cold metal as he looked at the sorcerer. "And if I don't? Will you flay me like the tired pony?"

The sorcerer balled his fists and nudged Ulvian sharply with his knee. "Don't be a fool!" he thundered. "The whole point of our escaping was to get my amulet back! It's of no use to you. Give it to me!"

Ulvian stood abruptly and presented the point of the trowel to Dru's throat. Reddish blood, the poisonous blood of the headstone spider, covered the tool's sharp tip. Dru blanched and turned his head away.

"You seem to forget that I am a prince," Ulvian snapped.

Dru swallowed hard and forced a smile. It was the ghastly expression of a grinning skull. "My friend," he said, striving for a soothing tone, "be at ease. I was—I am—very nervous about getting my property back. Did I not save you from the stone block?

Didn't my golem avenge the insults inflicted on you by Splint? We are free now, my prince, but vulnerable. Only my magic can protect us from the wrath of your father and the dwarf king."

The trowel was lowered a few inches. "I am not afraid of my father. I have no intention of hiding from him," Ulvian said slowly. "My only thought in aiding you was to escape those thugs in Pax Tharkas who seemed bent on murdering me. Now that we are free, I intend to make my way back to Qualinost."

"But, Highness," Dru objected, "How do you know your father won't simply return you to Pax Tharkas? Your supposed crimes are now compounded by mayhem, murder, and escape. I would not trust the Speaker's mercy. Better to return with me at your side, my prince, fully armed with all my black arts and ready to defend you!"

Ulvian bent over and lifted the wrapped amulet. Dru's eyes bulged. Color flooded his face, and his breath hissed out. Ulvian shook the silver cloth, and a single piece of onyx—the ring—fell out into Dru's hands. He put the cloth back in the box and closed the lid.

"What's this?" Dru all but shrieked. "The other—"

"I don't trust you enough to give it all to you. If you behave and do as I tell you, then I'll give you the other half. Maybe."

A scream of outrage welled up in the sorcerer's throat, but it died before it could escape his lips. Instead, Dru closed his fingers around the black stone ring, and his tight lips pulled back in a smile. "As you wish, Highness. I, Drulethen, am your servant."

The sorcerer told Ulvian that the onyx ring solved his transportation problem; he no longer needed a pony. The ring allowed its possessor to shape-change. Before Ulvian's wide eyes, Drulethen the elven sorcerer expanded like a water-filled bladder. His skin split, and feathers sprouted. His fingers curved into talons as his arms were transformed into wings. A ripping scream issued from his swollen throat, and a hooked yellow beak burst through Dru's face. The sorcerer's eyes, as gray as storm clouds, were slowly suffused with a yellow tint. The transformation was too horrible to watch. When next Ulvian looked, a giant falcon stood before him, preening his shiny, golden-brown feathers.

So warlike was the expression in the great bird's eyes, Ulvian fell back a pace. Uncertainly he asked, "Dru? Can you speak?"

"Har! Yes!"

Ulvian put the golden box under his cloak and walked to his pony, which was straining against its tied reins. The sight of the six-foot-tall hawk was unnerving it. As the prince mounted, he said, "Where shall we go?"

"Har! My home. Black Stone Peak. Har!"

So saying, the giant falcon spread its wings and lifted into the air. It was completely dark, but Dru's eyes glowed yellow, allowing Ulvian to mark his position. Calling out his harsh cries, the transformed sorcerer circled overhead, guiding Ulvian along the narrow path. A few hours ride, Dru promised, and they would reach his stronghold, the ancient pinnacle known as Black Stone Peak.

* * * * *

Twenty elven warriors, armed with lance and shield, formed ranks in the pass above Pax Tharkas with Kemian Ambrodel and Kith-Kanan at their head. Each warrior carried three days' worth of water and dried food, a thin blanket roll, and a clay cup. Kith-Kanan told his soldiers that the eyrie occupied by Drulethen was at the very highest ridge of the Kharolis, up a steep trail. The warriors would need to travel fast and light.

The peak of his conical helmet flashed in the clean mountain sunlight. No ceremonial headpiece, Kith-Kanan's helmet had served him all through the Kinslayer War and bore its hammered-out dents and broken rivets with pride. Mounted on his snow-white charger, the Speaker looked back over his small band of fighters, none of whom had served with him against the armies of Ergoth. He marveled at their youthful seriousness. When the young blades of Silvanesti had first gone to war against the humans, they had done so with singing and shouting and tales of valor ringing in their ears.

Every one of them imagined himself a hero in the making. But these warriors with their solemn faces—where did these pensive young elves come from?

He raised his hand and ordered Kemian to lead the warriors forward. Tamanier called out, "When will you return, Great Speaker?"

"If you do not see my face five days hence, summon all the Wildrunners," Kith-Kanan replied. "And find Verhanna. She must know, too."

Touching his heels to his horse's snowy sides, Kith-Kanan cantered to the head of the double column. The old castellan watched the riders go. The constant breeze sweeping down the pass fluttered the small pennants on their lance tips. Tamanier was afraid, but he couldn't decide whom he feared most—his own son, Prince Ulvian, or Kith-Kanan.

Leaning heavily on his staff, the castellan walked back to the camp. It was alive with the sound of saws and hammers, as the damage wrought by the golem was being speedily repaired.

* * * * *

The head of the pass gave onto three paths. One was the way down to Pax Tharkas; the one to Kith-Kanan's left, north, was the route to Qualinost; and trickling off to the Speaker's right, southward, was a narrow goat path that led to the higher reaches of the Kharolis Mountains. It was that way they must go.

"Single file. Tell the warriors," Kith-Kanan said in quiet, clipped tones. It was strange how easily the old ways of war and campaign came back, even after a long time.

"Who shall ride point?" asked Kemian.

"I will." The young general would have protested, but Kith-Kanan forestalled him by adding, "Drulethen and my son have had no time to set traps. Speed is the essential thing now. We must catch them before they reach the sorcerer's stronghold."

Kemian turned his horse around to spread the word to the others. He asked in parting, "Where is it this Drulethen is going? A castle?"

"Not exactly. It's called Black Stone Peak. The mountaintop was once a nest of dragons, who hollowed out the spire and made a warren of caves through it. Drulethen, with the help of his dark masters, took over the empty peak and made it his stronghold. You see, many years ago, during the great war, Drulethen extracted tribute from the dwarves as well as from any caravan crossing the mountains. He used to fly out on a tame wyvern and carry off captives to his high retreat. It took a concentrated assault by the dwarves and the griffon corps to overcome him."

"It must have been an amazing battle, sire. Why have I not heard of it? Why is it not sung?" he asked.

Unaccountably Kith-Kanan's eyes avoided his. "It was not a proud fight," he said, "nor an honorable one. I will say no more about it."

Kemian saluted and rode off to give the troopers their orders. The warriors strung out in a long, single-file line. The path was so narrow the riders' boots scraped rock on both sides as they negotiated the passage. Their lances proved troublesome in the close quarters as well. They were constantly banging against the overhanging wall of rock, making quite a clatter and bringing a barrage of pebbles down on the riders' heads. This narrow trail persisted for some hours, until Kith-Kanan emerged from it onto a small plateau. Once hemmed in by rock, the warriors were now exposed. The plateau was turtlebacked, paved with large stones worn smooth by centuries of wind and the runoff of melting ice. The heavy cavalry horses stumbled on the rocks. Dru's and Ulvian's ponies were far better suited to this terrain.

A cloud passed between the sun and the valley below. They were so high up, the cloud sailed along below them. The elves admired the view, and Kith-Kanan allowed them to rest for a few minutes while he scouted ahead. Kemian turned his horse to follow the Speaker.

"Any sign, Majesty?" he asked.

"Some." Kith-Kanan pointed to where moss had been scuffed off some stones by the hooves of ponies. "They are nearly a half day ahead of us," he reported grimly.

Water bottles were tucked away, and the ride resumed. They crossed the plateau to a steeply climbing trail. Kith-Kanan spotted a glint of metal on the ground. He raised his hand to halt the troopers and dismounted. With his dagger tip, he fished the object out from a cleft in the rocks. It was the broken lock from Feldrin's golden casket. A cold pressure constricted the Speaker's heart.

"They have opened the box," he said to Kemian. Standing, Kith-Kanan held the broken lock in his gauntleted palm and studied the surrounding slopes. "Yet there's no sign of any magic being unleashed. Perhaps Drulethen does not possess the amulet yet." Perhaps his son was smarter than he reckoned, Kith-Kanan silently added. The only hope Ulvian had for survival was to keep the talisman from the sorcerer's hands. The Speaker could only pray that his son realized that. Of course, Drulethen might be in such a hurry to reach his stronghold that he simply hadn't used the power he possessed.

The Speaker remounted and dropped the broken lock into his saddlebag. "Pass the word: Be as silent as possible. And quicken the pace."

Kemian nodded, his blood racing. This was far more challenging than rounding up bands of scruffy slavers. The chill air seemed charged with danger. The general rode down the line, conferring with the warriors in a hushed voice. The young fighters tugged at harness straps and armor fittings, tightening everything.

Kith-Kanan remained in the lead. He shifted his sword handle forward for easier drawing. Alone among all the rest, he was armed with sword and small buckler, instead of lance and full shield. His charger took the slope easily, its powerful legs propelling horse and rider up the hill. The warriors followed, but it was a slow process going up so steep a grade in single file. The column strung out until a half-mile separated Kith-Kanan and the last rider.

A covey of black birds started up in front of Kith-Kanan's horse. The animal snorted and tried to rear, but the Speaker's strong hands on his reins brought him down. With soothing pats and almost inaudible words, Kith-Kanan calmed his nervous mount.

The black birds circled overhead, twittering. Staring up at the ebony whirlwind, Kith-Kanan experienced a sudden flash of memory, of a time long ago when crows had watched him as he struggled to find his way through a deep and mysterious forest. They had led him to the boy, Mackeli, who in turn had brought him to Anaya.

A shout from behind snapped Kith-Kanan's head around. One of the warriors had seen something. He twisted his horse around in time to see the elf lower his lance and charge into a small passage Kith-Kanan had passed a hundred paces back down the trail. There was a fearful scream. The nearest warriors crowded into the passage. Kith-Kanan rode hard down the slope, shouting at them to clear the way.

Just before he reached the mouth of the side ravine, the warriors sprang apart, some losing their lances in the process. A dark brown form hurtled by, veered between the tall chargers, and bolted down the trail. Seconds later, a sheepish-looking warrior appeared, unharmed, from the narrow passage.

"Your Majesty," said the elf, scarlet to his ear tips. "Forgive me. It was a stray pony."

The warriors, keyed up for a fight or to face some unknown horror, began to chuckle. The chuckles grew into guffaws.

"Brave fellow!" "How big was the pony's sword?" "Did he kick you with his little hooves?" they gibed. Kith-Kanan called them down, and they rapidly fell silent. The Speaker glared at them.

"This is not a pleasure ride!" he snapped. "You are in the field, and the enemy could be near! Deport yourselves like warriors!"

He ordered the soldier who'd charged the pony to report exactly what had happened.

"Sire, I saw something large and dark move. I called out, and it didn't answer. When I challenged it again, it looked like it was trying to avoid being seen. So I couched my lance and went after it."

"You did correctly," Kith-Kanan replied. "You say it was a pony?"

"Yes, sire. Its mane was clipped short, and there was a brand on its left flank—a hammer and square."

"The royal brand of Thorbardin," Kemian observed. "The pony came from Pax Tharkas."

Kith-Kanan agreed. "It must be one of the stolen ones. Why is it free, I wonder?" he mused. It didn't make sense for two escaping prisoners to abandon one of their mounts. The animal must have gotten away by accident.

"Luck is with us!" he announced. "Our quarry has lost half its mobility. If we ride without pause, we should overtake them!"

The elves hurried to their mounts. Kith-Kanan scanned the sky. The sun was subsiding in the west, throwing long shadows across the western peaks. They moved on, traveling into the setting sun, which made seeing distant objects difficult. However, the lost pony was a good omen. Drulethen could hardly be in full possession of his powers if he let a small horse get away.

A leaden sensation hit Kith-Kanan's stomach like a hammer blow and his hands clenched the reins. Suppose the pony hadn't bolted. Suppose Dru simply didn't need it anymore. Because Ulvian wasn't with him. Because Ulvian was already dead.

Kith-Kanan's heart argued against it. The sorcerer had no reason to dispense with the prince yet. They had found no body, no sign of struggle, along the trail. Ulvian must be alive.

"Sire?"

Kith-Kanan turned to Kemian Ambrodel. "Yes?"

"The peak, sire. It's in sight!"

Kith-Kanan looked up. Glowering down at them from its towering height, Black Stone Peak rose above the surrounding mountains. Clouds clung to its lower slopes, but the spire itself was washed by the orange sunset. No details were visible at this distance; the peak was at least twenty miles away.

"Keep the warriors moving," Kith-Kanan said. The sight of the black pinnacle steeled his courage. For all their differences, there was a bond of blood between the Speaker and his son. If Ulvian had come to harm, Kith-Kanan would have sensed it. His son must still be alive. While he lived, there was hope. Separating him from the clutches of the sorcerer Drulethen, however, promised to be a difficult and dangerous task.

The Clash of Stars

14

Verhanna, Rufus, and Greenhands broke camp in early morning while heavy fog in the higher parts of the Kharolis still clung to the trail. It hampered their progress greatly. Fearing unseen crevices and crumbling paths, the trio crept slowly ahead, keeping their backs to the slope of Mount Vikris, the second highest peak in the mountain range. As the day wore on, the fog worsened, until the warrior maiden finally called a halt sometime in midafternoon.

"We'll walk into a ravine if we continue," Verhanna said, vexed. "It's better to wait out the fog."

"We don't get stuff like this in the Magnet Mountains," Rufus observed. "No, sir, we never get fog like this."

"I wish we weren't getting it here," was her waspish reply.

Greenhands passed his fingers through the drifting mist, closing them quickly as if snatching something. Bringing his hands to his face, he opened his fingers and studied them closely.

"What're you doing?" Verhanna asked.

"I cannot feel this gray thing around us, yet it dampens my hand," he said, puzzled. "How is that?"

"How should I know?"

As he turned his serene gaze on her, perhaps to respond to her rhetorical question, Verhanna stepped away from the steep wall of the mountain and peered upward into the murk. "I wish there was some wood about. We could go on if we could make torches."

There was no wood, so there was nothing to do but wait out the confounding mist. Patience had never been one of Verhanna's virtues, and she chafed at the delay. Greenhands perched on the ground, his back propped against a square boulder. Rufus took a nap.

Eventually the sky darkened and the air cooled. The fog fell as a heavy dew, soaking the travelers, their horses, and all their baggage. Rufus's hat sagged around his ears. Verhanna wiped futilely at her armor, muttering dire predictions about rust. Only the green-fingered elf remained unconcerned. His long hair hung in thick, damp strands, and water dripped from the hem of his poncho.

"Let's move," Verhanna said at last. "As I figure it, we're only a couple hours' ride from Pax Tharkas."

Once more Greenhands took the lead. He seemed to know where he was going, though he'd never been this way before. Verhanna and Rufus let their mounts pick their way several paces behind him. The violet dusk quickly changed to purple twilight. Solinari, the silver moon, rose above the mountains. The top of the pass was in sight, no more than twoscore paces ahead.

The warrior maiden jiggled her reins, urging her horse to a faster walk. Greenhands was nearly to the top of the pass. His right foot came down on the ridge of rock and dirt that marked the highest point in the pass, and he abruptly stopped. Verhanna pulled up beside him.

"What is it?" she asked.

"Wait," he replied. "It's coming."

"What now?"

She looked up and down the pass, alert for stampedes or rampaging goblins or anything.

Greenhands's placid expression had changed to one of great excitement. His eyes danced as he pointed upward and said, "Look!"

The starry vault of the sky was crisscrossed by brilliant streaks of light. Dazzling fireballs began at one horizon, streamed upward to the zenith of heaven, and vanished in explosions of color. From every corner, to every corner, the sky was gridded with fiery trails that left ghostly glowing imprints on the watchers' eyes.

Rufus halted on Greenhands's other side. "Shooting stars," he breathed, awestruck.

The celestial pyrotechnics raged on, utterly silent and blindingly brilliant. At times, two streaming fireballs would collide, making a doubly bright burst. Tiny streaks and broad, cometlike meteors were bom, chased each other, and died in every color of the rainbow. Red fireballs left yellow trails. Blue-white comets fell toward the ground, only to burst soundlessly overhead.

"What does it mean?" Rufus wondered, rubbing his neck, stiff from staring up so long.

"Who says it means anything?" replied Verhanna.

"Perhaps it's an omen, or a warning from the gods, my captain."

Greenhands smiled. "Do not always look for the worst, little friend. Perhaps this is simply the gods making merry. Maybe the gods need amusement, too. This might be a celebration, not a dire warning of doom."

No one disputed his words, but Verhanna and Rufus shared a vague feeling of apprehension. This seemed but one more of the inexplicable, and therefore frightening, phenomena that had afflicted their world lately.

"Well, I can see the lamps of Pax Tharkas from here," said Verhanna. "We'll be there soon, and you can hunt for your poppa all over the camp."

Greenhands pointed away from the site of the fortress. "No, this way," he said and set off on the steep southern trail.

Verhanna maneuvered her horse in front of him. "Look here," she fumed, "we've followed you across nowhere long enough. There's nothing up this way. If your father is anywhere in these mountains, Pax Tharkas is the place to look. Besides, we're low on food and water."

"He is near," said the green-fingered elf. Greenhands moved to go around the horse. Verhanna let her mount drift forward, cutting him off again. Finally the strange elf put his arms under the black charger's belly.

"Hey!" Verhanna said sharply. "What're you—?"

Greenhands planted his feet and lifted. Horse and rider together came off the ground. The animal remained strangely calm, though its feet dangled in midair. Verhanna remained quiet as well; she was dumbstruck. With a few grunts and only the slightest evidence of strain, the green-fingered elf raised the enormous load off the rocky ground, turned a half-circle, and set it down on the trail behind him.

"Yow! Do that again!" cried the kender. Greenhands was already on his way, climbing the path.

Stunned, Verhanna called for him to stop. When he didn't, she said, rather illogically, "Stop him, Rufus! Don't let him go that way!"

The kender gave her a look of supreme disgust. "How do you reckon I'll stop him, my captain? Shall I tell him a funny story?"

Verhanna spurred her horse after the rapidly disappearing elf. She rattled up the sloping path, and out came her longsword. She had no desire to hurt him, but his confounding actions and sudden display of strength had shamed her. Raising her weapon, the warrior maiden intended to use the flat of the blade to stun Greenhands.

When she was only yards from the elf, there was a sudden glare of blinding light. For an instant, the mountainside was as bright as noon. Rufus yelled shrilly, and Verhanna felt searing heat on her neck and upraised sword arm. A roar filled her ears, a sizzling sound hissed nearby, and all was white light and throbbing pain.

Eventually cool darkness returned, and Verhanna found herself looking up into the unhappy face of Greenhands.

"Are you all right, my captain?" he said worriedly.

"Y—Yes. Ow!"

Her sword arm burned and ached. "What hit me?"

"Nothing hit you," said Rufus, his head showing over the kneeling elfs shoulder. "One of those fireballs blasted into the mountain just above your head. The strike flung you off your horse and did this."

He tossed the stump of her sword down beside her. Verhanna numbly grasped the handle. It was still hot to the touch, and the blade had been melted off, leaving only a misshapen nub of iron above the crossguard.

"Where's my horse?" she asked groggily.

Rufus shook his head sadly and glanced over his shoulder toward the precipitous drop down the side of the mountain. He quickly said, "You can have mine, though. It's too big for me. I feel like a pea on a boar's back."

They hoisted the stiff Verhanna to her feet and showed her the furrow plowed over the slope by the fireball. The steaming slash was melted at the edges. It was a mere foot or so above where her head had been.

Verhanna peered down the steep slope where her mount had perished. Shaking her head, she whispered sadly, "Poor Sable. You were a brave warrior." Greenhands was supporting her trembling body. When she stumbled over a stone, he steadied her effortlessly.

With a healthy boost from Greenhands, Verhanna was soon mounted on Rufus's chestnut horse. Their mobility was severely reduced by the loss of an animal but the kender wasn't heavy and his horse carried the two of them easily.

"Do you know this trail?" the warrior maiden asked Rufus as they rode away from Pax Tharkas.

"No, my captain, though it seems to lead higher into the mountains." The kender scrutinized the stars through a screen of speeding meteors and announced they were headed south.

"Into Thorbardin," Verhanna mused. She cradled her sword arm, still numb from the shock of the fireball's near miss. For Greenhands' benefit, she said loudly, "Your father wasn't a dwarf, was he?"

Before the elf could reply, Rufus piped up, "Oh, that's impossible, my captain. He's much too good-looking."

Verhanna jabbed the kender in the stomach with her elbow—her sore elbow. Drawing in her breath sharply, she cursed and groaned, "Shut up, Wart."

* * * * *

Like one of the famed towers of Silvanost, Black Stone Peak stood out against the starry sky, tall, cold, and imperious. The darker openings on its face were entrances to its web of caves, first carved out of the hard, black rock by wild dragons some two thousand years earlier. Ulvian halted his pony and stared up at the forbidding peak.

Dru had once more regained his human form. Now he pushed past the Qualinesti prince, eager to be home again.

"You'll have to dismount," said the sorcerer, his voice drifting back on the night air. "There's no true path into the caves, only some hand-cut steps."

Ulvian swung down and led the pony by the reins. The night was fiercely cold, and his worn clothes provided little protection. There was no wind around Black Stone Peak, unlike every other mountaintop Ulvian had ever visited. Here the air was still and pregnant with menace.

The trail ended, and the two started up an uneven set of steps chiseled from the living rock. The pony went along reluctantly, tugging at its halter as the steps became steeper and narrower. Ulvian warred with the frightened animal until the pony finally snatched the reins from his hand. It clattered over the steps and quickly fled down the steep, winding trail.

"It's no matter, my prince." Dru said genially. "There's no place for the beast to go."

Ulvian turned to continue his climb. In the darkness, he took a wrong step and slid off the rock stairway. His sudden gasp and the sound of scattering pebbles echoed loudly.

"We'll break our necks trying to climb this in the dark!" Ulvian declared.

Dru held out his left hand. As the sorcerer muttered some words in an unknown tongue, Ulvian saw that the ring of black onyx lying in his palm had begun to glow faintly orange, then cherry red. In seconds, a crimson aura had enveloped the sorcerer. The prince, his cuts and bruises forgotten, shrank back as Dru turned toward him.

The sorcerer smiled. "Don't be afraid, Highness. You wished for light, and I have provided it," he said smoothly. He climbed higher, approaching the vertical side of the peak. In the glow of the amulet, an oval opening came into sight. Dru ducked into the low cave, and Ulvian, rather reluctantly, followed behind.

The cave smelled old and dry, with a faint background aroma of decay the prince couldn't identify. A dragon's den should smell fetid, he knew, but this one had been vacant for two millennia. The floor was remarkably smooth and doubly difficult to walk on since it sloped seamlessly up to join the walls and ceiling.

As they moved through the passage, the bloody glow surrounding Dru now and again illuminated some object on the tunnel floor: a dead, desiccated bird; a broken clay lamp; some tatters of cloth.

The two moved hunchbacked for some distance. Suddenly Ulvian saw Dru straighten. In a pace or two, the prince had emerged from the low tunnel into a vast cavern hollowed out of the very center of the stone spire. The sorcerer kicked among some debris near the wall and found a torch. He muttered a word of magic over it, and the ancient timber burst into flame. Dru circled the great chamber, lighting other torches still held in iron wall brackets decorated with metal spikes. The smell of burning tarry pine filled the cold air.

When at last all the torches were lit, Dru tossed his into a firepit in the center of the room. Some debris and wood there crackled into flame.

Lighted, the chamber was hardly less fearful than when dark. Most of the furnishings were wrecked, destroyed when the sorcerer's stronghold fell to the dwarves and elves. Glancing upward, Ulvian could see a few stars through the smoke hole fifty feet above him.

A more gruesome sight met his gaze when he looked down again. Resting in niches around the circular wall were hundreds and hundreds of skulls—white, empty, dry skulls. Some belonged to animals: mountain bears, elk, lions. Others were more disturbing. The light, airy craniums of elves nestled beside the thicker, smaller skulls of dwarves. In fewer numbers were human heads, recognizable by their wide jaws and small eye sockets.

"Lovely décor," the prince said, sarcasm masking his nervousness.

Dru had righted a broken chair that could nonetheless bear his weight. "Oh, these are not my doing," he said with mock humility. "The original owners of the peak collected these little mementos, and I didn't have the heart to throw them away when I took possession." A smile parted his thin lips. "Besides, I think they lend a certain air to my humble domicile."

Ulvian shrugged and kicked through the shattered remains of

Dru's former life. He threw a leg over a stove-in barrel and sat. "Well, we're here," he said. "Now what?"

"Now you must give me the other half of my amulet."

The small golden box was hard and heavy inside Ulvian's cloak. "No," the prince replied. "I have no illusions about how long I'll live once I do that."

"But, Your Highness, Feldrin will certainly send someone after us, perhaps even royal warriors of Thorbardin and Qualinesti! I cannot possibly defend us with only a half measure of my powers."

Half a hundred skulls leered over Dru's shoulders. Here on his own ground, the ragged prisoner of Pax Tharkas seemed to acquire new strength, greater self possession. "I didn't come here to withstand a siege. I am bound for Qualinost," Ulvian declared. "As far as I'm concerned, you've gotten all the reward you earned—escape from Pax Tharkas and half your amulet."

Dru folded his hands, twining his fingers together. "It's a long way to Qualinost, my prince. You have neither horse, nor pony, nor royal griffon to take you there."

From the corner of one eye, Ulvian saw the pommel of a sword lying on the floor, buried by torn parchment and broken pottery. "Am I your prisoner?" he asked coolly.

"I thought we were partners."

"A prince of the blood and a base-born sorcerer, partners? I think not, Master Drulethen. On the other hand, if you wish to become my servant . . ." Ulvian rubbed his beard thoughtfully. The sword hilt was just beyond easy reach.

"I would serve you gladly! But without my entire amulet, I am a poor spell-caster and not half the sorcerer I could be for you, Highness."

As Dru finished speaking, Ulvian hurled himself at the half-buried sword hilt. He skidded in the debris, and his fingers closed over the rough, wire-wrapped handle. By the time he'd rolled clumsily to his feet, Dru was gone. The broken chair was still there, but the sorcerer had vanished.

The prince whirled, searching wildly. Drulethen was nowhere to be seen. Then his voice boomed out, echoing in the vast circular hall. "You stupid half-breed! Do you think you can get the better of me so easily? How disappointed your father must be, to have such a worthless, stupid son. Will he weep, I wonder, when he learns of your death?"

"Come out and face me!" Ulvian cried, his eyes flying to and fro over the grisly trophies lining the wall.

"We could have worked together, you know," Dru went on. "With your name and my power, we could have forged a mighty empire. No one could have stopped us—not the dwarves, nor the Speaker of the Stars in Silvanost. But you had to be foolishly greedy. You thought you could command Drulethen of Black Stone Peak."

Ulvian stood by the firepit, turning constantly, keeping the sword always ready. It was an ancient dwarven blade, short and thick and rather rusty, but still lethal. The sorcerer's voice bounced off the walls.

"I am no one's tool!" the prince shouted. "Even my father will give way to me in time!"

Ten tunnel mouths opened into the central chamber at floor level, and Ulvian could see nearly a dozen more higher up. The prince didn't recognize the one he'd emerged from with Dru. Sweat formed on his brow.

"I have only to wait," the sorcerer said silkily. "When you fall asleep, the amulet will be mine."

"Liar! You can't touch the charmed box!"

"True enough, but I will have it, and I'll be rid of you. Good night, my prince. Sleep well. I'll be waiting."

Then there was silence, except for the soft crackling of the fire.

"Dru!" called Ulvian. No answer. "Drulethen! If you don't come out, I'll pitch the box into a gorge so deep you'll never find it!"

Still there was no response.

Furious and terrified, Ulvian strode to the nearest tunnel opening. As he stepped inside it, a wall of wind gushed forth, flinging him back into the circular chamber. It was impossible to resist the wind, as the slick, curving tunnel floor offered no purchase for his feet. Trash covering the floor whirled around him, and soon Ulvian was back by the firepit. The wind ceased abruptly.

The same thing happened when he tried two other tunnels. Dru wasn't going to allow him to escape with the box. Very well, resolved the prince silently. If he had to, he would smash the onyx cylinder himself rather than allow the sorcerer to possess it. The pommel of the dwarven sword was hard brass; it would do nicely as a hammer.

The torches blazed brightly in their wall sconces. Ulvian sank down by the soot-stained rim of the firepit, the sword held firmly in one hand and the golden box in the other. The cold of the mountain penetrated to his very bones. He huddled by the small fire burning in the firepit and tried to ward off sleep.

* * * * *

Twenty warriors and their leaders crouched in a cold defile, screened on three sides by slabs of upright stone. Some watched the wild aerial display, mesmerized by the dash and clash of shooting stars. Others gripped their lance shafts tightly, feeling the strain of impending combat like a hollow ache in the pit of their bellies.

"I don't like this—this marvel," Kemian whispered. "Do you think it's the sorcerer's doing, Majesty?"

Kith-Kanan looked up at the dance of comets and shook his head. "That is beyond the power of any mortal to orchestrate," he said. "More likely, it's part of the other wonders we've seen." For no reason he could name, the Speaker felt a surge of elation as he watched the stars racing and crashing over their heads. It seemed almost a celebration of sorts. He turned his attention back to the dark pinnacle just ahead. Dru and Ulvian must be inside by now. Still, they couldn't simply storm in. There was no telling what might lie waiting for them.

Though the Speaker hadn't been part of the attacking force that originally captured Drulethen, General Parnigar had. Parnigar had reported that Drulethen's wyvern had slaughtered many good warriors who tried to fight it in the tight confines of the tunnels. At last, Parnigar and the noted dwarf hammer-fighter Thulden Forkbeard had gotten behind the monster and cut its head off.

"Here's what we will do," the Speaker whispered. The young warriors forgot the shooting stars and listened intently. "You will separate into five groups of four, and each group will enter a separate tunnel. They supposedly all converge on the center hall, but be careful! Be as silent as you can, and if you find Prince Ulvian, subdue him and bring him out."

"What if we find the sorcerer?" asked one of the warriors.

"Take him alive if you can, but if he resists, slay him." Twenty heads nodded in unison.

"Sire," Kemian said, "what about you and me?"

"We shall go in the main entrance," Kith-Kanan announced.

The warriors left their lances with their tethered horses and formed into their assault groups, daggers drawn. Kith-Kanan raised his hand, and the ones destined for the farthest cave opening started up the trail. A moment later, the second group set out, and when they had reached the base of Black Stone Peak, the Speaker and General Ambrodel drew their swords and started forward.

In the cold, still air, every sound was as clear as crystal—the click of spurs on stone, the squeak of armor joints flexing, the rush of each elf's breath. The peak loomed over Kith-Kanan. Memories tumbled through his head, brief flashes of his past like the flare of the exploding meteors overhead. The scene he'd created by baring a weapon in the Tower of the Stars in Silvanost. Scaling the Quinari

Palace the night he left on his resulting exile. Arcuballis, his noble griffon, companion during his sojourn in the wilds. Sithas, his twin, whom he hadn't seen since the division of the elven nation. Flamehaired Hermathya. The vestiges of old shame still burned when he remembered how much he'd been tempted by her beauty, even though she was wife to his brother. His own wife, Suzine, who had perished in the war. Mackeli, his brother, if not by blood then by heart and soul. And as the black shadow of the peak covered him completely, Kith-Kanan recalled the face of Anaya, his first wife and greatest love, the dark Kagonesti woman he'd lost so long ago in the wild forest of Silvanesti.

The cave mouth was low, and both elves had to duck to enter. Kemian tried to go in ahead of his monarch, but Kith-Kanan gestured him back.

Compared to the brightly flashing display outside, the tunnel was velvet blackness. Kith-Kanan eased his feet along, sword point leading, as his eyes adjusted to the dark. The curving floor was like glass, and his iron-shod feet slid all too easily. Kemian lost his balance and fell backward, landing with a loud clang. Shamefaced, he rolled to his hands and knees and hissed, "Forgive me, Majesty!"

Kith-Kanan waved away his apology and asked, "Can you stand?"

The young general rose slowly. "Come," whispered the Speaker.

A yellow glimmer appeared far ahead. Kith-Kanan's breath froze on the chin guard of his helmet. The feeble light grew and picked out a thin coating of frost on the tunnel walls. No wonder it was so hard to walk! Kith-Kanan put out a hand to halt Kemian. The warrior stopped.

Carefully the Speaker replaced his sword in its scabbard. Tied to the upper hanger ring of the scabbard was a small leather bag, closed with a drawstring. Kith-Kanan removed the bag from its ring. It held powdered resin, which sword-armed warriors used to coat the grips of their weapons. During battle, blood and sweat conspired to make sword grips treacherous, so a generous layer of pine resin made a warrior's hold more secure.

Kemian watched, fascinated, as Kith-Kanan sprinkled resin on the soles of his metal-clad boots. The white powder clung to everything it touched. Kith-Kanan indicated that Kemian should imitate his action. The younger elf did so.

It was fortunate they applied the gum to their feet, for only a short way ahead, the tunnel floor sloped downward at such an angle that walking without the resin would have been impossible. By now, both elves could smell torches burning—and something else. They heard a low drone, not of conversation, but of a male voice singing.

The Speaker stopped short. He squatted, using his sword for balance. Far out in the center of the great chamber ahead, a lone figure huddled under a ragged brown cloak, rocking back and forth, humming.

"It's the prince!" Kemian breathed.

There was no sign of Drulethen, which worried Kith-Kanan greatly, though he was relieved to see his son alive. "Stay hidden, General. I will approach my son."

"No, sire!" Kemian caught the Speaker's arm. "It could be a ruse to draw you out!"

"He is my son." The Speaker's brown eyes bored into Kemian's blue ones. The general dropped his gaze and his restraining grip.

"The other warriors should be in position by now," Kith-Kanan said encouragingly.

He stepped down the passage, his sword still sheathed. Kemian braced his hands against the walls and waited in an agony of suspense, fearing something would spring out and attack the Speaker.

Kith-Kanan emerged into the chamber. The array of skulls, the detritus of Drulethen's former furnishings, failed to distract him. In a moderate tone, he called out, "Ulvian?"

The prince's sagging head jerked up, and he swiveled his neck to face his father. Cuts and bruises marred his bearded face. Ulvian's eyes narrowed. "Oh, that's clever," he said, his words slurred and rather high-pitched. "Assuming the shape of my father, eh? Well, it won't work!"

He slashed at the air with an antique short sword.

Kith-Kanan glanced at the other tunnel mouths. The dark circles were all empty. He saw no sign of his other warriors.

"Son, it's truly me. Where is Drulethen?"

Ulvian staggered to his feet. He needed two hands to keep the sword pointed at his father. "I won't give you the amulet," he snarled. "I won't!"

Kith-Kanan walked slowly forward, hands wide and devoid of weapons. "Ulie, this is your father. I've come to save you. I've come to take you home." He spoke soothingly, and the prince listened, his head hanging like a ponderous weight on his shoulders. The Speaker came within an arm's length of his son.

"You're not my father," croaked the exhausted Ulvian. Awkwardly he thrust at Kith-Kanan. The Speaker easily sidestepped the blow and grappled with his bleary son. Kemian and all the other warriors, still hidden in the tunnels, burst from the openings, believing their Speaker was in danger. No sooner had they shown themselves than a blast of wind roared down from the ceiling, flattening the warriors and sweeping them head over heels back into the tunnels. Their cries echoed from far up the passages.

The wind ceased blowing, and Kith-Kanan and Ulvian were alone in the chamber. Almost.

"Well, well," said the voice of Dru. "The sovereign of Qualinesti has come to see me. I'm flattered. I knew there would be pursuit, but I hardly dared imagine the Speaker of the Sun himself would seek me out."

"Show yourself, Drulethen," Kith-Kanan commanded. "Or do you prefer to hide like some eavesdropping servant?"

"Here I am!"

Kith-Kanan whirled awkwardly, supporting Ulvian in his arms. The sorcerer had appeared behind them, on the opposite side of the firepit. Drulethen now wore a crimson robe. A band of shining black silk flowed across his chest and over his shoulder, trailing on the floor behind him. A ruby pin glittered in the silk on the sorcerer's left breast, and his blond hair was shiningly clean and combed back from his forehead. All trace of the slave of Pax Tharkas called Dru was gone. He was Drulethen of Black Stone Peak once more.

"By your command, Great Speaker," he said mockingly. He wore the onyx ring portion of the amulet around his neck on a strand of braided black silk. He bore no obvious weapons.

"You will surrender now to the authority of the Speaker of the Sun and the Thalas-Enthia of Qualinesti," Kith-Kanan said. "Surrender or face the consequences."

Dru chuckled. "Surrender? To one elf and one halfbreed? I think not. Your troops are scattered, Speaker, and cannot enter this place unless I wish it. And you cannot compel me to do anything."

Never taking his eyes from the sorcerer, Kith-Kanan lowered Ulvian to the floor. The prince was unconscious from sheer exhaustion. The Speaker drew his own formidable blade.

"Swords don't frighten me! I have only to wish it, and I'll go where you'll never see me or find me. That will leave you and your worthless son to fall asleep or starve. In either case, you will be at my mercy."

The Speaker stared hard at Drulethen's face. He knew from experience that magical disappearance was an illusion, a misdirection of the watcher's attention. The sorcerer wasn't going to fool him easily.

"So why don't you go?" asked Kith-Kanan.

Drulethen stepped down from the hearth and circled around, coming closer. His scarlet raiment rustled softly. Kith-Kanan kept himself between the sorcerer and Ulvian. "I merely hoped that you could be reasonable," purred the Silvanesti. "Perhaps we can come to a mutually beneficial agreement."

Stall. Think, thought Kith-Kanan. Give Kemian a chance to do something. "Such as what?" the Speaker said.

"Inside your son's shirt is a small golden box. It holds the other half of my amulet, and I cannot get it myself. If you give me the rest of my amulet, I will swear to serve you for, say, fifty years."

"Serve me how? I do not traffic in black magic."

Drulethen smiled pleasantly. He looked sleek and well groomed in his new attire, not at all like the wretched prisoner who had hauled stones from the Kharolis quarries. "If it's definitions that bother you, then I'll stipulate that I shall perform only the whitest of magic, exactly as Your Majesty orders. Isn't that fair?"

Torchlight flashed off the ruby pinned to the black silk on Drulethen's chest. Kith-Kanan's eyes flickered to it and back to the sorcerer's face. What had the magician just said? Ah, yes. He remembered now. "So for fifty years' service to me, you get a lifetime of power for yourself," he said. "Assuming you even honor your oath to me. I don't think the world would thank me, Drulethen."

The sorcerer's gray eyes were flinty. "Then your answer is no?"

"It is no."

The ruby flashed fire again. This time Kith-Kanan's attention strayed too long, and Drulethen suddenly wasn't there. The Speaker crouched, ready for an attack, then cut through the air with his sword. From above came thin, eerie laughter.

"Father and son are so alike!" chortled Drulethen. "I shall leave you to a common fate. Farewell, son of Sithel! I only wish my wyvern were here. He did so enjoy eating the flesh of highborn Silvanesti!" The laughter took a long time to fade away.

Kith-Kanan knelt and found the hard lump that was Feldrin's box inside Ulvian's clothing. The prince never stirred.

Circling the room, the Speaker searched for a way out. No wind rushed in at him unless he got within a pace of an opening. Lying just inside the tunnels were daggers and helmets dropped by his lancers.

An idea came to him. Cupping his hands to his mouth, Kith-Kanan shouted, "Hello! Kemian Ambrodel, can you hear me?"

Nothing. He moved to the next tunnel, always standing back to avoid triggering the magic wind. "Hello, this is the Speaker! Can you hear me?" he cried. After trying six holes, he finally received a reply.

"Yes, we hear you," came the faint answer. It was one of his warriors. Soon the Speaker heard Kemian's shout.

"Get all the rope you have," Kith-Kanan ordered. "Tie it together, then tie one end to a large rock. Roll it into the tunnel. It should follow the downslope to me, then I'll be able to use the rope to climb out against the wind!"

"Understood!"

"It won't work," said Dru's bland voice. "No rope in the world can withstand the Breath of Hiddukel."

Kith-Kanan planted his fists on his hips and said sarcastically, "You don't mind if we try, though, do you?"

He returned to his sleeping son and gathered him in his arms. He lay Ulvian's slack form near the entrance to the tunnel where he'd heard his warriors. As he did so, Kith-Kanan recalled Drulethen's reference to Hiddukel. That must be the evil sorcerer's patron deity. Weeks ago, when Hiddukel had appeared to him in the Tower of the Sun, he'd given his name as Dru. Had the god been hinting at the part his infamous disciple would play in the lives of the Qualinesti?

"There's no way out for you." Dru's voice was sharp. "Give me my amulet, and I'll spare your life."

"My life? A while ago you offered to be my slave for fifty years."

The sorcerer said no more. Kith-Kanan drew a tattered piece of tapestry over his son and sat down to wait. His nerves were singing with tension, but he knew that if the warriors took too long, fatigue would surely set in.

And nothing would stand between Drulethen and his black amulet.

The Fertile Seed

15

"Are you sure this is the way?"

Rufus Wrinklecap's high voice split the cold night air. He, Verhanna, and Greenhands were following the steep, south-leading pathway up into the mountains. Verhanna had convinced Greenhands to let the kender take the lead to scout the narrow path for them. After some grumbling about having to walk instead of ride, Rufus complied. He quickly grew excited as he detected signs that others had passed along the trail very recently.

"Who were they?" asked Verhanna.

"Qualinesti, on shod horses," the kender replied. He sniffed the scant hoofprints, barely indented in the stony soil. "Warriors. At least twenty of them."

She scoffed, "How can you tell they were warriors?" Rufus stuck his small nose in the air. "I can smell their iron, my captain."

Verhanna pondered the significance of the warriors' presence. They surely weren't hunting runaways from Pax Tharkas; Feldrin Feldspar had dwarven brigades to do such work. Intrigued, she moved on, following the kender.

Greenhands had barely spoken at all since they'd begun to climb. Not even the continued panorama of fiery comets overhead broke his profound silence.

At last they reached a small level patch on the upward slope, and Verhanna called a pause for rest.

Rufus dropped where he stood, worn out by his nose-to-the-ground scouting. Greenhands remained upright, his eyes fastened on the slope before them. Now he started off again. Verhanna, chewing on a piece of venison jerky, called him back.

"My father is near," he replied, glancing back at her. "I must go."

Wearily the warrior maiden dropped her half-eaten snack in her saddlebag. "Come on, Wart. His Majesty is going."

"What's the hurry?" complained the kender. Verhanna offered him a hand, and he swung onto the saddle pillion. "Where are we going? That's all I want to know—and what's the hurry?"

"Don't ask me," Verhanna said, clucking her tongue to urge the tired horse forward. "But I tell you this, Wart— If we don't find something significant by sunrise, I'm turning back, and to Darkness with Greenhands!"

The trail made several sharp turns and climbed at an even greater rate, so that they lost sight of Greenhands, who was keeping some paces ahead of them. Verhanna and Rufus passed a deeply shadowed defile on their left, and the horse halted on its own. It danced and snorted, tossing its head and refusing to go on, no matter how Verhanna coaxed or used her spurs.

The sky went dark.

The sudden cessation of the darting stars was startling and left the landscape much blacker than before. No moons shone; only the glimmer of starlight illuminated their way.

Rufus tugged at Verhanna's elbow. "The horse is calm now," he said. "Let's go."

"No, wait. Don't you feel it?"

Her voice was a whisper, and Verhanna sat stiff and still in the saddle.

"Feel what?" the kender asked impatiently.

"Like a storm is about to break. . . ."

Rufus replied tartly that he felt nothing, and Verhanna touched her heels to the horse's flanks. They went on. Around a turn, the sharp spire that was Black Stone Peak jutted into view, blotting out an area of stars.

"I feel cold," said Rufus, wiggling closer to Verhanna's back.

"I hear voices!" she hissed, and urged the horse to a brisker pace. Up the final stretch of trail, kender and warrior maiden rode hard. They burst onto a scene of frantic activity. A score of white faces turned to her, and she recognized them as fellow Guards of the Sun.

Kemian Ambrodel appeared out of the night. "Lady Verhanna!" he exclaimed. "This is amazing! How come you to be here?" He offered a gauntleted hand to her.

She shook his hand and said frankly, "My lord, I'm no less shocked to see you. My scout and I were led here by an extraordinary fellow, a tall, flaxen-haired elf we call Greenhands. He must've passed you only moments ago."

"He is here. I put him aside, as we are too busy to deal with newcomers at present." Kemian lifted his chin to indicate a boulder a few paces away. On it was seated the green-fingered elf. His attention was not directed at the warriors or Verhanna, but at Black Stone Peak.

Verhanna dismounted, and Rufus hopped to the ground behind her. "What's going on here?" piped the kender.

The warriors were tying hank after hank of rope together. Most of it was in short lengths, used to tether horses on a picket line at night.

"Your father is in there," Kemian said gravely, sweeping a hand toward the black spire of rock behind them. Quickly the young general sketched the situation.

"Will two extra pairs of hands help, my lord?" she asked.

Kemian grasped her shoulder. "More than help, lady."

Verhanna and Rufus began tying what line they had to the end of the warriors' supply. While thus engaged, they didn't notice Greenhands slide off the boulder and walk straight up the ramp toward the caves in the spire. Rufus glimpsed him and shouted, "Hey!"

"Stop!" Kemian commanded. Greenhands was almost at the mouth of one of the cave openings. At any second, the awful wind would rise and sweep him back. It might also scatter their hard-won loops of rope. "Stop at once, I say!" bellowed Lord Ambrodel.

Greenhands spared a brief look at the elves and kender, then stepped into the opening. Kemian Ambrodel clenched his jaw, his body tensing in anticipation.

No wind boiled forth. The night was quiet and cold, and not a breath of breeze stirred.

Kemian gaped. "Who is this elf? A sorcerer?"

"A very strange fellow," Rufus said. He struggled with the rope he was tying. It was thick and stiff. "He's got all kinds of power, but he never works a spell."

Lord Ambrodel looked to Verhanna. "Wart's right," she agreed. "If anybody can reach my father, this Greenhands can."

"We can't risk the Speaker's life on some vagabond's tricks. Get the rope ready!" barked Kemian.

The warriors gathered up the rope and hastened to the main tunnel mouth. Rufus had wrapped the tough rope around his small hands, the better to wrestle with a last knot, and he was dragged all the way to the base of the peak.

Kith-Kanan tapped the flat of his sword blade against the palm of his hand. Dru had made no sound or appearance in an hour or more, and the torches around the great circular room were burning out one by one. Half were gone when he heard the distant ring of shouting outside. He called up the tunnel in reply, but all was silence once more. The Speaker didn't want to make too much noise for fear of encouraging Dru to think he despaired of his situation.

Ulvian lay completely immobile at Kith-Kanan's feet. Father regarded son with mixed feelings. It was Ulvian's willfulness and pride that had brought them here. He had not only dealt in slaves, but also had fled the Speaker's justice and helped an evil sorcerer to escape. Yet Kith-Kanan's expression softened as he watched him sleep, curled up on the floor like a harmless child. This was his son, the baby boy he and Suzine had rejoiced in. He might be fully grown, but his heart was as a child's—a boy who adored his mother and seldom saw his father.

Tiredly Kith-Kanan rubbed his temples and tried not to dwell on what might have been.

"You are not alone."

Kith-Kanan whirled. A quarter of the way around the room, a solitary elf stood. It wasn't Dru. This elf was tall, fair-haired, young. He wore a rough horsehair poncho and leather trews. His gaze on Kith-Kanan was intense.

"Who are you?" demanded the Speaker, stepping over Ulvian. "Is this another of your guises, Drulethen?"

The stranger didn't respond. Instead, he continued to regard Kith-Kanan with an unsettling stare. His face bore such a look of rapt joy that the Speaker was momentarily distracted from his own worry. With a shake, as if coming to himself suddenly, Kith-Kanan lifted his sword point a bit higher and demanded, "Answer me!"

"Who are you?"

"I am Greenhands. At least, that's what my captain calls me."

"Green—" Kith-Kanan's eyes traveled downward, noticing the colored fingers for the first time. The room was growing dimmer as more of the torches flickered and died, but the grassy hue of the elf's hands was plainly visible.

"How did you get in here? Why didn't the wind blow you out?" asked the Speaker sharply.

"I simply walked in. I have been looking for you for a long time." The stranger moved a few paces closer, and a smile lightened his face. "You are my father."

Kith-Kanan was taken aback. His first reaction to this astonishing statement was puzzlement. If this was some trick of the sorcerer's, what was its purpose? Perhaps this elf was some feeble-minded innocent, a dupe of Drulethen's.

Again Greenhands moved nearer to the one for whom he had searched. Kith-Kanan's shifting thoughts were stilled as he looked into the strange elf's eyes. They were brilliantly, shiningly green, brighter than the clearest emeralds. His face seemed familiar somehow—the full-lipped mouth, the high forehead, the shape of his nose. It reminded the Speaker of—Kith-Kanan rocked back on his heels, stunned by the thought that had exploded across his mind. Anaya! The tall elf reminded him of Anaya. The features, the eyes, were identical, even his green-tinged skin. Anaya's skin had changed just so when she had begun her transformation into a mighty oak. Lowering his sword, he moved forward to meet Greenhands halfway, near the now cold firepit. Their height was identical.

"Hello, Father," Greenhands said happily.

Kith-Kanan couldn't believe what he saw. It seemed impossible, yet he only had to look at this young elf to see his amazing resemblance to Anaya, to know that he spoke the truth. Somehow, by some miracle, his and Anaya's son had come here, to Black Stone Peak.

The Speaker's voice was uncertain, so strong were the emotions that gripped him. "Your coming was foretold to me centuries ago," he whispered. "Only I did not understand then. . . ." He lifted a shaking hand to touch Greenhands' face. The elf smiled broadly, and Kith-Kanan enveloped him in a warm embrace. "My son!"

The happy moment was brief. Danger remained all around them. Kith-Kanan wiped away the tears that dampened his cheek and held Greenhands out at arm's length.

There was a rush of air overhead, a beating of unseen wings. Alarmed, Kith-Kanan stood back and raised his sword. Only a quarter of the torches in the room still burned, and in the half-light he saw a winged thing circle and dip in and out of the fitful light.

"Son, do you carry a weapon?" he asked, swiftly donning his helmet.

Greenhands held out empty arms. "No, Father."

The Speaker kicked among the debris on the floor. The winged creature swooped near him, and he slashed hard at it, missing. The beast soared away, and Kith-Kanan squatted long enough to pick up a stout piece of wood, a leg broken from a dining table.

"Take this," he said, tossing it to Greenhands. "If anything comes at you, hit it!"

An eerie laugh floated through the chamber. Kith-Kanan glanced at Ulvian. The prince was still unconscious. Overhead, the laugh sounded again.

"A fine weapon for a fine-looking warrior," said Drulethen. His voice caromed off the stone walls, making it difficult to determine where he was. "A worthy addition to the House of Silvanos!"

"Indeed he is," Kith-Kanan retorted. "He got in past your spells, didn't he?"

"How do you know I didn't let him in intentionally? I'm collecting royal Qualinesti!" he snarled nastily.

With hand gestures, Kith-Kanan indicated that Greenhands should go around the other side of the chamber, away from him. The elf complied with commendable stealth. Kith-Kanan edged away from the unconscious Ulvian and talked to distract Drulethen.

"Well, great sorcerer, what do you intend to do with us?" he called out.

"My amulet. One of you is going to give me the other half of my amulet if I have to torture each of you in turn to convince you to do so." The sorcerer's voice had fixed in one place. Kith-Kanan peered at an upright, though broken, chair. A tall shadow had appeared there. He lowered his sword so the blade wouldn't gleam in the remaining torchlight.

"You cannot win, Drulethen. Ulvian might have helped you, but I will see to it you never have the amulet," he vowed. He stepped gingerly over some smashed crates, moving as silently as possible.

"Ulvian! That idle, untrustworthy wretch? He'll be the first to go, mark my words. I shall enjoy his torment."

Kith-Kanan's left shoulder bumped the wall. He was under one of the burned-out torches, and he slipped it from its bracket and sidled over to the next one, which still barely burned. He lit the stump and rushed toward the broken chair. As he did, the light from his brand fell upon Dru.

The Speaker froze in midstride, horrified. The thing perched on the chair was not an elf, nor was it a bird. It had golden-brown wings with red-tipped feathers, but instead of falcon's claws, two white elven hands gripped the back of the chair. Instead of a falcon's noble head, the thing was topped by a horrid mix, part elven, part bird. Dru's face and head bore feathers where hair had been. His eyes were large and black, like a falcon's, but set in elven eye sockets surmounted by feathery brows. Most hideous of all, instead of a nose, a large horny beak protruded from Dru's face.

"You see," hissed the sorcerer, "how much I need the rest of my amulet. The ring is the more powerful half, but it lacks refinement and control." He shuddered and hunched his head down between his shoulders. The awful face seemed to reflect a spasm of pain. "I find I can't control my transformations without the cylinder." The bizarre white fingers flexed over the broken chair's thick arm. "This is the last time I shall ask—give it to me!"

In reply, Kith-Kanan hurled the torch at the monster and lunged with his sword. Dru launched himself into the air, overturning the chair. He avoided Kith-Kanan's attack, but he didn't see Greenhands standing close by in the shadows, motionless. As he passed by, Greenhands swung his crude club. His strength was considerable, but his skill was not, and the blow was only a glancing one.

Nevertheless, Dru was sent spinning, to land in a flurry of loose feathers on the other side of the chamber, near Ulvian. "Get him! Don't let him get up!" the Speaker cried.

He outran Greenhands to the fallen sorcerer, and he prodded the strange creature with his sword tip, ordering him to stand and surrender. The pile of feathers writhed and shifted, and a piercing shriek rose up from them. Greenhands arrived, and before their astonished eyes, the sorcerer changed shape once more.

The body of the bird lengthened, and the wings shriveled into feather-covered arms. Dru pushed himself onto his back and cried out again in agony. The beak on his white face and his black falcon's eyes remained the same. Feathers covered the rest of his body.

"Stand up!" Kith-Kanan ordered again.

"I—I cannot," the sorcerer wheezed. Sweat ran down his grotesque face in rivulets, and his body shook as if palsied. "I am—undone."

Just then Ulvian groaned and shifted on the stone floor. He moved to push himself up, inadvertently distracting Kith-Kanan. In a flash, the supposedly exhausted sorcerer had tripped Kith-Kanan. The Speaker went down hard. Before anyone could draw another breath, Drulethen's fingers locked around the Speaker's throat.

The sorcerer stood, dragging Kith-Kanan to his feet.

Blood roared in the Speaker's ears. The fantastic figure of the sorcerer was lost as Kith-Kanan's vision was suffused with a red haze. He tore at the hands that were throttling him, but Dru's grip was like iron.

"I know you have it!" he shrieked, shaking the Speaker violently. "Give me my amulet!"

Just as Kith-Kanan was losing consciousness, there was a crash and a scream. He felt himself falling, falling, until the hard floor met his back. He rolled aside, gasping, and let his vision clear. When he tried to grab for his sword, just out of easy reach, a wave of dizziness brought him down.

Greenhands was grappling with Dru. The sorcerer wasn't as strong as the Speaker's son, but he was infinitely more cunning. Twisting his body and breaking Greenhands' grip, Drulethen managed to wrest the table leg club from him. The thick pine flashed down and snapped across Greenhands' shoulders. He went reeling. Shouting with triumph, Dru picked up the Speaker's sword, put its tip to Kith-Kanan's throat, and felt in his clothing until he located the other half of the amulet. Kith-Kanan had secreted it beneath the breastplate of his armor.

"Ah!" Dru said, taking the black cylinder in his hand. "At last!"

"What's happening?" Ulvian asked, pulling himself up to a sitting position. His short sleep had left him confused.

Dru had moved away. Kith-Kanan crept on hands and knees to his son. "Drulethen," he managed to gasp.

"Father," said Greenhands, moving stiffly to join them, "the evil one is changing again."

Kith-Kanan staggered to his feet, retrieved his sword, and turned to face Drulethen. The sorcerer was across the room. He'd fitted the cylinder into the onyx ring he wore around his neck, and now the complete amulet dangled against his chest. His face was slowly swelling and turning purple; his feather-covered limbs were growing longer and more muscular. A slow laugh escaped his twisted lips.

"What a bargain," he rumbled from deep in his throat. "A thousand years of power for a thousand years of servitude. That's the deal I made with Hiddukel." A loud snapping and cracking sounded. Dru clapped his hands to his head and howled with pain. "Now that I have my amulet whole again, the world shall tremble at my name!"

Hard, pointed plates erupted through the skin of Dru's back. The feathers on his body dropped away as a thick tail, covered with scales, grew visibly before the elves' astonished eyes. The sorcerer's elven form grew and grew, hardening and thickening, until a winged, scaly monster filled the cavern deep inside Black Stone Peak.

Ulvian dragged himself close to his father. "By the gods," he gasped, "he's become a dragon!"

"No . . . a wyvern," Kith-Kanan said. "Just like the one he rode before, terrorizing the countryside."

The wyvern reared up twenty feet tall, green-black and glistening. Its catlike eyes were a poisonous yellow, and from its fanged jaws flicked a blood-red tongue. Horns sprouted from its head. For a moment, it looked wonderingly at its own ivory-clawed forepaws, then its wicked gaze returned to the three grouped beyond the center firepit.

"We must get out of here," Ulvian wheezed.

"If we can. The wind spell may not let us," answered his father. Kith-Kanan flexed both hands around the handle of his sword. He had little hope of getting close enough to kill the wyvern before it mauled him to death. He glanced at his newest son. "Greenhands can get out, though," he said.

Ulvian looked at the unknown, white-haired elf before him. There was no time for questions or answers, as the wyvern opened its hooked, leathery beak and hissed a challenge.

"Spread out and try the tunnels!" Kith-Kanan ordered.

The prince started for the nearest passage. His limbs felt strangely leaden. To his surprise, no blast of air came out of the passage to bar his way. He ducked his head and disappeared into the tunnel.

"Go!" Kith-Kanan urged Greenhands. "Save yourself!"

"I will stay and help you, " he resolved. "I am strong."

The wyvern rushed the Speaker. Kith-Kanan backpedaled, slashing his sword back and forth to ward off the monster. From the side, Greenhands pried loose a paving stone in the floor and hurled it with all his might. The monster roared and hissed like a hundred boiling kettles as its left wing went limp. Its tail lashed out and swept Greenhands off his feet. The spearlike tail tip thrust at him, but the elf caught it in his hands and flung it back.

Kith-Kanan's sword scored a bloody line down the monster's torso. The wyvern returned its attention to the Speaker of the Sun. An iron-hard claw caught him in the chest driving all the wind from him. Had he not been wearing armor, every bone in his chest would have been crushed. Kith-Kanan hurtled back. The wyvern's claw came down, but the Speaker drove his sword straight through the monster's paw, pushing and pushing until black blood flooded down the blade. The wyvern bellowed in pain and snatched its claw back, taking the Speaker's sword with it.

Kith-Kanan shouted at Greenhands that now was the time to flee. Then he himself backed into one of the tunnels. The monster was shaking its injured claw, finally dislodging the sword from it. As the Speaker disappeared into the tunnel, the wyvern snaked its neck down and thrust it into the opening. Kith-Kanan retreated out of reach.

The wyvern turned on Greenhands, the only remaining target. The green-fingered elf was markedly unafraid, and he dodged nimbly about the chamber, throwing enormous pieces of stone at the monster. From the tunnel, Kith-Kanan shouted over and over for him to abandon the room, to make his escape.

Greenhands fought on. The power that had made him and given him great strength had also bestowed upon him lightning-fast reflexes and an instinctive knowledge of how to hurt the beast. After one near miss by the wyvern's snapping beak, Greenhands found himself flat against the curving wall. A torch bracket was by his ear, and he reached up and snapped the black iron holder off the wall. The holder was ringed with iron spikes. With sufficient force, the points could pierce the wyvern's skull.

Kith-Kanan saw his newfound son leap at the monster. The wyvern's tail slashed around, destroying the last few burning torches in the room. Darkness seized the scene, though Kith-Kanan could still hear the sounds of the struggle. Now and then the iron bracket held by Greenhands would scrape on stone, and a fount of red sparks flared.

The wyvern howled—in pain or victory? Kith-Kanan couldn't tell. He had taken a step back toward the room when the smell and sound of the monster filled the end of the passage. It hissed at him and began to force its way in. Only its yellow eyes, each as big as the Speaker's head, shone in the darkness.

* * * * *

"Try it again! Come on, put your backs into it!"

Verhanna, Rufus, and the warriors braced themselves against the back of a giant boulder, which they had managed to lever out of the mountainside. The scavenged rope was webbed about the rock, and now they were trying to roll it into the cave opening through which Kemian had heard the Speaker's voice. The boulder refused to budge more than an inch at a time.

"Weaklings!" Verhanna stormed, fear for her father manifesting itself in fury. And fear for Greenhands, to whom she owed her life. "You aren't true Guards of the Sun! The Speaker is in danger!"

Kemian snapped, "We know that! Do you think—?"

"Shh! Hear that?" Rufus said, interrupting Lord Ambrodel.

Strange sounds filtered out from the tunnel opening into the early morning air. They sounded like footsteps. Someone was coming out. The sun was a sliver on the eastern horizon, brightening the scene. Verhanna pushed forward to peer inside.

A slim figure staggered into view.

"Ulvian!" she exclaimed.

"Help!" he gasped. Two elves rushed forward to aid him. They supported him to the boulder and gently let him down. "Dru—he's become a wyvern! He's got both parts of the amulet!"

"Where's the Speaker?" demanded Kemian.

Ulvian closed his eyes and let his head sag against the rock. "Isn't he here?"

"No." Verhanna spat. "Neither is Greenhands!"

Kemian prodded the prince. "You left the Speaker to face a full-grown wyvern?"

"He told me to leave!"

The warriors and kender stared down at him. His face was still bruised from his beatings at the hands of the grunt gang, but his limbs were whole. Somewhere in the rear of the band, the word "coward" found voice.

Verhanna turned to Kemian. "The wind spell must be broken. We don't need the boulder and rope anymore. Let's go!"

"Wait. We can't just rush in. We must plan our attack!"

Kemian paused, then added more calmly, "Half will go in, the other half will stay and watch for the Speaker or Greenhands to emerge."

All except Ulvian volunteered to be in the contingent that went inside. In the end, Kemian made the choices. The attacking party included himself and Verhanna, who made it plain she was going in whether or not he chose her. She ordered Rufus to remain outside.

"But why? I haven't ever seen a wyvern before," he complained.

"Because I said so, that's why. And I pay you." She glanced at Ulvian, who sat leaning against the boulder, eyes closed. "You can guard Prince Ulvian," she said contemptuously. "He's an escaped prisoner, after all."

Chagrined, the kender watched half the warriors file into the yawning cave. He shifted from one foot to the other, looking from the tunnel mouth to the remaining elves. They were as anxious as he to be part of the fight, but they stayed where they were, tense and expectant.

When the last elf entered the tunnel, Rufus could stand it no longer. He sprinted to an adjacent opening and promptly collided with Kith-Kanan. "Your Mightiness!" burst out the kender. "We thought you were monster food!"

"Not yet, my friend. The beast is about twenty paces behind me."

"Yow!"

The kender darted around the Speaker to get a better look. The morning sun sent a roseate beam down the shaft, lighting the crawling monster's head and serpentine neck. Its mouth opened and a shrieking hiss reverberated down the passage.

"So that's a wyvern," Rufus said matter-of-factly.

"You'll get a much closer view if you don't get out of the way," Kith-Kanan stated. Kender and elf moved quickly away.

Kith-Kanan saw Ulvian scrambling to his feet by the rope-bound boulder. He also spied the unhappy warriors Kemian had left behind.

"Warriors! Get your weapons! The wyvern is coming!"

The ten elves ran to their horses and mounted, taking their lances from the conical pile they'd been arranged in. The wyvern's head snaked out of the cavern opening. It saw Kith-Kanan and hissed in outrage.

"Go in and fetch Lord Ambrodel," Kith-Kanan ordered the kender. Rufus saluted and dashed inside a tunnel.

A warrior brought Kith-Kanan a horse and lance. The tired, battered Speaker climbed into the saddle and couched his lance.

The monster's forelegs were free of the passage and it was wriggling the rest of its body out. The disk of the sun cleared the eastern mountains. The sky was bright blue.

The lancers charged the monster in ragged formation before it could get its wings, legs, and tail free. The first warriors scored hits on the wyvern's exposed chest, but it snapped its beak over their lance shafts and tossed the elves aside like dolls. One was thrown over the edge of the plateau, to vanish in the deep gorge below. A second was hurled against Black Stone Peak and slid to the ground dead, his neck broken.

"For Qualinesti!" Kith-Kanan shouted, charging forward.

Pushing with its powerful hind legs, the, monster freed its wings. One of the leathery flying limbs hung limp, injured by Greenhands in the chamber; the other swept to and fro, upsetting horses and blinding riders. Kith-Kanan buried his lance in the wyvern's neck but was knocked from his horse. Two warriors shielded him from the enraged beast. The wyvern snatched the closest in both foreclaws and shook him as a terrier worries a rat, then hurled his lifeless body to the ground. The other warrior succeeded in driving his lance through the monster's uninjured wing. The elf let go of the weapon, turned his horse in a fast circle, and offered a hand to the fallen Speaker. Sore but spry, Kith-Kanan mounted behind the warrior.

The wyvern bled from half a dozen wounds and both its wings were damaged, but its strength hardly seemed diminished by the time it worked its legs free. The warriors drew off a short way on the lower plateau in order to form ranks and charge again. Kith-Kanan took the horse of a fallen fighter.

"Try to get behind it," he told the elves. "I'll try to distract it." The warriors settled into tight ranks. "Now!"

They galloped at the beast, then split into two columns and surrounded the wyvern. It lashed out from side to side with its barbed tail, slaying elf and horse alike. The great beast suffered more wounds, but no one came close to piercing its heart. Kith-Kanan dueled furiously with its beaked head, slashing with his sword at the ugly, snapping mouth. At one point, the wyvern caught the crest of his helmet. Kith-Kanan frantically tore at the strap buckle, releasing it before the wyvern could tear his head off.

"Fall back!" he shouted. "Fall back!"

Four warriors were able to comply. The other six were either dead or seriously wounded.

The monster let out a howl and stamped its feet. It flung the bodies of fallen warriors at Kith-Kanan and the survivors, a hideous gesture of contempt. Panting, sweating in the chill mountain air, the warriors clustered around their Speaker.

"We must kill it!" Kith-Kanan said grimly. "Otherwise its wings will heal, and it will be able to fly away."

A sharp whistle caught the Speaker's ear. He looked up at the peak, toward the source of the sound, and saw Rufus Wrinklecap, Verhanna, and some of the warriors who had entered the cave. They were standing in several higher tunnel mouths, forty feet above the Speaker.

Verhanna raised a hand, and the warriors in the caves began to shower the beast with stones and debris from inside the peak. The wyvern hissed loudly and leapt at them. Even with numerous lance wounds, it was able to jump three-quarters of the distance to the caves. On the third such leap, the monster dug its four clawed feet into the rocks and clung there. With its injured wings tightly furled against its body, the wyvern started to climb.

Kith-Kanan's heart leapt when he spied Greenhands at one of the cave openings. His son lived, praise the gods! In his hands, he held a loop of rope. All the others in the high caves had weapons of some kind, but not Greenhands. What was he up to?

The Speaker and the remaining elves on horseback sat ready, lances couched. Slowly the beast clawed its way up the peak, its talons leaving gray streaks on the black rock. Loose stones and pieces of Drulethen's furniture thudded off its head and body from above. Thick, horny eyelids blinked shut every time an object hurtled at the wyvern's eyes. Sword in hand, Kemian appeared in the tunnel mouth next to Greenhands.

"The monster will cut them to pieces in those tunnels," said one of the mounted warriors. "Shouldn't we go in and help them?"

"Stand your ground," Kith-Kanan said sternly. "Lord Ambrodel knows what he's doing." In fact, the Speaker was extremely worried, but he had to trust his general's judgment.

Greenhands leaned far out of the cave opening, the loop of rope in his hand. The wyvern was only a few feet below, its attention on those hurling debris at it. The others suddenly ceased their attacks and withdrew deeper into their caves. Hissing and howling, the wyvern raised its head to see what they were doing and Greenhands dropped the loop of rope over its head, like a herder roping a wild bull. He and Kemian leaned hard on the rope, and it pulled taut around the monster's neck. The wyvern flung its head from side to side, trying to break the line. When that failed, it snapped its jaws in a vain attempt to catch the rope in them.

The beast decided to continue on in the direction it was being pulled. Greenhands and Kemian disappeared inside the tunnel just as the wyvern reached their level. The long, green-black neck snaked into the cave. All at once, the wyvern's four legs were scrabbling furiously on the peak and at the tunnel mouth, trying to find purchase. Its hideous shrieking cry echoed through the mountains. The massive muscles in its back arched as it tried to pull its head out of the tunnel. Kith-Kanan's breath caught when he saw blood washing out of the cave.

The violent scratching of the monster's limbs continued for a moment, and then it fell. The enormous beast hit the ground, and the impact shook the earth all around. Its legs continued to thrash and claw at nothing, and Kith-Kanan saw why. The wyvern had left its head inside Black Stone Peak.

They kept away from the raging, headless corpse until its dark blood had all leaked out. Its legs continued to twitch slightly. Kith-Kanan rode forward and drove his lance through the monster's heart. That put an end once and for all to the wyvern, and it lay unmoving.

Verhanna emerged with Rufus and the other warriors. Kith-Kanan asked, "Where's Greenhands? And Lord Ambrodel?"

"Here!" came the shout from above. Kith-Kanan looked up. Greenhands stood at the high cave entrance. He was covered with blood and held the head of the wyvern in both hands. As everyone watched, he hurled the head to the ground.

When Greenhands came out of Black Stone Peak, he moved slowly, carrying Lord Ambrodel in his arms. Two warriors came and relieved him of his burden.

"What happened?" asked Kith-Kanan, rushing to his son's side.

"The creature smashed him against the wall," Greenhands replied softly. "He has something broken. . . ." The green-fingered elf's legs folded beneath him, and he would have dropped to the ground but for his father's quick arms.

Verhanna ran to them. "He breathes," she reported anxiously. "I think he just passed out."

"No wonder," observed Rufus. "After seeing Lord Kemian cut that monster's head off!"

The young general coughed and lifted a feeble hand, "No," he said in a scratchy voice. "I didn't kill the monster. He did."

* * * * *

The wounded were cared for, and the dead were placed on a funeral pyre. Six young elf warriors had died in the fight, and Lord Ambrodel's life was hanging in the balance. Rufus bathed Greenhands with a bucket of water and found that, for all the black blood on him, he hadn't any wounds at all.

The wyvern's body was too heavy to move, so they piled what tinder they could find against it where it lay. The broken furniture from inside the peak proved useful, as did the lamp oil. Soon the beast was in the center of a roaring bonfire. As the sun passed its zenith, coils of oily black smoke darkened the sky, spreading an evil smell over the high mountains.

That deed done, the warriors dropped into an exhausted slumber. Kith-Kanan drew Ulvian and Verhanna a little away from the group.

"I have some news for you," he began, feeling a little uncertain how to go on.

Ulvian tensed. Verhanna glanced at him and then back at the Speaker. "What is it, Father?" she asked, her face serious.

Kith-Kanan looked toward Greenhands, who'd been sleeping since his battle with the wyvern. A feeling of tenderness warmed the Speaker's heart. Anaya's son. This elf was his and Anaya's son.

"I suppose there's no other way to say it than simply to say it," he said briskly. "Ullie, Hanna . . . Greenhands is my son."

Verhanna's jaw dropped in shock, but Ulvian's face remained as still as stone. Only the brightness of his hazel eyes betrayed his surprise.

"He's your what?" Verhanna exploded.

Kith-Kanan passed a weary hand across his brow. "You deserve the whole story. I know you do. Just now, though, I am weary to the bone," their father sighed. "Greenhands is the son of my first wife, a Kagonesti. I think the marvels of these last days were signs of his coming." He put a gentle hand on Verhanna's arm and was surprised to feel her trembling. "I know it's a shock, Hanna. It was to me, too. I'll explain everything later, I promise. It's been an eventful day."

With a fond pat on her cheek, the Speaker moved back among the sleeping warriors. He lay down near Greenhands, and in no time he was gently snoring.

Verhanna was astonished. Her brother! Greenhands was her brother! All at once, the absurdity of the situation struck her. After not thinking of marriage for centuries, now she chose a mate who turned out to be her own brother! The warrior maiden vented her spleen on a handy boulder, kicking the rock with all her might. All she succeeded in doing was making her foot sore. She simply couldn't think about this right now. She was worn out from battle and from all the worrying she'd done on behalf of her father and Green—her half-brother. Gods, it was too unbelievable!

The warrior woman stalked back to camp. At the edge of the sleeping mob, near the unconscious Kemian Ambrodel, she dropped down and slept.

Ulvian had also been surprised by his father's announcement. This unknown bumpkin, a son of Kith-Kanan? It was a startling bit of news. But the prince had too many worries of his own to waste much effort wondering how he had come to acquire a half-brother. He, too, lay down to sleep, but sleep was longer in coming. His mind was filled with thoughts of what his immediate future might hold. Some hours later, Prince Ulvian awoke with a start.

"Who is it?" he said. "Who's calling?"

He glanced around. The sun was low in the western sky, and its orange rays showed him the kender nearby. Rufus was curled into a ball, fast asleep, giving vent to his unique, high-pitched snores. The rest of the group also slumbered on. Just above them floated smoke from the funeral pyres, like a cloud of remembered evil. Ulvian grimaced at the smell and wondered how they had all managed to sleep in such a vile place.

Once more the prince heard the voice. It was soft and low, a feminine voice, he thought. It seemed to be coming from the direction of the largest fire, at the base of the peak. Ulvian rose and walked in that direction. Heat shimmered off the bed of coals. The voice, a faint whisper barely louder than the hiss of the dying flames spoke to him.

A stack of charred wood collapsed, sending sparks up into the cold, twilight sky. Ulvian listened to the voice and answered, "How can I reach you? The fire is still hot."

The voice told him. The words entered his head like smoke wafting into his nose. The words were caressing, the tone melodic and resonant. His tired, aching limbs seemed imbued with strength. Belief flooded his mind. He could do it. The voice said so, and it was true.

Looking into the charred remains ahead, from where the voice seemed to emanate, Ulvian strode into the cinders. His bare feet pressed down on glowing coals, yet he did not cry out. So great was his desire to find the source of the silver-toned voice that he no longer took notice of where he walked. In the center of the pyre, he found it. Thrusting his hand into the ashes and charred bones of the wyvern, the prince found the onyx amulet. Heat had fused the two pieces together. Now they could never be taken apart.

The voice spoke again, and Ulvian nodded. Though the amulet was still hot, he put it into his pocket and walked out of the fire. In minutes, he had fallen asleep once more. Though smeared with soot, neither his hand nor his feet were burned.

Four-Legged Cousins

16

Verhanna stirred from her slumber. Opening her eyes, she saw Greenhands sitting cross-legged on the ground a few feet away. The morning sun was in her eyes, and she lifted a hand to shade them. Greenhands was looking across the broad vista of mountain peaks.

It took the Qualinesti princess a moment to recall the events of the past days. The cold funeral pyres remained as mute evidence of what had transpired. She also recalled the news she had received regarding the white-haired elf before her. Her half-brother.

He turned to her, and she quickly looked away, embarrassed that he'd noticed her scrutiny.

"Hello, my captain," he said equably. "You have slept long—a night, a day, and a second night." Wind stirred his long hair. His green eyes were darker somehow, more muted than their usual vivid hue.

"By Astra!" Verhanna got to her feet and hurried to Rufus. She poked him in the back with the toe of her boot. The kender screwed up his wizened face and groaned.

"Go'way, Auntie! I wanna sleep," he grumbled.

"On your feet, Wart!"

Rufus's blue eyes popped open.

The warrior maiden and kender circled through the scattered sleepers, waking them. Kith-Kanan sat up, coughing and shaking his head. "Merciful gods," he muttered. "I'm too old to sleep on bare ground." Verhanna grasped Kith-Kanan's arm and helped him stand. He was very stiff from having slept in the open. "Is there anything to eat?" he asked. "I'm hollow."

Rufus approached Kemian cautiously. The general had been seriously injured by the wyvern, and the kender feared that he'd find him dead. But Kemian drew breath steadily. His brow was cool and dry, and after Rufus awakened him, his eyes were clear.

"Water," he said hoarsely. Rufus put a wicker-wrapped bottle to the elf's lips.

Gradually the whole party arose. They stood around, a bit dazed, taking in their situation.

Kith-Kanan saw Greenhands, still seated serenely on the ground. He stood when Kith-Kanan approached him. The Speaker held out a hand. His son looked at it uncomprehendingly, and Kith-Kanan showed him how to shake hands.

"My son," he said proudly. "You did well."

Greenhands' brow wrinkled in thought. "I only wanted to save you," he replied. "I did not mean to kill."

"Shed no tears for Drulethen, Son! His heart was as black as the onyx talisman he prized. He chose his path, and he chose his destruction. Be at peace. You have done a noble deed."

The elf didn't look convinced. In fact, he had a look of such sadness that Kith-Kanan put an arm around his shoulder and asked him what troubled him so.

"Before I found you, I often felt the presence of my mother," he replied. "She would guide me and help me. I have sat here a long time, reaching out to her, but she does not answer. I do not feel her near any longer."

"She must know that you're with me now. You're not alone," Kith-Kanan said gently. "When your mother . . . left me, it took me a long time to get used to not having her by my side. But we are together now, and there are many things I need to know about you and how you came to be here."

A disturbance erupted on the other side of the plateau. Kith-Kanan left his newfound son and hastened to the point of trouble. All the warriors were clustered in a group. They parted for the Speaker. In the center of the knot, he found Ulvian being restrained by two warriors. Verhanna and her kender scout faced them.

"What is this?" asked Kith-Kanan.

"My loving sister seeks to deny me a horse," Ulvian said, straining against his captors. "And these ruffians have laid hands on me!"

"There are twenty people, and only twelve horses," Verhanna snapped at him. "You're still a convict, and by Astra, you'll walk!"

713

"Release him," Kith-Kanan said. The elves let go of Ulvian. A smug sneer appeared on the prince's face, but his father erased it by adding, "You will walk, Ullie."

The prince's face turned red under his dirty blond beard. "Do you think I can walk all the way to Qualinost?" he exploded.

"You're going back to Pax Tharkas!" Verhanna put in.

"No," said the Speaker. The single quiet syllable silenced both siblings. "The prince will accompany us home to Qualinost."

"But, Father—!"

"That's enough, Hanna!" She flushed at this mild rebuke. "Has anyone seen to Lord Ambrodel?"

"He's doing all right, Your Worship," interposed Rufus. "But with those busted ribs, he can't ride." The kender suggested they make a stretcher from whatever they could find inside the cave. The stretcher could be dragged behind a horse.

Kith-Kanan gave orders for this to be done. Two warriors went in search of poles and cloth while the others collected their scattered gear and loaded for home.

The Speaker and his daughter went to see Kemian. The general was white-faced with pain, but he saluted gamely when his sovereign arrived. Kith-Kanan knelt beside him.

"The kender says you'll be all right," he said encouragingly. "Though he's not a healer, he does seem to have some knowledge of these things. How do you feel, my lord?"

Through clenched lips, Kemian replied, "I am well sire."

"Do you feel well enough to tell me what happened in the cave? How did you get hurt, and how did Greenhands manage to kill the wyvern?"

The injured elf coughed and almost fell back in pain. Verhanna got behind him to bolster him up. Kemian gave her a grateful glance over his shoulder, then launched into his account of the death of the sorcerer Drulethen.

"The green-fingered one reasoned that, with his strength, he could rope the beast and pull its head inside, where I would chop it off with my sword. I got the rope we'd gathered for you, Speaker, and tied off the end to a wall bracket in the great chamber. The warriors and the kender teased the monster into attacking, and Greenhands caught him in his snare." He paused to draw a ragged breath.

"We pulled the monster in, even though it fought hard against us," Kemian continued. "I've never seen so strong an elf, sire. Greenhands hauled in that wyvern as if it were a river trout. I stepped forward to finish the job with my sword, but"— he passed a hand over his chest—"the monster pinned me against the wall with its head. It meant to crush the life out of me and was doing just that when Greenhands took the sword from my hand and chopped the beast's head off. Two strokes was all it took, I swear. Then I swooned from pain."

Verhanna took up the water bottle Rufus had left and wet Kemian's lips. "Thank you, lady," he whispered. "You're very kind."

"That's not something I hear very often," she replied tartly.

Kemian coughed. Agony contorted his face. "Sire," he gasped, "is he really your son?"

"Yes. He is the child of my first wife, whom I lost many, many years ago."

Kemian grasped Kith-Kanan's hand. "Then you have a fine son, Majesty. With guidance, he would make a fine Speaker of the Sun."

It was the same thought that had just occurred to the Speaker. By common law of primogeniture, the eldest son was to inherit a monarch's crown. Even though Ulvian was born first, Greenhands had been conceived several centuries earlier. It was a legal and ethical riddle to try the brains of the wisest thinkers in Qualinost.

Verhanna interrupted his thoughts. "Father, I agree with the general. Greenhands is brave and good and has powers beyond what you have already seen." She recounted the experiences she and Rufus had had with Greenhands—his control of the herd of elk, her healing, their meeting with the centaurs.

The centaurs! She jumped to her feet, letting go of Kemian so quickly he slid sideways to the ground. He moaned, but Verhanna was already stepping over him and bawling for Greenhands. He and Rufus were standing at the edge of the ashes, all that was left of the wyvern's pyre.

"I'm calling you!" she said, planting her hands on her hips. "Why don't you answer?"

Rufus pointed to the object of their rapt attention. Half-buried in the cinders was the scorched skull of the monster. All the flesh had been burned away, and the horny yellow beak had turned a sickly gray from the heat.

"We was thinking that would make a great trophy," Rufus said.

"And on what pack mule were you planning to put that thing?" she asked pointedly. The skull was four feet long.

"I can carry it," Greenhands said softly, and Rufus beamed at him.

"Leave it. It's just carrion." Verhanna took hold of Greenhands' arm, pulling him away from the ashes. "Do you still have the horn that centaur gave you?"

"It's there." He indicated the rocks where their gear had been placed before the fight.

"Use it," she said. "Summon the centaurs."

"Why, my captain?" Rufus scratched his freckled cheek.

"We need mounts, don't we? Centaurs have four legs, don't they? If they're agreeable, we'll ride them right into Qualinost!" She grinned. "What an entrance we'll make!"

Rufus grinned back at her. So taken was he with her idea that he ran to the rocks and fetched back the ram's horn.

He inhaled deeply. Fastening his lips on the horn tip, the kender blew till his red face turned purple. A horrible wail escaped from the open end of the horn. Everyone on the plateau stopped what he was doing and put his hands over his ears.

"Enough!" said Verhanna, snatching the horn from Rufus's lips. He staggered away, winded from his effort.

She handed the ram's horn to Greenhands. He raised it high and blew.

A deep, steady tone issued from the horn. The unwavering bass note bounced against the mountains and echoed back like a phantom reply.

"Again," Verhanna demanded.

The second note took wing before the first had died. The two sounds chased each other all through the Kharolis and back again. Greenhands lowered the horn, and the two calls finally faded away into the distance. Everyone waited, but nothing happened. There was no answering sound.

Verhanna was disappointed, but before she could order Greenhands to sound the horn again, Kith-Kanan came up to them. "Son," he said quickly, "Hanna said you were able to heal a goblin bite she received. Do you think you could do as much for Lord Ambrodel?"

"If you wish it, Father," was Greenhands's reply.

They went to the general, and Greenhands sat down on the ground beside him. Kemian watched him expectantly, a fevered gleam in his gray-blue eyes.

Greenhands touched his fingertips lightly to each side of the warrior's head, cocking his own as if listening to something. "You must take off the metal he wears," Greenhands murmured, pulling his hands back. "It blocks the power."

"What power?" demanded Ulvian, who had joined them. Verhanna punched him in the arm to silence him.

Rufus deftly untied the armor that Kemian still wore and tugged it free. He removed every bit of metal the general had, even snipping the copper buttons from his haqueton. Those buttons found their way somehow into the kender's pockets.

"Now it begins," Greenhands said. He placed his hands flat against Kemian's ribs. After a few moments, it became obvious the breathing of the two elves was synchronous. Kemian's was short and ragged because of his injury; Greenhands also breathed in small gasps. The green-fingered elf slowly closed his eyes. Kemian's eyelids fluttered down also.

Their breathing came faster. All the color drained from Greenhands' face, and beads of shiny sweat broke out on his brow. At the same time, a flush of red blood came to Lord Ambrodel's face. His body went limp, his head lolling to one side. The green-fingered elf stiffened abruptly, his back and neck rigid. Now his breath came in harsh, loud gasps for air.

Verhanna cared greatly for Greenhands and hated to see him in pain. Her guilt was compounded by knowing that he had suffered for her also, when he'd saved her from the festering goblin bite.

Kemian cried out. His shout was echoed by Greenhands. The sound rose in intensity and was suddenly cut off. Greenhands' head hung down. His hands slid off the now sleeping general. He wrapped them around his own chest and moaned. Kith-Kanan and Verhanna gently lowered him to the ground.

"Rest easy," Kith-Kanan said, smoothing Greenhands' sweat-soaked hair from his brow. "Rest easy, Son. You've done it. You've healed Kemian." The general's chest rose and fell in deep, untroubled breaths.

It was early afternoon by the time the party was ready to go. Kemian and Greenhands had slept for several hours. Lord Ambrodel awoke fully recovered, and his healer had only some soreness and stiffness remaining. No centaurs had come to aid them, so they set out with ten riding and ten walking. Two horses were used for baggage only. Verhanna mounted up with Kemian and eight warriors. In spite of her protests, her father had chosen to walk, along with Greenhands and Ulvian.

"But you're the Speaker!" she protested.

"An even better reason to go on foot. My subjects should always know that I am willing to do without so that they may live better. Besides, down here I can talk with my sons."

Verhanna looked at Greenhands and Ulvian, who walked on each side of their father. Neither of them had spoken to the other. In fact, Ulvian seemed to be assiduously avoiding his newly revealed half-brother. With a last shake of her head, Verhanna reined about and galloped to the head of the little column, taking her place by General Ambrodel's side.

"How long is the journey to your city, Father?" asked Greenhands.

"On foot, we'll be many days walking," said the Speaker. "We'll have to pass through Pax Tharkas on the way."

Ulvian reacted violently to this. He halted in his tracks and stared hard at Kith-Kanan, who continued walking along with the rest of the group. The others on foot passed the prince, until he was standing alone on the narrow mountain trail, the rest of the party well ahead of him.

Kith-Kanan called out, "Coming, Ullie?"

He wanted to shout back, "No!" but there was no wisdom in resisting. His sister would merely insist he be restrained. His father had said he would be allowed to return to Qualinost with the rest of the group. All the prince could do was hope that was true.

*   *   *   *   *

They made good time that day, reaching the wider road in the lower elevations by midafternoon. Kith-Kanan halted them there for a rest and food. Cooking fires were lit under the flawless blue vault of sky. The Speaker commented on the fine weather.

"Strange," he mused, "the Kharolis in summer is usually beset by daily thunderstorms."

"Perhaps the gods are showing their favor," Kemian suggested.

Verhanna and her father exchanged a private look. "Some happy influence is at work," Kith-Kanan agreed. The Speaker believed that the shooting stars and this fine weather were all signs that the gods were pleased by the fact that, after four centuries, he and Greenhands had come together.

Rufus had dropped off the rump of Verhanna's horse when the column stopped and promptly disappeared into the rocks on the high side of the road. The group was busy, though, and no one paid any attention.

The soup was just beginning to boil when the drumming of hooves echoed down the road. The warriors, true to their training, dropped their pots and cups and grabbed their weapons. Kith-Kanan, more curious than alarmed, walked to the end of the road and looked up and down the mountainside, trying to see who was coming. Dust rose from the trail. He heard a high, broken yelp.

"Hi-yi-yi!"

Around the curve in the road appeared Rufus Wrinklecap, clinging to the back of a brown-skinned centaur. More wild horse-people followed, and they barreled up the road straight at Kith-Kanan. The warriors shouted for the Speaker to withdraw to safety, but Kith-Kanan stood his ground.

The lead centaur, carrying the kender, came to a stop just inches from the Speaker.

"Hail, Your Worthiness!" declared Rufus. "This is my friend, Uncle Koth, and these are his cousins!"

Kith-Kanan placed his right palm over his breast. "Greetings, Uncle Koth, and all your family. I am Kith-Kanan, Speaker of the Sun."

"Most happy to see you, cousin Speaker." The centaur's dark eyes, round like a human's, flitted quickly from side to side. "Where would be our friend, he of the green fingers?"

Kith-Kanan beckoned Greenhands forward. The centaur embraced him with both brawny arms.

"Little cousin! We heard you call, and have run hard all day to find you!"

"You were a day's ride away, and you heard him blow the horn?" asked Verhanna, amazed.

"Indeed so, sister cousin. Is that not why I gave it to him?"

Koth beamed, showing his uneven, yellow teeth. "We found the littlest cousin down the road, eating jackberries. He explained the boon you desire from us and led us back here."

Verhanna raised an eyebrow at her kender scout. "Jackberries, eh?"

Rufus gave her an ingratiating smile. "Well, there were only a few—"

"This is excellent," Kith-Kanan said. "Are you willing to carry us all the way to Qualinost?"

Koth scratched behind one ear. The stiff brown hair that fringed it grated loudly on his callused fingers. "Well, cousin Speaker, where might this Kaal-nos be?"

Kith-Kanan said, "By horse, it's an eight-day ride from here."

"Horse!" Koth snorted, and the band of centaurs at his back laughed loudly. "The sun and moons all know no horse can run like the Kothlolo," he boasted. "If it pleases you, cousin Speaker, we will have you in your Kaal-nos in six days."

This claim set the warriors buzzing with speculation. Kith-Kanan held up a hand for quiet. "Uncle Koth, if you can put me in my capital in six days, I will give you a reward such as no centaur ever dreamed of."

The centaur's eyes narrowed with thought. "Reward is good. I'll think on it, cousin, and so should you. When we get to Kaalnos, I'll find out if you think as big as Koth!"

There were only eight centaurs. Since it was claimed that ordinary horses would not be able to keep up, only the Speaker and his close party rode them. The rest of the warriors were told to proceed on horseback to Pax Tharkas, where relief and refreshment would be given them.

"Are we bypassing the fortress, Father?" asked Verhanna.

"If the centaurs can get us back to the city in six days, there's no reason to detour to Pax Tharkas," he replied. Verhanna looked at Ulvian and frowned but said no more.

There was much rough laughter and nervousness as the party climbed on the centaurs. Kith-Kanan rode Koth. Without saddles or stirrups or reins, the riders were worried about maintaining their balance as they rode. Rufus supplied the answer. His mount was a dapple-gray lady centaur who wore a buckskin halter over her small breasts. The kender took the wide sash belt from his formerly fine suit of clothes and tied it loosely around her human waist. This gave him something to cling to from behind, and it didn't impede the centaur's movements. In fact, she stroked the dirty yellow belt fondly, admiring its silky smoothness. The rest of the party quickly copied the kender's invention with whatever belts or braces they owned, and they were soon set.

"Ready, cousins?" boomed Koth. Together the centaurs chorused their assent. "You have a firm hold, cousin Speaker?"

Kith-Kanan shifted his seat slightly. "I'm ready," he said, gripping the leather baldric he'd converted to a centaur harness. Koth gave a wild, wavering yell and galloped down the road at breakneck speed. The rest of the centaur band thundered after him.

The Speaker had ridden some strange creatures in his life. His royal griffon, Arcuballis, had possessed breathtaking strength in flight and had once performed a complete loop in the air, but this! The riders' weight didn't seem to hinder the centaurs much; they bounded over low obstacles and careened around large ones with absolute abandon.

Kith-Kanan was above yelling from fright or excitement, but his followers were not so restrained. Verhanna, whose long legs nearly scraped the ground when astride her short-legged centaur, yelped involuntarily at every wild bump and turn. Rufus whooped and shouted from the back of his lady centaur and waved his big hat. Kemian tried to emulate the Speaker's dignity, but an occasional startled shout escaped his lips from time to time. Ulvian was tight-lipped, his thoughts on distant things. Only Greenhands seemed to take the ride with perfect equanimity. Despite the pounding pace, he held on with one relaxed hand and studied the scenery with total attention.

The landscape swept past at an astonishing rate. As surefooted as goats, the centaurs raced near the sheer drop that bounded the mountain road. Kith-Kanan gradually relaxed his death grip on the baldric and sat more erect.

"How long can you maintain such a pace?" he said loudly in Koth's ear.

"I shall be winded in a few hours," shouted the centaur. "Of course, I am old. My young cousins can run longer than I!"

Kith-Kanan cast a glance back over his shoulder. His children and friends bounced and yelped on the centaurs' backs. Red top-knot streaming in the wind, Rufus flipped him a salute. Verhanna gave her father an uncertain smile as she glanced at the cliff's edge almost below her feet. Greenhands waved casually.

The wind sang in Kith-Kanan's ears, and the day was fair and warm. He would soon be home in his beloved city, arriving on the back of a wild centaur. Throwing back his head, the Speaker of the Sun laughed out loud. His merriment echoed through the hills against a rhythm of centaurs' hooves.

* * * * *

By twilight, after half a day of constant motion—they even ate on the run—the centaurs were on the lower slopes of the eastern Kharolis, with the wide plain spread out at their feet. Kith-Kanan remarked on the abundance of flowers and the tall green grass, none of which had been present when he and his party passed through a week before.

"The flowers bloomed for Greenhands," Rufus said. He bit a wild apple, then offered the rest of the fruit to his mount. She reached back with one sun-browned arm and deftly took the fruit.

Kith-Kanan looked over Koth's human shoulder at the field of blooming flowers. He remembered a time long ago when he and his young friend Mackeli had journeyed to Silvanost through a land bursting with life. Pollen and flower petals had filled the sun-washed air, and everywhere there was a vibrancy above and beyond the usual growth of spring. It had happened because his wife Anaya had metamorphosed into an oak tree—she had joined the power that she served so faithfully. The ancient power had showed its rejoicing in an explosion of fertility. Now Greenhands' passage through the countryside was provoking the same reaction. It was one more bit of confirmation that Greenhands was indeed his and Anaya's child. Not that he needed much convincing. He saw his beloved every time he looked into his son's innocent green eyes and smiling face.

"Majesty? Majesty?"

Kith-Kanan snapped back to the present. "Yes?"

Rufus had guided his mount next to the Speaker's. "Your Mightiness, the others want to know if we can stop and stretch our legs."

The Speaker rubbed his numb thighs. "Yes, an excellent idea. Stop, uncle, if you please."

721

The centaurs drew up, and their riders stiffly dismounted. With many groans, they stretched their sore muscles. Kith-Kanan went to speak quietly with Greenhands. From the corner of his eye, he saw Ulvian stalking down the slope toward the plain, deeply shadowed now that the sun had set.

"Shall I fetch him back?" Verhanna asked, hand on her sword hilt.

"No. He won't get far." Kith-Kanan sighed. His delight in the fine day and his new son were tinged with worry for the problems of his other son. "Your people can catch up to him, can't they, uncle?"

A wide grin split the centaur's face. "No doubt, cousin Speaker!" Koth declared. "No two-legs can outrun the Kothlolo!"

They delayed a while longer, then everyone mounted up and Kith-Kanan pointed the way to distant Qualinost.

A Home Never Seen

17

Ulvian kicked his way through the waist-high weeds, batting heavy-headed flowers aside in clouds of yellow pollen. It was easy to see which way his father's mind was turning. Kith-Kanan was so solicitous of this newcomer, this upstart who claimed to be his son. Not once had he asked after Ulvian's health, asked how he had fared with the scum of Pax Tharkas. All his attention was for Greenhands. And the power this elf wielded! He'd defeated a wyvern, healed Lord Ambrodel, called a band of centaurs.

The prince didn't care whether Greenhands was truly his brother or not. All Ulvian was concerned about was making sure he received what he considered to be rightfully his—the throne of Qualinesti. The prince could see where this was leading—it was out with Ulvian, in with Greenhands. No wonder his father hadn't insisted he return to Pax Tharkas. With Greenhands in the picture, it hardly mattered now where Prince Ulvian went.

By now it was fully night, but the red moon, Lunitari, had risen and shone over the flowering plain, lighting his way. Ulvian knew that his father and the others, mounted on those mad centaurs, would catch up with him. He wasn't trying to run away; he just couldn't stand the sight of his father fawning over his supposed son. Ulvian was a prince of the blood, by Astra! Let the Speaker try to favor that green-fingered elf over him. Let him try! Ulvian had friends in Qualinost, powerful friends who wouldn't stand for such a usurpation.

He halted. Green-fingered elf. Elf. Greenhands was a pure-blooded elf, half Silvanesti, half Kagonesti. Humans, elves, and dwarves all lived together in peace now in Qualinesti, but there were always tensions among them. Ancient prejudices were hard to erase. What if Greenhands found favor among a majority of senators because of his purely elven heritage?

Ulvian realized he was stroking his bearded chin. The beard was just one more sign of his mixed blood, of the human heritage that flowed from the mother he had idolized.

If Greenhands were gone, everything would be all right.

So get rid of him.

Ulvian shook his head. It was as if someone had said those words in his mind.

Someone did.

"Stop it!" he said aloud. "What is happening to me? Am I bewitched?"

No, it is I who speaks to you.

"Who are you?" he yelled at the star-laden sky.

We spoke once before. The night Drulethen died, remember? You saved me from the fire.

The voice. Low and softly feminine. Inserting a hand into his shirt, Ulvian felt the onyx amulet there. It was warm from being next to his skin. He drew it out and stared at it in the red moonlight.

"Are you a spirit imprisoned in the amulet?"

I am the amulet itself. Once I served Drulethen. Now I serve you.

A slow smile spread over the prince's face. His fingers closed tightly around the stone. "Yes! Then your power is mine?"

It will be in time.

"Tell me what to—" Ulvian broke off suddenly. He heard loud swishing noises, as if made by many legs striding through the grass. He shoved the amulet back inside his shirt.

A pair of riderless centaurs appeared. The black one who had been Ulvian's mount said, "Ho, little cousin. We were sent to look for you. Uncle Speaker wants you back. Will you come?"

Ulvian regarded them with distaste but replied, "I will come."

The centaur approached him, and the prince climbed on his back. They went bounding away in the grass until they caught up to the rest of the party, hardly a mile distant. The other riders were slumped forward, sleeping. Only Kith-Kanan was awake.

"There's no reason to run away, Ullie," he said softly. "I'm not taking you back to punish you."

Ulvian gripped the belt that formed his centaur's harness. He forced himself to ask the difficult question. "Why are you taking me to the city, Father?"

"Because I want you there. Putting you in prison only taught you to make friends with criminals like Drulethen. I shall try to give you the guidance I should have given you when you were younger."

Guidance. He would give Ulvian guidance while installing that rustic on the Throne of the Sun.

"That won't be necessary, Father." Ulvian's voice was firm in the darkness. "I intend to pursue a different course once we get back home."

Kith-Kanan studied his son. Darkness and distance separated them from each other, and it was hard to read Ulvian's expression.

* * * * *

Verhanna and Rufus had ridden ahead to prepare Qualinost for the Speaker's return and to quell any panic at the sight of wild centaurs entering the city. Kith-Kanan, Kemian, and Ulvian rode together at the head of the little column. Behind them walked Greenhands and the other, riderless centaurs. The green-fingered elf had dismounted several hours earlier, claiming he needed the touch of the living soil on his bare feet.

They topped a treeless rise. Without being told to do so, Koth stopped. Kith-Kanan asked, "What's the matter, my friend?"

"That place yonder. Is that your city?" asked the awed centaur, pointing ahead.

"That is Qualinost," the Speaker replied proudly. "Have you never been to a city before?"

"Nay—the smell of so many two-legs is hard for us to bear."

Kemian raised his hand to cover his mouth and smiled. Five days with centaurs hadn't made any of them more used to the powerful aroma the creatures gave off.

In the clear air, the capital city of the western elves seemed close enough to touch. The soaring, arched bridges hung from the sky like silver rainbows. The Tower of the Sun was a molten gold spire, a flame leaping from the trees on the plateau. Kith-Kanan could feel the centaur's muscles tensing.

The sight of Qualinost had brought silence to the boisterous band. A feeling of joy filled the Speaker's heart.

"Onward, cousins," said Koth at last, lurching into motion. They descended the rise and soon entered a band of forest land. The centaur leader broke out into song. Rufus and Verhanna would have recognized it, for they had heard it before:

"Child of oak, newly born,
Walks among the mortals mild . . ."

725

Kith-Kanan was intrigued. He let the centaurs sing through the entire song once before he interrupted to ask, "Did you just make that up?"

"An ancient ode, it is," replied Koth. "Sung by uncles who died before I was a colt. Do you like it?"

"Very much."

The forest had given way to rolling hills, many tilled by farmers. The dirt road suddenly became paved with pounded cobbles. Other travelers on the road gave the caravan of centaurs wide berth. When they recognized Kith-Kanan, many set up a cheer.

The people grew more numerous. By the time the party reached the high cliffs overlooking the river that formed the city's eastern boundary, throngs of people had turned out to see the return of the Speaker of the Sun. The added spectacle of their Speaker riding on a centaur only increased their excitement.

The Qualinesti cheered and waved. Amused, the centaurs bellowed back their own hearty greetings. They came to the central bridge over the river, and the Guards of the Sun were drawn up in two lines, holding back the enthusiastic crowds.

"Hail, Speaker of the Sun! Hail, Kith-Kanan!"

Koth's front left hoof stepped down on the hundred-foot-long, suspended rope bridge. It swayed dizzyingly. He looked down into the deep river gorge and rolled his dark eyes. "Not good, cousin! We Kothlolo are not squirrels, to scamper on high!"

"The bridge is quite safe," Kith-Kanan countered. "It's used by hundreds daily."

"Two-legs are too foolish to be afraid," he muttered. "But a bargain is a bargain! He threw wide his thick arms and let out a bellow that silenced the assembled Qualinesti. Kith-Kanan tightened his grip on the strap around the centaur's waist, wondering what this yelling portended.

Still bellowing, Koth tore across the bridge at a blistering gallop, with Kith-Kanan holding on for dear life. The other centaurs set up a similar roar and, one by one, dashed across the bridge. By the time the last one reached the plateau and city gate, the crowds were cheering them on wildly.

"Who is brave? Who is strong? Who is fast?" roared Koth.

"Kothlolo!" answered the massed centaurs in deafening shouts.

Kith-Kanan slid off the horse-man's back. "My friend, I would walk to the Speaker's house now to be among my people. Will you follow?"

"Of course! There is a reward waiting. We traveled from Kharolis to city in five days!"

Kemian and Ulvian dismounted also. Flower petals and whole bouquets fell around them. Smiling broadly, Kith-Kanan drew

Greenhands forward. "Walk with me," he said in his son's ear. Ulvian waited for a similar invitation, but none was forthcoming.

Arm in arm, Kith-Kanan and Greenhands went down the street, trailed by Kemian, Ulvian, and the centaurs. The upper windows in every tower stood open, and elven and human women waved white linens as the Speaker strode past. The falling flower petals became so thick on the pavement that the underlying cobbles were lost from view. Elves, humans, half-humans, dwarves, and a kender or two cheered and waved all along the sweeping route to the Speaker's house. Kith-Kanan waved back. He looked at Greenhands. The younger elf seemed dazzled by the sheer size and magnitude of the greeting. The Speaker realized his son had never seen so many people before at once. The noise and outpouring of affection drew them on.

"Majesty, did Lady Verhanna announce the coming of your newfound son?" asked Kemian. Kith-Kanan shook his head. "Then why are they cheering him?"

"My people know who he is," said the Speaker confidently. "They can see it in his face, in his bearing. They are cheering the next Speaker of the Sun."

Lord Ambrodel grinned. Ulvian, just behind the general, heard every word his father said, but he plodded resolutely onward. Every joyous cry, every tossed bouquet, was yet another nail driven into the coffin of his desires.

They paraded past the Hall of the Sky. The slopes of the hill were likewise covered with Qualinesti, shouting and cheering. Each tree boasted several children who had climbed up for a better view.

In the square before the Speaker's house, Verhanna, Rufus, and Tamanier Ambrodel waited, flanked on both sides by the household servants and the remaining Guards of the Sun. Kith-Kanan went ahead of Greenhands, who hesitated at the foot of the steps. The Speaker stepped briskly up to the landing in front of the polished mahogany doors. He clasped arms with Tamanier Ambrodel and received a salute from Lord Parnigar, who had kept order in his absence. Kith-Kanan turned and faced the crowd, which gradually fell silent in expectation of a speech.

"People of Qualinost," he proclaimed, "I thank you for the warmth of your greeting. I am weary, and your affection makes me strong again.

"I have been to the high mountains, first to inspect the Fortress of Peace, later to put an end to an evil sorcerer who had long plagued those regions. Now that I have returned, I do not plan to leave you again any time soon."

He smiled and fresh cheers erupted from ten thousand throats. The Speaker held up his hands.

"More than that, I have brought with me someone new, someone very close to me. A long time ago, when I was merely the second son of the Speaker of the Stars, I had a wife. She was Kagonesti."

There were loud hurrahs from the wild elves in the crowd. "Our time together was short, but our love was not in vain. She left for me a most precious gift—a son." The multitude held its collective breath as Kith-Kanan descended the mahogany steps and took Greenhands by the hand. He led him up to the landing.

"People of Qualinost! This is my son," Kith-Kanan shouted, his heart full. "His name is Silveran!"

Through the roar that followed, Verhanna stepped close to her father and asked, "Silveran? Where did that name come from?"

"I chose it on the way here," said Kith-Kanan. He held his son's green-hued hand aloft. "I hope you like it, Son."

"You are my father. It is for you to name me."

"Silveran! Silveran!" the crowd chanted.

Kith-Kanan wanted very much to tell his people the rest of it. Silveran was his heir; he would be the next Speaker of the Sun. But he couldn't simply announce his decision, though he knew in his heart that Silveran was the best and wisest choice. Many people had to be consulted, even his political foes. The stability of the Qualinesti nation came first, even before his personal pride and happiness. He knew, too, that Ulvian would take the news very hard.

After receiving the cheers of the crowd for some time, Kith-Kanan led his family into the Speaker's house. Rufus and the Ambrodels, father and son, followed. The crowd began to disperse.

"Sire, what am I to do with the, ah, centaurs?" asked Tamanier, as the Kothlolo crowded up the steps to the double doors.

"Make them comfortable," Kith-Kanan replied. "They have done me a signal service."

Tamanier looked askance at the band of rowdy centaurs who filled the antechamber. Their unshod hooves skidded on the smooth mosaic and polished wood floor, but they moved in eagerly, delighted by the strange sights and sensations of the Speaker's house. As Kith-Kanan ascended the steps on his way to his private rooms, his castellan sent for troops of servants to deal with the centaurs. Amidst all the hubbub, no one noticed Prince Ulvian slip away from the royal family and disappear through the rear of the antechamber.

The prince strode furiously down the corridor that led to the servants' quarters, to a room used by the household scribes. The room was windowless and stood empty, as he knew it would be; everyone was in the streets, celebrating. When he shut and bolted the door, Ulvian had complete privacy. He turned up the wick on a guttering lamp and sat down at the scribes' table. With shaking hands, he took the amulet from his clothing and set it on the table before him.

"Speak," he said in a loud whisper. "Speak to me!"

Ulvian could barely form the words, so angry was he. Angry and, though he could hardly admit it even to himself, afraid. The prince was terrified by the adulation and acceptance Greenhands had received from the people of Qualinost. First he'd been banished to Pax Tharkas to be beaten and humiliated by the grunt gang, then he'd been terrorized by a lying sorcerer, and now, when all that he wanted should be within his grasp, now there was Greenhands.

The amulet was silent. The only voices Ulvian could hear were those of the people in the streets outside, still rejoicing.

"Are you trying to drive me mad?" he shrieked, flinging the onyx talisman against the far wall. It bounced off and rolled away. Ulvian buried his face in his hands.

I am not your servant. I do not come when ordered, said a haughty, cold voice inside the prince's head.

He raised up with a jerk. "What? Are you there?"

You must learn self-discipline. This anger of yours gets out of control and serves you ill. Drulethen did not lose his temper so readily.

Ulvian got down on his knees and felt under the shelves loaded with scrolls. His fingers found the amulet. It was warm to the touch, like a living thing.

"Dru wasn't so superior," said the prince, shifting around to sit on the floor.

Yes, I know, his killer is the one who has stolen your birthright.

Ulvian set the amulet on the floor. "Greenhands," he said with a sneer. "Now called Silveran—as if he deserves a royal name."

He is your father's son, but there is more to him than his ancestry. The power dwells within him. It is a danger to us.

"What power?"

The ancient power of order, which brings life to the world. It is not of the gods, but a more elemental force.

The prince shook his head. "This theology means nothing to me. All I want is what I was promised from birth: my place on the throne!"

Then Greenhands must die.

Put so bluntly, the idea gave Ulvian pause. He pondered the possibility for a long time and finally said, "No, Greenhands must not die. No matter how subtly it was done, suspicion would fall on me. That must not happen. I want this upstart discredited, not killed. I want the people, including my father, to want me on the throne." His jaw clenched, he added in a whisper, "Especially my father."

It was the amulet's turn to fall silent. Then it said, *You are a worthy successor to Drulethen.*

Ulvian smiled, basking in the praise. "I shall surpass that lowbom sorcerer in every way," he said smugly.

* * * * *

"I am most pleased to meet you, Prince Silveran."

Senator Irthenie bowed to Kith-Kanan and his son. They were in the outer hall of the Thalas-Enthia tower. The Speaker was about to present his newest son to the senators of Qualinesti, and he knew they weren't going to be as enthusiastic as the common folk had been.

The Kagonesti woman studied Silveran closely. He was dressed in a simple white robe, with a green sash at his waist. His long hair shone in the late morning sunlight that poured through the windows. "The public display yesterday was very clever," said Irthenie. "How did you accomplish it?"

The elf once known as Greenhands gave her a blank look and said, "I don't understand. I was very happy when I entered the city. The people were friendly to me. That's all I know."

"My son has certain gifts," Kith-Kanan remarked. "They come from his mother's side of the family."

Verhanna, standing back by the wall, raised her eyebrows.

"A very useful talent," Irthenie said. "But can he rule, Majesty? That is your plan, I know. Can this innocent in a grown elf's body rule the nation?"

Kith-Kanan adjusted the folds of his creamy white robe distractedly. "He will learn. I—we—shall teach him."

The rumble on the other side of the thick obsidian wall was the debate already raging about the Speaker's new son and possible heir. The Loyalists were outraged, the New Landers were doubtful, and the Friends of the Speaker were completely in the dark about what to say or do.

"Where is Prince Ulvian?" Irthenie asked. "Why isn't he here?"

"He's sulking," Verhanna snorted. "I offered to drag him here by his heels, but Father wouldn't let me."

"The Speaker has a kind heart and a wise mind. There is real danger in alienating Prince Ulvian and those who support him. I have not served this nation so long to see it torn apart by a dynastic war."

"Do you think it will come to war?" asked Verhanna, sensitive to the larger issues.

"Not really," the senator admitted. "The Loyalists want to exploit Ulvian in the name of tradition, for their own greed, but none of them would choose to die for him."

"I pray you are right," said the Speaker softly.

The ceremonial doors of the senate swung outward, and the steward of the chamber announced, "The Thalas-Enthia humbly requests that the Speaker of the Sun enter their house and address them."

The ritual invitation was a signal to Kith-Kanan that the fight was at hand. Adjusting the drape of his clothing once more, the Speaker said quietly to Silveran, "Are you ready, Son?"

The young elf was quite composed, having no conception of the fight that lay ahead. "I am, Father."

The Speaker raised an eyebrow at Irthenie. "Ready for yet another battle, my old friend?"

Hitching her wide, beaded belt off her narrow hips, the Kagonesti woman replied, "I say give them no quarter, Great Speaker." Her eyes gleamed.

Kith-Kanan swept into the hushed senate chamber, followed by Silveran, then Irthenie. Verhanna remained outside. As the steward moved to close the huge, balanced doors, she heard the first voices rising in anger from within. Unable to bear the suspense of waiting here but having no desire to sit in on what she considered pointless arguing, Verhanna left the Thalas-Enthia tower and returned to the Speaker's house.

There she was met by Tamanier Ambrodel, who looked harassed. "Lady," he pleaded, "if you have any influence with these vulgar centaurs, will you please ask them to get out of the house? They're wrecking it!"

She winked. "I'll have a word with Uncle Koth."

The antechamber was in chaos. The centaurs had camped in the open room, changing it from an elegant greeting hall to a fancy stable. Somewhere they'd found some straw, which they had strewn about on the floor to give their hooves better purchase. All the ornamental vases and artfully grown plants had been broken, uprooted, or eaten.

When Verhanna entered, four centaurs were playing catch with a globe of flawless emerald taken from the stair baluster.

She intercepted a toss and caught the emerald. It was weightier than she expected. "Oof!" she grunted, bending low with the ten-inch sphere in her arms.

"Hail, sister cousin!" cried Koth. He sat by the far wall, his legs folded beneath him. A heap of fruit was piled up beside him. On the other side was an equally large pile of gnawed cores. Koth's face was sticky with juice.

"Hello, uncle," she said, setting the emerald down on the floor. "You fellows are having quite a good time, aren't you?"

"This city of yours is paradise!"

The elder centaur burped loudly. "Why, only this morning, I

went to the big open place with cousins Whip and Hennoc and found all this lovely fruit!"

She surveyed the small mountain of pears, apples, and grapes. "Did you pay for this, uncle?"

"Pay? Why, as soon as we got to the two-legs who had the fruit, he yelled and ran away! He wanted to make us a gift of this, I am sure."

Koth polished a dusty pear against his hairy chest and bit into it.

"Look here, uncle. You can't let all the cousins carry on like this inside the Speaker's house. It's, er, causing a bit of a disturbance," Verhanna said in a kindly tone. "Why don't you go outdoors? There's a great deal more room."

He regarded her with sharp, intelligent eyes. "I think Kothlolo should live under the open sky," he declared. "City life is making us fat!"

With a few raucous words, he rounded up his band. He spoke a bit longer, and they began to file out of the antechamber.

"You're not angry, are you?" asked Verhanna as they headed for the doors.

"No, sister cousin. Why should I be? No uncle of mine ever went to a city. I am old and have seen more than I might have seen. I am content."

Outside, in the square before the Speaker's house, a group of four Kagonesti elves waited with a small, donkey-drawn cart. Tamanier Ambrodel was talking with one of the Kagonesti. When Verhanna and the centaurs appeared, the castellan approached them.

"Ahem," he said. "His Majesty Kith-Kanan would like me to present you with this gift."

With a sweep of his arm, Tamanier indicated the four elves and cart. "These Kagonesti are farriers. They will teach you and your people about shoeing. The Speaker thought that if your people were shod with iron shoes, you could travel farther and have less problem with worn and cracked hooves."

Koth descended the steps to the square and approached the chief farrier. "We will wear iron, like elf horses?" he asked with curiosity.

"If it pleases you," replied Tamanier, nervously stepping back by Verhanna.

The elder centaur lifted a horseshoe from the farriers' cart. The four Kagonesti farriers regarded the horse-man speculatively, as if already sizing him for shoes.

All at once, Koth yelled and lifted the horseshoe over his head. He spoke a long stream of centaur talk at his band, and they raised a cheer, crowding around the cart.

The four farriers got on their cart and led the band of centaurs away to their smithy. The Kothlolo followed with shouted good-byes and boisterous waves, except for one. A lone centaur remained behind. It was the dapple-gray lady centaur who had carried Rufus from the mountains to the city.

She approached Verhanna. "Sister cousin," she said slowly, as if searching for words in the unfamiliar Elven language. "Please thank for me littlest cousin Rufus!" She smiled triumphantly but Verhanna lifted puzzled eyebrows at her.

"Thank him? For what?" asked the warrior maiden.

In reply, the lady centaur patted a yellow sash she'd wound around her muscular human waist. After staring at it for a few seconds, understanding dawned on Verhanna. It was the same sash Rufus had used as a centaur harness on their wild ride to the city. The lady centaur had admired it, and the kender must have made her a present of it.

Verhanna smiled and nodded her agreement. The lady centaur whirled in a tight circle, her long white tail swishing out behind her, and trotted off to catch up to her comrades.

The warrior maiden stared after her. For some reason, she found herself wishing she could go back to the plains or the high mountains with them. They had no worries, no responsibilities, and ran wherever the wind took them. In the wilderness, you could fight your enemies with a sword, something Verhanna understood. Here in Qualinost, foes were not so clearly defined, and the weapon of choice was words. She had never mastered that form of battle.

Verhanna sat down on the steps. There were a few people moving across the square, and she watched them go about their daily affairs. To her left, the great spire of the Tower of the Sun glinted brightly. The dark stripe that was the tower's shadow crept across the square away from the Speaker's house. In a few hours, at sunset, it would blanket the entrance of the Thalas-Enthia. She wondered how long her father and Silveran would have to argue and maneuver with the crafty senators there. It could be hours or days . . . perhaps even weeks.

Yes, sometimes the simple life of the wilderness seemed very appealing.

When the meeting broke up, the news radiated outward from the senate hall in ever-widening circles, so that by a few hours after sunset, the entire city knew that the senate had accepted Kith-Kanan's testimony that Silveran was his true son. The last bit of convincing evidence presented to the senate had been the testimony of the scribe Polidanus, reading from the copied archives of Silvanos the tale of the elf noble Thonmera. Thonmera was one of the original members of the legendary Synthal-Elish, the council that had been the foundation of the first elven nation several millennia ago. It was written that he had been born sixty years after his mother's official death. Apparently the sorcerer Procax had cast a spell on Thonmera's mother because she had refused the magician's offers of love. Procax turned the elf woman into stone. Sixty years later, when Thonmera's father had the stone image of his dead wife moved to his newly built home, the laborers dropped it. The stone image shattered, and the living infant form of Thonmera was discovered.

The Loyalists were completely defeated. Indeed, the tale of Thonmera undercut their entire position. Senator Clovanos and his cronies had made a great show of proclaiming themselves loyal to the traditions of the elven race. What could be more traditional, Irthenie demanded, than the birth of a member of the great Synthal-Elish?

Throughout the debate, Kith-Kanan sat quietly, not indulging in the raucous verbal maneuvers. The Speaker left it to Irthenie and his other friends to put forth his case. He answered occasional questions put to him, but by and large he remained in the background.

In the end, by a vast majority, the Thalas-Enthia gave its approval to Silveran as the Speaker's son. Kith-Kanan did not press right away for the issue of succession, though everyone in the hall had no doubt that was his ultimate goal.

The dying rays of sunlight streamed in the high window slots in the chamber as the session ended. Senators stretched and yawned, rising from their hard marble seats to go to their homes. The Loyalists filed out silently, utterly dejected. Many of the New Landers came forward to offer their congratulations to Kith-Kanan for finding his long-lost son. He remained to speak to all of them, thanking each one personally for his or her vote of confidence.

Finally only Irthenie was left. Her hands shook and her legs were weak from the long, hard afternoon's work. Kith-Kanan put an arm around her tiny waist and supported her with his strength.

"You're about to collapse," he said, concerned. "Shall I send for a litter to carry you home?"

"I can carry myself home," she snapped, jerking away from his encircling arm. The Speaker of the Sun retreated from the old elf woman's ire. "I may be tired, but I'm not senile yet!"

"That you are not," agreed Kith-Kanan. He watched Irthenie's painful progress up the chamber steps to ground level, then out the open doors. A warm wind blew into the hall, flapping the Speaker's robe and stirring Silveran's loose, long hair.

"You've been very quiet," said Kith-Kanan to his son.

"In truth, Father, I haven't understood one word in ten." He pressed his hands to his temples. "Never have I heard so many words spoken at one time! It makes my head reel to remember it!"

His father smiled. "The good senators do like to talk. But the wellborn and the important should talk to each other and argue their points of view. It's far better than settling their disputes with blades, as was the case in Silvanost in my father's day."

"Talking is better than fighting," repeated Silveran, impressing the concept on his mind.

"And right now food is better than both," Kith-Kanan sighed, putting an arm across his son's shoulders. "A plump chicken, a loaf of fresh bread, and some fine Qualinesti nectar should do nicely."

"I'm hungry too."

Father and son mounted the shallow steps and passed out of the hall. The rose quartz outer walls of the tower burned in the setting sun, and the full weight of summer leaves tossed back and forth on the trees as the wind stirred through them.

"I will teach you all I know," Kith-Kanan promised. He held his head up, letting the sun wash over his face. His regal robe, rumpled by the long afternoon of sitting, flashed white satin highlights as he walked. "You will be a great Speaker of the Sun."

Silveran was quiet for several minutes as they crossed the square toward the Speaker's house. They were unescorted by warriors and unburdened by pomp. The green-fingered elf lifted his own face to the warmth of the sun and shook his hair out of his eyes.

"Father," he said, at last, "I believe this is what my mother wanted."

"I believe so, too," Kith-Kanan murmured. "I believe you were sent so that the nation of Qualinesti would not die. You are its future."

As the Speaker and his son moved through the people who were finishing the day's chores, they were greeted by bows and smiles and happy voices.

"Long live the Speaker," said a human woman whose arms were laden with freshly cut flowers.

"Long live Prince Silveran!" added two nearby elves.

It was a fine day, a fine evening. At the door of the Speaker's house, Kith-Kanan saw Tamanier Ambrodel waiting for him. He sent Silveran on ahead into the house. When his son was gone, Kith-Kanan asked his castellan why he was so happy.

"How do you know I'm happy, sire?" asked the surprised Tamanier.

"Your face is an open scroll," the speaker replied. "I can read your every emotion. Now, what is it?"

"The centaurs have received their reward and left the house," Tamanier reported.

Kith-Kanan sighed. "I'm sorry I wasn't able to bid them farewell. They were staunch friends when we needed them. Such allies must be treasured." He passed a hand before his eyes. "My head aches, Tam. Have the apothecary send up a soothing draft with dinner."

Tamanier bowed. He watched the Speaker ascend the stairs to his private rooms to join young Silveran for their meal. How old he seems this evening, the castellan thought. The expedition against Drulethen had taken a great deal out of Kith-Kanan. But with a new son and plenty of rest, he would recover quickly.

Onyx Dreams

18

In a small room adjoining the Speaker's bedchamber, Silveran lay sleeping on a simple pallet of blankets spread on the hard tile floor. He was too used to sleeping on the ground to be comfortable on the soft bed. Every night of the week he had been in Qualinost, he'd dragged his bedding onto the floor and spent the night there.

As often happens to those with untroubled minds, he fell asleep quickly and passed the night in harmless dreams of his forest birthplace. The heady changes in his short life had barely impressed themselves on his inner mind, and Silveran did not yet dream of glory or power or the adoration of the people.

The only troubling aspects of his dreams so far were the images of his half-siblings, Verhanna and Ulvian. They did not menace him, but he felt vaguely troubled whenever they appeared. Even the innocent Silveran could sense Ulvian's hostility, and he did not know what to make of Verhanna's strange behavior at all. Sometimes she got angry at him for no reason at all.

She loves you, whispered a voice in his dreams.

Like a child, Silveran took the voice for a normal part of his dreamworld. "I love her," he replied reasonably. "And I love Rufus and my father, too."

I could have loved, sighed the voice, *but you took my life*.

Silveran's brow wrinkled and he stirred restlessly. "Who are you? How have I harmed you?"

A face rushed at him in his mind's eye. With marble white skin over sunken cheeks, it stared balefully through bleary gray eyes.

737

Its mouth hung slackly open, and its breath reeked of decay and the grave.

Silveran uttered a soft cry and awoke. After some seconds of disorientation, he realized he was in the Speaker's house. A sigh of relief passed his lips.

The blanket over him twitched as if it were alive. Silveran grasped the satin hem where it lay on his chest and held on. The blanket billowed up, rippling from his legs up to his waist. The elf whipped it away to see what was making it rise. Silveran let out a much louder cry this time, for beneath the blanket, floating only a foot from his nose, was the disembodied face from his dream!

You killed me, whispered the white lips. *I was Drulethen of Black Stone Peak, and you murdered me.*

"No!l I slew a monster! It was a noble deed!"

The head floated closer. Silveran threw up his hands to ward it off. Scrambling wildly, he fled the room on all fours.

The connecting door to the Speaker's room stood ajar, and Silveran banged through it. Hearing his son's wild cries, Kith-Kanan sat up in bed. Beside his bed, a magical lamp in the shape of a small silver pine tree flickered immediately to life.

"What? What is it?"

It took him a moment to notice Silveran cringing at the foot of his bed. "My boy, what's the matter?" he asked sleepily.

"Make it go away!" Silveran pressed his face into the dark red drapes hanging from the corners of Kith-Kanan's bed. "I didn't mean to do it! I didn't know!"

The Speaker arose and drew on a light cotton dressing gown. He knotted the sash at his waist and knelt beside his trembling son. "Tell me what's frightened you," he said, gently removing Silveran's clenched fingers from the drapery. The elf related his dream haltingly, includeing how he'd seen the face of the sorcerer he'd killed at Black Stone Peak.

"It was only a bad dream . . . a nightmare," Kith-Kanan whispered soothingly. He stroked his son's sweat-damp hair. "You never saw Dru in human form, did you?"

"But I woke up and it was still there," Silveran insisted. "He looked so ordinary in my dream . . . so thin and frail. Is that who the wyvern truly was?"

"It is true, Son, but the sorcerer is ash and dust now. He cannot hurt you."

As he spoke, Kith-Kanan tried to ignore his own fears. The link between Drulethen, the sorcerer, and Dru, the manifestation of the god Hiddukel, loomed large in his mind. He didn't want to see enemies and conspiracies under every stone and in every shadow, but coincidence rarely applied when the gods were involved.

It was a strange scene, the father consoling his fully grown son, rocking the weeping Silveran in his arms. The commotion had reached the sensitive ears of Tamanier Ambrodel, whose rooms were only a short distance down the corridor. The disheveled elf appeared in the Speaker's doorway holding a candelabrum.

"Sire?"

"It's all right, Tam," Kith-Kanan said, waving a hand. "My son had a bad dream."

"I killed him!" sobbed Silveran.

Embarrassed, Tamanier quietly withdrew. The prince certainly seemed more overwrought than a mere bad dream would warrant.

Silveran's terror finally lessened, and he was able to compose himself. Kith-Kanan offered to sit up with him, but his son declined to return to his own room. "I would rather sleep here with you," he said, indicating the hard floor at the foot of the four-poster bed. With a slight smile, Kith-Kanan nodded. He remembered from many centuries past the hollow tree in which he'd lived with Silveran's mother, Anaya, and her brother, Mackeli. They had slept on the unpadded ground too.

Kith-Kanan climbed back into bed. He listened for a long time, but Silveran's only sounds were light, even breathing. The Speaker pondered the mystery of Dru and what the coincidence of names could mean. Was Drulethen really the god Hiddukel in disguise? Did the God of Evil Bargains torment Silveran's dreams?

*　*　*　*　*

The Speaker's house was haunted.

So the gossip went in the markets and towers of Qualinost in the days that followed. The strange son the Speaker had brought back from the mountains was being hounded by the dreadful specter of a severed head. It made the good folk shudder, yet they repeated the tale. The story was awful, but it was also fascinating.

No one else had seen the ghost—only Prince Silveran was tormented. The specter would not appear to him unless he was alone, and then it persecuted him relentlessly. The robust young elf soon lost his color and vitality as sleep was denied him by the vengeful spirit.

Verhanna and Rufus set themselves the task of always being with Silveran, since the ghost chose never to appear to others. For a time, this worked. With his half-sister or the kender always in attendance, Silveran's health improved. Then, after many weeks of this happy companionship, the haunting changed.

Verhanna, Silveran, and Rufus were in the garden behind the Speaker's house. A straw-stuffed sack had been set up, and the warrior maiden was teaching Silveran how to shoot a crossbow. With the passage of time, Verhanna had been able to accept him for what he was—her brother, and very likely the next Speaker of the Sun. She'd grown to enjoy his company immensely.

Rufus jogged back and forth, retrieving arrows that went awry. It was a balmy afternoon, with gray clouds scudding before the wind, chasing the last remnants of summer over the western horizon. The trees were just beginning to show a hint of their autumn brilliance.

Thunk! A quarrel stuck, quivering, in the target. Verhanna lowered the crossbow from her shoulder. She wore a sleeveless red tunic and thin white trousers. On her feet were dainty red slippers, embroidered in gold. These had been a gift from Rufus on her birthday a week before.

"You see," she said encouragingly, "it isn't so hard. Even Wart can shoot a crossbow."

"We kender think bows are cowardly," Rufus replied airily. "A real weapon is the sling. That takes true skill to use!"

"Sling, ha! Slings are mere toys for children," scoffed Verhanna.

Silveran sat on a marble bench cunningly shaped to resemble a fallen tree. He'd made a number of tries at the target, but his bolts always went wide. He couldn't understand it, but his lack of success didn't seem to bother him. It did, however, vex Verhanna.

"You have eyes like a barn owl," she grumbled, hands perched on hips. "Why can't you hit the target?"

"Weapons don't work well in my hands," Silveran replied with a shrug. "I don't know why."

"Nonsense. Warrior skills run in our family." She thrust the hunting crossbow into his hands. "Try again."

"If you wish, Hanna."

Silveran fitted a quarrel onto the bow stock. Verhanna stood off to his left, Rufus on his right. He raised the crossbow to his cheek and squinted over the wire-bead sight fixed to the end of the stock.

Murderer . . .

Silveran lowered the bow and shook his head, frowning. Verhanna asked what was the matter. "Nothing," he said, raising the weapon again.

Murderer . . .

The green-fingered elf knew that whispering voice all too well. Gripping the crossbow hard, Silveran tried to concentrate on the target, to banish all other thoughts from his mind.

He hadn't been bothered by the specter of dead Dru for over a month. His time had been spent with Verhanna and Rufus, or learning from his father the things that he needed to know as crown prince of the Qualinesti. His days were kept busy, and his nights had been calm since Rufus began sleeping on a small bed in his room.

However, hard as he tried to ignore it, the hollow sound of Dru's voice filled his ears: *Murderer. You killed me.*

Green robe flying, Silveran spun around, looking for the terrible face he knew would be hovering nearby. Rufus threw himself flat on the ground as the quarrel tip on the cocked crossbow spun by. He shouted, "Hey! Watch where you point that thing!"

The only sound the Speaker's son heard was the ghastly sighing of a long-dead elf. He swept around in a circle until he spied the horrible head suspended in space, just above his own eye level. The face of the evil sorcerer was even more decayed now than when he last saw it. The nose was sunken in, the eyes black sockets. The smell of death and putrefaction forced itself into Silveran's nostrils. He choked and aimed the crossbow at the dead elf's image.

"Silveran, don't shoot," Verhanna said evenly. The quarrel was pointing right at her forehead, only a half dozen feet away. A line of sweat appeared on her upper lip.

"Don't shoot the captain!" Rufus, still flat on the sod, added his plea to hers.

"Go away," Silveran quavered. "Leave me alone!"

"I'm not Drulethen," Verhanna said carefully. Keeping her hands spread apart in front of her, she took a step forward. She continued to speak in calm, soothing tones. "Turn the bow away, Silveran. It's me, Verhanna. Your sister."

In Silveran's fear-crazed mind, the words were different: *Time is short, murderer. When the last flesh rots from my bones, I will come to avenge my death on you. Time is short! Look into the face of your death!*

Maggots sprouted from the dead elf's skin. Drulethen's lower jaw fell away and vanished, leaving a horrid, gaping skull leering at him. Silveran shut his eyes and cried out for mercy. His hand tightened on the trigger bar.

Verhanna threw herself forward and knocked the bow aside. The square-headed quarrel leapt from the bowstring and hissed through the air, burying itself in a high tree branch. Silveran screamed and fought Verhanna, but she managed to pin him to the ground.

"No, no!" he ranted. "I'm sorry I killed you! Don't hurt me, Dru! I don't want to die!" Tears coursed down his cheeks.

Guards, servants, and Tamanier Ambrodel came running into the garden, alarmed by the cries. The guards restrained Silveran after Verhanna lifted him to his feet. The prince sobbed something about forgiveness and his own innocence.

"Did you leave him alone?" asked Tamanier quickly. "Did he see the ghost again?"

"We never left his side," Rufus protested. "My captain and I were teaching Greenhands how to shoot a crossbow."

Tamanier looked quickly to Verhanna. "Did you see anything untoward, Your Highness?"

She dusted dirt from her knees and shook her head. "I didn't see or hear anything but Silveran."

"He almost shot my captain," blurted the kender.

"Shut up, Wart."

Tamanier looked grave. "The Speaker must be told." He folded his wrinkled hands and pressed them hard against his lips. "Forgive me, Highness."

Verhanna bristled. "What do you mean?"

"His Highness could be ill in his mind."

Her eyes blazed. "You go too far, Castellan Ambrodel! If my brother says he's seeing a ghost, then by Astra, there's a ghost!"

"I meant no offense, Your Highness—"

"Well, you've offended me!"

The guards supported Silveran as they walked him back to the Speaker's house. Tamanier bowed and, white-faced, followed them inside.

Rufus picked up the crossbow and brushed the dirt from the bowstring. "You know, my captain, the old geezer could be right."

She shook a finger under the kender's nose. "Don't you start, too, you noisy beetle!"

The kender turned and stomped away toward the house. Shaking with fury, Verhanna watched him for a second, then snatched up a forgotten quarrel and broke it over her knee. She flung the pieces aside and stalked off into the garden. Soon the warrior maiden was lost from sight as she crashed through the bushes and descended the gentle slope into the deepest recesses of the peaceful garden.

From a window in the Speaker's house overlooking the upper garden, Ulvian watched the entire scene. He smiled. He was glad his rooms had such an excellent view.

* * * * *

Healers were summoned to the Speaker's house; priestesses of Quen came and worked their incantations over Silveran—all with no success. Clerics devoted to the worship of Mantis and Astra wove protective spells around Kith-Kanan's beleaguered son, but still the hideous corpse face of Drulethen tormented him, and him alone.

The Speaker met with the priests and healers. "Is my son bewitched?" he asked solemnly.

The high priestess of Quen, a former Silvanesti named Aytara, answered for all of them. "We have cast healing spells on your son, Great Speaker, and they do not affect him. The good brothers of Mantis have erected barriers to keep out elementals and evil spirits, and still he sees the dread specter."

Her wide, pale blue eyes never faltered as she gazed at Kith-Kanan. "Prince Silveran is not afflicted by mortal magic, Great Speaker," the young priestess finished.

"What, then?" he demanded.

Aytara glanced at her silent colleagues. "There are two possibilities, Majesty. Both are distasteful."

"Speak the truth, lady. I want to hear it."

"There are potions, poisons, that can corrode the mind. Your son may have been given such a potion," she said.

Kith-Kanan shook his head. "Silveran and I eat the same foods. No one knows who will eat or drink from any given plate or cup. And I have experienced no such visions. It cannot be poison."

"Very well. The last possibility is that your son has lost his mind."

Terrible, icy silence followed the pronouncement. Kith-Kanan gripped the arms of his vallenwood throne so hard his knuckles turned as white as the wood. "Do you know what you're saying? Are you telling me that my son—my heir—is mad?"

The priestess said nothing. A thought occurred to the Speaker. "My son has demonstrated magical ability in the past," he ventured. "Can this power not be used to help him?"

"He does indeed have great power, but he is completely untrained. Without much study and practice, he can't use these powers to help himself." Aytara's face was sad.

Kith-Kanan looked to each of the others in turn. All of them hung their heads and remained silent, having nothing further to offer.

"Go," the Speaker said in a tired voice. "I thank you for your efforts. Go."

With many bows and flourishes, the healers and clerics took their leave of Kith-Kanan. The Speaker turned away to stare out one of the windows. Only Tamanier remained in the hall.

"My old friend," Kith-Kanan said to him. "What am I to do? I almost think the gods have cursed me, Tam. I've buried two wives, found that one son was a criminal and another may be insane. What am I to do?"

At the far end of the small hall, the aged castellan took in a deep breath. "Perhaps young Silveran has always been troubled," he ventured. "After all, his early life and birth were not natural, and his powers are wild and uncontrolled."

The Speaker slumped back on his throne. He felt every day of his five hundred and some-odd years of life weigh upon him like stones in the folds of his robe, or chains laid in long loops around his shoulders.

"I followed all the signs," he murmured. "Has it all been a terrible hoax? It can't be. Silveran must be my true heir, I know it. But how can we cure him? I can't put my crown on the head of a mad person."

"Sire," said Tamanier, "I am reluctant to bring this up—especially now. But Prince Ulvian wishes to speak with you."

The Speaker started, his mind far away. "What, Tam?"

"Prince Ulvian has asked to see you, sire."

The Speaker gathered his wandering thoughts. With a nod, he said, "Very well. Send him in."

Tamanier pushed the doors apart. An eddy of wind from the porticoed exterior sent a handful of dead leaves skittering across the burnished wooden floor of the hall. The castellan admitted Prince Ulvian, then departed, closing the doors quietly behind him.

"Speaker," said Ulvian, bowing from the waist. Kith-Kanan waved for him to approach.

It took Ulvian twenty steps to cross the audience hall. In the months since his return from Pax Tharkas and Black Stone Peak, the prince had radically altered his looks and manner. Gone were the extravagant lace cuffs, the brilliantly colored and astonishingly expensive breeches and boots. Ulvian had taken to wearing plain velvet tunics in dark blue, black, or green, with matching trousers and short black boots. Heavy necklaces and bold gems on his fingers had given way to a simple silver chain around his neck, with a locket containing a miniature of his mother. Ulvian let his hair grow longer, in a more elven fashion, and shaved off his beard. Save for his broad jaw and round eyes, he could have been taken for a full-blooded elf.

"Father, I want you to send me away," he said after bowing a second time at the foot of the throne.

"Away? Why?"

"I feel it is time to complete my education. I've wasted too much time on frivolous pleasures. There are many things I want to learn."

Kith-Kanan sat upright. This curious request intrigued him. "Where is it you wish to go for this education?" he asked.

"I was thinking of Silvanost."

The Speaker raised his eyebrows. In a gentle voice, he said, "Ulvian, that's impossible. Sithas would never allow it."

Ulvian took a step forward. The toes of his boots pressed against the base of the vallenwood throne. "But I want to learn from the wise elves of the east, in the most ancient temples in the world. Surely the Speaker of the Stars would permit his own kin—"

"It cannot be, my son." Kith-Kanan leaned forward and laid a hand on Ulvian's shoulder. "You are half-human. The Silvanesti would not welcome you."

The prince flinched as if his father had struck him. "Then send me to Thorbardin, or Ergoth! Anywhere!" Ulvian said desperately.

"Why do you wish to leave so suddenly?"

The prince's eyes dropped before the Speaker's questioning gaze. "I—I told you, Father. I want to complete my education."

"You aren't telling me the truth, Son," Kith-Kanan contended.

"All right. I want to get away from this house. I can't bear it anymore!" He jerked out of his father's grip.

"What do you mean?"

Ulvian fidgeted with his narrow gray sash. Finally he turned away, putting his back to the Speaker. "His screams keep me awake at night," he said stiffly. "I—I hear him wandering the halls, moaning. I can't bear it, Father. I know he's your legitimate heir, and I can't expect him to go away, so I thought I'd volunteer to leave instead."

Kith-Kanan rose and walked to his son. "Your brother is ill," he said. "If it's any consolation to you, he keeps me awake at night, too."

The dark smudges under Kith-Kanan's eyes testified to the truth of his statement. "I wish you would stay and help Silveran, Ullie. He needs a good friend."

The somberly dressed prince knelt and gathered a handful of red and brown leaves from the floor. Slowly he turned them over, as if studying their wrinkled surfaces. "Do the healers give him any chance of recovery?" he asked, staring at the leaves.

Kith-Kanan sighed. "They don't even agree on why he is afflicted," he replied.

Ulvian dropped the leaves and stood. Turning to face his father, the prince said quietly, "If you want me to stay, Father, I will."

Kith-Kanan grasped his son's hands gratefully. "Thank you, Ullie," he said, smiling. "I was hoping you'd stay."

The prince had never planned to do otherwise. Back in his own quarters, Ulvian ran his fingers lightly down the front of his heavy quilted tunic. The hard lump of the black onyx amulet was there, sheathed in a tight leather bag hanging around his neck.

"My beauty," Ulvian rejoiced softly. "It goes well! Soon I will be sole and undisputed heir."

You deserve it, my prince, crooned the amulet for Ulvian's ears only. *Together we will rule.*

The prince busied himself putting the finishing touches to the speech he would give when he was made heir to the Throne of the Sun.

The Death of the Sun

19

Before the first frost, they moved Silveran to a room at the end of the south wing of the Speaker's house. In this secluded chamber, his nightly ravings wouldn't disturb those sleeping near the center of the great house. Tamanier, as keeper of the keys, had the duty of locking Silveran in his room each night. If his cries became too loud, a sleeping draft would be brought for him to drink. Only through powerful soporifics could they hold back the relentless specter that haunted the young elf. The strong medicines left him groggy and befuddled most of his waking hours.

When Solinari, the silver moon, first called the fingers of frost over Qualinesti, Silveran was sleeping fitfully in his pitiful cell. There was no furniture or lamp or anything else he might use to harm himself or others. Of his blankets, only two hadn't been shredded by fevered hands as he struggled to keep the hideous phantom at bay.

Greenhands, dead Dru called. *Rise, murderer. Tonight, you join me in the land of the dead.*

"No," Silveran groaned. "Oh, no, please!"

Your time is all used up. Rise! I am coming for you!

"No!"

With a sudden spasm, the elf jerked awake. His heart hammered inside his ribs, and his breath came in rapid, shallow gasps. "You'll not take me! You'll not!"

He scrambled to his feet. The door to his room was locked from the outside. Panic seized Silveran. He stood and kicked the locked door hard.

The thick wooden panel boomed but stayed firm. Knowing his son's great strength, Kith-Kanan had sadly ordered the door be the stoutest that could be found.

Greenhands, murderer...

In desperation, Silveran threw his entire body at the door. Under his frenzied assault, the jamb splintered, and the door flew wide. The dark hall outside was cold. Winter rugs had not yet been laid on the bare wood floor, and the elf's teeth chattered as he staggered out into the chill.

To his left were door-sized windows, shuttered. Through the slats of the seven-foot-tall shutters came a weird, yellow-green light. Silveran uttered a short, sharp cry and recoiled from the slivers of sickly light slicing in between the slats. Laughter rang in his head—Dru's laughter, mingled with the sound of rattling chains.

He ran down the hall, blindly blundering from one closed door to another. These ground floor rooms were unoccupied, as the Speaker was entertaining no guests. Silveran shook each door handle and pounded on each panel, but he couldn't get in. The chartreuse light grew stronger, until it cast Silveran's own long shadow to the end of the empty hall.

The light seeped through the closed shutters like oil through cheesecloth. As the petrified elf watched, it coalesced into the rough form of an elf. Silveran pressed his back against a locked door and stared in abject terror. The greenly glowing form assumed distinct arms and legs—but no head. The neck rose up, but where the head should be was only darkness.

Flee if you can, murderer! I have come for you! boomed the voice.

Silveran bolted from the shelter of the doorway and ran down the hall, crying out in horror.

He crossed the receiving room at the main entrance on the ground floor and seized the first available doorknob. This was the Speaker's trophy room. Here were displayed Kith-Kanan's various suits of armor, his personal weapons, as well as flags and standards captured from the Ergothians during the Kinslayer War. Silveran wove his way among the stands of halberds, swords, and pikes. The glint of metal gave him an idea, a mad idea. He would kill the wretched ghost again—for good this time—and be safe. Safe and free.

But the pikes and swords were held in their racks by strong loops of chain and wire, and none came easily to hand. Silveran hurried by them and went to the rear wall, scanning the trophies mounted there. These were not, properly speaking, weapons, but rather tools the Speaker had used in his long career. The saw he had wielded to fell the first tree when Qualinost was being built. The mason's trowel he used to lay the cornerstone of the Tower of the Sun. The hammer King Glenforth of Thorbardin had given him to carve out the first block for the fortress of peace, Pax Tharkas.

The hammer rested on a small pedestal under a crystal dome. The silver bands on its handle sparkled, and its gilded head gleamed. The dome was not sealed, and Silveran quickly sent it crashing to the floor. The hammer fit his grip as if made for him.

He exulted. The mighty dwarven hammer would smash diamonds to dust if swung smartly and struck fairly. Now he would deal with the monster Drulethen. His torment would soon be finished!

The door of the trophy room opened slowly. The elf huddled in the shadows, hammer couched on his shoulders. A pale yellow light filtered in from the open door, and a voice whispered, "Silveran? Are you in here?"

"Yes!" he shouted, leaping on the door and wrenching it fully open. He saw for a second a grinning, fleshless skull staring at him with empty white eye sockets, heard the mocking laughter in his ears. "Now I will kill you forever, Dru!" Silveran screamed and brought the hammer down in a smashing blow on Dru's skull. Bone yielded under the awful impact, and he smelled blood. The yellow light went out.

Silveran collapsed in a limp heap on the floor. He'd done it. He'd killed Dru completely. Now he was free. His eyelids fluttered closed just as more light filled the room.

Tamanier, Ulvian, and Verhanna lifted their lamps high. Behind them, sleepy servants muttered about their interrupted rest. The lamplight fell upon the scene in the Speaker's trophy room.

"By all the holy gods!" Tamanier cried. "He's killed the Speaker!"

* * * * *

The entire Guard of the Sun was roused and turned out of their barracks while the best healers in Qualinost were summoned to the Speaker's house. Kith-Kanan bore a terrible wound on his head where the dwarven hammer had broken his skull. But he was not dead. His heart beat, and he drew breath, but the Speaker of the Sun had not opened his eyes since the tragedy.

Strangely, Silveran was likewise insensible. His body was unmarked, yet he could not be roused, even when foul-smelling asafetida was waved under his nose. All signs of madness had left him; his face was peaceful, and the deep lines in his brow were smoothed out. He looked like a sleeping child, lying on the floor by his mortally wounded father.

Verhanna refused any help and carried her father to his bed. Tamanier explained how Kith-Kanan had heard the disturbance Silveran had caused and had gone, without summoning any guards, to investigate.

"I will never forgive myself," the old castellan said, wringing his hands. "I should have gone in his stead!"

"Never mind," Ulvian said unsteadily as they mounted the steps on each side of Verhanna. "No one knew this was going to happen. Silveran must have struck out at Father in a delirium."

In truth, the prince was much shaken by this turn of events. He had never desired Kith-Kanan's death, and he somehow realized the amulet had deliberately maneuvered father and son together for just this result. Now the evil talisman wouldn't have to wait long for Ulvian to receive that which he'd requested. In days—perhaps hours—Ulvian would be Speaker of the Sun.

Aytara and the entire college of Quen arrived, and they were put to work trying to save Kith-Kanan's life. Silveran merited only a passing glance. Aside from the fact that he couldn't be awakened, he seemed in perfect health. The high priestess didn't wish to waste a single spell or incantation on the uninjured elf; all the magic they could gather would be needed for the Speaker. Two of the guards carried the Speaker's unconscious son to a small room on the second floor of the great house. Their orders were to chain him and stand guard at his door.

Kith-Kanan was dying.

Soon the whole house was saturated with the smell of incense and the sound of chanting. The Clerics of Quen invoked their mightiest spells, and they succeeded in slowing the creep of death through the Speaker's limbs, but they couldn't stop it. Aytara admitted as much to Verhanna and Ulvian in the sitting room of their father's chambers.

"How—how long will he live?" asked Verhanna, silent tears trickling down her face.

"A day. Perhaps two. He is very strong. A normal elf would have died on the spot from such a blow. You should be prepared, my lady. The end could come at any time."

"Is there nothing you can do?"

Aytara bowed. Her white robes were wrinkled, her sky-blue sash loosely tied. She, too, was crying. "No, Highness. I am deeply sorry."

Verhanna nodded and the high priestess departed.

After a silent moment, Ulvian coughed. "There remains the matter of my succession," he said.

Verhanna. Glared. "What succession?"

"When our father dies, who will be the next Speaker? Certainly not our mad half-brother."

Snarling with outrage, Verhanna seized her brother by the front of his shirt and propelled him backward out the door and into the hallway, until he thudded against a pillar. "Don't talk to me about crowns!" she said through clenched teeth. "Our father isn't even dead yet, and already you crave his scepter! I tell you this, Brother, if you mention such a thing to me again before Father is gone, I'll kill you. I'll gut you like a wild pig! Is that clear?"

Mastering the fear that trembled through his body, Ulvian said that it was. He had no doubt she meant what she said. Though he clutched her arms, he knew he'd never break her grip.

Verhanna felt something hard under her wrist. She plucked open Ulvian's blue shirt, sending buttons flying. There was a leather bag hanging around his neck. Her brother's eyes were wide with fear and anger.

"What's this?" she hissed. When he didn't reply, she drew her dagger in her left hand and held it to his face.

For an instant, he thought Verhanna was going to slit his throat, but all she did was cut the thong holding the leather bag. Stepping back, she pried it open and found the onyx amulet.

"What are you doing with this?" she demanded.

"It's just a lump of carved stone," he said, his voice quavering. Ulvian prayed silently for the amulet to intervene. Nothing happened.

"This was destroyed in the fire when Drulethen was—" Verhanna stopped in midsentence. Her head snapped around in the direction of their father's bedchamber. Slowly she turned back to Ulvian, her face suffused with blood.

"*You!*" she breathed.

"No, Hanna, it wasn't—"

She seized her brother again, shoving him so hard against the pillar that his vision filled with stars. "Let me go! You'll regret it if you hurt me!" he babbled.

"I haven't got time for you now," she muttered fiercely. She let him go. Ulvian's feet dropped to the floor.

"Sergeant of the guard!" Verhanna bawled. A warrior with a fanlike array of horsehair on the top of his helmet came running down the corridor. "Post a guard around this room," she ordered. "No one is to enter but I myself, Tamanier Ambrodel, or the holy lady Aytara. Got that?"

The guard glanced sideways at the prince. "Is my lord Ulvian to be excluded, Captain?" he asked.

"He most certainly is. If I find out anyone else but the three I named has gone in there, I'll have your head."

The sergeant, a seasoned warrior, swallowed hard. "It shall be done, Captain!" he vowed.

A squad of eight guards formed before the doors to the Speaker's rooms. It was nearly dawn. Verhanna left Tamanier to make the announcement to the people. Already heralds clad in golden tabards were appearing in the halls, rubbing the sleep from their eyes and tugging on their ankle-high boots. The old castellan, strain and sorrow written into every line on his face, shepherded the elf boys and girls into an adjoining room. Minutes later, the heralds emerged, red-eyed and weeping. They raced out of the building to cry the sorrowful news to the waking city.

Verhanna went to see Silveran. The guards outside the chamber stood aside for her as she unlocked the thick door of his room.

"Captain," one of the guards said to her before she entered, "you'd best look at his hands."

She was weary and heartsick and still angry with Ulvian, and she told the guard she had no patience for riddles.

"Please, Captain," insisted the guard. "He was once called Greenhands, wasn't he? Well, his fingers aren't green anymore."

Verhanna's brows lifted at that. She went in and closed the heavy door behind her.

Despite the thick chains that encircled his arms and legs, Silveran was the picture of peace. It made her heart ache anew to see him lying so innocent and untroubled while their father was dying. What evil miasma had invaded his simple, guileless mind and made him go mad with fear? She still held the black amulet in her hand. Verhanna knelt on one knee and studied the elf's hands. Just as the guard had said, Silveran's fingers were now white, contrasting with his tanned hands.

Slowly, with much fluttering of eyelids, Silveran was waking.

"Hanna," he said happily. "Hello."

She stared down at him, incredulous at his calm manner. He sat up, and the chains draped heavily on his stomach. "Oof," he wheezed. "What's this? Why am I bound?"

"Don't you remember what happened?" she asked.

"Remember what? Won't you take these chains off? They hurt me."

"How do you think you came to be here?" she said sharply.

Silveran's brow furrowed. "I was asleep," he said thoughtfully. "I had some bad dreams—then I woke up, and there you were, and here are the chains."

In slow, deliberate words, she explained what had happened. Silveran cried out and retreated to the wall. The door opened and a guard poked his head in, but Verhanna waved him out. Silveran hugged himself and gasped for air.

"It cannot be," he said, shaking his head. "It was a dream, a terrible dream!"

"It is the truth," she said grimly. "The Speaker is dying."

He buried his face in his hands. "I am cursed!" Silveran moaned. "I have slain my beloved father!"

Verhanna sprang forward, grabbing his hands and dragging them away from his face. "Listen to me! You may have been cursed, but you're all right now. When father dies"— she choked on the word—"you must go before the Thalas-Enthia and demand that they name you Speaker of the Sun. Otherwise Ulvian will claim the throne. You must do it!"

"But I must be punished for slaying our father," he objected, sobbing. "No one could want me to rule. Let Ulvian be Speaker. I must be put to death for my crime!"

Verhanna shook him hard, rattling his chains. "No! It wasn't your fault. Ulvian used Drulethen's black amulet to drive you mad. He's the criminal. You are the chosen successor. Everything depends on you. Father believes you are the future of Qualinesti!"

Bells began tolling from the high towers of the city. The heralds' dire tidings were spreading fast. Verhanna listened to the doleful sound, knowing it was the Speaker's death knell. When the bells ceased ringing, it would mean Kith-Kanan was dead.

Quickly the warrior maiden unlocked the fetters on Silveran's hands and legs. "You stay here," she said. "I'll have the guards lock you in. You'll be safe."

"Safe from what?"

There was no time to explain. Silveran reached out for Verhanna as she made for the door. Whatever he intended to say died in his throat as he noticed for the first time that his fingers were no longer green.

"The power has left me," he breathed. "I no longer feel its touch."

Verhanna hesitated, her hand on the knob. "The magic? It's gone?"

He nodded. "Good," she said firmly. "Maybe that will be to your advantage."

The door slammed behind her before he could ask what she meant.

* * * * *

To walk among the green trees, to smell the sunwashed air, to eat what came to hand, and to sleep under the stars—that was the good life. The best life. For all his deeds and wisdom, it was this simple woodland existence that Kith-Kanan always hungered for. The myth makers, the legend builders, had elevated him into a hero, a demigod, in his own lifetime. No doubt after he was dead, their exaggerations would grow larger with each passing century. Perhaps Kith-Kanan might become a god someday in the eyes of his descendants. He did not wish it. A far more suitable tribute would be the continued happy existence of the nation he'd founded, Qualinesti.

Kith-Kanan walked in the shade of oaks. It was a remarkable dream he was having. Dreams were usually thin things, flashes in his mind's eye. This one, though, was magnificent. The smells, sounds, and textures of the forest were all around him. Wind whispered in the leaves high overhead. He heard birds and small animals calling and scampering in the dead leaves on the ground. Sunlight made sparkling patterns in the air. Remarkable.

Truly remarkable.

"Not so remarkable."

He stopped, as if rooted to the spot. Leaning against a tree, not five paces away, was his first wife and dearest love.

"Anaya," he sighed. "You visit my wonderful dream."

"This is not a dream, Kith."

She straightened and walked toward him. The green eyes, the dark hair, the Kagonesti face paint—it was all so real. As she scrutinized his face, he rejoiced in her every feature.

"This is not a dream," she repeated. "You are in a shadowed realm between the light of life and the darkness of death. Our son struck you down with a dwarven hammer, but it was not his will that put the weapon in his hand. Your other son used the Amulet of Hiddukel to bring him down, and you with him."

Sadness appeared in her eyes. "No one could prevent this destiny for you, my husband, but I have come back to tell you these things. Your son Ulvian must not sit on the Throne of the Sun. He has opened his soul to evil to further his ambition, and he will be the death and ruination of thousands if he is not stopped."

Kith-Kanan looked past her at the serene wildwood, feeling removed and remote from the terrible tale she'd just related. He didn't feel as if he'd been struck a mighty blow; instead, he felt as young and strong as he had when he'd first met Anaya. Tentatively he took her hand in his. It was warm and suntanned, and the tips of the fingers were delicately green. "How is it possible, my love? How can I be here with you?"

She lifted her free hand and caressed his cheek. "The gods you worship do not interfere with the ebb and flow of life. They are apart from it, and they allow life to follow its own course. But this place, and my existence, are not part of life or death. The power rules here in eternal balance with Chaos. Now, as a boon to me, the power allows me to see you and tell you the truth."

"What is this power?" he asked, pressing her hand to his lips.

"It cannot be named, like a flower or a beast. It is the property of order in all things, the counterpart of Chaos. That is all I can say."

Wind rustled through the closely growing oaks. Kith-Kanan held Anaya's hand. "Will you walk with me?" he asked gently. She smiled and said yes.

As they strolled down the path, he wondered aloud, "Will I be with you always?"

Green moss softened their footfalls, and the wind lifted Kith-Kanan's long hair.

"As long as you remember me, I shall be with you," she replied. "But you cannot remain here much longer. Even as we speak, your mortal body grows cold. You must go back and tell those you love and trust the true story of your death."

"My death?" Kith-Kanan mused over the idea, normally so frightening. "I've seen many people die, for all sorts of reasons. Is it a sad thing to be dead?"

Anaya shrugged and said with her characteristic bluntness, "I don't know. I've never died."

He found himself smiling. "Of course not. I'm not frightened, though. Perhaps I will find all those who have gone before me. My father Sithel, my mother, Mackeli, Suzine . . . ."

A large boulder appeared in the path, completely blocking it. Kith-Kanan touched the stone, feeling the lichen and watching a stream of tiny black ants march over it like soldiers conquering a mountain peak.

"This is the end, isn't it?" he said, turning to face her.

"The end of your time here." She regarded him solemnly. "Are you sad, Kith?"

He smiled and said, "No. I said good-bye to you long ago. This visit is a wonderful gift. It would be ungrateful to be sad."

Kith-Kanan leaned over and kissed Anaya softly. She returned his kiss, but already she was beginning to pale. Not daring to end the moment, he whispered into her mouth, "Farewell, my dearest. Farewell. . . ."

The forest became dark wooden walls and beams. Pain flooded his limbs, and he gasped loudly. There was a pressure on his cheek. Kith-Kanan opened his eyes and realized his daughter was kissing his face.

She drew back. "By Astra!" Verhanna cried. "You're awake!"

"Yes." Merciful gods, his throat was raw. "Water," he gasped.

Verhanna looked distressed. "Water? Will nectar do?"

She had a bottle of nectar beside her that she'd apparently been drinking from. Kith-Kanan croaked his assent, and she carefully put the bottle to his parched lips.

"Ah. Daughter, get some people in here. Witnesses. Tam, the guards . . . anyone. As fast as you can."

Verhanna called for help, and guards threw open the door. "Run and get Tamanier Ambrodel!" she said. "The rest of you, come in here. The Speaker has something to say, and he wants you to hear it!"

Seven warriors crowded into the modest bedchamber. Verhanna raised her father up and stuffed a pillow under his back so he could see the warriors. Then she lifted the nectar to his lips once more.

"My good warriors," Kith-Kanan rasped. The thick white bandage that covered the horrible wound on his forehead didn't dip low enough to cover his bloodshot eyes. "These are my last commands."

The elves all leaned forward to catch every sound he made. "My son," said the Speaker weakly, "is innocent. Silveran is not . . . responsible . . . for my death."

The guards exchanged looks of puzzlement. Verhanna, heedless of the tears that had once more begun to flow down her cheeks, prompted, "Go on, Father."

"He was bewitched . . . by the onyx amulet. The evil talisman struck a bargain with . . . Ulvian."

Puzzlement gradually turned to anger. Muttering, the warriors fingered their sword hilts.

"Ulvian will die for this, Father, I swear it!" Verhanna said. The guards seconded her vow.

"No!" Kith-Kanan said strongly. "I forbid it! Few are . . . the mortals who can withstand the sweet words . . . of Hiddukel. Ulvian—" He coughed hard, and fresh blood began to trickle down his face from under his bandage. "Do not harm . . . him. Please!"

Verhanna buried her face against her father's chest. "Father, don't die!" she pleaded.

"I am . . . not afraid. Is Silveran . . . well?"

She lifted her tear-streaked face. "Yes, yes! He has lost his magic, but he is himself again. The madness has left him!"

"I want to see . . . him."

Verhanna ordered a guard to fetch Silveran. He was gone several long minutes, so she dispatched two more. When they hadn't returned after quite a long wait, and Kith-Kanan's eyelids had begun to flutter closed, she got to her feet and stormed out of the room. Down the corridor at Silveran's door, she found the three guards she'd dispatched and the three watching the chained prince. Half of the warriors were howling for Ulvian's blood, the other half were protecting him.

"Get out of the way!" Verhanna said, shoving guards left and right. "The Speaker wants his son!"

"I'll go to him," Ulvian said quickly.

756

"Not you! Silveran!"

"But he's a murderer!"

Thrusting a finger at her brother, Verhanna cried, "We know the truth! You conspired to destroy Silveran so you could reclaim the throne. Did you also plot the death of our father?"

She whipped out her sword, and the guards stood back, leaving sister and brother facing each other. "I want to kill you so much I could—" She stopped herself. "But Father has forbidden it! Now get out of my way before I forget my promise to him!"

She sheathed her sword and unlocked the door. After hustling Silveran out, she and her half-brother ran down the polished wood floor. They were trailed more slowly by Ulvian and the guards.

Verhanna flew through the open doorway of Kith-Kanan's room. The four warriors who had remained behind were all kneeling around the Speaker's bed. His eyes were closed. Verhanna didn't need to ask; Kith-Kanan was dead.

Tamanier Ambrodel, his hair standing up on his head and his mantle askew, wept openly at the foot of the Speaker's bed. "I was too late," he sobbed.

The sergeant of the guard looked up at her. "He called to you, lady," he said chokingly. "And to someone named Anaya."

She had to swallow her grief, at least briefly. It was vitally important that her father's wishes were carried out. "Did you all hear what he told me before he died?" she said frantically.

"Yes, lady," said the sergeant. The other guards swore oaths that they had heard the Speaker's words as well. Tersely Verhanna informed Tamanier of Ulvian's plot against Silveran. Then she pulled Silveran into the room, and the guards rose to their feet.

"The Speaker of the Sun is dead," the captain said, her voice cracking. "Long live Speaker Silveran!"

"Long live Speaker Silveran!" echoed the warriors.

Silveran's face was bright as he tried to fathom it all.

"Your Majesty," Tamanier added, bowing to the new young monarch.

"Where's Ulvian?" Verhanna asked suddenly. He wasn't in the Speaker's rooms or the hallway nearby.

"Shall we search for him, lady?" asked the sergeant of the guard.

"It's for the Speaker to decide," Verhanna said softly, putting a hand to Silveran's shoulder. The warriors looked expectantly at him. The elf's eyes were calm.

The new Speaker gazed upon his father. "Let Ulvian go," he said.

Now that she had fulfilled her duty to Kith-Kanan, Verhanna allowed her wobbly legs to give way, and she knelt by her father's body, weeping uncontrollably. She had loved him and respected him with an intensity that approached worship. She couldn't bear the thought that he was gone, that she would never again see his face, never again hear his voice, teasing her for her seriousness. Her brother moved to stand behind her and placed his hands on her shaking shoulders.

"I need you, Hanna," Silveran whispered, for her ears only. "I need your help to rule Qualinesti."

Verhanna pulled her gaze away from the still face of her father and looked up into the solemn visage of the new Speaker of the Sun. Kith-Kanan had been right. Silveran, once known as Greenhands, would make a fine leader. He was good and kind and incorruptible.

Her voice shook, but the words carried to all those in the room as she responded with the same ancient oath she had once sworn to her father. "You are my Speaker. You are my liege lord, and I shall obey you even unto death."

With Silveran's hands still on her shoulders, Verhanna rose slowly to her feet. The guards surrounded Kith-Kanan's bed and came forward to raise him up. By ancient rite, a dead Speaker was carried to the Temple of Astra for prayers and purification.

"Stop," Silveran ordered, and Verhanna looked startled. For just that instant, his commanding voice had sounded exactly like their father's. Silveran held out a restraining hand. A hand no longer green. "This is my duty," he stated.

With great tenderness, he lifted Kith-Kanan in his arms and carried him down the central stair to the reception hall. Verhanna walked behind him and to his right, and the warriors fell into step behind her.

At the bottom of the cherrywood stair stood the entire household, down to the humblest sweepers. All cried openly, and their heads bowed as the body of Kith-Kanan, founder and first Speaker of Qualinesti, was borne past them. Poor Tamanier Ambrodel was supported by the strong arm of his son Kemian. The aged castellan was so grief-stricken he could barely remain upright. He had one last duty to perform for his old friend and sovereign, though. When Silveran, with his sad burden, reached the bottom of the grand stair, Tamanier lifted his right hand and signaled the group of heralds waiting by the front doors.

The heralds flew out the double doors and ran like lightning across the square and into every part of the city. As the second Speaker of the Sun stepped into the morning sunshine, their high voices could be heard crying the dreadful news.

Speaker Silveran paused, blinking in the bright light. Verhanna felt her own step falter as, one by one, the great bells throughout the city of Qualinost fell silent.

The Letter
Epilogue

To His Gracious Majesty, Silveran, Speaker of the Sun, from Kemian, Lord Ambrodel, currently at Pax Tharkas.

Great Speaker: I wish to extend my heartiest good wishes to you on this, the first anniversary of your ascension to the throne. All Qualinesti is proud of the great work you have done following in the mighty footsteps of your esteemed father, the late Speaker, Kith-Kanan.

Preparations of the vault for your father's final entombment here are nearly complete. The last touches are being applied, and Feldrin Feldspar is personally overseeing the tomb's completion. Before the autumn equinox, everything will be ready to receive the late Speaker in his final resting place.

Regarding the other matters you wrote about, I can tell you a few things. Of Prince Ulvian, we have no certain news, though many rumors circulate about him. One week we hear he is living in Daltigoth, the pampered guest of the Emperor of Ergoth; the next week I am "reliably" informed that the prince lives in direst poverty in Balifor. The suggestion of the General of the Guards, Lady Verhanna, to send her scout to Balifor to ferret out the truth is a good one. If anyone can find Prince Ulvian, Rufus Wrinkle-cap can.

The flow of travelers from the east continues to dwindle. Some of the Silvanesti who have lately come to us say that the Speaker of the Stars, Sithas, plans to seal the border and prevent

759

further emigration. Personally, I am not unhappy with this. The more people who leave Silvanesti, the more dangerous relations with the old country become, as they get more and more jealous of our wealth and success.

As Governor of Pax Tharkas, I can also report to Your Majesty that things go smoothly here.

The dwarves are admirable allies, and since the arrival of the Second Regiment of the Guards of the Sun, banditry has entirely ceased in the Kharolis Mountain region. The King of Thorbardin is greatly pleased. I enclose with this letter a missive from the king, in which he expresses his gratitude to Your Majesty for the garrison of guards. The king also hopes to begin mining nearby and says the mineral wealth of the mountains will greatly enrich both kingdoms.

Now, if I may, Great Speaker, I would like to beg a personal favor of you.

For many years, I have admired the person of General of the Guards, Lady Verhanna, but she has not returned my attention. Now that the period of mourning for Speaker Kith-Kanan has passed, I wonder if you would broach the subject of marriage to your esteemed sister on my behalf? I ask this for two reasons, Majesty. First, she is of royal blood and therefore requires your permission to marry, and second, she is my fellow officer, and I dare not approach her on such a delicate matter. It would be a breach of military discipline.

If you think it wise and prudent, Great Speaker, to do this for me, my happiness and gratitude would be boundless. I have loved Lady Verhanna for many years, but I dared not reveal myself to so formidable a warrior maiden. With you to sponsor me, I feel I may have a real chance at winning her hand.

That is all I have to tell you at this time. May the gods smile on Your Majesty, grant you wisdom, and continue the good fortune and happiness your young reign has already begun.

> Your Most Humble and Obedient Servant,
> Kemian, Lord Ambrodel
> Governor
> Pax Tharkas